LUCIFER'S SON

(Book One)
(The Temptation Chronicles)

By

Sergey Mavrodi

W & B Publishers
USA

W & B Publishers

For information:
W & B Publishers
Post Office Box 193
Colfax, NC 27235
www.a-argusbooks.com

ISBN: 9781942981329

Translated from Russian by ***Yuriy Chetverzhuk***

Book Cover designed by Dubya
Printed in the United States of America

CONTENTS

"Lucifer's Son"

JACK...

BEGINNING...

GAME. Day 1...

DREAM. Day 2…

DEAL. Day 3….

NIGHTMARE. Day…

IROCHKA. Day 5…

GIFT. Day 6…

SPELL. Day 7…

SECT. Day 8…

INTERVIEW. Day 9…

SHOW. Day 10…

SATANIST. Day 11…

PROPHECY. Day 12…

ROBOT. Day 13…

SHOW-2. Day 14…

VOODOO. Day 15…

FORUM. Day 16…

LETTER. Day 17…

MONEY. Day 18…

GENIUS. Day 19…

DIAGNOSIS. Day 20…

BOOK. Day 21…

Dedicated to those who seek the mystery of life. To them, there is no mystery, only the hunt. Be blessed.

Fallen angel, friend of mine!
Take me to your home divine
Bring me there, let me be
Hid with thee.

Over hill, over dale,
Over a river, tranquil and tame—
Sing me a song, tell me nothing is wrong
Today.

Tell me there is always hope,
Tell me to forget my woes,
That wrongdoing does no harm—
As it sometimes goes

Tell me all soon shall be well:
Problems will end, struggles will quell.
We'll arrive to our home to dwell—
Straight to hell.

Tell me, angel of the night
A tale of dreams broken in daily strife
Of traces of fortune left in the wake
Of a life that was fake.

Tell me a tale of betrayals and lie
How to cheat whom you love on the sly.
Let's talk of the filthiest human crud,
Of Judas' blood.

So, how are things in hell?
Are you, guys, all doing well?
I'll drop in on you some week
For a drink.

In a hurry? What a shame.
Please come back to me some day.
Check on me from time to time—
You're divine.

The Angel

A gentle whisper of a breeze—
Sound of an angel's wings.
He comes in and stands by me
Quietly.

Would you say at least a word?
Prophesy luck and reward?
Tell me I have earned some rest.
That I'm blessed.

I'm weary, my friend
Of the Earth's toil and regret
I have seen enough of strife
In my life.

I have sinned, I know my faults
My mistakes I can't recall
Go back to heaven's realm—
Fare thee well.

A gentle whisper of a breeze—
Flap another angel's wings
A black shadow comes to me
Quietly.

JACK.

1.

As tired as he was, Fedor sat still on a slim folding stool near the dying fire and stared into the red, twinkling embers while trying to fight sleep. His heavy eyelids were closing. All he wanted was to sleep. If he could only stand up and make his way to the tent, get inside, toss himself on an air mattress and go to sleep at once! Well, first he would have to kill all mosquitoes in the tent, although there were only a scant few of them around on that warm July evening.

Fedor felt that shortly he would do all that. He would go to the tent, open it…

He shook his head and stood up with a jerk, knocking over the stool. He staggered to the lavatory mounted on a tree nearby, bowed and started to wash up. A couple of handfuls of cold water on his face returned him to his senses. He still wanted to sleep. However, he was not allowed to sleep, not now; he had to go and check the leger fish trap rigs.

Had he come here to sleep or to fish? He could have stayed at home and slept there if he wanted; he had all the time of the world for that. Nonetheless, the days were too hot, and he had nothing else to do. And if he didn't go and check now, the live bait would be dead by the next day. Would that all have been in vain? Also, there just might be some fish in the rigs; if so, he had to collect them. He hadn't checked the rigs since early morning, so he had to go. Had to go—no bugging out!

Hurrying himself along with those cheerful thoughts, Fedor took a bucket with live bait which was standing nearby and started to slowly descend the path to the water. Jack, his huge black tame Great Dane who had been sleeping by the fire, woke up, jumped up and followed him.

Fedor approached his rubber boat, put the bucket on the grass and pushed the boat in the water. There was no wind, and the boat stopped, resting near the bank. Fedor picked up the bucket and, holding it carefully in his hand, placed one foot onto the boat. Then, trying to maintain his balance, he sat on the soft border of the boat—damn it, the boat needed some inflating but he could do that later, waited for Jack to hop in and then pushed off the bank with his other foot. Quickly, he sat down on the wooden bench—Jack was watching him attentively—put the bucket between his legs to keep it from turning over, put the paddles into the water and started rowing.

The current was very slow, so the rowing was easy. The boat traveled straight ahead. The brilliant golden moon was giving a lot of light, and Fedor could see everything around.

Fedor rapidly crossed the river, which was rather narrow at that spot, and entered a shallow sand bay where he had often been. When the boat shoved into the shallow bank, Fedor stood up and, although everything was still, he hurled a heavy stone anchor which was tied to the boat's prow onto the shore. Just in case—he didn't want the boat to be washed away. *You never know...I could step onto the bank and a strong wind could just take the boat away.*

He took the bucket with live bait and, stepping over the border, waded to the bank. Jack, who had already jumped out of the boat, was prowling around. With his free hand, Fedor pulled the empty boat higher up on the bank, checked his pockets: knife, fish-bag—well, bag for the fish, if any—fishing line, sinkers, plummets, fish hooks—it seemed he had all of it. He turned to his right, where there were a couple of rigs which he had put in earlier that morning.

Which one should I start with? Nearest or furthermost? I'm going to start from the far one, he quickly decided. *"It will take longer and give me more pleasure.*

The far rig was not anywhere close to his landing. Fedor had been walking for a long time; the sleepiness had vanished, and he was now in a good mood. It was very quiet, no mosquitoes. A full moon was shining from a sky with no clouds in sight.

Oh, my God! The stars are countless! Every inch of the sky is studded with them. And that scent...what is it? The grass? The soil? The night! Looking at the stars and at the scenery all around him and breathing the fresh, cool night air, Fedor suddenly came to the rigs.

"So, here it is?" he said aloud to himself. "It was too quickly. Somehow I thought it was a bit farther away. Oh, yeah, here is a familiar willow. Is it this one? Yes, for sure; it has a cracked trunk, and there should be a grave with a fencing—has someone sunk here? Yes, there it is; beyond the turn, there will be the bushes where the last rig was placed.

"These bushes? Or those? Or those? Well, let's see; no, those. Hmm, I thought I placed them here. And why didn't I place the rigs here? The spot is wonderful. Okay, let's do it now. Here's the bait. Or maybe I'll wait and do it tomorrow; maybe it's better to do it during the day. It's easy to mess up. Okay, I'll set the rigs tomorrow. If I remember. I'll try to." Fedor continued talking aloud, as much to hear a voice as the need to speak.

"There, our bushes. Where is the rig? Here—here it is, our rig. Well, what do we have here? I see. We don't have a damned fish here! What about the bait? Here it is, alive and cheerful. A very good one! Well, well, let's see. No one wanted you. Okay, there you go into the water."

"It's strange. Here we have a pit. Well, that's one heck of a start."

As if called, the huge black Great Dane came close to investigate the fish trap. "Jack! Go away! No!"

"Well, okay. Let's consider that the first pancake is always a failure, but you have to keep on cooking—or fishing. Heh-heh."

"Okay, let's check the other one. Darn. Nothing here as well! I thought... Well, it's high time for someone to be caught in here, with all this walking."

"Go away, Jack! Don't meddle! I'm busy."

"There, half this bait has been chomped off. Gads! Those must have been some teeth! Never knew that alligators lived here. But great—that's a good sign. Gonna catch this alligator now."

"Go away! Jack! Out!

"Here you go. There you go. Off you go." Fedor cast the rig out into the water once again. "Wonderful. Great. Nice throw—an expert one! Same spot as it was before. Well, that'll get the crocodile! Damn, I'm so excited that my hands are shaking!

"Well, well, well, well! So, where is the other rig? Oh, yes. There's nothing more here now. The other rig is around the turn. Over there, right in front of the grave with the floater.

"Hmm, has he been scaring the fish away while bathing at night? If I'm not wrong, they usually bathe during the nights with a full moon. Or, quite on the contrary, they come out of the water. Out of the grave! Well, it's not important. They come out, they bathe. The thing is, they trouble the water and scare my fish away. Maybe I shouldn't have placed the rig here, and that's the reason nothing was caught in the other two rigs. The damned floater scared away all my fish? Moreover, the moon is full. Hmm! But who ate off the bait on the second rig? The floater?"

Jack growled.

Fedor reflexively turned around, startled and froze. A subconscious horror took him, and, in the moonlight, he saw that someone—or something—was sitting on the grave. Fedor's heart sank, and his self-talk broke off.

Somehow, he clearly knew who that was. He couldn't perceive or explain the nature of his understanding, although he didn't need any of that. He just knew. He knew—that was enough. It was as if he learned something or remembered it—something he knew long ago, but forgot.

As if dark and grim memories of his ancestors that had been sleeping at the bottom of his heart came to awakening, as if a dam inside him was destroyed, and a cold, blind, thick and heavy horror, having occupied all his body, washed away all secret, age-long and ancient guards and talismans, cold took him, and he recognized the elusive, infernal posture—the icy, frozen restraint and the stillness of the ghoul who had just got out of the grave and that was impossibly clear and deadly light of the huge full moon in the sky.

It was as if he had already seen and felt this in his life, long, long ago, in some other life; as if all of that had already happened to him, somewhere there in the past. Far, far away, in the dark, grim and bottomless past.

He was flooded by dreams or memories. The bits and remainders of some wild, strange and scary events started their strange dance in his head: a sacred procession, bells ringing, haunting voices chanting, candles flickering. Strict faces of the priests, more candles; a coffin, shroud, crossed hands on the bosom of the deceased, his unnaturally alive, scary, red face with vivid, clear, viperous, red, and moist lips. They are putting down the coffin, burying it. Blood! Blood, blood, blood—a lot of blood. Coffins. Coffins. A dead child with torn throat, the tormented naked body of a girl, lying on the ground. More blood, new coffins. More, more. Empty villages with no people. More blood and, at last, alarm. Twinkling light of the torches, aspen stick, the roaring crowd tearing the grave.

All of it had happened before. It had, it had, it had—at this very spot, sometime long-long ago. Very long ago. Very, very, very long ago.

But it had ended then. It's all gone.

And now, today, it's all repeated, as if it were in some horrible, terrifying dream when you're falling down over and over again in a slowly whirling abyss that is sucking you down; you want to shout and wake up, but you cannot.

That wasn't the end. Nothing was finished. The sorcerer was back.

***

The ghoul turned up his head sharply. Fedor felt his body covering with sticky sweat, his legs giving way and a soft, nasty, sick weakness filling his body. He was frozen from the terrifying fear. A hideous emptiness appeared in his heart. The feeling of horror became almost unbearable.

He knew what was going to happen. The deceased would stand up and come to him, and Fedor wouldn't be able to run, to shout or to move under that empty and freezing glance. He would just stand still and wait, unable to do anything. Wait and look, look and wait. *Oh, God!*

The corpse stood up. The shroud was dim gray under the moonlight. Bony and slim bare feet were yellow under the shroud. Long hands with curved, gnarled fingers seemed clawed, as if they were clutches of a hideous bird of prey.

Fedor closed his eyes. He was shaking, trembling all over, and cold sweat was pouring down his face. He could not, he did not want to look. But the very thought that the ghoul would seize him right now, in this very moment when he was not seeing him made him shake with disgust. Fedor opened his eyes again.

The sorcerer was very near him. He was walking slowly, but, somehow, it seemed very quick.

Time stopped for Fedor. A step… one more. Right now.

At that moment, Jack leapt. Fedor caught a glimpse of some movement, and the next moment, a growling and shrieking tangle of the two bodies of the man and the dog rolled on the ground.

For some time, Fedor watched it blankly, then he clumsily turned away and started to run on his stiff legs. First he ran slowly but then went faster and faster. As he ran away from the grave, his strength came back to him, and he almost flew over the remaining yards.

In the boat! Forgetting about the tied stone, Fedor jumped into the boat and started to row frantically. He had never rowed like that before in his life. The stone was still tied to the rope and went after the boat, moving along the bottom of the river and clinging to it, but Fedor didn't notice it. He was just rowing with all the strength that he had.

Suddenly, a fish splashed at the side of the boat. Fedor thought that the floater was following him; terrified, he rowed even faster.

When the boat touched the shore, Fedor instantly jumped out and, having forgotten about everything, dashed to the car.

Ten minutes later, he was driving along an empty highway. At one of the turns, he lost control of the car and went into the opposite lane. The highway was empty; there were almost no cars at that hour, but that near accident was like cold water for Fedor. He reduced his speed and drove slower, trying to come back to his senses and calm down. He pushed the button of car stereo. The music filled the car.

Day started breaking. Summer nights are short, and the day was quickly coming into its rights.

There was a traffic police post ahead. The sight of sleepy and indifferent policeman cheered Fedor up.

Music, people, an illuminated post. All the night's events became bleak and blurred as he sat in a comfortable car. Quiet sounds of music wrapped around Fedor, and all that had happened during the night seemed distant and unreal, as if it had never happened to him.

"Maybe that was all a dream or a nightmare," he said aloud to reassure himself, but then he remembered it all—the night, the moon, the hideous white stain behind the fence. "It's impossible—nonsense! Living dead!"

Suddenly, Fedor felt his body start shaking, and his forehead covered with sweat. Immediately he pushed the button of the stereo. *Here you go. Louder, louder. Louder!*

It helped.

"Damn! I should stop and think about it," he told himself, making the music quieter, calming down but still shaking from time to time. "Where am I going, anyway?" Fedor turned around and slowly drove back. Already reaching the post, he went to the roadside and killed the engine. Here, with people near him, he felt more confident.

For some time Fedor stared bluntly at the post, then he relaxed and leaned back on the seat."I need to think it over," he repeated drowsily to himself and closed his eyes.

2.

When Fedor awoke, the day was full. Numerous cars were driving on the highway in each direction, and people were walking on the roadside. The police officers at the post were checking the papers of a truck driver. In general, life continued. Fedor yawned, stretched and got out of the car, trying to stretch his legs. It was a clear, sunny day, the birds were singing in the forest near the highway, the people were hurrying; but all of that was happening as if it passed Fedor, not touching him. He was watching it from the side, as if from a cold, dark, damp cellar or basement.

A heavy and hopeless feeling of horror and anxiety was hidden deep within him, and it didn't want to go away. It just simply went deeper for the time being. Reluctantly, it backed off, hid itself from bright rays of the sun, but it didn't leave him. It was here, at hand. A thin, icy crust of fear on his heart never melted down. He couldn't force himself to think of the previous night. All he wanted was to sit in the car and immediately drive away, far from this cursed place, to Moscow.

However, he had to go back. First, he couldn't leave behind his stuff—the tent, boat; it was all still there. *Bugger them! Why not*? the thought came suddenly to his head. *May they be damned!*

Second, there was Jack. How could he leave him again? He had already betrayed the dog, running away; how could he leave him alone in the wood after all that he had done, after dog had saved him?

What if he's wounded? What if he needs help? And how can I ever leave him? He's alone in the woods, he won't make it. He's a friend! How could he leave a friend? Fedor had to go back.

"Maybe I should leave him," he murmured faint-heartedly and wondered at his own cowardice. "I'll just drive away. What about a friend? I already betrayed him. How could I look into his eyes? But that's not the point. I just can't go back! I can't!"

Fedor waited in hesitation and looked at the sky. The sun was high and it was long past noon. It was already 2 or 3 p.m. He had to make an immediate decision. The road would take some time, then he would have to pack all the stuff. And maybe he would have to look for Jack. Fedor shook at the thought that he would probably have to cross the river again, but he made an effort and pushed those thoughts away. He would see about everything on the spot.

The day was long, but Fedor didn't want to wait until dark under any circumstances. He was dead certain about that. *Hell no!* Even if he had to leave and betray all he knew. He wouldn't even be able to make himself do it, even if he wanted to. That was just too much for him. He wasn't able even to think about that. So he had to go as soon as possible. Fedor already knew in his heart that he would go, so there was no sense in lingering. The sooner he finished it, the better.

Without further hesitations, he got inside the car and started the engine. It rumbled readily. There was enough gas. He had to go. Maybe he shouldn't. Eh? He had to. He had to, he had to, he had to. "Enough of that talk! Let's go! I'm a man, not a woman!"

Fedor signaled left and slowly started driving. He went past the traffic police post with all precautions—the police officer didn't pay any attention to him—and, going faster and faster, he drove back.

***

The closer he got to the camp, the heavier his heart became. All the fears of the previous night came alive and tried to get free. He used all strength that was left in him to fight off these fears. The last miles were especially difficult. A violent wish to turn around and drive away—drive away! drive away!—became almost unbearable. The only way he could make himself cross the bridge was to clutch the wheel with both hands and look straight in front of him. When entering, he accidentally looked at the river, and the terror that took him was so great that he almost bumped into the guardrail, trying to turn around on the bridge. After that, he didn't repeat that mistake and never lifted his eyes. He just dragged along behind a slow truck with local plates and stared at his dirty wheels. *Only at the wheels! Only at the wheels!* Convulsively clutching the steering wheel, he lowered the eyes and didn't look around him.

In his mind, he already felt that something was wrong. He shouldn't have come here. This was a bad idea. "Go away! Leave at once!" shouted voices in his head.

But he could not just turn around and leave; he just couldn't. He was taken by some blunt indifference; he acted mechanically, unwillingly and apathetically, as if in a dream.

Here. Right turn. Another right turn. Here's the arrow. Circle. Almost there. Here's the exit. Right here. That's it. Another turn.

He turned from the highway and drove onto the gravel. Little stones bumped at the bottom of the car. Forest to the left, field to the right, the river could not be seen from where he was, but Fedor easily discerned the forest on its opposite bank.

Without thinking, Fedor threw a glance there and immediately turned away. For a brief moment, he thought that he saw something white near the forest's edge—a little white spot. He didn't dare to look there again. He wanted just one thing—to finish it as soon as he could. He didn't understand at all why he was going there. He didn't care about his stuff or Jack. As he approached the river, his usual, normal, everyday human qualities and feelings—economy, shame, obligation, honesty—all of them just disappeared, dissolved, and gave way to the wave of familiar dark, blind, reckless horror which started to seize him again. He froze and stood still. There was nothing left in his soul, save great terror.

He had to leave! *Turn around immediately and leave!* Betrayal or no betrayal—he didn't care anymore. If only he could leave! *Leave! At once! Now! While you still can.* The thing was that he wasn't able to, as though he crossed an unseen line of an enchanted circle and could not get out of it.

The gravel road ended. Fedor turned right, down to the river. The road was dry, and the car slowly drove on the rough ground. It was the bank of the river. Further. Further. *Here is the camp.*

Seeing the tent, Fedor came to his senses. The feeling of fear and hopeless, sucking, deadly anxiety inside him grew, but now he could at least think and act on his own. He spoke aloud, hoping that the sound of his words would calm his fears. "Hmm. Where are the neighbors? There were other tents nearby and cars. Where have they gone?"

There was nobody on the bank. His tent was the only one. Not a soul around, not a living soul. Fedor looked around, and everything seemed ominous. Unruffled ribbon of the river, motionless sun in the sky, still, thick, and hot air—no wind at all. Dead silence around, haunted silence. Even the birds seemed to stop singing.

He got out of the car and looked at the tent. The thought that he would have to bother with it and stay here was absolutely unbearable. "Damn it! Let it go to hell!" He just wanted to leave as soon as he could.

Fedor knew exactly what he would do. He was taken by a feverish, furious haste and a wish to act. Now he would go down to the river bank, just for a moment, to clear his conscience, to make sure that there was no Jack on the opposite bank, then he would jump back into the car and leave for Moscow at once. At once! He would do it now and would not stop anywhere. He didn't care about the boat, the tent or other stuff. He had completely forgotten about all that. "Damn it! What about the boat?" *Away! Off! Now, at once!*

In the gleam of the afternoon sun, the opposite bank could be clearly seen from the spot where Fedor stood, and he didn't need to go down, but, somehow, he knew that he had to. Hastily, he went down to the water, slipping and tripping; the boat was where he left it, no one had taken it. He lifted his eyes and stood still.

On the opposite bank stood Jack. He silently watched Fedor, he didn't bark nor whine at his master's appearance, but just stood there patiently and looked as if he had appeared out of nowhere.

Fedor also looked quietly at the dog; the longer he did that, the more uncomfortable he felt. The stillness of the dog was unnatural. His stare seemed to be strangely conscious, as if Fedor was watched not by a dog, not by his favorite, beloved Jack, but by something completely different.

And that something chilled Fedor to the bone. He recognized that look—the empty and lifeless look of the ghoul, sitting immovably on an empty grave.

Fedor edged backwards. Jack was still watching him, not moving at all. Fedor continued backing until he suddenly bumped into the car. He couldn't even remember how he had ascended the hill, going backwards without falling down or tripping. Feeling the car behind him, Fedor continued looking at the creature on the opposite bank, slowly groped the door handle, opened it and bit by bit got inside.

It seemed that if for a moment he should lose the creature from sight, it would immediately re-appear near him. The thought filled him with unbearable horror.

Finding himself in the car, Fedor slammed the door and locked it, grabbed the wheel and pushed the accelerator. The car dashed on the uneven road, jumping on the bumps and constantly banging the ground with the bottom and bumper. But Fedor didn't notice it. He didn't notice anything.

Quick! Quick!! Out of here! He couldn't stand the sight of still black figure on the bank. Fedor suddenly realized that he couldn't call it "Jack," even to himself. It was not Jack. It was something completely alien. With brakes squealing, the car entered the highway and fled to Moscow, going faster and faster—75 miles per hour; 85; 100.

On a bridge, Fedor thought that he saw Jack suddenly appear front of the car and jump straight at the windshield. Frantically, Fedor turned the wheel. The speeding car crashed through the steel guardrail and fell down to the water from the height of some fifty feet.

***

When Fedor's body was dragged out of the water, one of the idling police officers who watched the perimeter, suddenly spotted strange wounds on the corpse's neck.

"Well. Those things look like marks from teeth." he said to his fellow policeman. Then he heard a noise and lifted up his eyes.

On the opposite bank of the river stood a huge black Great Dane looking at the motionless dead body lying on the ground. Noticing that it was being watched, the dog suddenly grinned and then growled loudly.

The policeman reflexively glanced at the monstrous fangs and then looked again at the wounds on the dead driver's neck. Then he looked at the now widely grinning jaws of the dog, now looking more attentively. For some reason, the officer felt weird. He looked again at the corpse, at the dog, then at the corpse again; suddenly, unexpectedly for him, he crossed himself.

When he looked up again, the dog on the other bank had vanished.

BEGINNING

1

Viktor stretched, yawned and turned off the computer. Then he looked at the clock and screwed up his face, annoyed. "Shoot! It's 2 a.m. already. I wanted to get to bed earlier. I won't have enough sleep again."

He moved away from the table, trying not to wake up his wife, who was sleeping in the adjacent room, and went cautiously into the kitchen. He opened the fridge, took out kefir and poured it into the cup on the table, filling it only half full. Viktor shook the empty paper bag, threw it into the dust-bin and opened the fridge to get another one. Having drunk the kefir—he used to have a cup of it every night—he quickly washed the cup and went into the bathroom to wash up. He didn't have enough time to return to sleep. He had to be at work at 9 a.m. on this day, promptly—they insisted—on time. In fact, Viktor was a programmer, and he usually worked at home, but he had to be at the office today! Sometimes, such unfortunate days did happen on occasion.

Viktor washed in a hurry, brushed his teeth, glanced at himself in the mirror and looked longingly at his bed. *Sleep, sleep, sleep!* How long did he have? *Six hours?* "It's okay." He said aloud. "Tomorrow I will go to bed earlier. Yesterday, I wanted to go to bed earlier as well. Damn it!"

Quickly, he returned to his study that was adjacent to the bedroom and clicked the light switch. The lights went out, and, at that moment, Viktor suddenly heard a faint noise behind him. He startled and stood still. Everything was quiet. Viktor lingered for several moments, listening, then turned on the lights again, turned around with an unpleasant feeling of slight fear, looked into the hallway—nobody was there, of course—and, calming down, approached the desk. There was a videophone on the table, near the computer. One camera was built-into the door instead of a peephole; a second camera was mounted above the door.

Viktor touched the screen, and it turned on. Within a couple of moments, an image appeared. There was someone in front of the door! It was so unexpected that Viktor almost jumped up from the sudden burst of fear.

"It's 2 a.m.; who could that be? What's he doing here?" Still, there was nobody ringing the doorbell. Coming to his senses, Viktor looked at the screen closely. The man in front of the door was unfamiliar to him.

The figure was a grim-looking old man with a sharp, unpleasant face and repulsive, sick-looking, unnaturally plump lips. The picture from the camera was black-and-white and not of a very good quality. The man's face was a bit twisted and so seemed even more ominous—malicious. Something in it made Viktor anxious, but he could not understand what exactly.

The eyes! he thought suddenly. *Oh, my God! His eyes are closed; he's standing with closed eyes.* Viktor froze and looked at the face of the man without eyes, and the more he looked at it, the more uncomfortable he felt. "Who IS that, anyway? Sleepwalker? Lunatic?" He muttered. aloud. "And just what is he doing near my apartment at this hour?"

Viktor realized that he was asking himself those reasonable questions in order to calm down, to explain everything, to get everything in logical and sensible order. As a matter of fact, he was anxious and scared because of the complete senselessness and algorism of the situation, of slight but obvious sense of ominous mysteriousness and mysticism in all that. Viktor had never believed in any kind of mysticism, and he had always been a reasonable and sensible person, but that, as it appeared, didn't change a thing. He was looking at that motionless, frozen face with closed eyes and felt the fear taking him. The fear, though, was without cause and so was even more frightening. voila

The door was safely closed. The strange old man didn't do anything wrong—he was just standing quietly—but Viktor kept looking at him and felt his fear grow. As if in a dream, he stretched out his hand and switched on the sound. He was shocked. The room was suddenly filled with a mournful, monotonous muttering coming from the loudspeaker. It was impossible to discern anything, but, nevertheless, Viktor thought that the muttering was not Russian. Amazed and confused, he looked at the old man's big mouth and saw that his lips—their sight was somehow repulsive—were, in fact, moving. There were no doubts; the old man was actually muttering something. That was a kind of a prayer or a spell.

Oh, God! What spell? Viktor thought wildly. *What crap is in my head?* Unaware, he hastily turned off the loudspeaker and switched cameras. From above, he could see the empty, illuminated hall, empty, that is, except for unmoving figure standing in front of his door. As a matter of fact, the figure was standing, not close to the door, but two or three steps away.

The man was clad in ridiculous white overalls. It seemed that he had nothing underneath. The overalls reached to his knees, and the man was bare-footed.

Viktor looked at the man's bare feet in wonder for some time. *What's that on him? Night-gown or what*? he thought. "I've got it!" He said aloud, snapping his fingers. "A sleepwalker woke up and came here. Tomorrow he won't even remember where he's been."

Suddenly, Viktor wished that it were true right now. He wished to see the anxious relatives who would take this strange, monstrous old man home. And Viktor would give a sigh of relief, laugh at his fears and go to bed. But, unconsciously, he already understood that nothing of that would happen. There would be no relatives. There would be no one; somehow Viktor was quite sure about that.

The old man didn't seem like a sleepwalker at all. He seemed an incarnation of something obviously evil, perilous, and strong, and he started to fill Viktor with superstitious horrors. It became more and more difficult for Viktor to look at him.

Suddenly, he thought that the old man might lift his head, stare at the camera with his unseeing eyes and somehow feel Viktor, find out about his presence. This thought scared Viktor, and he quickly stretched his hand and turned off the monitor. For some time, he sat staring at the dead monitor, not knowing what to do. Then, uncertainly, he reached to the monitor and stopped. He wanted to turn it on but didn't dare to do so at the same time. The wish to turn it on was almost unbearable, but the fear was stronger. He started with disgust and fear at the thought that he would see again that horrifying eyeless face with large, moving, plump, smacking lips.

"What's going on with me?" he tried to shout at himself. "Am I out of my mind? Well, there's a madman with closed eyes in the hall, and he's muttering something; let him stand there. Why should I care? The door is closed. Maybe I should call the police, tell them that there's someone in front of my door. Maybe he's a thief."

Viktor had never in his life called the police. "What's the number—02? What then? Wait for half an hour till they arrive? Then open the door in the middle of the night, explain everything? All of the neighbors will wake up. Should I wake up Masha? What if the old man should leave before they arrive? What then?"

Cautiously, trying to make no sound, Viktor sat in a chair and was still. He was fighting a strong urge to turn on the monitor and see what was going on in the hall and, at the same time, listened keenly and attentively. *Are there any movements, scrambles or rustles near the door? Are there any noises*?

However, everything was quiet—unnaturally quiet. The silence was deadly. Even the usual sound of the cars outside could not be heard. It suddenly seemed to Viktor that he was left completely alone in the whole world. There was no Masha, no neighbors, no police—nobody at all. All of them were sleeping tight and would not help, whatever happened to him. All of them had remained in another alive, normal world. The world from which he had fallen out, and every minute took him further and further away from it.

Viktor was seized by unnatural, wild horrors and a reckless, insane wish to save himself, do anything while he still could, while it was not late! He startled and turned the monitor on. It slowly lit up. The hall was empty!

Viktor didn't fully realize what had happened but felt an inexpressible, unspeakable relief inside. He quickly tapped the button to switch cameras. Nobody. There was really nobody in the hall. The old man had disappeared without a trace.

Viktor sat for some time in the chair in front of the empty monitor, trying to calm down and come to his senses. His hands were shaking. His head was burning, and the forehead was sweating. He was completely broken and devastated, but, at the same time, he had a feeling that he had miraculously escaped from great danger. He sat for some time, then stood up, turned off the intercom, set his watch at 8 a.m.—damn, no time for sleep!—and, taking the watch with him, went to the bedroom with his legs like lead. With difficulty, he took off his clothes and carefully lay on the side of the bed. Masha sighed in her sleep and turned over.

He fell asleep at once and had a nightmare. In it, he saw his mother, long deceased. Viktor had loved and respected her. She had been a woman of great kindness and humbleness; she had never complained about anything and had never lost her heart. She'd been a real saint. He had never seen her in his dreams before, and he was very glad when she appeared.

But what is this? What's with her? Enough! That's her? Why is she drunk and disheveled? Why is she looking at me that way and smiling so lustfully and suggestively? Where is she beckoning me; what do these shameless gestures mean? Why is she lifting her dress and spreading her legs lazily, as if unwillingly? Is she really trying to seduce me, to force me to coitus? Incest? Her own son? Just listen to her vulgar laugh and look at her red, sweaty, greasy face.

1.1

Viktor woke up abruptly and then lay for a while on his back with eyes open, staring at the ceiling. He felt as if a hideous blain had exploded in his soul and had filled everything with stinky and sticky pus—everything, even the most sacred and pure. Anyway, it was already clear morning. Viktor reluctantly looked at the clock. It was almost 8, and he had to get up. Quietly, he got out of bed, turned off the alarm clock with a quiet move—he didn't want to wake up Masha—gathered his clothes, slowly left the room and silently closed the door.

He put the clothes on the chair nearby and approached the desk. He hesitated for a second and then turned on the videophone. No one! There was no one in the hall. He switched the camera, though that was not necessary, and, having assured himself that no one could be seen from above either, he left the videophone, grabbed the clothes from the chair and went to the bathroom. Passing the front door, he felt a little prick of fear—a very faint one, but still fear..

Having washed up and breakfasted, Viktor once again gave a look at the hall on the monitor and, only after that, resolved to open the front door.

The residents of block were already up. The noise of the elevator, someone's muttering on the floor above him, voices—all of that was so familiar and usual that all events of the last night seemed for a moment like nonsense. But only for a moment! Viktor knew for himself that it wasn't nonsense. And then the horrible dream—something terrifying was happening. And somehow he felt that it hadn't finished yet.

***

At work, Viktor tried to distract himself and even tried to write a new program—high time! But his fingers were all thumbs. He was sleepy, felt crushed and out of place, and couldn't think at all. Events of the previous night sat firmly in his head. And the dream. Altogether, he was bewildered and dreary. How could he think about any programs? He trudged for an hour and then understood that it was all useless. He wouldn't be able to write anything today. He would only lose time and torture himself. He could see no sense in it. Tomorrow, it would take him an hour to do stuff that needed much more time today. He knew that from his experience. Damn! The most wretched feeling, as if he had a hangover. It was impossible to do anything. All he was left to do was to hang around. Maybe he could beg off and go home. And what would he do at home? Fight with his wife? However, he could have some sleep at home.

Viktor talked to the boss and explained everything. As Viktor was an irreplaceable specialist and a real work addict—he could stay at work for days if necessary—the relationships with management was great, and it was easy for him to beg off. For what it's worth, he had enough overtime leave. In brief, within half an hour, he was already at home. Masha was still sleeping. Viktor slowly took off his clothes and carefully, trying not to wake her up, got under the blanket.

This time, he didn't go to sleep at once. He tossed and turned, but, at the end, the weariness won. He slept soundly and didn't have any dreams.

***

When Viktor opened his eyes, the clock read 7:00. He couldn't understand—was it morning or evening? And, at first, he wondered where Masha was. But then the events of the previous night came crashing back to him, and he felt a dragging, blunt anxiety, and the fear of the previous day moved in his soul again. Soon it will be getting dark again. *What of the old man? No, it's better not to think about it.*

"I'm going to get up, have a shower, wash up, have breakfast—or supper?—and here I go. I'm going to watch TV and relax—an action movie, the stupider, the better. Where does Masha keep the TV guide? Okay, I'm going to find it later. First, I'm going to eat something." He needed to hear someone's voice even if it was his own.

Viktor got up, put on his slippers and, yawning, went to the bathroom. The way to it lay past the front door. Suddenly, Viktor wished greatly to go back and check the monitor to see if there was anyone in the hall, but he contained himself and forced himself from it. He didn't like passing the door, though. No, "*didn't like*" wasn't the word; he was plainly scared and could do nothing about it. He was just *scared*—that's it! Passing the door, he had an uncanny feeling and tried to tiptoe when he was near it. It seemed to him that the dreadful old man was standing in front of the door again, waiting for Viktor and listening to his footsteps.

Viktor took a shower, had breakfast-supper, drank some coffee and, curiously enough, felt even worse. He was fully awake, and the night fears were awake as well. Embarrassingly, he remembered that cursed dream; it was clear in his mind, in graphic detail. He felt sick. As a matter of fact, he had nothing to do in the kitchen, but, nevertheless, he washed the dishes for some time, wiped them, sorted the stuff in the fridge, and then washed his hands elaborately. Candidly still frightened, he bided his time, being unable to confess his fear, even to himself. He didn't want to go past the front door at all. He was wondering how he had done it so easily before. At last, it became impossible to linger. He had to make a decision.

Viktor tried to work himself up for a long time; he would decisively approach the door, then he would stop and come back to the kitchen. He was fighting himself and was trying to overcome, to conquer himself and his fear. But it was all useless. The worst part was that, with every unsuccessful attempt, his fear became stronger. Stronger, stronger, stronger—and, at last, it filled all his soul like the night before.

Now, he didn't even think about passing the door. The fear pushed away even the shame, and Viktor wasn't ashamed of his condition as he had been earlier. He just didn't care. He was anxious about one thing: how could he go past the door? He had to do it, because the growing fear was followed with a very strong wish to turn on the videophone and see what was going on in the hall. Was the old man in the hall?

All sensible and logical reasoning—it was too early, there was too many people in the block, nothing would happen till midnight—had no effect on him. He felt an irresistible desire to see everything himself, with his own eyes, and to make sure. He felt that it would help to calm him down a bit. In fact, he clearly saw that everything was falling down into an abyss. Not in the least was he able to control himself or the situation. The events were evolving all by themselves, independently from him. He couldn't influence them. As a matter of fact, he could only wait to see what would happen next, as if a merciless, strong hand grabbed him by the collar and dragged him away relentlessly; and he didn't even try to resist. He had just shivered a bit—that's all. All of that flashed in his head and instantly disappeared without a trace.

So I am just a weakling and nobody, Viktor thought with indifferent wonder and forgot about all that. It was not interesting for him anymore. Honor, shame. He just wanted to go past the door and turn on the monitor as soon as possible. Everything else was of no concern to him.

At last, he closed his eyes very tightly, held his breath and ran off like a guilty boy; he covered two yards, tripping in the end and nearly bumping again into the opposite wall. Dodging aside, he dashed to the intercom and turned it on with fingers that were shaking from the tension. The monitor showed the image of the empty hall. Viktor immediately pushed the button to switch cameras. Empty! Of course, there was no one.

"Who did you expect to see at 8 in the morning?" he said aloud, trying to calm down, and immediately grimaced with disgust. "You've already understood what you are, and you're still doing the same! What are you trying to make of you?" he told himself angrily. The memory brought him the dream of the previous night, and it became unbearable.

Well, high time to hang on! Find yourself at the end of the rope, do you? His thoughts tore through his frantic mind. *Uh-oh! Damn! What's the time? Last I checked, was it seven?*

Finding that it was already nine, Viktor felt even worse, though it seemed that it couldn't have gotten worse. He was scared. He was horrified, frightened to death. He was petrified that the yesterday's uninvited guest would appear again today. He was terrified and waited for him at the same time. He waited with a sick impatience. If he didn't come, Viktor would be even more disappointed. The anticipation was too strong.

Someone appeared on the camera screen. Viktor jumped up, but quickly got it together. It was just his wife. To his astonishment, he had completely forgotten about her with all the events. Now, seeing her on the screen, he sighed with relief and even calmed down for some time and cheered up. So everything was quiet, and there was nobody in the block or the hall. Maybe he's scaring himself in vain. *Well, an old man wandered in here. So what? He could be doing anything here, right? There are a lot of jerks out there. Right! And he was standing here all night, muttering something with closed eyes, bare-footed and in night-gown—wandered in.*

The door slammed and the lock clicked.

"Oh. You're at home," said Masha uncertainly, entering the room and seeing Viktor squirm in the chair. "Hi," she added carelessly, going to the bedroom.

Viktor hurried to turn on a computer for her to see, as if he had been working all along. He didn't want her to ask why he'd been sitting at the empty desk with intercom turned on.

Meanwhile, Masha got changed and went to the bathroom. Viktor could hear her turn on the water and close the door. The sound of the pouring water became more muted. He just sat without thinking, waggling in a cozy chair, glancing at the monitor from time to time and idly listening to his wife's sounds. She turned off the water, left the bathroom and went to the kitchen. Then the fridge door slammed. It seemed that Masha was going to have a supper.

1.2

As a matter of fact, the relationship between Viktor and his wife was complicated, especially in recent days. They had gotten married long ago—about ten years ago, when he was still in the institute. He had never been in love with his wife, but he did like Masha. At any rate, he didn't want to change anything in his life, and the problems that had recently appeared in his family were bothering him seriously. Actually, the main problem was that they didn't have any children. At first, they didn't think about children, with all the studying and working; but when they decided to have a child, they suddenly found out that Masha wasn't able to have a baby.

Rather, doctors said that it was very dangerous. She was diagnosed with some gynecological diseases. When Masha found it out, she was not herself. She came home, and she discussed that with Viktor for a long time. They were thinking about what to do and considering all the pros and cons. Masha was hesitating, and, as Victor understood later, she just wanted to be persuaded and to feel his support. Instead of that, he started to convince her to wait, to try some treatments, to consult other doctors—altogether, not to hurry and panic.

"What's the point? You're young,"—they both were 26 at the time—"you've still got time. We'd better wait a year or two, see what happens, take some treatment, and if nothing happens, if nothing improves, then we'll see. I want to do it, and you know it, but the doctor says that it's dangerous for you. I just care about you."

Truth be told, first and foremost, Viktor cared about himself, and he knew it deep inside. He didn't want to have children. The very thought of an infant in his apartment filled him with panic and horror. All the diapers, endless laundry, cries. In one word, all the normal life that he valued would go out of the window —moreover, it would be for many, many years. That thought was horrible!

And he would have to look after the baby, as well. His mother-in-law would be coming and going, trying to help. (Viktor's mother had died by that time.) No way! Crazy. Crazy. Well, that's the end of life. What about all his plans and dreams? No, no, he didn't want that! Not now. Later, sometime later—one day. Just not now—and then we'll see. Viktor was a quiet, homelike person. He loved his job, he loved to deal with software, to work on the computer, and everything was well in his life. He didn't want to change anything.

Deep inside, he realized that his attitude was very selfish and that Masha, like any other woman, needed a baby; such was her nature, an instinct. She was already very unhappy, she just didn't see that and didn't understand the true reasons for her problems. And he was using that, just because it was fine with him. He could see everything—her constant changes of mood and irritation. Nevertheless, he was acting as if nothing was going on, he was denying the problem, hoping that everything will be fine but later, when some time has passed it would go away. Sure, they must have a baby, but not now. Later. Later. In a year or two. Or three. Why hurry? They still had time. Many people have babies at the age of forty. That's not a problem.

However, it became clear that they didn't have time. A year later, in spite of all expectations, Masha got worse, and she had to have surgery—not a serious one, but she couldn't have children after that.

From that time on, their family relationships began to worsen quickly. Masha retreated into herself and started drinking. She had been drinking before that and sometimes very often, but not every day, until recently. And now she started drinking every single day. She answered all Viktor's questions unwillingly and briefly.

"What am I supposed to do?"

"Well, do something! Read a book. Watch TV."

"Am I supposed to watch TV all day?"

"Maybe you should find a job. You'll be communicating with people."

"What job? What can I do?"

"I could find a job for you in our company."

"No."

"Why do you drink so much?"

"It's not that much."

"Not much? Yesterday, you were drinking vodka, the day before yesterday, today. The day before yesterday, there were two bottles of vodka in the fridge, and now they're gone."

"Are you spying on me? Are you tracking how many glasses I have each day?"

"What are you talking about, tracking? I care about you, about your health."

"Yeah, I know."

They were having this type of conversations almost every day. Afterwards, Viktor had a strong feeling of complete helplessness and inability to do anything. He was afraid that Masha would simply go on a binge, but, at the same time, he didn't know what to do and how he should talk to her. It's easy to say, "Don't drink!" What was she supposed to do? What could he offer her instead? Watching TV? Embroidering? Handicraft? If only she had a baby. Damned be embroidering and handicraft. Hell! His life was crashing in front of his eyes.

Masha started to spend evenings away from home, and she made some strange friends and acquaintances, some Natasha's and Veronika's with whom she would talk on the phone for hours. She didn't talk to Viktor much. It seemed as if she was avoiding him. She used to get up at 12, when he was already not at home, then she went somewhere and came back at 9 or 10 in the evening.

"Have you been drinking again?"

"So what?"

It was an endless circle. He understood very clearly that by talking with his wife about drinking, reproaching her, and lecturing her, he was only making things worse, annoying her, and becoming irksome and unpleasant. But what could he do? Stop talking to her? Let her drink? And where is she in the evenings? At her friends'? Who are they, anyway? Don't they have any other business? And what are they doing there? Drinking together? He hoped they were married; did they have husbands? These and other questions were on the tip of Viktor's tongue, but he didn't dare ask Masha. He tried once and that was enough for him. He couldn't forget the argument that had happened back then.

***

"Don't meddle with my private life! Am I not allowed to have friends? Am I supposed to stay at home whole day? As if in prison? I'm not slave Isaura!

"What Isaura? That's bullshit! And what do you mean by private life? You're my wife!"

"For you, everything I say is bullshit."

"Not everything."

"No, everything! Everything I say is bullshit. And everything you say is not bullshit."

"But I'm talking business right now!"

"Right. Everything you say is business, and everything I say is bullshit!"

"Listen, let's have a calm talk. I just want to know about your friends with whom you spend all evenings."

"Well, I'm calm, anyway. You're the one who's yelling. You promised you would never raise your voice at me."

"I'm not yelling!"

"But you are."

Calm down, calm down. "Okay, I'm sorry. Maybe I did raise my voice. It's all because of the worry."

"See, you understand that you're wrong! I'm always telling you the right things. Why is it that I never yell at you, and you do?"

"I'm not yelling! We're not talking about that!"

"You're raising your voice again."

And so on.

So, in the end, Masha wouldn't talk to him for three whole days, and he had to ask her to forgive him. Eventually, he didn't find out what she wanted. As a result, everything just got worse. From that day on, Masha ceased to be soft on him and considerate for him. He felt much more like a husband who actually wasn't really one.

But he didn't dare to ask her anything and dwell on that topic. He was very afraid that, one day, Masha would leave him, and he would be alone. Solitude scared him. He spent all his time at work, he didn't go out, and he didn't know how to get acquainted with women. Where would he find a woman? How? Should he place an ad in a newspaper? And a man can't live without a woman, even such a man as him. It's unnatural. And he's too young—Viktor was 29. No, no! Let it be as it may. Things can probably get better. Everything's going to be okay.

One day, Masha came home very drunk. She had a fit of hysterics. She was crying and shouting that he had destroyed her life, that he was selfish and thought just about himself, that he had never wanted to have children, that she should have had a child and shouldn't have listened to him, and so on.

That scene had a large impression on Viktor. Moreover, he realized very well that many of those reproaches were true. Well, if only back then. If only he could redo everything. He didn't become Newton, and he failed to have a good family. If only he had had a baby, his life would have been completely different. Masha would have been different as well, and he would, too. Heh, no sense talking about it!

I.3

The phone rang loudly. Viktor heard Masha answer, say something quietly, and close the door. *Who is she whispering with?* he thought with the usual irritation. In such cases, he didn't use to feel jealous, but was anxious that his wife had her own life—secret to him—her own friends, and that she didn't need him anymore.

Anyway, he didn't care about that at the moment. When Masha came, his fears became weaker but still didn't go away. Viktor became sure of it when he saw someone for a moment on the screen. He immediately caught his breath, and his heart nearly leapt from the chest.

But it was just his neighbor from the opposite apartment. Relieved, Viktor watched him ringing the doorbell, saying something—it seemed it was, "It's me!"—the door opening and him going inside. The door closed. The hall was empty again. Viktor took a breath with an effort, leaned back in the chair and caught glimpse of Masha sneaking into the bedroom and closing the door. The carpet reliably muffled all noises, and he didn't hear her footsteps.

"Has she finished her supper and talked on the phone? Too quickly," Viktor wondered. He thought that she was drunk again. He waited for her to turn on the TV loudly, as usual, and winced with annoyance, but no sound came from the bedroom. Viktor listened, and his curiosity became stronger. The switch clicked. The lights in the bedroom went out.

"Has she gone to bed? At," Viktor checked the time, "11? What's with her today?" Masha never went to bed until 1 or 2 a.m. Very often it was even later. And 11?

"It's 11 already; midnight is close," flashed in his head, and he immediately forgot about Masha and everything else in the world. He somehow thought that if the cursed old man appeared straight at midnight, it would be a kind of proof. "Of what?" he asked himself at once with grim irony. "That it's an evil spirit? Devilry?"

Nevertheless, he grabbed that thought firmly. Viktor had an analytical, mathematical attitude of mind. Because of his profession, he was used to thinking systematically and consistently. He never believed in wonders and used to look for simple, sensible, and logical explanations. Moreover, he strongly believed that it was always possible to find such an explanation. In any case, he had strongly believed in that.

Until now.

He didn't believe anything and wasn't sure of anything after last night. All his beliefs crumbled into dust in the face of something supernatural and under the powerful rush of primal fear that had filled him the day before. All his beliefs turned to ashes. The first faint breath of the old, dark, and long-forgotten horror took all the veneer of civilization away, and he turned into a wild man who was waiting for a demon in awe. However, he was a wild man from the 21st century and that's why he tried to find a system in the demon's actions, a pattern which, maybe, would help to fight him. "Hide! Save yourself! Survive!"

"What exactly was supernatural?" Viktor thought aloud with despair. "Yes, I agree; it's all strange, no doubt, but what's supernatural in it? There was nothing supernatural in it. Why is it bothering me so much? Why is it so scary?"

Suddenly, it came to him that Masha hadn't fastened all the locks; she had closed only the latch. She just slammed the door and that was it. And what could the latch do? One would just push the door, and that was it.

Not giving a second thought, Viktor jumped up, dashed to the door, clanked with the keys and latches, then dashed headlong to the monitor and fell in his chair without any strength left. He was sweating, breathing heavily; his heart was pounding, and his hands were shaking. He didn't understand how he could do such a feat. He would never repeat it, not for the entire world.

Anyway, it was the last burst of activity from him. He didn't leave the chair. He sat in it, leaning forward and clutching his elbows. Now he would look at the screen, now at the clock. He didn't feel the slightest yearning, impatience or weariness. He could actually feel the slow flow of the time, and felt the seconds and minutes flow through him. He followed every one of them with a glance.

11:30. 11:31. 11:32. 11:33. 11:34. 11:35. 11:36. 11.37....

***

Viktor woke up and lifted his head. For a couple of moments, he looked blankly and confusedly around him—the chair, the screen, the clock—and then he remembered everything. Oh, God! Did he fall asleep? With his heart in his throat, Viktor glanced at the screen.

The old man was already standing there on his usual spot. His eyes were still closed, and his lips were silently moving, like the day before. With a stiff hand, Viktor switched the camera. An image from the above was not so scary .Suddenly his terror became so strong that he caught his breath and almost choked. The old man was closer! The distance between him and the door shrank. The day before, he had been standing almost in the middle of the hall, and now....

"Jesus, what does he want, after all? Why is it happening to me? Why?" For the first time in his life, Viktor felt a strong wish to pray, to utter the words directed straight to God, to seek protection from Him. He didn't know any prayers, but it seemed that the words were born in his heart, and he fiercely whispered them with great hope.

"Lord! Let him disappear! I believe now in You, Lord, and always will! I will pray, keep all the fastings, and do everything—but let him disappear! Right now! Save me, Lord! Save me, I beg You!"

"Let His enemies be scattered!" suddenly a difficult-to-understand quote—probably from the Bible—appeared in his head, and he repeated it loudly and profusely several times. "Let His enemies be scattered! Let His enemies be scattered! Let His enemies be scattered!"

Viktor saw that the old man started to lift his head—slowly, very slowly, as if in a slow motion or a nightmare. As if he heard Viktor and mysteriously smelled him, and now he was looking for him, trying to find him, to spot him, turning his still, motionless face of the corpse who had risen from the coffin towards him.

"That's it! A living corpse!" Viktor understood now what the old man looked like and why he was so scary. And those strange clothes—that absurd white long shirt to the knees. Maybe it's a shroud? Viktor felt his hair move. In one moment, his heart would burst, and he would die from fear. The words died on his lips. Frozen, with his mouth open, he stared at the screen with crazed look.

The old man's head stopped moving. A short pause, and he slowly lowered it and again stood still.

Viktor took his breath and sighed with a hysterical, convulsive sob. He didn't even think about saying or whispering anything. As if stiffened, he stared at the screen without thinking. Dark, cold, and hideous horror filled him completely.

Suddenly, the old man began to seem like a gigantic scary spider who was slowly and deliberately weaving its unseen, invisible-to-plain-eyes web with which he gradually covered Viktor. And he wouldn't be able to get out of it.

There was a noise behind. Viktor startled and turned around. When he looked at the screen again, there was nobody in the hall. The old man-spider had disappeared.

Freaked out, Viktor stared at the empty screen for some time, then he turned off the intercom by rote, slowly stood up and shuffled to the bedroom with a shambling, languorous gait. He felt sick and crushed. Taking off his clothes with difficulty, he lay on the bed and immediately went asleep.

He had a nightmare again. The whole world was covered by a grey, sticky web in which he struggled but only tangled more and more. He didn't see the spider itself, but he felt that it was near at hand and that it was crawling closer and closer to him with every second. The threads of the web trembled.

Viktor screamed and woke up.

I.4

He was wet. Masha wasn't there. The clock read half past four. Out of habit, Viktor called the office to say that he wouldn't show today. The boss grumbled something and hung up. Under other circumstances, Viktor would have a lot of emotions because of that, but now he forgot about it in a moment. He lay down again and started thinking. What was he supposed to do? He recalled all the events of the evening and night. His growing fear, then Masha came, then he waited till midnight, and then...

The further memories were painful; he just wanted to forget everything, to calm down, to wash everything out—be what may!—

to convince himself that nothing special had happened, at least for the time being, for the couple of hours that were left till evening. He knew that in the evening, when darkness came, the fear would return, but he made himself not give way to this dangerous and deadly—he was sure of that—mood.

"I have to fight! I have to fight!" he was repeating in despair. "Think! Think!" He still had time. It was not dark yet. He was capable of thinking more or less calmly. As soon as it started getting dark—he knew that very well—he wouldn't be able to. Fear would drive away all thoughts. He would stick tight to the screen and stare, stare, and stare. Like a zombie.

The thought of zombies stirred all the night fears and memories. *The old man. Zombie! That's what he had looked like—a character from the horror movie, the living dead. And what? Why not? Maybe they do exist—who knows?*

Okay, fine! Suppose it's a zombie. It's nonsense, of course, but suppose. So what—do I know how to fight zombies? From where did he come to the center of the city, this zombie? What the heck does he want from me? Eat me? Why me? Why did he cling to me in the first place? Where did he come from? voila

Viktor felt that his thoughts were going in circles, and he was simply losing time with those senseless speculations. He was losing precious hours that were left until evening. He tried to concentrate. "Okay, what have we got? An ominously looking old man." Viktor remembered the face that looked like a wax mask, closed eyes, large moving smacking lips, and he shuddered. "Some old man hangs out near my door for two nights in a row. Bare-footed, with eyes closed, in just a nightgown. And he's whispering something. Well.... So what? What? Let him whisper, if he wants to. Let him whisper. Like I care? Why is it bothering me so much?" Viktor remembered the old man, his motionless figure in white robe, freezing in the hall under the daylight fluorescent lamp, which could be clearly seen from the above camera, and he swallowed convulsively.

"No, that won't do! Logical explanations and reasoning are inappropriate and useless. I'm considering the problem from the wrong side. These are the facts. There's a strange old man, and this old man chills me to the bone, he scares me to death! Here's the dry fact. Why? It doesn't matter. That's not important. The thing is that he scares me."

"Now, what am I supposed to do in this situation? To be precise, can I do anything? I do want to do something. I may be a jerk, a fool, a panic-monger, and hysterical, and it all may be nonsense and superstition, but I'm scared! I'm scared, and that's it. I don't want to leave it unattended. If it's possible to do something, I'll do it. Anything stupid. I'll sprinkle everything with holy water, put garlic above the door—anything! But what exactly? What?" Viktor felt that he was starting to panic and that the wave of the past horror was covering him again, and he was quickly losing the ability to think reasonably. He tried to calm down.

"So, anyway, what? Well, holy water. I don't have any holy water. Nothing—at all. Next? Although, stop. I could go to the church and get some. Okay, I'll remember that. Garlic. No, wait, wait. Maybe I should move from here for some time, at least, for one night. How would I spend the night here tonight?"

This unexpected thought took Viktor and struck him with its simplicity; he immediately threw back the blanket and quickly sat on the bed. "Right! I have to go while it's not too late—get the hell out of here. Where will I sleep? Well, it's not important. At the train station. Who cares?" Viktor imagined a station, lights, instant hustle, crowds of people all day and all night long and almost laughed with joy.

"Right! Will do. I'll leave at once. Why should I lose time?" he muttered frantically, putting on jeans, being unable to hit the trouser leg and jumping with impatience. "I'm going to leave note for Masha. I'm going to write that I will be late at work and won't come home, not for the first time."

The thought of his wife was unpleasant—leaving her here, while she doesn't suspect anything. But he just shrugged that thought off.

"Well, nothing's going to happen to her," Viktor was buttoning the shirt quickly. "At least, I could wait near the entrance, warn her. I just have to leave the flat as soon as possible!"

His fingers were jumping, and little naughty buttons didn't want to fit. Finally, he left them.—"I'll button the rest outside!"—and almost ran to the front door. There he stopped short.

As soon as he saw the hallway, he realized that he wouldn't be able to leave the flat. He just couldn't! He didn't dare to open the door or even touch it, even under penalty of death. The thrill of joy that had filled him immediately vanished, giving way to deep depression. He realized that he was in a trap. For a brief moment, he even thought he saw the cold, dull shine of the thin light threads on the front door—the deadly shine of the web. From that moment on, the will to fight left Viktor completely. He started to wait for the evening, having no strength left. He didn't even try to think about anything, to consider or to make plans. He didn't try to fight at all. He felt as if he was a fly which was trapped in a web and was left to wait until the spider got hungry and decide to eat it, to drink its blood.

By the way, about drinking—Masha had to have some cognac hidden somewhere.

Viktor delved into the wardrobe and found an almost full bottle of cognac in the far end. "French. How could she afford it?" he thought in passing, pulling the cork and making several big gulps out of the neck of the bottle. Actually, he didn't like drinking, as he always had a headache in the morning after it, but now that wasn't important at all.

"Morning," he smiled grimly to himself. "First, I need to see the morning. What's going to happen to me in the morning? Maybe I will have no head, and there will be no headache. The cursed old man could eat me. He'd drink my blood and rip my head off." Viktor noticed that he got slightly drunk. He used to get drunk very quickly. "All the better," he took a couple more gulps. "I should get drunk, fall asleep and sleep until morning."

Viktor went to the next room, sat in a chair, put his feet on a table and started watching the clock hands while sipping cognac. He thought that, if he gave undivided attention to the hands, the time would go slower. Above all things, he wished that it would go on endlessly. Let the evening and night never come. And he would be sitting at the table while the clock hands barely moved.

However, time was passing quickly. It seemed as if he turned away just for a second—only to look out of the window—but 10 minutes already passed! He thought about something—half an hour more! Before Viktor knew it, evening came. The light slowly went out. There was no more cognac. "Damn! I shouldn't have drunk it. I should have kept it until night," he thought with delay.

By 8 o'clock, Viktor was completely sober, as if he hadn't been drinking at all. Though, curiously enough, he wasn't scared. He was tired of fear. He was filled with blunt apathy. He was sitting and staring at the screen, not thinking about anything. Ah, come what may.

At 10, Masha called and thickly and uncertainly told him that she wouldn't be home tonight and would stay at her friend's. After that, she hung up on him. This was something completely new. She had never before dared to stay at her friend's. However, at that moment, Viktor just didn't care at all. Somehow, from the very beginning, he was almost sure that something of that kind would eventually happen. The night before, she had gone to bed at unearthly hour, which had never happened; and today, she didn't come home at all.

It seemed that everything added up for his wife not to get in the way and meddle. Obviously, she was unwanted here today. All that was happening concerned only Viktor. He was a fly. The spider was interested only in him.

Meanwhile, it was almost midnight.

11:00. 11:10. 11:20.

"Maybe I should go to sleep again," thought Viktor indifferently. "It would be great."

11:30. 11:40. 11:50. 55, 56, 57, 58, 59.

The old man appeared right at midnight. He sprang up out of nowhere, materialized. Just a moment before, there was nobody there, and now he was standing in front of the door.

Viktor was looking at him through the monitor, almost with no worry. But that was the deadly calm of the prey silently going to the slaughter. He accepted his fate, realized that he would not save himself, and now was apathetically waiting what would happen to him next. Unlike the previous nights, he didn't even turn off the sound on the monitor. What for? What was the point? He didn't care. It seemed that he almost died.

Suddenly, the old man said a phrase in a loud, singing voice, stretched out his hand and touched the door. The next moment, his eyes opened wide, and he stared at Viktor. Viktor shrank back. When he looked at the screen again, there was nobody in the hall—nobody and nothing. Everything was ended.

Viktor didn't remember how he reached the bed. His eyes were closing, and his eyelids were like lead. He fell on the bed in his clothes and immediately went to sleep. He slept like a dog. He was sleeping tight and was smiling happily in his sleep as a man who's seeing very pleasant dreams.

1.6

The next day was Saturday—day off; no need to hurry. Waking up, Viktor lay with his eyes open for a long time and tried to remember what dreams he'd had. He vaguely recalled something simple, pleasant and nice. But exactly what it was, he couldn't remember. "A child!" suddenly came to him. He had a dream that he and Masha had a child. Right! He didn't recall all the details, but knew for sure that Masha was very happy, like him, that everything was changed and improved, as if by magic, with a wave of a wand. The child changed their life radically right away. Viktor wished he hadn't waked up. He wished that dream to go on and on, to continue over and over again.

Maybe everything's going to be okay. The devil may play any trick. Miracles can happen! To his own amazement, Viktor suddenly felt that he really almost believed in that. Believed in spite of everything. And that belief didn't go away, but became stronger with every minute. He felt a subconscious confidence that nothing was lost, that it was possible to change everything, do something, and he and Masha would be all right.

Change how? Do what? He didn't know that. Something should happen. Surely! A miracle. This would turn upside down his boring life, his grey, sad, and gloomy life. Oh! He and Masha would see more of the life. Yeah, surely! Nothing is lost.

"From under tired eyelids, a host of unsure hopes streamed at me," suddenly the sad and strange lines of some long-forgotten verse came to his mind. "What's with me today?" he thought with cheerful bewilderment. "Even verses come to my head. I'm definitely out of my mind!" He didn't want to get up. Viktor glanced at the clock lazily.

"Wow, it's already three. How long have I been sleeping?" He remembered the night and the old man, but all the memories were vague and unclear, as if half-erased; they seemed to be not important and essential and below his notice. They seemed to have nothing to do with him. It all was in the past, far, far away. There would be no continuation. Everything was ended. Ended, ended! Somehow, Viktor had no doubts about that.

The old man wouldn't come back. Ever. He had vanished, disappeared, died away. Forever, forever and ever. He sank without end into the same scary abyss from which he had appeared. Viktor couldn't even remember his face—well, a dim, blurred stain flashing from time to time behind a grey curtain and vaguely showing through a slowly swaying and trembling haze. Delusion. Mirage. Horror.

"Okay, I have to get up," Viktor stretched himself with great pleasure but didn't get up at once. He wanted to stay in bed and slug it. He felt a pleasant and nice slackness in all his body—sweet languor, bliss, contentment. Suddenly he wished that Masha was there with him. He imagined her lying there, naked, on her side. He cuddled up to her with all his body. His hands slide on her skin; they caress and stroke her and....

The front door slammed. He heard the loud voice of his wife. Viktor lay still and listened.

"Who's that with her?" he thought discontentedly.

Masha quickly entered the room. "Hi! Get up, sleepyhead! Come on, I want to show you something!" Masha was looking at her husband cheerfully.

"Come on," she added impatiently, as he stayed in the bed uncertainly and didn't move. There's someone there, and he's lying on the bed with only trunks on him.

Bewildered, Viktor stood up and followed his wife.

"He's handsome, right?" Masha was standing near the front door and was looking at her husband with shining eyes. At her side, there was a big black Great Dane. Seeing him, Viktor stood still at first, but then approached him with caution. Actually, he wasn't afraid of dogs, but that one was way too big.

"What's that, a hound of the Baskervilles?" he asked with a feigned cheerful voice, smiling frigidly. "Where did you find him?"

"Just imagine, he walked up to me on the street! I got scared at first but then saw that he probably got lost and was looking for a new master! He chose me himself!" Masha started chattering breathlessly, as if she were afraid that she would be interrupted. "Let him stay with us, okay? I'm going to walk him myself and see after him. Please?" she suddenly added with praying voice and a faint hope.

Greatly amazed, Viktor stared at his wife. When was the last time that she asked leave to do something? Begged him, and with such tone? She used to do what she wanted; that was it. Well! What's happening? The world has gone crazy?"

"Well, okay," at last he collected himself, "if you want to, I don't mind." Well, how could he mind? How could he mind? "But a dog is no joke." Like a baby, he wanted to add, but he held his tongue at the very last moment. "Only if you won't change your mind."

Viktor was speaking with an intentionally serious, grave, and reasonable voice, but, deep inside, he was rejoicing. For the first time in recent years, he was a master in his house, a husband, a man, and a head of the family. He wasn't a poor gruel and a mop whose opinion wasn't important to anyone and who was only used by his wife. He didn't care about the dog. He would have agreed to live with a tiger, if that would help him to get his family back! He was ready to accept anything.

"Oh! I knew you wouldn't mind!" Masha even clapped her hands and danced with joy. "I won't change my mind. You're the very best! I love you so much!" She clasped her hands around Viktor's neck, clung to him for a second and kissed him passionately. The dog lifted its head and watched them attentively.

"That's it! From now on, you'll live here. This is your new home. Make yourself comfortable," Masha faced the dog and patted his head tenderly.

"What name shall we give him? Have you thought about that?" Viktor asked her at once, just to keep the conversation going. And he didn't want to break the thin thread of trust that had suddenly appeared between him and his wife. He tried his best to keep that new, long-forgotten, sincere, and kind tone, and that mutual understanding. He wanted somehow to consolidate that change in their relationship which clearly was taking shape.

"Name?" Masha looked at the dog, thinking. "Jack! We'll call him Jack!"

II. 2

That night, Viktor made love to his wife for the first time in a very long time. Moreover, he was at his best, and he was relaxed and tireless. Masha had several great orgasms during the night and whispered with delight, looking into his eyes with admiration, "It turns out, you're the best. The best." It seemed she was absolutely happy. Viktor was happy as well. He probably hadn't felt so good ever in his life, even in his youth.

When he and Masha fell asleep in the small hours, Viktor had a strange and amazing dream. He saw that he, Masha, and Jack were making love. He was filled with ecstasy and bliss; he didn't know that such feeling existed! He watched as Jack penetrated Masha, and Masha screamed with delight; then Masha had oral sex with Jack. How? Absolutely shameless and incredible images appeared one after another, and Viktor didn't have an orgasm; it was something absolutely unthinkable and incredible!

It seemed as if he was floating on soft, rose clouds and swinging on the waves of a previously unknown, boiling and icy, lazy and furious ocean of bliss and passion. The bliss was so keen, so unbearable, that one could already hear and guess something forbidden and inhuman in it, something devilish and sweet! As if he was taken behind a forbidden curtain in the world of dreams and bliss where human cannot walk, as there is no return; and he was shown that which human cannot see, as he would long for it and yearn for something impossible. But the most amazing thing was at the end. Viktor saw in his dream that, after that insane night, Masha got pregnant and gave birth to a boy. He clearly saw that he was holding him, their baby; she was breastfeeding him and looking at him fondly with huge eyes that were shining with happiness.

"Like Madonna," he thought, and suddenly something caught his attention. In vain, he's trying to understand—what's that? And, at that moment, instead of Masha, he saw his drunk, disheveled and half-naked mother—a witch from his previous nightmare who's staring at him viciously and roaring with laughter.

When Viktor woke up in cold sweat, the laughter still rang in his ears for a long time. Masha lay at his side, and, as he could guess, she also was having a very pleasant dream; she groaned lasciviously in her sleep and sometimes stretched slowly and languorously, and her body shuddered. Viktor watched with amazement for some time and then turned over and closed his eyes. However, he couldn't fall asleep. Tossing and turning, he finally woke up, turned on his back, stared at the ceiling, and started thinking—recalling and restoring his dream. He couldn't tell what he felt. The dream left him with ambiguous feelings. Simultaneous shame, filth, abomination, disgust, and, at the same time, hideously, the sweetest and most inexpressible enjoyment. They got so mixed and mingled that it was impossible to distinguish and tell one from the other, as if, with your tongue, you taste something that seems disgustful and slimy which is floating in thick sugar syrup. The sweetness overwhelms everything, and there's definitely no way you can understand what exactly you're eating.

Viktor would give away everything that he had, just to feel something like that in real life—and then would give away everything he had to forget it! But he would never be able to forget his sensations. The sickly sweet, ineradicable taste of sinfulness, depravity, and viciousness would ever be part of his relationship with his wife.

"What's that?" he suddenly came to his senses. "I'm not going to do that, really—with a dog."

Viktor suddenly remembered his dream very vividly. Some of its episodes—painfully sweet feeling of enjoyment, contentment, bliss. "At any rate, Masha wouldn't agree to that," he thought dreamily and, right away, he was terrified by his thought. "So, this means that I would?" he muttered aloud and got confused against his will.

"Baby!" he suddenly recalled the end of the dream. "There was a baby! And something else in the very end, something unclear. What? What exactly did I spot there? Heh? Well, that's not important. So, the baby, a baby. By the way, yesterday, I had a dream that there would be a miracle, and Masha and I would have a baby, and everything would be okay. What if this is a miracle? Actually, why not? In fact, this miracle, to be honest, is strange, even shocking, but only in tales is everything nice and great—scarlet sails and white ships—not in real life. The most important thing in the real life is a result. Everything else doesn't matter."

"And treatment, tests, those dreadful procedures. Who cares? Who actually pays any attention? The most important thing is the result, isn't it? That's the only question. Everything else doesn't matter. One's got to do what he's got to do, if one wants to heal. Maybe it's the dog's sperm, indeed."

Viktor felt Masha, who had already woken up, moved closer to him. "Are you awake?" he caressed her hair gently.

"Go to sleep, it's too early!"

"I had an incredible dream."

"Me, too!' Viktor almost said it, but managed to stop. "About what?"

"Well, it was strange," Masha waited for several moments and smiled mysteriously.

"About what?"

"About us."

"Tell me."

"Are we going to do anything right now?" she didn't answer but cuddled up to him even more.

"Come on, tell me!"

"Later, later," she started to bite his earlobe lightly, "not now."

"Heh?"

"Shut up!" Masha shut his mouth with an impatient kiss, and Viktor felt himself becoming aroused. He turned to his wife and started to slowly and skillfully caress her. Masha moaned quietly.

Viktor didn't know how to handle women. He didn't have any experience, and he was awkward in bed.

But now, he felt as if thousands and thousands of women had passed through his hands. He knew exactly what to do; he felt every curve and every bend of his woman's body. His hands were acting independently. At any given moment, his hands only could bring Masha to orgasm, to the very top of bliss, but, instead of that, he was just caressing her—very slowly, very softly.

And when she couldn't endure it and wait any more, in that very moment—neither earlier, nor later—he penetrated her and started to move slowly.

Masha screamed, moaned and shuddered, and he screamed, moaned, and shuddered with her. He acted with the supreme art of love, with skill and tact, as a true master and virtuoso, but he was not a detached observer and a cold professional. No! He had the same feelings as she did: bliss, pain, passion, ecstasy—and he was hovering and falling into abyss; he was dying and resurrecting with her. They merged into one and then, when it was finished, Masha suddenly rose on her elbow, turned to him and said quietly in astonishment and even embarrassment, "I never knew that it was possible. I love you. No, I adore you—worship! You're my god!"

Viktor was confused. He wanted to turn everything into a joke and say something soft and tender, but suddenly, the words died on his lips. They stuck in his throat as if he choked over them. Suddenly, he remembered his obsessive and constant nightmare of the recent days—the sweaty, greasy, half-drunk, laughing woman, an old woman—his own mother or maybe a witch or a she-devil—and he startled and shuddered with disgust.

Something was wrong. All that was happening was filled with some unbearable, scary falsity, as if it was not him who made love to his own wife but someone else. Someone strange, someone who was more experienced and skillful than him. He wouldn't be able to do such stuff. It seemed as if he saw someone copulating with his wife in all thinkable and unthinkable ways, and he was watching it from the side and enjoying it. That show gave him unnatural, perverted and, at the same time, delightful and torturing enjoyment.

But, in that slow voluptuousness, in refined and vicious delight, he could clearly feel a subtle, even sweeter and sickening flavor. As if he already began devouring the disgusting, slimy pieces that were floating in the syrup—dead flesh.

II. 3

Masha gave him a smacking kiss and, twittering merrily, went to the bathroom. Viktor stayed in bed, trying to calm down and collect his tattered thoughts and nerves. He was ill at ease. He was frightened. Suddenly, he felt as if he was in a trap—a subtly made trap, a steel trap, a web. All the world was covered with a grey, sticky web, gleaming with damp, and he became more and more tangled in it.

Viktor had the unpleasant feeling that all of that had already happened to him. He was stung—web, spider. Something familiar, painfully familiar. Something of that kind already happened, didn't it? Eh? Damn! Why should he care!? Maybe it did, maybe didn't. All the same, he wouldn't remember it! Okay, forget it. He was totally confused. Masha—their new relationship, the actual reconciliation, what he had dreamt about the day before, endless nightmares, a baby. And, above all, his cursed dream.

He tried not to think about it, tried to drive it away from memory, but, subconsciously, he understood that it was useless. He wouldn't forget it. The feelings that he had in the dream were impossible to forget. He returned to them in his thoughts again and again. He was already poisoned, like a drug addict who tried the drugs once and now wanted to forget them, who tried to fight himself. It was obvious what the result of the fight would be. The result was known beforehand and easily predictable. Now it was a matter of time. How long would he endure? A day? Twelve hours? An hour?

The most horrible thing was that he clearly understood that everything depended on him. Masha didn't count. With his new talents and skills, he would be able to convince her of anything. He would make her do anything he wanted. She wouldn't resist. Nobody would be able to resist; no woman. By God's or the devil's will, from now on, he held an absolute power over the woman, over her body and her soul. He became the ideal lover who is an object of the secret dreams of every woman in the world.

He could drive them crazy and drive them to frenzy with one short touch or a fleeting caress. He could make a woman forget everything: honor, shame, family, and children. He could make her refuse everything for his look, for his kiss, or for one night with him—make her leave everything with pleasure and, closing her eyes, follow him. Anywhere, even to hell!

His new abilities and skills were somehow unnatural and devilish. It seemed that they had come from another, ancient world that had disappeared long time ago and was long and completely, completely, completely forgotten. A world filled with harems and odalisques; of lazy, enshrouding dreams and befuddling spice and thrilling temptations. Of sweet love's languor, and languishing, hot and reckless bliss. The world of Scheherezades, Shahs, beautiful concubines and tales of 1001 nights. Of Nebuchadnezzars and Gilgameshes, merciless Genghis Khans and Tamerlanes, satiated Chinese emperors and voluptuous Bagdad sultans. Of the lords of the universe. Of insatiable and lascivious Messalinas; seductive, graceful, fragile, irresistible, and vicious Salomes sliding in the eternal dance; majestic, queenly, divinely immovable, and indifferently mysterious Cleopatras. Of Tamara's grim castle. The world of wise Solomons, reckless Antonys, violently cruel Neros and Caligulas, and refined and exquisitely, coldly lustful Caesar Borgias. Of "thousands of thousands of wives I knew." Of the world of "Song of Songs," of "your breasts are two white goatlings, your womb…," of Babel and Sodom and Gomorrah.

Of the world of everlasting bliss and enjoyment; of infinite, boundless, unchecked, blind, and fiery passion; of the most sincere, clear, pure, devoted, and sacrificial loyalty and love—"strong like death"—and of the bottomless, the darkest, the most bitter and chilling vice, betrayal, sin, and lust—"and the heaven opened wide, and the fire rain started." For only there, in that world, in the kingdom of lust and delight, one could acquire the skills that he had, could earn all that he knew about a woman. The usual human experience would not be enough for that. Human life is too short.

In other words, what he wanted, what he sought, what he dreamt about, he could receive at any moment. He just had to reach out his hand. And the baby. The thought that he would be able to father a baby didn't leave him. Deep in his soul, he really believed in it, believed sincerely. "What if that's a miracle that I was dreaming about?" he thought again.

And if that miracle would happen, wouldn't it be an excuse for everything? For sex with a dog or even a toad? So, what about with a dog? It's not even a human. It's something rather like a dildo. If Masha were prescribed to take pills made of dog's sperm, she would take them without a second thought. She wouldn't doubt anything. Or, say, vaginal suppositories. So what's the difference?

Viktor felt again that he was in a trap, in a web. He was a fly, fighting in the web but tangling in it more and more. It seemed as if he was guided to a target and was helpfully given the means and excuses for that. Just reach out your hand and take it. Say yes, give way to temptation! Why do you resist? What for? He was offered everything for free, and he didn't have to give anything back.

Suddenly Viktor felt the wave of sweet insanity fill him again, and he couldn't resist it. He clearly saw Masha, himself, Jack. He watched Masha standing on her knees, leaning forward and bending, copulating with Jack, with her head lying on Viktor's lap and him caressing her and whispering something soft to her; he watched himself slowly turning her on her back, spreading her legs and....

Viktor startled and came to his senses. "No, it's wrong! Wrong—it's a sin! A great sin, a mortal one. He would never be able to forget it and neither Masha. Damned be all those excuses! They are from devil, the Evil One, Father of lies. No arguing with him! He should say, 'leave me, Satan,' like Christ did."

Yes, but what about the baby? Baby? What if? That is the last hope. Yes, that would be a miracle, but isn't all that happened to him a miracle? All those skills and talents which came out of nowhere—aren't they a real miracle? By the way, if they disappear as quickly as they came to him, what would happen to him? How would Masha react to that reversal and not-at-all-magical transformation? That he would again turn into an ordinary, wretched and guiltless loser, from an ideal lover, god, and Casanova! Viktor felt that the thought gave him cold sweat.

And a baby, again. Would he ever dare to tell her that there was hope, and he had refused it? He didn't use it and didn't seek her advice? Why would he seek advice? In order to lie to himself? In order to shift the responsibility onto her? She was completely in his hands, in his power. He could convince her of anything. He just had to caress her a bit, a pat here and there. "Damn it! Devil! Be gone, be gone, be gone!" So the lie would ever stay between them. So, what's the difference? And what is a better choice?

Viktor felt that he was completely confused and didn't understand anything. He didn't know what was wrong and right. He couldn't tell good from evil. He didn't know what he wanted. So, what does he want? Masha. Jack. Viktor fiercely shook his head, driving the delusion away. "No! No! No! It's wrong! He can't do this! Can't, can't, can't!"

"Darling, did you miss me?" Viktor didn't notice that Masha had entered the room. Jack was with her.

"Why did you bring him with you?" Viktor uttered with a faltering voice, looking at the naked Masha, at Jack and then back at Masha.

"Well, I thought that he was bored in there, alone," said Masha with an unnaturally low, languishing voice and suddenly, looking straight into Viktor's eyes, she slowly rubbed her thigh against the dog's neck. Growing cold with terror, Viktor looked at Masha. He knew that move. That was a move from his dream. "Right, Jack?" said Masha in a singing voice, still looking at Viktor. Then she slowly squatted, hugged Jack, cuddled him, rubbed her breasts against him and, still looking straight into Viktor's eyes, licked her lips with the tip of the tongue and very slowly spread her knees.

Like in the dream, Viktor stood up, approached his wife and put his hand on her head.

When Viktor penetrated Masha after Jack, he shuddered with surprise; deep inside his wife's vagina, he felt a burning, icy cold.

"Demons' seed is cold," the words from some old folio which he had read long ago came to his mind, warning him. Suddenly, as if with a stroke of lightning, Viktor saw and remembered the end of his dream. Masha was breastfeeding their baby and admiring him with quiet, motherly tenderness; suddenly, on the baby's head, Viktor saw a strange, dark mark—a patch of black, shining and stiff hair growing on the crown.

"Like Jack's fur," flashed in his mind, and the next moment, a wave of unbearable bliss flooded all his essence, and, rising up on his hands and pushing his head back, he screamed with ecstasy and enjoyment. And the next moment Jack, dashing from the side, tore his throat with one movement of strong jaws, and Viktor, not realizing what had happened, collapsed on his wife, covering her with blood.

Masha lay down for some time, then slowly pushed away her husband's body, stood up and, covered with blood, patted Jack's head on her way to the bathroom.

***

When the cops who came at Masha's call entered the room, Jack, who had been sitting quietly before that, leapt up, dashed to the window and, breaking the glass, jumped outside. The people, who ran to the window, couldn't see anything. The dog disappeared. Though, from the other side, it was just a second floor and a soft flowerbed below.

***

In nine months exactly, Masha gave a birth to a boy.

"He's going to be lucky!" the nurse told her, smiling. She passed the baby and pointed to the little dark hair on the baby's crown. "By the way, have you heard the news? Today is very strong magnetic storm. Even the northern light will be seen in the night! It'll be for the first time. So be careful!"

"Right," answered Masha slowly, and she glanced strangely at a woman in a white robe in front of her. The woman startled, turned pale and stopped smiling. "The light. I know, I know. I have heard of it."

LUCIFER'S SON. DAY 1.

Thus bespoke Lucifer:

Mine son, thou art mine own flesh and blood. I shall teach thee, and thou shall obey mine words if thou wish. I shall not concuss thee and protrude aught. Thou shall make a choice and thy choice shall be free.

Thou shall decide whom to follow: me 'r him.

And how thou shall decide, so be it.

But first thou shall answer me. Will thou hark to me? Will thou speak to me? Will thou be mine disciple?

Wherefore 'twas quoth'd. Satan is the father of lies. Thou shall not speak to him, thou shall not argue with him.

And his son answer'd to Lucifer:

— I will hark to thee. if I may hark to him, wherefore shall I not hark to thee? Art thou more convincing?

I shall speak to thee. If I may speak to him, wherefore shall I not speak to thee? Art thou more aureate?

I shall be thy disciple. I am a man and I shall distinguish between sooth and lies. And if nay—how can I make mine choice? Then thither is nay freedom at all! The blind cannot choose his own way.

Good,—answer'd Lucifer,—ask anon. And Lucifer was ask'd by his son:

— Christ, the son of god suffer'd and di'd on the cross. Shall I, thy son, suffer and die?

And Lucifer answer'd to his son:

— Christ knew that he was the son of God. So, what is his feat?

He only play'd. Death was a mere game f'r him.

He knew that 'twas not f'r ev'r and seriously. He knew he would come back.

Ay, he suffer'd and anguish'd on the cross, but one can stand all suffering and tortures, when thou wot that 'tis a mere game, a trial of strength of mind.

What is suffering? Thousands and thousands wast crucified, and thousands and thousands endur'd yea more cruel and devious tortures. And many of them behav'd with hon'r.

Yea in the face of death.

Real death, and not imaginary one.

And what?

Who can remember them?

Who admires them?

Whence art they?

They hast fallen into the abyss of time, leaving nay trace. In other words, the suffering and tortures itself art not worth aught. Thou shall not take it.

1

GAME.

"Judge not, that ye be not judged."
Gospel of Matthew.

Sidorov was awakened by a phone call.

"Yeah?" he asked quickly with hoarse voice, trying to talk quietly and covering the receiver with a hand, as he didn't want to wake up his wife who was sleeping near him. Half-asleep, he was slow to grasp and was acting with his brain on autopilot.

"Konstantin Viktorovich?" a pleasant and calm female vice asked politely.

"Right," answered Sidorov, being surprised a little and still trying to wake up.

"Hi! I'm a representative of the computer company," the woman on the other side of the line switched to English and said a long, complicated name which Sidorov didn't discern, although he even didn't try to—something international.

"I apologize for such an early call." Sidorov glanced absent-mindedly at the clock nearby—damn, it's seven! "But we were afraid that we couldn't reach you during the day," she spoke again in Russian. "Congratulations! You're a winner of our annual lottery, and you have won our main prize."

"You know, I didn't enter any lotteries," Sidorov unceremoniously interrupted his interlocutor. "I don't want any prizes, Don't call here, please!"

He hurled the receiver with rage and lay for some time, slowly cooling down. "Prize! Yeah, tell me about it! 'Our wonderful frying pan with a fantastic discount, just for you!' And they woke me up on Saturday, at 7 a.m., with this bullshit! Scum! They should be killed for that—with the same frying pan!"

The phone rang again. "Fuck!" Sidorov stared at it with rage for a several moments and then grasped the receiver.

"What's up, honey?" asked Nastenka drowsily and moved a little.

"Hello!"

"Konstantin Viktorovich, don't hang up, please."

"Listen," Sidorov opened his mouth.

"It's not a wonderful frying pan." Sidorov was still lying with his mouth open. "It's a real prize. And it's very expensive, by the way. About fifty thousand dollars," the company representative was still immovably calm. Sidorov stared at the receiver, shut his mouth and swallowed convulsively. "Just tell me where it should be delivered and when. Name the place and time."

"And what is it exactly?" Sidorov still didn't believe it, but the temptation was too strong. How could she possibly know about a frying pan? Did she just guess? Or have I said it aloud, half-asleep? Ahem, I can't remember. Well, okay.

"A brand-new game computer—a product of our company, an experimental development, modeling virtual reality."

With growing amazement, Sidorov listened to that slow and confident speech. "Well, it's too complicated for an ordinary bilk. But still.... No! No way! Are they going to present me with $50,000? Right! Sure! In your dreams! This can happen only in tales or in the movies." But a faint and timid hope already stirred in his soul, against his will.

"What if? Still, some people do win prizes, right?"

"However, the technician will explain everything to you in detail," his unseen interlocutor continued to speak dispassionately and calmly. "So, where should he deliver it and when?"

"Maybe I should come to you?" Sidorov made a last attempt. What if they are cons? He'd let somebody in. Though, on the other hand, they do not insist on coming to his place just to name any place. Damn! I don't understand anything! 'Where should we deliver $5,000 and when exactly? When is it convenient for you?' Bullshit!

"I'm sorry, Konstantin Viktorovich," he was answered indifferently from the other side of the line. "The equipment is sophisticated, and the technician has to set it up himself. So, where should he come?

"Okay," Sidorov gave up. "Let's say…hmm, er —today, at 2. The address is…," Sidorov told her his home address.

"Great. So, the address is…," the woman distinctly repeated the address that he had just told her. "The technician will come today, at 2 p.m. precisely. Have a nice day. Good bye."

"Good bye," Sidorov answered mechanically and heard her hang up. He carefully hung up, too, and leaned back on the pillow, feeling as if he was a man who was told that he suddenly became very rich. Fifty thousand dollars was an incredible sum for Sidorov. "If only that was true, and we will really be given this cool computer." This thought caught his breath. Surely, he wasn't going to keep it. He'd just play with it for a week and then would sell it; he could sell it right away—even if not for 50,000, but 40,000. If it costs 50, then he would easily sell it for f40orty. Forty thousand dollars! Crazy—damn!

Sidorov groaned and tossed and turned from excitement that filled him. Is it really true? Why did I tell them to come at 2? What a fool! I should've told them to arrive immediately, right now! This very moment! Bring it! Sidorov nearly moaned, feeling impatient and annoyed by himself; he looked around helplessly and then stared at his wife, who was lying at his side. He had an urge to have his say, to share his overflowing feelings with someone.

"Nastenka," he softly shook her shoulder. "Wake up."

"Eh?" muttered his wife in a sleepy voice. "What's up?"

"Wake up, wake up! I got great news!" Sidorov spouted words hastily.

"What news?" Nastenka asked, still drowsy and indifferent and going back to sleep.

"Don't sleep!" Sidorov shook his wife's shoulder a bit stronger.

She startled, opened her eyes, saw her husband leaning over her, and smiled softly.

"Yeah, honey?"

"Just imagine, I got the phone call, and I won $50,000!"

"Fifty thousand dollars?" asked Nastenka in amazement and looked at Sidorov with distrust. "What $50,000? Who called?"

"I don't know," he shrugged his shoulders in excitement, "a computer company. I think it's Americans. They say I won a lottery, and I got a prize. It's their cool, brand-new computer, worth $50,000! Can you imagine that?"

"So what?"

"What? Nothing. They will bring it today at 2. A technician will come to set it up."

"Today at 2? Where? Here?"

"Exactly! Right here! I told them our address and made the appointment. I should've told them to come earlier. How could I be such a fool? No, right now! Immediately!"

"Can you call them back? We got the Caller ID!"

Like all women, Nastenka was very practical in some situations. Somehow, Sidorov hadn't thought about such an easy and absolutely obvious opportunity.

"Good girl," he kissed his wife with delight, jumped up and rushed to the phone. "Bother it!" he said disappointedly a moment later. "The number didn't show."

"Don't get upset, honey. It's okay. Let's wait," Nastenka was smiling softly and looking up at him. "Come to me; I'm cold," she added softly and a bit playfully.

Sidorov also smiled. He was standing near the bed, looking at his wife and feeling the tenderness fill and overwhelm him. His heart was literally torn in pieces with love, and there was a lump in his throat. He was desperately in love with his wife, head over heels in love. He loved and worshipped her. No, that's not it. He felt that there were no words in human language to express his feelings, as there were no words to describe wind, fire, and water. It seemed to him that his wife, Nastenka, issued a soft, gentle inner light, emotional warmth. And he wondered sincerely when he used to notice that no one else saw and felt it.

He liked everything about her—every line, every move, and every gesture, how she talked, looked and laughed. They had been married for almost two years, and his love and passion to her hadn't weakened but, on the contrary, had become stronger. Beginning at their first meeting, he considered her to be a peculiar, high, heavenly creature that had come here from a completely different world—one unknown, mysterious and fair. She was altogether unlike any other usual, earthly women. It seemed as if she was made from some other stuff. Green… Assol... "Scarlet sails.".. No, some of his first early, piercing, and tender novels. The ones in which men and women are not called by the names—just He and She. Gumilev...

crystal and transparent verses, like ice in a glass, amazing and incredible:

Today I can see that your features are strikingly sad,
Your arms on your knees are as thin as dandelion stalks.
But listen, in far-away lands that surround lake Chad
A graceful giraffe softly walks

Sidorov used to repeat these beautiful, unspeakably sad and immortal verses, but he felt that even they were not enough. Even they seemed to be insufficiently deep and soft. His feelings towards Nastenka were even stronger, deeper and higher. He thanked the Fates that he was lucky enough to meet such love in his life; at the same, his happiness scared him. For, if something would happen to Her, to Nastenka... He couldn't imagine what would happen to him. He just couldn't imagine that. The world would fall, and the sun would fade! The time would stop and cease its flow.

No! That was impossible. God is gracious. He would not let this happen. He lay down near his wife, hugged her and started kissing, caressing and whispering the words which, at all times, men whisper to women whom they love. And they were intimate the way that two persons can be, the way that husband and wife can be. And they screamed with ecstasy, and they were young and happy. And he loved her, and she loved him. And nobody in the world was happier. And they believed that it was forever. Forever and ever. They believed that their happiness would not die away. For God is gracious. He would not let it happen.

2.

At 2 p.m. straight, not a minute earlier nor later, the doorbell rang. Sidorov, who was drudging since morning and waiting impatiently for that ring—and he stayed near the door for the last fifteen minutes!—opened the door immediately. Actually, he was excited all day, he couldn't do anything, and was just pacing the rooms. Never before did the time go so slowly for him. It seemed that the clock hands died, stuck to the clock-face and didn't move at all. And they completely stopped since 1 p.m.

In the meantime, Nastenka, curiously enough, took everything indifferently and calmly—she was busy with domestic cares and, from time to time, just kindly laughed at her husband, watching him running amok all day.

On the doorstep, there was standing a polite, well-dressed young man of about thirty-five years old with a box in his hands.

"Hello! Konstantin Viktorovich?" he asked politely, "I'm from the company," he said something long in English. It appeared that it was the same that Sidorov had heard from the woman in the morning. There was definitely the word "international" that he remembered very well.

"Yes, please. Come on in," Sidorov stepped aside, giving way to the guest. The man entered and stopped, looking at Sidorov inquiringly. "Up here, please. Come on in," he hurried, pointing at the door to the room, where his desk was and where he usually studied. Sidorov was a third-year student in one of the universities of Moscow. "No need to take off your shoes," he added, seeing that the guest stopped and was searching with his eyes for slippers. "It's okay."

The man entered the room, quickly looked around and, holding the box, went straight to the desk. "Here, right?" he asked half-affirmatively, pointing at the desk and glancing at Sidorov.

"Yeah, put it on the desk," said Sidorov readily, in a humbling voice. He was staring at the box and felt as if he was a child, who was visited by Santa Claus, with presents for him.

The man silently put the box on the desk and started opening it with careful, professional, quick, and precise moves.

"Hello!" Sidorov didn't notice Nastenka entering the room.

"Hi," the man stopped for a moment and looked at her. Nastenka came closer and stopped near her husband. The man stared at them for some time, then lowered his eyes and got busy with his box again.

A few more moves, and he carefully took out of it a strange black hemisphere. Struck with curiosity, Sidorov came closer and saw that it was something like a motorcycle helmet, though more massive and elegant.

"Where's a socket? Oh! Right, I see," the man unwound a cable, plugged it into the socket and pressed some buttons on the helmet, "Now I need to adjust it. Please, sit in the chair and put it on. Like this," he showed to Sidorov how to put on the helmet, "Yes, like this. Everything's Okay? Are you comfortable?" The helmet fit Sidorov perfectly well. He didn't feel it, and the helmet was very light. It seemed, as if there was nothing on his head.

"Okay, you may take it off. And now you, please," the man looked at Nastenka, inviting her. Smiling uncertainly, she looked at Sidorov at a loss, but he just shrugged his shoulders and nodded encouragingly. Still hesitating, she sat in the chair. The man gave her the helmet, and Nastenka put it on slowly and carefully in order to save her hairdo.

"That's it, you may take it off."

"That's it? You're finished?"

"Yeah, take it off."

Still carefully and slowly, Nastenka took the helmet off and gave it to the company representative in front of her. He took it, pushed something on it, and put it on the table.

"That's it, preparation is finished. The system is uploading now. It'll take about three or four hours. When it's done, this red light will go off... Yeah, this one. See, now it's on. When it goes off, you may start working. Well, what else? It operates from the mains or the battery. The battery will last for one day, then it needs to be recharged. Actually, it's better to keep it hooked up when you don't use it—for the battery not to discharge. You don't have to push any buttons. When you're finished operating—just take it off, put on the desk and that's it. The system constantly self-regulates and modifies itself according to the input information."

Sidorov was looking with awe at the wonder of modern computer engineering that was lying on the desk in front of him. "Just think about it: 'Self-regulates,' 'modifies itself"... I like that! Okay. We'll see."

"I adjusted the system for both of you. From now on, only you and your wife can use it."

"Damn!" thought Sidorov. "So, we won't be able to sell it? Okay, we'll see. We'll get it straightened out!"

"What's the drill? Is there any manual?" asked Sidorov a bit disappointedly. So, he'll have to muck about re-adjusting. More troubles and more expenses. So, he adjusted it for us only, moron! Why the heck did you do this?

"It's very easy to operate; you won't need a manual. Just put the helmet on, and that's it. If something's not clear, just ask the computer, and it'll explain everything in detail. In one word, you'll learn everything. I'm sure that you'll have no problems with it. In case of urgency, call us." The man gave Sidorov a card, then quickly packed the empty box, clapped it with his hands and looked around, trying to find a spot for it. "The crucial thing is—don't touch anything, and don't try to open a panel." (Right! Dream on!)

"Otherwise, you'll erase everything." (Come on, "erase!"... Perhaps, we won't. Our craftsmen can do it on wheels. More expenses, though.) "This is a new model, a know-how. You may use it, but don't open it. Well, you know what I mean," he didn't manage to find a good spot and left the box on the table, near the helmet.

"So, the system is mine? Does the company present it to me, or I can just use it for some time?" specified Sidorov, just in case.

"No, it's yours! It's yours," the man looked Sidorov straight in the eyes and, for some reason, smiled. "It's a gift from the company. It's yours from now on. You won it. Use it well! I hope you'll like it," he looked Sidorov in the eyes and again smiled strangely.

"What is it, anyway?" Sidorov exploded. "Indeed, what the hell does it mean—'you'll learn everything,' 'The computer will explain everything.' And what is he here for? Damned technician"

"I thought you'd tell us everything."

"A game! Didn't they tell you in the morning? A game. It's just a game."

3.

Three and a half hours later, when the damned red light went off at last—Sidorov already hated it! How long can you "upload?" What kind of system is it? Counter missile defense, heh? And where is it situated, by the way? Near the battery? The helmet is very small and almost weightless—Sidorov carefully took the helmet from the desk and, hesitating, fingered it over.

By that time, Nastenka was tired waiting, and she whirled away "on business," either to the hairdresser or beautician.

"Well? Let's put it on? Or maybe I should lie down in bed? No, at first, I'm gonna try it like this. In the chair. Well? Godspeed! Putting on!" With joyful impatience and expectation of unknown miracles, Sidorov put the helmet on with trembling hands.

At once, at that very instant, there appeared his recent guest in the opposite chair, the same man, a company representative, who came by in the morning and brought the helmet. Clad in the same suit, he lazily lay back in the chair with his legs crossed, and, staring at the ceiling, smoked a cigar of incredible beauty. The air was filled with the smell of expensive cigar smoke. Sidorov got wide-eyed and watched him in astonishment for some time.

"Well, well, well, dear Konstantin Viktorovich!" graciously smiled his unexpected guest, still not looking at Sidorov. "What's wrong, really? You shouldn't react so badly. You're merely in the game reality. Virtual reality. That's it."

"If you take the helmet off, I'll disappear. Do it!" he ordered harshly.

Without second thought, Sidorov obediently took off the helmet. The man instantly disappeared. There was nobody in the room. He didn't sense any smell. Sidorov was sitting alone at the desk in the empty room, holding the helmet in his hands and bluntly staring at the empty chair in front of him. Then he carefully put the helmet on the desk, stood up in prostration, approached the chair, and, without any reason, touched the upholstery. After that he returned to his seat again and, unknowingly, put on the helmet back.

Again, the man appeared suddenly, in the same spot and in the same position. It seemed that he hadn't disappeared at all. Tobacco smoke filled the room once more.

"Well, are you satisfied? Okay, let's get down to business," the man searched with his eyes for a place to ash, and, not finding anything appropriate, did it on the carpet.

All that time, Sidorov was watching his manipulations with certain mistrust. "Isn't it rude?" he thought involuntarily, "Shit, we've just vacuumed the carpet!"

The man caught his eye and smiled again. "Come on, don't worry about the carpet! All of this isn't real. It's a virtual world and a virtual carpet. Come on, don't get distracted! Let me explain to you the sense of the game."

"Wait, wait!" Sidorov gathered his thoughts at last. "Who are you, anyway? And how come you're here?"

"Me? I'm just a computer. You should have easily guessed, Konstantin Viktorovich," the man was looking at Sidorov, and a light ironic smile hovered over his lips, "Personal appearance and traits are just a whim of our programmer. Yet, if you want, I can change them. How do you like it now?"

Sidorov blinked. In the chair in front of him sat a gorgeous young beauty who seemed to have just come off the cover of the fashion-paper. She had splendid long iron-grey hair, which she was fiddling with one hand. She winked at Sidorov cunningly, with her dollish eyelashes half-lowered.

"And now?" she cooed in a sweet voice.

Sidorov wished to rub his eyes. Instead of the beauty, there was a very young, shabby guy. He seemed to be even younger than Sidorov.

"Hey, dude!" he began talking forwardly, addressing Sidorov, "I'll have everything sorted out for you. We wanna be straight here."

"No, no!" said Sidorov hastily. Then he sighed with relief, seeing the familiar figure with a cigar. "I'm fine with you," he finished firmly.

Well, let's say that the beauty would be "finer" for Sidorov, but, suddenly, he had a strange feeling that it was not a computer that took different images uploaded in it, but the man sitting in front of him simply turned into anybody at his own will: a girl... a guy.... It was him who was real and all the others weren't. Of course, it was nonsense, but Sidorov couldn't help it. Flirting with a girl, inside which there is a man... rather, with a man who turned into a girl... rather.... Bother it! In one word, hell with it!

"As you wish, as you wish!" the man blew a wisp of smoke, thoughtfully watched it rising to the ceiling, and then, at last, looked at Sidorov. "So, dear Konstantin Viktorovich," he began slowly, staring at Sidorov appraisingly, "the game is called…'Temptation.' Yes...'Temp-ta-ti-on'," stretching the vowels, he repeated slowly, as if tasting the word and smiling at his thoughts. "Exactly! Exactly "Temptation!" he continued merrily. "Well, it's about... by the way, how do you want me to talk about the computer? From the first person, about myself, like 'me,' or from the third person—'he'?"

"Me," allowed Sidorov.

"Okay. Well, today I scanned you and your wife. And now I know almost everything about you. Absolutely! Even more, than you do."

"That's nonsense!" thought Sidorov helplessly but becoming cold inside.

"Oh, no, Konstantin Viktorovich, it's not nonsense!" (Sidorov's jaw dropped.) "See, right now I'm reading all your thoughts. The latest development of our company... Well, that's not important. We'll skip the technical details. Just accept it as a fact, that's it. If you need any proofs later on, I'll gladly give them to you. So, the sense of the game is the following. You have to guess what your wife will do in an unusual situation that I'm going to model now."

Sidorov was blinking and felt like a fool. He was a humanitarian and didn't quite understand all that special terminology. "Model? What does that mean? And what "unusual situation?"

"To be brief, let's get to business and stop talking," it seemed that his interlocutor saw his condition and took pity on him.

Sidorov felt humiliating awkwardness—the one that you feel when you're talking to a person who's admittedly smarter than you, and you know that he realizes this, as well. That's why he's not expecting any objections. He's just patiently explaining to you, like to a small witless child, something that's seemingly obvious for him, and you can't follow him—you're ashamed to confess it, so you're just listening sagely and nodding obediently.

"Let's play once, and you'll understand everything. Deal?"

"Okay, let's try," Sidorov uttered reluctantly. A strange anxiety began to fill him. "What does all that mean? What kind of a computer is this? No such computers exist! Although, the deuce knows! Maybe, they already exist. Some ultramodern technologies. Super-duper! Artificial intelligence, damn it! When can I know about it? Nothing! I'm not a specialist." Sidorov didn't understand much in usual machinery, let alone computers.

"By the way—so, is he reading my mind now, too?" he thought suddenly, and he searchingly looked at the creature sitting in front of him. The man (or whoever he was) was watching him indifferently, but Sidorov had a very unpleasant feeling that he, Sidorov, was completely transparent. He was an amoeba or a slipper animalcule under a microscope, and it was slowly and thoughtfully examined from every side, in order to be diagnosed with presence or absence of cilium or pseudopodium or whatever amoeba has. Sidorov shivered against his will. The cheerful excitement with which he had put on the helmet several minutes ago was gone. Everything got mixed up in his head. He didn't know what exactly he wanted. Did he want to play such a game? Maybe it was better to take the helmet off and think a little?

"So? Are you ready?" his vis-à-vis asked politely. "Let's start."

"Yes," waving his hand, Sidorov muttered helplessly. Then he lowered his eyes and felt that he was making an unamendable folly or mistake, but he didn't have enough strength and was too ashamed to refuse. "Let's start!"

4.

The room disappeared. Suddenly Sidorov saw his wife, Nastenka, leaving their building. It seemed as if he was invisible and followed her several steps behind. Nastenka was in a hurry. She ran out on the road and started waving her hand, trying to get a ride.

Sidorov was watching her with unpleasant surprise. It suddenly struck him that, on the third hand, she looked like an ordinary chicklet, or babe, hitching on the roadside. He used to see hundreds of them on his way to work. She was ridiculously rushing and bustling, like a disturbed hen, only she didn't cackle and flap the wings. Altogether, she was gesturing too actively for Assol or a strange woman of Blok. For some reason, Sidorov used to think that his priceless, precious, and unmatched darling didn't walk on the streets, but slid quietly, with her eyes lowered, not looking to the sides, and smiling to her own mysterious and inconceivable thoughts. And she would never use public transportation and was somehow...she just would be where she wanted to. With a wave of a wand, she would fly like a fairy. It was nonsense, but he just realized that. He had never given it a thought before.

Suddenly, from the left lane, paying no attention to traffic rules, a luxurious white limo rushed to his wife. It seemed to be a Mercedes, though, no—it had different headlights. However, Sidorov was not much of an expert in cars. Such cars belonged to another, fantastic life. Another world. The world of tanned, well-groomed, and confident millionaires, yachts, three-storied villas, expensive restaurants, and chinchilla fur coats. The world where people are carefree, merry, and happy, and where there are no problems at all. The wonderful car stopped near Nastenka, squealing. The door opened. Sidorov peeped inside and was struck dumb.

A real prince from a fairy-tale was looking at him—or, rather, at his wife. Young, careless, free, handsome, and incredibly rich. He could feel it right away. An ideal one. A living dream. If Sidorov were a woman, he would immediately fall in love with him and throw himself on his neck. He hadn't even thought before that such people existed. That was just not fair.

Growing cold, Sidorov watched his wife getting into the car, merrily talking, and making eyes to this… this.... Choking with envy and jealousy, Sidorov wished to find a flaw in his rival that appeared out of nowhere, but he couldn't.

The stranger was flawless. Magnificent! Restrained, courteous, elegant, exquisitely polite, and, as it turned out, smart and witty. At any rate, Sidorov would never be able to have such a light, delicate, and rich talk about nothing special—"causerie," a French word that he had met somewhere, came to his mind—with a lady.

"With a lady! Shit!" cursed Sidorov to himself. He felt as if he was a clumsy, uncouth redneck, a churl, a commoner, who was puffing maliciously and watched a young count or marquis seducing his beautiful wife in front of him. Just for fun, he was laughing and according courtesies, being sure in his success and never doubting his irresistibility.

"Beauty! Right! She didn't turn out to be a beauty at all," thought Sidorov suddenly with anger, watching the sweet couple who were sitting close to each other. Indeed, against the stunning, brilliant, and splendid prince—Sidorov called him that against his own will—his precious Nastenka faded and molted and seemed to be a simple mud duck. Frankly speaking, she didn't look like a princess from a fairy tale at all. "Her features are very vulgar, though. And her nose... I've never noticed that before," thought Sidorov again. He felt that these thoughts were filling him with perverted and wicked pleasure.

"That's it! Some princess! Right! Sure! A pig in a bun shop! So, she wished for a damned prince, right? Wouldn't he be too much for her? Bitch! So, you were just beckoned and.... An ordinary whore. Like all of them. It's true that all of them are whores. Bitches and whores. Fool of a woman! Witless hen! He doesn't need you! Look at you!" muttered Sidorov to himself with a helpless wrath, watching his dear Nastenka setting a meeting in a restaurant in the evening, and then lying to him—a computer one—about some coiffeuse or manicurist who was working late, and he, dimwit and idiot, listens wide-eyed to this stupid woman bullshit and nonsense—what coiffeuse, pray, works at night!—with pleasant face, tucks it in and agrees with her cheerfully; sure, dear Nastenka! – moron! And…

All in all, it was finished in a week. A couple more dates, walks, restaurants—a "friend's birthday," "Mom asked me to come by in the evening" and so on – and his beloved and charming wife is holding a glass of champagne—"Asshole, damn it! Slut! Bitch!—hugging and kissing her new acquaintance and going up to his luxurious bedroom. The door of the bedroom chastely closes with a bang before Sidorov's face.

"Game over."

5.

Sidorov saw himself sitting in a chair at the desk again. In the chair beside him, the cursed computer man sat, crossing his legs lazily, leaning back and watching him unmoved. Sidorov stooped, looked with a vacant stare and felt completely destroyed, crushed, and lost.

Life lost all its sense. All that he believed in—wife, love, family—All of it collapsed. He thought that he heard the shards of his broken life tinkle, bumping into each other. The sound became more and more quiet. At last, it died away.

"Unfortunately, you have lost, Konstantin Viktorovich," a calm voice, that was familiar to Sidorov, broke the silence, "I watched you attentively. You managed to guess your wife's behavior only with a 20-percent degree of credibility."

Sidorov was listening, as if bewitched. The voice reached him as if from afar, through some kind of wool.

"However," the computer man made a pause and slowly let a couple of impeccable rings of fragrant cigar smoke, "I may congratulate you." Sidorov lifted his head. "You have a wonderful wife. An amazing woman! She held out for a week! Unbelievable!"

Sidorov looked at—the man? computer? game character?—well, at the creature that was sitting in front of him with sickly bewilderment. "Is he kidding?"

"No, no, Konstantin Viktorovich, I'm not kidding. Come on," he said soothingly.

"Yeah, right; sure, he's reading my mind," thought Sidorov drowsily. However, he didn't care anymore. "Let it be. So, what? He's reading my mind. It's even better."

"It's amazing, really," the man shook his head, "I've never seen anything like this. Actually, I never thought that it's possible!"

"What's the usual result?" asked Sidorov bluntly. "How long do they usually hold out?" He got curious. "Hold out—what a stupid word! So, it's a Brest fortress under siege, or what? 'How long shall we hold out?' Fucking shit!"

"Usually, a couple of hours. Day or two at the most. Though, two days is a very good result. But a week!" the man shook his head distrustfully "Amazing! Konstantin Viktorovich, you should make much of her. It's an exceptional woman. One out of million."

"This exceptional woman started lying to me from the first day!" thought Sidorov with a sudden anger. "And she slept with him in a week. With the next man in an expensive car, who just beckoned her. Shit! What's she doing with him, anyway? In his super bedroom? Is she sucking his dick, heh? His super dick?"

"Your wife isn't doing anything in no super bedroom!" said the man reproachfully. "It's just a game. A game. Virtual reality. Nothing of it really happened!"

"What if it did?" asked Sidorov stubbornly, "What if she really met someone... in a white "Mercedes?"

The man shrugged his shoulders in silence.

"I see. So, a week, right? She would hold out for a week? Is this her eternal love? Bitch! Bitch, bitch, bitch! And who's this handsome guy, anyway? Why is it him? Why is he looking like that? And in that fucking car? Is it some standard dream of all damned vile women?"

"No, that's a personalized image of an ideal man for your wife."

Sidorov was struck once more. "So that's whom she's dreaming about? So why did she marry me? Why didn't she keep waiting for him? A prince in a white Mercedes? 'No, I love you! Oh! my dear! Darling!' So what, she just wanted to marry as quickly as possible? Marry! That's it. She wasn't getting younger."

"Come on, you're acting like a child!" the computer again interfered with his sad thoughts. "There are no such people in real life. And no such situations. This is just a game situation, specifically made and modeled for your wife, an ideal situation. Nothing more. It could never happen in real life. You don't have to worry about anything."

"Well," thought Sidorov, "So, that's it... Of course, your wife is a slut, but don't worry. Your neighbors, drunks, can't afford her. And she wouldn't fuck with anyone for free. So you don't have to worry about anything!" Subconsciously, Sidorov was expecting to hear more consolations and objections, but the computer was silent. Sidorov lifted his eyes inquiringly. The man, sitting in front of him, watched him and smiled sardonically.

"Who are you?" asked Sidorov with a hoarse voice, and he licked his dry lips, "You are no computer!"

The man didn't answer. He stood up, came up to the window, put his hands behind his back and started watching the street attentively. "If you'd like to ask anything else, Konstantin Viktorovich, please ask," he said at last, "I'm listening."

"Ugh..." Sidorov cleared his throat hesitatingly. For some reason, he felt uneasy and didn't really know what to say and what to do. "How should he behave with… a human, well, not a human—with a computer, it doesn't matter! Okay, with a creature, that sees though you, sees all your secret, intimate, and innermost thoughts and dreams, which you considered to be yours only." He shouldn't talk to that creature, but run away at once.

As to the questions—he already had enough of them. That would do! He didn't want to learn anything more, about himself or his dearest wife. About his beloved spouse, damn her! About lovey-dovey and all mean women!

"So, you say, only with an ideal partner?" he mumbled after a pause, looking for a get-away and excuses for Nastenka. Frankly speaking, he didn't really see many handsome princes in white Mercedes in his district.

"Not at all!" the man took his eyes off the street and, half-turning, looked at Sidorov, "Did I say something like that? Nothing of the sort."

"What do you mean by 'nothing of the sort'?" Sidorov felt the walls of the room shake and the floor give way. "'Nothing of the sort'? So do you mean that? Do you suppose that? She could do it with an un-ideal one?" he whispered quietly, almost inaudibly, but he knew the answer, "With an ordinary man?"

"Surely. It's just a matter of time and efforts spent," the man shrugged his shoulder subtly. "Well, it'll take more than a week, of course. A week is a minimum period. And it's a very good result, believe me. Very good!" he repeated tightly, watching Sidorov attentively. "It's impossible to demand more from a woman. Take my word."

"Right… right." muttered Sidorov, "Alright... You know, I'm a bit tired. Let's call it a day. I'm gonna take the helmet off."

"Yes, sure," answered the man politely. Or the computer? "Good-bye, Konstantin Viktorovich."

"Good-bye," said Sidorov reflexively and took the helmet off.

6.

His companion vanished. Everything else in the room was the same. Sidorov saw something symbolic in that, as if it was a clear proof that the edge between the real world and the virtual one where he had just been was very unstable. And, very often, it was almost indistinguishable. It existed only in the mind. Just to imagine that a real man visited him and showed him real video of the affairs of his fair one... Sidorov almost yelled at that thought.

So was it real or not? On the one hand, he clearly understood, that it hadn't really happened—of course, it hadn't. But on the other hand, he clearly understood that it hadn't happened yet only because Nastenka hadn't had the chance. Nothing had just turned around. Nobody saw after her. No one had the time to get to her. There are many women around. And they aren't worse. "So, get in a line, ladies, get in a line! Come on, don't crowd. All in due time. What did the damn computer say? 'It's just a matter of time and efforts,' and 'a week is a very good result'!"

"Damn!" Sidorov pounded the table with his fist. The helmet bounced up with a bump and nearly fell down. Sidorov stared at it as if it was a rattlesnake. "Just to think about it! Only yesterday—what about yesterday? Only in the morning he was a happy man, the happiest of the living. He loved, adored, and worshipped his wife, fussed over her and considered her to be a high creature from another world! He recited her verses of Gumilev—shit!

You're crying?
But listen, in far-away lands that surround Lake Chad
A graceful giraffe softly walks

"She doesn't give a fuck about giraffes! Just tell her, where her dear boyfriend is. He's driving in a white Mercedes. So she'll stop crying, and she'll go suck his dick. Well, not at once, of course—in a week. 'A very good result'! Fucking shit!" Sidorov felt that his face was wet from tears. He sat a bit more and then went to the bathroom. Having washed up, Sidorov didn't go back to the room, but went to the kitchen, put on the kettle, came to the window and looked at the street. "Like the computer," he thought against his will. "And I should put the hands behind my back."

He was simply afraid to go back to the room. The helmet drew him like a magnet. He kept thinking about putting it on and talking to that unnatural computer again. He wanted to talk about his wife and all that situation. Let the computer comfort him.

"Let him say that all of it is not real. It's just a game, mirage, virtual reality. 'Why are you so worried, Konstantin Viktorovich? All in all, a week is a great result.'"

Sidorov felt the tears to well up. "Oh, Nastenka, Nastenka! Why, oh, why? Why? How could you? I loved you so much! And you...."

By the way, does love exist in the world at all? Real love! Eternal. "Strong as death." Or is this just fairy tales? I should ask this monster. He knows everything. He should know that. He'll explain and unscramble everything. I'll definitely ask him. But not now. I need to think a bit. I need to collect my thoughts and think. While I still got time. Before Nastenka comes home.

"So, how should I behave and communicate with her? I won't be able to do it as I used to. Do I love her? I don't really know. Same as before; no, I do not. It all remained in the past, and it cannot return. Ever. There's always going to be the damned helmet, and this dude between us... Damn him! What does he have that I don't?"

"Everything!" he answered himself mockingly. "And you know it. Fuck! Fuck, fuck, fuck!" Sidorov got outraged and spat on the kettle "Fuck the tea!" Then, cursing himself, he shuffled off gloomily back to the room. He sat in the chair and, with a sick and relaxed move, put —or rather slammed—the helmet on.

His new acquaintance was still standing near the window, with his hands behind his back, in the same posture as when Sidorov left him. It seemed as if he had been standing there all the time, not moving and going anywhere, while Sidorov was busy in the bathroom and kitchen. He didn't react to Sidorov's appearance. It seemed that he didn't even notice him.

"I just wanted to ask," began Sidorov with a stumbling voice, looking with hatred at the dark, immovable silhouette against the window. Actually, he didn't know what he was going to ask. "About eternal love? Does eternal love exist? Is everybody head-marked, or is it only him who's so lucky? As if the answer would help him! Maybe, maybe, it would. Well, no, it wouldn't. Nothing would help him. It's useless. Damn you and your devilish game!"

"You should be thinking about other things, Konstantin Viktorovich," said the man suddenly, still not looking at him.

"What?" Sidorov got lost. "Excuse me?"

"I said: you should be thinking about other things," the man unclasped his hands and faced Sidorov.

"Why?" Being struck with a terrifying foreboding, he asked quietly, moving his lips only. Oh, God! What? What else could happen?

"Because straight in," the man looked at the watch, "three minutes, eight seconds, your wife will come home, and she'll wish to put on the helmet. Yes, that will be her unexpected whim. You'll let her do it, right? You'll let her try it?" the man paused, glanced ironically at Sidorov and, without waiting for an answer, went on. "However, you won't be able to hinder her. It's better that you don't even try. A woman... what can you do when she wants something? So, your wife held out for a week. A whole week! And I'm wondering, how long you will, dear Konstantin Viktorovich? Eh? What do you think?" the man paused again and then looked at Sidorov inquiringly. He was sitting, gasping like a fish on the shore, and couldn't utter a word.

"Think it over; think it over, dear Konstantin Viktorovich! But not for too long. No longer than," the man glanced at the watch again, "forty-seven seconds. And then, after the game, if you'd like, we'll talk about eternal love. That's what you wanted to ask me, isn't it? Well, love, love," the man sighed theatrically. Sidorov was still sitting immovably.

"Well, good-bye. And, you know," the man suddenly winked at Sidorov and lowered his voice in a conspiratorial manner, "I'll tell you a secret. Somehow I think that your wife will lose, too. Like you did. But with a more, so to say, devastating score. You won't last a week. No! One hour at the most. Well, I doubt it. A couple of minutes! Right, we'll see. Good-bye."

***

In the evening of that day Nastenka packed her stuff, moved to her parents' house, and filed for divorce in a week. However, by that time Sidorov didn't care at all. He'd been drinking like a fish all week and had hardly understood what had been going on. The broken and crumpled helmet lay in the corner. Rather, not a helmet, but what was left of it. It was almost impossible to recognize a formerly beautiful and elegant item in a hideous, shapeless mixture of plastic pieces, scraps of metal and patches of cords.

***

And Lucifer was ask'd by his son:

— Wherefore did thou bewray it to me?

And Lucifer answer'd to his son:

— Thou live among men. And thou concerns art amongst them. Men art driven by feelings. Learn the price of the feelings—and thou shall wot the price of men. And thou shall hast what thou want.

And again Lucifer was ask'd by his son:

— Dost eternal love exist?

And Lucifer answer'd to his son:

— It's impossible to fill the soul with love only. Thither is place left f'r jealousy, and fear, and envy—f'r all of that, which maketh man a man. Sparkles of these feelings forev'r glow in a soul and art always ready to burst out from a wind. And again Lucifer was ask'd by his son:

— He teacheth love. What doth thou teach?

And Lucifer answer'd to his son:

— Love cannot be taught. It either existeth, 'r dost not. Otherwise—let him teach me.

And again Lucifer was ask'd by his son:

— And what doth thou teach?

And Lucifer answer'd to his son:

— Freedom.

And son of Lucifer took thought and ceas'd his questions.

LUCIFER'S SON. Day 2.

And the second day came. And Lucifer said:

— 'Tis said: doth not tempt. This is true. A man cannot intermit temptations. He is too weak. And Lucifer was ask'd by his son:

— What about Christ? F'r he resist'd all thy temptations, did he not?

And Lucifer answer'd to his son:

— Nay.

And Lucifer was again ask'd by his son:

— But he was able to object thee, did he not?

And Lucifer answer'd to his son:

— And wherefore did he object me? Wherefore did he speak to me at all? Did he hope to humour me? F'r he thought that he discern'd mine intentions and couldn't intermit the temptation to betoken me of it. That was a temptation of pride, and he didn't pass it.

And Lucifer was again ask'd by his son:

— And did he discern thy intentions? Thou show'd him the wrong ways.

And Lucifer answer'd to his son:

— Art thither any wrong ways f'r god? All ways art right f'r him. Christ couldst choose any path. but I made him make the choice and choose the one. And lose freedom.

And Lucifer was again ask'd by his son:

— But he didn't follow thy path, did he? He didn't go whither thou wish'd him to.

And Lucifer answer'd to his son:

— Is it so? If thou wish thy foe to go left, then betoken him to go right. So 'tis done. Christ went whither I want'd him to go.

And Lucifer was again ask'd by his son:

— But he didn't bow to thee, did he?

And Lucifer answer'd to his son:

— Wherefore not? Art thither any forbidden deeds f'r god? If so, he's not a god.

DREAM.

Lucifer's Son

1.

The very first night, when Alexey Gromov stayed alone in his apartment—he had taken his wife and kid to the summer cottage the day before—he had an incredible, amazing dream. As soon as he closed his eyes, there appeared a strange, inexplicable sound in his head—a whistle or a howl, that began growing... growing... and growing… And when Alexey thought that his head would burst and explode like an over-ripened watermelon, everything stopped short. It seemed as if a leap was made in time and space, and suddenly he was in another world. The world was changed, and he was changed as well. He had become different.

Slowly, very slowly, without sharp moves, he got off the bed and, moving slowly, as if in some jelly, approached the open window. He knew that it was just a dream and that he would jump out of the window and fly somewhere, but the feelings were so alive and real, everything around him was so detailed, visible and tangible, that, for a moment, he hesitated. "Come on! Is this really a dream?" But that was just for a moment.

The next second he was flying above the courtyard... higher, higher, higher…faster, faster, faster! The same strange, shrill sound appeared in his head again, and it was constantly growing! Suddenly everything stopped again.

Alexey found himself standing in an absolutely empty room. There was just a bed in the middle of it. Someone was lying on the bed. There was nothing—no rooms or doors—in the room. Just floor, ceiling, and naked walls.

If, up to that moment, Alexey's feelings were a little obscure and blurred—as it often happens in a dream—then, beginning from now, they became absolutely real. Alexey still knew that it was a dream but knew it only with his mind. His feelings were distinctly telling him that it was a reality. He could see, hear, touch, and smell. He pinched his arm, and nearly hissed with pain In one word, that was reality, the very real reality! Sheer reality—the sheerest reality it could be. Reality, and that was it! Whatever you do!

Alexey took some time to come into his senses. He was looking around him in great wonder, though there was nothing to look at—the room was empty. Then, hesitatingly, he approached the bed. There was a woman on it. Her head was on a pillow; she was covered with a blanket, and he couldn't see her face. Alexey went around the bed on the tips of his toes, trying to be silent, stooped, and carefully looked at the woman's face. He almost screamed with wonder. That was Ninka, the wife of his best friend, Vaska Zaitsev.

He and Vaska were friends since the childhood; they were joined at the hips. During all those years—they were almost 30—they didn't actually ever have a fight. Vaska lived overhead. He was a big, athletic, and handsome guy. Quiet, good-natured, and a little phlegmatic. By the way, he was always popular among women. Alexey even envied him because of this. Actually, now he envied him a little, but, in his youth, he envied him a lot. Alexey was stubby and skinny, and, overall, he was plain and unattractive. Correspondingly, he was never popular among women.

Vaska's wife, Ninka, was a remarkable and outstanding woman, like her husband. She was tall, proud, and, as Alexey thought, very, very beautiful —a gorgeous chick. He could never have such girls—neither in the institute when he was a student nor later. They simply never paid any attention to him. As it appeared, she loved her Vaska very much, and, as Alexey was her husband's best friend, she was very friendly with him.

But it seemed that she didn't see him as a man. One can feel it usually. At any rate, Alexey did feel it. However, he tried not to be offended. Well, how possibly could she see a man in him? Especially, comparing with her dear Vasechka. Firstly, he was much taller than Alexey. And, on the whole… Heh! Come on. There's nothing to talk about.

Alexey's wife had a very mediocre appearance. She was rather small and plumpish, like a barrel, with thin, straight, greasy hair. Well, as they say, not much cop. She wasn't beautiful in her youth, and after the marriage she just stopped paying attention to her looks. She got herself busy with the family, household, summer cottage; she gained more weight and became somehow coarse and old.

Recently, Alexey looked at his wife with slight disgust and abomination. That happened more and more often. Thank God, she was undemanding in bed. Otherwise, the situation would have been too bad. He actually married her because he clearly understood that he wouldn't have anyone better and he couldn't be picky; he was not too big for his boots! Though, generally, she was a nice woman—kind, merry, cheerful, and a good mistress, but….

At one time, Alexey wished for something completely different. He wished for real and serious love, real passion and true feelings. He wanted to find his dream, to meet Her—beautiful, mysterious, romantic. Once he thought that he'd met Her. There was a girl in his institute. Allochka. Interesting enough, but Alexey couldn't remember how she looked. Was she beautiful? What were her legs like? Slender? And her breast? Nothing at all! No details, no specific memories. Just a general image—one image. Some romantic veil that was enshrouding, covering, and surrounding her. There was something about her—something special. Reticence, maybe? no, not reticence, but abstraction. No—dreaminess, mystery, secret.

However, Alexey understood well enough that, probably, it was all his fantasies. In any case, the mysterious and dreamy romanticism didn't hinder her studying and attending all lectures and seminars and getting married during the last year of study to the most desirable guy of their class. She married a big guy, and he was smart, as well, from a wealthy family. He was merry, jolly, and had red cheeks. Well, as they sing, "I love military guys, big and ruddy." Seeing him, one would definitely think of the phrase "as red as a cherry." In one word, he was a great guy, as far as the whole male breed is concerned, but also earthbound and alien to romantic stuff, mysteries, melancholies, dreaminess, and other sentimental nonsense.

All in all, he was like his friend, Vaska. Alexey remembered well that he thought about this comparison straightaway. Later, when Vaska got married, his wife, Nina, subtly resembled Alla, though they were completely different in looks. Probably, the resemblance came from the fact that they both were indifferent and cold, and neither of them ever saw a man in Alexey. They were both unobtainable and inaccessible.

No! Alexey didn't intend to seduce his best friend's wife—God forbid! Never in his life would he think about hitting on her, thinking about her and flirting with her; however, there was something very offensive and insulting in her cold, scornful indifference and subconscious neglect, as if he wasn't a man, but something like a little dog. Her husband's pet, with whom she must be friends and tend well. But, if her husband would decide to kick it out or give it to someone—all the better. She wouldn't have to bother with it.

2.

And now, as he was standing in the middle of an empty room in his dream-reality, which was unlike anything that he had seen,

Alexey saw that the woman in the bed was Nina. Her eyes were closed, and her breath was still and regular; it seemed that she was in a deep sleep. Alexey stared at her in amazement for some time, then slowly and carefully reached for her shoulder and stopped, hesitating. He was absolutely stunned with the reality of what was happening. He was real, Nina was real, the bed was real, and the room was real. Everything was real. The only unreal thing was the situation in whole.

"What room is it? What is Nina doing here? Where's Vaska? Well, to be precise, it's not 'where's Vaska?' It's a dream; Vaska doesn't have anything to do with it! It cannot be a real Nina's bedroom—ah, shit!" Alexey was embarrassed. "What does all this mean? What should he do? Should he wake up Nina? Or not? Maybe it's not her at all? Maybe it's a monster or a demon, looking like her. And it's waiting for him to 'wake' it up. It's a peculiar world, the world of dream. It has its own laws."

Suddenly, Alexey remembered stupid horror movies about different nightmares which were happening in a dream and he shuddered. "Ough! Hell with her! Hell with Ninka, or whatever it may be. It's better not to touch her at all, not to touch anything here at all. Don't trouble trouble until trouble troubles you."

Still carefully and slowly, he took his hand away. Frankly speaking, he became anxious with all that was happening. Something was wrong. He should probably leave the dream as soon as possible. Run away. Take off. Scratch it. In one word, wake up. His consciousness, it seemed, made a mistake. He was in a wrong place. Fuck such dreams! What kind of dream is that, when he's standing and thinking as if he was in reality?

"Well, 'wake up'—it's easy to say. How should he do it? In the movies, someone would always wake up the hero. "Well, that's not the case. Nobody would wake me up. I'm all alone at home. All alone in the fucking world. Wife and kid are away. I took them to the summer cabin myself." Alexey was again amazed by the clear and vivid understanding of all that was happening. He remembered and understood everything—where he was, what he did, and how he got here.

"What the fuck is it? A dream! A hell of a dream!"

Nina muttered something indistinctly in her sleep and turned on the other side. Alexey froze in fear and then recovered his breath. Oh, my! Soon enough, he would be a stutterer. His heart was pounding, and his forehead was covered with sweat. "Phew! What am I afraid of anyway? What...? There's definitely something to be afraid of—when she would wake up and smile—there would be fangs in her mouth, the ones that fucking Count Dracula has. Or, maybe, iron claws, like… well... what's his name? Krueger. From that endless TV show, "Friday, the 13th?" No… "A Nightmare on Elm Street"? Right! A fucking nightmare. On Elm Street. That's it! The one where Krueger, with his iron fingers and dressed in a striped sweater, was chasing everyone."

Alexey looked at Nina cautiously. He could see only her head; her hands were covered with blanket. "Well, God knows if she has any claws. It would be better not to check. She doesn't have any sweater on, that's for sure. Well, however, she was lying under the blanket, and he couldn't see what was on her and what wasn't or if there was anything at all on her."

At the latter thought, Alexey got excited. "What's she wearing, really? Maybe… nothing? No! A night-gown, a short one, and that's it. No! A night-gown and panties under it—short panties—silk ones! Well, they feel smooth when touched. They are like a bikini, but they cover the ass a bit. Not completely, but just… Not a ribbon, like women love to wear, but there's something to cover the ass. And one could slip the hand under the panties."

He clearly imagined that he's slipping his hand under the blanket, touching Ninka's body, caressing it, feeling it; then he's slipping his hand—one finger at a time—under her panties. No! At first, he's touching her with his hand, with his fingertips. He's touching her leg near the ankle. And then his hand is going up and up…."

Fuck! Suddenly Alexey felt a very strong erection. Independently of him and against his will, it grew stronger and stronger. His fears disappeared in a moment, and suddenly he felt, understood, and realized that he was completely alone in the empty room with a sleeping woman in the bed—a young, beautiful woman, whom he liked very much. And, probably, she was naked. She was the woman whom he could only dream about up to this time.

"Fuck! But she's Vaska's wife! So what? It's just a dream—my own. There's nothing forbidden in a dream. A man isn't responsible for his deeds in a dream. There are different dreams. One could see things which are far worse." Alexey often saw dreams of which he would speak with no one. "What for? Nobody speaks about dreams. It's sub-consciousness. It's an uncontrolled process. It's purely private and intimate. What if Vaska's fucking my wife every night? I can't know for sure. Well, on the other hand, why would he? He's got Ninochka. Such a gorgeous woman—such beautiful… With such forms…" Still hesitating, Alexey touched the sheet distractedly. The sheet was real, as well, like everything else. It was an ordinary sheet—white, cool, and a bit scratchy.

Then, having collected his courage, he sat on the edge of the bed, trying not to wake Nina. He raffled the edge of the blanket; it was thin. Alexey felt that his lust and desire grew stronger with every second. He could barely control himself. As if accidentally and secretly, his hand slipped under the blanket —deeper, deeper…

Suddenly, Alexey was struck with the thought and snatched his hand back. What if she wakes up and sees what he's doing here? And she would laugh at his face in answer for his harassment. And she would tell Vaska everything! At this thought, Alexey flushed, and his essence was instantly filled with a hot wave of unbearable shame. It seemed as if it was a real humiliation. His cheeks were burning, his eyes were looking from side to side, and his thoughts were all amiss. He was feeling the edge of the bed convulsively. It seemed as if a whole century passed before he could calm down and collect himself.

"What the hell! She'd tell Vaska? What would she tell? It's a dream—a dream—my own. I'm a master here. 'Laugh!' I'd like to see her try! I'd show her—I would!" Alexey was screwing up his courage, but the very thought that Nina would wake up and look in his eyes… No way! Let her sleep. And he'd do it in her sleep, slowly, like this…

Alexey felt that he couldn't resist anymore. And he didn't want to. He decisively put his hand deeply under the blanket. But he didn't time his move and hit something hot and stiff. He immediately jerked back his hand, but, as Nina didn't react to it—neither moved, nor woke up—he touched her hot body with his fingertips, now more carefully and slowly. Nina kept sleeping tightly.

Having calmed down, Alexey caressed her hot and smooth skin; then, slowly, he took his hand from under the blanket and, trying to make no noise—though he was somehow sure that Ninka wouldn't wake up—it was his dream. Blast it! He can do everything he wants—moved closer to Nina's feet, and restraining and asking himself not to hurry, slowly and tenderly caressed her ankle and the outer side of her foot through the blanket. Then, still though the blanket, slightly touching her with his fingertips, he started going up her leg—calf, knee, up... up.. here…. He paused at her waist, just for a moment. Ninochka was sleeping on her side, having bent her knees, and, going lower, he touched her hip and upper buttock.

At first, he was slow and careful… just a little, barely touching…then he pressed his palm to her body and grasped her flesh through the blanket. It was very thin, and Alexey could vividly and distinctly feel everything—every fold, rubber thread, and stitch of Ninka's panties. He quickly moved his hand back to her feet and, forgetting about caution, put the hand under the blanket—he was leaning on the bed with the other hand—found Ninka's naked foot, grabbed it and went up. Up… up… up… a thigh… panties…. He slipped his hand under them and, feeling something soft, wet and hot, put his middle finger inside. Then, unable to think straight and losing control, he took the blanket off her, quickly lay near her and, unable to unbutton the trousers with trembling fingers, began taking them off.

His desire was so great, that, penetrating her, he did only a few moves. Then he jerked convulsively and, clenching his teeth, closing his eyes and putting back his head, moaned tensely and woke up. He was still lying in a bed in his room, at home. His underpants were wet.

"Oh, my God! Did I just have a pollution! Holy Mother of God! When did I have it the last time? When I was 15, right?" Alexey turned on his back, put his hands behind his head and listened to his feelings. He felt easy and cheery. And a bit sad. It was a pity that everything ended so quickly. He wanted to get back into his dream. He began recalling all the details with pleasure.

He's grasping her with his hands… her body… hot and stiff… He's penetrating her… between her legs… from behind… lowering her panties… between her long and slim legs… Alexey felt that he was getting aroused again. Shit! If only he could go back there… This time he would do it slowly… Slowly… Easy… With feeling… wit.. and punctuation… As is right and proper.

"Fuck! What a dream! It was so damn real! It was even more than real. Even better than in life. Fuck! As if he really was fucking Ninka!" Alexey deliberately tried to think about everything that had just happened to him in an earthly and rude tone; thus he wanted to hide and conceal from himself his own secret and intimate thoughts and feelings. He felt good—very good—very. He had never felt so good before; not with his wife, Verka, not with anyone. Let alone Verka! Phew! Forget about her. And Nina! Now she's one hell of a woman! Yeah… that fool Vaska is a lucky bastard!"

Curiously enough, but the thought that he actually raped his best friend's wife, although in a dream, gave Alexey pleasure. It added a special, extra savor to his sweet memories. Sharpness.

Poignancy. If only he could have this dream again…again. Alexey even closed his eyes with pleasure, like a fat cat, dreaming of a new portion of sour cream. He almost began purring. "Oh! Again…but this time in another way… Slowly… Easy… Put her on her back… Hot chick… Ooh! Put her legs on my shoulders… and…and then put her on her belly…slowly spread her legs… gently… gently….

Alexey suddenly realized that he was thinking about Nina, Vaska's wife—a healthy woman whom he knew very well—as if she were a thing, a heartless blow-up with which he could do everything he wanted. He could raffle her, bend her, and make her take any positions he wanted. However, that thought was pleasant, as well. The thought that he owned her, that he owned her body and had absolute power over her. He could do with her everything he wanted…everything he wanted…everything he could think of. He didn't have to ask her, he didn't have to be ashamed at all. He didn't have to think about her reaction. Eh! Alexey even fidgeted in the bed with desire. One more time…one and only time!

3.

Alexey had a logy day at work. He couldn't do anything properly. He was absent-minded and inattentive, he answered the questions inappropriately and, as Olenka, an acrimonious and bad-tempered secretary, said, he was "in the clouds." "Gromov is in the clouds today!" she said.

Hell with the work! Alexey couldn't stop thinking about his dream. He was dreaming, drooping, and recalling various thrilling details all day long. When he… and then… and she was like…

All these memories were thrilling him very much. They were so clear and real, so alive, that it seemed to him that he had indeed spent the night with Vaska's wife. Shit! He should have put the underpants on. Now he couldn't leave the table!

Alexey could barely wait until the end of day. He wanted to see Vaska as soon as possible; the very idea was bothering him from the morning. The thought that he would see Nina, that he would talk to her as if nothing happened, look in to her eyes, smile politely, knowing about the night before. This thought was so thrilling, so tempting that he barely restrained himself and didn't leave earlier. Under any excuse. He had a headache. Maybe a sore foot and an ear… Fuck them all! Let them think what they want!

Coming home, Alexey threw his briefcase on a sofa, and, without changing, rushed to Vaska. He rang a doorbell and started thinking quickly what he would tell him "Listen, Vasya!" but suddenly the door was opened by Nina. Seeing her, Alexey nearly choked over with surprise and felt that his face blushed. All his night memories came back to him with renewed strength.

"Hi, Nina," he said, stammering, "is Vaska at home?"

"Hello. No, he's on a business trip. He'll be back by the weekend," said Nina politely and indifferently, not bothering to invite him in and waiting for him to turn around and leave.

"I see," said Alexey slowly, trying to bide time. "And why are you here and not at the summer house? I already took my wife and kid there." His and Vaska's houses were near each other.

"I don't have the time, really. Maybe, we'll go there this weekend, if everything's okay." Nina clearly wanted to finish the conversation.

"Okay, I see. When Vaska's back, tell him to call me."

"Okay, I will."

"Bye."

"Good-bye."

Alexey stood for some time in front of the closed door, then turned slowly and plodded to the elevator. The usual feeling of humiliation, which he always had when talking to Nina, was mingled with a strange disappointment. He couldn't explain to himself its nature. It seemed as if he subconsciously waited that he and Nina would already start an affair that she would feel something, take him differently or behave herself in some other way. That maybe she had seen the same dream as he had. That she'd been there, in his dream. She was real. In his unnaturally real dream.

Alexey realized the absurdity of his delirious, sexual fantasies, but the usual indifference of Nina was like a bucket of cold water for him. His cheeriness and excitement vanished, giving way to inner emptiness and scorn to himself, to his worthlessness. It seemed as if suddenly all his long-forgotten adolescent issues regarding his unpresentable looks woke up and came back to him.

"Who could ever want you? Ugly as sin. Poor. What are you dreaming about? 'Affair!' Right! Don't bet on it! She's ignoring you completely! You're like a louse to her. As if you didn't exist at all! And she's right. You are a louse. You're nobody! You should do something worthy in your life and then start hitting on women. Freaking Don Juan! A fucking demon and seducer from downstairs on the wings of love. Mother-fucking Casanova."

All these thought made Alexey lose his spirits. He was wretched and depressed, despicable and filthy. It seemed as if there was dull, gray, endless, cold autumn rain outside. "Maybe he should drink, eh? Drown his sorrows? How does Apollon Grigoryev sing?"

Sad... Hearts of pain died away.
A glass of vodka?

"That's it! A glass of vodka? Right, vodka. No chance I would drink. I have to go to work tomorrow. And I have nothing to drink, anyway. I don't wanna go out. And if I do? Would it help? No, it'll just make it worse, that's for sure."

Alexey wandered aimlessly between the rooms, not knowing what to do, and then switched on the TV. He channel-hopped. Nothing—endless shows and 30-year-old, ancient movies. "Fuck you all! I came home from work, and there's nothing to watch. One could easily go on the bottle. So, what shall I do? Go to bed, eh? At half past seven? So, what's our dear Ninochka doing right now? Eh? And what's she wearing? It's summer, and it's hot... Maybe she's wearing the same night-gown? And panties... By the way, does she really have such lingerie? Same as she had in a dream? Hm, that would be interesting to find out! But how? Anyway, what am I thinking about! What crap is in my head? Enough! I had a dream, that's it. Enough! Forget it."

"Heigh ho! So what shall I do? Eh?" Alexey yawned two times in a row and felt his eyes closing and his eyelids becoming like lead; he had a deadly wish to sleep. It was irresistible, Already falling asleep, he managed to take off his clothes and lie down on a bed, covering himself with a blanket. "I have to wash up," he thought, before finally falling down in a black bottomless abyss.

4

Alexey found himself standing in the same room. Near the same bed, on which there lay a woman. Ninka! Alexey started sweating with excitement. "Is it real? Is it?! Thank you, God! Is she really here? Like yesterday? No, not like yesterday... Now he doesn't have to hurry... What for? Now I know everything. I have time."

Slowly and deliberately, trying to prolong the pleasure and thinking about all details of what he would do now, he went around the bed, stopped, and still slowly, as if thinking and hesitating, grasped the edge of the blanket with two fingers and started quietly, inch after inch to draw it, draw it, draw it off Nina.

Slowly at first… slowly… very slowly… then, having lost his head upon seeing an intolerably seductive image of half-naked woman's body—so close and obtainable; just reach your hand—and having forgotten about his reasonable decisions and intentions not to hurry, he pulled the blanket with a jerk. At that very moment, Ninka woke up. For several seconds, she just stared bluntly around her, then suddenly sat on the bed, pulled up her naked legs, and, covering her breasts with her hands, looked at Alexey with saucer eyes.

"What are you doing here?" she asked with low voice which was trembling with fear and surprise.

Alexey stood with the blanket in his hands. He was embarrassed and couldn't utter a word.

"Ahem, Ninochka! It's just a dream. See? Just a dream…."

"What are you doing here?" repeated Nina, not listening to him, still looking straight at Alexey.

"Nothing," he got completely embarrassed under her stare. "I'm just standing. Going… looking. I saw you lying here; I thought I should find out what's going on? Maybe you're sick? Maybe you need help? Maybe I should call first aid?"

There was complete mess and mayhem in Alexey's head. His thoughts got confused, he kept saying some nonsense and bullshit—he knew it but couldn't do anything about it. He was just jabbering and jabbering and couldn't stop. His ears and forehead were burning, he had a cobweb in his throat, and his tongue was producing unimaginable twaddle against his will. It seemed as if he lost his wits and couldn't think at all. He was very ashamed, as if he was a boy caught spying in a girls' changing room. He dreamed about one thing only—he wanted to sink into the earth at once.

"Give me the blanket!" Nina interrupted him in a commanding voice.

"What? What, Ninochka? Blanket? What blanket?" Alexey hustled, trying to understand what she wanted from him, rushed about and twisted his feet, "Oh, the blanket! Where's Vaska? Right, he's on a business trip. You told me that. Yeah, the blanket…blanket…blanket—where is it? I've seen it somewhere."

"It's in your hand!" Nina interrupted him coldly again. "Toss it to me! Now! And get out of here immediately!" she added in a commanding voice. Nina clearly saw Alexey's state and, it seemed, she almost calmed down, recovered herself, and stopped fearing him. Moreover, concerning the situation, she wasn't going to be soft on him or even to be polite.

"Polite?" How can she be polite? What's he doing here anyway? In her bedroom, near her bed? With her blanket in his hand? How come he's here!"

"Right, I'll," shrinking, mumbled, or, rather whimpered Alexey, in a weak voice, "I'm gonna leave now."

"And where would I go?" He suddenly came to his senses. "There are no windows or doors. It's a dream! My dream. I'm seeing it in my sleep. Ninka and this fucking blanket. Dream…it's my dream. I'm the master here! I can do whatever I want…everything I want! What's the matter with me?"

Alexey halted, waited for a couple of moments, then plucked up his courage, slowly straightened up, looked into Nina's eyes narrowly, and sneered imposingly. Under his gaze Nina froze, cowered, and somehow shrank. Her eyes opened even wider, she got very pale, and suddenly, she slowly began to move away from him, as if trying to flatten herself against the back of the bed.

Alexey, still sneering with a scoff and staring at her, opened his hand, and the blanket fell softly on the floor. Nina threw a look at it, and it seemed that she became even more pale.

"What's the meaning of all this? What are you going to do? Are you out of your mind?" she said, almost whispered, in a stiffened voice.

Alexey could physically feel her growing fear and brutal horror. He almost smelled it. The scent of prey's fear, the feeling of complete impunity, and limitless, absolute power over the woman sitting in front of him besotted him. They strengthened his desire, lust, and growing passion. Slowly, he went forward, and his grin became wider and undisguised. He openly stared at Ninka's body, devouring it with his eyes; and, under that sticky, shameless, explicitly lustful, and unambiguous gaze, she was shrinking and jiggetting, trying to hide and cover her nudity.

"Come on, Ninochka! What are you afraid of? I'm not gonna do anything wrong to you. Well, I'll just put you to good use, and that's it. Be a good girl, like yesterday, and everything's gonna be fine. You'll even like it. You liked it yesterday, didn't you?" the sound of his own voice and the possibility to say to a woman's face such incredible things got Alexey even more aroused.

"Stay away from me! Don't touch me! Help! Vasya!" Nina screamed suddenly in a loud voice, being scared to death.

"Come on, there's no need to scream! Vasya's not the only one, who… I should use you as well," Alexey got aroused even more. He couldn't restrain himself anymore, but he didn't want everything to finish very quickly. "Maybe, I'm even better, eh? You'll have the opportunity to compare. You'll see who's better," he suddenly remembered an unambiguous and dirty phrase from a French novel and even laughed with pleasure.

"What? What? Whom will I compare? You and Vasya? Look at yourself in a mirror, you freak! Monkey!" Nina's scorn was so sincere and strong that it seemed to Alexey that he was stung and burnt; blood went to his head, and everything reeled before his eyes.

"You bitch!" he screamed in rage, rushed to her, and grabbed her hands. Then, feeling her resisting, almost immediately let them go and, taking a big swing, smacked her with all strength that he had, first with right hand and then with the left one.

When the body of the stunned woman slackened, he quickly pulled her panties down to the middle of her hips, tore the gown on her breast, took Nina's legs up under the knees and, grabbing her naked breast with one hand and her hair with another one, fell on her with all his body and began to rape her furiously. Pressing her face against the pillow, he hissed viciously in her ear, "So what, bitch? You like it? You like it? And now? Now? You like it, right? Right? And now? You like it? Like it? Li-i… i-ke? Li-i..!

Alexey moaned loudly and woke up.

His underpants were wet again. He just had a pollution.

5.

During the day, Alexey started to feel a strange anxiety. At first, it was very weak, but then, as the day went on, it became stronger and stronger.

"So, was it a dream or not? Hm… dream. In any case, it's not just a dream; it's as plain as it can be. If so, what if she'd remember everything, too? What if we share this dream, and she's seeing the same?"

"Though yesterday she didn't tell me anything, when I visited her. Idiot! Yesterday, she was sleeping—and she woke up today! She saw me today. So what? It was a dream. Dream! You never know what you can see in a dream! It was her dream, what does it have to do with me? I have nothing to do with it at all. I don't have the faintest idea! It's like in a joke. "It's your own dream, madam!"

Alexey tried to cheer up and calm down but felt heavy-hearted. "It was a dream, right, but what if it was not a dream at all? It was too real, this dream. Too real. Instigation of the devil, but not a dream! Well… However, why should I care? I'm okay with it. The more instigations, the better. And more often. Yeah!"

"What was I saying? Well, right… So, instigation—I mean, a dream. If I'm having doubts about it, so she must be having them all the more. Especially if she's feeling everything the same real way, as I do. Sure! She's definitely having them! Who'd like it if somebody fucks you in a dream, as if for real? Various jerks." Alexey screwed up his face involuntarily. "Bitch! And if they beat you up, as well. Fuck!" Some details of the previous night came to his mind, and his anxiety became even stronger.

"She'll definitely tell Vaska! So what? First, he's not here yet, and secondly, fuck him! It's just a dream. What's my fault that your wife's having nightmares? Sexual ones. Maybe she's a masochist, and that's the way her subconsciousness works, as Freud says? Suppressed desires, shoot. Libido, actually. In one word, stay at home and forget about business trips! Fuck her more often, and she won't be having such dreams. All her whore-like libido will go away. Like this! Well, but it'd be better if she didn't remember anything. Fuck! Should I call her? How's your precious health, dear Ninulechka? How are you? Do you miss me, darling, when you sleep at night alone? How's your beloved Vasechka? Does he have any sign of the horns? I mean, is he back already? It's a pity! I need to talk to him. As soon as possible!"

"Oh, well; or maybe it's better not to call? She'll probably think, 'he fucks me in a dream, bothering me in a real life, and now gets used to calling! He got to me! He fucked me up! Literally and figuratively. Whether I wake or sleep.'" Alexey smiled to his own smartness. "'And it's strange. He has never called before. It's very suspicious! Eh? But why is it "suspicious," really? It's a dream! A dream! So what; should I call or not?" Alexey looked at the receiver, hesitating, reached for it, but stopped his hand halfway.

"Come on, I'll do it!" Resolutely, he grabbed the phone and, being afraid that he would change his mind, dialed the number.

"Hello!"

"Hi, Nina, it's me."

"Oh… hi."

"Listen, has Vaska called?"

"Nope."

"If he calls, tell him to contact me immediately. Okay? I need him badly."

"Alright, I'll tell him."

"How are you? Everything's okay?

"Fine."

"Well, you seem to be tired."

"No, it's okay."

"Yeah.. Okay, bye. Don't forget to tell Vaska about me."

"Okay, I won't."

"Okay, bye."

"Bye."

With great relief, Alexey carefully put down the phone and wiped his sweating forehead with a shaking hand. "Well! She didn't tell him anything. And she spoke to me in a good way. Though, her voice was a bit… Well, well, well! What's the meaning of it? In any case, it's good. That's wonderful! Either she doesn't see any dreams and, naturally, doesn't remember anything, or she just thinks, 'that's only a dream.'"

"Well, right. What should she be thinking? She's probably surprised; why is she seeing me in her dreams? And so often. You see, I'm not her type of guy. Ouch! But that's your problem, madam. You need only to spread your legs, for it would be more convenient for me, the monkey. Yeah, that's good. Very good. Haw-haw! Adieu, darling! I hope, this night, we'll meet again. Ciao!"

The rest of the day, Alexey was in a wonderful mood. He laughed, made fun, and almost danced and hopped around. Having come home in the evening, he went to bed at once. For some reason, he was almost sure that he'd have his wonderful, fascinating, and charming dream again. His foreboding was right. As soon as he closed his eyes, he found himself in a familiar room. Nina was sitting on a bed and looking at him with horror, like a prey. This time, she wasn't sleeping.

6.

During the next few days, Alexey almost got the hang of his wonder-like dream. Moreover, he actually learned how to control it. First of all, he found out that he could get in it not only in the night, but during the day, as well. He could do it whenever he wanted to—at any moment of day and night. He only had to close his eyes and concentrate in a special way.

But it was not the most important thing. The most important thing was that he learned to stay in the dream during orgasm. Now, when he cummed, he didn't wake up like before. On top of it, he was able to start all over again straightaway.

This new revelation, these new, alluring, and limitless horizons and prospects that opened before him besotted, surprised, and befuddled him. He almost lost his head. Moreover, he had never been a sex bomb in real life. Actually, he had never had any particular talents in this field. Well, he was at average level—nothing special.

As the result, for the last two days Alexey almost didn't leave his dream. He abandoned his job —"fuck it! fuck them all! I'll think something out later!"—and didn't eat much, but kept raping and raping Nina, continuously and relentlessly. With his new, truly limitless and fantastic capabilities, he was able to do it freely and unstintingly hundred times a day—and he did it!

He lost count of his endless orgasms, and he thought that his honeymoon with Nina would go on forever, and ever, and ever. That his life would turn into one continuing and never-ending pleasure. Into eternal, fantastic, and lustful paradise. Naturally, it finished when, by the end of the second day, he understood that he had enough of Nina. She was like an old, used lover with whom you just keep sleeping by inertia—only because there's nobody else. He didn't use to take pleasure in the intimacy with her anymore. And it wasn't interesting for him to rape her. The charm of novelty vanished—and, as a matter of fact, there was no rape. "What 'rape' are you talking about?"

Being exhausted and scared because of his endless abuses and beating, Ninka collapsed by the middle of the first day and didn't even try to resist. Nothing was left of a proud, independent, arrogant, haughty, and confident woman. Now she turned into an intimidated, cowed, limp, humble, and speechless creature that was eager to do everything, as long as she wasn't beaten and tortured. And she did it upon first request. Alexey looked at her and sometimes it made him sick. Now, he used to think about her as something impersonal and nameless, something neuter. ‘It’. So what ‘abuse’ and ‘rape’ are you talking about?

***

Bored as he was, Alexey looked around the room and snapped his fingers lazily. The woman, who was sitting in a corner, darted off, rushed to him, stood on her knees, and began doing a blowjob. Recently, he entertained himself by training her like a dog. One flip - a blowjob; two flips - position number one, and so on. It was fun at first, but then it became boring as well. Alexey watched her for some time listlessly, then he stretched with a crack and yawned. "Ugh! I’m sick and tired of it! Nothing new. This bitch who’s eager to do anything—she’s like a young fucking pioneer. Yeah, she just lacks a tie around her neck. A red one. And a horn with a drum."

She sucked to him tight. One wouldn’t be able to tear her off. She likes it, probably. Yeah, she’s doing her best, fucking madam. "That’s because she’s scared," he smiled cynically to himself. "She’s like a sewing machine. Fucking ‘Zinger’, actually. Right. Go on! Do your best. Probably, I’ll cum."

"If you don’t do it properly again, you’ll be the one to blame, bitch," he said quietly and menacingly, and saw with pleasure that Nina startled and moved her head faster. "Well, we were so proud!" thought Alexey with malice, looking down at the woman who was standing on her knees and trying to please him. "Gee! Come on! Listen, you! How dare you?" A couple of slaps was enough—big deal. That’s it with the pride—off it went. That’s a price of any human and of all his so-called dignity. Well, maybe, someone needs a bit more. A couple of them. But, as a matter of fact, it’s all the same. The result is the same. A dime a dozen—that’s our price.

"‘Monkey!’ ‘Freak!’ So, now you’re sucking freak’s and monkey’s dick! You like it, right? Slut!" Alexey suddenly recalled some humiliating details and moments of the memorable scene when he raped Nina for the first time, and he felt the old, heavy insult and rage move in his soul again. So, he didn’t forget anything! "Freak!" Bitch! Hey, what are you doing, slut! Can you suck properly? Did you forget how I like it? Close your fucking mouth!" he shouted in rage, grabbed Nina’s hair with two hands and started moving her head back and forth, trying to find the necessary pace.

Then, feeling that he couldn’t do it, he hurled the scared woman away and, breathing heavily, stared at her in wrath, with his eyes filled with blood. "Cunt! Fucking bitch! What should I do to her? She must remember, bitch, for the rest of her life, who's a freak here!"

Alexey looked around helplessly. Nothing! Just a stupid bed. He needed a stick! Or a lash. Or, even better, a whip! No. He didn't know how to handle a whip. A lash would be better.

"Spank this slut! Blow off his steam! Right! Spank! He'll do it right on this very bed!" Suddenly, there appeared a lash in his hand. He glanced at it—and he wasn't surprised. "Right! I see. He's the master here. The lord. The king and the God. The lord of the dream! Naturally, all his wishes must be fulfilled at once. Right. That's the only way! Why didn't I think of it before! Well! And now, my dear Ninochka, we'll play a game. A real game. It will be fun."

Alexey imagined how he would spank Nina—lash her spine… her naked spine; her ass—stiff, shaking ass. Purple, fiery scars swell on her skin; she screams, writhes, twists, and shrieks with pain… burning, wild pain. And he felt that he was literally shaking with desire. He lingered a bit and then, freezing with anticipation of something completely new, unknown and that which he had never experienced before—a poignant, forbidden, previously unknown pleasure; unexplored, inaccessible, fascinating, bright, glamorous, and fantastic feelings—provocative, scorching, and dizzying—he slowly began to approach Nina, who stood still, being scared to death. He stared at her with a feverish, dancing, fiery, and at the same time attentive and evaluative look. Coming very close to her, he stopped.

Ninka cowed in her corner, covering her head with her hands. Seeing the lash, her eyes became completely insane, like she was an animal, scared to death.

Alexey came closer.

"Well! It's not convenient to beat her! All strokes are gonna fall on hands and head. I should probably put her on the bed. And someone should hold her. But who? Servants! I need servants!"

He flipped his fingers impatiently. Ninka startled and rushed to him reflexively, considering it a command, but then again hid in her corner."

Near the woman, who stayed in the corner, there appeared two silent figures in dark shapeless robes and hoods which covered their eyes. The figures took her up and dragged her to the bed.

Nina didn't have the time to understand anything and started screaming only when she was already lying on the bed, with her face down, as Alexey wanted. Burning with impatience but trying not to show it, he slowly and lazily approached the bed, playing with the lash. Trembling as if with fever and hearing a drawling and hooting noise or ringing, he looked greedily and impatiently at her extremely long, slim, and naked legs, ass, back—choosing a spot for the first blow and trying on. Then, suddenly, as if he remembered something or even changed his mind, he approached the woman, who was lying on her belly, grabbed her hair, pulled up her head with a jerk, and with a convulsive move, put his stiff dick, which was trembling with hyper-arousal like a string, into her mouth, and did several short thrusts.

After that he stepped away, aimed carefully, did a wide swing, and, with all strength that he had, lashed the naked shoulders of Ninka, who was lying on the bed. She shrieked piercingly. Alexey's desire was at its peak. He did several similar blows and then, feeling that he cannot stand it and restrain himself anymore, threw the lash away, jumped on the prostrated Ninka, saddled her, spread her buttocks wide open, and, with a sharp and strong move, plunged his stiffened dick into her ass. He immediately groaned, twitched, and wriggled, shuddering in sweet convulsions.

Then he lay for several moments, catching his breath. He put his head on the back of the woman, who froze beneath him, and rested, listening to his feelings. Finally, he stood up slowly and reluctantly and, breathing heavily, stepped away from the bed and ordered his servants to rape Ninka in front of his eyes. Then he flipped his fingers and, creating the third servant, told the three of them to do it.

This sight got him aroused again, and he joined them. Cumming on her face, he lifted up her chin, covered with sperm, and said quietly, looking straight into her eyes, "From now on you will call me 'my master, the Lord of the Dream'."

7.

Beginning from that moment, the room of the dream, as Alexey called the place, where he went in his sleep, began to turn quickly into a real torture chamber. Lashes, whips, knives, various thongs, pincers, and red-hot canes... Alexey didn't even know where they were coming from—maybe from some dark, dense mazes of his subconscious. Days and days on end, he tortured and tormented Nina. He liked to hurt her, and he delighted in her sufferings. It got him aroused, lashed him, and thrilled his sensuality, which started to fade quickly. Every time, the tortures were more and more devious. He tormented her, raped her, then tormented again, then raped once more, and felt insane, incredible, and unparalleled pleasure. During these moments he was an overman!

The wounds and injuries that he dealt her were of no importance, for, as he soon found out, they could disappear at any moment at his will, and the prey's body was again ready for new tortures and new torments.

Pain. Only pain! Pure and refined. Without any annoying accompanying additions, like unavoidable deformities, wounds, scars, injured organs, and broken bones. Nothing! Pure pain only! Nothing, but pain! The traces of tortures would disappear, but the memory of them won't. Both Nina and Alexey kept good memory of everything. All the details—what had happened the day before and an hour before that. Nina remembered her pain, her fear, her horrors, and all her horrible feelings. She remembered everything in smallest details—every minute, second, and every moment spent in the room of the dream.

Alexey remembered everything, as well. He loved to travel, refresh, and savor certain moments of his pleasures which were most vivid for him. Very often, he recalled them with joy, like common people recall the scenes and episodes of their favorite movies, which they liked and remembered. But that was not a movie. Everything in the room of the dream was real. Blood, flesh, and pain—all of it was real. And the pleasure was real, too. And the stronger one's pain, the sharper was the other's pleasure. That theatre of two actors didn't have any insincerity. Each of them played the role, and the game was serious, like in real life. And nobody could leave it. It was impossible—like in real life.

The last few days, Alexey stayed in his dream without any breaks. As a matter of fact, he wasn't interested in a real life. If he could, he would live constantly in the room of the dream. Unfortunately, he had to return to the real world from time to time. He had to eat and drink, and he had to answer the phone. On the whole, the reality reminded of itself from time to time. Alas! He couldn't get away from it completely.

By the way, sometimes it happened in very inappropriate moments—like when he began to enjoy the process. You just fly into a passion and... like, for example, today. Alexey just felt, at last, that he…

At this moment a phone suddenly rang. Wrested from his dream, Alexey looked around bluntly with crazy eyes, then reached out for the phone and found it only at the third try. His ears were still filled with a divine music of tortured Ninka's moans and screams.

"Yeah!"

"Hi, it's me," he heard Vaska's voice and got a little surprised.

Well, well! It was like a message from hell! He completely forgot about Vaska's existence. It seemed that everything had been left in another world, and he was living on another planet, and all those vaskas-petkas-sashkas-mashkas-wives-jobs had stayed somewhere there… in the past… on Earth… in another, old life.

It turned out otherwise! Not at all! It turned out that they were still here, near him. They were still rusting and pottering around; they were living their common, gray, ordinary, and worthless lives of rats.

It blew his mind—unbelievable! During that time, he had turned into a God, an overman, into the Lord of the Dream! One universe died away for him, and another one emerged. He became another man. He'd been in hell and in paradise. He had learned about man and his soul, about his worth—he had learned things that he would have never found out during all his life! No, not his life—a hundred lives—a million!

He remembered Ninka in the room of the dream, her crawling at his feet, groveling, and fulfilling his orders at the flip of his fingers. He remembered her copulating with a group of his servants, with all of them—together and apart—in front of his eyes. She did it voluntarily, just to entertain, distract, and amuse him a little, He remembered her…

"Hello! Do you hear me?" reality forced itself obtrusively in the form of Vaska.

"Yeah, hi! So, you're back already? Something's wrong with the phone," Alexey quickly came to his senses.

"Yeah, I came back yesterday. I called you, but nobody answered."

"I switched off the phone; I didn't want to get any calls from work."

"Oh, I see. What did you want from me?"

"Right! Yeah, there was something, some stuff. Well, it's not urgent anymore. I'll tell you when we meet. Have you got news? Everything's okay?"

"Not really… Ninka's got problems."

"What problems?" asked Alexey, freezing. What does he know?

"She had a miscarriage."

"Miscarriage?" Alexey was sincerely surprised. "Hmm… How come I didn't know? Interesting—very interesting! Well, well! So, my dear Ninochka, you have your own secrets? Well, well! We're gonna have a little chat today—very interesting."

"So, she was pregnant, right?" he asked, just in case.

"Yeah, on the sixteenth week," Vaska spoke in a sepulchral voice, "We wanted to have a baby so much!"

"Yeah, I see. Listen, you have my sympathies. There's nothing to say. Take it easy, both of you. You'll definitely have a baby. What do the doctors say?"

"Doctors? She didn't consult them."

"She didn't? Why?"

"Why? She's having strange problems with sleep." Alexey's heart skipped a beat. This is it! "She sleeps all the time. Listen, I don't wanna talk about it on the phone. Could you come to my place now?"

Suddenly Alexey became suspicious and concerned. "Why is he inviting me? What if he knows everything? No, it's nonsense. It's impossible. Well, even if he does, so what? She can see anything in her dreams? What does it have to do with me? Sorry, man, but that's not what I see in my dreams!" But these words were empty. Alexey felt the real fear filling his body. "What if he knows? So what? What if…no, he cannot know anything. I'm just scaring and working myself up! What if he does?"

"Frankly speaking, I was going to bed," he mumbled and blanched. "What am I saying? What is the time, for God's sake? 'I've been having headache all day,'" he corrected himself. "What's the matter?"

"Nothing special. I just wanted to have a beer and to chat. You know, I'm all fucked up."

"Yeah, sure, I'll come by," Alexey suddenly resolved.

"He seems to be calm. I'll find out, what's happening. By the way, that's a chance to see Ninochka. My dear girl. We're gonna talk in a civilized manner. I already forgot what she looks like when dressed up. I'm used to seeing her only in a position number one recently—and in crowd scenes, as a rule—for the most part."

The thought that he would come to Vaska's place, see Nina there, and talk to her in a very polite and attentive manner—"Oh, hello! Please excuse me"!—keep up a fucking small talk; and she would quietly sit on a stool in front of him, putting her knees together modestly—"oh, dear!"—and in a couple of minutes, half an hour at most, he would recreate the very same room, in the smallest detail; with the stool and Ninochka, sitting modestly on it, and he would fuck her right away—without taking her clothes off—on that very stool, having spread her knees, pulled up her dress and moved her panties aside. And then, maybe, he would order two or three of his servants to fuck her, while she'd be dressed, too, very carefully. She should be dressed; it's more provocative! And she should show some blush, she should play hard-to-get and mince, and blink her eyes shyly, "Oh, I'm so ashamed! You're so bad!" And then, suddenly, she would ask them, "I want two of you to fuck me! And then three of you, like I'm a whore! Like this, with my clothes on! Come on!"

"Right, well, we'll see; it depends on my mood!" The thought thrilled Alexey very much; he even forgot about his fear. "Indeed, why is she always naked with me? I can dress and undress her easily. It's in my power. And that horrible torture room—iron! I should change the interior from time to time. Sometimes, at least, just for a change. Why did I cling to those pincers? Blood and more blood. No, it's boring. I'm tired of it." "I should take a day off. I should be a fucking gentleman. 'Pardon me, madam! Would you mind?'"

"Surely, monsieur. Go ahead, please!"

Well? In a very polite and civilized manner—politesse; you know it! "Down! Suck! Look in the eyes!" It's no good! One would surely grow fucking wild! And one would forget how to talk like a human.

"Sure, I'll come by," Alexey added cheerfully, "No problem. Do you want me to bring anything?"

"No, it's okay. I've got everything we need."

"Okay, deal. I'll be there in 15 minutes."

"Deal."

"See you." Alexey hung up the phone and rubbed his hands with excitement. "Well-well-well-well-well-well! Excellent! Wonderful! Very good! Atta girl, Ninochka! Darling! Hey! How're are you? Waiting for me? Are you making up? Are you powdering your nose? Maybe I should spend a couple of minutes and fuck her once? Just to warm up? While I still have a boner? No, no, no! All in good time. Later! Later. La-ter. We'll wait. We'll prolong the pleasure. And then we'll stretch Ninochka on the bed. Why the hurry? Why would I bother my girl over trifles? Otherwise, the poor girl won't have enough time to make up before I come. Well! She's gonna be ugly. It's not gonna be pleasant to look at her; I'm not gonna want to fuck her. No, I don't want to ruin everything. I need to give the girl the time to prepare. She should come before me in all her beauty. Show herself. Enchant and bewitch me. She's incredibly beautiful! Incredibly proud! Incredibly inaccessible! Incredibly… It's even scary to look at her. Let alone touch her accidentally. Especially for such freak as me. Heh!"

"All right. I need to wash up quickly and take a bite. I forgot when I ate the last time. Working and working. Yeah… Did I eat yesterday? Yes, it seems… Or, maybe not. Maybe, that was not yesterday. Heh… okay! I'll eat something. I don't want a bottle of beer to make me drunk. I don't want to drink with an empty stomach."

Cheerful and excited, Alexey cast the blanket away, jumped off the bed and rushed to the bathroom joyfully. There he washed up and shaved—"Fuck! I'm so scruffy! When did I shave the last time? It wasn't long ago, right?"—brushed his teeth carefully, and, yawning and stretching, went to the kitchen. "Well, what do we have here? Nothing at all! As bare as the bone. And what's in the fridge? The same… 'Winter, cold winter,' I see. So, what am I gonna eat? Maybe, fuck it? No, I should eat something. It's a must! Right, but what exactly? Should I have some porridge? I got cereal here. Come on, what fucking porridge? I should grab a bite, and that's it! Well… well… Fuck! Nothing at all! Nothing. Empty. Void. Zero."

"Okay, if there isn't any, we must do without. Fuck it! I'll have something to eat at Vaska's. No, I should eat something here. Just a fucking little. Do I have anything at all in this fucking flat? It can't be that I have nothing at all! Oh! I do have bread! I forgot about it. Well, all right. Wonderful! It's stale, but hell with it."

Alexey grabbed the first saucepan he could see, poured some cold tap water into it, and threw in pieces of stale brown bread which he had found in the kitchen. Then he caught them with a spoon, minced them on a plate and, choking, started to eat that cold soup, not being able to feel any taste. Having finished it, he wiped his mouth with a rag and nearly ran back to the bedroom to dress up. He was eager to go to Vaska as soon as he could.

8.

Vaska opened the door at once. Usually he was cheerful and merry, but now he looked somehow crestfallen—depressed and concerned. In one word, he looked bad. Alexey hadn't seen him in such a state. He even felt sorry for him, and something like a late remorse moved in his soul. "Well, he's my childhood friend, after all. He's the only one left. Fucking life paths, damn them! It's all because of the women. Fucking women. All evil comes from them," he thought insincerely and prudishly, like Tartuffe; grimacing, jesting and buffooning to himself; following Vaska to the room and looking eagerly for Ninka with his eyes. If she had let him fuck her, nothing of that would have happened, probably. He would just be fucking her secretly, like all normal people do, and that's it.

But no, she wouldn't do it! "No way!" "Look at yourself, you, freak! Ouch! Sure, I was offended! And who wouldn't be? Who? Who would stand it? I'm an ordinary man. How could I listen to all this stuff? So..."

"And here we go! I began to fucking enjoy it. I liked that she didn't let me do it. It's a pity that she couldn't resist for long with all her abstinence. But now, this bitch is letting everybody fuck her," he smiled cynically and sat in a chair offered by Vaska. "In all holes. She turned into a real yes-girl, that's it! She's providing sexual services, like they do in the best houses of London. At the first request and to a high standard, from the front and from the back."

"By the way, where is she? I can't see her anywhere. Is madam resting? Gathering strength? For future feats? That's good. She's going to need her strength. Yeah, she's definitely going to need it. I feel it in my bones! And I'm never wrong. So, where is she? I'd like to have a peep at her. What's she going to be wearing when we fuck her all at once? Negligee again? Shit, I'm fed up with it. Fuck! I'm a poet already! Pushkin, motherfucker!" Alexey's spirit rose even more.

"And where's Nina?" he asked innocently, "Sleeping, right? You told me that she's got problems with sleep?"

"No, she's not sleeping right now. She'll join us later, I think," answered Vaska.

"So, what's wrong with her?"

"I don't even know what to say," Vaska touched the chair upholstery shyly. "She says that she's seeing the same dream all the time. And it's very real, life-like, as if it's not a dream. And someone's torturing her constantly in that dream. Some bastard!

He's beating and tormenting her. Can you imagine that? That's terrible, like in a horror movie."

"No way!" exclaimed Alexey, explicitly showing that he was surprised and concerned with the news, and, at the same time, glancing stealthily and inquiringly at Vaska. "So, what does he know? It seems that nothing. 'Some bastard?' What do you mean 'life-like'? Is it so real, this dream of hers? How is this possible?"

"How should I know? She says it's very real. Like in real life. As if it's not dream at all."

"And what is it then?"

"How should I know? I'm telling you her words. How should I know what it is?"

"So, she's taking a beating there? Who's beating her? Who?" Alexey held his breath.

"She can't remember," sighed Vaska helplessly. (Phew!) "'It seems,' she says, 'as if I know this scum,'—Alexey startled reflexively—'I know him, but I can't remember who it is! Sometimes it seems that a little more time—just a moment, right now—and then it goes away again!'"

"Fuck!" thought Alexey anxiously. "So, maybe I shouldn't see her? What if she remembers me? What then? Well, he's definitely serious about all that 'bastard' and 'scum'." His anxiety grew, and he was sitting on thorns. "Fuck! Why the hell did I come here? Fucking demons guided me! I should have stayed at home and gone to sleep. I should have already been with Ninochka in the room of the dream. In a polite and civilized manner, quietly and safely. No! He wanted to experience new feelings, moron! Yeah, you're gonna have them! The whole nine yards! There'll be hell to pay! Fuck!"

"This brutal beating was the reason of the miscarriage," meanwhile, Vaska continued. "She's really living through it, like in waking life. I can't understand anything!" He suddenly exclaimed sadly. "What should I think? Maybe she's off her nut? Because of the miscarriage? Because of the baby?"

"Well, you should consult a doctor," said Alexey carefully.

"How can we consult a doctor if she's sleeping all the time? And, by the way, she can fall asleep at any moment, at any place, unexpectedly. And I can't wake her up."

"Right!" thought Alexey, "I see. That's the way it is. So, when I go to sleep, she does ~~it~~, too. And until I wake up… Surely, that's the only way. Okay, that's good to know."

"That is the reason I wanted to see you. Can you take us to a hospital tomorrow? My car broke, as luck would have it. Troubles never come singly!"

"No problem! At what time exactly?"

"Fuck! Why the hell should I do it? For you and your bitch, who can't have a baby? Why the hell did I come here? Fuck a duck!"

"Is it okay at twelve?"

"Ur… at twelve?"

"Well, whenever you want.

I see. No fucking way to get rid of him. "No, no—twelve is okay. No problem."

"If you want to change the time, it's okay with me."

"No, no! Let's make it twelve. Twelve is all right." I don't want us to spend half an hour arguing. Okay. Good. Your bitch is gonna pay for that. That ride of ours. She's gonna pay good! 'Bastard and scum,' you say? Fine!"

"By the way, where is she? Did I drag here in vain? Only to take this bitch to the hospital tomorrow? Where is she? Though, what if she recognizes me? Fuck her! I don't care! It would be even more interesting. How would she be, looking into my eyes? Yeah, that would be fun! She's gonna be shy, right? She's going to blush. She's going to be as red as blood. Like bonny lass. 'Lass,' damn it! Of general use. Actually, that's her dream. I have nothing to do with it. So, where the hell is she?"

"So, you're saying, she's taking beating in her dream. So what—just beating, and that's it?" he asked incidentally, watching Vaska attentively.

"What do you mean by 'just?'" he asked him again uncomprehendingly. "Yeah, she's taking beating and tortures."

"I see! So, she's being whipped ass in all her holes, together and apart, and your dear wife hasn't told anything about it. Nothing about taking a position at the flip of the fingers. Yeah, right, why would she disappoint her beloved husband? It's not worth mentioning. Why would she hurt his soft mentality? Why would she harrow his feelings? Well, somebody's fucking her—so what? Nothing to talk about. It happens very often in life. She's not greedy. Women are specially created to be fucked in all holes! "Well done, Ninochka! Well done!"

"Maybe she's got a lover, by the way? Eh? That would explain her lying to Vaska so easily. But if you're in love with someone, you shouldn't lie, right? You shouldn't conceal anything. Well?

Maybe, that's the way it is. Well, that's the love between her and Vaska! Yeah, the pure one! And I was a fool to listen open-mouthed. How come I didn't think about it at once, about such a possibility? You never know! Maybe she really has a lover? Well, that may well be the truth. The husband is often away, the madam is alone. She's bored.... That may well be the truth."

"She must have a lover! So what? Everybody else has a lover, and what about them? Are they angels, or what? Fucking love, right. Sure! Our madam is a particular one. Untouchable! Bitch! Surely, the father of her fucking unborn baby wasn't Vaska. well, it's all guesses. I'll ask her later today. I'll take interest. Well! So, we're gonna have a very substantial conversation, a heartwarming one. I'm looking forward to it. I cannot stand it any longer! I'd very much like to peep at her live, once. With one eye only. Just for a moment! Eh? And then I can say 'good-bye' and leave."

"I'll tell them that I need to check my car, prepare it for tomorrow's ride. 'Everything should be hunky-dory tomorrow. I want to take you and Nina to the hospital safe and sound. I don't want her to get sick in the car. She's suffering enough already!'"

"So, fuck him and his beer! I already have an entertainment for today. Much more fun!"

"No, I meant—maybe, they want something from her?" patiently explained Alexey to his slow-witted friend. He felt very sorry for him. Why isn't she telling him everything, really? "They're just beating her, you see?"

"Not just beating, madam, not at all. It's not all that sad out there. They have some fun."

"Do they demand anything? If only in a dream. Even in fairy tales, wicked creatures always want something from their prey. And they take it."

Suddenly, Alexey wished to remove scales from Vaska's eyes, to plant a seed of doubt. He wanted Vaska to think a little—is his wretched wife really taking just the beating? Are they doing anything else there with his poor and miserable wife? Or are they just torturing her? If everything in a dream is like in real life... And if they do something else—why isn't she telling him about it? Is she concealing it? Lying? Telling tales? "

"So, she can lie to you? Is she ashamed of it? Listen, buddy, that's the universal explanation; it's good for all occasions! So, probably, she's ashamed to tell about her lover, as well. And about any other shameful stuff. That's why it's called so—'shameful.'"

"I'm a butcher, monster and 'bastard and scum,'" you see—and she is an angel! Martyr! So why is she lying to you, this fucking martyr? Saints do not lie. Come on, let her tell you, in detail, how she sucks a dick at the flip of the fingers. How she plays different roles. How she prances, like a trained pony. And I would listen to that! Saint! We're all saints here, we're tarred with the same brush! I'd like to see that saint in the room of the dream! See how she dances and twists with my servants. It's a real pleasure! That's it! That's it, my dear Vasenka! I'm really sorry for all of that, but your wife is a whore. A real, licensed whore, and there's nothing you can do about it, whether you like it or not. She will never forget the experience of the room of the dream. She has crossed the line, and there's no way back!"

"It's a pity, but it doesn't matter whether she did it on her own will, or she was made to do it. It's like a disease. AIDS! Whether you got infected yourself, or it happened by chance—say, during blood transfusion - it doesn't matter. The point is, you're infected now. And the virus doesn't care. It doesn't care that you were beautiful and healthy, extremely honest, high-toned, and noble. It doesn't care that you haven't done it with anybody. That was in the past. Before the disease. And now, I'm sorry. The end is same for everyone."

"So, your precious Ninochka... She's already infected. That's it! She already has a mentality of a whore. She sucked my dick at the flip of the fingers and sucked my numerous servants' dicks—and she would suck anyone's dick with pleasure! She'd like to, say, make some easy money. The husband is away. Well, she wouldn't even think about it! Come on! One more... She had them a lot already! She just wouldn't like you to find out—that's it. But she has no moral barriers and principles. They all remained in the room of the dream. See, she's already lying to you through her teeth. From the very beginning! And it'll get worse and worse. Mark my word! It has been well said that 'the rust eats iron, and the lie—soul.'"

"Saint!" She's an ordinary whore, not a saint! Scum! Cunt. Filthy clout, hedge-born trash! An ordinary cock-sucker."

"And who's beating her? A woman? A man?" Alexey hoped that now the thoughts of this slowcoach, Vaska, would go in right direction.

"I don't really know. I think, a man," said Vasya, confused. It seemed that this question simply hadn't occurred to him. "What's the difference?"

"Well, never mind," Alexey immediately pulled out. "You'll figure it out, if you're not an idiot!"

"Listen, Vasya, I'm gonna get going, okay? I need to check the car. She's been playing pranks recently. You know, a car is like a woman; one must get into her, and she won't play pranks! Get under the hood!" he laughed, losing control.

Vaska glanced at him strangely, and Alexey quickly checked himself. "Shit! He should be more cautious! See, recently all of my jokes are about one thing only."

"We'll have a beer another time, Okay? That's not our last meeting, right?" he tried to amend the awkwardness that had appeared. "Deal?"

"Well, okay. It's up to you," said Vasya slowly, still looking at him with a certain doubt.

"Say hi to Ninka!" passed Alexey, rising from the chair. "May she recover as soon as possible. It's a pity I didn't see her," he added with sincere regret. "For some reason, I'm embarrassed. I'd like to say something to her…comfort her, for example. With such problems that you have… and with a miscarriage… that's horrible! Crazy! I can't imagine myself in your place."

"Bring her in, moron! Let me feast my eyes on her! On a cold lady. Snow Queen. Extremely strict, cold, and completely inaccessible. Like fucking Mont Blanc."

"Wait a moment," said Vasya with emotion and rushed to the adjacent room.

Alexey, burning with impatience and biting his lips, was ticking over. "Come on! Come on!"

A minute later, Vaska came back and lifted his hands in guilt.

"You know, she can't see you. She's feeling sick. She's in bed, and she doesn't want you to see her like this, undressed and bare-faced. A woman, you know…"

"It's all right! No big deal. I'll see her tomorrow, anyway."

"Bitch! Scum! By the way, she could dress up before I came, but she didn't want to! So, you don't respect me? You don't respect me as a man? Oh, yes, 'freak and monkey.' Hold on, bitch! I'll dress you up! I'll do your hair and dye it as well. Dye it red—in scarlet! It's very popular in the room of the dream! Bleeding edge? You're gonna bleed as well. You're gonna squeak and chatter! And you're gonna feel good—very good! You bet! You're gonna have enough doctors at your side! The whole group of them. I'm gonna be the first, and then the rest. On a first-served basis. We're gonna tend you until you recover. We're gonna tend you as usual. A very good method! And then, my dear, we'll chat a little. Vis-à-vis, in an intimate atmosphere—the one that would dispose to openness."

"For example, about your fucking child. How come I didn't know about it? I'm not your husband, and you shouldn't be playing these games with me! All these gasps and groans! You shouldn't be ashamed with me. Hold on, bitch! You'll get it!"

A poor mimicry of a smile appeared on Alexey's face. His lips were trembling and twitching. During last few days, he completely forgot how to control himself, and now, he restrained the wrath that was bursting out of him with a great effort of will. His eyes were covered with a pink veil. He felt that in a few moments he would completely lose control.

"Okay, bye! Off I go! I need to grab some tools. Bye—see you tomorrow!" he grabbed the hand of Vaska, who couldn't even open his mouth, shook it, and, not waiting for his answer, turned around, shot out from the flat, and ran quickly down the stairs. He was blazing inside.

"Bitch! What a bitch! So, I'm nobody to you? You don't even have to dress up for me? Hold on, scum! I'll show you! I'll show you the dance of the little whore-like swans. With ballet shoes. You're gonna dance and sing! In chorus. I'll give you doggy-style hell! You're gonna know, who's the monkey—you or me?" Alexey dashed into his apartment, slammed the door, quickly took off his clothes and jumped in the bed. Then, catching his breath, he tried to calm down. The hot expectation of close revenge didn't let him concentrate and get the necessary condition.

At last, after a few vain efforts, he did it. The world reeled before his eyes, and the growing ringing came in his ears. One last effort! And…

9

There was someone else besides Ninka in the room of the dream—a strange young man in his mid-thirties, dressed elegantly. He was sitting in a chair which had appeared out of nowhere, and he looked around him with lazy curiosity. Judging by his bored looks, all these unambiguous accessories and attributes of the torture chamber didn't impress him at all.

"Here you are, dear Alexey Petrovich!" he exclaimed cheerfully, seeing Alexey, who was a bit surprised and embarrassed.

"Who the hell is that? What's he doing here? Maybe I created him myself accidentally? Like all other homunculus? As a result of my hyper-arousal?"

"Please, have a seat," the man pointed to another chair that appeared behind Alexey's back. "Come on, sit down!" he added, seeing that Alexey was hesitating. "Take the load off your feet. We are going to have a very long talk."

Alexey sat down, still hesitating. He didn't know how to behave. "Who is that, anyway? Why can he dare to give me orders? 'Sit down,' 'don't sit down!' It's none of your business! Fuck you! I'll do what I want. Fucking captain, go to hell! May I see you in a coffin! It's my dream! I'm the master here. The Lord of the Dream. I probably created you myself accidentally. By mistake. You moron! Otherwise, where did you come from? I'm gonna flip my fingers. and you're gonna disappear!"

Alexey almost did it, but something stopped him. Something was wrong. The stranger was too confident. He was too independent. And these chairs—where did they come from? Alexey didn't create them; he was sure about that. "Fuck! Who the hell is that dude? Okay, let's calm down for a moment. I don't need to do anything rash. Let's wait and talk. Let's see what's gonna happen next. I don't wanna make a mess. Come on! Keep talking while you can. Everything in due time. In the end, he can set his servants on him if anything crops up. Okay, we'll see."

Though Alexey put on a brave face, he felt uneasy. He could physically feel the steady, studying gaze of the man sitting in front of him. A slight panic started to fill him. He could feel, with his skin, the approach of some unknown but apparent and menacing danger. He could feel a pressing threat from his guest, as if a cobra or a viper in a human form was sitting in front of him. And it could attack him at any moment. Though it could stay where it sat, as well. Who knows what it is thinking about? Alexey's panic grew. For some reason, he had no doubts that this unexpected meeting wouldn't bring any good to him, as well as these "talks."

"There's nothing to talk about! I need to run away while I still can. I have to return to real life. Probably that's the real master. He has come at last, shit! Speak of the devil—is he a demon, or what? I may well see the scene from the fairy tale about Masha and the three bears. 'Who slept in my favorite bed?' In one word, I have to leave!"

Alexey tried to restrain himself secretly, wishing to wake up at once. Far from it—he was still in the room of the dream. The stranger was still sitting in front of him and staring at him. It even seemed to Alexey that a slightly mocking semi-smile appeared on his lips. Feeling that it was all useless and losing control completely, Alexey started to flip his fingers, chaotically and openly, trying to bring his servants. Nobody! Nobody, naturally, appeared. The room remained empty, like before. Just him, the stranger, and Ninka in the corner; he almost forgot about her. No time for her. He was busy.

The stranger sniffed distinctly. His smile became wider. He was clearly playing, observing Alexey.

"Shit, he's looking at me like a boa at a rabbit," he thought suddenly, "before swallowing him!" Alexey didn't like the role of a rabbit at all, but it seemed that nobody was going to ask him. He could only sit and wait for what would happen next. "What does he want from me? My soul, eh? 'It's high time, Alexey Petrovich, you paid for the pleasure received!' I got nothing else! Come on! Start talking!"

"Come on, Alexey Petrovich, calm down!" said the stranger apologetically, breaking a pause that had become inappropriately long, "I just wanted to talk to you, that's it. Face to face, in quiet atmosphere, without all your Frankensteins. How come you can't stop thinking about them for a moment? Haven't you had enough fun with them?" he glanced at Nina, then ran his eyes over the room and the walls, which were covered with different whips, rods, and lashes, and coughed delicately. "Well... Ugh... Well, okay. We'll get back to it."

"So, dear Alexey Petrovich, I just wanted to explain something to you and maybe give a piece of advice. See, you're not using your current gigantic capabilities rationally. Why do you do everything by yourself? Torture is a great art! It is a whole science with a millennial history. You can't even imagine the progress that it has made during this time. The people were rather inventive in this sphere. Very inventive!" the man smiled at something and shook his head thoughtfully. "And all of this," he pointed scornfully at the tools, created by Alexey, that were crowding the room and winced with disgust, "Excuse me, but it's dilettantism. "You could have got a first-class specialist, a professional executioner; and he would teach you quickly all that you want. He would have taught you a lot. A lot, believe me, dear Alexey Petrovich—a hell of a lot—that which you have never dreamt about!" the man laughed merrily at his own joke. "Funny, isn't it? A pun. Ho, ho, ho! A pun.

"Though, on the other hand," he added slowly, cutting his laugh and staring at Alexey with a strange, odd look, "very few people can be really cruel. One needs much more strength for that than it's usually considered," he glanced at Nina again and smiled quietly. "Ugh… It doesn't matter, though. Well, enjoy yourself. I won't keep you.

"Yes! One more thing. If you decide, after all, to use my advice, I recommend Asia to you. Well, exotics…new feelings…you'll like it. China, for example, age of Ming. There are wonderful specialists. Wonderful! Fantastic ones! By the way, the Chinese are great experts and plotters in this sphere, as well as in the sphere of love, too. Did you know about the trick with a goose? No? Very interesting one. Really! It is beautifully described in one of the Old Chinese treatises.

'A goose is beheaded at the moment of copulating with it. The throes of the decapitated fowl give, according to the author of the treatise, 'exalted and unparalleled pleasure.' I recommend you to try it with your lady," the stranger again glanced at Nina, who froze with terror and looked at him with unnaturally wide eyes, and smiled gallantly to her.

Holding his breath, Alexey listened carefully to his guest—and the more he listened to him, the more scared he became. There was something unnatural in the behavior of the man who was sitting in front of him, completely relaxed. An ordinary man wouldn't react like that to all these pincers and horrible saws. No wonder, no fear, and no disgust nothing at all! Just lazy boredom. "'Dilettantism!' What the fuck! A nice 'dilettantism,' shit! Is this a human, really?"

"And a last 'advice?' 'Try it with your lady?' So what, do I have to cut her head during copulation, right? Like a goose, right? And the throes of the decapitated body would give me 'exalted and unparalleled pleasure?' Really 'unparalleled?' Ugh…curious enough… really interesting. Is it 'unparalleled on earth,' indeed?"

Suddenly, Alexey felt that this thought seized him. He imagined vividly how he's approaching Ninka, who's standing on her knees and bending forward. He's going round her, coming from the back... And then, during copulation, in the very last moment, when this is it—he swings a sword—zing! And then, with both his hands, he squeezes the decapitated naked body of the woman which in throes and convulsing.

Interesting! As a matter of fact, these feelings may be really interesting. What does the author say? "Exalted and unparalleled on earth?" Ugh… Maybe that's true. And mind you, that's just a goose!

A woman would serve this purpose better! Not simply better—night and day! Well… "So, how can I do it in practice? Technically. Heh? I can't wield a sword, and I definitely wouldn't be able to cut a head with one blow. I would more likely cut my own hand. Zing! Maybe I should try it with a servant? No! He would just be a nuisance. Distraction. I should do it myself. Right! I can do it with a guillotine! I'm gonna fix her head, and then press the button at the right moment."

"Interesting! I need to think… Right! So, what would happen to her? To Ninka? Would she come back to life again? So what, I chop off her head? And that's it? Finita la comedia? I'll have to fuck a corpse without a head? I'll have to be a necrophile?"

"No, not a corpse!" Alexey suddenly heard a calm voice of the stranger and looked at him. Is he reading my mind? "Surely, she'll come back to life! Don't worry! It's your dream, you're the master here. You may burn, drown, and dismember a hundred times per day; you may do whatever you want! She's in your power completely. Absolutely. Enjoy yourself!" the stranger left the chair and looked around, searching for something.

Alexey stood up, too, and he was shifting from foot to foot in hesitation, not knowing what to do and how to behave. Maybe he should say good-bye? Thank him for the advice?

Not finding anything, the stranger lifted up his eyes at Alexey, who was standing bolt-upright, and, without changing the tone, continued in an ordinary voice, "You've still got time. A whole hour."

"Why an hour?" asked Alexey surprisingly. "And what then?"

"And then everything will come to an end." Out the corner of his eye, Alexey saw a slight movement from where Ninka was sitting.

"What end?" he asked bluntly and looked at Nina reflexively.

Nina leaned forward, pressing her hands against her breast and stared at the man, trying to catch his every word.

"Yes. A week precisely," the man found at last what he was looking for. It appeared to be a cane with a massive head that was standing against the chair. Alexey hadn't even noticed it.

Playing carelessly with the cane, the stranger turned away from Alexey and went to the opening that appeared in a wall.

"And what now?" asked Alexey, confused as he was, with a wretched, trembling voice. He felt as if he was a child who had to part with his favorite toy. "Won't I be able to ever come back here?"

The very thought that that's it, tale is over, he's not a God anymore, nor a devil or the Lord of the Dream; that he had only daily routine waiting for him—gray daily routine! That thought made everything inside him shrink, and he almost cried.

"And that depends on Nina Nikolayevna!" the man halted on the doorstep, faced Alexey, looked into his eyes, and gave him a dazzling smile. Then, still smiling, he looked at Nina, who was still staring at him. "Now she is going to be the Lord of the Dream and your mistress, Alexey Petrovich. For a week, as well. You're going to switch places. It's only fair, right?"

"What?" Alexey sank slowly on the floor, clinging to the chair. "What! You can't do this! You can't do this to me! Why didn't you tell me at the very beginning? Why didn't you warn me?

"Farewell," the stranger stepped into the opening, and the door in the wall disappeared.

Alexey still sat on the floor, staring at the wall, holding on to his chest, and feeling a nasty, wobbly weakness fill all his body.

Then, very slowly, he looked at Nina. Nina was sitting upright and staring at him. Her eyes we filled with such cold hatred that Alexey flinched convulsively.

"Come on! Come on, degenerate!" she whispered in a hissing voice, "what are you waiting for? Come on, fuck me, chop my head off—enjoy yourself for the last time, fucker! Feel the 'exalted pleasure'! Come on, what are you waiting for? The clock is ticking! The Lord of the Dream." Nina swore, threw her head back and started laughing wildly and frantically. Tears were running out of her eyes, she was choking with them—but still she kept laughing, laughing and laughing, and she couldn't stop.

***

Next day, Alexey Gromov committed suicide, having jumped out of the window.

***

It happened when Vaska, being concerned that his wife had been sleeping for a very long time, dared to wake her up. Though the day before she had asked him not to do it under any circumstance, she had told him that she hadn't been seeing any nightmares any more, and she just had had to sleep well for a week and restore her strength.

And Lucifer was ask'd by his son:

—Can a man withstand a temptation of the absolute power?

And Lucifer answer'd his son:

—Nay.

And Lucifer was again ask'd by his son:

—Thou spoke of justice. And thou gave the woman the power ov'r that man. What for?

And Lucifer answer'd his son:

—I just gave her a possibility to choose between his and mine justice.

And Lucifer was again ask'd by his son:

—And what is his justice?

And Lucifer answer'd his son:

—Whosoev'r shall smite thou on thy right cheek, turn to him the other also.

And, being silent f'r a while, Lucifer's son again ask'd him:

—What did that woman doth to that man?

And Lucifer answer'd his son:

—Thou art too young to wot it.

LUCIFER'S SON. Day 3.

And the third day came.
And Lucifer was ask'd by His Son:
—Wherefore is it said: meiny of devil, but slaves of god?
And Lucifer answer'd His Son:
—F'r mine meiny art free people. I don't ne'd slaves.

DEAL.

"*Whoever desires to save his life, will lose it.*"
Gospel of Matthew.

1.

Igor was sitting on a bench in a square and looking around distractedly. He had nothing else to do, as a matter of fact. He didn't want to go home. *Maybe I should buy a beer?*

Suddenly, a girl, looking like a business lady, appeared on the opposite side of the alley and caught his eye. The girl was followed by a guy with a camera; it seemed he was a cameraman—TV crew. The girl halted, said a couple of words to the operator and started saying something into the camera. Igor was watching her with lazy curiosity. At any rate, that was kind of entertaining. So there was the girl, rather stylish, dressed in flossy denim dress and sunglasses. Yeah, a nice girl. Eye appeal. Igor liked the girls of her kind.

Meanwhile, the girl stopped talking, turned around, and, with a microphone in her hand, headed to Igor. The cameraman, with a switched camera on his shoulder, followed her. Igor just didn't have the time to understand what was happening; the TV crew was already near him. The girl sat down by his side freely, gave him a professional smile, and started jabbering.

"Hi! It's 'Religion in Modern World'. You're live on television. We'd like to ask you a couple of questions. Do you mind?"

"Okay," answered Igor a bit irrelevantly, being embarrassed. Never before had he had any business with TV, and he actually was at a loss. The camera which was pointed at him constricted him, and he couldn't think properly. He somehow felt as if he was infatuated.

"Present yourself, please," continued the girl cheerfully, "Name, age, profession?"

"Igor, 40, designer."

"Wow! Your profession is very actual!" the girl brightened up, "That's wonderful! That's exactly what we need! We want to know the attitude of a modern man towards religion, like you, Igor! Lately, there has been a steep turn in the society towards religion, church and belief in God. Religious holidays are celebrated, and our leaders take part in it publicly. What do you think of it?"

"Well, I think positive, for the most part," mumbled Igor. *What do I think of it, really? Nothing! Fuck these holidays! I've never been in a church, actually.*

"Do you think it's normal?" asked the girl with a very concerned look.

"What exactly is 'normal?'" repeated Igor, like a parrot.

"That everybody's turning back to religion," patiently explained the journalist.

"Yes!" answered Igor, smiling foolishly and looking askew at the camera. He felt stupid.

"Why?"

"What 'why?'" Igor asked her bluntly again.

He couldn't turn away from the camera and concentrate. All thoughts fled from his head.

"Why do you think that turning back to religion is good for society?" the journalist repeated her question with angelic patience. Her smile, though, became a little tenser. It seemed she began to suspect that she ran into an idiot.

Finally, Igor got mad and threw off his daze. *What am I doing, really! I'm a grown man, but behave like a like a prim young lady. I'm embarrassed by the camera. Get it together! Don't disgrace yourself in front of the people!*

"I think that a man must believe in something. In something good," picking the words with care, he answered slowly—*Like this? Right. Exactly!* "In God, or in communism—it doesn't matter. But one must believe in something."

"Yeah, I see. Tell us, Igor, do you believe in God?"

"Me? No, actually," laughed Igor. He finally recovered from the confusion, got the hang of it, and felt free and relaxed. "Nobody implanted the faith in me in the childhood, and now it's too late, I think, to change my beliefs."

"Right! Excellent!" the woman brightened up again, "So, you do not believe in God?"

"No," answered Igor with a smile.

"And, naturally, you do not visit a church?" the girl showed nothing but pure curiosity.

"No, of course." *What does she want from me?*

"Very well. One more question which may seem strange to you. So, if you don't believe in God, you don't believe in the Devil, right? Well, that he exists?"

"Devil?" asked Igor in wonder. *What fucking devil is she talking about? What's with all these questions? Maybe it's some kind of provocation? Like when they ask people various stupid questions with a hidden camera, watching their reaction? What does the devil have to do with it?*

"Certainly, I do not."

"So, we see a modern man who, supposedly, does not believe in anything," the girl turned to the camera, "neither in God, nor in devil. Now we are going to check if that's true! Igor, did I understand you right—you do not believe in anything?" she asked Igor again.

"No," Igor didn't know where she was going, but felt that there was some trap. Actually, he was tired of the journalist's importunity. He started to feel that he was plainly used to be shown as a fool to the viewers. They were making fool of him for the delectation of the respected public. *What the fuck is that? Do I look like a buffoon to her?*

"Very well. Would you mind signing this paper?" the journalist was holding a paper in her hand. Igor didn't actually see where she had taken it from.

"What is it?" he asked, almost rudely.

"Let's read!" the journalist turned to the camera again and started reading aloud. "Contract: I, such-and-such, sold my soul to the devil for $10,000. Date, signature. Igor, if you really do not believe in anything," she said to Igor in a voice of a professional provocateur, with a subtle smile on her face. "Sign it. It really doesn't matter to you!"

"Why? Why should I sign it?" Igor tried to joke it away. He got embarrassed with such a turn of events and now was thinking frantically, what could he do? Actually, he was worried not with the meaning of what was happening—*What soul is she talking about*?

It's obvious that that's bullshit! Honeypot!—but he was afraid to become a fool, to get into a stupid situation, and to allow somebody to make idiot of him, in front of all people. *Fuck! What's the trick here?*

"In order to receive $10,000!" said the journalist cheerfully, watching his reaction with great interest.

"So, if I sign this piece of paper, I'll get $10,000?" Igor joined the game with a merry look on his face, trying to show that it amused him a lot. As a matter of fact, he wasn't amused at all. It was pretty clear that he would see neither hide nor hair of $10,000, and nobody was going to give it to him. So what was the joke? *This skank is probably waiting for me to get scared, to refuse to sign it.*

"Yes!" the girl got even more cheerful. "Sign the paper, and I'll give it to you right now!"

"Well, maybe you would show it to me at first," asked Igor kiddingly, "I'd like to know what I'm selling my soul for."

The girl laughed, too, and, with the knack of a conjurer, suddenly produced a thick envelope out of somewhere.

"So, there's exactly $10,000 in this envelope," she said loudly into the camera. "Let's see," she opened the envelope, took out a pack of C-notes and showed them to the camera.

Igor's eyes popped out. The joke was going too far.

"As soon as Igor signs the contract, I will give it to him. But everything must be serious," she looked at Igor cunningly and winked at him saucily. "You need to sign it with your blood! Boo! Like it is done in all scary tales. In my hands, I have a single-use needle—well, not a needle, actually, but a device for stabbing when drawing a blood sample. I am going to stab Igor with it, he's going to press a finger against the contract, and, thus, it will be signed with his blood. Are you ready? Sorry for familiarity; I'm a bit nervous!" she said briskly to Igor, holding a needle in cellophane.

Then she added with a laugh, "The needle is very thin; you won't feel any pain, I promise. We already tested it on our cameraman, Kostya," she pointed at the man with the camera that didn't react to her gesture and continued doing his job, as if nothing had happened.

While Igor was staring at the cameraman, Kostya, bluntly, the journalist grabbed his hand, wiped his forefinger with a piece of wet cotton-wool and stabbed him slightly with the unwrapped needle. Igor didn't have the time to realize what was happening; he just watched everything and did nothing at all. She grabbed his finger, wiped it, stabbed.... By the way, he didn't feel any pain. Before he knew it, everything was finished, and there was a tiny scarlet drop on the pulp of his finger.

"Press it here, please," the girl held out the paper. Igor pressed his finger against it obediently. "So, dear viewers, Igor wasn't afraid to sign a contract with the devil concerning the sale of his soul. And he even bound it with his blood!" The journalist held up the contract and showed it into the camera for some time. "Could you dare to do the same? Write us or send your messages to e-mail. Our e-mail is the following," the journalist said something quickly.

Igor could discern only the word "at." Actually, he didn't care about that. He was in a kind of a trance. *Contract... blood... money...*

He looked at the envelope, and then cautiously peeped inside it. *Dollars! Bless me, dollars!* He touched them with his hand. *Dollars! No sense touching them. Did they really give them to me? Are they mine? Or it was just for an image, and they're going to take them back?*

He lifted up his eyes. The journalist disappeared. Igor just caught a glimpse of her and the cameraman getting into a van that, obviously, had been waiting for them. It started and vanished in the queuing traffic in a second.

That's it! Everybody's gone—the journalist, the camera, and the cameraman. He was left with the envelope and a piece of wool on his forefinger. Everything else around him was the same, as if nothing had happened to him. As if Igor had just been sitting on a bench for 15-20 minutes, looking around him. And yet, it had happened! The money and the wool clearly proved that. It had! There had been that unreal interview, and that foolish contract, as well as the show with finger-stabbing and blood-signing. And 10,000 real American dollars which he got as the result of this phantasmagoria. He got them in the most fantastic way.

It's a fucking lot of money! People would kill for such sum of money! Nobody just gives away ten grand. But they had given it to him. Igor looked at his finger. The blood was real. And the money was real.

Fuck, what is the meaning of it? Did I really sell my soul to the devil? What fucking devil? There's no devil! And the money? The money is here. So why did they give it to me? Ten thousand dollars. It's no laughing matter!

Igor turned the envelope over in his hands and then put it into his pocket. Then, without hesitation, he stood up and headed to the bus stop. He was going home.

2

First thing at home, Igor hurried to watch the TV program. *Well, first channel... NTV... Where is it? She said that it was live. Where is the program? What is it called? 'Religion,' 'Modern society...' Where is it? Is there anything of the kind? Nothing. Nothing of the kind. What religion are we talking about? In the modern world. Who wants to know that? Usual talk shows and TV series—an endless draw and pandemonium.*

Well, well, well! So what? Where is my interview, heh? Interview in a square? Where is that program? Maybe it's on a satellite channel? On a leased channel? Or cable? Maybe. But unlikely. Nobody would show such bullshit on a leased channel! Nobody would watch it, even for free. But they gave me the money! They did. And I signed with my blood for it. Fuck! I kinda don't like it. I don't like it at all!

Umph! What did they demand from me? Nothing! That's the point—nothing. Nothing at all! Just the 'soul.' So what now? Don't I have my soul now? Or is it just after death? Like with Faust? Fuck, I should have read the contract, at least. Contract! It's a useless scrap of paper, not a contract! Why, the patent is an ordinary contract. They read it to me and then offered to sign—and I signed it at my own will. With blood. Everything's right. In a proper fashion.

God damn! So it turns out that I really sold my soul to the devil! What if he really exists, this devil? What then? Then it's a fucking disaster! The one you couldn't tell in a tale or write with a pen! The most fucking disaster. Unheard and unseen before. I'm gonna burn in hell—that's what's waiting for me! Forever! Amen.

Igor tried to get his thoughts together. All right, enough for showing off, mocking and playing with nice words. Enough for flirting and playing hide-and-seek as he used to do all his life when he talked about faith. *'Useless scrap of paper!' 'Fucking disaster!' I should cast away this playful tone. The matter is serious enough. Calm down! So, what have we got? A while ago, in a square, I was approached by a girl and a guy with a camera. They looked like a*

TV-crew, and they said that they were from some TV program, and offered me to make a deal with the devil, to which I agreed, like the dumbest moron. I agreed to it of my own free will. And, supposedly, I sold," Igor was quick to say this reservation, "supposedly—supposedly sold my soul to the devil for $10,000 which was passed to me immediately with corresponding jokes and tips. After that, the guy and the girl quickly got into a van which had been waiting for them, and drove to an undisclosed location. Together with fucking contract signed with my blood!"

Well, calm down! That's it? No. There is no such program on TV. At least, I couldn't find it in TV listings. Well! What 'at least?' There's no such program! It doesn't fucking exist! Doesn't exist! Here I have TV listings before me. Devil! Though, I shouldn't mention the devil in vain."

"Well, well, all right! Let's stay put. What do we have in the end? Let's unscramble and analyze everything.

Variant number one: It's complete nonsense, but let's assume it isn't. I was followed and tracked down—by whom? Why? Who the fuck needs me? —they caught a moment when I sat down on a bench; they couldn't possibly know about it—I didn't know it myself—and approached me as if they were from TV. On a purpose, to officially give me 10,000 foreign dollars. Wonderful! Yeah, and they got me to sign some piece of paper for everything to look plausible. How else could they have given me ten thousand bucks? They needed a reason—a plausible one. Otherwise, I wouldn't have taken it; I have my pride.

"So they were mysterious well-wishers. They mysteriously and secretly care and look after me. For forty fucking years. they didn't care—and then appeared out of the box! They arranged a real play with outfit change and stuff. With singing and dancing. With camera and van. And with needle therapy. Igor looked at his finger. The small wound was almost healed. *A cheap vaudeville.*

And the contract with blood doesn't mean anything! It's nonsense! It's just for the credibility. For mystery and conspiracy. The contract doesn't mean anything! Probably, they have already thrown it out into the nearest trashcan. They didn't want to litter. Well, a very interesting version—very! It explains everything beautifully. And, what matters—it's credible! Okay, let's leave it for the time being. Let's leave it in store. As a last resource. Let's move on."

Second variant. Everything's the same, but they are not well-wishers, but quite on the contrary. Ill-wishers. Mysterious and very secret, as well. And, by the way, I'm curious, what do they want from me? What the fuck do they want from me? I'm poor as a church mouse! What can they take from me? Well, it doesn't matter. So, there is a reason for that. They have already lured me and made me—by deceit! by deceit!—take the money under some pretext! They shoved it on me by force! They pushed it on me, and, soon enough, they'll appear again, show their teeth and demand to work the money out. 'Please, dear Igor Ivanovich, face the collection! If you dance, you must pay the fiddler! The beauty of a debt is its payment!' And so on. Ten grand... Well, in one word, it makes sense.

It's rubbish and bullshit squared! Cubed! Bullshit, bullshit, bullshit! The only relief is that I sold my soul, not to the devil, but to some hopeless morons who, for some reason, decided to take up with me. They showed their folly. Yeah, that's better! Well! Okay, let's move on.

Third variant. In fact, what about the third variant? There is no third variant! That's it, right? All the more or less sensible—"sensible!"—variants are accounted for. Well... well... Yes! That's it! No more sensible variants, right? There are only supernatural ones left. To be exact, there's only one supernatural variant. The only one. The only one that's real. That is: it's all true. The devil does exist, and I did sign a contract with him. I sold my soul.

"Nonsense! Nonsense—nonsense—nonsense! Nonsense—nonsense—nonsense—nonsense—nonsense! There is no devil. No! No devil at all! I don't believe it! I don't! How does he look? A girl in jeans? With a microphone? Bullshit! Bullshit! It's impossible! Impossible! It's impossible, and that's it! Okay, it's impossible, but what about the money? Does the money exist? Where is it from? Here it is." Igor fingered over the envelope and took a pack of dollars out of it. *"Is it real? Yes. So what?"*

"Motherfuck!" Igor felt that a cold, black emptiness appeared inside him. A vacuum. No matter what he said, no matter how he bristled up, rattled, jested, trifled, and played the buffoon—it wouldn't disappear and diffuse. Moreover, it would get darker and darker. He felt as if he had made a terrible and unamendable folly or mistake and now started to realize that and to wise up.

Why the fuck did I need these cursed dollars? Why the fuck did I get involved in that? I should have said no, and that's it! Excuse me, but I'm afraid of blood! Yeah, I could have said whatever I wanted! No, and that's it! That's enough! End of conversation.

Guys, you take your contract and go to fucking hell! Sh... Oh, right! No more "sh" and "d!". Oh, my God! It's the 21st century! And I believe in all that? Me? Who has never been in a church! Oh, God! It's the 21st century! We're living in the age of computers and internet! And, you see, I sold my soul to the devil! Eh? Yeah, I kinda did it! Good gracious! Unbelievable!

Igor did his best to keep his presence of mind, but that was difficult for him. He felt more and more uncomfortable. He felt as if he was kicked out from the world of men. As if he was no more a man at all! All of them had a soul, but he didn't! He sold it. To Satan. And there was no way back. That's it! Everyone, even the most terrible and tough criminals, murderers, and abusers - they were humans, bad humans, but still humans—everyone had hope for God's mercy, and he didn't! He was the only one who didn't have it! He was not a human anymore! Castaway! He had a seal of the Satan. Devil's mark."

Igor walked around the flat aimlessly. He felt more and more sad. Not knowing what to do, he took the phone and called his old friend from the institute, one of the few with whom he still kept terms. Luckily, he was at home. After the usual greetings and exchanging the latest news.

"Did you know that Mashka got divorced?"

"Really?" Igor passed to the main subject of the conversation—the one that was the actual reason for his call. "Listen, Dima. Recently I read a very interesting book. The main hero of it is offered the chance to sell his soul to the devil."

"What? Sell what? His soul?" the friend asked him in wonder. It seemed that the pass from Masha's divorce to a selling of a soul was too quick for him.

"Right. Well, that's the plot!" Igor tried to explain him quickly. "That's what the book is about!"

"So what?"

"Well, I got curious. What if, say, someone would offer me to do that—would I agree? And why not? I do believe neither in God nor in the devil. Why not? Would you agree to that, if you were offered?"

"Offered what?"

"What what? To sell your soul to the devil! If they offered you, would you agree?"

"No!" the friend's tone was completely categorical.

"Why?" asked Igor, freezing, "Do you believe in the devil?"

"Do you want to buy my soul or what?"

"It has nothing to do with me. It's just in general. Hypothetically."

"Well, I wouldn't agree to that."

"But why?"

"I wouldn't, and that's it!" He clearly didn't want to dwell on this subject. Igor talked to him for several minutes more and then hung up the phone.

After this conversation, he felt very dreary. He hadn't expected such a straightforward reaction. Well, actually, he had suspected that his friend would refuse, but, nevertheless, he had thought that they would discuss it, go through all pros and cons. Well, he had hoped that they would have a real talk. But not that way! "No," and that's it. Interesting. Surprising! He was a clever man... Educated... And such a strange reaction. "No!" And why "no?" Without any discussion. *Blow me tight! It's strange.* Igor mumbled all these words, smiling sarcastically and shrugging his shoulders eloquently, but he was not cheerful at all. He started to feel more and more that he was kind of a renegade, a castaway, and a betrayer. A man who had committed such an unheard-of wrongdoing that he didn't have any excuse or forgiveness, and all explanations were senseless and useless. Suddenly, the rhymes of a half-remembered song came to his mind. It seemed to him it was Galich.

Seeing that here is no sense in excuses,
That dishonor is utter and there's no way out,
Our ancestors...

Song! A nice fucking song! What next? What about 'our ancestors?' Oh, hell, I can't remember! Hell again? All right, all right! Be calm! So what about 'our ancestors,' heh? What did they fucking do in such situations? Kill themselves, right? Yeah! Exactly. In the end there is "and a gun to the temple!" I see. Fuck! Okay, we'll keep it. And I don't have a gun yet. And what's the point? It's not a way out for me. On the contrary—it's a way in! Into the hell. To all demons and eternal torments. Into the underworld. Into the fire of hell. Yeah, that's the only way I have. I have already bought the ticket. Actually, it's a one-way ticket, but it's cheap. It has a discount for foolishness. Reduced tariff for morons. Just ten thousand bucks. Well, I'm curious, what circle would be that? Probably, the last one—the ninth? Yeah, that's the only choice.

I'm fucking shocked! I mean it; I'm fucking shocked! For just freaking $10,000! However, what's the difference? What difference does it make? Ten thousand or a million? The sum doesn't matter. If the devil does exist, the sum doesn't matter. There is no sum of money for which one could—no, one could do it for any money, like I did!—for which one would sell his soul. And then one would burn in the hell forever. Forever! The only hope is that it's a stupid joke. Fucking TV crew. Their balls should be cut off for such stuff! We're living in the 21st century! What fucking devil are you talking about?

Igor trudged until the evening, waiting for his wife to come home. He had a strong desire to immediately, now, call his other friend, Kostya—by the way, he knew him from the institute, as well,—but he managed to restrain himself and didn't do it. *What's the sense? If Dimka refused... It seems that Kostya is a real believer. He actually got married in a church. So...*

He realized clearly that it would be useless to talk to his wife about that. Women are usually very superstitious and mistrustful in such matters, but he couldn't restrain himself. He had a painful urge to talk about it, and he needed to talk all the time! He had to get back to that topic over and over again.

He couldn't wait until his wife started the supper and he didn't let her wash up; he attacked her with questions when she hardly had stepped into the apartment. However, like he thought, they couldn't have a decent conversation.

"Vera, what if you were offered to sell your soul to the devil—would you do that?"

"What is that stupid question!"

"Why is it stupid? A good question. Would you agree? If they gave you a lot of money?"

"Stop bugging me with your nonsense!"

"Come on, would you agree? For money? A lot of money?"

"I don't want to talk about that."

"Why?"

"Leave me alone! What is the sense of talking about it!"

"Well, it was just a question."

"So, leave me alone. Don't we have anything else to talk about? By the way, have you bought any bread?"

And so on and so forth.

***

As a result, Igor's spirit sank after this conversation. He couldn't sit still. He wanted to go somewhere, to do something, to amend everything, and to give this fucking money back. (He had wisely hidden the envelope with the money for his wife not to find it. And he didn't want to see it, either! He just couldn't! Let alone touch it. The money literally burned his hands. But he had nowhere to go and nothing to do. He couldn't amend anything. That was it. Everything failed. Something very terrible had happened—so terrible, that his mind refused to believe it. It was impossible! *No! No! No! There is no devil and no Satan! No! No and no! That's bullshit! Bedtime stories!"*

"And what about the money?" his subconsciousness reminded him sarcastically. "Where does the money come from?")

"The money? It's just... It's from the TV crew. Talk shows and stuff. Rich sponsors. They have a lot of money. Easy money! Ten grand is nothing for them! Ha-ha! 'Ten grand!' Do you know what you're talking about? 'Ten grand is nothing for them!' They gave it to the next man and left. Are you out of your mind? Come on, I neither know nor care! But there's no devil! No, no, and no! This I know for sure. And if he exists, let him appear! Right now! Then I would believe in him! So, where is he? No devil?"

3

Suddenly, in a chair near a table, there appeared a young man in his mid-thirties. He was sitting with his legs crossed and looking patiently and lazily at Igor, who became pale and was utterly speechless. "Did you want to see me, Igor Ivanovich?" he asked calmly and politely after a pause.

"Umgh," Igor opened and closed his mouth without uttering a word. The man waited patiently.

"Who are you?" Finally, Igor managed to say something, "How did you get here?"

"A strange question," the man shrugged his shoulders. "Let us not lose time and get to business. So, Igor Ivanovich, why did you want to see me?"

Igor was staring at the stranger who sat in the chair, and couldn't understand what was happening. *Is that really a devil? Demon? Satan? So, it appears, he does exist? And hell and all that's described in the Bible—so, it's all true? Wait-wait-wait! I'm not thinking straight! Something important... important... something that... Oh, yeah! Soul! Soul! I did sell him my soul!*

"I want to have my soul back," Igor said suddenly in hoarse voice. "I didn't know what I was doing!" he added with a complaint and almost whimpered, he was so miserable.

The stranger's expression didn't change, but Igor thought that he could see a fleeting scorn in his eyes.

So what? I don't have to be ashamed with him! He sees through me anyway. The whole schmeer. He knows that I'm no hero! I just want to have my soul back! I want it back!

"You're a grown man, Igor Ivanovich," the stranger was examining Igor as if he was a rare insect. "What do you mean that you didn't know?"

"I thought that you didn't exist," mumbled Igor. "I thought that it was a stupid joke from the TV. Am I really talking to the Devil? Well, it's complete nonsense!"

"So, why did you take the money, Igor Ivanovich?" the stranger asked him softly, "if you thought that it was a joke?"

"Well, why shouldn't I? They just gave it to me!" explained Igor hastily, trying to find an excuse for his deeds, "How could I know? Maybe they wanted me to take it? That's not my problem."

"Sure!" the stranger agreed willingly. "Same with me—when someone's selling a soul, why shouldn't I buy it? How could I know? Maybe you want me to buy it? That's not my problem!"

Igor was confused. He didn't know what to say to that.

"Well, however," not waiting for an answer, the stranger continued cheerfully, "that's not the point. We all make mistakes. So, I'm gathering, you want to cancel our deal, right? That's it?"

"Yes, yes!" nearly screamed Igor, "I do! Cancel! Give the money back! Here it is, please!" Igor started to take out the envelope with the money.

"Wait a minute, Igor Ivanovich!" the man lifted up his hand, trying to calm him down. Igor froze, "You don't need to get the money. Not now, at least. The point is…," the man paused, staring at Igor. Igor was listening to him, holding his breath and trying not to miss a word.

"You know what? Today or tomorrow, you will be contacted by a man. His name is Igor—same as yours. He will have your contract. If he gives it back to you by tomorrow's midnight, we shall deem it cancelled. He must give it to you voluntarily, Igor Ivanovich! Remember that! Voluntarily! If he doesn't—alas!" the stranger threw up his hands, "then everything will be in force. So, will you keep it in mind? He must give you the contract voluntarily by tomorrow's midnight. And then you will be free. And, please, be more wary in the future. If he doesn't… You got me?" Raising his eyebrows, he looked at Igor inquiringly.

Igor nodded hastily.

"Very well. You'd better try to come to an arrangement with him. And now allow me to say good-bye," the man glanced at the clock on a wall. "I'm in a hurry. Got a lot to do. Well, Igor Ivanovich, all the best." Saying this, the man disappeared. Igor stared bluntly at the empty chair for some time and then slumped on the sofa. His thoughts were all mixed up, and he couldn't think straight. At the same time, he felt a huge, terrible, and unparalleled relief.

"He is saved! Saved! He had only to arrange everything with Igor. Yeah! We'll arrange it! He is a human, after all! Flesh and blood. And two men will definitely find a common language. It's not like talking to the Satan, whom you don't even know where to look for."

So, Satan does exist! And God, and the Bible... It's all true! And hell exists, too. Oh, my God, how will I live with that? That's... That changes everything completely! I'm going to start attending church tomorrow, and I'm going to start a new life. I'll learn all prayers by heart. Maybe I will retire to a cloister and pray for forgiveness. Well, no, the cloister is too much; I just mentioned it out of despair. Forget the cloister! Probably that's not for me; but I'm pretty sure that my life will be changed. Tomorrow, I will buy the Bible! And something else, maybe. A psalm book, or what's it called? I really don't know anything about it. What holy books are there?

Fuck! By the way, I should stop swearing, especially when I think about God. Mother... Shit! Fuck! That's enough! Three words, and three blasphemies. All right, I'll get used to it, a bit at a time. I've been swearing and cursing for forty years; I can't just stop doing it in one minute, right? I can make mistakes from time to time. Right. At first. I can forget about it. God will forgive me. Even the devil forgave me. "What did he forgive me, actually? Heh? What, really?"

It seemed that Igor's pleasant thoughts suddenly halted, having hit an unseen obstacle. Right away, he felt that the black emptiness that had disappeared came back again.

"Indeed! What did... HE?

Even in his thoughts, Igor didn't dare to utter such words as Satan or Devil. Demon was alright; demon was neutral and not dangerous and somehow a funny, harmless creature with a tail from

"Evenings on a Farm near Dikanka," who was mounted by a smith, Vakula, and who spoke pleasantly to Solokha, but Satan or Devil—that was different! That was no joke!

"It seems, HE doesn't do anything without purpose? Never! So, why is HE letting me go? Why is he giving me my soul back and talking to me like a friend? Though, why do I think that HE is actually giving me my soul back? I need to talk to that Igor first. What did HE say? If Igor voluntarily—HE emphasized it—gives me that cursed contract by tomorrow's midnight. And what if he doesn't?" This thought was so horrible that Igor banished it, almost wavering his hands.

He will definitely give it back. There's no choice! How could he not give it back? Then I will show him! I will! And what will I show him? How exactly? He must give it to me voluntarily. Voluntarily! HE repeated that several times. And then repeated once more. Voluntarily! This means that I cannot take it from him by force. It's useless. And I cannot trick him, no way. Nobody plays cunning with the Devil.

"Oh, my God! So that's... What if he tells me to give him my flat? Or I'll have to kill someone? 'And eat!' he added a phrase from a famous joke. *Oh, God! No reason to be excited yet! Out of the frying pan into the fire! What would that Igor ask of me? An authorized representative of... of the... well, it's clear. Probably, he's the same, but only in human's look. Some maniac. Chikatilo. What should one do to meet him, actually? I can't even imagine that. There are no crimes one can make to meet him! Hitler or Joseph Stalin himself—it doesn't matter. Maybe a sectary? Satanist? Head of a sect? No, it's unlikely that he would talk to the Devil himself. I doubt that the Satan talks to anyone at all. Yeah, but he did talk to me! Well, I wish he didn't. Should I pray? 'God almighty and merciful!' I don't happen to know a single prayer. And it's all useless. I should have done it before that. And now..."*

Igor started to realize clearly that the situation was hopelessly horrible. He, Igor Ivanovich Fedorov, being of sound mind and memory, voluntarily sold his soul to the Devil and sealed the contract with his blood! For no reason! Just because of foolish naughtiness and empty bragging. He just showed off in front of a young chick and a camera, an old fool! *See, I'm a hero now! Half seas over me and I'd take on the devil himself! See this, good people! It would be better if I got infected with AIDS in front of the camera. Or with bubonic plague. Or just would hang myself. For delectation of good folk. And it would serve me right! Especially, it would have been really much better than what really happened. And now this Devil comes to me and plays cat-and-mouse and his other devilish games with me. I don't understand what he needs me for, but soon I'm gonna find it out. Yeah, this would be easy to do. But, for some reason, I think that this knowledge won't make me happy. At all! And it all will end with a horrible nightmare, like it always does when people try to make a deal with the Devil.*

Will I burn in hell forever?" he suddenly thought desperately and nearly groaned with blind terror *"'Abandon hope all ye who enter here?' Forever? Without hope? No! I don't want to! Oh, God! What did I do? Save me, God! God forbid! You saw everything! I'm no monster and no villain—I'm just an ordinary, harmless fool with common sins, nothing more. God forgive! I didn't know what I was doing! Save your slave!"*

Involuntarily, Igor glanced at the chair, where his recent visitor had been sitting, hoping desperately that, if he was such an important person that HE himself talked to him, then he would be protected—and his protector would appear in the same chair—if not by the God himself, then by, at least, the Archangel Michael in shining white armor and with fiery sword in his right hand, and he would comfort him and tell him, Igor Fedorov, to sleep well and not worry about anything at all. Satan is shamed once again, and his works are ruined. 'Let His enemies be scattered!' Amen."

However, no one, alas! appeared. It seemed that nobody needed him, except... The chair remained empty.

Igor sat in front of the ill-fated chair for some time, then stood up and paced the room. Everything was happening too quickly, and he couldn't fully realize the reality and seriousness of the situation. He just didn't have enough time to think it over. He couldn't catch the events. They were changing with such a kaleidoscopic speed and were so incredible and unbelievable, that they actually resembled an amusing and exciting game. A show. Like a movie or a play. A musical. Something would happen right now, everything would change, and decorations would be switched. Several times in a row. And in the end, no matter what adventures a main hero would have, there will be a happy end. And everybody would be happy. Everybody would hug, kiss, jump with joy, slap each other's back and scream, "Wow!"

At that moment a phone rang. Igor answered indifferently. Probably, it's a friend of his wife's calling. They would talk for an hour, instead of cooking the supper. She just fucking came from work!

"Hello!"

"Igor?"

"Yeah," answered Igor reflexively and felt his heart sink. He knew who it was.

"I'll be waiting for you at my place tomorrow at 3. Write down the address." Igor wrote down the address without a grumble. "Got it?"

"Yes. Who is it?"

"You know who it is," someone giggled nastily on the other end of the line. "And one more thing. Bring your kid with you. He is at a summer cottage, right? So, go there and bring him back. You'll do it by 3."

"What for?" asked Igor in a dead voice.

"What for?" the other man showed surprise. "Guess yourself."

Igor didn't say a word.

"Boys are one of my vices," explained the talker and giggled again, "Especially young ones. Yours is 5, right? Just the thing! So, tomorrow at 3. Grab some Vaseline or cream—I think I've ran out of it. I will, certainly, tell the guys, but bring some, just in case. Okay, bye. See you."

Igor heard the short dials. For some time, he just stared at the phone, and then, as if he was afraid to break it, put it down carefully. He just couldn't believe that everything that happened was real. That was just impossible! It was a horrible dream, and he would wake up now. was it really happening to him? For real? It was just a joke, a show, a musical, an action movie with a happy end. *Where is the end? This nightmare can't be real*! What does his five-year-old son have to do with it? What did he mean by 'I like boys?' 'Just the thing?" 'Grab some lubricant?'"

Every phrase fell down to his soul like a huge weight.

So he wants me to bring my only son for him to entertain? My five-year-old son? Does he really think that I will do that? And what did he say about 'guys?' There are a couple of them? You bastard! I'm gonna call the police! They're gonna close your stinking den, scum! What's your address? Outraged, Igor grabbed the paper with the address on it. His hands were shaking, and he couldn't discern the words.

So! Where should he call? 02?

He reached for the phone and halted. *"What then? What am I going to do? What shall I do, if I hand him in to the police? He's my only hope. Right, but my son, Valerka! Shall I bring him for amusement of these degenerates? No, I would rather die! Or better, kill these bastards. These scums! I don't give a damn what would happen to me then! And what would happen to me? I would burn in hell forever—that's what. Forever! Everybody, even the most terrible sinner, has hope, but I do not have any. I sold my soul to the devil. That's it! My only chance is to make a deal with that bastard. And how can I have a deal with him, if he wants my five-year-old son for his entertainment? For now—and I don't know what he would want later. Maybe my wife. Maybe me. Maybe something else. Oh, God! What should I do? What? There should be a way out! There should be!"*

***

Next morning, Igor went to the summer cottage. There, he told his mother-in-law some bullshit about an interview in the school—ha! made everything up—which demanded Valerka's and his presence, took his son, and drove away.

His mother-in-law listened to him in great wonder, lamented, "He's five years old!" and glanced at Igor with suspicion. But, as Igor was completely sober, she couldn't say anything against it.

The night didn't pass in vain for Igor. He had thought about everything. He seemed to age a hundred years. And, as the result of his thoughts, he was going to the given address, and his five-year-old son was with him.

He knew that address very well, and he quickly found the right building. He still had about 40 minutes; he bought Valerka ice cream, and they sat on a bench in the yard. He was looking at his five-year-old kid, who didn't suspect anything and trusted his father completely—so helpless, and he loved him a lot—and was thinking; he just couldn't say to himself what he was thinking about and what he was feeling. However, he was going to the place. And he brought his child with him.

At 3 o'clock straight, Igor was standing in front of the door. He waited for a second, looked at Valerka, patted his head for some reason, and pressed the doorbell. Its sound hardly died away, and the door opened. On the doorstep, there stood the same man, his yesterday's visitor—the Devil, Satan, or whoever he really was. All in all, it was HIM.

Igor hoped to see anyone else—some monster, maniac, a beast in a human form, or even group of beasts—but not HIM! He was so embarrassed that he froze in front of the door, clutching Valerka's hand.

All is lost! the thought suddenly came to him. *He's changed his mind.*

"Come on in, Igor Ivanovich!" the man stepped aside and gave Valerka a friendly smile. He smiled back, trustfully. Still shocked, Igor entered the flat, moving like a sleepwalker, stepping with wobbly legs and dragging Valerka with him. The man closed the door behind him, smiled at the kid who was looking at him upwards, and spoke to Igor.

"So, Igor Ivanovich! Now you will go home and tell your wife, Vera Valentivovna, the whole story of yours, from beginning to end, in every detail. About you signing a contract with me yesterday, and then wishing to cancel it at any price. Why you came here, and why you brought your son with you. You will tell her everything—without concealing anything," the man smiled, "All your most secret thoughts. If you do that, your contract will burn right at midnight."

The man handed the contract to Igor. He took it with a lifeless hand. "If you conceal anything, exaggerate, hide, or try to cast yourself in a positive light, it'll remain intact. And that will be it! This is your last chance. The only chance. You won't have the second one. Do not forget that. When you'll be confessing to your wife," the man smiled again, "the smallest falsity, and everything's over! Now go. You're free. I won't take any more of your time. You have a nice son," he added in the doorway and closed the door.

Igor went to the elevator and pressed the button. Coming out on the street, he went to his car, opened it, set Valerka near him, buckled him up, and drove home. He didn't have any thoughts, didn't hesitate, and had no emotions. He acted mechanically—as if he was a robot, or a zombie. He felt as if he really was a zombie—the living dead, seemingly living. As a matter of fact, he was long dead or, rather, rotten alive.

For a live man couldn't do what he had to. He just didn't have enough strength for that. He had to die at first. He had to kill all that was alive: feelings, shame, and conscience. Lose his soul. Though it seemed that he had lost it already—the day before, on a bench in a square.

5

Curiously enough, his wife was already at home. There was something wrong at work, and she was able to come home earlier. However, Igor was not surprised; he took it for granted. Surely, that was the way it should be! For HE told him, "Go home and tell your wife the whole story." So, his wife had to be home already.

Seeing Valerka, she was taken aback at first, but then got very anxious and rushed to Igor. "What happened? Why have you brought him? Is everything all right? Something wrong with Mom?"

"I need to talk to you. Immediately. Right now," said Igor in a dead, monotonous voice, "Go to the kitchen. I'll be right back. I'll just run cartoons for Valerka; I don't want him to hear us."

"Do you want to watch cartoons? About a wolf?" he asked his son playfully and, not waiting for the answer, dragged him to the bedroom. He put the videotape into the VCR and switched on the TV "Sit here and watch cartoons. Mom and I will talk in the kitchen. All right?"

"Okay," answered Valerka, laughing. He was watching the adventures of his favorite cartoon characters.

"Sit calm and don't mess around," said Igor, before leaving, and he went to the kitchen.

His wife, who was scared to death and chalky pale, was sitting behind the table and staring at him silently. Only God knew what she could have thought about everything. "Something's wrong with Mom?"

"I wish!" Igor looked at her, breathed air in his lungs, and, plunging into an abyss, began talking.

"Your mom is all right, don't worry. Valerka is okay, too." His wife gave a sigh of relief. "You don't need to worry about that—just listen to what I'm gonna tell you. It's very important.

"Yesterday, I left work early. I didn't know what to do—the weather was fine—so I went to a square and sat on a bench. And when I was sitting there, I was approached by a TV crew, a girl with a microphone and a guy with a camera. "I liked the girl. She was stylish, up my alley," he added after a pause, recalling that his talker wanted him to tell only the truth without concealing anything. Certainly, the impression which a female journalist had on him, was not that important—that detail was harmless and completely insignificant—but, nevertheless, under other circumstances, Igor would have never told his wife about it and would have concealed it. That was the reason that he didn't dare to conceal it now. Who could know what was significant and what wasn't. He had been told to say everything—that meant everything. The stakes were too high.

"Don't be surprised, and don't interrupt me. You're gonna understand everything now," he added indifferently, seeing that his astonished wife was going to say something.

However, she wasn't going to be silent. "What am I going to understand? That you like chicks in denim dresses? You old jerk! Aren't you ashamed to tell me that?"

"I am," said Igor in a watery voice.

"So why are you telling me this?" asked his wife in astonishment, staring at Igor and feeling already that something was wrong.

"You just listen to me, and you'll understand everything," answered Igor in the same lifeless, monotonous voice and then continued in a second. "So, I was approached by a TV crew: a guy and a girl."

"I already heard that!" his wife couldn't suppress an acrid commentary. "The girl was stylish and up your alley.

Igor waited until she went silent. "They presented themselves as the hosts of a TV show about religion and told me that I was live on TV. Well, that meant that they were broadcasting everything live. They started asking questions."

"Who? The girl in the denim dress?" his wife asked acidly again.

"Yeah, the journalist," Igor answered patiently. The stupid women's foolishness of his wife began to irritate him, in spite of everything. "What does the girl have to do anything with it? I completely forgot about her. I don't care about her. And it turns out that she wasn't a girl. She… ough! Listen, if you keep interrupting me, I won't be able to finish,"

"You haven't finished in a month! Right, I see! You're thinking about stylish chicks."

"Motherfuck! Motherfuck!" yelled Igor, outraged. But he remembered at once what was happening and why he was telling her all that, and calmed down. "Vera, would you listen to me, okay?" he asked her wearily, "Compared with what you're gonna hear… You will forget about chicks. Just listen to me quietly for some time, and you're gonna understand everything. Okay? You'll understand why I'm telling you about such unflattering things about me. You'll get it—just wait a bit and listen." Igor paused again and scratched his forehead, trying to calm down and collect his thoughts. "Well… So… They started asking questions. Do I believe in God? I said that I didn't. And in the devil? If you don't believe in God, so you don't believe in devil either?

"Whom?" asked his wife suspiciously.

It seemed that she couldn't forget Igor's confessions about the sexual appeal of the young interviewer in the denim dress, and she kept listening to the rest of his story inattentively, thinking that he was trying to dupe, distract and fool her. And finally, it would turn out that he had fucked that chick, and he would tell her about that. He would repent, so to say.

Right! thought Igor irritatingly, *in front of the camera, on a bench, ~~in the~~ downtown, in broad daylight. Live on television. Silly woman, what's she thinking? Long of hair and short of brains. A clone. When hearing about a possible rival, a genetic program of her nest and breed protection is automatically switched on, completely blocking a capability to perceive the reality adequately. Women!*

Nevertheless, she was alarmed at him mentioning the devil. Firstly, she was afraid of the devil, like any other woman; secondly, it didn't match a quite simple scheme that was built in her head.

"In the devil? Oh, now I see why you were bothering me with your stupid questions about…." Even irritated, his wife didn't dare to say HIS name.

Before that, Igor always considered that to be stupid superstitions and women's whims, and he used to kid her a lot, sometimes in a very wicked way; and now it turned out that she was right, in fact. Yeah, he shouldn't say his name in vain. And he was smart, educated, and modern—and, in the end, he came to the same result, and he was afraid of all that. He ended up in a jam, he was in a tight spot, and all that situation was very stupid and foolish; and he didn't know how to get out of it—and she, being so ridiculous, unlearned, and superstitious, understood everything well from the very beginning and didn't even wanted to talk to him when he foolishly tried to speak of HIM. And she was absolutely right, by the way. He wished he had had her women's foolishness on that bench! Heigh-ho!

"So that was the reason? I knew straightaway that something was wrong! And you just told me, for no reason! for no reason! I can feel it at once!"

"Yes, that was the reason. And 'for no reason'? That was a lie. I didn't dare to tell you at once," said Igor honestly.

He couldn't lie, even on minor issues. An argument with his wife shook him a bit, and he woke up. But that revival was imaginary. Like galvanization of a corpse. Like contraction of frog's leg under the influence of electrical discharge. Illusion of a real life. In fact, he was dead. Even his wife felt it at last and became silent.

Rather straight and unnaturally honest answers of her husband started to scare her. The living felt the dead.

"So, they… she asked me if I believed in the devil. Naturally, I told her that I didn't. Then she offered me the chance to sell my soul and to sign a contract. 'So, if you do not believe in anything, neither in God nor in the devil, what's the difference? Why not? And we'll give you money—$10,000.'" His wife groaned softly. "'So, you need to sign it in front of the camera, and we'll give you the money. That's what our show is about.' The point is whether you are afraid or not to sign a contract. Everybody can talk a lot, but when it comes to business… Well, I wasn't afraid," Igor smiled sadly, "And I signed it. With my blood."

"With blood?" asked his wife in astonishment.

"Right! With my blood. She had a special needle with her for drawing blood samples. She stabbed me with it; I didn't even realize what was happening. Actually, I did realize everything—she just stabbed me very skillfully, and I didn't even feel the pain," Igor corrected himself. "He didn't realize,' you see! I fucking realized everything!"

"So, she stabbed my finger, I pressed it against the contract, and she gave me the money. Here it is," Igor produced the envelope which he had brought beforehand, put it on the table and pushed it to his wife. He was thinking about showing her the contract but decided not to do it now —all in good time.

"Is this real dollars? Ten grand indeed?" asked his wife in surprise, staring at the pack of money which she had taken out of the envelope.

"Yeah, real. Downright real. Exactly ten grand," said Igor. "I checked in a currency exchange office." That was true. Igor indeed had visited a currency exchange office on his way home. Luckily, it was situated near their building, just around the corner.

"So, in brief, she gave me that envelope, got in a car, together with her cameraman, and drove away with the contract. And I was left with this envelope."

Igor was telling her everything in the smallest detail, being afraid to miss anything. He remembered that he had been told, "In every detail!"

"So I got worried. Up to that time, I thought that it was a silly joke—well, you know, the guys from TV usually make such jokes with hidden cameras and stuff—'self-made cameraman' and so on—but I suddenly realized that that was no joke. What joke? Ten thousand bucks is no joke!

"So I started thinking about what I had done. I don't believe in the devil, but still… The money is real. And there was a reason why they gave it to me. I reckoned this way and that, I thought about different explanations, but it all was useless. It just wasn't right… Whatever I would think—here it is, ten grand! And there's no escaping them. Did they actually present it to me? Just like that? Bullshit! They didn't say that it was a gift They told me honestly: we're buying your soul. And I was a fool to sell it. Voluntarily. And signed with my blood," Igor caught his breath and looked at his wife.

She was sitting with her mouth open and staring at him, as if fascinated.

A fucking soap opera for her! Adventures. Don Pedro gives the envelope with the money to Donna Juanita, thought Igor sadly and continued after a groan.

"Well, when I realized that, I got anxious. I called Dimka Sokolov. I asked him if he would have agreed if he had been offered the opportunity to sell his soul. He told me that he wouldn't. No way! Without any explanations. I was very surprised; I expected that we would discuss it, and he just reacted in such a way. Then I got very anxious. I tried to talk to you, but you didn't want to!"

"Of course," interrupted him his wife, "How could you possibly ask me that? Sell my soul!"

"Come on, Vera, wait," asked Igor, "don't interrupt me, okay? I need to get a load off my mind. It all makes me sick. I wish…! Yeah, I know that I'm an idiot."

I wish I were just an idiot, he thought hopelessly and sadly. "This is only the half of it; there are more treats in store. Well, I got scared. What if HE really exists? And I indeed sold HIM my soul? What then? So, I began comforting myself. Well, that was just impossible! We're living in the 21st century, and I was scared by some old wives' tales. There is no devil! Well, if HE exists, let HIM appear! And HE did appear."

"Who appeared?" whispered his wife, looking at him with round eye. "Are you out if your mind?"

"Vera, I know that it sounds crazy and I know what you're thinking, but I'm not insane. HE did appear, and I did talk to HIM. HE just appeared in a chair in the form of a young man, spoke with me—and vanished."

"You're sick! You need to go to the doctor! You're hallucinating!"

"And the $10,000? Are they also a hallucination? And the contract? Is it a hallucination as well?" Igor produced the contract that had been hidden in a newspaper. She grabbed it mechanically and began reading, confused. "So what? Do you believe it now?"

"So what with the contract?" she looked up at him. "You're seeing devils because of it, because of the stress. You worried too much, and that's why you're just imagined all that stuff. You just fancied it!"

"What fucking stress are you talking about?" hissed Igor in wrath. "I'm telling you—I talked to HIM! Just like I'm talking to you now. All right, then. Just let me finish, and then you may believe it or not. It's up to you. If you don't believe it—all the better. Just listen."

"And why should I listen to you? Why are you stuck on it?" It seemed that she began suspecting something again. *"Maybe I'm right—maybe, he's trying to pull my leg. And now he'd start talking about that young journalist again."*

"Because HE told me to do that," said Igor hopelessly.

"It's useless!"

"I need to tell you everything from beginning to end, in every detail and not concealing anything."

"Well, you're insane! Right! You got a mania. Yeah, I saw it on TV."

Oh, God! She is such a silly woman! thought Igor in wonder. *How come I didn't see it?*

"Vera, can you just listen to me? Well, just listen quietly, and that's it! Like you're listening to a crazy talk. No one argues with insane people. One must listen to them and agree to everything. Just listen to me, that's all. You may not agree and listen at all, but just pretend to be listening. I don't care. All the better. Just don't interrupt me."

"All right, go on," his wife chattered in a sweet voice. Obviously, she paid no heed to his wish not to interrupt him and was ready for further arguing and commenting as he spoke.

Maybe it's for the better, suddenly thought Igor. *Maybe, she won't see the trees for the forest? Maybe she won't understand anything because of her foolish questions? Maybe she wants to prove to me by any means that she's right, that she "always feels it" and that I've got a 'mania,' and I'm an idiot who just got too anxious. Maybe I'll get away with it. Heh?*

"So? Where did I stop?"

"You saw a devil," his wife helped him, "in the form of a young, handsome man. It's good that it was not a woman. A stylish one, in close-fitting jeans—you like such girls, right?"

Silly woman! thought Igor with anger. *Dumb. One-celled animal. With only one wrinkle.*

"Right," Igor decided not to pay attention to his wife and not to react to her retorts, but to tell her without concealing anything, like he was advised from the very beginning, addressed directly to an unseen higher confessor. And his wife…

All the better that she's such an idiot. Probably she won't even understand, with her pea-brain, what I'm gonna tell her. She's not gonna grasp it. She didn't get it when I told her about HIS order. That I'm supposed to tell her only the truth. Bare truth. Unadorned. Naked. And it doesn't matter whether I'm crazy or not. What matters is that she can ask me whatever she wants. Whatever. Own it! Whatever you ask, I will give you an answer. I'll give you chapter and verse. As if confessing. Just ask!

She didn't pay attention to that detail at all. She missed it completely. She was drawn far aside. To some new stuff. 'That's bullshit! I saw it on TV!' Well, great! Why should I dissuade her? I'm fine with it. Let her split along. Godspeed! She's trying to prove that I'm an idiot. I'm fine with it. I do agree. I'm fine with idiot, insane—whatever she calls me! It's really better than what it is. For, actually, there is no word for such scum as me. The word is not invented yet for such scum. My own son! And... Well, let's hope that it won't go that far. To this topic and further explanations. Maybe I'll be able to get away with it, if I'm lucky enough, and if I build up my story cleverly. I'm gonna tell her the Forsyth Saga. About Don Pedro and Donna Juanita.

If you conceal anything, exaggerate, hide, or cast anything in a positive light, a formidable warning suddenly came to his mind. The thoughts ran through Igor's head. *"And that's exactly what I'm going to do,"* he thought. *"'Conceal, hide, and exaggerate. Cast in a positive light.' Using the pinheaded stupidity that my fool of a wife suddenly showed. Vera fucking Valentinovna. How come she's suddenly become so stupid? Exactly today. I've never seen her so stupid. Well, she used to be an ordinary woman, sufficiently clever and sufficiently silly. Sure, she isn't Sophia Kovalevskaya or Marie Curie, but she is a rather sensible and rational woman. She used to understand everything pretty well."*

And today, she looks as if she were crazy, as if she broke loose. She doesn't want to listen to anything and doesn't let me say a word. I talk about Thomas and she talks about Jonas. She's harping on about her 'mania,' and she wouldn't change her mind! All in all, as if it wasn't her. As if someone pushes me and makes me lie to her, trip her up, distort the facts! 'Hide and exaggerate!' It's so simple! Someone tempts me.

"The Evil One tempts me, I saw him another time," suddenly an ancient quote came to his mind.

Well, don't hide; I wouldn't dare to do that, but simply cast everything in proper light. Why should I ruin my life? Just change the angle and light, and that's it! A ripe matter—a picture would be shown in proper tones. And I would be no villain or monster but, on the contrary, a sufferer. What did I endure during that time? How I suffered! Was it really easy to do it? My own son! It's a real tragedy. Emotional drama. Emotional, fuck? And nothing really happened!

"And she will believe me. She will take it at face value. She will get it the way I show it to her. Technically, there's no lie. I've told everything just like I was asked. I didn't hide or conceal anything. Well, I dwelt on some of the details, and the others... well, just mentioned, but it's still..."

Well, whom am I going to play these games with? With HIM? Who do I want to fool? HIM?

"Probably it's one of HIS temptations. The last one. A temptation which I almost yielded to. No way! Nobody's gonna argue and explain everything to me. The paper won't burn at midnight; that's all that would be explained. Stay with your wiles. Go on with them. No way!"

"By the way, is it by chance that I'm telling her everything in detail? I'm wagging my tongue, beating about the bush. I just need to tell her the point of it, but, instead, I'm trying to conceal this point with all means I have. I'm trying to drown it in the sea of useless details. In the ranting about denim dresses of some girls."

"Vera, listen to me!" Igor slammed the table with his hand to draw his wife's attention, "Listen to me carefully. Here is the thing. It doesn't matter whether HE did appear, or whether it is my imagination. The thing is that I believed in it. And I asked HIM to cancel the contract at any cost.

"And HE said that the cost would be Valerka. I had to bring him to the designated address for the entertainment," Igor swallowed but recovered himself and continued, "for the entertainment of the whole group of child molesters. I did that. If they had tortured and killed him there, I wouldn't have done a thing.

And if they had demanded you, I would have done that, also. I would have done anything! Anything at all. I would have killed him myself! And you as well! With these hands. And I would have killed anyone else. Just to save myself. I betrayed all of you. All and sundry." *That's what matters,"* he thought a bit and added, "And I would have betrayed you now, if I had had to make a choice.

" One more thing. Actually, I gave HIM an oath to tell you the truth and not conceal anything. Not to hide or exaggerate. You may ask me whatever you want; I will tell you everything. HE promised to me that if I do it, my contract will burn today at midnight, and I will be free. And I agreed to everything for that."

Igor went silent. Vera didn't say a word as well. He looked up at her. Vera was staring at him. It seemed that she couldn't fully realize what she had just heard. No wonder!

"So, you were ready to bring there… Valerka?" she said very quietly at last.

"You didn't get me. It's not that I was ready. I did! Earlier today. Just now," answered Igor in helpless voice, staring at the table.

"What? What did you say? So, he…? Answer me! Now! What? What did they do to him?" his wife yelled in terror.

"Nothing. They did nothing," Igor tried to calm her quickly. "There were no rapists there," he added bitterly. "The same man, from yesterday… well, HE waited for me there. HE told me to go home and tell you everything. So I came home."

"So nobody touched him?" asked his wife in anxious voice, being unable to calm down.

"No."

Vera gave a sigh of relief. Then her eyes widened. She began to understand.

"So, was it the same man?" she said hesitatingly, stumbling at every word, "That you saw yesterday? You saw him today?"

"Yes. And Valerka saw him, too. You can ask him."

"And yesterday… you say he just appeared in a chair?"

"Right. I called for HIM, and HE appeared out of nowhere. And then he vanished the same way. He spoke with me and vanished."

"And you saw him today again?"

"Yes."

"Holy Mother of God! Save me!" his wife crossed herself and muttered a prayer.

Then she looked at the contract and quickly moved away with the stool, trying, obviously, to keep as far away from it as she could. "So you really sold your soul to the devil?" she whispered quietly, as if to herself, still staring at the piece of paper with a brown stain at its bottom.

Igor was silent. The woman sitting in front of him, who had been his wife in some other, mortal life, began to slowly realize what was happening. The stream of information that rushed down on her—especially *such* information—wild, incredible, and supernatural, which she couldn't perceive seriously at once—astonished and perplexed her; but now she began to comprehend and digest this information slowly, coming to her senses gradually. At last, she started to understand what exactly her husband had told her. Igor was waiting.

"Wait, wait! So you brought Valerka there, knowing that he would be raped? Abused?"

"Yes."

"And you…and you say that if he had been killed there, you wouldn't have done anything?"

"Right."

"And you would have killed him yourself? With your own hands? Your own son? How? With a knife? Like Ivan the Terrible?"

"Don't torment me!" Igor nearly screamed. ("Don't try to hide or exaggerate anything!") "I'd have done what they had told me to. A knife? Okay, a knife it would be."

"And you would have killed me as well?"

"Yes."

"But why? Why! I just don't get it! I'm your wife! And he's your son. How can you talk about such things so easily? I just don't understand, what's happening! What's wrong with you?"

Igor went silent. Then, still staring at the floor and not raising his eyes, he started talking.

"Listen, Vera. Try to understand me," he stumbled, looking painfully for the right words to clearly express his thoughts. "Yesterday I found out that the devil exists. And hell exists, too. Some people believe in God, some don't—but even the people who do ever have a grain of doubt. At least, so it seems to me. Come on, what with "seems?" That's the way it is! It's one thing when you believe abstractly and completely another when you just know. These are different things. There is a good reason that all who saw Christ, spoke with him, and saw him resurrected—all of them became apostles, saints and so on.

"For, if you know exactly that paradise exists, that the afterlife exists, you may not be afraid of anything on earth and may endure any tortures—if you know for sure that there will be retribution in heaven. So that's probably why neither God nor the devil appears to anyone. And there are no wonders. Because that would change everything. The world would be different. There would be no free will. Nothing would exist at all! No one would sin, and, probably, no one would do anything at all. Everybody would just pray and dream about getting to paradise. That's why our world is such as it is—and it exists; that's all, because there is that grain of doubt. Even the saints have it. Who knows what will happen after death and if there is anything after it? Maybe there's nothing at all! No one has come back from there. And we live only once. That's the foundation of everything.

"Maybe it's all rather confusing because the topic is complicated," Igor was silent for some time, thought a little, and then continued. "So, yesterday, I did find out that the devil exists. I found it out. And the hell exists, too. And I did sell my soul. And for that, I will burn in hell forever. Forever! Just think of it—forever! I'm gonna die in 30 years and forget after death about you—about yours and Valerka's existence! It seems that souls do not remember their earthly bondings. And what if they do? Well, how long would I remember you there? Ten years? One hundred? And we're talking eternity here!

" What am I talking about? What 100 years? I'm gonna die tomorrow; and, in a year or two, you'll get married again and forget about me, as if I never existed, especially if you got a nice new husband."

"And if I die tomorrow—will you forget me straightaway, too?" asked Vera quietly, "And will you marry again?"

"I forgot you already. I feel that I'm dead among the living. And I am dead, really. I came back from hell. I know for sure that there is an afterlife, and mortal life is just a moment before the eternity for me. It's a forbidden knowledge, because a man is not allowed to know it. I realized it. I don't know why God punished me with it."

***

The minute hand inevitably approached the twelve. Igor was sitting behind the table in the kitchen and staring at the paper in front of him. His wife had already gone to the summer cottage with his son. She was afraid to talk to Igor or even to stay with him. She was afraid to be anywhere near him, as if he had really turned in a terrible monster, a demon.

Right at midnight, the paper blazed up brightly. Igor was sitting with his head on his hands and watching mindlessly the flame eating the paper with printed words. "...Soul," he suddenly saw the last word, untouched by the fire. The next moment, it was gone in the flames. Only a small pile of ash was left on the table.

And Lucifer was ask'd by His Son:

—'Tis said in the Apocalypse, the Revelation of St. John the Divine: "And I saw another mighty angel come down from heaven, cloth'd with a cloud; and a rainbow was on his mazzard: and his face, as the travelling lamp, and his feet as pillars of fire. and he set his right foot upon the flote, and his left foot upon the earth, and he cri'd with a loud voice as when a lion roareth; and when he had cried, seven thunders utter'd their voices. and when the seven thunders had utter'd their voices, I was about to write; and I heard a voice from heaven saying to me: Seal up the things which the seven thunders hast spoken and write them not." What did those seven thunders utter?

And Lucifer said thoughtfully with a strange look, repeat'd after him like an bruit:

—Angel strong...

And instantly the mind's eye of His Son saw fragments of some image, strange and obscure. As if he had turn'd into someone else and saw everything with other eyes:

— ...Cold scorching wind. And his garments vanish'd under the breath, and its rags wast drawn aroint and disappear'd.

His shoulders wast clad with coal-black armour, and it cover'd all his corpse. He sat in a saddle, and, narrowing his eyes, look'd ahead, at the still, endless, and perfectly straight lines of sharply white riders with long spears atilt—the host of angels from the heaven... the army of the servants... the meiny of the god—looking with his eyes f'r the captains, his former allies and cater-cousins: Michael, Gabriel, Uriel... however, nay one of them was to be seen. Belike, they wast at the back, at the rear, protect'd by the endless chains of the front-rank warriors.

Fair enough...—he thought with scornful indifference, and then blindly patt'd a fighting raven that was sitting on his left shoulder—the bird shook and croak'd with annoyance; then he look'd to the right, at a huge black dog that was tense as a string and star'd ahead, at the motionless, endless, snow-white ranks of the foe, and, softly touching the horse with the spurs, pull'd away...

4.

LUCIFER'S SON. Day 4.

And the fourth day came. And Lucifer was ask'd by His Son:

—'Tis said in the Bible: "And ov'r all these virtues put on love, which binds them all together in perfect unity." What dost that cullionly?

And Lucifer answer'd to His Son:

—I shall bewray thee, what it means, Mine Son.

NIGHTMARE.

"Give not thy soul unto a woman."
Wisdom of Jesus, Son of Sirach

Diary of Valeriy Vitalievich Zaslavskiy.

Today is my birthday. I'm 40. A milestone birthday. I'm in a very bad mood. So what? What have I achieved in life? What have I spent it for? What did famous Abdullah tell Vereshchagin in "The White Sun of the Desert?" "A good wife and a nice house—what else does a man need to face the old years?" Exactly! It's too right! It's said about me. Bingo. It's all that I have,—"a good wife and a nice house"—I have all that, and there's nothing more to wish for. What next? Waiting for old age? What next, eh?

At one time, I wanted to become a millionaire. Well, I did that. So what? Nothing! Same boredom and depression as everyone else has—yet, I can spoon up caviar. It's the only pleasure. And then… Well, I surely can comfort myself that everybody else doesn't have what I do. They don't have caviar. They have spoons only.

***

Someone knocked at the window of Zaslavskiy's luxurious limo. He turned his head. A slender girl—she was probably no older than 15—smiled at him and gave him a promotional leaflet. Zaslavskiy opened the window a little bit, and the girl slipped the leaflet through the hole. He took it and looked at the paper mechanically; and, when he lifted his eyes up, the girl was gone. Zaslavskiy looked around, trying to find her, but, at that moment, the green light switched on, someone honked from behind, and, cursing fate, Zaslavskiy pulled away.

He liked that girl. Very much. Actually, "liked" was the wrong word. He was struck by her.

Diary.

Oh, my God, what a girl I have seen today! Oh, God! I've been thinking about her all day. I've never felt anything like this. I see her face in front of my eyes. Her smile… It's nonsense, of course, but I think that I fell in love with her. At first glance! No, I don't think—I know it for sure. I'll find her! At whatever cost! I'll find her, whatever it takes. I'll find, I'll find, I'll find her! Without doubt! Darling…

***

Zaslavskiy hardly found the address from the leaflet. It was some shithole. He didn't know Moscow that well, and that place was surely a hellhole. He hardly found it with a map. However, if he had had to go, not to the other side of Moscow, but to the far-off lands, Zaslavskiy would have done it. He would have gone to the ends of the earth! He couldn't understand what was with him.

Middle-age crisis, he smiled wryly to himself. *No fool like an old fool.*

Diary.

I've been to the lecture—the one from the leaflet. Strangely enough, I got a nice impression, seeing that I was rather skeptical before it. Naturally, I went there not to listen to all that crap about Space and Supreme Forces, but with only one purpose—to find Her.

Well, if she distributes their leaflets, then she's somehow connected to them. It means that I can find her though them. I can even stop by their office and wait in the car until I see her, however long it might take—even a week or two—as long as necessary.

Well, I think that, probably, that won't be needed; I'll find some other ways, but, still, if it's necessary, then I'll do it. One must do what one must do. I have to find her—that's what matters. Price is no object. I'll find her! She won't escape me. No! That's a rude thing to write about her. It's kind of humiliating. I'll find her and propose to her. Pah! I just can't read this nonsense and vulgarities that I write. So, I'm in love indeed. Love, love, love! People become stupid when they're in love. Well, I'll find her, and then we'll see. We'll have to see about that. I have to find her first.

So, concerning the lecture. Strangely enough, as I said, it wasn't stupid. It was pretty good. Very clever, one may say. Even I—considering that I was in a kind of exaltation—was very impressed. I was impressed a lot. Actually, we spoke about interesting stuff, and we exchanged interesting ideas.

Shit! This is clumsy writing—well, it doesn't matter. Actually, I'm feeling embarrassed, exalted (did I spell the word right? I think so—exaltation, exalted). My head is a complete mess. I want to sing and laugh with happiness. I'll find her, I will!

So, concerning the lecture. Interesting stuff was discussed there. Really interesting. You don't usually think about such stuff. I'll try to write down what I could memorize. I'll forget it soon enough, no doubt. And this stuff is really interesting. So, I need to sort out my remarks. I even began taking notes during the lecture. Yeah! Wonders will never cease. I never wrote anything down in the institute. And now it really reached to me!

So…So… Remarks! Yeah, I do lack practice. Actually, it seems that my notes are no good. Some strange names. Bergson, Whitehead, Mach… Oh! Obviously, these are the authors that were mentioned during the lecture. I marked it so I could read them later. Here we have a phrase in Latin. "Ignoramus et ignorabimus—We don't know and shall never know," by Du Bois-Reimond. Interesting… So what? Is that it? And where? Okay, I got it. I'll try to recreate it from memory.

So we talked about the supernatural stuff. Does it exist or not? Yes. There is no single scientific fact. But what does that mean? That nothing supernatural exists? Not really. This means only that all methods of scientific investigation cannot be basically applied to such events. That's it. For all scientific methods are based on the recurrence of the event. It's always possible to repeat an experiment. That's a keystone. Only such events can be studied. The simplest ones. It's impossible to use scientific methods for irregular events.

For, if the event is unique, and it doesn't recur or recurs only at unpredictable moments, then it's impossible to study it.

Take a ghost. It appears unpredictably and disappears the same way. How can it be studied? It's not a pendulum which you always have with you. Just swing it, and you may study it as long as you can. A ghost cannot be dragged to a laboratory. So, this means that it's impossible to study it. The only thing that can be done—his presence may be recorded—a picture taken, for example. Even then, by chance, if you're lucky enough. But it's impossible to study it systematically. But that doesn't mean that ghosts do not exist. What if a devil appears before me tomorrow? I can talk to it as long as I want, but, from the scientific point of view, it doesn't exist. Because it's impossible to "study" it. Even the fact of its presence cannot be "scientifically" recorded —to take a picture, for example, and so on, if it doesn't want it itself. But does that mean that he doesn't really exist?

Well, and so on and so forth. Causality, determinism… In one word, the conclusion is the following: Science can study that which can be technically perceived, but that's not all our world. It's just a part of it, and it is very small. A very huge layer of the events cannot be studied and perceived in essence. For example, everything regarding private mental experience…

Interesting….Very interesting….The most curious part is that all of this is obvious and beyond doubt when you think of it seriously. How is it possible to study a devil, indeed? On the other side, you never think of it. From the very childhood, we were taught about science. Science! And what about science? According to Mach, science gives us useful rules for acting and nothing more.

All in all, it was a very powerful lecture. Powerful. Very powerful. By the way, I mentioned a devil for a reason. For, actually, I didn't understand who they were. What was that organization? Group? Sect? I don't even know what word to use. Well, that doesn't really matter. So, they talked about the devil too much. And, by the way, in a restrained and respectful tone. Satan… Beelzebub… Prince of Darkness…and in that manner. And all examples one way or another were connected to him. Not just "supernatural," but "Satan," etc. Well, that's strange. Are they devil-worshippers? Though, why should I care? I don't give a crap whether they are devil-worshippers or not. Whatever! I'm not going to join them. I just want to find Her, my girl.

By the way, I don't know how to find her. At any rate, I haven't seen her there today. I just spent a whole day there in vain.

First, at the lecture, and then, in a car near their office. I was just waiting for her to appear. Well, all in all, I'll wait for a day or two, and then I'll have to do something else. Ask someone and such stuff. And what would I ask? "There's a girl who shoved your leaflet at me; do you know, where I can find her?" "And why do you ask, pervert?" Well, it doesn't matter. We'll cope with it. It's just a question of money. And I have plenty of it, thank God.

And if there is no lead here —say, she just had a one-time job—I'll start looking for her seriously. I'll hire people to check the schools, to take pictures of all 14- to 16-year-old girls, to pick up all the more or less pretty ones to narrow down the field of search—she was beautiful, gorgeous, wonderful—the best in the world!—and bring them to me. And then I will check them myself. How many of them? Thousands? Tens of thousands? It doesn't matter. So be it—tens of thousands. Even hundreds! But I will find Her. I will find her anyway. By any means. At whatever cost. Whatever! Absolutely.

***

The whole next day, Zaslavskiy spent in the office of the sect—so he called that group to himself. He listened to another lecture, got acquainted with a ton of totally strange and wild people, from Krishnaites to middle-aged women of his circle who didn't know how to occupy themselves. Everything was great, and the lecture was very interesting again—"Order and chaos"—but he hadn't come for that. The girl was still not there. It seemed that his hopes to meet her here were in vain. He had to do something. He had to change his tactics.

Diary.

I spent a whole day in that sect again—no result. Oh, God! What have I heard? What are all these people thinking about? It's a completely different world. A guy said, "So I was in trance, and God and devil appeared before me at the same time. And they started to pull me in different directions. Then God says: He shall go to paradise. And the devil: He can't go to paradise because he committed a lot of bad acts. And God: He committed them from the best of motives. And a bright tunnel opened above, and I started flying there, but woke up."

Well, a real madhouse. One would become an idiot here. I met a girl—actually, a young woman in her thirties. She's got a kid. It appears that she doesn't lack money. And she told me that she attends all of these seminars, just to kill time. Blue murder! The people do different stuff when they're bored. They're interested in God, or devil—just to kill time.

Well, okay. I don't care about that. Right! The lecture was interesting again. "Order and chaos." Though, bugger the lecture! As a matter of fact, I don't care about these problems. Yeah, I'm interested in them but not to such extent as to come here for that. Would I drag myself in the early morning to the end of the world to listen about "order and chaos" and talk to some freaks? Sure! God dang them all! They have their own life, and I have mine. Which I like, by the way. Well, maybe I don't like it very much, but I'm not that disappointed in it so as to visit such gatherings of boredom. Well, phew! I'm all messed up with these stupid speculations. And I'm thinking about other stuff. I've run though my recent notes; it seems as if I didn't write anything at all. Just a stream of consciousness.

Where is She, eh? Where! Where, where, where? Where, where, where, where, where, where, where, where? Where?

I can't think about anything else, and I can't do anything. I'm just in a twit! All my thoughts are about her. About her! About her! About her! Where is she? Where's my bird, my darling? My girl… beloved? I think about her, and I want to weep for tenderness. I couldn't even imagine that it's possible. I thought that this was possible only in books.

I think that, if I saw her now out of the window, I would jump down; I wouldn't want to lose her again. I'm losing my mind! I would give everything I have for her look! I would leave everything and go with her up hill and down dale.

P.S. Though, would she want all your "everything?" Just like you.

P.P.S. I tried to write her a love letter. Of course, it's no good. And I cannot really write, and there are no such words. If only I could express in words all that I feel now. By the way, that's the proof of the yesterday's lecture. Private, individual mental experience, feelings, emotions and love cannot be studied and perceived. So, from the point of view of modern science, they do not exist at all. Then why, when I say that I love, does everybody believes me, and when I say that I saw a ghost at night, everybody smiles skeptically, at the best? So, actually, what's the difference? The one and the other cannot be proved.

***

The next day was Saturday. Zaslavskiy hadn't thought about that, so this event, ordinary as it was, caught him unawares. He lingered for some time at the closed door of the office which he knew already all too well and, without having got what he wanted, went home. He was in a terrible mood. The thought that he wouldn't see Her neither today nor tomorrow was completely unbearable. He felt as if a gaping two-day emptiness appeared suddenly in his life. An abyss which he couldn't fill with anything.

Diary.

It's Saturday. The office is closed. It's horrible. The life lost its sense. I don't actually know how I'm going to live through these two days. All my thoughts are about Her and Her only. I can't think about anything else. And I don't want to! There's nothing else. There's nothing else in the world. Just Her. She's the only one in the world. And there's no world. She is the world, and nothing else exists. I would die for Her look, for Her word. If she ordered me, I would die. And I would be happy. God! If you exist, let me see Her once more! Just let me glance at her, just one time! However, I'll try to write her a letter. I cannot restrain myself. I will, probably, never send it, but…

LETTER.

I love you! Love, love, love, love, love, love! I always loved you; I just didn't know that, but now I do. And I will always love you. Forever. I will never leave you. If you send me away, I will just die, like a man dies without food and air. I don't even know your name, but I'm thinking about you, and my heart is bursting with tenderness. You smile, and everything around you smiles, the whole world smiles; you frown, and the whole universe becomes dark.

You are my universe. There isn't any other, and I don't need it. I felt terrible without you. Very terrible! It's true. True, true! I don't know how I could live all these years. And I didn't even live. I just led an aimless life. I was going somewhere by inertia. For some reason, I got married, then divorced, then married again. I dated women. Will you forgive me? That was not me. It all doesn't matter now. Only you matter. Only you. You, you, you. And nothing else. Nothing, just you.

***

On Monday, Zaslavskiy hurried to the office at an ungodly hour. He was there approximately an hour before the opening. He could have come even earlier but got stuck in a traffic jam. He had hardly parked his car when somebody knocked on the window. He startled, as the situation resembled the one at the traffic light when he had met Her.

However, this time it wasn't her. A young man in his thirties was standing near the car and smiling politely. Zaslavskiy pushed the button, and the window-glass went down.

"Valeriy Vitalievich?"

"Right," answered Zaslavskiy, being surprised a little.

"We need to talk. About Nightmare."

"What Nighmare?" asked Zaslavskiy, freezing. He guessed already whom they were going to talk about.

"Well, the girl at the traffic light. You're looking for her, right?"

"Get in," said Zaslavskiy quietly, still staring at the stranger, and he licked his dry lips.

The man opened the door and sat at the front seat. He was looking at Zaslavskiy intently and wasn't hurrying to start a conversation.

"So, what *did* you want to tell me? And how do you know me?" asked Zaslavskiy, looking coldly at him. He knew his worth very well and could let anybody know it, too.

However, it didn't work this time.

The man sitting near him just smiled patiently and answered calmly, "Valeriy Vitalievich, I'm going to explain everything to you. Just listen to me, and you'll understand it. The thing is that I'm a leader of this organization," the man pointed at the doors of the office, the opening of which Zaslavskiy had been waiting for so long. "My name… well, for obvious reasons, let's omit the names. You don't need it. Why would it matter? So, on Thursday, a girl came to you at the traffic light and gave you our leaflet. Since then, you've been thinking only about her. Right?"

"How do you know?" asked Zaslavskiy with astonishment and ever fear. He lost his usual confidence at one stroke.

"It's Nightmare," answered the man calmly.

"Is Nighmare her name?" asked Zaslavskiy in excitement.

"Yes. For you."

"What do you mean, 'yes' for me? And for others? Is it her fake name?"

"For you, it's real."

"Listen!" Zaslavskiy blew up at last, "stop talking in riddles! 'Yes, for you'...'real for you'—that's nonsense, really! How childish, indeed!"

At the last words from Zaslavskiy, the man frowned a little and said apologetically, "Valeriy Vitalievich! If you just listened to me, like I asked you at the very beginning and didn't interrupt me and asked counter questions, you would understand everything very quickly.

"All right, I'm listening to you," said Zaslavskiy, calming down, and he got ready to listen.

"Nighmare is, according to Dal dictionary, an illusion, spell, dream, reverie, phantom, ghost."

"What 'ghost'?" asked Zaslavskiy in astonishment, forgetting about a promise not to interrupt. "Are you kidding?"

The man smiled softly and shook his head reproachfully.

"All right, all right, I'm sorry. Go on, I'm listening to you," Zaslavskiy went silent. For some reason, it seemed to him that, in spite of his seeming youth, this man was a hundred, or even a thousand, years older than him.

"You see, Valeriy Vitalievich, our organization is not quite ordinary. We study supernatural and unusual things. Devilry… black art… magic… voodoo… sorcery… Actually, a lot of stuff. It all exists in our world, and it's not unreal, like many people think. Well, you've been to our lectures, and you know what I mean. Irregular events, if you wish. Breaches of causality and determinism. In one word, all the stuff that is impossible to be studied by the scientific methods. You can't study a devil, right? If it didn't want it itself," the man sniffed.

Zaslavskiy felt an unpleasant cold in his heart, realizing that he actually quoted a phrase from Zaslavskiy's diary. "What is this? A subtle example of the limitless possibilities of the dark magic?"

"Well… So, we've come to the most important stuff. Nighmare is, in our language, a creature of the opposite sex which was properly…well, enchanted, one may say—though the procedure is a bit different, everything is a bit complicated. Well, it doesn't matter! So, it is enchanted, so it may charm and make a certain person fall in love with it. The person, for which it all, actually, is done. In our case, it's you, dear Valeriy Vitalievich. This girl was specially prepared for you. The strength of the Nightmare's charms, which affects the object, is so great that he cannot resist it. He would think and dream only about her. Well, you feel what I'm talking about!"

Zaslavskiy listened to all that, and his head was spinning. *Magic... sorcery... nightmare...* "Wait," he finally got to the point of it. "What do you mean, 'prepared for me?' By whom?"

"Us," the man smiled softly, "us, Valeriy Vitalievich. By our society."

"Did you follow me or what?"

"Sure, Valery Vitalievich, we did."

"What for?"

"Money! Money, money, money. And nothing else. It's all very simple. We need money, and you'll give it to us. By midnight tomorrow, you'll transfer it to our account," the man gave Zaslavskiy a piece of paper. He took it mechanically and started reading, confused.

"What is it?"

"Our account details. The account number to which you must transfer the money."

"Twelve million three hundred seventy-five thousand eight hundred fifty-nine dollars and seventy-five cents," read Zaslavskiy aloud and looked at the man inquiringly.

"Yes, that's right," he said with a smile.

"Wow!" smiled Zaslavskiy ironically. He felt cold rage rise in his heart. Is he being blackmailed? "75 cents?"

"Exactly!" the man laughed merrily, "Exactly 75 cents, Valeriy Vitalievich. In other words, all that you've got. Down to the last cent."

"How do you know the exact money in my account?" Zaslavskiy hissed in fury. The man continued smiling brightly. "Oh, right, black magic! All right, I'll find it out today what kind of black sorcerer I've got in the bank. Okay, we'll deal with that. Now back to business. I just don't understand something. Why do you think that I'll give you all my money? And what does that girl have to do with it?"

"You don't have to do it," the man answered indifferently. Zaslavskiy looked at him in amazement, "It's up to you."

"And what then?"

"Tomorrow, at midnight, the spell will disappear."

"What?"

"I said that tomorrow, at midnight, your spell will disappear," the man smiled brightly again and looked straight in Zaslavskiy's eyes. "You will be free again. Free as a bird!" He waved his hands playfully. "You can go wherever you want. You can get back to your previous happy and calm life with your millions, mansions, and your beautiful wife. She was a Miss of some city, right?

"Penza," answered Zaslavskiy reflexively.

"There now! She also got a prize at the Russian national contest, right? Didn't she? She was second, right? Between you and me, she should have been first, but you actually didn't want that. You didn't want the girl to become too excited. And you were right, as a matter of fact. All in all, Valeriy Vitalievich, you're very lucky. Money… house… and such a wife! A good wife and a nice house—what else does a man need to face the old years?" Zaslavskiy startled again, hearing another quote from his diary.

"Hang on, hang on," he tried to concentrate, "And what will happen to… her? To Nightmare?"

"To her? Nothing. She won't notice anything. You'll just cease to love her. Once and for all."

"And that's it?"

"That's it."

The thought that he would lose Her forever tomorrow filled Zaslavskiy with a wave of cold fear. *Calm down! Calm down!* He tried to check himself. *He's just a blackmailer. He intentionally talks about such a short time. I shouldn't yield to him. I shouldn't take my cue from him.*

"You're lying!" he said harshly, harnessing his willpower, and, in his turn, he looked straight into the man's eyes. "Once and for all, right! If you bewitched her once, then you would do it again. If you need it. 'Tomorrow, by midnight?' Why the hurry? So I wouldn't think it over? I wouldn't do something?"

"You see, Valeriy Vitalievich," answered the man, calmly and immovably, without turning an eyelash, as if he hadn't noticed the provocative tone of Zaslavskiy, "The creation of Nighmare is a very complicated and delicate matter. One needs to take into account and consider a lot of different factors. Alignment of stars, time of birth, and so on and so forth. It's very tricky and subtle stuff, mind you. It needs a lot of skill. So, in your case, the creation of Nightmare was directly connected with your 40th birthday, Valeriy Vitalievich. It wouldn't be possible to create her at any other moment. Forty years is a very special date for a man, believe me. A landmark, a line. So, it won't be possible to create a second Nightmare for you. Ever. This is the only one. The first and the last one."

The only one? Ever? Zaslavskiy felt that he was falling down into a black bottomless abyss. *He's lying! It's impossible! And what if he isn't? What if it's true?* The very thought that he would lose her forever made him almost scream with pain.

"All right, let's assume that—well, if we could make a deal with you? What then? Would I see Her?" The man nodded.

"Would she love me?" At this thought Zaslavskiy felt that if the man said "yes" then he would agree to everything at once. Not only would he give him all his money, but he would also give him himself, if needed. He would clean the floor in their office for free.

"No," answered the man, looking at Zaslavskiy with sympathy.

The world crashed. Zaslavskiy realized, very clearly, that everything that he was told was true. These were no jokes and no game concerning Nightmare and everything else.

"Nightmares never fall in love with the objects of their influence. But it doesn't matter. You will love her forever, anyway. Just like now."

"Even when she gets married and grows old?" softly asked Zaslavskiy, as if to himself, staring in front of him.

"She will never grow old for you. You will always see her as she was back there at the traffic light the first time you saw her."

Diary, several months later.

I haven't written anything for some time. I didn't have time. A divorce… Property… Troubles. I gave everything away, but still…

Well, that doesn't matter. I don't care. I don't care about anything. Except for her. When I see Her… I see Her very often. Every day. My darling, my dear… He didn't lie to me. I will love you forever. Whatever may happen. Forever. In this life and after it. I don't need anything if you're not around. I don't need a paradise or a hell. And I will always see you as you were back then at the traffic light the first time I saw you.

And Lucifer's Son told him:
—I doth not wish to talk anon. I ne'd to think.
—Very good,—Answer'd Lucifer to Him.—Think. Think.

LUCIFER'S SON. Day 5.

And the fifth day came.
And Lucifer was ask'd by His Son:
– How shall one make a right choice? How shall one betoken good from evil?
And Lucifer answer'd to His Son:
– Thy heart shall betoken Thou, what is white and what is black.

IROCHKA.

"Flowers and sweet dreams bloom there!
All my dreams and your dreams are there!"
Modern pop-song.
"Seen then that ye walk circumspectly,
Not as fools, but as wise..."
Epistle to the Ephesians

"He that is without sin among you, let him first cast a stone at her."
Gospel of John.

1.

Oleg Viktorovich Krasin couldn't explain to himself later why he suddenly wished to respond to one of the many ads which had filled all main newspapers: "Sorcery, black and white magic, breaking hex spells" and so on and so forth. Something like this—it all happened accidentally. Intuitively. He had never responded to any ad, and now he just called, as if he was possessed to do it. As a matter of fact, he didn't even know what he would say. What was he calling for? He just dialed a number.

However, the conversation exceeded his expectations.

"Hello!" he heard a pleasant male voice answer him.

"Hello!" said Krasin after a short pause. "Hi, I'm calling concerning the ad."

"Right, Oleg Viktorovich! I'm listening to you."

Krasin almost dropped the phone, being astonished. For a short moment, he thought that he called the wrong number and, instead of the ad, had called a friend of his. But what friend? The voice of the man wasn't familiar to him at all.

"Ugh, I'm sorry; I probably got the wrong number. Who am I talking to?"

"No, Oleg Viktorovich, there's no mistake here. You got the right number, and you called the right man. You're calling concerning the ad, right? 'Clairvoyance and sorcery?'"

"Yeah…"

"So, that's it. That's the right number. No mistake."

"But how come you know me?" muttered Krasin, being embarrassed and bewildered.

"How come? You're calling concerning the ad about 'clairvoyance and sorcery.' Clairvoyance? So what did you expect?" the man on the other side of the line was clearly enjoying himself.

"Yeah," mumbled Krasin, getting even more embarrassed.

He got completely lost and didn't know what he should do and how he should act in this situation. All that was happening started to seem somehow unreal. A daydream. No, it's not possible. The alarm-clock will go off in a moment, and he will wake up. The alarm-clock wasn't in a hurry, though. The dream continued.

"You know, Oleg Viktorovich, I'm actually not far from you. Just around the corner. Next door."

Krasin looked at the number reflexively. Yeah, right. How come he didn't pay attention to that?

"Well, the bakery—first hall, fifth floor, Apartment 20. The code to the door is 382—3-8-2. Got it?" Krasin automatically repeated the numbers aloud. "Right. Okay, I'm waiting for you. Come on—you won't regret it," added the man vigorously and finally hung up the phone.

Krasin stared at it for some time, confused, then shrugged his shoulders and put the phone down. The conversation had a very strong impression on him. He said at once, "'Hello, Oleg Viktorovich. Here is a vivid example of my clairvoyance for you.'"

Well, very impressive—very. Well, there's no doubt about it. Who could expect this? Here is both sorcery and clairvoyance. I always thought that it's cheating. Well! This stupid "Well!" was the only thing on his mind. Frankly speaking, Krasin was still completely embarrassed. The session of sorcery and clairvoyance had caught him unawares.

"Just like Bulgakov said," he thought. *'The Master and Margarita,' right. The famous scene in vaudeville, a session of black magic with its following unmasking. I wonder who's waiting for me in that bad apartment No. 20? Woland and Co.? Though I'm not Stepa Likhodeev and that... What's his name? Well, that sound director. The one who sat in a loge with his wife and a lover and demanded the unmasking? Apollon, I think.*

"Would you mind telling me, Apollon Grigorievich, where you were yesterday evening? Well, Apollon Grigorievich was at the meeting of the sound committee yesterday, but I don't understand what it has to do with dark magic?"

"Come on, madam. Of course, you don't understand. And you're completely mistaken concerning the sound committee. Having dismissed the driver, Apollon Grigorievich took a bus and went to visit the actress Militsa Prokobatko, where he spent about four hours."

Oleg Viktorovich was a well-read man, and he was secretly proud of it. He could quote whole passages of the classics, and he had a very bad habit of doing it in season and out of season and at every given opportunity. The fact that he couldn't remember the surname and patronymic of Apollon was very unpleasant.

So what was his surname? Sempleyarov? Shit! What am I thinking? He came to his senses. *Bulgakov is great, of course, but what am I supposed to do? Should I go there or not? And why shouldn't I? It's interesting! What else will he tell me, this dark magician or whoever he is? Clairvoyant sorcerer. Moreover, I don't need to be afraid. I don't have a secret lover—alas and thank God! I'm not used to visiting Militsas on a bus. Well, okay, I'll go there. Sure—just think about it—a real clairvoyant. 'Hello, Oleg Viktorovich!' Bloody hell! Really? Crazy!*

Krasin mumbled the last words while dressing up quickly. He became filled with the frantic excitement that usually takes someone when dealing with something wonderful and supernatural. With something unexplainable. The very thought that soon he would talk to a real sorcerer fancied his imagination.

"Through fields and seas, a sorcerer guides the bogatyr!" He hummed aloud, closing the door. "Or is it 'through woods?' Well, woods, woods! 'There're marvels there: the wood-spite roams!'"

The anticipation of the close meeting with a secret became almost unbearable. Krasin almost ran to the elevator.

2.

The door to the apartment No. 20 opened immediately. On the doorstep, there stood a young man in his mid-thirties who smiled politely. "Please, come on in, Oleg Viktorovich," he moved aside.

Krasin entered silently, having decided not to be surprised with anything. *We'll see what's going to happen next. What's he going to offer me? It was he who invited me here.*

Actually, frankly speaking, Oleg Viktorovich tried to be skeptical and independent, but, nevertheless, he felt as if he was a child in a puppet show. He strongly believed that the fairy would wave her wand, and… But why would they show it beforehand?

"Please, here," the man pointed at the room with his hand. "Have a seat, please."

Slowly and with dignity, Krasin sat in a massive leather chair and waited for continuation. *And? Wave and? Say if you started. Don't drag your feet. What are you going to offer me? 'You won't regret it!' So, here am I. I came here. What next?* "

"And next, Oleg Viktorovich, is the following."

Krasin jumped in his chair with amazement. "Did I say the last phrase aloud?" he asked himself, bewildered." The anticipation of a wonder became even stronger.

"I studied your astral card, while I was waiting for you."

Oleg Viktorovich frowned fretfully. "Astral card?" Due to the numerous performances of various charlatans in mass-media, especially, on TV, he had a strong idiosyncratic response for such terminology.

Though, on the other hand, he could clearly see the results here. 'Hello, Oleg Viktorovich!' *Alright, what's the difference, really? Let it be the card. Maybe it's the way it should be.*

His memory eagerly produced an appropriate image from "Faust." The witch is preparing the elixir of youth and creating some insane spells. "What is this performance for, tell me? Fool, that's just to laugh! Enough, oh wise Sivilla."

Shit! It seems, I mixed up two different translations—Pasternak's and Holodkovskiy's.

"Do you want to become younger?" he suddenly heard a question which appeared to be an answer to his thoughts.

This time, Krasin was really struck. He was smitten. He stared in awe at the man who was sitting in front of him. *Second coincidence in a row! The first one could be attributed to a mere chance, but the second one? Is he really a clairvoyant, devil take him? But clairvoyants do not exist!*

Oleg Viktorovich was really scared. *It's impossible! He's an educated and well-read man. Of course, he's not a specialist, but he watches TV and read newspapers. It's impossible! He can't read my thoughts as if they were written on paper. What's the meaning of this? Is it some kind of session of dark magic in the house near the bakery? Maybe, Azazello and Begemoth would appear in a mirror, and I would feel the scent of earwax?*

"Excuse me?" he froze, finally realizing the sense of what he had just heard. *Alright, damn his clairvoyance, but what's he offering? What's he talking about? What does he mean by 'become younger?' Is it really possible? Indeed?* A wild hope that filled him drove away even his fear.

"What do you mean by "become younger?" Really? Is it really possible?"

His mind was working furiously. His thoughts were tumbling. *Is it true? No, it's impossible! If it were possible, everyone would become younger. It's definitely some kind of charlatanism. Hocus-pocus. Bubble scheme. Now he's going to offer me a magic potion for incredible price. Or cream.*

Like Azazello gave to Margarita, suggested his memory. *With swamp odor. Just spread it, and you're fine! A woman in her twenties, with natural curly hair, was looking at her from the mirror. By the way, I have natural curly hair, too. I used to have it.*

Krasin reflexively touched his head that was bald like a cue ball, for a long time.

"Well, it all depends," the man smiled ambiguously. Oleg Viktorovich heart sank.

I knew it! It's a piece of crap. As usual. Phew! And I almost believed him, like a fool!

"No, no! Don't get upset, Oleg Viktorovich, it's not due time. Unfortunately, it's impossible to become younger, but you can go to the past for a couple of hours."

"What do you mean, go to the past for a couple of hours?" Krasin didn't understand him. "I just don't," he wanted to say "don't get," but had scruples about using this slang word. For some unknown reason, his companion inspired him with respect, "get the picture."

Shit! It's even better! Even-Steven. Hell of a scholar. Bibliophile. Expert in Russian polite literature. Krasin got completely embarrassed.

"Well, you may choose any day of your life, and I'll send you there for about two hours," explained the man calmly and with exquisite politeness, as if not noticing his involuntary slip of the tongue and embarrassment. His cold, immovable, and polite tone made Krasin even more embarrassed. He felt as if he was a toerag. A plebeian, talking to an aristocrat or a patrician.

"I don't get it! Don't get the picture!" *What the hell is that? I've got a vocabulary of a boy at the disco. Like a poor vocabulary of Ellochka the Cannibal! Shit!"*

"I'm sorry! I'm sorry!" Krasin finally overcame his embarrassment and tried to get to the point. "Would you be so kind to explain everything to me in detail, if you please." Gathering all his erudition, carefully choosing the words and minding the correct phrase building (that's why they immediately became somehow clumsy and graceless), he said cautiously, "I think I probably do not understand completely what you're saying."

"With pleasure, Oleg Viktorovich!" he gave him a wide smile and looked kindly at Krasin.

He didn't even present himself, he thought suddenly. *Our conversation is rather strange. Well, it doesn't matter, actually. It's up to him. Maybe the sorcerers don't do it. 'What's in your name?' Or 'my' Well, I don't remember! My, your — what's the difference? As a matter of fact, I need to quit quoting at every given opportunity. Fucking quotation! Fucking intellectuality! I just can't concentrate on anything. I always 'let the thoughts flow over the tree.' Or is it 'thought?' Where are they flowing, exactly?*

Bother it! It just clung to me! It's a phrase of Rollan Bykov, by the way. From the movie 'Two Comrades Were Serving.' With Vysotsky in a leading role. Well, almost a leading one... Phew! No, it's just impossible to think at all! Shit! What crap do I have in my head? It's not a head, but a...

"You know, you shouldn't get distracted, just listen to me!" said, or rather ordered, Krasin's strange companion in a tough, commanding tone.

Like Joshua told Pontius Pilate, thought Krasin. After that, all quotes and verbal crap immediately disappeared from his head. His thoughts became unusually clear and vivid, as if he had had a large cup of strong coffee; being a little surprised by the edge of his conscience with that fact, he obediently prepared to listen.

"So," the man paused, looked at Krasin more closely, made sure, that, from the look of it, he was listening to him attentively, and continued. "You shall choose a day from the past. It's recommended that the day would be emotionally rich, for you must remember it very well. And then I shall send you there. So your current conscience will get into your young body."

"You may do whatever you want there. It will not have any influence on you as you are now. Well, you know, the twin paradox which is admired by fantasy authors; they say that you may change your future with some act and, thus, return to a different world. Well, nothing of that kind will happen to you. You may do whatever you want and not be afraid of anything. Even if you die there, it's okay. You'll just wake up, and that's it. Oh, by the way, everything will happen the following way. When do you usually go to sleep? Eleven, right?" Krasin nodded reflexively. "Great! Tomorrow you will go to sleep, as usual and then go to the past. Make sure that nobody bothers you during the sleep, at least in the first half of the night, until three in the morning. You can turn off the phone in the bedroom. Otherwise, your time travel may be interrupted. If nobody wakes you, you'll spend two or three hours in the past. Maybe a little longer. Well, it depends—as the occasion demands. It's not that bad, actually. Especially if you use that time wisely. Right?" the man stopped for a moment and smiled.

"You'll have some unusual skills there, but you won't be able to handle them. It's not complicated. You'll just feel them in you, and that's it. There's no need to explain anything beforehand. But just be careful with them. Don't be carried away. Don't misuse them," he paused. "Now the most important thing. Where would you go? What day?" the man paused again and looked at Krasin closely. He was listening to him, catching his breath.

"You see, Oleg Viktorovich, the best travels happen when you choose a day when you made a mistake or had a failure, and then, for long years or even your whole life, would think of it and would want badly to correct it. You know, it's easier to remember negative emotions than the positive ones. Such is the nature of men."

The word "men" sounded very strange, as if he was speaking not about himself, as well, but about something strange—that which didn't have anything to do with him. A Martian, for example, would talk in such way.

"Well, like I already told you, the events *there* do not have any influence on the events her, so it's completely useless to go there, to the past, with a desire to change something in your present life. Say, invest money or, on the contrary, save it. You would think, 'What great a life I would have then!' Nothing of that sort would work. So it's useless to do anything serious in the past.

"But talking about something playful," the man stopped talking and winked at Krasin openly.

He was so surprised that he didn't even have time to smile back. He was just sitting, staring at his companion bluntly and blinking his eyes.

"Say it didn't work out with a girl you liked, she dumped you—sometimes it happens—and now you may change everything. Replay, make up for the lost time. You'll come back here with a lot of nice impressions and unforgettable memories. This is quite possible."

"You had situations of that kind in your life, didn't you?" He again winked at Krasin, who was completely embarrassed, as if they had a conspiracy. "Like everyone else has. Well, you remember it, in the institute? Irochka Belyaeva?"

Krasin did remember it. He remembered very well the scene near the institute, when he plucked up his courage, caught up with the girl who was hurrying home, and, blanching and blushing, offered to meet her somewhere today. And her scornful and indifferent answer, that she's busy today. And the next day, her boyfriend, a very big guy who was taller by a foot than Krasin and heavier, probably by twenty kilograms, approached him and, smiling boldly, told him than he and Ira were talking merrily yesterday.

Krasin, the winner of all-institute sambo championship, offered him to talk about that in detail, but the guy, however, calmed down and disappeared into thin air. Krasin remembered that with malicious joy.

Somehow, he could remember a lot of stuff. Well, a lot of time had passed, and he's long married, he's got children and almost grandchildren! Irochka got married a lifetime ago—to the same guy, it seems—and it turns out that he didn't forget anything. Well, it's not 'turns out!' He recalled and replayed that scene hundreds of times—thousands, or even more.

This clairvoyant sorcerer was right; it's impossible to forget negative emotions. Well, maybe he didn't say exactly that, but it doesn't matter. That is the point. The same one. It's impossible to forget. It seems that they are stamped in a fiery letters on the scrolls of the heart. They are burnt out on the living flesh for the rest of the life. Shit!

"So," continued the man, smiling subtly, "you can change everything with your present experience. And, moreover," he made a dramatic pause, "you can go there together with her!"

"What do you mean: together with her?" repeated Krasin after him, being astonished. He couldn't understand anything.

"Come on!" his companion abandoned the aristocratic manners completely and switched to an unceremonious and almost histrionic tone. "Tomorrow, you will meet her and offer her to go together to that memorable day. I'm sure that she remembers it very clearly. Women do not forget such things. And, surely, you will talk to her concerning conditions," he smiled cynically. Krasin was still blinking crazily.

"Why are you looking at me like this? Aren't you getting anything? She's an older woman, one may say, and here is such an offer! She could be a twenty-year-old girl again. Naturally, any woman will agree to that! And you will set the conditions yourself, whichever you want!" He again winked playfully at Krasin, who was smiling foolishly. "Come on, think faster! Are you going to wait and mumble forever?"

"Well!" said Krasin in amazement. He began to understand slowly what exactly he was offered. "Well! Of course, it's... And how am I going to find her?" he realized suddenly. "I got only one day. I don't have any of her contacts."

The man silently gave him a piece of paper.

"What's that?" asked Krasin, surprised.

"Home number of Irina Nikolaevna Davydova. It's her current surname."

"Right," thought Krasin. "So, she did marry him back then."

"Tomorrow's Sunday, and she's going to be at home all day. You should call her in the morning and arrange everything. Actually, you've still got some time today. All in all, you'll cope with that!"

"Listen!" said Krasin suddenly, "How do you know all that? And you already had the phone number; how is this possible?"

"Well, it is!" the man answered indifferently. He was looking for something with his eyes. "And it's not a problem to find out the phone number nowadays." He looked up at Krasin, "You just need a will. If you wanted to find it, you'd have done it long ago. You can buy databases at every corner."

"Yeah, but how did you find out about her?"

"Well, Oleg Viktorovich," the man's tone became a bit tougher again, "get in touch with her by the phone, arrange a meeting, and discuss everything with her. She has to be in bed tomorrow at 11. That's very desirable. Otherwise, all your travel may go down in flames. Go down the pan. And don't ask silly questions! Whom did you call? A clairvoyant? So why are you surprised?"

Well, Krasin shook his head in his mind, *here it is.*

"And one more thing," the man's tone changed subtly and became a bit more businesslike, "don't worry about the money. It all will be free. The thing is, your astral card is very interesting. Consider it your luck."

Oh, well, thought Krasin with even greater doubt, *oh, well! Free—that is, at no charge? I got an interesting card, right? Uh oh! There's no such thing as a free lunch, so I was taught.*

The man glanced at Krasin and smiled softly.

"Alright, don't worry so much! Everything will be okay, I promise. You'll come back in fine fashion and full of impressions, unforgettable ones," he added with a strange tone after a very short pause. "Yeah! One more thing." Krasin grew suspicious reflexively. "Concerning your future skills," the man took thought for a second, "well, it doesn't matter. It doesn't matter," he finished confidently. "So, are you in?"

"In what?" asked Krasin bluntly.

The man didn't answer anything but kept looking at him silently.

"Oh, yeah, sure," Krasin came to his senses. "Sure, I'm in! Of course," he added quickly.

"Wonderful. All the best! I wish you to have a great time," the man stood up, implying that the conversation was over. "Good-bye."

"Good-bye," Krasin stood up, too. His head was spinning. He had a lot to think about.

3.

Coming home, Krasin went to the kitchen and started making coffee, deep in thought. He didn't drink instant coffee, so the process of making it usually took a lot of time and became a kind of sacred action, a ritual. Gristing, water boiling… then he should see that the coffee doesn't boil over. Altogether, it was not a simple matter.

He was doing all that mechanically, and, at the same time, he was thinking about all that he had just heard. And the more he thought about that, the more he understood the sense of the offer made to him and all incredible perspectives that appeared before him thanks to all that. At first, he didn't grasp and perceive them, but now it began to get through to him. Of course, a lot of stuff remained obscure and vague—what did the sorcerer say? "You'll handle it?" Eh! "You'll cope with it!" But even that what he had clearly grasped…

Well, that's something! Well, go back to the past! How old was he back then? 19? 20? No, 21, it seems, it was third year of studying—or not? Was he 20? Well, it doesn't matter; 20, 21, what's the difference? I wonder if I would feel like a 20-year-old? Well, sexual vigor and stuff? Otherwise, it would be a tale of the lost time. Children and old people. You still can, but you don't want anything for a long time. No, no! You still want as well. You want! I wouldn't mind to… Irochka. Well, the 20-year-old one, of course. Probably I would be disappointed, as it usually happens when you wait for too long for something and want it badly, but still… I've been dreaming about her for such a long time!"

So, regarding Irochka. I should call her and arrange a meeting. Why should I beat about the bush? I'm going to finish my coffee and call her.

To his own amazement, Krasin found out that he was nervous. *Come on! It was a lifetime ago. Oh, my God! Well! First love never grows old, indeed. It does not rust!*

Well, let's say, it's not the first one. To be precise, not actually the first one. To be more precise, it's not the first one at all. But it's the most memorable, so to say, that's for sure! The most memorable. All other girls were skanks. nameless and faceless. Common. All those Manechkas-Valechkas, freaking Mashkas and slutty Natalkas. Sucking Natalkas. And the like of them. Their name is legion. Well, maybe, not a legion. I made that last bit up. For the sake of a witty remark. Hey, what's all this stuff with phrase-

mongering with myself? Why am I indulging in verbal masturbation; why am I whacking off? Am I afraid to call her?"

Krasin took a paper with a phone number out of his pocket. *Well, what district is that? Hell knows. I don't know. Well, it doesn't matter. I shouldn't be thinking about that. So, what shall I say to her? Eh?*

Hi, Irinochka! It's me. Come on, it's me! Yeah, yeah! Got it? I have an offer for you. Do you want to go to the past for a couple of hours, to fuck with me, to when you were 20? Well, do you remember the time when you blew me off? Hahaha! Yeah, right! To the same day. But this time, fair and square! We'll do it immediately upon arrival. We'll go to an empty classroom and... So what? Are you ready for a sex-tour? Okay, see you tomorrow! Meanwhile, study some new positions."

Okay, enough with the jokes. So, I'll do the following. I'm going to call her, arrange a meeting, we meet, and then I'll explain everything to her. What that's all about and where we're going. Just like this.

Krasin noticed just now that, with all these endless and empty thoughts, speculations, and mental monologues—masturbating monologues, fuck… musing…milling… the wind—he drank all his coffee. He was staring at an empty scoop in embarrassment. *How did I do it so quickly?* Then he sat behind the table and, still nervous, took up the phone.

Alright, why should I bother now? He tried to calm down. *Hell of a Romeo! I need to arrange a meeting for now. That's it. If her husband picks up the phone, I'll just hang up,:* he decided at the last moment. "*Then I'll call her later."*

"Hello!" a familiar low female voice answered. Krasin's heart skipped a beat. He broke a sweat at once. It was her! He recognized the voice. No doubts it was her!

"Can I talk to Irina Nikolaevna?"

"Yeah, just a moment.'

"Mom, it's for you!" he heard a second later. *It was her daughter? Bless me! She was a grown woman. And she had the same voice. Well, no wonder...*

"Yeah!"

"Hi, Ira!" said Krasin hoarsely and cleared his throat. So much time has passed. "Listen, you may be surprised. That's Oleg Krasin. Well, do you remember me? We studied in the institute together? I tried to pay court to you on the third year of study?"

What if she doesn't remember? The thought made him panic.

"Yeah, hi," Irochka said it in a surprised tone, but there was no doubt that she remembered him at once. She didn't call him by name, but that was alright. Probably her husband was around.

"Women never forget such things," Krasin remembered the dogmatic statement of that mysterious sorcerer-clairvoyant (Krasin didn't have any doubts about his competence in these matters as well), and he felt more confident.

Unpredictability disappeared. Inconceivability too. The aura cleared away, so to speak. She was an ordinary woman. She was a vauntful and inquisitive daughter of Eve, just like all of them. Suddenly, he knew how to behave himself and what to say. And he knew that everything would be alright. And they would arrange a meeting. And then he'd see.

"Ira, I need to see you as soon as possible," he said confidently. "It's better to do it today. No, right now. It's very important for you. At my job, I actually found out something concerning you. It's very important—extremely important. But we shouldn't speak of it on the phone. I'll tell you everything when we meet. Tell me where to come, and I'll be there. I'll drive in a car," Krasin paused. "Oh, but don't tell anyone about this call and our meeting—not your husband or children," he said quickly.

I don't want her to come with her husband. She may well do that. She'll think that it's a business meeting, concerning all her family.

"I take a lot of risk, calling you. Well, you'll get it when I tell you everything!"

Shit! Did I go over the top with all these scary secrets? She's an old woman. She's not 20 anymore. She'll just get scared. She may feel sick, by the way. Maybe she's got a dicky heart. Shit! It's like in '12 Chairs.' Ilf and Petrov. An image from the exhibition. 'Union of sword and plow'. Hungry Ostap, feeling the scent of the money, passionately instructs the conspirators. 'Complete confidentiality! Everything should be in secret! It's to your interest! Take courage!' Phew! Quotes again? I promised myself!

"Well, I'm not sure," he heard Irochka's uncertain voice. "Well, alright; let's do it. So, what's up really?"

"Ira, we'd better not discuss it on the phone," Krasin felt that he was a master of the situation. "You'll get it when we meet. Don't worry, it's all right," he relented, after all. "Quite on the contrary! I'll have very important news for you. Just for you. A kind of surprise."

"Okay," it seemed that Ira had made a decision, "Can you come to the metro station Sviblovo in an hour?"

Oh! So that's where she lives—Sviblovo.

"Yeah, sure. Is there only one exit?"

"No, I think, there are two."

Ira started to explain him, muzzily, where she would be standing, but Krasin wasn't listening to her.

What's the difference? I'll find it. Are there a million exits? It's one or another.

"Alright, Ira, you just wait near either of the exits, and I'll find you myself. Okay?"

"Okay," she yielded easily.

Onset! Speed and onset! That's the key to success. It's an old and reliable recipe for attacking women and fortresses. Assault! Shit! Why did I mollycoddle ~~with~~ her in the third year? I should have grabbed her and... Heh-heh... Well, youth... It's okay! I hope we'll catch it up. Everything's waiting for us. We'll show...

"So, in an hour," continued Krasin aggressively, exploiting the success and consolidating the grain. "So when shall we make it exactly? Now it's twenty past three. So, let's make it half past four. Deal? Straight at half past four, near the exit."

"Okay. I'll be wearing..."

"Irisha," interrupted her Krasin gallantly, "I'll recognize you, whatever you may wear."

"Well, okay," she yielded completely, being flattered, "we'll see. Bye."

Krasin waited until Ira hung up and, only after that, put down the phone. He felt a huge inspiration. Everything had gone easily and smoothly!

I'm really a ladies' man, he thought with humorous pride. *I trapped the woman in one stroke, made her agree to a meeting. I talked her ear off. Shit! How come I fell on deaf ears myself? I should have called her twenty years ago, given a long song and dance, lured her out to a meeting, and then... It is a matter of technique.*

It turns out that everything's so simple! You're a fool, idiot, loony. So much time is lost. Though, on the other hand, maybe it's for the better. Maybe it's not lost. Whatever God does! Alright, we'll have to see. I need to shave. I don't have time to harp on and whack off again. It is what it is. Stop talking! Ahead and up! And then? And then we'll see. God will guide me! Ahead!

4.

Krasin recognized Irochka at once. She had grown old, withered and had put on some weight, but that was her, no doubt.

Well, he thought with hopeless sadness, *probably I look like her to onlookers.*

He was even afraid to approach her. However, he recalled what he wanted to offer her and cheered up. *She's going to go for it, surely. She's got no choice. So, tomorrow night I'll... she...* 'Yesterday, with God's help, Kern had sex,'" he suddenly recalled a famous vulgar phrase from the notorious letter of Pushkin.

Ugh! So, tomorrow, I will, with God's help... At last. Well, well, we'll see. Of course, with God's help it's easy to fuck anyone. Well... So, should I go? Godspeed! Stop talking!

Krasin got out of the car and, without hesitation, went to Irochka, who was standing all alone. She wasn't paying attention to him until he came close to her, almost within a hairsbreadth. Obviously, she didn't recognize him.

"Hi, Irisha! Don't you recognize me? You haven't changed a bit," he briskly greeted his might-have-been mistress, who now was rather battered, worn out with life, and ecliptic. An elderly, overweight woman, to whom these sacramental words were addressed, stared at him for some time in embarrassment and finally said tentatively, "Oleg?"

"Yeah, it's me! Have I changed much?" smiled Krasin wryly.

Well. it was unpleasant for him that she hadn't recognized him—very unpleasant... very! There was no doubt about it. Ugh! *Do I really look bad to onlookers? Like her? Maybe I look even worse than her; I recognized her at once! Well, how would I talk about sex with her? It's just awkward; I don't have the heart. It would probably make her eyes pop! When I start talking about this crap, she'll take offence. She probably already forgot how to do it and what for and what it is. Probably, she's all hairy there. With moss. Cobwebs. Alright, we'll see.*

"Well, Ira, let's talk in the car." Not waiting for an answer, he pointed at his car and went ahead, leading the woman. She followed him obediently.

Getting into the car, Krasin waited a bit, staring in front of him and gathering his thoughts; he chewed his lips and then turned to the woman sitting near him.

"First of all, Ira, I need to apologize," he began talking calmly. "Actually, I haven't found out anything important and secret about you. I just played cunning a bit. Just a smidgen. I made it all up so you would come to this meeting." The woman shifted, and he continued hastily, "However, I really have something to tell you. And it's very important. Just listen to me carefully, and you'll understand everything."

He realized that he had started the conversation muzzily and was too talkative. He could feel the growing anxiety of the woman sitting near him. It seemed that Irina Nikolaevna began to regret getting into his car.

"'I made it all up so you would come?'" *What's the meaning of this? What does he want from her? What has he contrived? What if he's a maniac? Who knows what he's been doing all these years! And now he pulls a rabbit out of a hat!*

Altogether, everything went wrong. He had to do something quickly. Change something. Krasin decided not to drag it out anymore but to take the bull by the horns, to force events and cut to the chase.

"Listen, Ira, do you believe in sorcery?"

"What?" The woman froze and looked at him even more warily, as if he was insane. And she had been possessed to get into the car of an insane person.

"Come on, don't be afraid," Krasin said in a more convincing and reasonable tone. "I'm not insane or a lunatic. I'm a normal man. I'm just asking—do you believe in sorcery, omens, magic? Well, everybody believes in it a bit. It's a usual question. Nothing special. Why do you get nervous? Do you believe in it?"

"Well, I'm not sure," said Ira, still cautiously, "I think, I don't… I believe in omens. Why do you ask?"

"You see, Ira," said Krasin, in a more calm voice, "Yesterday I responded to an ad in a newspaper."

Why the hell did I lie to her? It was today. Well, it doesn't matter.

"About sorcery and clairvoyance."

"And?" asked Ira with genuine interest.

"Guess what—that sorcerer called me by the name and patronymic, though I hadn't introduced myself! I just dialed the number from the ad, and he said at once, 'Hello, Oleg Viktorovich!' Can you imagine that?"

"Really?" asked Ira again with even greater interest. Her eyes became bright.

She seemed to calm down completely and showed vivid interest in what was happening.

True daughter of Eve—thoughtless and inquisitive. *At any age,* thought Krasin with involuntary irony, looking at her.

"Yeah, I nearly went crazy, too!" He tried to play up to her more. "I wouldn't believe it myself, if anyone told me that! So, we met—he lives just around the corner—and he made me an incredible offer! It rocks! Travel to the past!"

"What do you mean, travel to the past?" asked Ira, fascinated.

In front of Krasin there sat a little girl, listening to a fairy-tale about a good magician with her mouth open.

"Right! Travel to the past. Although it's just for a couple of hours. I may choose any day in the past, and he will get me there. Actually, the present me will go to that day, and I'm going to be in my young body. Besides, he assured me that nothing that happens there would influence the present. So, it would be happening in a parallel world. So, even if you die there, you'll just wake up here, that's it!"

Krasin felt that he was still talking in a confusing manner, and he shouldn't have mentioned the word "die," but that didn't matter.

It's alright. That will do. The most important thing is that she's listening. And she's not scared anymore. She'll ask me, if there's a need. And how can I talk consistently? Talking about this is a hell of a mess! Frankly speaking, he didn't even fully believe in all this and didn't understand everything.

"So," Krasin tried to gather his thoughts which were running away. "So that's it! I chose the day when I tried to ask you on a date." Ira looked at him in amazement.

"Yeah, right. Why are you surprised? I was never blown off in such way ever again in my life," he laughed sadly. "Yeah, I remembered that. So, actually, I chose that day. It doesn't matter why and what for," he tried to smooth the awkwardness with the mockery. Ira was silent.

"I couldn't forget you—all these years," he said quietly, unexpectedly even for him, and lowered his eyes. "Yeah, I often thought about that. All my life. Yeah, that's it," he gathered his thoughts again,. "This sorcerer says to me, 'If you want to go to that day, you should meet the girl'—well, you—'and arrange everything with her beforehand. Offer her to go there with you.' That's why I called you—to arrange everything. And I made up all these scary secrets for you to come, secrets of the Spanish court. What was I supposed to do? I badly needed to see you, and what if you refused?

I had to play safe. *Come on, it's not important! We're talking crap! Let's get to business,"* he made himself lift his eyes up.

Ira was still staring at him silently.

"Alright, stop fooling around!" Krasin suddenly got angry. *"Enough of these love comedies. And of pastorals as well. Uh-oh! Daphnis and fucking Chloe. A boy and a girl."*

"Why am I dying in front of her like a precocious boy? I almost beg her. She must beg me, if that is the case! Such an offer! And I'm blushing and wavering here, you see. I'm prim, see, as if it's me who needs something from her. Come on! I don't care if she agrees or refuses."

"So what? Do you agree?" he finished firmly, looking straight in Ira's eyes.

"I don't care if she refuses! All in all, I can try to get together with her when she was 20. There and then. Right off the bat. 'With God's help,' just like Alexander Sergeyevich advised.

Ira blinked. It seemed that she had been listening to Krasin's whole story as if it had been a beautiful, romantic love tale about a passionate and unrequited love of her former admirer, which he bore through the years. A story which was beautiful and wonderful, but didn't have anything to do with her present life. And now this simple, clear and completely concrete question caught her unawares.

Krasin felt her halt very well and began to convince her ardently.

"Listen! For several hours, you'll be a 20-year-old again! Can you imagine that? Just imagine that for a moment! You're young! You, present you, move to your young, 20-year-old body during a sleep. Tomorrow evening, you'll just go to sleep as usual and get into another world. Moreover, whatever may happen there will not influence you now. In any case, you'll wake up in the morning, as always, in your apartment, in your bed, near your husband."

As Irina Nikolaevna didn't react to his remark, Krasin understood that this was true; she slept with her husband indeed. "With that… what's his name? So, she loves him! Well, well! Let's hope…'With God's help.'"

"So, it's like time travel," he finished vigorously, "like in a movie. It's free and there's no risk. A lot of pros—just think of the feelings – and no cons at all! So? Are you in?"

The elderly woman's eyes opened wide and became bright, and Krasin saw that she began to realize what he was talking about.

"I really don't know what to say," she said slowly and distrustfully. "Are you serious? Do you believe in all that?"

"Listen, Ira, what's the difference? Whether I believe it or not, it doesn't matter. They do not demand anything from you, right? Well, if nothing happens—you'll just go to sleep and wake up, as usual. This would be it. I just need you to go to bed no later than 11, and that nobody wakes you up in the night. And you'd better turn off the phone. Just do all that, and that's it. And don't worry about the rest. It's all that you have to do."

"Alright, alright!" laughed Ira. "Okay, deal, if you insist."

As her last humorous remark was said with a more playful and familiar tone than the previous ones, Krasin resolved at last.

"Of course, I insist!" he said with the same humorous familiarity and winked at Ira, who was looking at him and smiling. "It's not that simple. I have my reasons!"

"Really?" asked Ira in an even more playful tone. "And what would they be?"

"What, what? Like you don't get it? 'With God's help!' Well, I hope that, at last, you wouldn't blow me off there. Why would I go there, if you flip me off again? I'm not a masochist!"

"And why do you fly there?" Irochka looked at him saucily. Her tone became even more familiar and trustful.

Here, things are looking up, thought Krasin with joy. *I hoped she would be an easy lay. Right! Exactly! I think she's getting everything pretty well,"* he thought. *"As a matter of fact, we're talking clear with her. We've almost arranged everything. She almost spread her legs!"*

"Though, on the other hand, what does 'easy lay' mean?" he thought suddenly. *"And how is it connected to 'things are looking up'? What's the meaning of this? Would she be a 'lay,' or would she be 'looking up'? Or, on the contrary, 'down'? By the way, does it mean that she would be an easy lay from both sides? She would do it from the front and then turn over and do it from the back. Phew! That's a lot of crap in my head! Linguistic gibberish. That's because I'm nervous. Nervous! I'm nervous, like a 15-year-old boy, who's trying to fuck a girl. A 'girl', fuck! Quite the contrary."*

"*We* fly there! *We*!" he said tightly. "Just think of it—we're both young, we're 20. By the way, the sorcerer said that we would have the feelings and desires of the 20-year-old. So we would have no problems with that. Krasin paused meaningfully and looked at Irochka straightforwardly. Irochka was still smiling toward him, and it seemed that she was fine with his tone and behavior.

Maybe we would do it here? thought Krasin suddenly. *Maybe I should offer her to go to my place straightaway? I got some cognac at home,"* he hesitated. *No, it's no good,* he decided finally. *I'll just make things worse. She might be scared. She'd become tense. And then I would spend two more hours convincing her.*

"And I don't really have the itch. I don't want to shame myself. Actually, I don't have a boner, and it's not worth it. It's pretty simple. One should do it, if he has a boner. So, I would better fuck her in the other world. When I had a boner, and she also was worth it. Back then, when she was still young. Apple-cheeked. Unspoiled! And what is she now? Used. Second hand. Recycled."

"And no one would ever find it out," he gave her his main and decisive argument, "Well, can you imagine that?"

"Well, I'm not sure, said Irochka moodily, like a child. She pouted her lips, looked at him askew, and screwed up her eyes.

Her glance was so explicit, so dreamy and so evaluating that Krasin sweated. He suddenly had an erection, and, moreover, he thought that Irochka saw that, too, and that she was not displeased with that. Quite on the contrary, she liked that. It flattered her female ambition. Actually, Krasin suddenly understood that he didn't notice the age of his might-have-been lover any more, as if she had become younger right before his eyes. Without any sorcery. In front of him, there sat the same 20-year-old girl, beautiful and desirable.

Shit! Maybe, I should try? the thought flashed in his head. *I should just offer her!*

"You know, Ira," he said slowly, still looking explicitly into her eyes, "I'm looking at you and still see that twenty-year-old girl, young and beautiful." The woman blushed. She was obviously pleased to hear that, as if so many years didn't pass.

"Maybe, we would work it out? Eh? After… after a date in that world? What do you think?"

"I don't know," said the woman voluptuously and hotly and shrugged her shoulder slowly.

For some reason, Krasin thought that she was a bit disappointed. *Shit! I was a ditherer, and I remained the same. I should have dragged her into my bed immediately. But I'm still hesitating. And I should definitely do that in another world!*

"Alright, we'll wait until tomorrow," summarized Irochka, looking a bit mockingly at her admirer, who was sitting near her. Krasin felt ashamed under her stare. *He is a grown man, and he's sitting, jiggeting, and drooling over me Well, what else should I do? Maybe he's going there because no one would sleep with him? And then we'll see.* "Okay, let me out, I need to go. (Krasin unlocked the doors obediently.) I don't want my family to worry. I told them that I would be back in an hour."

"So, tomorrow go to bed at 11," Krasin briefed the woman one last time, "Better yet, even earlier. And don't forget to turn off the phone in the bedroom."

"Okay, I got it. Bye."

"Bye. Oh, let me give you a ride home," he said suddenly.

"No, no, there's no need," Irochka was already opening the door. "I'll go on my own. It's not far from here."

"Okay, as you wish."

"Alright, good bye."

"See you tomorrow. I hope!"

"We'll see," Irochka smiled at him cheerfully and saucily for the last time and got out of the car. For some time, Krasin watched her going away from the car, approaching the bus stop.

She's got nice legs, he thought with delight. *And her ass — very nice altogether. I put my eye on her back then for a reason. First quality product, extra grade! It's a pity that everything went so stupid back then. Actually, it was not her fault. It was my fault. I behaved like a dumb head. Like an idiot. What's all this fuzzy-wuzzy? I wonder what she was thinking about me back then? I should ask her that.*

"We laughed so much," he remembered the words of her future husband, and he felt flushing with shame.

Alright, we'll fucking deal with it. And I'm gonna meet this jerk, by the way, he thought suddenly. *Great! We'll have a chat. We'll talk closely. We didn't finish our conversation back then. So, we'll see 'who's gonna sing, and who's gonna cry.' And who's gonna laugh last.*

5.

All the next day, Krasin felt as if he was in a fog. Time stopped. It seemed that the cursed 11 p.m. would never come.

"What's wrong with you?" asked his wife compassionately. "You look weird today."

"Yeah, I feel sick," he told her, as usual. "I think it's blood pressure. The weather has changed."

"Yesterday, I felt bad, too. And magnetic storms are underway, they say," his wife started her favorite topic, but Krasin wasn't listening to her anymore.

During the long years of marriage, he learned to go out in such moments. and then he would just check in periodically and remind of himself with various indefinite phrases like. "Right!" "I see," "Got it," and so on. This was more than enough to support the flow of conversation with his wife. He never needed anything else.

Closer to half past ten, Krasin began preparing for sleep. His wife, of course, fancied to watch TV today. She was watching some crap—a show or a quiz. In short, fucking bullshit about the life of happy morons. Krasin went in for dramatics because of that. He was so excited and outraged that his wife even got scared.

"What's wrong with you today?"

"I'm feeling bad. I've got a headache. I want to go to bed earlier. Do you get it? Do you? And don't wake me up, for any reason! Don't you dare! I took a pill. Got it?"

Finally, straight at 11, he was already in bed. His wife was sleeping at his side. She seemed to go to sleep once her head touched the pillow.

It's strange, Krasin was surprised. *She usually tumbles for half an hour, at least; she can't fall asleep.*

He listened again to her measured breathing and sniffed distrustfully. *She's sleeping, indeed! Well, that's great but somehow strange. Have the wonders already begun?* he asked ironically his new acquaintance, the clairvoyant sorcerer, and closed his eyes.

II.

"The ships are in my haven.
No flight—we'll go by sea.
The clock hands go 2 hours -
Back!"
Modern pop-song

1.

Oleg Krasin, a third year student of one of the prestigious Moscow universities, was hurrying after a slender red-haired girl whose dress was waving in the breeze. It was warm, almost hot, so Oleg was lightly dressed. He was wearing a short-sleeved shirt, light pants of archaic fashion, and light shoes of the same archaic style.

"Well, just look at me," thought Oleg Viktorovich, who ran a few more steps by inertia and suddenly, stopping dead, began looking and touching himself, as if in some sickly bewilderment. He even forgot about the girl who was going in ahead of him. In fact, the same thing happened to her, too. In any case, she was behaving same way as he was, like in a mirror. She stopped suddenly, too, and looked at herself and felt herself mistrustfully, embarrassed.

Incredible thoughts filled Krasin's head. Like he was Kisa Vorobyaninov, who stared at his chairs in the window of the thrift shop. The bells were ringing and fanfares were singing. As if he won a million dollars in a lottery and, for a moment, couldn't think straight with joy. No, no! He could remember everything clearly: the sorcerer and his instructions; he understood everything very well—where he was, why, and how he got here. But understanding theoretically and abstractedly is one thing, and feeling in waking life is completely another! All these new feelings that rushed at him unexpectedly and overwhelmed him—freedom, strength, youth; all of them were so unlooked-for and vivid that they literally dazed and blinded him, knocked him off his feet. They caught him unawares. It seemed that he was staggering, as if drunk.

Finally, he came to his senses a little and looked up at Ira Beliaieva, who was standing several steps away. She was holding a small mirror in her hands and staring in it tensely.

"You're pretty!" said Krasin playfully in a low voice, approaching the girl. He had almost no doubts that this was same Irochka whom he had seen the day before. Everything that the girl in front of him did proved that incontrovertibly. Absolutely. Clearly and unambiguously.

"So what? Impressive?"

"Is this?"

"Me!" confirmed Krasin, grinning broadly. "Hi from the future!"

"Crazy!" whispered the girl and looked at him bottom-up. "Is this really you, sir?"

"Yes, that's me! Did you forget how old we are now? And yesterday we were talking like close friends, right?"

"Right. But it's so incredible that I can't come to my senses. So, am I sleeping now in that real world?"

"Yes, you are. I explained everything to you yesterday; no, the day before yesterday. Remember?"

"Yeah, I remember, but I didn't believe in it completely, to be honest."

"Frankly speaking, neither did I," confessed Krasin. "How could one believe in it? But, as you see…"

"Yeah…"

How long would we be 'yessing' here? thought Krasin, irritated. *Clock is ticking. Every minute and second counts; they're like gold dust, and we're standing here and chatting! As if we didn't have the chance to chat enough. 'Closer to the body!' as Guy de Maupassant said. Time is money!*

"Listen, Ira," he said in a measured tone, looking straight into the girl's eyes, like back then in the car. "We're losing time, precious time, and we haven't got a lot of it. Just a couple of hours! The only hours in life! And they would never repeat. Ever!"

"I don't quite understand you," she blushed and moved away a bit from him. "I think I didn't promise you anything."

Krasin got embarrassed for a moment with her cheeky behavior. Then he felt rage slowly rising inside him. *Fuck a duck! Holy Christ! What do you mean by 'didn't promise?'Does she want to shaft me for a second time? 'See, I don't understand you!' Yesterday, she fucking understood me, and today she doesn't! What the hell is that? What's the meaning of all this? Did I come here from another world for this? And dragged this bitch with me so she would shaft me for a second time? To make me absolutely happy, so to say.*

No way, darling, you're not gonna do this trick for a second time. Thank God, I'm not 20 anymore. So, let's... 'With God's help!'

"Oh, you don't understand? And you didn't promise anything?" he asked her mockingly and gave her an unambiguous and sexually explicit look. She blushed even more and moved further away from him. "Frankly speaking, I didn't expect this from you; I thought that we had a deal yesterday. And it seemed to me that you understood everything very well. So, I was wrong? It's a pity, yeah. What a pity! Alright, I'm sorry," he finished floutingly and shook his head sadly, "It's a pity that it happened again, for a second time, but that's that! I'm sorry."

Ira looked at him coldly, as if he didn't exist at all, turned away silently and went along the street.

What the fuck! thought Krasin in amazement. *Is she really going to leave, just like this? In acknowledgement of all that I have done for her? I've brought her here! Come on, what the fuck!*

"Wait a minute, Irina Nikolaevna, just wait a minute," he called the girl who was strolling off quickly. She just quickened her pace in return.

What a bitch! Krasin was amazed again. *She's clearly going to run away, and that's it! She's going to jilt me, like I'm a chump. Well, well!*

"Stop running away!" he shouted to her back. "You won't be able to run away! You don't know anything about this world. I didn't tell you everything yesterday. I've got something in stock, just in case. And I was right, as it turned out! I just want to warn you about something."

The girl startled and halted. Then, slowly and reluctantly, she turned to Krasin and stared and him inquiringly.

He slowly approached her, grinned boldly straight in her face, and said in an instructive and mocking tone, "Why are you in such a hurry, dear Irina Nikolaevna? I haven't come yet to the point."

He grinned again, now at his involuntary joke. It seemed that Irochka got it very well, and her face froze.

She's not actually going to let me fuck her! Krasin understood at last. He just couldn't believe in what was happening and in the devilish treachery of the woman that stood before him.

'Woman,' fuck! A fucking snake! By no means! And she's trying to show her insulted innocence, like she's a tight-ass! Tight-cunt. Well, well! Just look at it!

"So, lassie! If you don't like it in this world, it'll be my pleasure to send you back to the future. Right now! How do you like it? I can do it at any moment."

Irochka blanched and staggered back. He hit right on the mark. Obviously, she didn't want to go back. She stared at Krasin for some time, as if she wanted to find out from his face, if he was telling the truth, and then she hissed, like a furious cat, "I don't believe you! You made it up. Why didn't you tell me that yesterday?"

"Well, bitch," Krasin was amazed yet again, *so did she come up with this plan yesterday? From the very beginning? She planned to dump me and leave. Take offence at something, for example. And she was flirting with me in the car. She was scrambling my brains*

and making eyes at me. She wanted to find out as much as she could, and she didn't want me to abort mid-deal.

"Well, women, women! And I was a wretched fool to fluff my feathers. I was proud as a peacock, as an Indian cock. 'I'm gonna... her..!' 'She's ready for anything!' I'm gonna! And she's gonna! Uh oh! Atta girl, Irochka! Ball buster! I'll be damned! That is too much!"

"You can check, if you want!" he grinned, looking straight at her and added after a pause, "Oh! I see we're talking as friends again? That's promising. So, what?"

He saw in her eyes that she faltered. She was still hesitating for a second, but then said firmly, "Well, alright. What do you want from me?"

"Right! I see. We're gonna bunny-fuck hurry-scurry, and that's it. We're straight. Right! You wish!"

Krasin felt a real rage starting to burn inside him. He was irritated by the fact that, undoubtedly, Irochka Beliaieva wasn't interested in him as a sexual partner at all.

She just wanted to get rid of him quickly and get away. It was a huge blow to his ego. All those beautiful and wonderful illusions in which he had taken comfort all these years—"I was behaving like a jerk;" "She got embarrassed"—were shattered at once. He didn't have any more doubts about that.

"Why the hell did I come here? A nice day have I chosen! That fucking sorcerer gave me a hell of advice—clairvoyant."

"You know very well what I want from you," he answered rudely. "Enough of fooling around! If you don't want to listen, find out the hard way."

Why should I be too soft on this bitch?

"It seems you thought that you could set terms for me. Bargain? Forget it! Forget it now! Either you do, what I tell you, or good riddance to you! "

"Here is the choice. And I need you only for sex work, as a blow-up to suck and spread your legs when I've got a boner. That's it! So, what do you say? And stop playing hard-to-get," he shouted in rage, seeing her blinking, as if she was going to cry. "Lady Nevershit. Either you blow me here, or bog off! So what?"

Ira was at a loss. She clearly wasn't ready for such turn of events. But, to her credit, she didn't hesitate for too long. Krasin remembered that she was a dreamy and sentimental girl, but now he saw her in completely another light. A moment—and a decision was made.

"Okay, I agree," she said firmly. "I want to stay here."

"That's it," answered Krasin malevolently. His irritation still didn't go away. "And one more thing. Don't play Zoya Kosmodemyanskaya here, like you're facing torments for a higher aim, with the corresponding face. Like me or not, but you should pretend that you do, that you're high on me and that you can't live without me. That you dreamed all your life that you would blow me here. And I must believe it.

"Otherwise, it's your funeral! If you annoy me, I'll send you back. There are a lot of women here. So try not to annoy me. It's in your best interest. You got it?"

"Yes, my lord!" Irochka did a playful curtsy. Then she smiled softly. The tears on her face disappeared completely.

Krasin opened his mouth in wonder. *Oh, my God! Are all women like this? Bless me! Save me from this! It's not Irochka, but the devil incarnate! A demon in a skirt! Satan. Tempter.*

Krasin realized clearly that she was playing, bluffing, boggling, and dodging, but, at the same time, he looked at her and felt his desire grow. He just couldn't resist it. It was created in him as an instinct, like a program in a robot. It's a usual reaction of a male for the call of a female, ready for mating. Reason and sense are useless. It's impossible to resist. For that, one must stop being a male. Stop being a man. Betray his marrow and nature.

He came close to the girl, devouring her body with his eyes. There was nobody on the street, and Krasin felt an unbearable desire to touch her, grab her breast, pat her ass… tushie—so seductive, beckoning, and tough—but he didn't dare to do that. They could be seen by someone—some auxiliary police, young fucking communist geeks—they could be arrested for violating public morals, and then they would spend two hours in jail. And they would beat him, as well. That would be a nice travel to the past. Flights waking and sleeping.

There's no need to hurry, by no means. I have to look around a bit. See what's going on. Assimilate into environment. And then I could play pranks. Shit! I want her! Awfully! Young blood is up. It's roiling.

He grabbed the girl's hand and literally dragged her into the first building that he saw. However, Ira wasn't resisting. Thank God, the door to the hallway didn't have a coded lock. As soon as it closed, Krasin came at Irochka and started grabbing and groping her body. Breast… buttocks… Then he pulled up the hem of her dress with one hand and, shaking, put his other hand there, into the depth between her legs, into the place of dreams. As he touched her body, hips, thighs, dress, and lingerie, his desire became so strong that he felt that was it. One more second—and he would cum! Right now! This very moment! Right into his underpants!

He let Irochka go and started unbuttoning his fly. Irochka squatted down quickly, moved close to him, and opened her mouth.

As soon Krasin handled the buttons at last, she came even closer to him, grabbed his hot, tense and unnaturally hard penis which was like a stick, with her right hand and put it deep into her mouth at once. Krasin cummed almost immediately. The pleasure that he felt was so great that he literally passed out for a couple of moments. Everything reeled before his eyes. When he came to his senses and looked down, he saw that Irochka was still squatting in front of him and staring at him with a smile. He patted her head gently, her smile became bigger, and then she carefully, very carefully—almost tenderly—took his soft dick with her both hands, thoroughly licked the cockhead—the sensation was very sharp, and Krasin startled lasciviously several times—and only after that stood up lightly.

Krasin fixed himself up quickly, and they left the hall. Everything that happened took several minutes. Krasin was completely happy at that moment. In seventh heaven! His wings were sprouting. He was in empyrean. He was just blown by a girl whom he had dreamed about all his life.

2.

"So, where shall we go? To the institute?" Krasin, beaming with happiness, asked Irochka, who was looking at him inquiringly. "Oh, God! I feel good!"

She smiled softly and nodded. He looked around and squeezed her buttock with his palm. The girl almost didn't resist.

"Come on, Oleg! Don't. People are watching!" Her dress and pants were very thin. Krasin felt that he wouldn't need much time to recover strength for the future feats.

Hooray! Hail to youth! So, I'll be able to do it two or three times at least, he thought with joy. He wanted to sing and dance. Everything was wonderful! The weather, his spirits, and Irochka at his side. *Just reach out your hand. Life is great and wonderful!*

"Look here! Life is great, comrades! And it is short—that's the most important thing!" he sang or, rather, bleated. He never had an ear for music or the voice. Irochka glanced at him but didn't say anything. However, his last phrase threw cold water on him.

Oh and speaking of "short."

"We don't have a lot of time, indeed. We need to hurry. We have to see our fellow students with new eyes. We can already guess what's waiting for them. And we know for sure what's waiting for certain students. Sashka Shabanov will die in a car accident in a year. And Zheka from our group… Shit! Am I really going to see all of them now? Crazy!"

He looked askew at Irochka, who was going by his side. She was deep in thought. Her lips were touched by a vague smile. A strange smile… Either dreamy or a curious smile, in one word. Odd.

"What are you thinking about?" he pushed the girl with his elbow playfully.

She slowly turned her eyes on him, "What is the best way to spend this time?" she said quietly and thoughtfully, as if thinking aloud., "These two hours, the only two hours in life. They would never happen again. I will never be young again. Ever. Ever."

"Well," said Krasin, not knowing what to answer her.

He was bewildered by the serious tone of the girl. *What's wrong with her? However, on the second thought, she's right. Never again. Two hours of youth, an incredible gift of fate. And how am I going to spend it? Fuck Ira a couple more times? Is that the supreme goal?*

And how should I spend it? Thinking about sense of life? Thinking that everything in life is changeful and circular? Well, I can think about that at home when I'm back. Fortunately, I've got nothing else to do there at my age. Just sitting and thinking until I'm blue in the face.

And here, I don't have to think, I need to act. I need to go on the racket while I'm still young. I have to love while I still can. I have to fuck, while I... Yeah...It's not a saying, really. I made that up. Well, it doesn't matter. All in all, while I'm still young, while I still have a desire, while I still can have a boner. And then? Damn it! 'And later you'll have to pay, But that would be later!' It can go to blazes! I have only one youth! I think, it's the only thing that I realized in my silly and lousy life. I learned it. A bit too late, of course, as usual, a bit too late, but fate is giving me one more chance. I can be young for two hours. Probably that old witch just had a nice mood. She was satisfied, she was full. She porked out.

She ate some poor bastard and got sluggish. She relaxed. She thought, 'I should do a nice thing, I'm bored. Just for a change.' And here..."

"In one word, I'm fucking lucky! I won in a lottery, the lottery of life. For the first and the last time, I hit the jackpot! So use it!"

"Together with Irka. She's probably thinking about the same stuff, and she's scratching her small head. What's the best way to use the prize? To use the gift of fucking fate. Its unexpected present. 'Beware of Greeks bearing gifts,'" a proper quote came to his mind.

"Which, in Russian, means, 'beware of Trojan horses,'" he thought gloomily. "And the treacherous fate usually slips the likes of them, bitch. Trojan ones. With a secret inside. With a surprise. It looks like a horse from the outside, and there's a fuck-up inside, waiting for its time. Inside, there are loony Menelauses-Odysseuses, fuck them!"

"Well, alright! Fuck it! We Russians have another saying for that. We got it in store, so to say. It's our inheritance. 'Never look a gift horse in the mouth.' Even the Trojan one. We'll deal with it!"

"Alright, cheer up!" he pushed Irochka again. "If you think too much, you'll be too sad. You can't change anything with your thoughts. Let's score a full ride, and that's it. You may think for hundred years but won't come up with a better idea."

Irochka looked at him in surprise, and Krasin checked himself.

Why am I talking in sayings only, like a skomorokh on a fair? I read too much fucking crap during my life. And now it's pushing out of me. Belch of education. I don't have my own thoughts. All of them are borrowed. It's very convenient. On the least occasion, here I am—a quote or a saying! Fucking joke or a catch-phrase. Shit, these silly thoughts make my spirit sink. It was so great. I need to quit these speculations, this digging inside me. This fucking Dostoevsky style."

"Listen!" he suddenly stopped short, looking at Ira mistrustfully. She stopped, too, and stared at him, bewildered.

"What? Why are you looking at me like this?"

"Look at yourself in a mirror."

"What for?"

"Just do it!"

Irochka shrugged her shoulders and opened her purse.

"Don't you notice anything?"

"What do I have to notice?"

"You don't really see anything?"

"I'm not sure."

"You changed!" said Krasin with excitement; he almost screamed. "You've become more beautiful, much more beautiful. Indeed, you've become a real gorgeous girl. Like in a fairy-tale. Irina the Beautiful. Upon my word!"

He stepped back a little, swept his eyes over her in amazement and even tut-tutted with delight.

"Well, well! You have a hell of a body! Super! Nice. You're a real goddess. a Venus of Milo. Aphrodite. Cypris. You're just not from this world!"

Irochka listened to him for some time with her mouth open, then she grabbed the mirror and started looking at it devouringly.

"Right, it's impossible! Really—it's me and not me. Here I have and…yeah! Everything's gone. What does it mean? What's the meaning of it?" she stared at Krasin with burning eyes. "And my body as well?"

"Just look at your legs! Legs for days!" Suddenly Krasin came close to the girl and grabbed her breast. She staggered back in surprise and fear. "Right! What breast size did you have? B cup?" The girl got shy and nodded with reluctance. "And look what you've got now!"

Irochka felt herself hastily and looked up at Krasin with crazy eyes.

"My aunt!"

"You're a sex-bomb, no doubt," he laughed. "Frankly speaking, I thought that your breast was a bit too small. Well, just a bit. And now it's a perfect fit. Dead-on! Just the job. The very thing. It's what I like."

Krasin paused, listening to himself and his new feelings, and then continued more calmly and even thoughtfully.

"You've become a woman which I always wanted you to be. A perfect girl of my dream. Ideal Irochka Beliaieva. Your appearance adjusted to my wishes. It had become better," he paused again, "but you haven't changed inside. It's strange—not a bit! You're the woman whom I met yesterday. Sorry, the day before yesterday. Why am I confusing them? Second time in a row. Right, you're the same. Not better and not worse."

"How do you know it?" asked Irochka in astonishment.

"I just know," answered Krasin thoughtfully. "I just know, and that's it. I feel it. The sorcerer warned me that I'd have new and strange—well, unusual—capabilities here. It seems that they do appear."

"He told me, 'You will feel them.' So, I do feel them. But, for some reason, I think that it's not the end," he paused and then added even more thoughtfully. "I'm gonna have more of them. There's gonna be a continuation."

Somehow I'm not pleased with this, he continued to himself. *Hell knows why. I'm not pleased; that's it! I'm sick in heart... Sick. "What are all these tricks for? What games are they playing with me? It would seem—what would be easier? If her appearance changed so easily, she could adjust to me inwardly as well. She could fall in love with me, like a cat, follow me on a leash, and hang upon my lips."*

"However, that's not the case. She used to be a bitch inside, and she remained a bitch. She became even worse. More dangerous. A very beautiful bitch. Super-bitch. And that's a spice storm! Nuclear sex-bomb. Fucking neutron bomb. It can kill all that lives in vicinity. No one would have a desire for her!"

Though, why should I care? How could she leave me? She's still afraid that I would send her back. And she's gonna be even more scared after she sees that it turns out that I'm great and powerful. After she sees with her own eyes, so to say. By the way, can I really send he back? Hell knows! Maybe I can, maybe I can't. I don't really know yet. Alright! She's not gonna escape me. That's pretty clear.

Just to think of it! She should feel at least some gratitude and thankfulness, right? I made her such a beauty. Does she have any conscience? Though why would women have conscience? They've got fake eyelashes instead of conscience. They put them on and off when necessary.

Well, I'm thinking about the wrong stuff. Wrong! There was something else important. Something... The sorcerer from the bakery told me something else. Fucking clairvoyant. Or did he warn me or caution me? What was that?

Oh, right! 'Be careful with your new skills!' Or 'don't misuse them?' Well, I can't remember; it's not important. It is as broad as it is long. So what? What does this dream mean? What do 'careful' and 'don't misuse' mean? Maybe I shouldn't have made Irka a Miss World, so that all local communist girls would envy her? I was satisfied with her when she had her previous looks. If that is the case...

And how would she go home? Would she turn into an old woman again, after being Irina the Beautiful? A goddess? Women react very badly to such things. "Though, what does it have to do with me? I didn't do that. Not in the very least. I've got nothing to do with it. Or did I actually do it? I did want it, right? And here you are. Dinner is served!

Shit! I can't understand anything, with all these fucking psychological whims and intricacies. Freaking puzzles. 'Did!, did not; wanted, didn't want!..' Fuck you with your magic tricks! Yes, I wished for that! I did! So what? What next?

I'm an ordinary man. I like Irka more now, with her bigger boobs and slender legs, not to mention everything else. It would be more pleasant for me to fuck her as she's now. That's it—end of story. And I don't give a damn about anything else. Fuck it! I don't give a toss about anything else. I couldn't care less. Fuck it all! Bollocks to that! I'm on a sex tour.

Well, let's ask her, for example? Is she pleased that she's become more beautiful? Come on, let's ask her! 'Irochka, honey, do you want to be ugly again so that the travel back would be less painful? Eh? I could do it, no problem. So, by mutual consent; it's better for her, and it's better for me. The issue is over. I'm absolutely right. Right! Shit! But why am I so wretched then? As if I lied to a kid. My heart aches.

'Heart!' Why am I moaning here, heh? What kind of human am I? Neither fish nor flesh. A chimera. What does it look like? Head of lion and body of goat? Or vice versa? I don't remember! All in all, a goat with lion mane. An old woman was turned into a gorgeous girl. Fucking Cleopatra-Nefertiti—she's young and beautiful! Just fuck her and be content. No! Something's wrong again. Well, I'll be damned! Someone else in my place would be jumping for joy! Like a goat. With a lion mane. And what am I doing?

I'm just thinking, you see. I'm just losing precious time. I got a woman at hand, but I'm still whacking off. I'm pulling her leg. Fucking thinker. Sophist. Freaking Hamlet. 'To be or not to be?' 'To boink or not to boink?' And if I do boink, who would it be? Of course, to boink! Boink, take out and boink again! Pop it in this Ophelia balls deep! These Ophelias are created for this. To be boinked. Otherwise, they drown out of despair. Don't refuse a gift! While you're hesitating, she'll sleep with someone else. Do I want it? I told her not to think much myself!

And yet! Did I do it or not? Quite honestly? Well, me! Me! me! me! I just felt that I was able to do it, and I couldn't resist. I decided to try it at once. To improve the breed, so to say. Well, I didn't ask her; I just didn't have the time. It happened in the spur of the moment. One—and a princess instead of a frog. I'm sorry! Guilty as charged.

"But what does it change? What? So I could ask her. Would she refuse? Is there a woman in the world who would refuse it? Is there? Show her to me! No! No, no, and no! There are no such women and there can't be! No! So, the result would have been the same. Enough! That's it! "We'd better start using the fruit of righteous labor. Trying the new Irochka. Skimming cream off her. Stripping her down. Checking if everything in her is fitted for me. Did I do it in vain, or what?"

Shit! I really shouldn't have done that. The mutual consent is bullshit. Women are like children in this matter. They lose their heads immediately. A child would reach his hand to a candle. I shouldn't have shown her such a toy. No! I shouldn't have tempted her. Fuck! Damn it all! Did you want to be God, you fucking moron? You were warned! Fuck!

"Alright, let's go, we shouldn't be idling around," Krasin tossed his head, driving off gloomy thoughts. "Let's go separately; I don't want us to draw attention. You go ahead, and I'll be following you. I can't really walk alongside you. You're beaming like a spotlight. People see you from far off."

Approaching the guard desk, Krasin lingered, searching for the student ID in his pockets. Meanwhile, Irochka had already entered the institute. Krasin found his ID at last—it was in a lapel pocket of his shirt; he looked at his photo with delight—he was so smart and serious on it; Sure, future learned scholar, fucking Archimedes—and then entered the hall, too.

Oh, God! Everything's so familiar and, at the same time, so strange! Krasin was looking around and twisting his head. *All these hammers and sickles.* He noticed that Irochka stopped in front of him and was chatting with two girls, unfamiliar to him. *Are they her friends or what? It seems they're not from their year of study.* He didn't see any of his friends yet.

Irochka clearly drew attention to her. She was standing in the center of the hall, like a small sun. This sight made Krasin feel even gloomier. *Yeah, a nice Cinderella tale have I made. Clock is striking twelve and... But, unlike the tale, it's forever.*

As a matter of fact, he had a restless, itchy feeling that he was losing time. "The clock will strike twelve soon, indeed. It's better to act. He should spend these precious minutes in another way. These truly precious two hours. And how is he going to spend them? Empty talk with his fellow students who never were interesting for him, and they are not interesting for him now. They didn't manage to achieve anything in life. By the way, neither did him. *Alright, what's the difference? Achieved or not. I shouldn't be thinking about that. I need to do something! Now. Right now. I'm losing time, like a fool."*

By the way, if this is really a kind of parallel world like that sorcerer explained to me, and it doesn't cross our world, then I can do here whatever I want. I just don't want to be caught during these two or three hours. I could kill someone. They won't have enough time to find me. It's impossible to do it in just two hours. And then I won't be here anymore; I'll disappear. And, even if they do find me.... It just would be a shame to spend two hours in the police precinct like a moron. But then, I'll disappear anyway. I'll come back into my world. All in all, I don't have to be afraid of anything.

As a matter of fact, I should pick up a girl that I like, take her somewhere, fuck her and then strangle her. I wouldn't want her to kick up a racket. A lot of new experience! "No! It's some kind of crap again. Bullshit! First, how would I take her somewhere; second, where? Third, why do I need it at all? Why do I need some undesirable chicks, if I've got my beautiful Irochka. She's incredible and absolutely virgin. My beloved pussycat. I came here for her. She's my first love. Untouched. Unspoiled. Well, she blew me once, but it doesn't count, one may say. It's just warming up, training. With an old model."

And now we should pass on to the basic action. Event. With an improved one. I want her again. I do, I do, I do! Where is she? Enough chatting. Actually, we shouldn't have started this crap, all these walks with her ahead and me behind. We don't have the time for this nonsense. Whom should we be ashamed of? All of these? They're gonna just disappear forever in two hours. They're not real. They're just alive for the time being, like in "Faust," second part. Okay, that's it! Enough of this double talk. Come on, come on! At first, I should deal with Irochka. So, where's she?

Krasin found her with his eyes and headed to her without hesitation.

"Excuse me, Ira, can I talk to you for a second?" He came close to the three chicks, which were chatting enthusiastically, and addressed Irochka unceremoniously. The other two girls went silent all together and stared at him with funny indignation, as if he had done a crying indelicacy. As if he had interrupted a fucking important conversation. Like which panties they would have put on tomorrow.

"Silly women! Fucking dummies. Single use—just for two hours," thought Krasin with hateful irritation.

Irochka looked at him, surprised, exchanged looks with other girls, shrugged her shoulders a little like she didn't understand what that squirt and churl wanted from her and, only then, slowly and reluctantly, approached him. *Fucking Tsar Maiden! Whore-like swan.*

"Listen, enough fooling around," hissed Krasin furiously. "How do we spend the time? Walking in single file, so nobody would notice anything? Like joined at the hip. Talking to these living ghosts? Why would we pay attention to them at all? They're not humans! They're shadows! Ghosts. They're gonna disappear in two hours. Without a trace. Forever. Fuck them! Fuck what they think! Are you in your mind? Two hours! The only! Never again! How should we spend them? So you took thought and came to this—to chatting with your friends? And they're not really your friends, they're nobody. They're dummies, God forgive! Phew! I knew that all women are silly, but to such an extent! I thought that you're a bit smarter.

"In one word, I want you again. I just can't resist it! But now I want to fuck you properly. Seriously. The whole nine yards. Let's find an empty classroom. And then we'll see!" He rushed to the stairs leading to the upper floors.

"Wait, Oleg!" begged Irochka, "I need to excuse myself to the girls. I feel awkward."

"Whom do you feel awkward with? What girls?" Krasin nearly yelled in answer. "Wake up and look around you! Do you know where we are? They do not exist! It's just illusion, created for two hours. Hallucination! Why should we talk to them at all? We've got only two hours! Can you understand it?"

Irochka fell silent in fear. He almost ran up the stairs, covering two steps at a time. Irochka was lagging behind.

Well, second floor... Let's check here at first. Occupied... Occupied... 'I'm sorry!' Why the fuck do I apologize? To whom? 'I'm sorry!' Phew! What a crap! Well, indeed... ... A psychological barrier. It's my education. Its influence, fuck it! It seems that it's not that easy to be rude. Even with ghosts. 'I'm sorry!' 'Excuse me!' Okay, fuck them! So, what? Where? Shit, it's the last room. That's it! Fucking disaster! Holy shit.

I have to go to the third floor. Fucking shit! Am I going to run up and down for two hours at the drop of the hat? Jumping and hopping on the stairs like some gigantic fucking grasshopper, like a jumping dragonfly? 'Well, how was your trip, dear Oleg Viktorovich? Did you like it? Did you use the time well?' I did use it fucking well! Wonderful! Fucking shit! I'm just fucking shocked! What the fuck? What the fuck, really?

Someone called Krasin between the second and third floors.

"Hey, Oleg!" One of his institute friends stood before him. As chance would have it, it was the same Zheka who was supposed to die in a car accident next year.

Oh, God! Get lost! Save us!

"Hi, Zheka," said Krasin reluctantly. He almost crossed himself instinctively.

"Why are you staring at me like this?" his friend asked him in surprise.

"Well, well… no, it's nothing. It's okay. Everything's fine. Wonderful! "

Shit! What they used to say back then? What phrases did they say? Idioms? 'Fine'—where's it from? From back then or from here? Maybe I should just swear? Swearing didn't change, that's for sure.

Fucking crap! Forget it—everything's fucking great!

Though, 'forget it.'? Shit! What am I thinking again? From there, from here!

By the way, about 'fucking great.' It seems, I won't be able to fuck enough the way things are going. I would be fucked up myself, that's for sure. They fucked me up already. I'm just like Ruslan near the Head, messing around for a solid hour. 'I ride along and no grudge bear you, but cross my path, and I won't spare you!' But, quite the contrary, I do grudge, but can't really ride. I can't spare. No one can actually do it with a head.

Shit! Shit! Shit! Shit! Away from me! Enough talk!

It's high time I did real work. It's high time to cum once, unlike this impotent Ruslan. He probably just didn't have a hard-on. So he's complaining to the Head. 'Help me! Recently I can't do anything in bed, I just ride along and cannot reach, and I don't have a boner; and if I do reach, if I do have a boner by chance, I just can't come. I can't ejaculate.' And, instead of helping, the man just started laughing. So, one thing led to another. Well…funny. Fucking humor. Childish humor. I'm a hell of a comedian. Whistler. Nightingale the Robber. I whistle and whistle.

"I'm sorry, Zheka, I'm in a hurry."

I need to fuck Irochka! We'll talk later. In hell!

Zheka looked at Krasin strangely, then shifted his glance to divinely beautiful Ira who was standing nearby, but didn't say a word. However, Krasin already forgot about him as soon as he turned away. There is no time! He's not in the mood for ghosts. He's busy. Busy.

However, there's something strange in all this. Unnatural. This is such an event, travel to the past, to another world, and all I want is to fuck a girl. Yeah, I've been dreaming about her for a long time. But, don't I really have any other interests? Higher or more important ones? It's somehow insulting, really.

And what 'other interests?' Of course not! Love! Love! Lovey-dovey, stick in and out—it's the most important stuff in life. 'Aimons, dansons et chantons. We love, dance, and sing.' That is life. Everything else is showing off. Devil's tricks. Oh, it seems, there's 'buvons —we drink.' If I'm not mistaken, I could have forgotten French. That's right, too. But, in any case, aimons" at first! Aimons, aimons, aimons! The more the better. And then everything else. All these chantons and dansons. We'll sing and dance after that. Being pleased by the fact that I fucked her at last. At last, hmm?

Fucking shit! It appears that I'm a chatterbox! Verbal prattler! Whore-hoper. I've got verbal incontinence, oral diarrhea. Brain-poisoning. Time acclimatization. The sickness of all travelers and tourists. I must have thought about some old stuff. About these zombies, how pretty they will be in 20 years. Enough! ENOUGH! Enough.

And now just fucking. Fucking, fucking, and fucking! As great Lenin told us. And no nails! Like Mayakovsky added.

Right. I need to beware of nails. Probably, I'm gonna fuck her on a table. Where else? Or on the chairs. No, what am I talking about? What chairs? 'What dog?' They would sprawl in a crucial moment. I don't want to break my... something. Because of my folly. I would definitely not fucking want that! How do they say? 'One can break his dick when fooling around.' Exactly!

It's quite possible. Falling off the chairs. Facedown. Like upturned Buratino. I'd be ashamed to look into the sorcerer's eyes. 'So, how did you like Irochka?' Well... I... see...

In short, on a table!

Actually, 'short' doesn't mean that you can have a short penis when fucking somebody on a table; as you've got more room to maneuver than with chairs, or that sex on a table is more comfortable, but that... Shit! There now! When you're too blotty, you think about it all the time, and all the words become potentially sexual, like they acquire second meaning. Attain. Second breath. Implication. Even the most trivial, neutral, and harmless, at first sight. Ordinary.

"Amazing! I've never noticed it before. I just haven't paid any attention. Maybe because I was never too blotty. Or, maybe, because I was content with imitations. Stand-ins. Whether she puts out or not, what's the difference? Actually, I didn't want it that much. And now I do want it. I want it badly! Very badly! Hell, yeah! I mean, I want it. Literally. That's for sure. No implications and second thoughts, under no circumstances.

Though, 'under' is a very sexual word. Ambiguous... It has two meanings. And the second meaning is under the first one; and it's using the both, concerning the thoughts at the back of the mind. That's it! I seem to go crazy. Temporary insanity because of sex. Blue balls. Or what's the right word for it? When sperm goes to your head? And slams it with a hammer. Right! Third floor. So, what do we have here? Occupied... Occupied...All in all, on a table. 'All in all' is okay, right? Except for the hint to love-in... Orgy... But it's a strained interpretation, an obvious one. The—what's it called?—'meaningful hallucination.' That's a name of a band, and they have this song—'Forever Young.' From the movie 'The Brother.' It's exactly about me. In a certain sense, I'm 'forever young,' too. Well, okay, maybe not forever. Temporarily. Temporarily young. For two hours only. Which run away, flow away, and escape without a trace. Drip drop! 'I could drink a sea...' I could fuck Ira...

I could, if I found a fucking empty room in this freaking institute! Which is jam-packed with stupid morons who entrenched themselves in almost every room! Come on! I'm sorry. All these fucking scientists. Well, what an idiot I was back then! I was sitting here, as well. I was pounding the books. And what did I get in result? A bald head? Right! From... Fuck you all! Jerks! Well, what was I saying? Oh, yeah. So, on a table. Excuse me. Pest on you all! Drop dead! With all your computers. Though they didn't have computers back then. Just the big ones. Stationary ECMs. I'd put her, my darling, on the edge of a table, spread her legs...or we could lie down. The table is big enough. No, it would be skeezy. Someone could walk in on us, some freaks. And that would be the end of sexual feats. I would spend the rest of the time fighting with local authorities. With a fucking dean or someone else.

Oh, oh, oh! Empty! An empty room! At last! We found it."

Krasin moved aside, letting Irochka enter, then took the first chair he could find and put its leg into the door-handle, blocking it. "Let them break in, if they want. Darn them! I want not to care a damn about this!" Shaking with desire, he almost pushed Irochka to the nearest table and set her down on it, lifting her dress and spreading her legs. When he saw her naked thighs and sharply white panties, everything swam before his eyes, like earlier in the hall.

"Wait," whispered Irochka and waved him off. She jumped down lightly, bent down and took off her panties, put them in her pocket, and then, stretching her dress, quickly sat on the table and spread her legs wide. The stiff and curly hairs between her legs were red, also.

Krasin lost his head at this seductive and beckoning sight which he had seen thousand times before that in his secret and intimate dreams. Unable to turn his eyes away from it and to understand or hear anything around him, he took down his underpants and trousers, and, being caught in them—naturally, the trousers fell down on the shoes—limped to the table, moving his straight legs clumsily.

Irochka was staring with her shining eyes at his shaking and utterly tense penis, which looked like a clock hand, pointing at half past two.

As soon as Krasin came close to her, the girl moved her body back and, leaning upon the table behind with straight hands, put her legs around his waist. Using his right hand, which was shaking with excitement, Krasin lavishly moistened the head of his dick with saliva and ran it tightly—up and down! bottom-up!—along the yawning narrow pink slot that beckoned him in the woman's body. Irochka was panting and watching all his manipulations. At last, holding his breath, very slowly he put his whole cock—the whole; nothing remained out of it—into something very soft and very tender. Irochka sobbed and dropped a sigh, "A-ah!" and closed her eyes in sweet languor, feeling him at last inside her, in her womb. He paused a bit, trying to extend that blissful moment as long as he could, and then, slowly and smoothly, moved his waist back—Irochka again gave a soft sob, "A-ah-ah!" feeling that move inside her—forwards... and backwards again... and then with rising speed, trying not to hurry and, at the same time, being unable to restrain himself. The girl gave a deep sigh, opened her eyes, and embracing

Krasin's neck with her arms, huddled up impulsively to him, shaking and screaming voluptuously with every new thrust, "A-ah-ah! A-ah! A-ah!"—quietly at first, but then louder and louder.

"Oh-oh-oh-oh-oh! Honey!" she whispered-moaned-whirred, feeling that Krasin cummed, and, at the same time, the chair fell down, and the door opened. It seemed that somebody had been trying to break in for some time, but the happy lovers couldn't notice anything around them for the past several minutes.

On the doorstep, there stood a furious teacher, and behind her there was a whole group of merry students, looking into the room over her shoulders. It appeared that the group was supposed to have a class in this room, so they actually came here.

Krasin, caught unawares, was standing in the middle of the room with his pants down, embarrassed and filled by wild panic. He looked at them in dismay and felt at that moment that something changed. He couldn't explain to himself how it was, but he clearly could feel all of them, as if he was holding invisible threads which controlled them. He could do with them whatever he wanted. If he wished, they would die or move again. From that moment on, he controlled them completely.

"You'll have some unusual skills there. You'll just feel them in you, and that's it," he remembered at once the words of the sorcerer.

Right! And he felt it. Again. Like he expected. He anticipated. Back then. When he had turned Irochka into a beauty. Well. Wonderful! Really wonderful! Incredible. Krasin gave a deep sigh, "A-ah-ah," recovering his breath. By the way, he felt for the first time that he could also send Irochka back home at any moment. Back to the future. He'd been bluffing before that. Though, actually, now it was the least of his concerns. He wasn't going to send her anywhere. Especially now, when all these cursed zombies were dealt with, once and for all, and there would be no problems with them. Finally! God be thanked!

They're as meek as lambs. They're just standing and staring. That's it!

He bent over, pulled up his trousers and started freshening up. Shit! His dick was wet and sticky. He should clean it.! He needed a handkerchief or a napkin. Suddenly a funny thought came to his mind. He glanced at Irochka. Being scared, she stood dove-eyed at his side. Her dress and everything else was neat and clean. It could seem that she had been studying with her fellow student in a vacant room. They just locked the door so nobody would interrupt them. They were too busy with scientific outputs. And inputs as well.

Krasin wouldn't be surprise, if she already put on her panties. Ladies could do a lot of tricks and miracles in times like this. Copperfield would really envy them!

Krasin looked at the teacher who was standing in front. She was nice, young. He moved his eyebrow a bit, and the woman moved to him. Irochka cowered in fear. The woman came close to him, kneeled down, carefully took his dangling dick in her hands, and started licking it. Krasin looked at Irochka. She was staring at that scene like a stuck pig and couldn't utter a word.

"Take it easy," said Krasin casually. He smiled and winked at her. "It appears I can control all of them. Actually, the sorcerer told me about that, but I didn't understand him. And now I see what is what. I got a hang of it. It's probably, because of the affect," he smiled again, "a big fucking shock!" He took the liberty of using swear words with Irochka for the first time. It just slipped out. Irochka was silent. She didn't pay any attention to that. She seemed not to notice it.

Well, well! thought Krasin ironically. *Maybe her life experience is richer than it may seem at first. I was caught in the act, with my pants down. A very piquant situation, actually. It was hard to get my bearings. I could really become a wiener for the rest of my life.*

"Alright, enough," he said quickly to the teacher. The woman stood up obediently, turned away, and went to her initial spot on the room's doorstep.

Irochka watched her go and then turned to Krasin in astonishment. "So, you really can do with them whatever you want? You just tell them, and that's it? Nothing else?"

Krasin felt a touch of jealousy. After all, just now... *in front of her... another woman. She could fucking take some offence in common decency! Does she really care? And what about all these gasps and groans? 'Oh-oh-oh! Honey!' Is this a game, or what? Did she feel anything at all?"*

"Yeah, I don't even have to tell them anything," he answered with reluctance. "I just did it, for the sake of result," Krasin paused. "I can do it in my mind," he finished absently, trying to sort out his new super skills. As a matter of fact, he didn't understand them fully.

"Listen, Olezhek," said Irochka with hesitation. Krasin looked at her with surprise. *Olezhek! Well! Wow! Soft words. That's something new. She never called me that.*

He saw that the girl was hesitating and wanted to say something. "Come on," Krasin cheered her up, "what's the matter?"

"Listen! Well, you know...don't be offended, okay?"

"Come on, fire away," he encouraged her again. He got curious.

"Do you promise me not to be offended?"

"With what?"

"No, first you must promise."

"Alright, I promise! So, what's up?"

"No, not 'I promise,' but promise really. Do it properly."

"Oh, God! Alright. I promise that I won't take offence. I mean it. I solemnly swear. Are you glad?" Krasin's interest was at its peak. *What's she up to?*

"Do you mean it?"

"Oh, God! I do mean it! I won't take offence! Out with it! What's up?"

Irochka glanced at him, lowered her eyes and, blushing—Krasin was pleased to see it—said very quietly, "Kiss me."

"What?" asked Krasin in amazement.

"Come on, kiss me! Hug me."

Without a clue, Krasin hugged and kissed her obediently. He wanted to step back, but Irochka nuzzled close to him, so the kiss was passionate and long.

"Do you love me?" she whispered quietly.

"I do," lied Krasin, without a moment's hesitation. "I love to fuck you," he added to himself.

"Really?"

"Really."

What does she want of me? 'Really, truly?' I'm curious what she wants to tell me after such a long prelude. She can't actually resolve to do it. 'Aye me, what act, That roars so loud, and thunders in the index?' Does she want to confess to something? Interesting!

"Do you feel good?"

"Sure. And you?" he couldn't but ask the question.

"Yes, very good," Krasin smiled smugly and patted the girl's head. "I mean it! You're the best man on earth. The very best, honeybunch." Krasin patted her head again.

"So, what did you want to tell me, darling?" he asked after a pause. *'Honeybunch.' It's not masculine; the proper word would be... I don't know!*

"Olezhka, can I... do it with someone here? Someone from them? Can you give them an order?"

"What do you mean 'with someone?'" asked Krasin in amazement. He couldn't believe his ears and just stared at the bewildered girl.

"Well, you're not able to do it right now, and they're not real, anyway."

"No, they're not real. They're fucking children! But they can fuck like adults," an old joke came to Krasin's mind.

"Haven't you cummed?" Not knowing, what to say, he asked the first question he could think of.

"I have, of course! I've cummed," Irochka hugged Krasin, who was standing like a stock, and kissed him on the lips. "But you know that women feel it otherwise.

Yeah, thought Krasin.

"I want again," she said very quietly and shyly.

Wow! So much for Irochka. Goody-goody. She's talking now. Explicitly. I want a man, and you haven't got a hard-on. And that's just for starters, just out of courtesy. Because she needs something from me. Because she has to ask leave to do it. Because she's not gonna be able to do it without me.

"And, as a matter of fact, I want a man, and a new one. Fresh one. I got a choice. Just for a change. However, darling, when you got a boner again, I'll be ready for you. You are always welcome. I'll serve you out of turn, with great pleasure. I love you, and you know it! Best of all! All-all-all! Honeybunch."

Well, while my honeybunch is resting and recovering his strength, why would I be idle? I could practice at the same time. For now. And, really, why should she be idle?" thought Krasin suddenly. *She's right. We don't have a lot of time; why should we spend it for hugging? And with whom? Who am I to her? Nobody. We haven't seen each other for a lifetime. At first, she even wanted to escape from me. And all these 'darling' and 'I love you' are just part of the price. Part of the deal. I told her myself, 'pretend,' so she's pretending. She's doing her best. She's working off. But when she's free from pretending, why wouldn't she entertain? Take pleasure? Relax. Relax her mind and body. Let her imagination run free!*

Moreover, she's got such a chance, a fantastic one. The one that would never happen again in her life. You're young, beautiful, and desired! You're full of strength. And all men are yours for two hours! They're in your power completely. You may do with them whatever you want! You may even fuck them yourself. And no one would ever find it out. And, as a matter of fact, it's all unreal. It's like a dream. You'll always have an excuse for yourself. In case you're that fucking honest. "Well, if I were her—if I were me, I would fuck all women, one by one, in all holes and with all methods, but, unfortunately, I can't. Fucking physiology! It catches your eye, but you can't catch it. Well, yeah, I must wait for a boner, really. Shit!

Well, let her fuck! Like a cat. With all of them. Why do I care? In good health! I'm not her husband, after all. It's even good that she'll cornute him, one more time, in my presence. And it would be interesting to watch. Yeah, I'd like it. Maybe I'll join them, the thought made Krasin feel pleasant excitement. He wasn't jealous at all—quite the contrary. He suddenly turned on the heat.

Exactly! Love-in. Orgy. Orgy-orgy-orgy! I need to roll her for a love-in. Though, probably, she won't agree to a love-in at first. Although, we'll see! So, she should just start and warm up. She'll get into the process, and then we'll see. We'll see how it goes. How it goes in and goes out. Why would I be losing time? I'll get what I want, anyway. I'm pretty sure that she'll be able to satisfy everybody. But I doubt that all of them would satisfy her. She's a serious girl. Though there are a lot of people in the institute."

And I'll get a direct benefit, by the way. I'm going to enjoy watching it, and I'll drool sooner. Yeah, I'll have a hard-on. Which is actually soft now. As a matter of fact, I do want her. But my dick doesn't. Alright, enough talking. Am I doing it again? Did I think of something old again? God, I've got more 'agains.' Five in a row! Or four? Well, it doesn't matter. It's because I'm nervous, probably. Overexcited. So did I think about something bad again? So, here is the fifth one. Something rotten? No, I don't think so. Oh! about a love-in. Sexual orgy. About episodes and crowd scenes. It's too hot. It has the same effect on subconscious. It makes your mind weak. It digests badly. At first. And then it's alright. You get used to it. Him, him, you and me — it's our happy family! It's alright. I'll get used to it. This thought is rather pleasant. Hot... and savory... spicy. It refreshes the main course. Like a sauce. It adds a new taste. A new flavor. Rise for the fight against the unsavoriness! All of you." Krasin was eager to begin. "Why linger? Time!"

He looked at Irochka with a new approach. He imagined that she's standing on all fours… *the first one is beneath her... as usual! He's boinking her... fucking her... in a usual hole... the boy is working! He's doing his best. Traditionally, so to say... right... the second one is behind her, he's fucking her in the ass... slowly... sniffing with pleasure... with feeling, wit, and punctuation! It would better be their mutual friend; it's more provocative. And the third one is fucking her in the mouth. In the mouth! She's blowing the third one. She's licking...licking. With her tongue! Yeah... yeah! Right! like this! Atta girl! My beloved smackdown... Darling!*

And I can approach from the front when I'm done watching them. Then I can let her suck and lick a bit, just to arouse me. I touch her soft and silky hair and then make a pause and bend to whisper some gentle words into her ear. Then I straighten again, put my dick into her mouth slowly and, without a pause, ask her with a gesture—by pointing to the...—can I? Please? I beg you... And only then she understands and nods shyly, allowing it. She lowers her eyes, blushes, and answers with the look of her eyes. 'Yes, do it!' No sooner—he comes from behind. He drives that zombie away—enough! He gives him a mental order, 'You can fuck her in the mouth,' and he takes his place. He's got a beaten path before him.

In her ass... into the ass of my sweet, young, beloved, and tender girl! My beauty... Sweetie! In her ass! She's the most beloved and desirable girl! Tender...slowly...without ruffle. I enjoy watching this. Beneath her, with a frenetic pace. I kiss her back... her thighs; I tickle them a little. I touch her with my lips and fingertips. Oh! Oh-oh! Here and here, my sweetie... and here... Yeah! Yeah! Then I wait until she starts to suck our mutual friend's dick. She's looking up at him at the same time and smiling. He's the one whose dick she sucked at the very beginning. I bring that one closer; let him join, enough idling. Let her work with both of you. Let her gain experience...like this! Yeah! Everyone's busy now. Her ass is smooth, tight, and sharply white like virginity itself, like winter snow, He spreads her buttocks carefully and tenderly. He puts his dickhead, which was nicely licked by her a second ago and which is still wet with her saliva, to her small pink butt pussy. He pauses a bit... chooses the right spot... grabs her by her hips... tightly but not roughly. He squeezes them with his hands, her well-turned hips, ideal and flawless. Like this. He takes a breath, and bang! Until the end, with one thrust! One sharp move of his waist! A-ah!

Pop it in! Put this bitch on my dick! So it goes into her ass completely at a whack! The whole of it, balls deep! Take it out—and then again! And again! Recalling at the same time how this bitch, this whore, was fucked in the ass by our mutual friend, the one whom she's blowing right now! He took his dick out and then put it in again! He took it out and put it in again! Again and again! He was panting and drooling over with happiness, right before my eyes! He put his dick in her like a spit, like a stick! Slut! Whore!

Again! Again! Until the end! While this bitch was serving other two at the same time. And this cunt was shrieking and yelling, she was twisting and twitching beneath all of them, and she was cumming! Cumming! Cumming! She was looking back at the one who was fucking her in the ass, and this slutty bitch was happy. She tried to reach him with her hand. She was eager to see his dick penetrating her, penetrating her ass. Full-length! She was insanely aroused by the sight. This whore enjoyed it. She enjoyed watching her friend fucking her. She enjoyed touching him with her hand. Now she seems to enjoy sucking his dick. She's looking into his eyes, like a faithful dog. Right! It's good to please a nice man. Come on, cum on her face! Both of you! At once! Come on! Right now! Do it! Whack off into her open mouth! Come on! Like this! Yeah! Yeah! Oh, God, it's too much! Her face is covered, and her mouth is full. Oh, she's smacking her lips and smiling, bitch! Do you like the taste of it? Cheap whore! Cunt! The dirtier, the better! Thus the pleasure would be more acute! As a contrast!

Hey, you, the one beneath! Faster! Faster! Move it! Come on! Cum! Straight in her! Fuck this cunt! Come on! Do it, or her screams would tear my ears! Yeah! Good! I see it! It's spilling. And this bitch has cummed, too! She's shaking and kissing the one beneath her, like she's crazy. She's crying and moaning. What a bitch! She's shuddering with all her body, and the contractions of her ass! I can feel them with my dick. Again... Again... Again! Oh-oh-oh! Oh-oh-oh-oh! I'm gonna cum! Now! I'm gonna cum in her ass! In my first teen-age love! My dream! I'm gonna fuck her in the ass! Yeah! Right now! Yes-yes- yes- yes- yes! Ah-ah-ah-ah! AH-AH-AH-AH-AH-AH-AH!! Yeah! Yes! yes! yes! O-oh-oh-oh-oh-oh... Oh, God... God... Irochka! My sweetie! Irochka! You're so... You're so....You liked it, right? Did you? Right, honey? I liked it, too. I liked it a lot. Your ass is so sweet. Oh! O-oh! I don't really want to take it out, to leave you, to leave you beautiful body, to take it out. Oh-oh-oh! S-s-s-s-s! Yeah, great! Wow! Top class!"

It seemed to Krasin, as if he came to his senses, the images that he saw were so vivid and clear, as if he saw all of it in reality and experienced it. He was still panting. *And I haven't really tried to fuck her in the ass,* calming down, he smiled to himself. *I should do it! With such an ass. I have to try all dishes, the whole menu, according to the price list. And with such a sauce! Curious! Very curious! Extremely curious! Shit! Shit, shit, shit! Come on, come on, come on! Time! Time-time-time! Time!*

"I'm fine with it!" said Krasin cheerfully to Irochka, who was looking at him inquiringly and waiting for his answer, and she didn't even suspect what was happening with him.

She seemed to be scared with his unexpected enthusiasm. She looked at him curiously at first, but then smiled with relief, took a breath, and relaxed a bit. Obviously, deep inside, she had been afraid of his reaction to her prank in "enfant terrible" style—in a style of a terrible infant. She'd been afraid of the consequences. "Oops! And the next moment you're at home, near your stupid, snoring husband."

Krasin noticed all that, and he was flattered. He liked it. Right! She should be afraid of him.

"Let's try it, if you want! I would like to see it myself, actually, when you're…." Irochka glanced at him, smiled softly, blushed, and dropped her eyes.

"Well, let's pick them up," he was nearly rubbing his hands with anticipation. "Or, maybe, you want to do it with, well, with your future husband?" it dawned on Krasin. "What was his name? Andrey? Sergey? I don't remember. Hell knows." The thought about her husband was unpleasant for him.

"That's a decided preference, dear. You can easily go back, with trumpets and stuff. Sex for the sake of sex is one thing, and a specific partner is another. Moreover, the future husband… Are you doing it again? If you want a lot of sex—please! In good health! Sexual gymnastics. I'm not jealous of your sex with a lot of other guys. For me, they're like descendants of Alexander the Great, unable to hold together that which was owned by him alone. Fucking Diadochi! Here's one! Well, come on?"

"No, no! Not at all!" Irochka nearly waved with her hands, "My husband will… Well, I'll have time to do it with him. The whole life."

"Oh, I see," Krasin relented, "That's right. So, let's go. We've got little time. We can do the bride-show right here. I'll be bringing them in one by one, and you're gonna choose. By the way, you've got the furniture here," he pointed to the tables. Irochka smiled shyly again and looked at the corner, to which Krasin was pointing. Her embarrassment aroused Krasin even more. "We can move them together if necessary. You don't want to do it on a floor. So what? Let's start?"

Irochka glanced at the door and nodded.

"One by one?" asked Krasin.

"Yes, let them come, one by one," asked the girl timidly.

"Are you going to look at them, or touch as well?" Krasin winked at her cynically. "Like they're stud-horses, or breeders."

Irochka blushed again.

Krasin picked up in his mind the first male that he saw and ordered him to come in. To be precise, he didn't "order" him. Somehow, he entered the conscience of this young man and, still being himself and staying in his body, saw everything for his part and with his eyes. He couldn't describe that feeling, as one can't describe any feeling—sight, touch, smell—but that feeling was definitely present. It was. Now he understood why the sorcerer didn't explain anything to him. How could one explain it? How would one explain to the congenitally blind, 'From now on, you'll be able to see?' He doesn't know what vision is. What is 'to see?' He will understand when he recovers his sight."

The man entered. Irochka stole a glance at him, turned to Krasin at once, and shook her head negatively. She seemed to be still embarrassed.

"Next?" asked her Krasin in a loud voice. Irochka nodded.

"Don't be scared!" Krasin told her. "They don't understand anything right now. They're like living dummies, like robots. Though, if you want, I can return some of their feelings," he reassured her, "hearing or sight, for example. Or speech. Everything's in our power. Why would you fuck with dummies, really, blow a robot? You're not a calf."

You're a cow, he smiled to himself. *There should be feedback here. One shouldn't only derive pleasure, but give it, as well. I know...* Saying these thoughtful sententiae, Krasin was at the same time watching everything with the eyes of the dark-haired guy that stood in the middle of the room.

A slender, red-haired girl—She's beautiful, very, extremely, fantastically! Incredibly beautiful, unnaturally beautiful! An ordinary guy at her side, a plain guy—wow! What's wrong? I'm not that handsome to onlookers. Well, I'm a moron. Do I really look like this? Now I understand why she blew me off. And why she wanted to run away. Fuck a duck! I never thought that I'm such a frump. I'm so unattractive. But I work out...

Krasin looked closely at his arms with the other guy's eyes. He took pride in them. He couldn't see a fuck—no fucking muscles, no muscles at all. *Why the fuck do I work out every day? I'm a freaking tadpole! How come she let me fuck her? I wouldn't do it, if I were her. Though, what could she do? Well, why am I fooling around? 'How come she let me fuck her?' And how could she not let me fuck her? She did what she could, and I clung like a limpet to her! Produce it on the spot! I was so impatient! I mean, I'll produce it, and you'll take it in your mouth. Produce and take. In the nearest building. So what? What could she do? She wanted to be young, if only just for an hour. At any rate, I don't have any more illusions about her loving and adoring me and stuff. All her moans... 'Oh, fucking darling!' Everything's clear to the court. Alright, maybe, it's for the better that I don't have any illusions. And jealousy. Sex! Just sex. Pure sex. Naked sex. Well, let's see, what our girl is capable of?"*

Saying this to himself, Krasin involuntarily tried to look at that scene with Irochka's eyes. He tried to enter her like that guy. He didn't mean that at all, when he said "let's see" in his mind; he just thought it unknowingly. But the phrase itself told him what to do.

***

Shift! An immediate mental break, a click, and he became... *Oh, God!* He was overwhelmed with a stream of new striking feelings. Now he could see that scene with her eyes, too. That guy still remained in him, he didn't go anywhere; or he remained in the guy—he couldn't quite get it, but he moved away and shifted aside, on the back burner, on the periphery of perception. Now Krasin was in Irochka's subconscious. He was inside her. He could see everything with her eyes and feel it like she did. Probably he could even control her, like those on the corridor, but he didn't do it. He didn't even try. What for?

Meanwhile, he was just looking around with amazement, listening to his senses and the feelings of the young girl, trying to understand them. All that stuff was incredibly interesting for him.

First of all, he was surprised that, in her eyes, he was more attractive than in the eyes of that guy. *Oh, that's probably because she's used to me. Her eyes are blurred. I usually make such a dismaying impression only on new people. They think that I'm a screwed-up jerk. And she already took a measure of me; she doesn't notice anything anymore. It turns out that she's got affection for me. Really... Well, well! She considers me a buddy. Or even a friend. A close person, so to say, almost a kindred,* he couldn't but smile ironically to himself. *However, friendship is all very well, but spread the legs! Well, yeah! That's interesting! No hostility at all.*

And I forced her to be intimate with me. Yuck! What turgidities we're using! It turns out we're so chaste and shy. Who would have thought? Fucking chaste! Yeah, we can still fuck. But if it's going to be like this. if I'm going to force the missuses to be intimate with me, fucking force them—yuk! 'Forced her into intimacy!' 'Oh, earl!' And how should I say it? 'I made her fuck?' That doesn't sound well. 'Suck?' Ugh! Alright, alright, it doesn't matter. I need to stick to the point. So, what now? What about intimacy?

Actually, the fact, that I forced her—she seems not to care at all. She doesn't think about it. She doesn't bother. She takes it for granted. Well, I fucked her, that's it! Moreover, she liked it the last time. Upon my word! Let's assume that she didn't have an orgasm—she's lying through teeth about that—but she liked it. She did. Well, to some extent... But that's nice, anyway! Hah! So far so good. Frankly speaking, I was expecting it to be worse. Much more worse! I thought that she couldn't stand me. That she almost hated me. 'Yuk! that bastard!'

Krasin felt an unwilled pride. His nice feelings towards the girl, which appeared and strengthened in him in spite of her innocent pranks and small cheats, became even deeper. Above all else, he really liked her as a person. He liked her toughness and resolution. In his opinion, she behaved in a good way and showed her worth. She could adapt very quickly, like a chameleon. That's a dear. And when she tried to shaft him. *Well, everyone has a right to defense. She just didn't want to do me a blowjob. So it goes. I'm not Apollo!*

All in all, he was glad to help her and to bring her pleasure. He was glad to make compensation for psychological damage. For communicating with him. *Yeah, I saw myself from the sidelines!* He was sympathizing with her. They became a single whole for some time. A single organism. Symbiosis.

By the way, when she's going to fuck now, I'll feel everything, too. I'll feel what she feels during sex. During fuckery. When she's being fucked. Krasin felt a strange, urgent, and surprising need to use rude, dirty words. They aroused him. *It's strange! I think I never...* Or her? He couldn't get it. He tried to set his heart on it and grow into sexual feelings of the girl, trying to comprehend, perceive, and embrace them in full and to separate them from their own ones. He didn't understand yet why he was doing that.

Warmth below his waist is gradually filling all his body with sweet languor. Stiff, almost irritable nipples—they needed kissing and caressing. And desire, desire, desire! Sharp and unbearable desire!

Krasin had never felt this before, even when he had been taking Irochka to a hall of the building. He realized now that, back then, it was only a faint shadow of the woman's desire.

And I can make it even stronger, he thought suddenly. *Right! I can! I can make her feel everything a hundred, a thousand times stronger! Keener! I can make her have feelings that are impossible in the real world which even don't have any names. It's not orgasm; it's something unthinkable! Super orgasm! Arch-orgasm! Super, super-orgasm! Mega-orgasm! I can make her go crazy, burn with passion and unbearable desire! And cum, cum, and cum without a pause! Yeah, it's all in my power. And I'm gonna feel it with her! Yes! Yes!*

***

Now she wanted to be caressed, caressed, caressed, caressed by a man—by a couple of men—they touch and kiss her naked body. And then they fuck her! Fuck her! They're penetrating her toughly and tenderly, and she's twisting and screaming with unthinkable pleasure, she's shaking with endless orgasms, and the men are cumming one after another, they're screaming and shaking with her in sweet convulsions. She's feeling their hot sperm everywhere—inside her, on her body, on her face, and in her mouth. She's swimming and melting in the ocean of passion, delight, and bliss. And there are other men around her, a lot of men, and they're watching it. They're masturbating on her. And they all want her, they're growling at each other and trembling with desire, they're ready to do anything for her. for intimacy with her. They're ready to jump down each other's throats, to tear each other asunder! They' re males, mad with lust, and she's their female—the only one and the desired one.

But she wasn't cruel! Oh, no! She loved them all, every one of them; she wanted everyone to be pleased—this one, and that one—all of them! All! 'Why are you fighting? Don't do it. Don't you want me? Come on, take me. Don't hurry… Carefully… Yeah! Yeah! Like this.. Take me, take me! Do you feel good?'"

And women—there were women. Oh! How do… How great they are! They're undressing her slowly, slowly, slowly, slowly. They're feasting their eyes on her lingerie, her dress, her body. They're whispering her compliments; they're caressing her, laughing, admiring her flawless style—ah, men don't understand anything about it – and they're removing all her clothes, all of it!

Her dress—and she's twisting with all her body when they're taking it off through her head, then the bra, panties—ah – and they're kissing, kissing, kissing all her body! All! Everywhere, everywhere, everywhere, everywhere! Even there — oh-oh-oh — in the way that only women can kiss. They're caressing her like only women can caress.... caress.. softly... tenderly... tenderly... without hurry... Men can be so rough at times, and only a woman can completely understand another woman... the beloved one."

And she's already shaking with a growing, growing, growing, absolutely unbearable desire which is taking her somewhere—carrying her... and she's swimming, swimming, and swimming in its hot and fiery waves. And a huge hush, a whole tsunami of overpowering and crazy desire takes her softly and carefully and lifts her up, higher, higher, higher, to the deep, clear, and dazzlingly blue sky. And out of there, out of transparent aerial abyss, she hears a beckoning, crystal voice, as if belonging to an angel. It's calling her... calling her... him...

***

"Oleg! Oleg! Oleg!"

"Uh! What?" Krasin startled and opened his eyes.

His wife bent over him and was shaking his shoulder, alarmed.

"Wake up! Are you alright?"

"What happened?" he sat up on the bed, looking wildly around him, unable to understand anything half-awake. He couldn't understand where he was and what was happening. Irochka... hall... institute... all the fuss... room... anticipation... A scary guess dawned at him. He looked slowly at his wife.

"You were sleeping so strangely," she explained to him calmly, seeing that he was awake. "You didn't move at all, as if you were dead. I got worried!"

"Stupid cow!" yelled Krasin in rage, clenching his fists fiercely. He had never raised a hand on his wife, but now the desire to smack her stupid face was almost unbearable. "You woke me up! I asked you not to do this! Not to wake me tonight! Didn't I?"

"Don't yell! You're gonna wake everyone up," babbled his frightened wife. "I woke up myself and saw that you looked like a ghost. Your face was white as death."

Krasin slumped on the pillow. What's the point of talking to her? It's over! Everything's gone. Youth and strength, the desire which he felt just now with Irochka was raging in him like a volcano. Vesuvius! He wanted to hit the ceiling and kick himself! He had to do something! Now! He couldn't even think about lying down near this old woman—he looked at his wife with disgust—and falling asleep.

Act! Act! Act! But what can he do? Maybe he should call the sorcerer? *What's the time? It's twelve. Motherfuck! I've spent there only an hour! Only an hour! Because of this stupid bitch. Did the fate send her to me, so she would spoil my life?*

So, what can he do? Right! He should call that sorcerer. *Maybe he's not asleep. It's not that late, and he wanted to keep track of my journey. So he's definitely not sleeping. Well, I'm gonna call him—that's it!"*

Krasin grabbed the phone. No signal. "Oh, right! I turned it off."

He put the phone down, fount the socket, and turned the phone on. It rang at once. Krasin nearly jumped with surprise.

"Hello!"

"Hi, it's me!" he heard Ira's crying voice.

How does she know my number? Probably, I told her in the car. I don't remember.

"What's wrong?"

"My wife woke me up!" His wife was looking at him with round eyes. Krasin didn't care.

"Do something, anything you can! I have to go there! I have to! It's not fair! Only an hour passed! If you wish, I will do whatever you want, like I did there. I'm ready to do anything. Anything you want! Just help me! Help me!" Irochka was choking with tears.

Jeez! She's hysterical! And where's her husband? Though, what husband? He's gone. She doesn't care about him now. And I'm not feeling better. I would howl with the pack! I would beat my head against the wall. And she's feeling even worse, I bet. There she was, and here she is. She was the most beautiful, passionate, desired, and sexy girl in the world, and she turned in a flash in an ordinary, worthless, and washed-up old woman. Oh, God! She's having withdrawals, like drug-addicts. Clucking! And it's all because if this stupid cow! Fucking snake!»

"Please, Irishka, calm down!" said Krasin, trying to sound confident and firm. "I'm gonna call that sorcerer and find out everything, and then I'll call you back. Alright? Wait for my call. Okay?"

"Alright," sobbed Irochka jerkily.

"Okay, then wait. Stay near the phone."

"But be quick!"

"Okay," said Krasin and hung up the phone.

"So where do I have his number? Shit! It's in the newspaper. And where's the newspaper?" He got scared that the newspaper could be in trash and got coated with cold sweat. "No, here it is! Phew! Well, well."

"Who's this Irishka?" he heard suspicious voice of his wife.

"Shut up," he said coldly, dialing the number.

"What do you mean "shut up?" What freaking Irishka is that? At midnight?"

"I told you to shut up!" said Krasin louder, paused with the phone in his hand, and looked at his wife with a stony stare. "We'll talk later. I need to make an urgent call," he said, dialing the number. His wife went silent.

"Hello!" Krasin nearly screamed when he heard someone pick up the phone.

"Hello, Oleg Viktorovich," said a calm familiar voice.

"Do you know?"

"Sure, I'm completely aware of it. Did I ask you?"

"Yeah," began Krasin, but checked himself, realizing that his explanations were completely useless. "*What's the difference, why? It's over! That ship has sailed. What shall I do?"*

"And what now?" he asked, freezing.

"What now?" asked the man ironically.

"You know, Ira just called me," Krasin began telling him haltingly. "She's got hysterics. She's crying on the phone."

"Yeah, I wouldn't like to be in place of Irina Nikolaevna," the man smiled again, "but I warned you, Oleg Viktorovich. You shouldn't have misused your new talents. Did I warn you? Why did you do that to her?"

"Yes, but," muttered Krasin, "I thought it would be better."

"For whom?" the man paused and, without waiting for Krasin's answer, finished calmly, "Unfortunately, nothing can be done. A second travel is impossible."

"But…"

"All the best, Oleg Viktorovich. Good-night."

Krasin heard short dials. He waited a bit and then dialed another number.

"Yeah?" he heard Irochka's tense voice. "It's you? What's up?

Oh, God! I haven't even said a word, thought Krasin, being amazed with such rush. *Yeah, she's definitely feeling bad. It seems she put balls on her husband and children. She's gone berserk.*

"Ira, I've talked to him," Krasin held his breath, unable to continue. "He says that nothing can be done. A second travel is impossible. I'm sorry that it went like that," he added, not knowing what to say. She was silent. "Hello! Hello! Irisha, do you hear me?" Krasin said in a louder voice.

"Yes. I can hear you," answered the woman in a cold, lifeless voice.

"I..."

"I got it. Bye."

Krasin heard the short dials again. He kept holding the phone for some time and then put it down slowly.

***

Early in the morning of the next day, Krasin came to the familiar door in a building near the bakery. The door opened, and he saw a sleepy old woman.

"Excuse me, I was here yesterday concerning the ad," said Krasin.

"There's no one here," interrupted him the woman rudely. "They moved out."

"When?" asked Krasin in amazement.

"Probably this morning. Or yesterday."

"But I called them last night!"

"I don't know nothing; I'm here just to clean up. I was told that the tenants had moved out, and I had to clean up the apartment."

"I'm sorry," said Krasin.

"It's okay," said the woman indifferently and closed the door.

Krasin waited a little and then went home. Closer to the afternoon, he resolved to call Ira. She must have already got up.

"Hello," he heard the voice of her daughter. "Oh, God! Well, she sounds like Irochka, exactly like her. But her voice is somewhat strange today."

"Can I talk to Irina Nikolaevna?"

"Who's asking?"

"A friend of hers. I called her on Friday."

"You know, she," her voice trembled, "died."

"What do you mean 'died'?" asked Krasin in astonishment. "When?"

"During the night. She got poisoned with sleeping pills."

Holy Mother of God!

"I'm sorry. Accept my sympathies," said Krasin quietly and hung up the phone. He sat for some time, staring blindly in front of him, then stood up slowly, approached the window and leaned on the glass with his forehead. There was a book on the window-sill.

Antoine de Saint-Exupery. "The Little Prince." It was probably his daughter's. He automatically took and opened it.

"We are responsible for those whom we tamed," he saw the underlined phrase. Krasin threw his head back and bit his lip so it bled. Tears poured down his face. "But I didn't want that! I didn't want that! I didn't know! I'm sorry, Irochka! I'm sorry! I didn't know, what I was doing! I just meant well… I meant well! I meant well!"

"For whom?" he seemed to hear the mocking question of the damned sorcerer, "For whom!"

And Lucifer was ask'd by His Son:
— Whence did the soul of that woman go: to hell, 'r to Elysium?
And Lucifer answer'd to His Son:
— To hell.
And Lucifer was ask'd by His Son:
— Wherefore?
And Lucifer answer'd to His Son:
— F'r she is not need'd in Elysium.
And Lucifer's Son said thoughtfully:
— I don't deem it fair...

LUCIFER'S SON. Day 6.

And the sixth day came.

And Lucifer was ask'd by His Son:
— 'Tis said: let the dead inurn the dead. What dost it cullionly?
And Lucifer answer'd to His Son:
— I shall bewray thee.

GIFT.

"Blessed are they that mourn: for they shall be comforted"
Gospel of Matthew.

1.

Ilya was sitting on a bench in a hospital yard. He was staring bluntly in front of him in a complete prostration. The sentence that he had just heard was still in his ears, "About ten days, no more." According to the firm conclusion of the doctor, this was all the time that his wife had.

He was recalling a completely unreal nightmare of the last days; he got a call and was told that his wife had been hit by a car and that she was in Sklifosofsky institute. He remembered very well the feeling of total disaster that filled him. The world shook. If she dies… Ilya couldn't even imagine that. He married for love, he loved his wife, and he loved her very much; well, maybe not like an exalted, romantic hero of a TV show, but he loved as much as he could. At any rate, he couldn't imagine his life without her. The very thought that… he shrank and froze inside. How could she not be? *It's impossible. It's just impossible!"*

And now…'ten days at most?' What did the doctor say? 'Medicine is helpless. Try to consult psychics. Maybe, they would help you. Here, call this number. Tell them that I sent you.'

Ilya was eager to consult anyone. A psychic, a devil, or even a demon! But it's all nonsense, all these psychics. He never believed in them and even teased those who tried to tell him about them. And now he was going to call them. However, he didn't care about logic. He was ready to believe anything, if there was a single chance, the only one. One chance out of a million or a billion—he would make a call. He would call a psychic, a Yakut shaman, Dalai Lama, or even Pope. Anyone! If there's a smallest chance, the tiniest chance that it would help his Natashenka! He will make the call!

Ilya startled, reached into his pocket, took out his Nokia and a paper with the number, and started dialing the number quickly. The realization that he was doing something gave him relief. He heard long dials. If only he were at home!

"Hello!"

"Hi! Stanislav Yurievich?"

"Yeah," answered the man.

"I'm from Vartan Eduardovich. He told me that I could call you. I've got," Ilya faltered and swallowed, "my wife… she's…"

"I see, I see," interrupted him the man. "Have you got a pen?"

"Yeah, just a moment," said Ilya hastily, grabbing the pen. "Yeah, I'm ready."

"Alright, then write down the number," the man on the other side of the line started dictating the address.

Ilya wrote it down carefully on the same paper with the number. There was still much space left on it.

"Got it?"

"Yes."

"When can you be there?"

"Right now!"

"Then I'm waiting for you. How much time do you need?"

"About two hours."

"Alright, then see you in two hours. Bye!"

"Good-bye," said Ilya and ended the call.

.

***

Ilya came to the designated place in one and a half hours. He called from the outside and said that he was already there. "Should I go in or wait here for half an hour?"

"Come up, come up," invited him the psychic kindly.

Ilya entered the building and took the elevator to the ninth floor. Nobody opened the door for some time. Ilya even began to doubt that he had the right apartment; maybe he had written down the wrong address? When the door opened at last, on the doorstep he saw a girl about twelve years old.

"Is Daddy at home?" asked her Ilya in embarrassment. She's probably his daughter.

"Yes, come on in. Daddy, you've got a visitor!" she called.

Out of the room, there came a man with a phone in his hand who beckoned Ilya. Ilya entered.

Still talking on the phone, the man pointed to the chair, standing lonely near the table which had obviously been put there for Ilya. Ilya sat down.

The man finished the conversation quickly.

"Yeah, alright. Okay, bye. I'm gonna call you," and, smiling cordially, he said to Ilya, "Ilya?"

"Yes," confirmed Ilya.

"I'm listening to you."

Ilya began his story. It was not easy. There was a lump in his throat which was hindering him, so Ilya would pause from time to time, heave a sigh, and only then continue. However, the man was listening to him very attentively without interrupting.

"You see," Ilya swallowed. "Recently my wife was hit by a car; it was on Friday. Her internal organs are seriously injured, she's got a ruptured spleen," he yawned nervously, "numerous fractures, concussion of the brain," he yawned again. "Here, look at the diagnosis," Ilya gave the man a paper that he brought with him. The man took it, ran through it with his eyes, and looked at Ilya again, offering him to continue.

"Doctors say that she's got only ten days," whispered Ilya coarsely. He inhaled some air with a hiss, exhaled slowly, and continued after a pause. "Vartan Eduardovich advised me to see you."

Ilya was staring at the psychic and waiting for an answer. Actually, he didn't know what he wanted, what answer he wanted. He seemed not to believe him, not to believe in all those miracles, and, at the same time, he wanted badly that he would help him. He wanted him to say, "Yes, I can do it! Your wife just has a disturbed karma, so we're gonna recover it, and your wife will get well!" Or something else of that kind, something similar. That is the nature of man. When something's wrong, he's grasping at a straw.

The man paused, staring at Ilya, and then said slowly, "I can help you." Ilya caught his breath.

"My wife isn't gonna die?" he asked with his lips only, feeling a desperate and reckless hope waking up in his soul, believing and not believing it at the same time.

"No, she won't die," answered the psychic calmly, still staring at Ilya, "not until you want it."

"What do you mean, 'not until I want it?'" asked Ilya, embarrassed.

"I can arrange for you to be able to control inner wattage of your relatives—your wife, mother. You will be able to retain their inner energy as long as you want. Simply put, you can keep a person alive."

"I'm not getting it," Ilya shook his head "So Natasha isn't gonna die?"

"No."

"And she's going to get better?"

"No, she's not. The decay process will simply stabilize on a certain level. And it's impossible to foresee what level it would be. Maybe she won't be able to walk. Maybe she will walk, but she'll have some serious disease. I can't tell you anything now. Her current insignificant life energy will simply be redistributed optimally, so it will sustain the activity of her organism. Well, her brain, most likely, will function fully; I looked at the diagnosis—there're no organic injuries—but the rest… Most likely, she'll be bedridden. Maybe not completely, but something like that. By the way, she won't have any children, so keep that in mind!"

"I'll take it," Ilya interrupted the man.

"Wait, wait! Listen to the very end," he lifted his hand. "So, thus you'll be able to sustain life in any person. In your parents… well, in anyone you want. Whether they live or die will depend completely on you. Do you understand me?" the man looked at Ilya in a strange way.

"Yes, sure," he looked back at him, being surprised a little. *Why is he looking at me like this? If everything's like he's telling me, saving lives of my relatives? There's nothing to think about.*

"Alright," said the man after a pause. He was staring at Ilya with an almost basilisk look. Ilya felt ill at ease. "I feel that you really want that now. Great! Then we'll do the following. I'm going to hold a ceremony of your initiation, and you're going to feel what it is. You're going to feel this gift for a moment. But it will depend on you whether it will be developed in you. It will depend on your wish. If it's not developed within 24 hours from the moment of initiation, it will mean that the seed died. Now it's," the man glanced at a watch, "ten to three. If, at this time tomorrow, you don't feel the awakening of the gift, it will never develop in you. It will be the end. Do you understand me?" he asked Ilya.

"Not completely," answered Ilya in embarrassment. He was a bit lost in all these "awaken—not awaken," "wish—not wish." "So, I should feel something tomorrow at three? Did I get you right?"

"Exactly," the man nodded.

"But it's possible that I won't feel anything, right? So, it may work out or it may not?"

"Yes."

"And what does it depend on?"

"It depends on you only, whether you want it to happen and the gift to awaken."

"But I do want that! I told you that!" Ilya stood up in excitement.

"You want it now. And there's still time until tomorrow. Maybe you're going to change your mind."

"No, I will not!" Ilya nearly shouted.

"Well, if you don't change your mind, it will be great. Why are you worrying so much?" said the man apologetically. "I repeat—everything's going to depend on you only. So close your eyes, relax and try not to think about anything."

Ilya closed his eyes obediently. The man started muttering, and Ilya suddenly felt that something happened to him. Something changed in him for a moment. For an infinitely small moment, he could feel the gift that the psychic had spoken of. Like a woman who feels her child move for the first time. He couldn't describe or explain to himself what he felt, but he definitely felt something. Now he knew that it was true. All that he had been told was true. He really was able to save Natasha. And that was the most important thing. Everything else didn't matter. And all these psychological mindsets, "If You want it," that wasn't really for him. That was nonsense. He was troubled a little by the fact that he didn't understand the sense of the problem. *What does it mean, 'you won't want it?' I won't want to save the most close and beloved person? Why? What is this nonsense?*

2.

Ilya was literally flying home. He felt a great load off his mind, the load that had been there for several recent days. The world was again in color. *Natasha is not going to die! She's going to live! I will save her! I will!*

He was overwhelmed with emotions. He wanted to do something. He wanted to save everyone at once, make them happy. He imagined how he would tell his mother and Natasha's mother about his gift and laughed with joy. They probably won't believe him. *No, they will. They will see Natasha's diagnosis, and they will believe it. How would one not believe it? By the way, Natasha's mom strongly believes in psychics. It doesn't matter; they will believe it. I'm going to hear a lot of moans and sighs when they find out everything.*

The fact that he should wait until tomorrow was unbearable. In order to release his raging energy and occupy himself, Ilya started the full-scale cleaning of his apartment. He was sweeping and vacuum-cleaning. He defrosted the fridge and washed all the dishes. In a middle of cleaning up the phone rang. Ilya, who was busy with the fridge at the time, wiped his hands quickly and rushed to the phone.

"Hello!"

"Hello, Ilyushenka, it's me," he heard his mother's voice "How's everything? Have you been to the hospital? Why haven't you called me?"

"Oh! Hi, Mom. I have."

"And what did they tell you?"

Ilya faltered. He didn't want to lie. But, on the other hand, what should he tell her? About the psychic? She won't believe him. She would think that he's gone crazy out of grief. And Ilya was rather superstitious. He didn't want to tell her beforehand; he didn't want to jinx it and to scare off fate. He had got nothing yet.

And when it's going to be in me, when it's going to awaken tomorrow, then I'll tell her. And for now, it's better to touch wood. For luck. Just in case.

"They said that there are still some concerns," he said after a pause, forcing himself to speak. "Tomorrow, in the afternoon, everything will be clear."

"But what are the doctors saying?" asked his mother again, worried. "How did the surgery go? Why do I have do force the words out of you?"

"Well, tomorrow, everything will be clear; I told you," answered Ilya with slight irritation, "Most likely, she'll live," he added, unable to restrain himself.

"So, is she going to recover?" asked his mother cautiously. The pause before the last word was barely noticeable, but Ilya caught it. For some reason, he felt his irritation grow stronger.

"I didn't say that she would recover," he said almost rudely. "I said that she would live."

"So, she's going to be an invalid for the rest of her life?" his mother asked even more cautiously.

"Mom! What are you talking about?" shouted Ilya in irritation. "We don't even know if she is going to live. Do you get it? Why does it matter whether she will be an invalid or not? She could possibly die! Don't you understand that?"

"Sure, I do, I do understand that! Calm down, Ilyusha, don't worry," his mother backed down at once and began comforting him. "I know how difficult it is for you. How do you feel?"

"Alright," he grumbled almost calmly.

"Has Vera Ivanovna called you?" Vera Ivanovna, Natasha's mother, lived in another city.

"No."

"Well, she's probably going to call you. Say hello to her for me."

"Okay," answered Ilya reluctantly. For some reason, he wished to end the conversation as quickly as possible. "Alright, Mom, I'm in a middle of full-scale cleaning. I'm defrosting the fridge. Let's talk tomorrow. I'll let you know if there is any news."

"Call me at once, as soon as you find out anything. I'm going to be worried."

"Alright, alright! I will call you as soon as I leave the hospital," Ilya's voice rose to a shriek again. "I won't forget it!"

"All right, then, Ilyusha! Calm down, don't shout. Are you really okay?" asked his mother anxiously. "Maybe I should come to you?"

"No! Don't come here!" Ilya almost shouted again. That's the limit. "I'm feeling absolutely normal. Alright, we'll talk tomorrow. The fridge is dripping ."

"Well, alright, alright. Don't forget to call tomorrow!"

"I won't!" Ilya hurled down the phone in rage. His perfect mood was gone. The conversation with his mother left a strange, heavy, and unpleasant feeling. He couldn't understand it and find out what was the reason of it. It seemed they just had a usual conversation.

Having cleaned up, Ilya turned on the TV at full sound. Until the dead of night, he sat and stared bluntly and thoughtlessly at the shimmering blue square screen. He seemed to be trying to escape the thoughts and questions that were growing in him and scaring him and which he didn't want to be thinking about. He switched off the phone wisely, right after the conversation with his mother. He didn't know why he would do that. To be precise, he didn't want to know. He pretended not to know. He preferred not to ask himself that question, as well as many others. He felt that this ostrich behavior, the attempt to hide head in the sand and not see anything or think about anything, was foolish, shortsighted, and very offensive for himself.—Is he afraid? Is he afraid to face the truth? What's wrong?—but he couldn't help it. He was afraid, indeed. He was afraid to think. He was afraid of himself. If only tomorrow would come sooner!

3.

Ilya turned off the TV about four in the morning and went to bed. He didn't normally go to sleep so late—or so early—so he was hoping that the fatigue would do its job, and he'd fall asleep at once and that he would sleep until twelve or even until one in the afternoon. And then he would wash up, have breakfast, and it would be three already. However, his expectations didn't prove true. He couldn't fall asleep. As soon as he lay down, the thoughts which he had been drawing away came at him from all sides.

Indeed, what if she, he was somehow avoiding calling his wife by her name in his thoughts, *"is going to be an invalid for the rest of her life? Bedridden? Well, not if, but for sure. She's in such a condition that she has almost no life energy left. All I can do is to redistribute it, so she would have a half-vegetative life. Eating, drinking and other stuff. By the way, about other stuff; most likely, she's gonna soil herself.*

Ilya never liked to think about such earthbound topics; it was unpleasant for him, like it was for any man, but now was not the time for disgust and sentiments. *Like it or not, but someone would need to clean up after her. There is no way out. Surely Mom is going to help me, but she can't live here. And I don't want it.* At any rate, he didn't want it until now. They wanted to live separate from parents.

Oh, dear God! Should I hire a nurse? And where would I get the money for her? And I'm going to need not one nurse, but how many of them? Three nurses, right. Yeah, one for an eight-hour shift or a day here and two days off. Or even four nurses? Well, all in all, it's clear. I won't be able to make so much money. And will I have any money at all?"

He'll have to quit his job and look for some homeworking, right? It's still not clear. And where would he look for such a job? It was hard enough to find a usual job. Unemployment rate is rather high.

Alright, then! If I eventually deal with financial problems, my and her parents will help him. I've got some money in stock, though, what stock? It wouldn't be enough for the whole life, but it doesn't matter. Let's assume that I'll be able to make a living. But just make a living; that's it. I may give up on life. I may give up on career, plans, and perspectives—on everything. Even on family and children. What family are we talking about! What children?

From now on my life will look like tending her. Struggle for existence. Forever, by the way. Until the end of her days.

The thought gave Ilya shivers. His future started to look more and more desperate. It looked more and more hopeless. The most unpleasant was the fact that he turned out to be not the man that he considered himself to be his whole life. He was not so noble, good, kind, sincere, and honest. It was bitter to realize, but he had nowhere to turn. He had to acknowledge the obvious. A noble person would never have such mean thoughts. He would just do what he needed to without a word. He wouldn't leave a loved one in the lurch.

Right, thought Ilya in anger. *Noble! I used to think until now that I was noble, and it turned out otherwise when life nailed me. How did I come to this? I just hate to look at myself. I turn out to be a selfish rabble. And no, not like this. These filthy thoughts about my bitter fate do not reflect well on me, that's true. But still, it's not that simple. If Natashka had become an invalid after a car accident, I probably would have been tending her the rest of my life without a word. I'd have been changing potties. But that's different; that's God's will. First, you do not have a choice in this situation; a tragedy struck you, and that's it. Nobody would ask you if you like it or not; and, second, as they say, God giveth and God taketh away. This situation may be solved in a natural way, with the death of the sick. God decides whether a person lives or dies.*

But here I am, the one who decides; I decide. I take over the functions of God. And I'm just a human. A human! This burden is too heavy for me. What can I decide? Can I kill the loved one, can I kill my dear wife? Can I let her die, knowing that I can prevent it, that I can prevent her death, that I can help her. Can I? Can I? It's clear that I can't. I can't do a freaking thing. Otherwise, how would I live with that? And, oh, God! My parents—they're gonna live forever, too. Sick and feeble, but they're not going to die. As long as I live, I won't let it happen.

Suddenly, Ilya was covered with cold sweat and even sat down on the bed, being terrified. He remembered that mother of one of his friends had died of cancer. She had been all swollen and scary and hadn't left the bed.

Surely my mother would be in such condition one day, too. But she's not gonna die, because I'll be able to stabilize the process and stop the decay of the organism on the last stage of the disease.

During the moment when the psychic was doing his passes in front of Ilya, initiating his gift, he managed to realize that he couldn't work with a healthy organism, only with sick one. And only with organisms in last stages of the disease, when a person doesn't have any more life energy left. That was probably because it's easier to control such small flows of energy. He couldn't control large flows. He couldn't help his mother while she was healthy.

So Mom will get sick, Ilya looked around wildly. *What's wrong with me? What am I thinking about?* But he couldn't stop. *Her condition will become terrible, but I won't let her die. She will live forever, swollen and horrible, until my death. And Daddy as well... And Natashka... I will go crazy! This very thought is turning me crazy! I'm shivering! I don't want Mom and Dad to die, do I? I don't wish death on them, do I? Of course not. So, they're not going to die!*

It's a curse, not a gift; it's a devilish trap. It seems that everything's in your power, you can make decisions on your own, but, as a matter of fact, you're cornered. What can you decide? You're not God; you can't handle death and life. You can't take the life of your loved one.

Finally, Ilya feel asleep at eight. He was seeing nightmares: his mother and father, deformed and swollen, and his bloodstained wife with broken bones that stuck out of her body. They all were limping towards him slowly and reaching their hands, and he wanted to run away! run away from them, but, as it usually is in dreams, couldn't move at all. They were closer… closer… Ilya screamed and woke up.

The clock said four. Ilya was carefully listening to his senses. Well? Nothing. The gift didn't awaken. Ilya got up, yawned, and went to the bathroom. He was at ease and free, like a man who had just escaped a great danger.

And Lucifer was ask'd by His Son:

— Is it hard to lose the lov'd ones and cater-cousins?

And Lucifer answer'd His Son thoughtfully:

— Aye.

And his son again saw a flash, and he was clad again in black armor, sitting on a horse. And he saw the same plain, and the same sharply white endless ranks ahead. But anon all space between him and those ranks was cover'd with heaps of bodies in white arm'r. Thither wast a lot of bodies, and they cover'd the ground as far as eye couldst see.

He lift'd his left arm, bent in the elbow, and the bird, which was sitting on his shoulder, jump'd clumsily to his gauntlet. The raven was wound'd. Its wing was broken, and the left clutch was almost severed, dangling on a piece of skin. He look'd ov'r a bird and breath'd softly—and the wounds wast healed, and the bones wast grown together. But the raven need'd time to heal completely.

He put the bird on his shoulder again and, paying nay he'd to the endless ranks, that froze in front of him with numerous spears, jump'd off the horse lightly, bent ov'r to the dog and patt'd its mazzard. the dog yelp'd with pleasure and wagg'd his tail-stump. 'Twas injur'd badly as well. Very badly. yea more, than the bird. They wouldn't last another hurlyburly.

A horse... and... a wound... another one... and another chopp'd wound...

Then he turn'd aroint from the ranks and went but soft aroint, leading the horse. The bird was on his shoulder, and the dog ran at his side. The angelic horns blew a clear melody in the back, signaling the attack. Abrupt orders couldst be heard. But the ranks didn't move, and nay warri'r rush'd fia.

Hearing these sounds behind him, he halt'd f'r a moment and turn'd but soft back. The horns and shouts di'd aroint. Thither was dead silence above the field. The ranks wast fill'd with terror, and they stagger'd back and shook under his unwinking stare.

Lucifer linger'd f'r another moment, then turn'd aroint and went aroint but soft and deliberately, surround'd by the ringing silence.

LUCIFER'S SON. DAY 7.

And the seventh day came.

And Lucifer was ask'd by His Son:

— 'Tis said, "Either make the tree good, and its fruit good; 'r make the tree bad, and its fruit bad; f'r the tree is known by its fruit." Is it so?

And Lucifer answer'd His Son:

— What doth thou deem good and bad? That is the main problem.

SPELL.

"I find more bitter than death the woman
who is a snare, whose heart is a trap and
whose hand are chains."
Ecclesiastes

SATURDAY.

From PR to x13: Hello, x13!

So what? Did you try to contact them?

From x13 to PR: Hello, PR! Yeah, I was up all night! I'm pissed off by the time difference. Moreover, I don't know the language that well. I write as I understand it. If I don't get anything, I put it in brackets.

A human is like a drop in the ocean of other humans. The ocean is huge, and the drop is small. Its energy is small compared to the energy of the whole ocean. That's why all that happens to a certain human, all fluctuations inside the drop, influence only the nearest environment—the adjacent drops. And then these fluctuations are extinguished, and they fade away.

That is only clear and natural. But the ocean, like any other system, has so called resonating frequencies. And when the drop starts fluctuating in these resonating frequencies, its fluctuations do not fade away, but are strengthened, and they pierce the whole ocean, as if reality adjusts to them, or, rather, they adjust the reality to themselves.

That is the mechanism of influence of the great people—Alexander the Great, Caesar, Napoleon; the actions of one human, the fluctuations of one small drop with a tiny amount of energy, compared to the whole ocean, have the colossal influence on the whole ocean. These are the fluctuations in the resonating frequencies.

So, the spell of happiness changes something inside you [I didn't get everything clearly here—some "inner essence," or what?] and switches your frequencies to the resonating ones. That is, from now on the reality [world] will adjust to you.

Well, maybe, you're not going to become Alexander the Great—the adjustment is not precise—but, still, from now on, all your actions will influence not only the adjacent drops, but the huge layers of water around you. And it's more than enough to make you happy. You will be able to influence the reality actively.

Something of that sort. And they wrote that the spell is very dangerous, and one must be extremely careful with it. But it was 6 a.m. there, and I couldn't think straight, so I didn't find out anything about it. Why is it dangerous? What's that exactly about?

From PR to x13: So, when are you going to contact them?

From x13 to PR: Not earlier than Monday night. They don't usually work on week-ends.

From PR to x13: And did they send you the spell?

From x13 to PR: Yeah. A sound file.

From PR to x13: Did you listen to it?

From x13 to PR: Yeah. It has strange words in strange language, with pauses. One must repeat them distinctly. That is, a word, and then a pause. During the pause, you should repeat the word precisely. Well, you should try to reproduce it.

From PR to x13: Did you try it?

From x13 to PR: Do I look like an idiot? No, these games are not for me. Hell with them!

From PR to x13: Do you believe in it?

From x13 to PR: I don't know.

From PR to x13: So, you won't go for it?

From x13 to PR: What?

From PR to x13: For the reading of the spell.

From x13 to PR: No.

From PR to x13: At all?

From x13 to PR: No.

From PR to x13: Why not? It's the happiness spell. Don't you want to be happy?

From x13 to PR: I'm pretty fine without the spell.

From PR to x13: Alright, then send me the file with the spell. I'm looking forward to hearing it.

From x13 to PR: Okay. Are you going to read it?

From PR to x13: I'm not sure. Maybe not. I'm going to wait until Tuesday and find out about the warning. I'm not sure.

From x13 to PR (5 minutes later): Got it? Everything okay?

From PR to x13" Yeah. Everything's alright. Thanks. Speak to you on Tuesday. What are you going to do on the weekend?

From x13 to PR: I don't know yet. Probably I'll go to the summer cottage. And you?

From PR to x13: I don't know either. I'll stay at home. Got a lot of work to do. Okay, bye.

From x13 to PR: Bye-bye!

TUESDAY

From PR to x13: Hello! How are you? How was your weekend?

From x13 to PR: Hello, PR! Same as always. I stayed at home. And yours?

From PR to x13: The same. Did you contact them?

From x13 to PR: No, they've got problems with the server. There's a notice on the site that they will be back at the end of the week.

From PR to x13: Shit! So, we must wait until the end of the week?

From x13 to PR: What's the problem?

From PR to x13: What's the problem? I wanted to read their warning concerning the spell.

From x13 to PR: Did you listen to it?

From PR to x13: Sure, I did! About ten times, I think.

From x13 to PR: And?

From PR to x13: It's gibberish. Nonsense!

From x13 to PR: So why did you listen to it 10 times?

From PR to x13: I don't know. It seems as if you're looking into an abyss. You know that you shouldn't, but you can't help it. You can hardly keep from doing that, as if someone's pushing you: come on, say it!

From x13 to PR: So say it. You think that it's nonsense, anyway.

From PR to x13: Right! It's nonsense, but still, I'm afraid. The deuce knows!

From x13 to PR: Exactly! So wait until the end of the week, until they get back.

From PR to x13: Alright. Speak to you tomorrow.

From x13 to PR: Okay. Bye-bye!

WEDNESDAY

From PR to x13: Hello! I couldn't help but read the spell.

From x13 to PR: Hello, PR! Really? When?

From PR to x13: Just now. A minute ago, before I wrote you.

From x13 to PR: So? Are you already happy?

From PR to x13: You bet!

From x13 to PR: Well, well! Listen, I'm very busy. Let's speak at the end of the week, when their site starts working again. I really have a lot to do. A lot!

From PR to x13: Oh! The reality is already changing! It's nice to know that someone else is busy!

From x13 to PR: Okay, enough of these self-made jokes! I have to go. Bye-bye!

From PR to x13: Alright, alright! Go back to work. Bye.

SATURDAY

From PR to x13: Hello! Where are you? Are you up? Are they working already?

From x13 to PR: Hello, PR! Up? I've been as busy as a bee since morning! Working hard. Unlike some happy fellows who, as it appears, take no account of time, and sleep until 2 p.m.

From PR to x13: Hey, stop pulling my leg! A bee! Tell me, did you contact them?

From x13 to PR: Yes, I did, I did! Hey, mind your tone! Do you think that you can give me orders now, when you're producing a wave on a resonating frequency? Okay, I'm kidding! So, I contacted them and asked them to send the warning like you told me. And I added that one of my friends had read it. By the way, they took it seriously and asked a lot of questions. Who are you? How old are you? What do you do? When did you read it? And so on. Well, I actually don't know anything about you. And I wouldn't tell them anything behind your back, anyway. In one word, they sent me a rather long questionnaire. I'm gonna send it over to you, and you should answer these questions. I'm gonna give you their e-mail. Okay?

P.S. Rather interesting questions, mind you! At any rate, some of them. They said, if you don't want to answer, just put a dash.

From PR to x13: Okay, send it over. And the warning?

From x13 to PR: They said, considering that you have already read it, the warnings are useless. They could make it even worse. It's impossible to change anything now. You just have to see how the spell begins to influence you.

From PR to x13: And how would I see that?

From x13 to PR: They asked to keep track of everything that's happening with you and tell them about all events in detail. Well, they want to observe you as if you were a patient in a hospital. They want to observe your health.

From PR to x13: By the way, concerning health. I've been a bit sick for the last few days. I'm feeling… tired… I'm not really sure. I just want to stay in bed. So just send me the questionnaire, and we'll talk tomorrow. I'm gonna lie down. I mean, we'll talk on Tuesday.

From x13 to PR: Okay, go down on someone, if you want! I'm kidding! Alright, take rest. Have a drink or something. Bye-bye!

P.S. It appears that happy people may get sick, too! Well, well! Who could have thought?

From PR to x13: Bye. Talk to you on Tuesday. Don't forget about the questionnaire. E-mail from box@pr.ru to letter@magia.xx

Name:Pavel

Surname:Rostotsky

Age: 38

Date and time of birth:July 17th, about 12 p.m.

Monthly income: (below \$1,000, \$1,000-10,000, \$10,000-50,000, more than \$50,000) (underline as necessary)

Profession: Businessman

Marital status: Married

Children: No

Age of wife: 19

Is your wife beautiful? no, beautiful, very beautiful

How many times a week do you have sex with your wife? ________

How many times during the night can you have coitus? ________

What is the average length of your coitus?________

Does your wife usually have orgasm during the coitus? ________

Are you satisfied with your sexual life? no, yes, I don't know

Is your wife satisfied with her sexual life? I think, no; I think, yes; I don't know

Do you have a lover? no, yes

Do you want to have a lover? No, yes

< more than 100 questions following >

TUESDAY

From x13 to PR: Hello, PR! How are you feeling? Look, I'm pissed off by them, by these warlocks. They want to know how you're doing. I told them that you're sick, so they went insane! They asked me to contact you immediately and ask you how you're doing. I just can't understand what's going on. You read the spell of happiness, right—the resonating frequencies and stuff? So, where is it? Where is happiness? Maybe you're going through adaptation?

P.S. They received your questionnaire. Everything's okay.

From PR to x13:Hello! You're surprisingly early today. How am I feeling? Frankly speaking, it sucks. I'm sick, and that is no joke. I'm weak, and my head is dizzy. I've never experienced anything like this. I'm staying in bed all the time—and not going down on anyone! My wife's worrying. She's staying by my side. I already had 10 doctors visit me, but there's no result. No fever, nothing. They say that it may be over-fatigue. So, it's unclear. It seems that the cursed spell really got to me. It's nonsense! I'm worrying about my wife. Poor woman, she's… Well, alright. Contact those warlocks and ask them what to do. I need them to remove their voodoo. Maybe I read the spell in a wrong way, and it's influencing me in the way it shouldn't? In one word, they have to do something! Why the hell did I read it at all? Everything was great in my life. I just lived and… The best is the enemy of the good, and that is true. See, he wanted more happiness. From the warlocks. On the resonating frequencies. Alexander the Great! Gaius Julius Caesar! So, you must contact them immediately! They must do something! They make everything as it was. I'm no Caesar, like Ostap Bender was no Count of Monte-Cristo. It's high time to retrain as a house-manager.

From x13 to PR (15 minutes later): I wrote them everything in detail—about your health and wishes—and that you want the spell to be removed. They told that they're gonna have a council, and the answer will be tomorrow. So you should wait. Well, maybe you should consult other doctors? I don't really know what to advise you. Cheer up! I will tell you tomorrow, as soon as I receive a message from them. Deal? Talk to you tomorrow. Cheer up. Bye-bye!

From PR to x13: Alright, got it. Talk to you tomorrow. Bye.

WEDNESDAY.

From x13 to PR: Hello, PR! I just received a message from the site. I translated it quickly, and here it is. No comments. It's up to you to decide. I can't help you here.

P.S. Translation is a bit clumsy—for you to know. I was in a hurry; the letter is rather long, and I've got no time to edit it.

Dear Mr. Rostotsky,

We studied your questionnaire and the whole situation attentively. We deeply regret that you read the spell of happiness without previous consultation. If you did that, it would be possible to avoid the current problems. Nevertheless, we must face the present situation.

It's very unpleasant for us to say things that may upset and aggrieve you, but we have to do it, for the situation is very serious. We count on your reason and good sense, and we are sure that you will understand with what you are going to read now. Briefly speaking, your problem is that you love your wife, and she, as it appears, doesn't love you. Surely, that is only our guess, but, frankly speaking, the answers that you kindly sent us, confirm it completely. Actually, your situation is ordinary and common.

You are rich, and your wife, as you wrote, is very beautiful and younger than you. Don't you think that, if you were not so rich, you wouldn't be able to find such a young and beautiful wife? In other words, it's unlikely that she married you for love, and it's more than likely that it was just a marriage with an eye to your fortune. You must agree that this guess comes easy. Your problem is that you really love your wife. And when one loves someone, one wants his beloved to feel good. That is the happiness.

In other words, you change the reality that surrounds you, so your beloved would feel as good as possible. You try to fulfill all her subconscious dreams. And her subconscious dream is that you wouldn't exist. That she would be rich and free. We emphasize that it is her subconscious wish. Your wife may be a very good woman, and, probably, she doesn't wish you anything bad consciously. And if you told her that, she would be scared and even offended. However, one cannot resist nature. She doesn't love you. And, like any other human, she wants to love someone and to be happy, and you are an obstacle for her.

These problems are commonly found in many families, but, in ordinary life, the subconscious wishes are suppressed and unrealized. But, having uttered the spell of happiness, you involuntarily lifted the lid and started the mechanism of realization. That is the main danger that we wrote your friend of and which you have neglected, being eager to utter the spell. You said that doctors can't find the reason for your disease, and that your wife is worried and doesn't leave your side. It means only that she's really a good person, and she doesn't wish you anything bad consciously.

Subconsciously, she wants you die not from some terrible cancer or AIDS, with pain and torments, but that fade quietly, go away from her life, die on her hands, blessing her before death; and she would tend you selflessly, without sleep and denying everything to herself. And everybody around her would sympathize with her and be delighted with her big heart and her strong love. And she would be honest to herself. She would have done all that she could. All that a man can do.

We deliberately describe everything so roughly and cynically, but the situation is really very serious, and you shouldn't indulge in illusions. If nothing changes, the end may be very bad for you. The process will develop very quickly and with growing speed, for your wife felt that her secret dreams may come true, her freedom is close, and this feeling of freedom makes the suppressed wishes stronger, the mechanism of their realization, that you have started, continues working—you're feeling worse, the proximity of the freedom becomes stronger etc. Well, it's a classic example of the feedback. Figuratively speaking, a snake bites its tail.

What is to be done? It's impossible to lift the spell. The problem would be solved if you ceased to love your wife or if your wife would fall in love with You. Unfortunately, it's impossible to fall in love or cease to love on order. Actually, we may advise you to exclude your wife from your will; thus, she would be afraid to lose you and remain with nothing, but, in this case, it's useless as well. It would just make things worse. First, as you love her, you probably won't be able to do this; second, as long as you love her, everything would be in her favor, and she would make you change the will, and after that, she would wish your death all the more, but now, probably consciously. Now that you're capable of such things. She's thinking about you all the time, she's tending you and doing everything for you—and, in acknowledgement of all that, you would leave her without bread and butter. Why did you get married then? And you must agree that she would be right, in a way. She doesn't wish you anything bad consciously. She doesn't know what she's doing.

Now, when you understand, as we hope, all seriousness and tragedy of the situation, let's sum up. Our resume. As long as the spell is in force, it's impossible to do anything. Whatever you do, everything would turn against you. That means that you don't have much time. Let's call it like it is.

You must immediately leave your wife and go as far from her as you can in terms of distance, to the other side of the world. You are rich, and it wouldn't be difficult for you. After you have read this letter, buy a plane ticket and leave at once. We are not sure if you would make it; maybe the car breaks, or you're late for the flight, but that's your only chance. Maybe the spell would be weaker when you're far from her. For even on the resonating frequencies, your fluctuations of your drop have a limited sphere of influence, not the whole ocean. This sphere is huge, compared to an ordinary person, but it is still limited.

All in all, leave at once—now. And when you're far from your wife, you will be able to heal, and then you'll decide what to do next. Don't lose a moment! Maybe every day counts, or every hour! It is a very strong spell. Everything may happen very quickly.

With sincere respect, wishing success and good health, MAGIA.

Listen, what are you going to do? Write me as soon as you can. Do you need help to make ticket reservation or anything else? Maybe you need a ride to the airport. Name it. We're friends, though just virtual friends for now. We can meet in person. So, you must tell me what you need. Don't be shy.

From x13 to PR (10 minutes later):What's wrong? Why are you not responding? Do you want me to make a reservation? Just tell me the destination. Or should I pick up the place myself? Ticket and hotel. I've got money; that's not a problem. I'm not poor, as well. And I can arrange a visa. You can go to Kamchatka; thus, you won't need a visa. It's far from here. Just tell me your personal data, and I will arrange everything. I can even send a car for you, to get you to the airport.

From PR to x13: Thanks for caring. I'm deeply touched. No kidding.

From x13 to PR: So what about a ticket? Will you make a reservation, or should I make it? Do you need help? Don't be shy.

From PR to x13: I'm not flying anywhere.

From x13 to PR: What? Are you out of your mind? Why?

From PR to x13: You know, I can't… I think… It's difficult to explain… Well, I think that, if I leave, I would betray my love. It's impossible to leave the one you love.

From x13 to PR: Are you an idiot? It's the influence of the spell! It doesn't let you leave her. Aren't you getting it?

From PR to x13: It's not the spell. It's… Maybe, that's the reason. You know, it really works. I was never so happy in my life. It seems as is fate sent me a horrible trial, and I passed it. With honor. My love passed it. I love her, anyway, no matter what. She's happy, and I'm happy as well. If she's unhappy, I will be unhappy, too. Why would I leave her? Why would I hurt her? Why would I torment her?

From x13 to PR: You're thinking so because of the spell! Spell! Spell! Don't give up! Fight! Leave! Leave now! Fight!

From PR to x13: Did you know these verses? I didn't understand them, but now I do:

Oh, God, my end should be like this:
Having tasted all the pain
I want to look outside and wave my hand
When death is on the doorstep.

Probably, a few people can feel it. And the God let me feel it. And I would be forever grateful to him for that. For this is true happiness, the higher happiness. I wish for nothing more.

My Lord, I got it all.
Where should I sign?
I beg you: save me from hatred.
I'm not entitled to it.

That's it. Bye. It's difficult for me to write. The letters are blurred. What was I talking about? Yeah… Hatred… I'm not entitled to hatred. No! Love… Just love… Love only!

From x13 to PR: What's the matter? Answer me! Please, answer! Please.

ONE MONTH LATER

From Romka to x13: Hey, dude! I'm pissed off by your e-mails. There's no PR here. Don't write me anymore! Do you need problems? *Romka.*

And Lucifer was ask'd by His Son:

— Can this woman be blam'd f'r the death of that man?

And Lucifer answer'd His Son:

— Nay. He wish'd f'r happiness—and he receiv'd it. She gave him happiness, she let him die, when he was happy. Thither is nothing moo that one man can doth f'r another one.

LUCIFER'S SON. DAY 8.

And the eighth day came.

And Lucifer said:

— Miracles cannot endure happiness. They violate the harmony of the ordinary. The strong doth not ne'd miracles, and they art hilding f'r the weak.

And Lucifer was ask'd by His Son:

— But don't they help a man to receive what he wants?

And Lucifer answer'd His Son:

— A man cannot receive more than he possesses. If a man dost not possess aught—he dost not deserve it. Everyone receives in life as much as he's worth of. Nothing more n'r less. Winners art not appoint'd. A man wilt become a winner. A wolf cannot be made a pack leader. Otherwise, the wolf and the pack shall die.

SECT.

"Some time later, he fell in love with
a woman in the valley of Sorek whose name
was Delilah."
Book of Judges.

"I found one upright man among a thousand,
but not one upright woman among them all."
Ecclesiastes.

Lucifer's Son

1.

He had a terrible headache. Moreover, he felt sick and was thirsty. Well, everything as usual. The whole package.

Oh, God, I was so drunk yesterday, though Igor Rudnikov sadly, filling the glass with mineral water and taking out a green pill of aspirin from a pack. *Maybe, I should take two of them?* He hesitated and took out one more after a pause.

Rudnikov swallowed the pills, washed them down, lay back on the pillow, and closed his eyes. Now he should lie still and, what's better, fall asleep. That would be perfect. So there's a chance that, after he wakes up, he wouldn't have headache. Aspirin is good. It always helps. Especially if you take two pills.

However, he couldn't fall asleep. Oh yeah! Falling asleep. No such luck! He barely dozed off, when the phone rang suddenly.

"Yeah," answered Rudnikov.

"Hello," he heard the drunken voice of Sashka Petrov. "Are you up?"

"Yeah, I am," said Rudnikov with an effort, trying to speak less and quietly. Every word was a blunt prick to his head.

"We've been continuing since the morning," said Petrov merrily. "Come on, we're waiting for you! Where did you go yesterday?"

"No way, I won't come to you!" grimaced Rudnikov. The headache became even stronger. Hell with him and his conversations! "I'm literally dying here."

"Come on! You should cool your coppers. Everything's gonna vanish as if by magic," Sashka laughed on the other side of the line "We'll drink a bit."

"Are you in your mind? I will die, if I get up! Leave me alone, for Christ's sake!"

"Well, you're displaying no team spirit. You don't respect us," summarized Sashka humorously.

"Well, I have a team spirit!" So it began! He could probably take offense while he's drunk!

"You know very well how I take it. For you boozers, it's like water off the duck's back, but I'm gonna be fucking recovering myself for the whole week."

"Well, I see. Yeah, Gari, you're not one of us! Alright, if you change your mind, welcome. We're at Fedorich's place."

"I won't change my mind. I'm gonna be in bed all day, trying to recover. I already took two pills, I got a terrible headache."

"Well, as you wish. We'd be happy to see you," Sashka halted for a moment "Alright, bye," he gave up finally.

"Bye," almost groaned Rudnikov, put down the phone, and poured more mineral water. His head was killing him. *Shit! I should take a third pill. Why did he call? Are they bored there? Can't they live without me? Holy shit! I have no words for that. I haven't felt that way for a long time. I could beat my head against the wall. I have to lie down and be still for fifteen minutes, without thinking. And I should turn that fucking phone off. Why didn't I do it before? I wouldn't have those conversations.*

Rudnikov pulled the cord out of the socket with rage and hurled it on the floor. He somehow calmed down after that. It gave him the feeling of comfort and safety. Now he should just lie down, and he would feel better.

In about fifteen minutes, the headache was gone. The pain began to fade and go away and finally disappeared. Rudnikov was lying for some time and enjoying the absence of pain. He felt good. *Well, aspirin is a nice stuff. It always works.*

He lay down peacefully and without thinking for ten more minutes. Then he became completely sure that the headache was gone. After that, he started to slowly recall the evening of the day before that.

Well, there's nothing to recall! Everything was as usual. We got sloshed with booze. We were very drunk. And the recollections were somewhat snatchy with a lot of gaps and lacunas. He wasn't showing off and wasn't teasing anyone, and thank God! So far, so good. Last time before that he fucking... *It's still embarrassing to recall that. Yuk! Shit! I just blushed. What was I whispering in the ear of that silly girl? Oh-oh-oh! It's good that nobody noticed that. Or maybe someone did. Ah! Alright, forget it! Why should I think about that crap? People do a lot of stuff when they're drunk. I may well forget it. I just shouldn't do anything like this in future. I must remember that I'm a fool and an idiot when drunk. I need to stay away from women, as far away as I can!*

Who knows? You can fucking wake up in the morning, and see an aurora with pink tits. Yuk! Yuk-yuk-yuk! I shouldn't be thinking about that. Everything what I'm thinking about comes true, as if by the book. All fucking disasters! You think about this fuck, and here it is! Right on cue! 'How can I help you! Did you want to see me, master?' What are these silly thoughts? Why am I distracted? What happened yesterday? Something happened, right? I was going to recall it. In other words, I was going not to forget it. So, what?

Rudnikov tried to concentrate.

Well, drinking...drinking...toasts and pep talk...drinking. Pep talk and toasts...drinking...Semin and Tatyana. Well, that's alright. Markin singing... Gap. Drinking again... Another gap. And another... Stop! And here there was something. Well! So, what was it? There was something. Something important...well...important...

So what? What fucking important could be there? I hope I didn't fuck anyone wham-bam? Maybe that is important stuff? God forefend! No, no! Well, so, what? Will I remember it or not in the end? Oh-oh-oh! Conversation with Frolov. The man of the day.

Rudnikov started to recall something obscurely. *Table, ruckus... and drunk*—Frolov is telling him something. *In great secret, drunk secrets. Is he flipping the coin? I don't remember! What does the coin have to do with it? Alright, from the very beginning.*

Well, we're sitting and talking, and he starts boasting. Then a coin... Fuck the coin! What's he saying?"Oh! Yeah, right.

Rudnikov drank some more mineral water and remembered everything at last. He remembered what Frolov was telling him. He was speaking about his current promotion, which they had actually been celebrating the day before that.

"Why do you think they promoted me? For no reason? No! Nothing happens for no reason. This is just the beginning. I joined the sect, and, from now on, everything's gonna be great in my life. Honky-dory! I'm gonna have luck in everything—in everything!"

Right! And then he started flipping the coin to check if he was lucky. Curious! Umph! Very curious! Rudnikov even forgot about his hangover.

What sect? What was he talking about? It is true? A sect? Frolov? Frolov is a sectary? This drunkard? What the hell? On the other hand, he couldn't make this up. First, he was drunk as a skunk, he was dead drunk, too drunk to make such stuff up; and, second, it's actually impossible to make this nonsense up. Umph... Well, is it true? A sect...

Shit! What a nasty condition! My head seems to be stuffed with cotton wool with fucking cuttings. Like Winnie-the-Pooh. 'My head is filled with cuttings...' Yeah, yeah, yeah! It's alright. And such stuff. Yeah, yeah, yeah! So, what was I thinking about? Oh, right, about Frolov. Yeah, yeah, yeah! And such stuff. About sect and sectaries.

His promotion was strange, indeed, by the way. Nobody was expecting that. It was out of the blue. The next moment, he was promoted. What the fuck? Umph... Sect... I wouldn't fucking mind to join such a sect. By the way, I did tell him that. I want to join it. And he gave me a drunk smile and answered that he was a bugger.

Rudnikov recalled the self-contented mug of drunk Frolov and smiled involuntarily. "Bugger."

Laugh if you want, he checked himself, *but compare his salary to yours. And if you're so smart and merry, why are you so poor? Heh? As poor as a fucking church mouse! As our wretched tongue-tied prime-minister with huge brows. An ambassador in Ukraine. I'm curious, who's doing the translation for him into Ukrainian? This serves the khokhols right! That's for Crimea.*

Alright, what was next with this bugger? What interesting stuff did he manage to tell me? But there was nothing more. Then someone came to us, and thus, our interesting conversation ended.

So what? A very strange conversation... Umph...very strange. I'm curious if all the stuff about the sect is true, or is it just the drunk talk? Well, no, it doesn't seem to be the drunk talk. Quite the contrary, it seems that he spilled the beans, and now he's probably regretting that. In case he remembers anything, of course.

Curious...very curious. What kind of sect is that, which could help with the career? Some kind of Masonic lodge, right? Yeah! Why should I care? I don't believe in all that, anyway. Neither in Masons nor in lodges, the devil or demon. Masonic or not, it must be real! They must bring some benefit. You don't wanna fucking join some wretched and poor guys—morons like me, foolish ones who don't have a nickel. Fuck it all! We don't need such sects! I'm poor and miserable like them. I'm fucked up by my light purse. Surely, poverty is no vice, but give it a rest!"

And the main thing is that there's no future—no future at all. That's really terrifying. No connections, no relatives; I've got fucking nothing! Like Luka Mudishchev—The fate gave him a dick, but didn't give anything fucking else!' Same with me... I would join any sect, against my will. I would go to the other side of the world, out of fucking despair and hopelessness. It's like jumping feet first, a swallow dive. What could I lose? What if this is true? As far as I know, masons did exist in all social classes, as well as their lodges. So...heh-heh.... Yeah, people may do a lot of strange stuff when they are bored. Fuck a duck! They may be fooling around a lot. They've got a lot of money, they're bored, so they have nothing better to do.

They're playing children games. Lodges and sectaries. Carnivals and outfit change. Just for the sake of time-killing.

Well, it doesn't hurt to try, as Lavrentiy Palych used to say. Something may come up at any moment. I could meet the right people and stuff. The main thing is to be in the right place at the right time. It seems I said something wrong, no? Eh? Oh-oh! I just can't think straight. Alright, I need some sleep. On Monday, I'm gonna twist Frolov's arm, and he has to introduce me to that sect. Otherwise, I can do it the bad way, if necessary. I can intimidate him, for example. He definitely doesn't remember that he told me anything yesterday. Well, we'll see! I shouldn't think too much about this now. I'll decide later what to do. He won't escape me. He's going to fall in love and get married. And if he doesn't want to do it the bad way, it would be much worse, if we do it the good way!"

"That's it! I need to sleep! Sleep, sleep, sleep..."

2.

First thing on Monday, Rudnikov visited Frolov. *He also wanted to see his new office. Big daddy! A private office, a suckretary and stuff. And here... fuck a duck!*

"Hi, Dima," he greeted Frolov a bit unceremoniously. He was sitting behind the table with an intent look and obviously dealing with very important papers.

Well, he fucking became so businesslike, wrapped up in work since the morning! What the hell? As if he didn't puke all over the water closet at Petrovich's. What are you busy with? You definitely can't be feeling well after Friday and Saturday. Actually, I don't know what you were doing on Sunday. Probably 'resting,' drinking some other stuff, as usual.

"Oh, hi," he nodded carelessly.

It seemed to Rudnikov somehow that Frolov wasn't glad to see him. Either he didn't wish to talk to his co-workers, as he used to, or he recalled something that had happened in Friday, and that was the reason he didn't want to talk to Rudnikov. Probably he was afraid of the questions. *Well, let's check that!*

"Listen, Dima, I see that you're busy. I won't take a lot of your time," Rudnikov gabbled, "Concerning our Friday's talk...."

At these words Frolov startled and tensed up. Rudnikov couldn't but notice that.

Well! I see, he thought. *So, buddy, you spilled the beans on Friday. You gave away all your secrets foolishly. And now you regret it. I see, I see! We'll write it down.*

"You wanted to see me today. So, what?"

"Ugh—what 'what?'" asked Frolov hesitatingly, looking distrustfully at his unexpected visitor. He clearly didn't remember anything. *Great!*

"So, should I make a call?" asked Rudnikov with an innocent look.

"What call? I'm sorry, Igorek, you know…on Friday… I was," Frolov smiled strenuously. His eyes were flickering uneasily, "Remind me what I was talking about."

"What do you mean?" Rudnikov was genuinely surprised. "About the sect." Frolov turned pale and staggered back. "You told me everything," Frolov's eyes popped out, and his mouth opened, "and gave their phone number."

Frolov's eyes were filled with real terror, and his jaw dropped. Rudnikov got scared a bit himself, being astonished with such a reaction.

What's wrong with him? Maybe I shouldn't meddle in it? Maybe I should just fucking forget it? Forget all these insane sectaries. There's a chance that I won't be able to leave them later. It's like a grave. There's no way out. Do I really need it?

I do! He made a decision in anger. *I need it badly! I don't want to stooge for some Frolov for the rest of my life. I don't want to be a helpless pawn while he's relaxing in his office and fucking his suckretaries. Why is he better than me? I want all that, too!*

"Have you got it here?" asked Frolov dully, looking sideways.

"What exactly?" Rudnikov answered, pretending that he didn't get it.

"The number."

"No, I left it at home. Why?"

"Nothing," Frolov sighed helplessly, tapping the table with his fingers, "Never mind."

"So, what have you decided?" asked Rudnikov more insistently. *He won't be able to get rid of me!* "You told me not to call them. It would be better if you talk to them first. You told that you would think it over and tell me your decision on Monday morning. So, what? Should I call them or wait?"

The whole of Rudnikov's plan was based on the firm belief that the members of the sect must—well, if this sect really existed, though he had no doubts about that, for Frolov was too nervous—use the elementary caution and conspiracy. And, therefore, they wouldn't be pleased with Frolov when they found out that he gave away their phone number to everyone, being in a sizzled state. To his drinking buddies.

All the more so, the people in that sect must be really serious—they were able to put such moron as Frolov in this office without effort. It's really cool; it's no mean achievement, while I'm busting a hump here! I'm working for someone else... shit, everything in life is totally unfair. And the main thing is that he has a look as if he really deserves all that, with his ball-breaker. Hey, you, wretched drunkard, what ball-breaker are we talking about? You're fit just for lifting a glass with booze and outdrinking someone. A boss-man, shit! Moron.

"No, you did the right thing not to call," Frolov tried to smile with his trembling lips, threw a quick look at Rudnikov, and his eyes started flickering again.

Rudnikov even pitied him. *Well! The matter is really serious, it seems...all the better!*

"I think I'll... talk to them... first," Frolov was literally choking on the words.

It was obvious that the conversation was unpleasant for him, and he was dreaming about one thing only—that it would be great if Rudnikov disappeared into the depth of hell. It would be great if Rudnikov died from the heart attack this very moment. Or he was hit by a car on his way home. A lot of people die in car accidents every day. No man, no problem!

"Otherwise, if you call...ugh...ugh. I shouldn't have given you that number!" he snapped out sadly and stared at Rudnikov. "Did I really give it to you? Aren't you lying to me, good man?"

However, Rudnikov passed this unexpected test with honor; he didn't shift his eyes, and he kept a shielded look.

"Well! Ugh!" Frolov fidgeted and grunted again. He hid his eagle eye and started studying the surface of his table. "Well, I'm gonna talk to them myself," he sighed heavily after a pause. "And after that I won't be able to do anything. I'm a small person there."

"Well, for how long should I wait?" Rudnikov asked insistently.

"How do I know?" answered Frolov listlessly.

"Well, approximately—a week? Two weeks?" asked Rudnikov again, wishing to lean on him. *"It may be that he won't do anything, and then he's gonna say, 'Well, they didn't contact you? So, they didn't want to.' Yeah, I know that kind of stuff. We've been there. We act the same way.*

"I don't know!" Frolov shouted, "I already told you! I don't know! They will find you, if they want to."

"Come on, calm down!" Rudnikov settled down. "I just asked; I just want to know for sure," he halted for a second. There was a question on the tip of his tongue which he wanted to ask him badly—"And for how long did you have to wait, good man, until they contacted you?" But, after a bit of thinking, he decided not to ask it. Enough for today; he shouldn't cross the line.

"Alright, Dimon, take care. I'm gonna go. Time," he glanced at the watch. "Yeah, listen," he turned back on the doorstep, "what kind of trick did you show me with the coin? I just couldn't get the drift. Did you talk about some numbers?"

"What numbers?" Frolov leaned forward. "What did I tell you?" he almost shouted, "What?"

"Well, I don't remember, actually," Rudnikov was embarrassed with such unexpected effect. As a matter of fact, that was a simple question. "I was drunk as well."

"You're gonna learn everything in due time," Frolov sank into a chair. "They will tell you everything. If they want to."

3.

Having returned to his department, Rudnikov surrounded himself with papers and pretended that he was lost in work. As a matter of fact, he was deep in thought. The conversation with Frolov had a great impression on him. There were no doubts that the sect really existed, that Frolov was one of its members, and that, thanks to it, he got the promotion, became a manager, and got a private office. Moreover, Rudnikov realized something additionally. Frolov was scared. He was clearly afraid of the possible consequences of his drunken rant. That was obvious. It was impossible not to notice it.

And what about the last episode with the numbers? He almost had a stroke when I started talking about that. He began trembling.

I'm curious what these numbers are. He did tell me something. But what exactly? And he was flipping the coin..."

No, I don't remember. Something distracted me. Oh, yeah! A free show! Our dear tight-ass Olya from another department raised to reach for salad, and Maksimov, who was sitting near her, was drooling with happiness and touching her ass secretly with an idiotic smile. She was reaching and reaching for salad and just couldn't get enough of it, poor woman. She just couldn't get back to her seat. She was looking for a spoon.

Rudnikov smiled unwillingly, recalling that merry picture. He wished that he had had a camera then. He would have made a nice shot. *Shit!* He became sad suddenly. *I wish I was listening to Frolov and not watching that silly woman being groped. As if I haven't seen anything of that kind before! And it turns out that he was talking serious stuff. I won't be able to fucking draw anything out of him.*

Just think about it—they will tell me everything tomorrow! Sure, they will, but it's good to know beforehand, just in case. Well, I can't do anything about it. I should wait until they are kind enough to contact me. If it happens at all, of course. So, for how long should I wait? Well... two weeks. Right. Two weeks at most. If they don't show up in two weeks, I'll have to shake down Frolov again. Though, it would be fucking hard to do it then. He's snorting already, and he's probably not going to let me in his office in two weeks. Yeah, right! He's a big boss now. Fucking bugger. Fagot."

The thought that some wretched Frolov was sitting in his private office and not giving a damn, and Rudnikov, who's a hundred times smarter and more talented than him, was still rotting away and vegetating on his office as a simple clerk, was completely unbearable. It was stinging him.

"What a life! Why am I so damn unlucky/ Everybody finds the place in the sun eventually. Everybody! Some join the sect, and others get a lucky marriage."

Rudnikov thought about his friend from the institute who had recently married a daughter of a large businessman. Her daddy had bought them apartments and a car—well, the full package. She was kind of ugly, actually, but looks aren't everything. One would marry an old witch for such money. Yeah, a real old witch. Or, rather, marry the money. Daddy's money.

So, everybody finds the place in the sun, and I'm the only one who's still goofing around. Square peg in a round hole! Nobody fucking needs me. Soon I'm gonna turn thirty, and what have I achieved in life? Well, what? What do I have? Nothing! Zero! Neither house nor home. Poorest of the poor. I'm drinking myself to death with local drunkards from the institute, with same losers as me. I would gladly join a sect or knock my head against a brick wall! I'd do whatever it takes to get out of this swamp, at any cost!

***

For the next few days, Rudnikov stayed in his department without going anywhere. He had a lot of work to do, and he was as busy as a one-armed paperhanger. *Where did it all come from? Never before had he had so much work. Fucking disaster!* He didn't have time to think of Frolov. When he went for a smoke, his boss would scowl at him. He would look asquint at him, as ill luck would have it. What could he do?

Rudnikov put out the cigarette with a grim face, threw it into the dust-bin, and headed for the exit, when the door to the smoking room opened, and on the doorstep, "like a fleeting vision, like a spirit beautiful and pure," there appeared Zinaida Yurievna herself, magnificent and unparalleled. Also known as Zinka, or Lady Ziu, she was a gorgeous platinum blonde in her mid-twenties. She also was a manager of one of the departments, a dragon lady, a social animal, and the object of endless envy, gossip, and worship of all local females.

"Broads," according to Vitka Ivanov. "All our broads have gathered to pick Zinaida to pieces. 'Zinka has a new fur coat.' 'Did you see the Mercedes in which Lady Ziu drove to work?' and so on and so forth."

Rudnikov almost opened his mouth in surprise. *Oh, God! What's the meaning of this? It appears even the respected people do visit our filthy smoking room. What's wrong with her today? Does she have a wish to talk to ordinary folk? She's actually somewhere there—in heavens, up there—very high! In higher spheres, so to say—she's living there, right? She's hovering there, among brilliants, fur coats, and Mercedeses. And she doesn't smoke, as far as I know. What's she doing here at all?*

There were various rumours about Zinaida Yurievna, though nobody knew anything for sure. Either her daddy was a big shot or her boyfriend. "Either daddy or a stick!" Local females used to make this rude joke.

So, it was unclear, though everybody knows about such things usually. And here...it was obvious that there was something or somebody; otherwise, how would a 25-year-old girl become the manager of the department, let alone own numerous fur coats, dresses, and cars. There definitely was someone, but who exactly? No one ever picked her up at work, no one saw her home, she didn't seem to call anyone while at work; all in all, she was a mysterious woman. Secret and mysterious, like Galley's comet.

How come we have such people in our native swamp? And, above all, what's she doing here with such looks? As a matter of fact, she should be walking on a runway and shining at the beauty contests. She should be relaxing with millionaires in night clubs and expensive restaurants. She should be enjoying the sun on islands and cays. But she...

These thoughts used to visit Rudnikov, when he saw this magnificent, well-groomed and cold beauty—*Zima*ida, as he sometimes called her to himself when running into her in the corridor from time to time. He even was soft about her secretly, like, probably, almost all local guys, but it was somehow...abstract and platonic. As if she was a movie star, a goddess or a beauty from a magazine—Marilyn Monroe, for example. It was like dreaming about something impossible and inaccessible. Just look at her and then at me. *Hah—too funny for words! I'm like a bug for her. A cockroach, whisking along the corridors. There's nothing to be talking about here. Enough to make a cat laugh!"*

And now brilliant Zinaida Yurievna slowly approached Rudnikov, came very close to him. Rudnikov involuntarily glanced at the unnaturally deep neck of her stunning dress. Looking serenely through him with her large, bottomless, and ultramarine eyes, she said softly, "Today, at seven, at the metro station Frunzenskaya, underground, in the center of the hall. Sit on a bench. You will be approached." Seeing his absolutely mad astonishment, which, obviously, was shown on his face, she added softly and serenely, "That's concerning your recent conversation with Frolov." After that, she turned slowly away and proudly left the smoking room.

She's like a princess, a swan of Tsar Gwidon, thought Rudnikov, coming to his senses and gazing after her. *In the sea, in the ocean, on the island of Buyan. But I'm no Gwidon at all. Gwindon! Someone must be fucking her! Yeah...very curious...*

He scratched his chin thoughtfully. He shouldn't come out of the smoking room now. *We're gonna wait. We shouldn't be in a hurry, right? Let her sail far from here. We shouldn't be seen together. It would be no good. No good at all. We don't want to scare the folk.*

Why do we need all these bad sensations? Thank God, there was no one in the smoking room. Otherwise, the people would start talking. She may not care, but I do. What does it mean? Our Zinaida Yurievna is a sectary, too? Well, well! That is too much! One really can't tell in a tale or write with a pen. It blows my mind. Why does she need it for, with her looks and exterior? She can have whatever she wants without any sects. Though the deuce knows! Maybe it just appears so? And, as a matter of fact, these women are more complicated than we think. Looks are great, of course, but you can't have Mercedes and brilliants using your cunt only. Well, certainly, you may get lucky. They've got fierce competition, as well. She's a presentable lady, that's for sure; she's got everything she needs, according to our institute standards, of course, comparing to local skanks. But, on the other hand...

No! What am I saying? I'm not blind. I do watch TV from time to time. She could teach any television slut a thing or two. Though these freaking females are very unclear. All this female business—who would fuck whom? And where? Back or front? It's a hell of a mess if one goes too deep into a problem."

"So, Zinaida Yurievna is a sectary? Unbelievable! It's a wonder, a turn-up for the books. Well! Umph... . And that means that the sect is serious, very serious. Such a hardened vamp, such a white shark, as our Lady Ziu—oh, exactly, "white shark"—I should show my wit when I have a chance! Anyway, such a tough broad wouldn't join some morons. No, she wouldn't deal with them. No way, she's not like that drunkard Frolov! So, if even she is there...well! Rudnikov shook his head in amazement.

He just couldn't believe this unexpected turn of events. He wouldn't be surprised with anyone, but divinely cold Zinaida... He just couldn't imagine that she was a sectary. He simply didn't have enough imagination. Sectarianism—it's something imperfect, something hysterical. A frowsy of uncertain age with disheveled hair, her mouth open in mute scream and her eyes angry. Or, quite on the contrary, prudish and ascetic—black kerchief, sharp nose, shy withered eyes, thin, colourless lips, hair brushed back with a knot on a top of a head. All in all, it's something repellent.

But a magnificent beauty like Zinaida? Is she used to coming to the sect meeting in her Mercedes S-Class? However, the fact remains. I can still smell her perfume in the smoking room. So, maybe, she's gonna want me later somewhere? A naughty smile came to Rudnikov. *During one of their sabbats? She's a sectary, and I'm a sectary as well. I'm a member of a sect. 'Are you a member of the party? No, I'm its brain!' Though, that's unlikely. She's probably there just for the management, for the narrow circle. For certain members who have special merits. Well, we'll see about merits. Who's got a larger one? Such women always carry a value. Like real property in Moscow and everywhere. Private property, authorized personnel only. No ordinary members, so to say."*

What an outrage! Injustice is everywhere, even in sects. Everywhere, everywhere! Where one should look for justice? Where... By the way, there's a good rhyme as an answer. In... In Zinaida's one! What do they call women in a sect? Men are members, that's clear, and who are women? She-members? Female members? Memberettes? It's curious that there's no word like sheath for members. Well, sheath is for sabre, and what is for members? Nothing? Alas. Oh! There is, there is—vagina!"

Rudnikov recalled when Vitka Ilyin brought the Explanatory Dictionary of the Russian Language and read aloud the meaning of the old Russian word "vagina" while they were smoking.

"A container, a thing for putting other things in it; bag, purse, case, sheath, box."

"So, it is derived from the verbs 'imbed' and 'enclose' and not from the noun "moisture," as it appears." The ladies were thrilled.

So, how should I call all these vaginas? Somehow shorter and sweeter? Oh, right! Sectaries-sextants-sextaries! Sextaries...yuk! Jawbreaker! Alright, enough fooling around.

***

Rudnikov came back to the department. His boss stared at him in anger."Did it take you ages to have a smoke?"

"Am I cursed or what?" Rudnikov exploded. "I've been working like a nigger for the last few days! Don't I have a right to smoke for two minutes?" He sat behind the table, took another thick book so everyone could see it, and pretended to be reading it. His boss was silent. The other employees nestled their noses in papers.

Fuck you! thought Rudnikov, being irritated. He felt somehow free and easy, as if he was a man who didn't have anything to lose. *All the same, there's nothing good in this hole. No future. You can kiss the boss's ass, or screw him—all the same! There's no difference, same result. And they wouldn't fire you; for where would they find another fool who's gonna work for such salary? And they don't want to give you a raise. Raises are only for employees who have connections.*

Or for those who have a cunt, like Zinaida. A method of vagina. 'A thing, for putting other things in it.' Though, probably, she isn't using her vagina; at least, not with local bosses. No doubt, they're eyeing her hungrily, as do all of them. No entrance for him, as well. No way. This vagina is a top one—only for high-ranking members. The one who can properly put something in it! Hah! So, then I'm entitled to it, too. My member is, in certain aspect, with such a chick, high-ranking. I can show you. No problems! I have no issues with that so far. Thank God! It reacts even to local skanks. The aboriginal inhabitants of our native institute swamp. And it's no joke!

And our frogs' spells are stronger than the ones from the fairy tales. They can't be unspelled with kisses. They turn into princesses only after the third glass. Even then, not always and not for long. But before that, you may kiss or fuck them—no use! They're just quacking. Yuk! And it's disgusting to recall everything in the morning. It turns the stomach, especially when you've got hangover. You may wake up near one of them—a sleeping Frog Princess, en years older, than you...Pah!

Well, what about the meeting today? What did she say? Seven o'clock at Frunzenskaya? Umph, right, the exit at Park. Yeah, I can do it. Is there one station only? Yeah, it seems so. Only one, that's for sure. And there are benches in the center—'sit on a bench.' So, they must know me by sight. Curious... Well, it doesn't matter. Let them know. I'm really interested in another thing. Is this sect legal? Why do they appoint meetings in the Metro? What's with all this secrecy? Whom are they afraid of? Authorities? That's the only option. They're definitely not afraid of me."

Well, 'it's even more interesting.' Like Alice said when she entered Wonderland for the first time. Or did she say something else, in a more figurative way? Well, that doesn't matter at all. I really don't want to go to Wonderland with all these sectaries. I don't need any problems. And it matters! It's very important for me—very! It's the most important thing. It's very easy to get caught, during some anti-terrorist operation, for example. They're gonna cuff you, and that's it—enjoy your time in jail. They're gonna show your various miracles in a police department. It rocks! You won't find it funny. Alice didn't even dream about it. Yeah, we know that. Rogue cops. Save and protect!

All the more so, as I don't know anything about them, about these sectaries. What if they are really indulging in some illegal activities? What if they're preparing for acts of terrorism? Like

Aum Shinrikyo, explosions in Tokoyo underground, gas attacks? Touch wood. I'm already sweating.

"No way! There's no need for panicking. What explosions? If that were true, Frolov wouldn't be dealing with them. Fucking terrorist. Drunkard. And Zinaida! She's definitely not of that kind. Why would she need bombs? She's a sex bomb herself. It's a piece of crap! Terrorists! It's a piece of crap, no doubt, but where are they hiding? Why wouldn't they invite him to their office, to tea? They would drink some tea together or coffee; they would talk—the whole shooting match. 'On metro station Frunzenskaya, on a bench in the center of the hall; you will be approached.' And he's gonna be asked, 'Do you sell Slavic wardrobe?'

Yuk! Eh-heh-heh...yeah, hell of a life! If it's not one thing, it's another. If I go, it would be a fucking disaster; if I don't go, the same. Well, alright, I'm gonna go. Maybe everything will be okay. What can I do? I have to risk it, come as it may. That's the motto of our life. One fool makes the ropes, and another one throws the loop. I'm gonna do it! "And they're not idiots, are they? They understand everything perfectly well. All these fucking conspiracies. If they weren't nailed before, why would that happen now? Well, in that case, I would turn very unlucky. I shouldn't be thinking about that. It's useless. It's like walking on a street and being hit by a falling brick. It's possible, but so what? Do I have to stay at home all the time? Or wear a helmet? It doesn't have any sense. No purpose. There's no insurance against it. You may be wearing a helmet but still fall down an open manhole. And you may break your neck there.

"So, I'm gonna do it! I'm gonna go there! To metro station Frunzenskaya. A bench in the center of the hall. I'm gonna sit there until they approach me. Or until the metro is closed. To the max. I got nothing to lose."

Absolutely!

4.

Rudnikov arrived at Frunzenskaya ten minutes early. He sat on a bench and began waiting. Ten minutes went very slowly. His fears woke up again. It seemed to him that the whole station was filled with special-service agents.

That guy, on a bench in front of him—what's he doing here? He was sitting here when I came, and he's not going to leave. It doesn't seem that he's waiting for someone. And that man—why is he glancing at me? Right. And that one, with glasses and moustache; he's staring at me. And when I look at him, he looks away. That's it! I got it. I'm in trouble. That's for sure—again!

"Well, well! Calm down! I've still got time. What will I say if they take me in? 'I don't know anything at all?' No, that won't work, probably. Should I turn Zinaida and Frolov in? Fuck! Fucking disaster! In that case, I'll have to quit the job. They won't forgive it. Nobody likes rats.

But what will I tell them? What was I doing here? 'I've got a meeting?' 'With whom? Who else is involved? Ah-hah... did you forget it? Do you think we're idiots? And now? Now you remember it? Sit! Look in the eyes!' Fucking hell, another one! And this one's staring at me all the time. That's it. It's over. Keep me posted. Who is this, anyway? FSB agents or ordinary cops? What cops? Terrorism... sect... It's definitely FSB. So, Lefortovo. Fucking hell!

At that moment, the main FSB agent, the one with glasses and moustache, was approached by a woman, and, talking and laughing merrily, they headed for the exit. Rudnikov felt a great relief, like he was born anew. He took a handkerchief out of the pocket and wiped his sweating forehead with a shaking hand.

Ugh! It's easy to pass out with this stuff! Drop a cue because of the emotional stress. Nerve cells do not reproduce. And I'm too old for these spy games. Old! I'm not a boy. I don't wanna play cops and robbers in the metro. Or spies and scouts. James Bonds and Stierlitzes or Mata Hari. Well, well! What a meeting! On a Black river. The beginning is great. Let's see what comes next. Is this what sect life is about? I thought it would be different.

"Igor Ivanovich?" he heard someone ask him and nearly jumped in surprise. Maybe not even nearly; he probably did jump. At least, the woman near him looked at him with apprehension and surprise and even moved away. Rudnikov lifted his eyes and saw a young elegant—this word somehow came to his mind at once—man in his thirties. Actually, he was a bit older than Rudnikov.

"Yeah?," answered Rudnikov, looking at the man expectantly and standing up.

"Let's talk outside," the man pointed to the exit invitingly, and they headed to the escalator together.

The man was silent. Rudnikov didn't speak either. He wanted to make a nice impression and tried to behave decently and with honour from the very beginning. Having left the underground, they turned left at once. The man clearly knew where to go. Rudnikov was following him silently, asking no questions.

Maybe, we're going to their office? he thought. *That would be great.*

However, his hopes were not destined to be fulfilled, alas!

Metal fence… gates… past the public toilet… and they're walking on the paved alleys of a park or a square. *No, that is no square; that is a park, a big park with alleys and benches. Wow! There is a pond with ducks and elegant curved bridge in the middle. Well, well! I've never been here before. I didn't even suspect that there's such a big park here, straight in the middle of the city, not far from the metro. Though Luzhniki is not far from here. Park of Culture, Sparrow Hills. Well, right. It's almost the green area. Elite district.*

Meanwhile, the man headed confidently to one of the vacant benches near the pond. "Igor Ivanovich, let's sit on the bench and talk here," he offered in a deceitfully soft voice. However, his tone left no doubts. It was impossible to refuse his offer, and Rudnikov realized that clearly. "A beautiful place… nature… clean air… And nobody is going to distract us."

The spot was really wonderful in every respect. It was nice just to be sitting there, with water and swimming ducks at hand, and the nearest bench was almost on the other side of the pond. And there were no alleys near it. No one would come there. All in all, an ideal spot for a couple of lovers. Just like Manilovsky temple for solitary thinking. Well, the architects who planned this park were really smart. They thought about everything. It was a very old park; that was the reason. It was founded long ago, in days of yore. In times when they built for people, not for…

"I'm listening to you, Igor Ivanovich," the man interrupted his lyrical thoughts and looked at him with expectation.

"Ugh!" grunted Rudnikov involuntarily. The question took him unawares. He didn't expect such a beginning of the conversation. For some reason, he was quite sure that he would be persuaded, asked, and convinced; all in all, they would be trying to entrap him. And he would be just sitting, listening, and making mental notes while demonstrating that he is having doubts, hesitating, and, overall, he hasn't made the final decision yet. And that would mean that he could subtly escape their cunning trap. For example, he would go to another sect. That's even better. The other sect is waiting for him with open arms.

You bet! He's so precious object—no one fucking needs him at all. Fucking exotic fruit! Goldfish. And everybody's just dreaming to catch it and then eat it without sitting on anything, as a famous proverb says.

All these thoughts came to Rudvikov's mind at once, and he suddenly realized clearly that it was the most important time of his life, a turning point. His fate is being determined here and now. No one was going to convince or ask him—quite on the contrary. At whatever cost, he had to ask, beg, convince, and persuade the man who's sitting in front of him to admit him to the sect. He must prove that they need him."

And why the fuck do they need me? he thought in panic. *There's a lot of fish like me in every pool. Various kinds of them—dime a dozen, hojillions. The only relief is that they decided to meet me. So...*

Shit! How should I behave? What should I say? There's no sense acting high and mighty and puffing my cheeks when he probably knows everything about me—who I am and what I am. From Frolov, maybe, or from Zinaida. Maybe there are more sectaries at work. I don't really know anything about them at all. So, if I try to show off and act like D'Artagnan, I'm gonna find myself in a very silly situation, I'm afraid, at the very beginning of it. And it will all end without even starting. "'Thank you,'" they'll say. "'We'll consider it,' and that's it. Or they'll simply screw me. 'We don't need any morons. We have a lot of them - all the best!'"

"Well, you know, I thought that you would tell me about you," began Rudnikov carefully. "I don't know anything about you."

The man smiled.

"Well, I'm sure, you know everything about me," added Rudnikov intuitively, giving way to internal impulsion. It was surprising even for himself.

The man smiled broader, and Rudnikov realized that he had chosen the right tone. He should be speaking sincerely. It appeared to be the most sensible thing in this situation.

"We know a lot, Igor Ivanovich, a lot; not everything, of course, but a lot," the man was more than friendly. "So, why do you want to join us, actually?"

"You know, I just want to build a career," Rudnikov decided to break through, to go all in. Ah—no guts, no glory! "As far as I understood, Frolov, you can help me with that. I just want to achieve something in life. That's it."

"Even if you have to betray your principles, beliefs, and religion?" asked the man with interest.

Rudnikov hesitated for a second. The mention of religion struck him unpleasantly. Maybe he wasn't true to any religion, but he didn't want to turn Muslim, for example. This is somehow... But he didn't hesitate for long.

Ah-ah! If I must become an Islamite, I will! Dash it all! I will become even an idolist. That's just a matter of money. Why would I argue? One should sell himself easily and at a high price.

"As a matter of fact, there's nothing to betray," he said sadly. "I don't have any religion, let alone principles and beliefs."

"Good on you, good on you," the man's smile became even broader and more radiant. "That's very good. It's a great pleasure to speak with a sincere man. Alright, Igor Ivanovich, then I'm going to be sincere in response to your sincerity. I'm not going to torture and mystify you anymore, but will put you in the picture, and you're going to make a decision whether you will join us or not. Deal?"

"Yeah, sure," Rudnikov shrugged his shoulders. "Of course. I'd be very glad to listen to you. As a matter of fact, that's why I'm here."

"Well, that's great!" the man looked at Rudnikov intently. For some reason, Rudnikov felt ill at ease and even shivered, and then the man continued after a short pause.

"You see, Igor Ivanovich, our organization is rather unconventional. My story will probably surprise you, but you're an educated man with a university degree, so it will be a bit easier for you."

Rudnikov studied at the physics department of Moscow State University. *Just to rot alive in this hole*! he thought with rage. The mentioning of his education made his passionate wish to join any party, any organization, any sect, just to get out of this dead end, even more stronger.

"So, as you probably know, according to the general notion, if you, say, flip a coin..."

Rudnikov startled involuntarily. He recalled drunk Frolov at once, who also had been doing something with a coin.

"...half the time you're going to have tails, and the other half, heads, on the average. In other words, both these events are equally possible. By the way, it is natural and obvious that the result doesn't depend on the person who's flipping the coin, be it Petrov or Sidorov. The probability is the same for everyone.

"As a matter of fact, this is not quite true. Every person brings individual distortions in the informational and statistical field, and, consequently, the results of the series of flips would be different. Of course, the deviations are very small, about centesimals and millesimals of percent, but, nevertheless, they do exist.

"By the way, that explains the well-known fact that some people are lucky and others aren't. Modern science denies it, yet, it's very simple—personal deviations of informational and statistical field. By the way, it's very easy to discover it experimentally, but it didn't occur to anyone to make such experiments. In other words, every person has his own stable probable distribution. It's not true that all people have 50 to 50; rather, some have 50.001 to 49.999, some have 50.003 to 49.997, etc.

"And we've come to the point. The individual distribution may be changed. We can make it even; for example, 0.6 : 0.4. Or even 0.8 : 0.2. As a matter of fact, we can make it whatever we want. In other words, it's possible to make a person lucky, and he's going to have luck in everything. He's going to succeed in everything, whatever he does. Happiness will always be coming to him."

Rudnikov was listening with growing amazement. He was an engineering expert himself. He had a degree in theoretical physics and, professionally, he knew the theory of chances and statistics. Therefore, he could worthily judge the sense and originality of what he had just heard.

Just to think of it! Nobody thought about that before! Every person brings individual distortions to probable distribution. And, as a result, the results of the series would be individual. But it's a scientific discovery—a revolution! A breakthrough in informatics! This is worth a Nobel prize. And, what's important, it's all very simple. It's possible to check it experimentally. Holy Jesus! 'Sect'—who's sitting in front of me—a new Einstein or what? In his own person? Norbert Wiener?

Right! Well, what was he saying about the changing? I was so amazed that, obviously, I didn't hear the most important stuff. Holy Christ! I'm really shocked. I'll be damned.

"By the way, that is the reason of the promotion of your friend, Frolov," continued the man meanwhile.

Fucking 'friend!' I don't need such a friend, thought Rudnikov gloomily.

"We didn't make any specific efforts for his promotion as you obviously were thinking. We just improved his statistical characteristics and made him more lucky and fortunate, and, after that, everything happened of its own accord. 'Natural force of events,' as the ancients used to say. By the way, it's a very nice old term which is now forgotten.

"Well... By the way, he shouldn't have demonstrated to you his luck with a coin," added the man suddenly, staring at Rudnikov.

"What do I have to do with it?" he shrugged his shoulders mentally. "I didn't drag it out of him. He was wagging his tongue."

"Such demonstrations are strictly forbidden by the rules of our organization, so we'll have to deal with your friend."

"Well and good," smiled Rudnikov with malevolence. "You deal with him. Give him the bum's rush! I'll be pleased with that. Right. How could one have business with drunkards? They know better, though. Now I understand why he got so nervous when I mentioned the coin in his office. And then he was glad that I didn't remember anything. He surely felt the shoe pinching!"

"And, actually, one can frighten the luck away. Believe me!"

Oh-oh-oh! thought Rudnikov. *So he was scared that he could frighten his luck away. I should have fucking told him that I did remember the numbers. I wish he was worried.*

"So, what next?"

The man continued his explanations. "Your luck will grow, but it'll happen by means of the people that surround you. Consequently, they will become unlucky."

Well, fagot! thought Rudnikov about Frolov in astonishment. *So, he became a boss at my expense? At the expense of all of us?*

"Well, as you know, the law says, if something's increased in one place, then it's decreased it another place," the man smiled. "But, as we found out, Igor Ivanovich, you don't have any relatives, and, as you just told me, you do not have any particular moral and ethical problems with that. Do you?" the man looked at Rudnikov questioningly.

"No," he replied briefly.

What moral and ethical problems are you talking about? I don't give a fuck about surrounding people. Let them go to hell! Fiery hell! Blast it all! I'll be glad of it. It serves these morons right! Surrounding people! Rudnikov imagined for a second that, from now on, everything was gonna be great in his life, unlike the others', and he even closed his eyes with pleasure. *The higher justice does exist in the world. It does! For how long are they going to use me? Yeah, they like it. I'm a fucking sacrificial goat for them! And not one scum! Not even Frolov, freaking scumbag! Alright. You're gonna find out what it's like. You're gonna fall on hard times. You're gonna be in my boots.*

"Alright," the man nodded, "now you may ask questions. If you don't understand anything, feel free to ask."

Rudnikov took some thought. "Tell me," he began timidly, "You said, 'by means of people that surround me.' And what if I want to get married?"

"Then it would be better for you to leave us," answered the man calmly.

"And is it so easy?"

"Sure," the man shrugged his shoulders. "No problem. You can do it at any moment."

"Without any consequences for me?" asked Rudnikov, with even bigger astonishment. He was still suspecting that there was some trick. *How could one just leave? Maybe then I would become a constant loser? Would I lose everything that I earned during my stay in the sect? Would some fucking disaster happen to me? Can it be so easy? It's not that simple to leave such an organization.*

"Absolutely!" answered the man with a smile. "Well, your luck would become as it was before, and that's it. It would be as it is now."

"But won't it decrease?" Rudnikov couldn't calm down. "Won't it diminish? I'm not going to become a loser, am I?"

Though, who am I now? A lucky one? If so, why am I joining the sect?

"No, no!" answered the man. "You would become an ordinary man with ordinary, statistically average characteristics. That's it."

"Oh," Rudnikov faltered, "And all my acquirements? Well, all that I will have earned during the stay in your organization? When I'm still lucky. Will all of it stay with me? Or will I have to give them away?"

"No, there's no giving away," the man lifted his right hand kiddingly. "You will keep everything. Use it well!"

"You know," Rudnikov resolved to be completely sincere, "these are truly remarkable conditions. I can't really believe it. It seems that it's some kind of a trap, so to say. Please, don't get insulted. You see, I'm speaking openly."

"Yes, I can see that, Igor Ivanovich," said the man softly, looking straight into Rudnikov's eyes. "I see that. Well, take it easy. There are no tricks, traps, or half-words. Everything is as I told you. Neither better nor worse. So it's up to you to decide."

"Well, I don't have to give it a second thought," muttered Rudnikov. "Surely, I'll do it with great pleasure with such conditions. Right! So, concerning conditions," he startled suddenly. "You said that Frolov shouldn't have demonstrated his luck. It's forbidden. And is anything else forbidden? What are the rules?"

"Two things are forbidden," the man explained calmly. "First, showing the trick with a coin. Second, wishing ill to the whole organization or its certain members."

Rudnikov was eager to ask what would happen if he broke one of these rules—~~well,~~ just to know it, to have an idea—but he didn't resolve to ask that question. He just didn't have the heart. He understood intuitively that it would be better not to touch that topic. Hell with it!

That's the same thing as to ask terrorists, "What will happen if I betray you?" 'Why? Are you going to betray us?'" Hell with it! No need to play with fire.

And these conditions are not scary, actually. Quite on the contrary, they're really acceptable and clear. There's no need to boast under the influence that you're a hero and a lucky one now. Don't draw attention to yourself. Don't bite the hand that feeds you. Don't wish ill to the people who have made you a lucky one. So, is there anything peculiar in all this? These are common human requirements; they're quite natural. But still, what will happen if I do break them? I want to ask that badly. I have a great mind to do it. It goads me to do it. Well, away from me—the devil is tempting me.

"I see," he lowered his eyes "I've got it. Tell me—you said that you're going to make me luckier, so to say. You will improve my individual statistical characteristics." The man smiled approvingly. "And what it will look like in practice? Is it some kind of a ritual? A procedure? How will it be?"

"You are going to see it yourself," the man stopped smiling and stared at Rudnikov. "Don't worry, nobody's going to make you do anything. You may leave at any moment. Nobody's going to stop you, and there will be no consequences for you. You'll just return to your usual statistically average life—that's it.

"Our weekly meetings are usually held on Fridays. So, you can visit them every Friday, if you want, or every other Friday. Or once a month or a year. It's up to you. But, the more often you visit them, the better your statistical characteristics will be and the luckier you will be. Very long breaks won't bring any good. During the meeting, you kind of receive the boost of special energy, and it's going to disperse in time. You must do a regular recharge in order to keep that energy. You must visit our meetings."

"Excuse me," asked Rudnikov with interest. He was a physicist, after all. "You said 'a boost of special energy.' So the phenomenon has an energetic essence? And what is this special energy?"

"Dark psychic energy—voice of pain and torments."

"Well, well!" mumbled Rudnikov, hiding his eyes.

He was deeply disappointed. *Yet another freak. dark psychos. And I was a fool to believe them. Serves me right. Though, the idea with a coin is a good one, concerning the individual distribution.*

"So, dark energy…pain and torments? And can it be detected with any devices? Can it be measured?"

"No," answered the man immovably. "It can't be measured. There are no such devices."

Rudnikov chuckled to himself. *Of course not... **for now!** There are no such devices, you see, **for now!** The science can't reach the level of your sectarian inventions. Sure, what can science do? How can it reach the span of sectarian thinking? We're already 100 years ahead of it. Or even 200 years.*

Oh, God! How many idiots are there? Unrecognized geniuses, greatest ever, with their fucking inventions. Every day, they tell about it in mass media. The same ignorant journalists, the same morons. An engineer, Ivanov, from Elabuga, proved wrong all the works of Einstein and a technologist, Petukhov, from Konotop, made telepathic connection with Tau Ceti. And now he's communicating with them all day long. He has already fucked up the local inhabitants. They don't really know how to get rid of him. Still, the idea with a coin is a good one, but it can be recorded."

Rudnikov looked up at his companion with a scorn. "Hmph! There are no such devices, but it can be recorded. And how exactly?"

"Oh, right! 'Our telepaths!' They're devices themselves. They feel how it fucking goes through them, through their bodies, bringing pain and tortures. In a very dark city! In a dark company! Dark energy! Bother it! Though what can they say? They're insane. I'm curious how they came up with the idea about a coin. Though that should be checked, too. Right, but Frolov! And Zinaida?

"You see, the sources of dark psychic energy, the energy of pain and torments, are naturally the places where the people feel pain and torments. First of all, prisons and hospitals. All these establishments, as a rule, are situated within the city limits, in residential districts.

"So, if we statistically study the inhabitants of the adjacent buildings, we shall learn that the quantity of diseases, deaths, and accidents among them is essentially higher than in ordinary districts. In other words, these establishments are a constantly working negative factor like, for example, radioactive waste damp. The principle of the study of the influence to the environment is the same—comparative statistical study of the potential objects of influence."

Rudnikov was listening to that with his mouth open. His skepticism vanished, giving way to some superstitious awe. *Incredible! It seems that this man is a genius, if he's really a human at all! He has inhuman ideas. 'Individual probabilistic distribution,' 'dark psychic energy;' it's from another world. It seems to be incredible, but the approach is purely scientific. That's really amazing! It's easy to check everything with experiments. Please, do it! Incredible! And has anyone gathered such statistics?*

"Excuse me, has anyone conducted such statistical study?" Rudnikov even craned his neck with curiosity.

"Yes. Our organization did it," the sectary answered briefly.

Rudnikov wanted to ask and specify a lot of things. Selection criteria... specific numbers... Suddenly he became a scientist and a researcher. But he glanced at the man near him and realized at once that all these questions were at least inappropriate. It was no scientific symposium.

Why is he asking all these questions? What's the use of it? Oh, he needs numbers and graphs; he's a scientist, you see—a fucking researcher. He's no researcher at all. The researcher must go where it came from. When did you study it? When exactly? How many years ago? It doesn't matter that you got a degree in something. Cut it out! Think about business, not about graphs. Ask a serious question, the one that concerns you, moron. You don't know when you're gonna have such a chance. Maybe this manager has only one interview with a newcomer. So, ask him serious questions.

Cut this bullshit out. Numbers and graphs! Wretched dummy! Fucking theoretical physicist. See, you remembered too much! Come on! Well... well... What should I ask?" Rudnikov was at a loss.

"So, as far as I get it, your offices are situated in the close vicinity of prisons and hospitals—well, of the sources of dark psi-energy," he said aloud, "and I recharge myself with it by visiting the meetings. Right? Could you explain the whole mechanism of influence in detail?"

Why the fuck do I need this mechanism? he thought in panic. *Why did I cling like a limpet to him? Why would I care? He's probably gonna get mad! You've been told—you're gonna be lucky, just visit the meetings—and that's it! No 'how' or 'why?' Now tell him about the mechanism. Well, don't go there, if you don't want to.*

"See, I have a degree in physics," he asked, smiling humbly. "I'm just curious."

"I see, I see," the man responded merrily. "Well, in short, it goes like this. Yes, you understood everything right. By visiting our meetings, you're recharging with dark psi-energy. You become its carrier. And you draw the luck of the ones who surround you, you draw their positive, white psi-energy, like negative and positive charges are being drawn to each other."

"Wait, wait!" Rudnikov interrupted him in excitement, without even noticing that. "How is this possible? It turns out that everybody—well, the inhabitants of the adjacent buildings—are influenced by the dark psi-energy negatively, and the members of the sect—positively, right?" The word "sect" popped out; Rudnikov didn't mean to say it.

"That's right," confirmed the man, paying no attention to Rudnikov's slip of the tongue. "That's the sense of ceremonies and ritual acts which are held during the meetings—to make the dark psi-energy safe and even useful for our members, to make it work for their good!" he laughed.

His laugh somehow made Rudnikov's ears tingle.

So, I'm gonna built my happiness on the unhappiness of the others? the obvious thought came to his mind. *That's a bit... Though, why would I care?* he recovered himself. *Why would I care? They have warned me right away concerning moral and ethical problems. Well, you may live on your small salary, if you wish. Serve Frolov, if you're so high-toned. And then he's gonna built his happiness on you. He's gonna forge it. He's in the sect. Together with Zinaida, by the way. And I'm sure that they've got no moral issues. They're sitting in their offices, in apple-pie order, and they're not giving a hoot about any morals. They fuck it from their Mercedes."*

The thought about Frolov, Zinaida, offices, and Mercedeses cheered Rudnikov up.

"Alright, I've got it. I'm in," he said firmly and looked straight in his companion's eyes. "What should I do next?"

"Here's our address," the man gave Rudnikov a piece of paper. "The meeting are held, as I've already said, on Fridays, beginning at ten. Come when you wish. But try not to be late," he added, standing up. "Alright, you probably are heading to the station, and I need to be in another place. Good bye," he nodded to Rudnikov and quickly paced into the depth of the park.

Rudnikov followed him with his eyes, then opened the paper slowly, and read the address written on it.

"Well, where is that? Oh, I see. How late is it? Past eight. Well, I can make it. It's Friday today. So maybe I should go there now? Why should I wait?"

He folded the piece of paper, put it in his pocket, and headed to the metro station. *So, what? Should I go or not? Or maybe I should go next week? And why next week? Well, it's somehow strange, going there straightaway. I need to prepare myself mentally, psychologically. Or should I go? Eh?*

"I'm gonna flip a coin," he resolved. "If it's heads, I'm gonna go!"

The coin went high up, spinning, and fell on the ground with a thump. Rudnikov bent over with a sinking heart. Heads!

5.

At 8:48 p.m., Rudnikov was already at the address written on the paper. *Shit! What should I say? Who am I? Well, at least, I can show them the paper with the address,* he thought and pulled the door. Near the entrance he saw a young man, sitting behind the table. Either a guard or security; it was unclear.

"Excuse me," said Rudnikov, without even knowing what he should ask. He really couldn't say, "Where are the meetings of the sect held?" Maybe this guy is not one of them? "I was given this address."

The guy glanced at the paper and pointed to the stairs, "Second floor. Wait a second," he reached with his hand under the table and gave Rudnikov a black mask with slots for mouth and eyes, like the ones that Special Police Force wears.

Rudnikov stared at it, bewildered. "Do I have to wear that?" he looked at the guy inquiringly.

"As you wish," he shrugged his shoulders. "It's up to you. You may not wear it."

Rudnikov hesitated a bit, fingered the mask, and then, feeling stupid, put it on his head with a silly smile. The guy was watching all his manipulations indifferently. It seemed that he had seen all this many times.

Curious enough, the mask was very comfortable and didn't obscure him. *It's a pity there's no mirror here,* thought Rudnikov and began ascending the stairs.

**

A strange platform… A door…

Rudnikov pushed the door and entered a hall which didn't seem to be one—a lobby, probably. There was a door to the left, to the right, and ahead. To the right of the large door, there was another guy, sitting in a chair.

"Are you for the first time?" he asked politely, seeing Rudnikov.

"Yeah," he answered with a slight irritation. "Is it written on my forehead?"

"Change into this," the guy put his hand into a large duffle bag which was on a table, took a bundle out of it, and gave it to Rudnikov. "Leave your clothes over there," he pointed to the right door.

"Is it a must?" asked Rudnikov grimly, "or at will, like with the mask?"

"It's a must," answered the guy immovably, staring at Rudnikov with gray, steel eyes.

Rudnikov was somehow uncomfortable under his gaze. It was unpleasant and savage. He shrugged his shoulders defiantly and headed to the right room with an independent look.

"Take off all your clothes! And underwear, as well," said the guy coldly to his back.

Rudnikov slammed the door angrily. *Fuck! Every under-strapper wants to be a boss! A big boss.*

"Don't wish ill to any of the sect members!" he recalled the directive which he had received in the park, and startled involuntarily.

"Alright! Come on! I was just kidding," he asked for pardon from a mythical main sectary and all of them at once, with an obvious humbleness. *Oh, God! I haven't yet joined the sect, and I'm breaking the rules already. I almost had a fight with security. The beginning is kind of unlucky. It shouldn't be so. Why would I demand my rights here? When in Rome, do as the Romans do. Do what you're told to and be silent. You're were told to change, so do it. Why do you ask any questions?*

Rudnikov looked around. It was a dressing room. There were benches along the wall and hooks for clothes. He could see pants, shirts, and underwear on the hooks. *I see. It's a men's change room, and the left room is obviously the ladies' change room. I got it. He opened the bundle. Umph, what's that? A cassock? A gi? A black wraparound robe without buttons, but with a stupid thick rope instead of a belt. Do I have to put this thing on a naked body? Well, a fucking medieval monk in a cassock and police mask. And what are women wearing? The same as men? Well... Slippers. Black ones. Oh, and slippers. Great! A candidate to a nut hospital. A client of a psychiatrist. Why is everything black and gloomy? Oh, yeah! It's dark psi-energy! Everything's pretty serious. Adult-like.*

Rudnikov tried to make himself take everything that was happening; ironically, but he couldn't do that well. *All these fierce guards, cassocks, and masks... I hope nobody's gonna steal my clothes. I don't want to go home, dressed in this robe with nothing under it, in a mask and slippers.* Rudnikov giggled involuntarily, imagining how he enters the underground in this outfit. It would be like Vysotsky said, 'It's a laughing matter, but there's nothing to laugh about!'"

No! Everything's strict here, I can feel it. And the clothes here is rather expensive, much more expensive than mine. Who would need my stuff? Rudnikov got undressed quickly, put his clothes on an empty hook, and put on the robe-cassock hastily, trying to handle the sleeves. Having wrapped up the gown and tied up the rope, he felt more confident. He didn't want anyone to enter and see him while he was changing. He felt uncomfortable. He raked around for a mirror. Nothing! No freaking mirror! It seemed that the sectaries didn't need ~~no~~ mirrors. *Judging by the cassock and the rope, they are very rough people. Shit! I'm late! I need to go. It's almost nine. Maybe they won't let me in. This cursed guard...*

Rudnikov left the dressing room quickly and headed to the central door. The guard followed him with his eyes but didn't say anything. Rudnikov pulled the door and entered.

A huge through-hall without furniture, but with a carpet on the floor and a strange dais in the center. *Is it a podium, or what*? On a dais, there stood a huge cabinet clock with an unnaturally massive pendulum. The pendulum ended with a crescent beneath.

What kind of axe is that? thought Rudnikov involuntarily. *Zing! Zing!*

The dais was half circled by men and women who were dressed in the same way as Rudnikov. To be precise, almost the same way. They were wearing robes. Many of them didn't have any masks. And they all were bare-footed. Rudnikov looked around and saw at once an orderly row of slippers near the door. He took his slippers off, too, and put them near the others', remaining bare-footed. *How will I find them?* he hesitated for a second, but then decided not to think about such stuff. *Ah, we'll see about that. We'll deal with it. I'll do like the others.*

As nobody was paying any attention to him and wasn't going to give him any orders, he thought that the best thing to do would be to try mingling in the crowd. He should just behave like the others. That's why he immediately entered the circle, mingling with other people. Wearing a mask, he felt confident and wasn't shy at all. The sectaries were standing quietly and waiting for something. Probably they were waiting until 9 o'clock, when everything was supposed to begin. Rudnikov recalled what he had been told in the park.

"*The meeting begins dead on 9. Don't be late*." Dead on 9 was supposed to come, according to Rudnikov's calculations, at any minute. Just in a moment.

Oh! Here is the clock. He looked at the large clock-face. *Nine! And what are the strange figures instead of the numbers?*

The distant door opened. Three persons entered the hall. They were wearing the same robes as everyone, but theirs were red and with hoods. Cowls—or what is the right name for such things, worn by the monks? One sectary was going ahead, and the others followed him. The front one was definitely the leader. A rope on his robe was red as well, while his companions had the yellow ones. *So, it was the main priest and his servants—ostiaries, as they are called in the monasteries.* The analogies with monks and monasteries were constantly coming to Rudnikov's mind; probably that was because of the robes.

One ostiary was holding a bag in his left hand and, in his right hand, was a prop like a tripod or a high stool. Rudnikov couldn't see what it was exactly. The second one was carrying carefully in his outstretched arms a strange shiny bowl which was obviously filled with something, with some liquid. Rudnikov heard a loud meowing from the bag and was astonished. *A cat? Is this a part of the ritual?*

The three of them appeared in the center of the hall and ascended the dais. The servants installed the tripod, put the bowl on it, and took a big yellow spoon, a tray and a plastic bag from another bag which Rudnikov hadn't seen at first. The contents of the plastic bag were put on a tray. Rudnikov couldn't see from afar what exactly it was. Balls? Well, it was unclear. The main sectary took the spoon in his hand and intoned a long phrase in Latin. At least, Rudnikov thought that it was Latin. He was a more or less educated man, and he could imagine how Latin would sound, with all the distinctive endings "is" and "us."

One of the sectaries from the circle approached the priest and kneeled in front of him. The priest drew something with a spoon and put it to the lips of the kneeling man. He drank it. The priest took the ball from the tray and put it in the sectary's mouth. He chewed and swallowed it. It was clear from the movements of his jaws, muscles of the throat, and Adam's apple; then he stood up and returned to his spot. His neighbor, a young girl without a mask, immediately headed to the center of the hall, and everything repeated. Then another sectary… another one… in full circle.

When Rudnikov's turn came, he did the same without hesitating. He approached the priest, kneeled, drank a spoonful of some ropy sweet liquid, and swallowed the ball that was put in his mouth. To his amazement, it was meat. A cutlet or a dumpling—he didn't know the right name for it. Chopped meat shaped as a ball. Rudnikov couldn't understand what kind of meat it was. Its taste was very strange.

Actually, the atmosphere started to be very pressing. A ring of immovable bare-footed sectaries in robes and masks; red priests with their hoods in the center, chanting Latin verses; a sinister pendulum with a crescent—it appeared to be not a crescent but a sharp blade of an axe—and all this was accompanied by the constant loud meowing of the cat.

Meow! Meow! Meow!

"What kind of meat was he eating right now? Its taste was very strange. Sweet. Though maybe it was sweet after the syrup from the spoon. *Well, the taste is strange. I have never tried such meat. Maybe it's a cat?*

The thought made Rudnikov sick. *Well, let it be. Why do I care? Everyone was eating it. And nobody got poisoned. Come on! Well, a cat—so what? It's nothing. Maybe it's not cat's meat; maybe it's rabbit meat with a sweet sauce. I don't care. Let it be a cat or a mouse. I don't give a damn! I need the result. The result from the eating of cats and kneeling to Latin chanting... Well and good! I can stand or kneel; I'm not that proud. I'm used to anything. I'm patient and learned. I've been in different situations.:*

Meanwhile, the last sectary stood up and went to his spot. The priest lifted his arms and said a couple of phrases in Latin.

Enough! Is it really Latin? thought Rudnikov suddenly. *It seems it's not Latin at all. It's some strange and obscure language.*

For some reason, he felt uncomfortable at once. The comical side of what was happening, which had been prevailing up to that time and had been helping to maintain a certain distance, tranquility, and cold blood—all these rituals, changing; they are adults, after all—receded into the background and lost any importance. He suddenly became terrified. It seemed to him that it was no demonstration or a play for world-weary and bored men and women who were pretending to be sectaries, but it was something real and sinister. And all these motionless people in black robes and with glazy eyes began to scare him.

It seemed that some evil magic brought him to the Dark Ages. He couldn't imagine anyone of these people in usual, normal life, in normal surroundings, in usual dresses and suits. He couldn't imagine that they were laughing, talking, playing with children, or watching TV. They seemed to be real, genuine fanatics and bigots. Inquisitors. The robes fitted them well; they looked natural in those cassocks.

Suddenly Rudnikov felt an urge to leave immediately, to run away. It seemed that evil in that hall was flowing in the air.

Dark psi-energy! thought Rudnikov convulsively. *The energy of pain and torments! Probably I'm charging with it. I came here for that.*

The priest lifted his arms again and started chanting. The sectaries began swaying from side to side and monotonously repeating together with him the ends of the phrases. Rudnikov repeated with them.

"Norus extum. Tractum versis."

He was filled with a strange, unexplainable feeling, as if he were mingling with all of them and becoming a part of a huge, single whole. He was dissolving, dissolving, dissolving in it.

The sectaries swayed more and more. The priest suddenly shouted a loud phrase, and music came from somewhere. A strange music—strong, powerful and, at the same time, pinching, sad, heart-stirring, and mournful. *Is it an organ?* Rudnikov hadn't heard such music before—nothing of the kind. At the first accord, all the sectaries, as one man, joined hands, stepped to the left, and then made two steps to the right. A pause. Then again—a step to the left and two steps to the right.

Rudnikov was moving with everyone.

The circle of the people started moving counter-clockwise. A step to the left and two steps to the right. A step to the left and two steps to the right. Slowly at first and then faster and faster. To the left—and to the right. To the left—and to the right.. To the left—and to the right! Faster, faster, faster. Accordingly, the music went faster and faster. Louder and louder. And the people were moving in time with the music. It was setting the rhythm. Faster! Faster! Faster! To the left—and to the right! To the left—and to the right! Again! Again! Again!

The ropes got untied and the robes unwrapped because of the moving. Rudnikov could see the naked bodies of men and women under the robes—their breasts, thighs, black triangles at the bottom of the women's bellies, men's penises, some of which were hard. Rudnikov felt that he had an erection, as well.

To the left—and to the right! To the left—and to the right! Again! Again!

Suddenly, in the center of the hall, there was a wild, heart-rending scream of a cat. Rudnikov lifted his eyes in answer to that strange sound and saw that the cat, which had been brought in the bag, was wriggling beneath the pendulum with its legs tied. With every move of the pendulum, it cut the cat with the sharp crescent, bringing a great pain to the animal and making it yell.

Swing, yell! Swing, yell! To the left—and to the right! To the left—and to the right! Faster-faster-faster-faster!

Suddenly, one of the women broke the circle, came inside it, and twitched and wriggled on the floor, being taken either by the hysterics or convulsions, and, at the same time, the circle broke, the light almost went out, and an incredible and horrifying orgy began. Everyone was copulating with everyone. By twos, threes, or fours. Men with women, women with women, and men with men.

Everybody was filled with madness. It was not sex as we understand it. It was something else. An obligatory part of what was happening. A final part of the ritual.

Rudnikov felt that it was really necessary, that it was very important, indeed. The huge amount of sexual energy, evolved by the men and women, was interacting through the spells with the pulsing dark psi-energy of pain and torments and dissolving it. It was neutralizing it, making it safe for the people in the room. For the sectaries.

The red twinkling twilight, inhuman organ music, voluptuous screams, and moans from everywhere, desperate wild screams of the cat, and the figure of the priest in the center, clad in red and somehow illuminated, with his hands aloft and head thrown back, chanting prayers, or spells, in a state of trance…

***

When Rudnikov came to his senses, he found himself standing in a circle of people. The robes were wrapped and the ropes were tied; the lights were on, and, what was the most important thing, it was silent. No music and no screams of tormented cat. He looked at the pendulum. The wretched animal beneath it was cut in half. The poor cat was dead.

The priest, who was standing in the center of the hall, said a final phrase, turned away, and headed quickly to the distant exit, followed by his two servants. As soon as the door closed after him, the circle broke and the sectaries rushed randomly to the nearest door. The same door through which Rudnikov had entered the hall.

Rudnikov moved with them. He was completely wasted, like a squeezed orange. Obviously, the rest were feeling the same. Their eyes were lowered, and they were staring at the feet. Nobody was talking at all.

Rudnikov left the robe and slippers in the dressing room, taking the mask with him. He just looked what the others were doing, and followed their example.

When he was in the metro coach, he recovered a bit and started to recall the details of the event in which he had just taken part.

Robe… he's standing in the circle… sacrament…so, what kind of meat was that? Alright, it doesn't matter. Music… the movement in the circle which was becoming faster… orgy… He didn't remember the orgy that well, and it was worrying him.

Shit! Probably, the liquid contained some drugs, and I took it. I don't remember anything! How is this possible? Just some episodes.

Completely wild ones. I'm fucking someone in a very quick tempo, like it was my last time. And who was that? What? Where? Was it at least a woman? No, it was definitely a woman! I think... Fuck, it's better not to recall it! If I do, I would fucking hate myself for the rest of my life!

By the way, wasn't I fucked by someone? By chance? Did someone fuck me accidentally? Didn't I do to someone? No, no! What 'no, no?' If it's' "no, no,' indeed, that's because I was lucky. I couldn't think straight at all. I was filled with madness like everyone else. Who was I fucking? A woman... Maybe that was some 100-year-old witch? There were some of that kind; I did notice them. They couldn't stand up when they were taking the sacrament. The ostiaries were lifting them up by their arms. And how did they dance with everyone? Fucking hell! I don't give a damn how they were dancing. Dancing! And how did they? And, what's more important, with whom? Actually, it's horrible. It's a common sin in its pure form. Fucking Sodom and Gomorrah. Thank God that they didn't make me fuck that wretched cat! First when it was alive, and then - dead. They just made me eat it," he thought gloomily. *"in the form of balls and cutlets. So what? I didn't care who to fuck and who'd fuck me. I don't like it at all. If I wasn't fucked by chance, I'd be definitely fucked the next time. For sure! I'd be fucked in the heat of the moment—and that's it! Fucking heat! Give up all hope. Farewell to virginity! I'm not a cherry anymore, Mom. Well, fuck these orgies! I value my honor. And I didn't like it at all! It's unpleasant to recall it. As usual. Yeah, and what's the use of it? What's the use? What did I eat the cats and endanger myself for?"*

Rudnikov became uneasy again and moved restlessly, trying to find out if his anus was wet. *What if? No! It seems not. Right, 'it seems'. Alright, even if it is, one mistake does not an anti-Semite make. A plague on you for saying such jokes! Dash it all! I need to come home as soon as possible. I have to take a shower and wash away everything. They could make a shower in the sect. Well, fuck them with their shower! What shower are we talking about? A public one? For men and women? Is someone going to be ashamed after such a crowd? We're all friends. And the men—I have seen them already!"*

Rudnikov again recalled some of the most vivid images and spat involuntarily. *Yuk! Filth! Curious... Is Frolov a virgin? Or a seasoned woman? A fucking whore. Yuk! I have to keep away from him, just in case. From that whore. I don't like faggots. It's a pity I haven't seen Zinaida. Next time, I'm gonna look for her with purpose. I'll hunt her down. When the lights go out, I need to find her. And, after that, everything's gonna be easy. As far as I understood, no one would say no. Go ahead. Use it as you wish. Do it where you want to. Please! Right. It's the only pleasant thought. A ray of light in the realm of darkness. In the realm of the dark psi-energy. Even then... While I'm looking for Zinaida, they would do it with me a hundred times. It's impossible to say no. Alright, I'm going in circles. Yes! So what's the use of it? Have I become more lucky? How can I check it?*

Suddenly, Rudnikov realized that he knew how to do it. He had to flip a coin a hundred times. The result of the first flip—heads or tails—would be his luck, and he should count it. If the first one is heads, he would count heads. If it's tails, he would count tails. The excess of the statistical average of 50% would be his current luck, the level of his fortune. Rudnikov didn't remember how he learned it—maybe someone told him?—but he knew exactly that it was true. He just knew it. He barely checked himself and didn't start flipping the coin straight in the metro coach. Waiting for his station, he rushed outside, sat on a bench, and flipped the ruble which he had found in his pocket.

"Heads! All the better! We're gonna count the heads."

Heads Heads Heads Tails Tails Heads...

So 62 to 38. Not bad, not bad at all. For that I could risk—risk, but nothing more. Thank God, nothing happened yet. Alright, we'll see. Now I can only wait. Wait, wait, wait! I'll see how my luck will show itself. Maybe gifts will fall down from the sky. We'll see!

6.

During the next few months, the life of Igor Rudnikov changed drastically. He was promoted, he won in a lottery and a casino—by the way, he won a huge sum of money in a casino, and he became an anniversary visitor in a famous supermarket into which he came by chance—he was just walking by and thought, *Why wouldn't I come?*

All in all, the luck chased Rudnikov hotfooted. He succeeded in everything that he was doing. He bought a car and a lot of clothes, and he started visiting night clubs, restaurants, and casinos—not that often, but he did it. Actually, all his life became somehow better. Out of a chronic loser, which he had been all recent years, he suddenly turned into a strong, handsome, and confident man, and everybody could feel that—everybody who surrounded him at work and in restaurants and casinos—everywhere he appeared. He was emitting the aura of confidence and strength. He was followed by a trail of success. And everyone likes to communicate with such people. They are very rare nowadays. Actually, not only nowadays. They were always rare. At all times.

As it is known, a man gets used to the good stuff very quickly, and soon Rudnikov couldn't imagine that, at one time, everything had not been so. He tried not to think about it. What for? A small, gray, timid, and screwed-up man which he was in another life, hundred years ago, died and was completely forgotten. He became a leader, a winner, and a child of fortune. There were only victories, victories, and victories ahead! From now on, there were only luck and success. Always and everywhere! Ahead!

So, in the fumes of success, the first year passed. And then came the collapse. Actually, rust, scold, and dark stains had appeared in his life from the very beginning. Everything was falling down around him. It seemed that he was succeeding on the shatters of the lives and fates of other people. Different things were happening to the people who surrounded him; they were followed by strange, constant griefs and misfortunes: someone would die, get sick, drink a lot; another would be dumped by his wife, another's summer cottage would burn, etc.

Rudnikov was aware of all that—he wasn't blind—and, frankly speaking, he was tormented by that, always, from the very beginning. And the further it went, the more torments he felt. It appeared not to be as easy to carry such a burden as he had thought before that. Moreover, with the flowing of the time, he took all of his success for granted. But all those disasters and cataclysms, being a monster which is bringing grief and pain around him —drinking with the man that you like, knowing that his friend or relative would soon be sick or even die. That was horrible! Rudvikov began to feel as if he was a devil incarnate, a hellspawn who couldn't live among humans. He was a werewolf and a ghoul who was drinking the luck and happiness of the others. He was taking their lifeblood. He was feeding on it. And all that he touched would die.

And the meeting of the sect, which he visited regularly, were the sabbots of the same inhuman beings as him. They were cursed. Ghouls. Probably the other sectaries were feeling the same way. At least, they almost didn't talk to each other. After the meeting, they would put on their clothes quickly and leave for their holes until next Friday.

Rudnikov recalled with an unpleasant surprise that, about a year ago, he wanted to find Zinaida at the meeting and fuck her. Today, she seemed to him a beautiful, painted, exotic, and tropical snake or maybe a water lizard or a frog. She was dangerous and treacherous, and she carried a deadly poison. And he had to keep away from her. He didn't think about her as a sexual object. What object? After he had seen her in action during the weekly orgies, he had a real, purely physical hatred of her. It was a kind of pathologic disgust!

As it turned out, Lady Ziu was a lesbian—an active and dedicated one, as it seemed. At least, Rudnikov didn't see her with men—neither during the orgies nor in life. He saw her with women only. To be precise, with young girls—as a rule, with very young girls. It appeared that they were the main object of her passion. What would she do to them, and what would she conceive? It was a sight to behold. Actually, quite on the contrary. Rudnikov couldn't forget the most impressive images for a long time. He just couldn't efface the memory of it. He was almost impotent due to that. He almost began hating all women. *Fucking women! I wish you saw these women! Bitches during estruation. Lustful females. Whores. Chippies. Crap. Women are very mean creatures, especially when they get out of hand and lose all sense of shame. Wretched lesbians without any limitations! At least, a man is a restraining factor for a woman. Even in bed, during the time of intimacy, a woman remains a flirt, she's playing a role, she's trying to impress him and take his fancy. And, as she can't fully understand a man, who's of opposite sex, she's somehow restrained and stopped, and it makes her stay within the bounds of propriety. She's afraid to do something wrong. But when women... between themselves... looking through each other... with all their filthy physiology... throwing away shame and decency... Pah! That's horrible!*

Actually, men shouldn't be at these orgies in the first place. It was good that they were not allowed to them in ancient times. Very wise. Well, it's like a famous ad says, 'Women have their little secrets.' So let them stay with their little secrets. Hell with them! It's better not to delve in them. You're definitely going to come across a used tampon, at the best case.

Well, women! Broads, though, what about broads? Are they the only ones to be blamed? What about men? They're really not any better. Or even worse. There were more than enough gays at the meetings. Rudnikov saw too much of them. He was fed up with them. All positions and views. Full-face and half-face. *"It's right that everybody hates them! It's a fucking disaster!*

He wasn't afraid for himself. Nobody was hitting on him like he thought at the very beginning. And nobody was making him do anything. *Everything's up to you. Nobody's gonna rape you.* Mutual agreement. Maybe, it was somehow connected to the strict rule of the sect not to wish ill to any of its members as he was warned from the very beginning—maybe. Rudnikov wasn't sure about that and didn't really tried to find out. What for? Why? What's the difference? They may have a lot of rules. There are rules; that's what matters. And he was satisfied with those rules. That's it! What's more? What else did he need?

As a matter of fact, Rudnikov took these orgies for granted, as if they were an inevitable evil with which he had to live. They didn't attract him at all. He realized very quickly that it wasn't that pleasant to make love in the company of other people, however friendly they may be. After all, it is very private and intimate stuff. Nevertheless, he clearly felt that these orgies were necessary as a part of the ritual, of the ceremony. Sex provided a relief. It was impossible to stay in the hall, filled with dark psi-energy, without sex.

His luck was now at the level of 80-82%. It was an average number, neither lower nor higher. Though, if he missed one meeting, his luck would immediately be lowered by 10%. Rudnikov tried it once. He made an experiment. After that, he was recovering the coefficient for a whole month. But, on the other hand, his luck never went higher than 82%. It was his top limit. He attended all meetings after that event. All of them! Consciously and diligently. It was like a job for him. He attended them, no matter how he felt. That was sacred!

By the way, about sacred. In these latter days, Rudnikov started to think what kind of sect it was. Religious or not? Was it a sin to be part of it? Such questions had not come to his mind before, especially when he was a loser. What religion? What sin? Success—success at any cost, and everything else didn't matter. But now—now all was changed. All these dark energies he hadn't believed in it before, neither religions nor dark energies, neither god nor devil. But the facts were obvious. He became a lucky one. A child of fortune. Suddenly, he achieved everything in life. *What was it, if not a miracle? And if it was miracle, then there should be...who? God? Devil? Who? There was definitely someone. But who?*

Umph! Who? So, what God could be here? Dark psi-energy ritual killings of animals, all these terrible orgies. What God? "And the meat, meat balls. What are they made of? What kind of meat? What is this strange sweet flavor? If Rudnikov had been afraid that it was a cat, then now he only hoped that it was only cat. "*Cat meat. Just cat meat. And not... God bless me! I'd better not be thinking about that!"*

All in all, Rudnikov didn't become a zealous sectary at all. He held out the first year, being drunk with his success and new possibilities, but then came a hangover. As the time went, he was sicker in heart. Nothing could bring him pleasure. No casinos and restaurants. And the meetings began sitting heavy on him. All these orgies—faggots and lesbians And that was not really the point. He was a doom for those who surrounded him. He carried a curse. Yeah, he even had nightmares due to that. The last straw was the death of 2-year-old son of one of his colleagues. It happened all too quickly, unnaturally. He got sick and died. And Rudnikov won in a lottery again; he was now doing all the lotteries.

After that, he was struck by a severe psychological crisis. Depression, collapse, insomnia—he was in a low mood actually, he realized—that was it! He couldn't do it anymore. He had to leave. He had to quit all those psi-energies. Curse them! He didn't want to deal with it. It turned out that he was too positive for these negativities. He remained an outsider. Probably that was the reason that his index never went over 82%. He had too much white energy in him. He had too much compassion, softness, and sentiments All of this useless crap. *A real hero should be tough, firm, and confident, like a Doberman Pinscher. And what's this? A standard gentleman's set of classical loser. A sissy and hodad. A teddy pugdog. A silly dog from one of Disney's cartoons."*

In brief, I've made a good start. I was promoted, I won some money in casinos and lotteries, I bought a lot of cloths, I got a car; it'll be enough. Never mind the Mercedes; I can do without them. Their price is too high. I have to pay with blood, the blood of other people. The blood of children. Let them go to hell! I'm too weak for such entertainments —too weak. As usual. Like in everything else. Well, alright. Maybe it's for the best. Fuck all these bloody winnings! I'm not a ghoul who's drinking blood. Fuck it! Let it go to hell! I'll live without it. I have lived without it before.

As a matter of fact, Rudnikov made a decision. Now he had to start acting. He had to bring his decision to life. He had to quit. He had to stop attending the meetings.

One would think that it's easy—just don't go there if you don't want to. Nobody's making you do it. Well and good—do as you please. Go back to your swamp. Go back to your ooze, to your nothingness. Have flag, will travel! You can be a nought again, but this time - forever. Rudnikov realized all that, and that's why he was postponing it. After each meeting, he was irritated and promised himself that it was the last time.

"I'll never visit them again!" But next Friday came, the memories of previous meeting lost its keenness, and he came again to the familiar building, hating himself for his weakness and lack of will. Moreover, now he knew what one pass was worth. It would be very difficult to recover after that. It was a serious restraining factor for him, as well. How would it look like? He was attending the meetings for the whole year, he was eating the cats, and now he would be up the spout!

As a matter of fact, Rudnikov was quite ready for the break, but he still needed one little push, so he could resolve to do it. Without that push, his hesitations could last for a very long time. Only God knew for how long!

And that push came in time. It seemed that fate itself interfered and made a decision instead of him. Rudnikov fell in love suddenly. Actually, he fell in love at once, at the spot. He fell head-over-heels in love. He had a crush. He fell hard. He fell in love with a very young girl. She was 16. Actually, he preferred more mature women, but here! This girl cut to his heart, maybe with her vulnerability or her trustingness, maybe with her childish innocence. Or, maybe, with reticence or dreaminess.

She wasn't silly—quite on the contrary! He had a lot of chances to check it, but, unlike most of Rudnikov's female acquaintances, she preferred to be silent. She preferred to listen attentively, staring at her companion with her large, dark almond eyes. Rudnikov liked that a lot. It seemed to him that there was a secret in this silence. He was even confused a bit with her mysterious look of Mona Lisa, a mysterious look of the Sphinx.

"What are you thinking about?" he would always ask her during such moments.

"Well," she would shrug her shoulders and smile with her eyes only, "nothing."

Ksiusha. Her name was Ksiusha. Actually, Rudnikov called her that. Her proper name was Kseniya.

7.

Rudnikov was smoking thoughtfully near an open window, ashing his cigarette outside. He had to make a decision. Ksiusha was supposed to arrive any minute.

"Well, it can't go on like this. I have to do something. Now, immediately. She's in great danger while she remains with me. She's in terrible danger. Something could happen to her at any moment. Or wouldn't it, given that I love her? What kind of luck is that, if she's hurt? No, no; that sectary asked me about that at the very beginning, whether I had any relatives. So, my luck doesn't care. It strikes everything and anything to the maximum, everybody who's near me."

It's only natural. The poor girl is not protected from this dark energy of mine, like all others. I do trick the nature with all these devilish rituals, together with other scum like me. Rudnikov thought about terrible dances, orgies, and strange sweet balls, and felt disgust. *And she's an ordinary human. She's not allowed to stay at my side. It's better to be in a cage with a tiger or a crocodile. Well! Oh, God, we're all sinful!*

So, what? What shall I do? Eh? I need to make a decision. It's obvious that I'm gonna leave the sect. I already did that. I'm not gonna go there again. Ever. That's it! Dim the lights, the show is over! We're like ships that pass in the night. That's clear. But that's not enough. I still need time to discharge. I have to cast the remains of the dark psi-energy to the others. I'm charged like a capacitor, a battery or an accumulator.

Well, I need time. Time, time, time, time! Nothing would help me except time. I has to wait. Wait? And how long? How long should I wait? Hell knows! How long—a week? A month? Yeah, right, a week! Dream on! A month at least, as sure as sure can be, or maybe even more. Well, I got a special device. A portable Geiger counter. I could check myself at any moment. I could check my radioactive background and find out when I cease to glow.

Rudnikov put a hand in his pocket automatically, took out a coin and flipped it with a usual move.

"Heads! Great. Heads, heads, heads, tails, heads—83 to 17—a record! Though it's inappropriate time, as usual. It's not a good time for fucking records. I'm glowing with dark psi-light; I'm literally burning with it, like a nuclear reactor. Like a gloomy 1000-watt lamp of pain and torments. People should be avoiding me like

a plague. And nobody should meet with me. Oh, God! Why have I invited her here? I should have checked myself at first. Moron! Idiot! Fucking goblin! Bandar-log. What if something happens to her because of me? Later! Well, it's better not to think about that. I don't want to draw it before time.

Well what shall I do? Eh? What's the decision? I have to leave her for the time being, at least for four or six weeks, until my level is normal. Until it becomes as usual. Like others'. 50 to 50. Shit! How? How would I leave her? What excuse shall I think of? I need to make something up. I'm going on a business trip. She's gonna believe me.

Rudnikov ashed his cigarette outside. He didn't want to lie to Ksiusha, even in details, even for the sake of it. He loved her, indeed.

Well, I need to tell her everything. Everything—about the sect and stuff. I need to tell her how I built my happiness on the torments of the others. It's better to do it now. And I'll have to do it anyway. I can't let this lie stand between us. I don't want that. It's wrong. Even if she understands and forgives me, I won't forgive myself. Never! I could lie to her; it's easy, she's a child, but I couldn't lie to myself. What does the Bible say? 'A corrupt tree bringeth forth evil fruit?' Well, something of that kind. And it's right. I don't want our relations to be built on lies. We need to set the record straight. We need to cut the fucking Gordian knot. Otherwise, it will tangle more and more with the time. As always, one lie brings the other one. The next moment you're in it completely. You're trapped in these lies which were supposed to serve good goals. 'Dirt remains dirt, whatever color it's painted in.' Well, I have to tell her."

The thought that he had to tell Ksiusha about the orgies and the death of the 2-year-old child—about everything—made Rudnikov sick. *It's curious; how she will take it? Maybe she'll get scared and run away? Will she hate me? Will she despise me? She's very young, inexperienced. She's a teenager. And everything's black and white for the teenagers, right and left, good and evil. But life is complicated. There are many flowers in it and many shades. How shall I explain that to her? It comes with the life experience, the understanding. It comes with time. And what shall I explain to her? What understanding? That right is really left? And black is white? That the sect is good? All this dark psi-energy of pain and torments. Shit!"*

Rudnikov took a pull at his cigarette.

And these fucking orgies! An interesting topic. Maybe I shouldn't mention them. It can wait. Then, some time when we get married...or, at least, without unnecessary details. Well! In general, I don't want to shock her; she's probably still a virgin.

Strangely enough, Rudnikov didn't sleep with Ksiusha. It just didn't happen. He didn't insist, and she was completely inexperienced and ignorant in these matters. However, Rudnikov was pleased with that. He wanted to arrange everything as others do: wedding, wedding night, then children. He was fed up with these quick animal matings.

Come on, enough! I had enough of them. Thank God! I am full to the throat with them, at work and at orgies. Enough.

That's probably why he fell in love with Ksiusha. Her youth and virginity, her sincerity, naivety, and spontaneity. *Well, of course, not only because of that. But these are part of the reason, and not the least important. And discussing all the filth with her—uh-uh! Talking about this stuff, well, it's clear that it's not the 18th century, and she's not a prim young lady, she's not from the moon. She's a modern girl, she watches TV and she uses internet. So all the same! I just don't want to talk to her about that; I don't want to do it, and that's it. Later, sometime later—after the wedding."*

The bell rang. Rudnikov startled, quickly put out the cigarette and rushed to the door.

"Oh, hi! Come on in," he stepped aside, letting Ksiusha in.

"Hi!" the girl entered the hall. "You hid my slippers again?"

"Don't take your shoes off!" Ksiusha looked at him in surprise "Come on in. We need to talk."

The girl looked at him intently again, without saying a word, and then went to the room. Rudnikov followed her. He wanted to do it as quickly as possible—talk to her and send her home at once, far from him, while he had such a huge radioactive background. *87:13! No way! She should stay away from me. We'd better not see each other for some time. We'd better not talk, even on the phone. I don't really know how this dark energy works. The mechanism is completely unclear. It doesn't necessarily include the physical contact.*

I mean, territorial, he corrected himself, smiling. *Umph! Physical. Alright. So, probably, a usual communication is enough to expose a person to risk. Maybe I'm exaggerating, but it's better to be too cautious. I don't want her to...well, it's better to be too cautious. Well, we won't talk for a month. That's easy. It's alright.*

As a matter of fact, the thought that they wouldn't talk for a month—the whole month—was terrifying. *But what can I do? I have to do it. What's the other option? What if? Well, that's it! The issue is over."*

"Listen, Ksiusha, I want to tell you," he winced and scratched his temple, not knowing where to begin. The girl was still silent. "Shit, I don't really know where to begin," mumbled Rudnikov. "So, we need to part ways for four to six weeks. We need to stop seeing each other and talking to each other, no communicating at all."

"Why? Are you leaving?" asked Kseniya in surprise.

"Yes, I mean, no. No, I'm not going anywhere," he said again.

"Why then? What's the matter?" she got even more surprised.

"What's the matter? What's the matter? You see, well...what's the matter? You see, I'm a member of a certain organization," resolved Rudnikov at last, "a sect."

"What?! You? A sect? What sect?" the girl was staring at him with eyes which were round with astonishment. "Are you a sectary?"

"Yeah. Actually, I was. I decided to quit."

"So, you're really a sectary? A member of a real sect?" the girl was looking at him as if she saw him for the first time. "So what?" she asked after a pause. "They don't want to let you go? Is this some kind of mafia?"

"No! What mafia?" said Rudnikov discontentedly. *Mafia!" You watch too much TV! All these modern shows.* "No, Ksiusha, it's not mafia. And nobody's holding me there."

"So, what's the problem?" asked the girl with a shrug of her shoulders.

"Alright, look," Rudnikov took a coin out of his pocket.

I'm not allowed to show it to her, I can scare the luck away, he remembered immediately. *Right, it's for the best. Maybe I'll scare it away, indeed. And I won't have to wait for a month. All bridges are burnt.* He flipped the coin and caught it in the air. *Heads!*

"See, it's heads?"

"Yeah, I see," the girl looked at the coin and then at him, "so, what?"

"Now look," Rudnikov put the coin on the nail of his bent thumb. "Now I'm gonna flip it 100 times, and heads will be no less than 80 times."

"Is this a kind of a trick?" asked Kseniya.

"Look!"

Rudnikov started flipping the coin quickly. "Oh, God! How many times did he do it for the last year? He didn't flip so many coins during his whole life!"

Heads…heads...heads...heads...tails....heads...heads. *90:10! Oh, God! Murder! What's happening?*

"That's it! You have to leave now!" Rudnikov bounced out of a chair.

"I'm not going anywhere!" the girl was outraged. "Can you explain to me what's happening?"

"Alright! Listen carefully, we haven't got much time," said Rudnikov hastily. "So, it's like this. A year ago, I joined a sect. Well, I thought that it was some kind of Masonic lodge where various powerful people grow fussy. They're disguised—black masks, secret signs. Well, it's fake. It's a game. So I decided to join them because of mercantile reasons. I wanted to make useful acquaintances and stuff. So I joined them.

"It turned out that they were no Masons. And it was not fake and play. It was all very serious," Rudnikov gave a heavy sigh. "I'm not sure how they do it, but their members become very lucky, everywhere and in everything. Did you see how many heads I had?" Kseniya looked at the coin on the table. "Ninety times out of 100—90! —while the average rate is 50. That is my coefficient of luck. I succeed in everything I do. I got a promotion, I'm winning in lotteries, everything's okay in my life. Everything's absolutely fine," Rudnikov caught his breath and continued. "But the problem is that it's happening by the means of other people, by the means of those who surround me. They begin to experience bad luck—in everything! They start to be sick, die, get into accidents. Well, it doesn't matter. I'll tell you later. Later, when it's all over," Rudnikov faltered, looking for words.

"When what is over?" asked the girl quietly, using the pause.

"When everything's over, when my curse is lifted," Rudnikov almost screamed. "I told you—it's dangerous for you to me near me! At any moment, something may happen to you, like to other people. And I'll just win a lottery. That's why I want us to part ways for some time."

"And what will happen then?"

"Well, you see, then it will all disappear. With time, it'll just go away. I'll become an ordinary man. I have to attend the meetings in order to keep my luck. And I have to take part in these satanic rituals. But now I'm quitting!"

"Did you take part in satanic rituals?" asked Ksiusha, looking strangely at him. "What did you do—dance around the fire in some forest?"

"Why in the forest?" Rudnikov was surprised. "What fire?"

"Well, I saw it in a movie," explained the girl. "'Chases with devil'. There were sects, Satanists, and human sacrifices. They were doing walkarounds near the fire."

"Well, walkarounds," mumbled Rudnikov, rolling his eyes. "No, Ksiusha, we're doing it in the center of the city, not far from the metro station Sokolniki, in the school, by the way. It's not like in a movie."

"School? Why school?" the girl was surprised.

"Well, I'm not sure," Rudnikov smiled and shrugged his shoulders. "Maybe the layout is convenient for the meetings. The school hall—it's very convenient. Well, that's it!" he hurried. "Enough talking! Did you understand me? We have to part ways for some time, until everything's fine with me. We have to stop talking on the phone and communicating at all, just in case. And, when everything's fine with me, I'll give you a call. Alright?"

The girl nodded and stood up, too.

"Alright, off you go. I'm not showing you out, okay? For the same reason. You need to stay away from me. I love you," he added, standing on the doorstep and looking at the girl's back. She halted and turned back. "Have a good time," he smiled to her.

"Alright," she smiled back, turned away, and headed to the elevator.

Rudnikov slammed the door and came back to the room. Fuck! He took the cigarette out of the pack with his shaking hand, clicked the lighter, and took a deep pull at cigarette. "Now I have to wait for a whole month! I'm gonna turn crazy—the whole month!"

8.

The whole next day, Rudnikov stayed at home being bored to death. He didn't have anything to do; he never liked to read books, so he could only watch TV. During that time, he learned the TV program by heart, watched a whole bunch of idiotic movies, and listened to a lot of modern pop songs on the music channel. *Fucking music videos. What a crap!* Well, he substantially raised his cultural level and widened his musical horizon.

All this time, he was constantly flipping the coin. He was checking; the coefficients were falling down. Slowly, but surely—very slowly!

0.86:0.14; 0.8:0.2; 0.65:0.35…

Finally, at the end of the month, they stopped at the level of 0.5 0.5—0.499:0.501.

"Fuck! They could stop at 0.501:0.499 why not?" thought Rudnikov gloomily, making sure that the dynamics stopped, the process of discharging finished. He didn't have the background. "So, I've been a loser, and I remained him. 0.499 : 0.501! A whole tenth of percent—it's not even a centesimal! Fuck!"

Now he could call Ksiusha.

"Hello," he heard her mother's voice.

"Hello. Can I talk to Ksiusha?"

"She's not at home."

"Not at home? And when she's gonna be back?" Rudnikov chilled. *Not at home?' And where's she? It's 11 p.m.!*

"I don't know," her mother said indifferently. "She said that she'd be late."

"I'm sorry," mumbled Rudnikov and hung up the phone.

Ksiusha lived with her parents, and she didn't get on well with them, so he didn't want to leave any messages. And it wouldn't be good to call after half-past eleven.

Rudnikov called about 5 more times before it was half-past eleven. Ksiusha still wasn't at home.

"Alright," he started calming himself. "She could be anywhere. Tomorrow, I'm gonna find it out."

Above all things, he wanted to leave everything, rush to her building, hide himself somewhere, and wait for her until the morning, if necessary. He would wait for her return and see who'd be with her. Jealousy sparkled in him and burned like a fire.

"Jealousy is fierce, like hell, and its arrows are made of fire," he recalled a phrase which came to his mind out of somewhere, and only now could he understand its meaning. Before that, the sentences of that kind were only nice words for him and nothing more. Literature. Fiction. But now he could feel it himself, he could feel it with his own skin. *I was fierce, indeed!* He hurried and scurried about the apartment and couldn't sit still.

He took the phone a hundred times and threw it down again, not resolving to call. "Fucking parents! They go to bed too early!"

Where is she? Where? Where could she be at this hour? At night? With whom? She isn't walking alone on the streets; she's with someone. With whom? With whom? So, is she seeing someone? Does she have a boyfriend? So she found a new boyfriend during this month?

He was falling, falling, and falling down in a black abyss. His heart turned cold, until it became a piece of ice, a block of ice. He couldn't stand it any longer. Cursing everything and despising himself for weakness and wimpishness, he rushed outside, got into his car, and drove to her house. He felt better when he started driving. Actually, he was doing something. He just couldn't stay at home and wait until morning. It was impossible, unthinkable. "And its arrows are made of fire."

Fifteen minutes later, Rudnikov was already near her house. He parked his car far from it, for he didn't want Kseniya to see it—that would be embarassing—and hid himself in a hallway between the second and third floors.

What if she's at home already? he thought belatedly, *and now she's sleeping in her bed. It's already half past twelve. And I made the last call at half past eleven.*

But he couldn't just leave his look-out. He would rather stand here all night than stay at home, doing nothing and knowing nothing.

"At least, I'm gonna know that she came home between half-past eleven and half past twelve," he made a decision. "If she doesn't come back during the night, it will mean that she's already at home."

He tried not to think what would be if she didn't come back during the night, and he found out that she was not at home. The very thought was terrible.

He was standing, smoking a cigarette, and looking out of the window. *Yeah, like this. If I turn away, she might slip in quickly. And I can't see who's standing near the elevator on the first floor. Maybe it's her or maybe it's someone else. I could check where the elevator goes*—Ksiusha lived on the 9th floor—*but that's not for certain. And if I go outside to check in what apartments the lights are on, then, first, I could miss her if it wasn't her in the elevator, and, second, I could run into her near the hall. I'd be very ashamed if she realized that I'm spying her. And she would definitely realize that. What am I doing near her house at night? Well, I'd better stay here, look down, and not move at all. That's the best option. I'm not producing any noise, so the neighbors won't raise a stink and call the cops—'What's he doing here at night? Is he a killer?' Right! Fucking killer! Arbenin. Othello. 'If a had a gun, I would kill you! But if I had an axe, I would chop you! You'd better poke at me with your horns!'—and I wouldn't miss her."*

Moreover, he was okay with waiting. He was so nervous that he didn't notice the flow of time; it rushed like an arrow. He was a hunter, waiting in an ambush. *Hark! A twig cracked. Is it a sound of a car? No, that's not it. Again!*

Ksiusha came home at about 3 a.m. She was alone.

Rudnikov made sure that she entered her apartment—the elevator went to the 9th floor, the door slammed, and he could see from the outside that the lights in her room went on—and drove home with a great relief. Of course, he had to find out where she had been until 3 a.m., but she came back alone. Alone!

9.

Next day, Rudnikov called Ksiusha and set a meeting. Ksiusha was very pleased to hear from him. Feeling her tone, Rudnikov melted down and didn't do an interrogation with tricky questions as he had previously wanted. He just mentioned that he had called her the day before, and she hadn't been at home.

"My friend was celebrating her birthday," said the girl calmly, "and I got home late."

Well, 'my friend'. Until 3 a.m And what were you doing there, eh? With your friend. Just talking? Well, alright. If you say friend, let it be so. Why would she be staying at home all the time while I'm doing hell knows what? I'm getting rid of the dark energy, God forgive! A fucking accumulator! Who'd have thought? As a song says, 'My friend's (though, it was 'sweetheart,; it seems) in a high palace, and nobody can enter it!' In a very high one! 'Palace!' On the 9th floor. Alright, forget it.

Jealousy is humiliating and offensive. For the both—for her and for me. If you love someone, you have to trust them. And if you start suspect and spy on them, you're giving them a moral right to lie to you. If you can do it—spying is lying, as well—then why can't they do it? Alright! That's it! Enough! Stay where we are. Forget it! I don't wanna dig deeper.

For the next two weeks, Rudnikov saw Ksiusha almost on a daily basis. They were attending exhibitions and concerts and just taking walks. Rudnikov didn't care how exactly he was spending time with her. He just wanted to be with her.

At the end of the second week, he came across a coin. He came home from a date with Ksiusha and was changing when a coin fell out of his pocket. Rudnikov halted and looked at it, then put his pants on the bed, bent over, and picked up the coin. He wasn't checking all this time, for he wanted to get rid of the obsessive habit which he had acquired during the last year. He used to flip the coin everywhere—at home and on the street. He used to constantly check his luck. Now, when he quit the sect, there was no need to do it. His luck stabilized on the statistical average level—even lower; Rudnikov couldn't but swear—what's the point of checking? Now he was an ordinary person, like everybody. An average moron.

Rudnikov held the coin between his fingers thoughtfully and then flipped it with a habitual move and caught it in the air. Tails! Alright. Let it be tails.

Tails. Tails. Heads. Heads. Tails. Heads.

Rudnikov stared at the coin in amazement.

"0.38 : 0.62! How is this possible? What's the meaning of it? It's impossible." He was told in the park that his luck wouldn't become lower if he quit the sect, right? He was assured in that. *What's happening*?

He squatted and conducted another quick series.

0.37 : 0.63!

He had no more doubts. Something was wrong with him, completely wrong. He didn't think that the sectary was lying to him in the park. He recalled the man. No, he could see that such a man wouldn't lie. He was too powerful for that. He didn't have any need to lie. Rudnikov could feel it at once. So the reason was in him. Maybe, he did something wrong? Eh? Did he break the rules of the sect? What rules?

"Don't show a trick with a coin to anyone and don't wish ill to a sectary."

Well, it's clear with ill-wishing. What ill, if I haven't been seeing them for a couple of months? And a coin? Shit! Actually, I showed it to Ksiusha. Could that be the reason? But everything stabilized after that. I did check it several times. I just can't get it! I don't get it at all! What the hell? I could easily fall off a balcony. Or some other fucking disaster could happen to me. Such coefficients 0.37 : 0.63! Fuck me! Well! Well, well, well! What am I supposed to do? Eh? What am I to do? I need to do something, right? What? What?

Rudnikov grabbed the coin, dropped it in excitement, bent over to pick it up, and conducted another series.

Again 0.37 : 0.63.

"That's it! Snafu! Epic fail!"

Rudnikov felt a wild terror rise from the depth of his soul. He knew how it could happen. He saw enough of it. Next moment you're in heaven. You got under the wheels of a dump truck. Or you're in a hospital with a tumor which has appeared out of nowhere "I slipped, fell down, came to my senses, and there's a plaster!" Or, or, or, or! *What should I do?*

Well! Well! Calm down! Calm down; I need not to panic. Nothing's happened yet. It's possible to amend everything. It is, it is. How? How would I amend it? How? Well, calm down! Think! Think, think, think! So, what do we have?

My luck coefficient suddenly went down. It fell down to the critical point." Rudnikov felt that he was filled with panic. "I don't want it! I don't! Why? They promised! They guaranteed! Why?

Alright, calm down! Well, well. Why has my coefficient dropped down? Wait a second! Wait a second? What is the difference, why? Why can't I go to the meeting and raise it again? Right! Oh, God! Phew! Of course! What a fool am I! It's all very simple. What did the sectary tell me in the park? I haven't seen him after that, by the way. 'At least, once a year.' Phew! Well, well! It's much better. Well! Fuck a duck!

When is Friday? Today! Today is Friday! Shit! What is the time? Eight? Well, great! I've still got time. It's good that I didn't stay with Ksiusha too late. I have to go now. I need to change and take a shower. For I... Rudnikov winced, thinking of what was waiting for him. *Alright! I have to endure it. Forget about the disgust. I have to return everything to the usual level. And then we'll see. Eventually, I will be able to ask someone from the sect. Maybe I'll talk to the management. What the fuck is this, really? Why did it fall down? It shouldn't be so, right? It seems that they taking it easy that I decided to quit. I'm gonna tell them that I'm getting married. Well, you see. It doesn't matter. We'll deal with that. Now I need to get back to the usual level as soon as possible. And then we'll see.*

Rudnikov took a quick shower, changed, and rushed outside. He still had a lot of time until 9 if he drove. But, after a thought, Rudnikov decided not to drive. *No, I don't need that! With such a coefficient, I'd better go by metro.*

He crossed the street carefully and, looking around frightfully, prowled to the station. *Are there any hooligans? What about mad dogs Though a mad crow could fall from the sky and bite me. Peck me in the eye or two eyes and then peck at the top of the head with its huge beak. It would fucking peck me. And bye-bye! Sleep peacefully, my friend! Well, it's quite possible.*

I need just to get to the sect! If only I could get there! Save and protect! Oh, God, I'm sinful; I'm going to charge with dark energy. But what can I do? Eh? I'm weak, my Lord. Men are weak. And I want to live! Oh, God, if only I could get there! If only the metro doesn't explode, if only the coach doesn't run off the track; if only, if only, if only! If only I could get there!

What if they moved? I haven't been there for a couple of months, the thought made Rudnikov stand still and stare in front of him, and he covered with cold sweat. *No way,* he continued walking. *It's impossible. What am I saying? Why the fuck would they move? What if?*

Having entered the metro station, Rudnikov calmed down a bit. *Well, if the coach doesn't explode, if there's no fucking terrorist or a shakhid or some Mason or an alien. Well, so why did my coefficient go down? What is the reason? Well, there's no point thinking about that now. We'll deal with that there, in the sect. They're gonna explain everything to me. They're gonna unscramble it. I just need to get to them.*

Help me, Lord! Hallelujah! Or what is a right prayer? Amen? Well, if only I get there. Amen, hallelujah—whatever! If only I get there! If only I don't fall on the tracks. If only I don't fall off the escalator or from the stairs headlong, straight onto a mad dog which is running there by chance.

Well! Here we are. Thank God! Amen, hallelujah! Now slowly, without haste - though, I don't want to be fucking late!—without haste and after a prayer, let's leave the coach like this, walking along the platform carefully, carefully. It's better not to come close to anyone. Right, like this. Well, the escalator... stands still. Freeze—don't look around; don't provoke anyone. We're close. Right, like this; that's it. Now, go slowly to the doors right outside—carefully, without haste. Everything's okay? Yeah, it's alright; great. Let's go on this familiar street; let's go. I know this place; everything's good. Watch the step. Don't get distracted; stay focused. That's it; it seems we're on the spot, a familiar place. So? Are they still here? Godspeed!"

Rudnikov entered a familiar door. "Oh, my! Thank God! Phew!" He wiped his wet forehead.

Nothing had changed in the hall during that time. It seemed that time stopped here. A familiar guard was sitting on his usual spot and looking at him indifferently. Rudnikov almost rushed to embrace and kiss him. It was so pleasant that there was something stable in this world. Rudnikov nodded to the guard, just in case, letting him know that he wasn't here for the first time, and he knew the drill. The guy didn't react to it.

Everything was the same on the second floor, as well. An empty hall, and a second guard near the door. Rudnikov was already late. He grabbed a robe from the guards, rushed to the dressing room, changed quickly, and, tying the rope, entered the familiar hall.

It turned out that the quantity of the sectaries had grown. Substantially. The sect was obviously developing and expanding. The circle of the people was so thick that Rudnikov could hardly find a spot for himself. As soon as he stood in the circle, the opposite door opened, the priests entered the hall, and the ritual began. Sacramental music, slow movement of the circle—to the left and to the right; to the left and to the right.

Rudnikov had been to the meeting quite some time before that, and he felt that he was filled with the common madness. To the left and to the right. To the left and to the right! Faster and faster!

During the recent times, when he visited the meeting very often, he acquired a certain immunity and learned to control himself, but now, after a long break, that immunity disappeared, it seemed.

To the left and to the right! To the left and to the right!

The circle of people was moving faster and faster. Faster and faster! Faster! More! More!

A-ah, that's even better, thought Rudnikov. *It's good that I can't control myself. The more I can relax, the more energy I'm gonna get; that's what matters.*

***

When Rudnikov came to his senses, everything was over. The circle broke, and the sectaries went to the exit, reluctantly. Rudnikov dragged along with them. He couldn't remember anything at all. He'd gone out. What had he been doing? Or what had they done with him. Only God knew.

Well, it doesn't matter. Forget it; it's over. What are my coefficients now? That's what matters. Did I come here in vain? And, for the rest, I don't give a damn. That's okay. One time...

He entered the dressing room and, without looking around him, changed and got out hastily. The sectaries didn't use to stare at each other. Everybody tried to change quickly and leave unnoticed. Down the stairs, the door with the guard—*And who are the guards? Are they sectaries or not?* he thought suddenly. *They don't take part in the meetings*—and he was already outside.

Biting his lips with impatience, Rudnikov turned into the first yard, squatted, and took out a coin.

"Well, heads! A good sign. I didn't have heads for a long time."

Heads. Heads. Tails. Tails. Tails—fuck! Heads—see? Heads. Heads.

"51 : 49! 51 : 49!! Hurray! Viva! Victory! I didn't do it in vain. Oh, shit! Now I can catch a break. I can go home and not be afraid of anything. Well, I almost...yeah," Rudnikov noticed that his hands were shaking. "Fuck, I got too nervous. My hands are shaking wildly. Frayed nerves!"

He tried to smoke a cigarette in order to calm down. His fingers were shaking, and he broke all the matches. He lighted a cigarette on the fifth or sixth try and stood for a while, closing his eyes, lifting his face to the sky and drawing on the cigarette. Then he threw it away and went slowly to the metro.

10.

On Saturday, Rudnikov's coefficient dropped to 45 : 55; on Sunday, to 34 : 66; and on Monday, it was already 23 : 77.

Something terrible was happening, something strange. Rudnikov was sitting and staring at the coin on the table. Tails! 22 : 78! Even worse than during the previous series. Before that, he had at least 23 to 77.

So, what's happening? There should be an explanation to this nightmare and nonsense. It's unthinkable and beyond any limits. 22 : 78! It's an outrage! I won't last until the end of the week. No, I won't; that's for sure. As sure as death. That's obvious. Come on, think, think! You're a scientist. You're a theoretical physicist, after all! At least, you were one. Think! Look for a reason! You were taught to do this—to analyze and to summarize facts. You must consider it a scientific experiment which has somehow failed due to an unknown reason. And now you must find this explanation and reason in yourself. Now! Badly! Otherwise—memento mori. And that's tough.

Strangely enough, this time Rudnikov was calmer than he'd been on Friday when everything had begun. At least, he kept the ability to think clearly. On Friday, he was filled with terror and couldn't think at all.

A man can get used to anything, thought Rudnikov philosophically, *even to fucking disasters. And he can't be reached by anything. Okay, so what have we got? The coefficient shouldn't be dropping, but it is. It's dropping, dropping, and dropping, like winter snow, like it's scum! I was told in the park that it shouldn't be dropping, during the first meeting. Sure, I wasn't given any guarantees, but somehow I think that that man wasn't lying to me. What for? Well, anyway. I can't check anything, so I have to believe it. It's an axiom. It shouldn't be dropping; however, it is dropping."*

"So, what does it mean? There's a reason, an additional reason which I cannot understand right now. I cannot figure it out. I cannot calculate it. I cannot grasp it. And it's constantly active. Continuously. It's been constantly active recently. I didn't use to have it before."

"Stop! Wait a moment. All of my troubles began when I decided to leave the sect. Right? Right. Before that, everything was okay. And when I decided to leave...No, as soon as I decided to leave, everything was okay, as well. My coefficient dropped to statistically average and stopped there. It froze, it stabilized. So, everything happened like I had been warned from the very beginning. I became an ordinary moron, like many others—crowds of morons. Cattle. And then something went wrong, and my troubles began. The coefficient went down—down a hill like a snowball."

Well! When did it happen? When exactly? Eh? Well, well when? I'm quitting, telling Ksiusha about needing to stop seeing each other I'm staying in front of TV for a whole month, like an idiot. Well, everything's still alright here; the coefficient is dropping, of course, but slowly, as it should, as I'm not attending the meetings and, finally, it stabilizes at the level of 49. I do recall that I was sad because I considered myself a loser. Fucking loser! If only I had known then!

Well, alright. What was next? What? Nothing. After that, everything stabilized, and I started seeing Ksiusha again.

Rudnikov suddenly felt that something broke inside him.

I started seeing Ksiusha again! So what? What does Ksiusha have to do with it? Well, we started seeing each other; what's the big deal? What does Ksiusha have to do with it? And excuse me—everything was fine before that. We were dating before that, before all these fucking disasters, when I was still visiting the sect, and it was okay. My coefficients were great. Sure, I was charging during the meetings, but it doesn't matter. They were not dropping down. So, Ksiusha wasn't a constantly active negative factor. So, stop it! Stop it! Stop laying the blame on somebody else. Ksiusha has nothing to do with it.

Well, let's start from the very beginning. Why am I swinging from one extreme to another? I have to think logically, consistently, and systematically, like I was taught. So. What can be the reason for the coefficient's decrease? That's the main question. That's the most important thing. What's the reason? First, the breaking of the sect's rules. At least, I have heard some unclear threats about that. Nothing specific, but let's assume that this may be a reason. Oh! Nothing specific? I was told, 'don't drink the water, or you'll become a goat. Don't show a trick with a coin; you may scare off luck.' But I did. I showed it to Ksiusha. Shit, Ksiusha appears everywhere!

Wait a second! After that, everything stabilized on a usual level. And then it went down when we started dating. Fuck! What's the meaning of this? Do I have to keep away from her or what? Because I told her everything? No, it's nonsense. It's just impossible. This happening has a purely energetic nature. Dark psi-energy. How can she draw luck from me? For that, she has to charge with dark psi-energy constantly. She has to feed with it. She has to attend the meetings."

Rudnikov was filled with a real terror. He even stood up.

What day it was, when I waited for her in her building? When she came back home at 3 in the morning? Friday! It was Friday night, the day of the meeting. Well, wait a second. Wait a second, wait a second! Stop it—no hasty conclusions! How could she find out about the sect? From the address? By chance? From someone else? During the month when we were not dating? Umph; it's possible theoretically, of course, but unlikely. First, it would be a strange coincidence; second, she knew that it was deadly for me. I couldn't be seeing her, especially if she were a sectary. She would have warned me, at least.

Wait a second! It's not important. If she had been interested in the sect, why wouldn't she have asked me? Where and what? What have I told her then?

Rudnikov began recalling his conversation with Ksiusha. He showed her the trick with a coin. *Right. The conversation was completely neutral. She didn't even ask anything. She was silent, as usual. Or did she? What were we talking about, anyway?*

Well, I started flipping a coin. She asked, 'Is this a trick?' I tell her, no, that's not a trick, and I told her everything about the sect. Well, fucking Satanists and stuff. So, what was next? Then she recalled a movie; well, she saw a movie about a sect, and they were doing walkarounds near the fire in the forest. And she asked if we were doing the same in the forest. I told her that we were not—that we were doing it in the downtown, and I told her the name of the metro station.

The terror vanished, giving way to some dull, desperate sadness. And he told her that it was in a school. Near metro station Sokolniki, in a school. So she could easily find it if she wanted to.

Are there many schools near Sokolniki? There's definitely only one—the one and only. Well, two at most. And that's unlikely. Well, you go there on Friday and observe; if it's not the one, then it's the other. And it seemed that she knew about Friday. Or didn't she? That doesn't matter—if not Friday, then Saturday. When else could the meetings be held? One could wait there for the whole day, if necessary, given the will. And there's definitely only one school there, not two.

But why? Why? Why didn't she warn me?

"Why, why? Because she didn't know how you would react," said a cold and ruthless voice inside him. "Does she need any problems? And she doesn't give a damn about you. It's even better if something happens to you, and you just disappear. Why would she need you now? She's a master of her life now. Like Lady Ziu."

The mention of Lady Ziu made something click in his mind, and an invisible barrier fell down in his memory. He remembered everything. The last orgy—a tangle of naked twisted bodies, of men and women—and a very young girl in a mask in the center of it; she was copulating furiously and frantically with everybody and in all possible and impossible positions.

Seems like exercises in sports acrobatics, thinks Rudnikov, looking at her.

Lady Ziu, who's waiting for her turn in her harness with a fastened dildo, makes eye contact with him, smiles mockingly, and, still staring at him, walk slowly towards the girl, grabs her roughly by her hair, and lifts her head with a jerk.

Rudnikov licked his dry lips. *It was Ksiusha! That young girl was Ksiusha!* Rudnikov felt that he couldn't breathe. *Is this true? No, I just imagined all that. That whore was in a mask, that bitch. How could I know that? It wasn't her!*

"Why wouldn't it be her?" the same relentless voice told him floutingly. "If she attends the meetings, then it's obvious. Like everyone else .That's an essential part of the ritual. The more, the better! So, the girl's doing her best. She's raising her coefficient. It's good that she's young, and she's got a lot of strength. Otherwise, what's the point of going there?"

"But she's... I haven't done it with her—she's a virgin. She's a child. Did she sacrifice her virginity for that?" Rudnikov tried to deny it, grasping at a straw.

"Why would you say that?" he heard the voice in his head. "Why would you think that she was a virgin? That's just your imagination. You simply wanted to believe it; that's it. 'I haven't done it with her!' And did you ask her? If you had asked her at the very beginning, you would have received it. She would have done it, still smiling, and without a word. Right! What's the point of talking too much?"

"Shut up! Shut up! Shut up!!" yelled Rudnikov at himself, enraged. "Shut up! It's not possible! It's not possible!"

Well, alright, he started thinking frantically, calming down a bit. *Alright, well. Let's assume that. It's nonsense, but still, let's assume that for a moment. Can I find out anything? Can I make sure or check anything? Can I find out anything about her?*

Suddenly, out of nothingness, there appeared in his mind Vitka Ilyin, who was holding up his forefinger.

"Well, he was a good chap. He was diagnosed with cancer; I was already attending the sect. So, what was he saying? Something on this matter..."

He wrinkled his forehead, trying to remember.

A smoking room, clouds of gray smoke Vitka is saying something in an instructional tone.

"Buddy, it's very easy to find out anything about a girl nowadays. Piece of cake! Of course, if you have some wits, you should just go to her female counseling center, give some money at the register office, and you have her medical treatment record for an hour. And everything's written in it, in plain sight! You see everything, what's inside her. You see her endometrial stuff."

Rudnikov jumped up and, having dressed up quickly, rushed outside. He was filled with a sickly urge to act; he needed to make sure in stuff that was, actually, clear to him. He didn't know, and didn't think, what he needed it for and what he was going to do after that. He was so excited and worried because of all these findings that came crashing down on him that he, actually, couldn't think straight. He had only one goal in front of him—the female counseling center. He had to go there and read her medical treatment record. *I need to do it, and then we'll see. Now I have to deal with this. I don't have any facts. Just guesses. What if it's not true?*

He rushed outside, got in the car and burned rubber.

***

Having approached Ksiusha's house, Rudnikov stopped, got out of the car and, seeing a woman who was walking out of the adjacent building, went to her.

"Excuse me, could you tell me where the nearest female counseling center is? The one serving this district?"

The woman halted, looked at him with a bit of surprise, and took some thought. "Counseling center? Oh, that would be," she named the street. "I just don't remember the number…"

"Thank you," interrupted her Rudnikov, turned away, and rushed to the car. For some reason, he knew clearly what he had to do. 'I know this street. That's it! I'm gonna ask someone there or just check the whole street. I will find it!

However, it was not so easy in practice. Nobody knew where that damned street was. Finally, he found out that the building was on the other side of the avenue. Rudnikov didn't want to go a compass, so he parked his car, crossed the avenue, and began his search on foot. At last, he got lucky. The first passer-by told him exactly where the counseling center was.

Rudnikov entered the building and, without hesitation, approached the first old lady in whites that he saw. It seemed that fate itself was guiding him.

A hundred bucks, and he was thumbing a medical treatment record of Samoylova Kseniya Evgeniyevna with his shaking hands. *Date of birth... well. No, no, what's that? Two abortions? The first one at the age of fourteen... The second one..."*

Rudnikov felt that he wasn't able to read it further on. His head throbbed, and his eyes were filled with tears. He waited a little bit, came to his senses, and, holding the record in his hand, told a nurse, who was waiting for him, in a shaking voice, "You know, I'm gonna make copies of some pages at the post-office, and then return it to you in an hour."

"No, no! It's strictly forbidden to take the records out!" the woman got scared.

"Just one hour," assured her Rudnikov, taking another C-note out of his pocket. "Well, you know, so I can read it in a quiet atmosphere. And here, with all this hurry..."

"Well, alright," resolved the nurse, taking the money, "but no longer!"

"Alright, alright! Don't worry! I'll be back in an hour."

Rudnikov was already rushing to the door, putting the record in his briefcase.

He had to cross the avenue in order to get to his car. He almost reached the middle of it when the light went green, and queuing traffic started moving. Rudnikov thought at once that he could still run across the street, and he dashed towards the moving cars. Suddenly, his briefcase opened, and all the papers fell down to the ground.

Rudnikov halted in embarrassment, turned away, and bent over. Loud squeaks of brakes bump! Pain—and the world went dark for him forever.

A coin fell out of his pocket and dropped to the ground with a clink. Tails.

***

"Hey, Ksiukha!" Kseniya Samoilova, a pupil of the ninth grade, was called by her classmates, Borya Shvetsov and Valerka Znamenskiy.

"What?" Kseniya halted and looked at them inquiringly.

Borya didn't say anything, but took out a Grant and showed it to the girl.

"Wow!" she smiled. "Where's the cash from? Did you bust a car again?"

"Right!" answered Borya, smiling. "We did. And there were dollars in the glove compartment. We got lucky."

"Lucky," repeated the girl with a strange look, "I see. You got cock socks, boys?"

"No," answered Borya with hesitation, having exchanged looks with his friend.

"Then skull fuck only!"

And Lucifer was ask'd by His Son:

— Wherefore did that woman betray that man?

And Lucifer answer'd His Son:

— Because he was weak. And Lucifer was again ask'd by His Son:

— Is it right?

And Lucifer answer'd His Son:

— If someone betrays thou, then he dost not value thou. So, ye are worth nothing. Everyone receives what he's worth. Neither moo, n'r less.

LUCIFER'S SON. Day 9.

And the ninth day came.

And Lucifer said:

—If thou want to make a man unhappy, just give him all that he wants.

And Lucifer was ask'd by His Son:

—Wherefore?

And Lucifer answer'd to His Son:

—Because a man always wishes f'r too much.

INTERVIEW

"If you live long, you will often
marvel. For a grain of evil seed
was sown in Adam's heart from
the beginning."
Third Book of Ezra.

Host (H): "Hello, dear viewers! Today our guest is the most famous and, probably the most mysterious writer of our days—Sergey Eduardovich Barinov."

Writer (W): "Hello."

H: "Sergey Eduardovich, I'm your sincere admirer and fan, and I have read all your books—several times. I like them all a lot; I admire your talent and consider it to be something extraordinary in its power. I think that your works are a happening in literature.

"When I'm reading your novels, it's very easy to feel a connection with a hero and to become him. How do you do it?"

W: "Well, any literary works, any creation of something new is always a secret. It's impossible to explain how I do it. Let's recall the ingenious words, "I keep in mind that marvelous minute." That's several words. But write them, and you'll become Pushkin. And these are not secret or special words which are open only to certain people. No, these are usual, ordinary words which are known to everyone. But try to create something of that kind!

"Such examples are very convincing. For, if we're talking about a big novel, like "War and Peace," everyone knows intuitively that he can't create something of that kind. Only Tolstoy could do that. Here we have too many words which must be placed and composed in a correct order.

"The scale of the action itself is a part of its greatness. But here we have several words only—several. The secret is at hand; it's teasing you, it's beckoning you with its accessibility. You may think that you can catch it, grab with your hand. Nothing of the sort. It always slips away in the last moment. Like sunlight. Here it is. But try to catch it!"

H: "So, you think that there are no laws in creating?"

W (thoughtfully): "You know, at first, I wanted to agree with you. Completely! No, there are no laws. But suddenly, I thought about a famous line of our second ingenious writer, Gogol, 'Dnieper is marvelous in calm weather.' Pushkin's 'I keep in mind that marvelous minute.' Gogol's 'Dnieper is marvelous in calm weather. 'Note, that both lines have the word "marvelous." "Marvelous minute." "Dnieper is marvelous." So, the most famous lines of two of our geniuses—very short lines, just a couple of words—contain the word "marvelous." By the way, this word is not that popular, it's even rare. It's not a personal pronoun, like "I, he", or something of the kind. Not at all!

"If this is a coincidence, then a very interesting one! So, probably there are some laws. But, at any rate, they cannot be perceived, at least, now. So, 'marvelous are Your deeds, Lord!' By the way, it's again 'marvelous!" It's one of the most popular lines of Bible. Note that it's "marvelous.' Not 'wonderful,' but 'marvelous.' 'Marvelous,' 'marvel.' So, probably there are some laws.

H(a bit embarrassed): "Well, indeed. I haven't paid attention to that. Very curious. Well, alright. You mentioned Pushkin and Gogol. Who else do you like? Tell us your favorite writers."

W (confidently, without hesitation): "Saltykov-Shchedrin."

H(surprised): "Saltykov-Shchedrin? Actually, I…oh! 'Essays of a Province,' 'Tales,' 'The Golovlyov Family?'

W: "No, I think that these works are among his weakest creations. 'The Diary of a Provincial in Petersburg,' 'Abroad,' 'The Letters to the Aunt,' 'The Molchalin Family,' 'Tashkent Men.'

H (even more surprised): I haven't heard of those. (After a pause.) "Alright. Saltykov-Shchedrin. And who else?"

W (takes thought): "That would be it."

H (astonished): "That would be it? And Dostoevskiy, Tolstoy, Chekhov? Don't you like them? Or Pushkin?"

W: "When did you read 'War and Peace?' Or 'The Brothers Karamazov?'

H (a little embarrassed): "Well, frankly speaking, Natasha Rostova. Back in school, I think."

W: "And did you read it after that?"

H (still embarrassed): "No."

W: "There you are. And, at the same time, you say that Tolstoy is a great writer, and 'War and Peace' is an immortal book. So, why is he great? Nobody seems to read him. It's a pure insincerity. We consider the writers great, but no one reads them except for literary critics. It's nonsense! It's veneration of images.

"There are no immortal works, like there are no immortal men. And that's the higher wisdom. If the humans were immortal, we would still be under the power of Genghis Khan or some Nebuchadnezzar who would never abandon their power. There would be no progress, or it would slow down in thousands and millions times.

"Forget Nebuchadnezzar! Just think—what if Stalin was immortal? Or Lenin. We would have still been building Belomor Channel. And that's at the best case. And, in the worst case, we would have conquered the whole world and stopped history and progress. The time would have ceased its flow. Disaster! Collapse! Closed system. Anabiosis. An organism which has fallen into a coma but maintains the minimal life-sustaining activity and metabolism and which can exist in such a state as long as you please. Forever!

"Death is an essential condition of progress. The great must die. Otherwise, sooner or later, they inevitably become an invincible obstacle to life and development. A flow of life goes away and rots. Everything's covered with mould of centuries and drowns in an abyss of indifference, having tasted no fruit of life. Apathy and fatigue. No one is interested in anything, no one pities anything, nothing is happening, and no one can do anything. Tomorrow is the exact copy of yesterday. Dead end. Finish. A swamp with quacking toads which are ceaselessly praising their master. Their lord.

"Same with literary works. They grow old and die, like people. Eventually, only memory remains. A tomb which one can visit—but nothing more. In this respect, any modern comic is better than all the works of Tolstoy, like a living donkey is better than a dead lion."

H: "But why is it dead? People do read Tolstoy, though I agree that they read him less than they used to and less than it's believed. And I'm sure that people will be reading him a hundred years from now. And the comic will be forgotten tomorrow. It's going to die, indeed. It's a short-lived thing."

W (laughing): "That's right! I give up. You had me. I overreacted a bit in the heat of discussion. 'War and Peace,' for example, is not dead yet. It's an old man who's not interesting to anyone, but he's still respected due to his age and gray hair. Aqsaqal, long-liver—he's going to creak for another hundred or two hundred years. It's some kind of half-asleep tortoise Tortilla. It's slumbering in ooze on the bottom of a pond. And comics are ephemeral day-flies which are frisking above its expanse. They won't be here tomorrow, but their place will be taken by others. New ones. Myriads and myriads of others. And then they'll disappear in their turn. But Tortilla will still be slumbering in its mud.

"But tell me honestly—is this a real life? Some time ago, it was a beautiful butterfly, the fairest of all! And everyone was admiring it. But now, it's all in the past. 'The days and deeds of days gone by'.

H: "Alright, let's talk about you again. Or no, wait! But you did name Saltykov-Shchedrin, right? So, how is he different from Tolstoy, in your opinion?"

W: "He can be reread. I think that he's the only writer whose works can be read over and over. Constantly. There's always a volume of his complete works on my table, and I reread it. In circle. I finish it and then start all over again. I don't know any other authors like him. Though, it depends. It's a purely private matter.

"The only problem is that I've almost learned him by heart. (Laughs.) Soon I'll have nothing to read. However, I don't read much recently. (Darkens.) I have no time for this. I mainly write."

H: "So, let's talk finally about your own works. As I've already said at the beginning of our show, I'm your biggest fan; I admire your talent, and I adore your skill, and I'm not afraid of these high words and pompous epithets. In my opinion, they're well-deserved. But, you know, your novels leave a strange impression. To be exact, not each one of them in particular, but all of them in general. Your evolution as a writer. A choice of topics.

"All your novels are ingenious! very ingenious!.. It's an incredible skill—all of them. And they could be reread over and over again! If this is a criterion of skill—it is beyond doubt. But the subjects of your first novels were light and clear, they were filled with the wish for good, and all the heroes were positive. They were strong and brave people, and the readers liked them a lot.

"But further on, they became darker and gloomier. The last ones are an endless horror, an abyss of human mentality. It's impossible to read it, and it's impossible to get away from it! Why is that? What is the reason?"

W (after a long pause): "I will tell you a tale, a very interesting one. Once upon a time there was a man. Quite an ordinary one, like me. I began writing very late. Probably, you know that."

H: "Yes, sure! And you wrote ingenious and serious stuff. It seemed as if you came out of nowhere."

W (with a wry smile): "Well, not exactly. Not from nowhere. Actually, I was writing before that."

H (with astonishment): "You were?"

W (with the same smile): "Yeah, I was; been there. But under another surname, under a pseudonym."

H (With a greater astonishment): "But why has no one heard about these works of yours?"

W (smiling with embarrassment): "Because they are worth nothing. They're bad. Trash, rubbish! An ordinary graphomania. Well. However, it doesn't matter now.

"So, let's continue with our tale. There was a man; he struggled desperately for a living but to no purpose. At last, he couldn't stand it, tore his clothes, and yelled, "Oh, Lord! Why, oh, why am I so wretched and poor? How long? Save me, Lord! Save me! Help me! Send me talent!"

"And the Lord pitied him and sent to him his angel. And the angel came to him and said, "Be glad! For the Lord heard thy prayers. From now on thou shalt be talented. Ingenious. Overingenious! Thou shall become a writer, the likes of whom the world has never seen! So be it!

"From now on, the Lord shall speak with thy lips. Go thee, bring light, good, and truth to the people. Open thy soul for the people. No one shall resist the strength of thy word!"

(The writer went silent.)

H (quietly, staring intently at the writer, who is smiling sadly to his own thoughts): "And what was next?"

W (still smiling sadly): "What was next? The man, naturally, started to write. At first, he felt easy and happy, and his novels were good and cheerful. They were full of goodness, light, and positive heroes.

"But a man is not a god or an angel. Everything is mixed up in him, good and evil alike. There are light and dark sides of his soul. Various secret thoughts and vile wishes. When the first euphoria passed, his dark side came to life. And the man realized with fear that he couldn't but write about it, as well. His genius became his curse. He could not but write. He could not but turn himself inside out to the public. He couldn't but open his soul to the people.

"And what was in that soul? A petty soul of an ordinary and common man—the same thoughts and wishes. Mud and slush. After all, talent and genius can't appear out of nowhere. They can't appear on their own. It's an essential part of the personality. And here, a hen was given wings of an eagle. What does a hen need them for? Where would it fly with them? The hen would continue to dig in the soil as it has been doing before. And the wings would only be a nuisance. The wings make it look silly. For, as it turns out, it must fly now that it has them. It must hover in heavens. For all beneath it must admire the cackling hen. Everybody else must see it hovering in all its beauty.

"Eagle wings belong to the eagle. You can't ask anyone to turn you into an eagle. That's the same as to ask for death. You won't be yourself. You will be different. An eagle. A different bird. There's nothing from a hen in it."

H (more quietly): "And then?"

W: "He had problems with his wife. It happened when he first described his male sexual fantasies. As the power of his influence was not a literary one—it was reality, pure reality—like the angel had promised him, and his wife didn't react to it; he suspected that she didn't love him. As a matter of fact, he cheated right in front of her eyes. All the sexual scenes were described very vividly. And it seemed that she didn't care."

H (interrupting): "Right, your descriptions of sexual scenes are very powerful. I was just going to ask you about that. How do you manage to do it?"

W (indifferently): "Well, it's very easy. I just try to imagine that scene, and then I describe it thoroughly with maximum details. It's a kind of eye-witness report. A literary painting. And, as a description may be a bit idealized, it may be exaggerated, and I can describe ideal sex, when everything is great and both partners do everything simultaneously - so, the impression is, correspondingly, even stronger, than in real life. For, in real life, one of the partners may have bad spirits, something's wrong… well, you get it. And here, everything's the right way, a realization of a dream."

H (curious): "So, can you imagine and describe everything?"

W (still indifferently): "Of course. For example, sex with you, now, here in the studio. (Staring intently and appraisingly at the host): you stand up and approach me slowly."

H (with seriocomic fear):"Umph! That's enough! I believe you. Let's get back to your tale. So, what happened next?"

W: "And where did we stop?"

H: "Problems with wife. He started describing his sexual dreams, and she didn't react to that. And he suspected that she didn't love him. By the way, what if she reacted to it?"

W: (shrugging his shoulder and smiling): "I don't know - it's a tale. She didn't react in the tale. However, I think that nothing would change. He would suspect her in something else. For example, that she didn't understand him, she doubted him, so she didn't love him. All in all, I don't know. Again, she didn't react in the tale, and he had doubts about her sincerity.

"It got worse. Jealousy appeared, as well as suspicion. She had to have a lover. If she didn't love him, why wouldn't she leave him? He was a wealthy man. His novels were very popular. Well, all those problems—money, jealousy, suspicion—are common. They're usual for a lot of husbands, and they exist in many families; but, unlike other husbands, he had an absolute weapon, and, certainly, he used it. He was a savage, a Papuan with a Kalashnikov, and he used the assault rifle to deal with his Papuan problems without a second thought.

"Temptation was too strong. And he wouldn't have been able to resist it, even if he had wished. He had to write. Write, write, and write—about what was going on in his soul. And he wrote a new ingenious novel. It was about that, what troubled him at that time. About adultery. About marital infidelity. About a married woman who had a lover. The novel was explaining and justifying her behavior. He did it on purpose—to see his wife's reaction. She liked it, of course. To be precise, she didn't say anything, but he saw her reaction. And how could she not like it, if it was impossible not to like his work? And who was his wife? She was not Joan of Arc, Maid of Orleans, resilient and firm.

('Resilient,' the Host giggled unwillingly.)

"No, she was an ordinary woman with a common, average morality, the likes of which are described in the Bible: "Do not tempt!" And he was tempting her! He was making the readers feel the same that his negative heroes felt. He did it with the power of his unnatural talent. He was making the readers understand them and sympathize with them and, correspondingly, justify them. Thus, he was changing the morality of a reader; he was breaking its foundations. He was making a reader accept the point of view of a rascal and a criminal. A reader would become a rascal and a criminal for some time. The man would awaken dark sides which exist in everyone.

"For, if you can feel the psychology of a criminal, then you have something criminal in you. Every woman can play a whore or a bitch—she can understand her psychology, mentality, and the pattern of her behavior. But try, for example, to understand the pattern of behavior of a ground beetle. There's nothing from a ground beetle in you, but there's definitely something from a bitch or a whore.

"In short, if he wrote a novel about amenities of cannibalism, about the pleasure of eating men flesh, a reader would like it, too. On the one hand, he realized that very well, but he understood that the reading of his novel was like a reality or an action. And since his wife read it, it was similar to taking a poison. 'Evil blood flowed through my veins.' As if a snake, tarantula, or scorpion bit her. Then it got worse. He began doubting everyone—his friends, relatives, and all his loved ones. He imagined what they would do in different situations, however unnatural and impossible it had been in real life. Everybody thinks about such stuff from time to time—'Would anyone sell me for a million'—but these thoughts usually leave ordinary people very quickly. But, in the case with the man, they started to become real in his devilish novels.

"Their success led to a new wave of rage and desperation, and a new novel would appear, even more terrible and desperate than the previous one. A desert or a vacuum appeared around him, without friends and relatives. For they were ordinary people, and they had their limits of trust, friendship, and honor. They would not pass those unnatural tests and temptations which were offered by him in those unnatural novels. There's a strength limit even for steel, let alone people. There are abysses in which a man should not look into, for there's nothing in them save treachery, dishonor, and lies. There are temperatures that melt everything, even love, honor, and faith.

"Being alone, he started to take revenge on all people. Perverted sexual scenes, orgies, and violence—all of that flowed like water. He awakened the vilest and lowliest instincts, and he was gloating, seeing that editions of his novels grew. It seemed that Satan himself was speaking with his lips. And it is well known that it's forbidden to talk to Satan and listen to him.

"But there was no book-printing and no mass media"—suddenly laughed the writer—"when this saying appeared. No TV, in particular."—he added after a pause, looking ironically at the Host.—"But nothing is said about 'reading'. Reading is probably allowed."

H (after a long pause): "And what was next?"

W (laughing again): "Next? There was nothing next. It's just a tale!"

H (after another pause): "Well. A tale. You know, this tale left a somehow strange impression. Could it be about you, by any chance?"

W (smiling): "Wow! That's a compliment! Are my novels so popular? Like the novels of the tale's hero?"

H: "Well, I don't know… Maybe… I think they are. And you described vividly the change in the themes of your novels."

W(smiling again): "It's a game. I'm playing with you and the viewers. I'm provoking them in order to raise my ratings and interest in me and my works. Now my novels will be interesting even for those who have never read anything except for price labels, checks, and bottle labels. For they would want to talk to Satan. It's very interesting. It's irresistible. Tell a man about a forbidden book, and he will read it."

H (embarrassed): "Are you being serious?"

W (with the same irony): "No. Yes. Yes... no. I told you that's just a game. And the game of the fact that it's a game. And so on, into infinity. Recursion. An endless row of nest-dolls. A Mobius strip in which inner side is outer one, as well. And truth is lie. So, it's impossible to understand where the one ends and the other begins. Take a famous saying: 'I'm lying!' If I'm lying, then I'm telling the truth; and if I'm telling the truth, then I'm lying. This saying is true and false at the same time."

H (even more embarrassed): "I'm at a loss."

W (mockingly): "It's alright! I'm speaking on behalf of Satan, and he likes paradoxes a lot."

H (gathering her thoughts): "Are you a believer? Are you a Christian?"

W: "Do I believe in the existence of Christ? Sure!"

H: "Sure?"

W (shrugging his shoulders): "Of course. Christ existed."

H: "Well, you're saying this in a strange manner. So surely…"

W (still looking at the Host mockingly): "Every true believer must be sure in that. Right?"

H: "It seems that you're telling the truth, but…"

W (interrupting): "Well, well! This scene was already described by Goethe. We shall not repeat it. I'm not Faust, and you're no Margarita. (Slowly, after a pause): It you like my novels so much…"

H (smiling frigidly): "That's it! Our show has come to an end. Please answer the questions of our viewers. There a lot of questions, but we have no time. Answer at least one of them. So, the question (looking at the paper and choking): What was Christ like?"

W: "Too serious. He didn't have a sense of humor at all."

H: "That's it! Our time is over, and our show has come to an end. Again, today we spoke with a famous writer, Sergey Eduardovich Barinov. Good-bye, Sergey Eduardovich.

(The writer nods.)

Good-bye, dear viewers. See you next time. Take care!

And Lucifer was ask'd by His Son:

—And what was Christ like?

And Lucifer answer'd His Son:

—He was dull. He was too busy with his mission. Marry, he had nay sense of hum'r at all.

LUCIFER'S SON. DAY 10.

And the tenth day came.

And Lucifer said:

—The feelings of average people art average, as well. As a rule, they doth not pass yea the simplest tests. The happiness of the average man is in his humbleness—in the fact, that these tests rarely happen in his life.

SHOW.

"Who has been tried thereby, and found perfect?"
Wisdom of Jesus the Son
of Sirach.

Kolia (K): "Hi to everyone who's listening to us! So, it's 12:15, and, as usual on Mondays, our famous radio "Prank" is live. Today's hosts are the famous Olia and Kolya. I'm Kolya, and Olya is at my side."

Olya (O): "Hello! Well, Kolya, you won't die from modesty. Actually, there was no need to say that you're Kolya. I'm pretty sure that we won't be mixed up."

K: "Who knows, who knows! Things happen. It's better to introduce myself. So, today's guest is Alexandr. Hello, Alexandr! As far as I know, you're a student, you're 20, you got married recently, and you love your wife very much, etc. So, you're exactly who we need!"

O: "Oh, youth! Newlyweds, wedding, veil, wedding night! It's so romantic! I do recall, I—"

K (interrupting): "Well, I can't imagine you in a veil. However, we'll talk about you later. Let's listen to Alexandr."

Alexandr (A) (a bit embarrassed): "Hi! I'm really a student, I'm studying in the institute (names an institute) on the second year. Two weeks ago, I had a wedding, I got married."

K: "And who's your wife? Is she studying with you?"

A: "No. She studies, but in another institute."

O: "Where exactly?"

A: "In a medical school."

K: "Right! So, she's a doctor! Well, Olya, if we get sick, we'll have a doctor to consult. I hope Alexandr's wife will consult with us for free. By the way, what's her name?"

A: "Ella."

O (giggling): "Ellochka the Cannibal."

K: "Alright! Olya, your jokes! So, Ella. A beautiful name. I like it."

O: "I like it, too. Did I say otherwise? Every woman has to be a bit of a cannibal."

K (with humorous fear): "Really? So she can bite something?

O (with feigned indignation): Kolya, you always vulgarize it! I didn't mean that!"

K: "Really? And what did you mean? Alexandr, are you afraid of your wife? Can she bite something off a man?"

A: "No, I don't think so. She's a very soft and kind woman."

K: "And you're not afraid of her?"

A (laughing): "Of course, not."

K: "Well, you should be! Every man should be afraid of his wife. Women are unpredictable. You never know what to expect from them!"

O: "Well, it begins! Don't listen to him, Alexandr. He's simply jealous. He doesn't have a wife. Tell me, do you love your wife?"

A: "Yes, a lot."

O: "And when did you say you get married?"

A: "Two weeks ago."

O: "And how long have you known your wife?"

A: "Since the fifth grade."

K: "Oh, a school love!"

A (a bit embarrassed): "Yeah."

O: "And did you love her all this time?"

A (still embarrassed): "Well…yeah…"

O: "See, Kolya! Here's an example for you. And they say that there are no real men! Since the fifth grade—if you fell in love in the fifth grade, by now..."

K: "Well, I didn't fall in love in the fifth grade, and it's too late now. I'm too old to be falling in love."

O (speaking with the tone of Saakhov from the movie 'Kidnapping, Caucasian Style'): "That is never soon and never late, by the way!"

K: "And there's no one to fall in love with. Except for you."

O (with dignity): "No, that's not allowed. For your information, I'm a married woman."

K: "Well, then all is lost. There's no happiness in life! Not everyone is as lucky as Alexandr. Meeting your love in the fifth grade! Alexandr, so you say that you love your wife?"

A: "Yes, a lot."

K: "And does your wife love you?"

A: "Of course!"

K: "Are you sure in that?"

A: "Certainly, I am."

K: "That's wonderful! Great! For today's show trick is dedicated to that topic: Does Your Wife Love You? We'll try to play her up, in order to check that. Aren't you afraid? Are you sure in your wife?"

A (after a very short pause): "No, I'm not afraid. I'm absolutely sure that my wife loves me."

K: "And you don't doubt it at all?"

A (firmly): "Not at all!"

K: "Well, you'd better not rue your words. Do you remember what Olya said? Every woman is a bit cannibal. So, you're not afraid?"

A: "No."

K: "Alright. Then I'm announcing the rules of the game. Now we're going to part for a week, and, next Monday, we shall gather in this studio and share our impressions. Deal?"

O: "Well, I'll be here, anyway."

K: "Alexandr?"

A: "Me, too."

K: "Well, no need talking about me—I can't leave Olya alone. So, see you on Monday. Then we'll have the game's final act. Don't miss it! All the best!"

O: "All the best! We'll be waiting for you!"

(Theme song.)

One week later

K: "Well, hi to everyone. Today's Monday, it's 12:15, and, as we promised, we have a final act of the show "Prank". Again, the topic of the today's game is "Does your wife love you?"Our game's participant is Alexandr, a newlywed, and he's 20. He's married for two..."

O (interrupting): "It's three already!"

K: "Oh, pardon me! He's been married for three weeks, and he's been loving his wife a lot since the fifth..."

(To Alexandr): "Since the fifth one?"

A (embarrassed): "The fifth what?"

K: "Do you love your wife since the fifth grade?"

A: "Yeah, since the fifth one."

K: "So, he loves his wife since the fifth grade."

O (languidly): "I wish I had such a husband!"

K: "Hush!"

O (indignantly): "What do you mean by 'hush?'"

K: "Hush means "don't hinder me!" We have a game final, and we don't need your jokes. See, Alexandr is very nervous."

A: "No, I'm not nervous..."

K: "You're not? That is good. That is right—no need to be nervous. It's just a game."

A (smiling frigidly): "Why?"

K (interrupting cheerfully): "No, no! It's nothing! Nothing at all. Don't worry. I'm just whipping up tension. I want to intrigue our listeners, to keep them from leaving our radio show. Attention! The final of our famous radio show trick!"

(Theme song playing.)

"Well, Alexandr, here are the rules of the final. Now we're going to listen to the recording of certain conversations and phone talks of your wife, which were made during the last week, and then I'll explain to you what is going to be next. We didn't waste any time, and we contacted your wife on behalf of various invented persons. Well, we were playing her up, as the rules of our games suppose, and now we're going to listen to the results of that. Alright? By the way, didn't she tell you that we were calling her? Didn't she tell you about strange calls?"

A (confused): "No..."

O: "I wouldn't do it, either. Any woman has a right to innocent secrets."

K: "Well, it's clear with you. But we're talking about another woman."

O (with humorous insult): "What's going on? I will take offence."

K (supporting her): "And keep silent until the end of the show! That would be great!"

O (offended): "Blackface!"

K: "Enough! Hush! It's a final. Don't forget it! So, Alexandr, shall we listen to the records? Again, according to the rules of the game, you may refuse to participate at any moment. In such case, we're not going to listen to anything."

A: "Will you give me the records?"

K: "No. According to the rules of the game, they will be destroyed, and you will never listen to them. So, what?"

A (confidently): "Let's do it!"

K (in a voice of a tempting snake): "Are you sure?"

A (still confidently): "Yes!"

K (with the same tone): "Are you sure?"

A: "I am."

K: "Alright! Attention, a recording!"

***

Record 1.

Click. Short signals, as of a long-distance call. Someone picks up the phone.

Female voice (F): "Hello?"

Male voice with distinct foreign accent (M): "Hello! Hi!"

F(surprised): "Hi."

M: "Excuse me, are you Ms. Avdeeva Ella Borisovna?"

F(even more surprised): "Yeah."

M: "I'm calling from New-York, the law firm Goldberg and Co. I'm its representative. I have to speak to you. We're working on a case regarding the estate of Mr. Husief. Is your maiden name Guseva?"

F: "Yeah."

M: "Good. Mister Husief is your relative, and he mentioned you in his will. Would you mind if our Moscow representative contacts you and explains everything to you?"

F (embarrassed, after a pause): "Well, alright… But I don't know no… But when?"

M: "As soon as possible. Would it be convenient for you to meet tomorrow at 12, Moscow time?"

F: "Yes it would… But…"

M: "Alright. But I have a small request. Please, don't say anything to your husband until you meet with our representative and speak to him. Your husband is mentioned in the will, as well. And there are financial—what's the Russian word?—issues. Right, issues. But we shouldn't speak of it on the phone. Our representative will explain everything to you in person."

F (hesitantly): "Well, okay… alright. But I'm afraid that it's a misunderstanding."

M: "No, missus, it is no misunderstanding. Our representative will explain everything to you tomorrow. Good-bye."

F (embarrassed): "Good-bye."

(Short dials. The sound of the woman hanging up the phone.)

***

Record 2 (phone conversation)

The same female voice and a confident male voice without an accent, belonging to a Russian; no doubts, it's the host Kolya.

F: "Hello?"

M: "Hello! Could I talk to Ella Borisovna?"

F: "Speaking."

M: "I'm the Moscow representative of the New-York law firm Goldberg and Co. Yesterday, you received a call from them."

F: "Right."

M: "We need to meet today. Could you come now to hotel (names the hotel)?"

F (after a short pause): "Yes."

M: "Great! Say, in one hour? Is it okay?"

F: "Yeah. And what metro station that would be?"

M: "Oh! You haven't got a car. Then I'll pick you up. Tell me where, exactly."

F (after a pause): "Well, let's meet near metro (names the station)".

M: "Great! I know where it is, I can park just in front of the entrance. Black Mercedes, number plates (says the number). Got it?"

F: "Yes."

M: "So, at 1 o'clock straight?"

F: "Yeah, alright."

M: "Good-bye. See you soon." (Hangs up the phone.)

***

Record 3 (apparently, in a car)

F: "Excuse me, are you waiting for me?"

M: "Ella Borisovna?"

F: "Yes."

M: "Right, get in, please! By the way, I haven't introduced myself. Semen Viktorovich Marchuk. Here's my card. So, Ella Borisovna, let's get to business. Recently, your distant relative on your father's side, Mr. Husief, died in New York. You are his only heir."

F (nervously): "I don't know nothing about relatives in America. My dad never told me about them."

M: "Well, he emigrated there a lot time ago, right after the war. He was taken captive and then stayed in the West. He was officially considered missing in action. That's why your father hasn't told you anything about him. He didn't know anything about his grandfather himself. Well, a man was missing in action during the war—that's it. For his part, Mr. Husief was looking for you all these years, but he managed to find you only just before his death. Your father was already dead. That's why you're the only heir. Here's a copy of the will. (Rustling of papers.) Can you read in English?"

F (hesitantly): "No."

M: "Here's a translation. Read it."

(Pause.)

F (amazed): "Ten million dollars?"

M (calmly): "Right. Precisely ten million. As a matter of fact, Mr. Husief's fortune was bigger, but he donated a part of it to charities, as is common in America. And tem million was left."

F: "And what now? Can I get it?"

M (still calmly): "Sure. But note the… can I have it for a second… this item of the will. (Reads): 'The heir may give any part of the sum to her husband.' That's why I asked you not to say anything to your husband until I informed you of that."

F: "I don't get it…"

M: "It means that the inheritance may be divided between you and your husband, as you wish."

F: "What do you mean by '*divided*'?"

M(patiently): "In this case, part of the money will be transferred to your account, and another part - to his account. And you are to name the proportions. You can divide it in half, or you can give him only four million, or three, or one. It's up to you to decide."

F (embarrassed): "I'm not sure… It's so unexpected..."

M (soothingly): "You know, you shouldn't be in a hurry. The matter is rather serious… It's a lot of money, and you must make wise decisions. You should think it over. I know that you've gotten married recently, and, surely, you love your husband a lot, but life is a very complicated thing. You never know. Love is love, and money is money. You never know, mind you! Believe me, for I have seen a lot in life as a lawyer. So, you should think it over without a hurry, until Monday, and I'll call you on Monday, and you'll tell me your decision. Alright?"

F (still embarrassed): "Well, alright."

M: "One more thing! Keep in mind that, if you decide to give a part of it to your husband, he will find out about the whole will. He'll find out that there is ten million and that you have decided to give him a certain part, and the rest you kept for yourself. Well, there it is. According to the law, we'll have to show him the will in full. But, if you decide not to give him anything, he won't find out about it at all. Think about that, too."

F: "So, if I give a part of it to my husband, he'll know about the whole inheritance? And he'll know which part I left to myself and which part I gave to him?"

M: "Exactly. So think about that. Actually, you really should either give a half of it, five million dollars (the man pronounces the number tightly), or nothing. I'm afraid, if you give him a million or two, it'll make the things worse. He'll be insulted and stuff. Though that's my own opinion. It's up to you to decide. So, again, think it over, and I'll give you a call on Monday—say, between 12 and 1 p.m.—and you will tell me your decision regarding your husband. We have to decide quickly. And, depending on that, I'll tell you what to do next. Deal?"

F: "Deal."

M: "That's great! Can I give you a ride?"

F: "No, thank you. I live not far from here."

M: "See you on Monday?"

F: "Yeah."

(Some rustling and then a door of a car closes.)

***

K (in a cheerful voice): "So, Alexandr, you heard the recording. Today is Monday, and the time is between twelve and one. What shall we do? Shall we call? You say your wife didn't tell you anything?"

A (in a lifeless, dull voice): "No."

O (interrupting): "She didn't tell anything—so, what? She wants to surprise him."

K: "Right, *'surprise'*… So, what? Shall we call? Again, we can stop at this point. But then you'll never find out what your wife has decided."

A (in the same dead voice): "Make the call."

K: "Are you sure? Alright." (Dials a number).

The same female voice as was in the records (F): "Hello?"

K: "Hello! Hi, Ella Borisovna. It's Semen Viktorovich calling. So, what have you decided? Will you give anything to your husband?"

F (firmly): "No. Let them register everything on me."

K: "Great! Alright, I got it. I'm going to pass your decision to New York, and then I'll contact you. Will you be able to go to America for a couple of days, if there's a need? I mean, without your husband, considering your current decision?"

F (still firmly): "Yes, I will."

K: "Wonderful! All the best. Wait for my call."

F: "Good-bye."

K: "Good-bye." (Hangs up the phone.)

***

O (sadly): "*'Wait for my call!*'" We have lied to a poor woman. As usual. What can we wait for from men?"

K: "Unfortunately, Alexandr, you've lost. Your wife didn't pass the test. However, take it easy. It's just a show!"

O: "I wouldn't give a cent to my husband! Why would I? Let him earn it."

K: "I don't doubt it. So, dear listeners, our show has come to an end. The trick is going to be next Monday, at 12:15.Once again, today you were entertained by the hosts Kolya…"

O: "And Olya!"

K and O (together): "See you next time!"

(Theme song playing.)

***

And Lucifer was ask'd by His Son:

—Art thither distaff who can pass this temptation?

And Lucifer answer'd to His Son:

—Aye. But it doesn't matter. F'r thither art nay men who can fully believe it and nev'r hast any doubts in it.

'Tis very easy to plant a se'd of doubt in the heart of a man. And once 'tis planted, it shall grow after that. Sooner 'r later.

***

K: "Hello, hello, hello! Hi to everyone, who's listening to us! We're live again, and today is the long-expected final of our famous radio show trick. Let us introduce the participant of today's final. Roman, 22, a manager of the company, married for less than a year. He's very happy in his marriage; he loves and adores his beloved wife. And so on and so forth. Let's greet Roman. (Short record of applauses and greetings.) So, the topic of today's show is 'Do you trust your wife?' Roman here trusts his wife fully. Right, Roman?"

Roman (R) (firmly): "Yes."

K: "So, you positively and absolutely trust her? So recklessly?"

P (still firmly): "Absolutely! Recklessly!"

O (with envy): "Real men do exist. They exist! Right, Roman. If you love someone, you have to trust him, in spite of anything. Especially if it's a woman. (saucily): My husband trusts me, too!"

K (with doubt): "Really? Now I understand why he asked me recently when our show usually ends. Alright! Take it easy. Calm down. We're live."

O (indignantly): "Hey, what are you pointing at?"

K: "Come on! I'm not talking about you!"

O: "About whom then?"

K: "Can you remember when we had a winner of the show for the last time? When did anyone win?"

O (thoughtfully): "Well, I can't really remember."

K: "Neither can I remember." (Short pause, then decisively): "Well, we're going to do the following. Let's listen to the record of the previous final. Do you mind, Roman?"

R: "No, actually."

K (still decisively):" Great. Attention—recording of the previous final—begin!"

(Music theme, then Records # 1, 2, 3.)

K: "So, Roman? Now you know how everything went for your predecessor. By the way, did your wife tell you anything?"

R (after a pause): "No..."

K (regretfully): "I see, I see. Well, shall we continue or stop at the runner-up prize? If you tell me now that you still trust your wife, we shall stop at that."

R: "Let's continue."

K: "You still have no doubts about your wife?"

R: "I don't."

K: "And what about the fact that she hasn't told you anything? Well, it doesn't matter. Well, wonderful right? Wonderful! Umph…"

(A short halt).

"Listen, Roman, I need to talk to Olya now. Music pause."

(Theme music playing.)

"So, attention! I announce Roman the winner of our show, without listening to the records! You passed the test, you didn't doubt your wife, and you were ready to go to the end. Your confidence wasn't disturbed even by the example of your predecessor or by the fact that your wife hasn't told you anything. And, actually, it's…well, it doesn't matter. That's it. That's enough. Let our game have at least one winner! The topic of the show is, "Do you trust your wife?" In spite of everything, you still trust her, and that is enough! That's wonderful! You're a winner of our show—congratulations! Our goal is not to find out the truth—whether your wife is capable of lying. Our goal is to make sure that you trust her, no matter what. And we made sure in that. Congratulations, you passed the test!"

R (dumfounded): "Wait a second! I don't get it. So, we're not going to listen to the records of the conversations with my wife?"

O (at once): "No!"

K: "What conversations?"

R: "Well, like in the previous final?"

K: "And who told you that there were any? There were no conversations. We didn't call her at all."

O: "Sure! What for?"

R (embarrassed): "But how…?"

O (discontentedly): "Roman, don't ruin everything. You trust your wife, right?"

R: "I do."

O: "That's great! Wonderful! So, trust her—you have won. What else do you want?"

R: "But...."

K: "No, no, that's it—enough! Our time's up, the show has come to an end. Roman, you're a winner! Congratulations! You've won some prizes: T-shirts with our logo and two tickets to a restaurant. You should visit it with your wife whom you trust so much."

O: "And you're right about it! If only all men were like you!"

K: "Congratulations again! And again, dear listeners, today you were entertained by the hosts Kolya…"

O: "And Olya!"

K: "Good-bye! All the best. See you next Monday."

(Theme music playing.)

And Lucifer was ask'd by His Son:
—Is it possible to intermit the temptation of doubt?
And Lucifer answer'd to His Son:
—Nay. It's against human nature. A man is prone to doubt everything. Whence a doubt ends, fanaticism begins.

LUCIFER'S SON. DAY 11.

And the eleventh day came.
And Lucifer was ask'd by His Son:
—Wherefore didn't Christ want to speak to thou in the desert, but said, "Get behind me, Satan?"
And, smiling, Lucifer answer'd to His Son:
—F'r he had nothing to say to Me.

SATANIST

"Blessed is he that readeth this prophecy
for the time is at hand...
He that overcometh shall
inherit all things."
Book of Revelation (Apocalypse).

Host (H): "Dear viewers! Our topic today is 'Destructive sects.' And our today's guest is a leader of one of these sects. As a matter of fact, it's not an ordinary event; I'd say that it's completely unique. For, usually, the leaders of such sects prefer to stay in the background, and they never give public interviews. The more was our surprise that there is one among them who agreed to do it. By the way, the sect which he heads is one of the most odious and sinister—the sect of the Satanists. So, again, today our guest is the leader of this sect. The sect of the Satanists. Please introduce yourself."

S (a man in his forties) (calmly and even lazily): "There's no need of that."

H: "How shall I be addressing you then?"

S (still calmly): Just *'you'*. It's more than enough for the normal communication during the interview."

H (shrugging his shoulders): "Well, alright, it's up to you. By the way, aren't you afraid to go live, like now? As far as I know, the destructive sects are forbidden by the law."

S (with the same lazy tome): "I'm not. Well, shall we begin at last? "

H (a bit indignantly): "Alright, alright! Let us begin. (Pauses for a second.) You worship Satan. Why?"

S: "Because Satan is the true father of the world."

H (looking at the speaker with astonishment): "How? Excuse me? God created the world, right? Or do you think otherwise?"

S: "I think that the world that we live in exists thanks to Satan. If it were not for Satan and the fall of Eve, we would still be pasturing in the paradise, like domestic animals, naked and blissful, of the Lord."

H: "And do you think that it would be bad?"

S (laughing): "I don't know. I haven't tried it. Ask cows, sheep, and other cattle. I think that they like it. So, maybe it's not that bad. Maybe. For the cattle. But personally, I, as a human, like the world where I live now—the world of computers and Internet. And I don't want any other world."

H: "But is this world perfect? Are there no grief and torments in it? Is there no evil? And is this evil and torments not from devil? Are they not from Satan? Or, maybe you like evil?"

S: "Again, I simply like a beautiful and sinful world where I live. And I need no other. And evil is an essential part of this world. It exists thanks to it. It exists thanks to the eternal fight of good and evil. That's the way the world wags, whether we like it or not. You're afraid of evil. But imagine for a moment—what if the good wins tomorrow? Have you ever considered that? The kingdom of Heaven will be on earth. The end of the world—the end of everything. The end of the world, as we know it. And, as is predicted in Apocalypse, it would be another world. Maybe it would be better, but not the same. Another heaven and another earth. "And I saw a new heaven and a new earth: for the first heaven and the first earth were passed away.

"Time will cease its flow. And it is a very meaningful remark. "There shall be no time." What does it mean? Only that there will be no events, ever. From that time on, everybody will pray to God and praise him. There will be nothing else! "The throne of God, and his servants shall serve him." That's it! Dead end. The end of progress. The end of civilization. Do you wish for that? I don't. Again, I like this world, though it is imperfect, sinful, and wretched. This is my world. And I don't know any other world, and I don't want to. And our world exists thanks to Satan, thanks to the fact that he is still fighting, and the good hasn't won yet."

H: "Right, but what if the evil wins? What if Satan wins eventually?"

S: "Oh! So, you actually admit it? Beware! It is a blasphemy. And God does not like jokes. He's very revengeful and resentful, and he never forgets nor forgives anything. So, for this question, you're going to burn in hell for a couple of extra centuries! However, don't lose courage. (Laughs.) I'll ask the master about you. (Points downwards with his finger.) I promise. And I'm on very good terms with Him."

H: "Ugh…Well! Umph…"

S (laughs again): "I'm just kidding, don't worry! God doesn't have time for us, he's got a lot to do. Well, maybe you should pray one more time. Concerning your question—note that, in the Apocalypse, there's no word that the kingdom of the Beast, the triumph of Satan, means the end of the world, great and numerous disasters and grievances of humans. Not at all! Quite the contrary. It appears that all people were rather happy under the reign of Satan. And they were pleased with that reign. But, surely, God didn't like it. He was outraged and sent "seven angels having the seven last plagues; for in them is filled up the wrath of God" upon men. So, it turns out that Satan won, he reigned upon earth, and men under his reign were prosperous, happy and pleased with everything, and then God, seeing that he lost completely, destroyed the world, unleashing the angels upon men. He sent the punishers.

"Moreover, men didn't want to leave Satan' they didn't betray Him, and they were protecting Him to the end. Just look what was happening. *'And the fourth angel poured out his vial upon the sun: and power was given unto him to scorch men with fire. And men were scorched with great heat, and blasphemed the name of God, which hath power over these plagues, and they repented not to give him glory.* 'What do men have to give Him glory for? For plagues? For the deaths of their own children? And it would be even worse.

'And the fifth angel poured out his vial upon the seat of the beast, and his kingdom was full of darkness, and they gnawed their tongues for pain, and blasphemed the God of heaven because of their pains and their sores, and repented not of their deeds." What

deeds? That they worshipped the Beast? '*And his kingdom was full of darkness.'* So, everything was good before that? Everything was light and joyful?

'*And the seventh angel poured out his vial into the air. And there were thunders and lightnings and there was a great earthquake, such as was not since men were upon the earth. And every island fled away, and the mountains were not found, and there fell upon men a great hail out of heaven every stone about the weight of a talent; and men blasphemed God because of the plague of the hail; the plague thereof was exceeding great.'* Again, what are all of these punishments for? For the fact that men wanted only to live as they deemed right?

And men tried to protect themselves, and Satan gathered them in one place which is called Armageddon in Jewish. But, according to the Apocalypse, men, alas! lost and were defeated. For God is powerful and almighty. And ruthless."

H: "Is it written so in the Bible?"

S (shrugging his shoulders): "Of course! In the Apocalypse. In the Revelations of St. John. You should read it when you have time."

H: "Well, actually…well, alright… So, you think that the Kingdom of the Beast was the golden age?"

S: "At any rate, men were defending that kingdom until the end for some reason, with all strength that they had. And they didn't '*come to reason*' and didn't betray it, in spite of the horrible heavenly plagues and torments sent upon them by a cruel and ruthless God. So, there was a reason for that. They had that which they would defend. They loved it. So, it was the golden age. The age of overall happiness."

H: "And are you sure that this kingdom shall come?"

S: "Once again, according to the Bible, it shall come. However, recall the New Testament, the second Temptation of Christ. '*I shall give to you all this power and their glory; for it has been handed over to me, and I may give it to whomever I wish,'* says Satan to Christ. In other words, He's already ruling the world, and it's quite natural, for, as I've said, this world was created by Him."

H: "Excuse me, but what does it mean: Satan is ruling the world? What do you mean by that?"

S: "Were you in the army?"

H: "Yes."

S: "So, you certainly took the oath. Did you swear the allegiance to the flag?"

H: "Of course. Why?"

S: "And what does the president—or any ruler of the modern country—do, when taking his office? What is his first step? Does he take the oath on the Constitution?"

H: "Yeah! But I don't understand what you're pointing at."

S (lazily and leniently): "What am I pointing at? The Bible says: an oath is the act of Satanism."

H (astonished): "Where is it said?"

S (smiling): "It is. For example, Gospel of Matthew, *'Do not swear. All you need say is 'Yes' if you mean yes, 'No' if you mean no; anything more that this comes from the Evil One.'* What other proofs do you need?"

H (embarrassed): "But the Church doesn't deny temporal power, does it? Christ says explicitly: *'Render unto Caesar the things that are Caesar's, and unto God the things that are God's!'"*

S (still smiling): "And whose is Caesar? That is the main question. So, regarding the abovementioned, this statement may read somewhat different. *'Render unto God the things that are God's, and unto Devil the things that are Devil's.'* That's it. And that's right. That's the way the things are."

H (after a certain confusion): "So, you're saying that any temporal power is from the devil?"

S (calmly): "Of course. Recall the Gospel of Luke: *'All this power is delivered unto me; and to whomsoever I will, I give it.'* So, the devil had the power in the first place, and he gives it to whoever he likes."

H (passionately): "And what about the church? There's the church—the Church of Christ."

S (looking at him ironically): "The church. And whom is it founded on? On Simon and Peter? *'And I tell you that you are Peter, and on this rock I will build my church.'* It is founded on the man who later denied Christ three times—a traitor! And again, *'Make a tree good and its fruit will be good, or make a tree bad and its fruit will be bad, for a tree is recognized by its fruit.'* Gospel of Matthew. And what fruit shall a traitor bear? Snakes bear snakes only. And scorpions bear scorpions. *Neither doth a corrupt tree bring forth good fruit. For of thorns men do not gather figs, nor of a bramble bush gather they grapes.* Gospel of Luke. (Thoughtfully): And Christ himself—he's a man, too. And, so, there's a fight between God and devil in his soul. And if he wished good upon men, he'd have to make his choice in the end.

"Maybe he's already made it. Do you remember how he fed five thousand men with five loaves of bread? What is it, if not a change of stone into bread? It is what the devil told him to do in the very beginning. At first, Christ denied that path, but it turns out that he took in eventually. And what could he do, if such is the way of the world? Would it be better, if men were hungry?"

H (with superstitious awe): "What are you talking about? Are you saying that Christ eventually became Antichrist? And the Second Coming of Christ will be the coming of Antichrist?"

S (screwing up his eyes mockingly): "Well, well, well! Why would you say these horrible words? Why would you scare yourself and our trustful viewers? Christ took the only right path, for he wished good upon men. That's it. He took the path which Satan told him for the simple reason that he didn't have any other path. The other path meant seven angel-punishers, plagues, and an earthquake. Death and torments.

"The path of Satan: men are weak—help them, feed them and turn the stones into the bread. And they shall appreciate that, follow you, and appreciate your humanity, justice, kindness, and generosity. The path of God: let men earn their bread themselves, and if they can't, let them and their children die from hunger. *'Cursed is the ground because of you; through painful toil you will eat food from it all the days of your life; It will produce thorns and thistles for you, and you will eat the plants of the field. By the sweat of your brow you will eat your food.'* The Book of Genesis. Which path do you like better? Which one would you prefer?"

H (after a pause): "I don't know. I'm not God. I'm just a human."

S: "Well, alright. You don't know What if something happens with you—for example, you have a desperate disease? What then? You're definitely going to seek help of sorcerers, magicians, and psychics, when all doctors abandon you, aren't you? Eh? Aren't you? (Winking.) And all of this is sinful. From the Evil One. All these magicians and sorcerers. The Church condemns it, and it is clearly said in the Bible. But you will do it anyway. Of course, you're going to place a candle in the church. Just in case. On the principle, *'Render unto God the things that are God's, and unto the devil the things that are the devil's.'* Maybe, some of them would help you. What? Is it not true?"

H: "I'm not sure I've never consulted sorcerers and psychics. I'm a Christian, and I don't believe in all these miracles."

S (mockingly): "You don't. And your wife doesn't believe in them either, does she?"

H (embarrassed): "What does my wife have to do with it?"

S (looking at him intently): "Your child is seriously ill, isn't he?"

H (quietly, in a hoarse voice): "How do you know?"

S (calmly): "He shall die in 7 months."

H (shocked): "What?"

S (looking at him with a smile): "You may keep placing candles in the church. And your wife may keep talking to psychics. Still, it won't help. You can tell this to your wife. It's of no avail. He's going to die anyway. As you know, everything is God's will."

H (with awakened and desperate hope): "And what will be of avail? What will help? Maybe you would be able to help?"

S (after a long pause, with the same smile): "What if I would? Would you deny God? Is that all your faith?"

H (not listening, with the same desperate hope): "So, are you able to help me? "

S (indifferently, standing up and moving the chair aside): "No. The interview is over. All the best."

And Lucifer was ask'd by His Son:

—Would that man deny God, if he was given hope?

And Lucifer answer'd to His Son:

—He already deni'd him in his soul—when he ask'd that question.

LUCIFER'S SON. DAY 12.

And the twelfth day came.

And Lucifer said to His Son:

—Men art not capable of resisting the temptation of curiosity.

Knowledge of thy fate is a beshrew, but not a blessing. It makes a man miserable.

PROPHECY

"What fills them with foreboding
and their hearts with fear is dread
of the day of death."
Wisdom of Jesus
The Son of Sirach.

Notice on the door of registry office.

ATTENTION, NEWLYWEDS!

Do you want to know your future? Visit our website <site address>. New methodologies and modern computer technologies guarantee an excellent result! Absolutely free! Welcome!!

***

Notice at the website.

ATTENTION, NEWLYWEDS!

If you want to know your future, please fill in the questionnaire and send us your wedding photos, and we shall send you our prediction within 24 hours. Don't hesitate! We will not disappoint you! To receive detailed information about us and our methodology of predictions, click here.

Do you want to fill in the questionnaire? Yes. No.
Our e-mail for contact: <link to e-mail>.

***

The page which appears after clicking the link <click here>.

Hi! Thank you for visiting our website.

First off, a couple of words about our center and the methodology of predictions creating.

A lot of people are surprised by the very thought that the future can be predicted, and they take such predictions with skepticism and consider them to be charlatanism. For fatalism, predeterminacy, doom, and fate—at first sight, it seems to be incompatible with free will. As a matter of fact, how can my deed be predicted? Well, do it, and I will do it otherwise! And what then?

Yes, at first sight, this objection seems to be rather convincing. But only at first sight, As a matter of fact, this contradiction is imaginary.

From the scientific point of view, life is a random and stochastic process, a flow of accidental events. These events have been well-known for a long period of time; they are perceived, studied, and they have their own laws of development, and, consequently, they may be predicted. Sure, every particular event of this process is accidental, but the general outcome is naturally determined. Say, flipping of a coin. It's impossible to predict the result of a particular flip, but, nevertheless, the result of the whole process is known beforehand. Half the time it's heads, and another half, tails.

Same with the predictions of future. Sure, every particular deed of yours cannot be predicted—well, free will—but the result of the whole life process, its approximate development and passing—all of that doesn't have a random nature. It obeys the laws of statistics, and so it can be easily calculated and predicted. Moreover, not all events in real life are equally possible, and it limits a lot the quantity of the possible variants and makes the task of prediction even easier. Of course, theoretically, one can leave a room through a window, but, in practice, it is usually done through a door.

Or, for example, if you're lost in a wood and, having wandered there for a couple of hours or even days, you strike a wide path which is clearly leading to a human abode, then it's clear that you're going to follow it, although no one makes you do this. And you're still free to go wherever you want—to the four winds. You may keep roaming in the wood for a couple of days. It's up to you. But, in the end, you're still going to find that path, and you're going to take it, for there are no other roads here. The same is in life. It seems that there's freedom of choice. You may go wherever you want. However, even with all this imaginary "freedom," it's very easy to predict where you will be in a couple of hours. You will be in the spot which you can reach during the time that you've got. That's all the freedom that you have.

That is a general situation with predictions, essentially. We hope that you do realize now that predictions are real. It's not difficult to guess that you will follow the path. But, certainly, that is in general, the fact that you will follow the path. As a matter of fact, accurate and individual predictions are a very complicated, subtle, and delicate thing. How will you go? With what speed? Will you rest? Whom will you meet? And so on and so forth.

In order to make such a prediction, one must try to do an accurate psychological profile of a person that you're interested in; you should try to guess his character, personality features, will, emotionality, sympathism, etc.; you should make a card, or a formula, of his personality in order to understand what you should be waiting for from him in the future. For there always will be people who leave a room through a window. And in that case, one should pay attention, not to their speed and the window, but to what floor this window is on. It's necessary, in order to understand and predict what exactly the individual is going to break in a moment, and if he's going to stay alive at all.

So, the future of a person, as we see from this very simple example, is certainly defined mostly by his character, mentality, and psychics. And right in this sphere, in the field of study of human mentality and psychics, we have achieved the most impressive and revolutionary results. We have advanced here a lot. Actually, we have made a real breakthrough!

As a result of long-term, comprehensive, and laborious scientific research, our specialists—and there are many internationally known specialists—developed, introduced, and successfully tested a unique and exclusive psycho-table, an analogue of the famous Mendeleev's table. This table allowed us to combine and systematize hundreds and hundreds of fundamental types of human characters and personalities, as well as helping us to define and comprehend the fundamental laws of formation, establishing, and development of the personality.

Like any element in the nature, be it liquid, gas—anything—consists of some elementary bricks, atoms, and is, in its essence, just a combination of these atoms. For example, the usual water, H2O, is a combination of two atoms of hydrogen and one atom of oxygen; so, any human personality, however complicated and seemingly mysterious it may be, is, after all, a certain combination, a mixture of some elementary psycho-bricks: fear, shame, libido, etc. All these features exist in it in various proportions.

All of us, idiots and geniuses, however unique and special we may seem, are made of the same psycho-material, like a fair Gothic cathedral and a primitive farmyard are built of the same stone. Classification of the basic characters and their combining into one structured table became a decisive and the most essential step on the road of studying of the human personality. It gave us an instrument to explore it. It pointed out an approach. It was a kind of introducing of the integrated system of coordinates in psychology. For, from that time on, any real character could be described as a more or less complex combination of the basic ones which are already thoroughly studied, and its formula is well-known—what exactly is mixed up of the psycho-bricks, and in what proportion. And, as we know the formula of every element of the combination, so, needless to say, we know the formula of the whole combination—that is, the formula of the real human personality. This method of successive simplification allows us to find it eventually.

So, this is the methodology in general. The only serious problem is how to get as much information about a personality as to be able to start a systematic work on its identification. But this problem can be solved with our special, carefully designed, and detailed questionnaire, which is available at our site. You should fill it in if you want to get our prediction.

As a matter of fact, all these conclusions and reasonings are not quite new, for similar researches and studies have been conducted for a long time, by different people; but, up to recent time, their results were only theoretical and purely scientific, and they didn't have any applied significance. or they had only limited one. For example, the famous IQ tests, which are filled in by the employees while applying for a job. These tests allow the evaluation of a professional suitability of a certain person, but nothing more. The issue of predictions of the future and forecasts of fate was never raised—most notably, because of the technical and computational difficulties of these kind of predictions.

The thing is that a real formula of the personality of any real man is so complex and complicated in practice that unavoidable errors in its calculation make any predictions made with its help absolutely useless. They are too general, ambiguous, and uncertain. One may read coffee grounds with the same result. Not to mention that it's not enough to calculate the formula of personality. In order to receive any accurate prediction, one must take into account and make allowance to the influence of many outside factors, and it may be very difficult sometimes—first of all, because of the purely technical reasons.

In other words, the corresponding scientific methodologies of predictions and forecasts of the future do exist; they are developed, explored, and well-known, and they are based, by the way, on various sociological polls and surveys, statistical studies, economic and social characteristics, and indexes of society development—of course, with the allowance to the personality of a certain man; but purely technical and calculational difficulties of their practical use and realization were unconquerable up to recent time. As a matter of fact, they deprived the prediction of any sense.

That was the situation until recently, up to the present time. But now, the situation is changed completely! With the invention of modern superpower and super-quick computers, it has become possible to bring the errors of the calculations—primarily of the personality formula—almost to zero, and, correspondingly, to make predictions for the future without mistakes and with a very high level of accuracy and truthfulness.

This is a way you should treat our predictions, if you certainly decide to take part in our project and fill in the questionnaire. These are purely scientific predictions, based on the elaborately designed methodologies, which are calculated on the modern supercomputers. They're almost absolutely accurate and faultless. It's not a game or charlatanism which may amuse you later and be easily forgotten. No, it's your future, indeed, whether you like it or not. Keep that in mind. We want to emphasize that our project is purely scientific and non-commercial; we don't charge our predictions. Financial benefit or interest from our side is not an issue. We're making predictions for free. Keep that in mind, as well, when you're reading and analyzing them. So, we'd like to warn you one more time.

OUR PREDICTIONS ARE ABSOLUTELY REAL!
THEY ALWAYS COME TRUE!
ALWAYS! BY ALL MEANS! WITHOUT DOUBT!
THIS IS YOUR FUTURE!!

That is how you should take them; you should accept it as a given. Hurry up to fill in our questionnaire and find out your fate!

Aren't you interested? Don't you want to look behind the magic veil of Isis, where even gods cannot reach? Fill in our questionnaire, and we will tell you what's behind it!

Good luck!

***

E-mail from Center Newlyweds to Fomin L.D.

Dear Leonid Danilovich:

First of all, thank you very much for you and your wife's participation in our project and for kindly answering our questions. We hope to see you on our site in future. Now, regarding our prediction.

Unfortunately, we have bad news. According to our prediction, in two months, you're going to die in a car accident and be buried at the cemetery (name of the cemetery). A year after your death, your wife will get married again. She will marry a very wealthy man, about her age, who's going to passionately love her. She will be very happy with him, and she'll live to very old age. In that marriage, she'll have three children: two boys and a girl. After her marriage, she will not visit your grave at all.

As we realize clearly what impression on you our prediction may have, we took the liberty—in order not to lose time, and without your consent—of calculating the possibility of you avoiding this fate and the means of doing so. Fortunately, yes, you can do it! Our calculations show that if you get divorced at once, you're not going to die in a car accident. Alas! We can't see how exactly your fate will develop in this case, for here, everything depends on how quickly you get a divorce. The following two months are a critical period of your life; every day is of a great importance and has a great influence on the next course of events. As the date of your presumed death comes near, it will be more and more difficult for you to avoid it.

Figuratively speaking, this car accident may be compared to a large heavy stone that is lying on your life course, and you have to get rid of it, whatever it may take. You still can do it today; you have a strong and powerful lever of two months' time which you may use to lift and move aside that heavy stone. But with every passing day, the lever in your hands is going to melt down and become shorter, until it disappears completely at last. So, beginning from a certain moment, it may become so short that you won't be able to move anything with it; you will simply have no strength. Bear that in mind and do not linger. You have little time. It's almost impossible to predict when the lever will become too short. And the error of a couple of days may be crucial.

We inform you that, in case of your divorce, your wife will never get married, and, overall, her future life won't be successful. She will have a great need of money, she will start drinking, go down, and grow old; actually, she will become a miserable person.

We are fully aware, how difficult for you is to make a decision concerning the divorce. It's very unexpected and just after the wedding; and considering how it's going to influence the fate of your wife whom you love very much. We know that from the formula of your personality.

That's why we offer you the chance to make a little psychological experiment. We're going to send you another prediction for your wife, and you'll see, how she reacts to it. Will she tell you about it at all? If she doesn't, it'll be easier for you to divorce her. As a matter of fact, you'll have a moral right to do it. After that, you can ask your wife if she received the prediction from us for you to be sure that she concealed it and didn't just ignore it.

Let us assure you that we would never advise you this, if it were not for the extreme nature of the situation. And the situation is extraordinary, indeed. It is a matter of days already. Today you can change it. But tomorrow… However, it's up to you to decide. We won't do anything without your consent. So, please, tell us your decision as soon as possible. So, shall we send your wife the following e-mail, or not? Waiting for your answer.

P. S. If you're having any doubts as for the truth of our prediction, we can make a new detailed prediction for you for the following month. So, you will be able to wait for some time and make sure that it's accurate. It is very complicated and time-consuming work, and we do not usually make such quick and very detailed predictions, but, as your case is peculiar, we're ready to do that. However, we want to warn you that it will take some time—apparently, a couple of days. Frankly speaking, we're not quite sure that it is a wise decision in this situation

At any rate, it's up to you to decide. Anyhow, please tell us your decision concerning the e-mail to your wife. Shall we send it or not?

ASSUMED TEXT OF E-MAIL FOR YOUR WIFE:

Dear Anna Petrovna:

First of all, thank you very much for you and your husband's participation in our project and for kindly answering our questions.

We hope to see you on our site in future. Now, regarding our prediction.

Unfortunately, we have to inform you that your husband is going to die in a car accident in two months. A year after that, you will get married again. You will marry a man of your age, a very wealthy one who's going to love you very much. You will be very happy with him, and you'll live to very old age. In that marriage, you'll have three children: two boys and a girl.

Concerning your current husband, Leonid; it's still possible to save him. If you want him not to die in a car accident, you should divorce him immediately. However, we warn you that, in this case, you will never get married, and, overall, your future life won't be successful. You will have a great need of money, you will start drinking, go down and grow old; actually, you will become a miserable person. Decide for yourself.

With compliments,

Sincerely yours, Center Newlyweds

***

E-mail from Fomin L.D. to Center Newlyweds

Send it.

***

Petition for a divorce (filed the next day).

I, Fomin Leonid Danilovich, ask to dissolve my marriage.

***

And Lucifer was ask'd by His Son:

—What if his prediction was ordinary? Without any disasters in future? Would it doth any good then?

And Lucifer answer'd to His Son, smiling:

—Well, I shall bewray Thee that, as well.

***

E-mail from Center Newlyweds to Zharikov S.M.

Dear Semen Mikhailovich:

First of all, thank you very much for you and your wife's participation in our project and for kindly answering our questions. We hope to see you on our site in future. Now, regarding our prediction.

Please accept our heartiest congratulations! You are going to be very happy in your marriage. You will have two children: a boy and a girl. Your life will be peaceful and untroubled, without any disasters and commotions.

Actually, you'll have problems with alcohol before you turn 40, as is usual for the most men of this age; and you'll have a feeling of dissatisfaction; you'll think that the life is going by, that you're not living, but lead an aimless life etc. All in all, it's a usual middle-age crisis in its light form—nothing special. There will be a period when you'll think about having a young lover, but you'll never resolve to that. Peace, laziness, big belly, summer cottage, wife and children, vodka and beer, TV; as soon as you're 50, all these signs of the crisis and all your silly thoughts and tribulations will disappear without leaving a trace, and you will spend your last days in peace. You will die at the age of 66 from a heart attack. Your death will be easy and painless. Your wife will outlive you for seven years. The last six years she will spend at the summer cottage with your neighbor—the same lonely, retired old man.

The following are the pictures of you and your wife, starting from this moment until both of your deaths, with five-year intervals. These pictures are made through computer modeling, and, considering the newest developments in that sphere, their accuracy is almost absolute. The error would be up to the thousandths of one percent. You may feast your eyes on them, for that is how you and your wife are going to look at that age. You may put them in your family album at once. So, accept our heartiest congratulations one more time. One can only envy you! Other people suffer torments, die, and grieve. They fall under the blows of the fates, rise, and fall again. They keep looking for something and never find it. They scream in pain, weep in happiness, and choke with tenderness. They love passionately and hate fiercely. And what's the meaning of that? That is vanity of vanities. The end is the same for everyone. All shall end in ash.

But you will lead a quiet, calm, and peaceful life. You'll bring up two children, you'll have faithful and loyal wife, and you'll die quietly and peacefully in your bed. Would anyone wish for more?

We're happy for you!

Yours faithfully, Center Newlyweds.

P. S. As a gift, we send you a more detailed prediction of your life for the next 3 years. You'll also be able to check the accuracy of our predictions. Good luck!

And Lucifer was ask'd by His son:

—What shall that man doth?

And Lucifer answer'd to His Son:

—He shall get divorced, too. But later. In a few years. When he's absolutely sure that the predictions art true.

And Lucifer was again ask'd by His Son:

—Wherefore?

And Lucifer answer'd to His Son:

—F'r a man can't live, knowing his future. That is death f'r him.

LUCIFER'S SON. DAY 13.

And the thirteenth day came.

And Lucifer said to His Son:

—Death is the higher judge in life. Only the final battle with death shows a man's worth. There's nay place f'r pretense hither, and one hath to speak the sooth. Everything else may enwheel a disguise.

ROBOT

"Peter took him aside and began to rebuke him.
"Never, Lord!" he said. "This shall never happen to you!"
Gospel of Matthew.

***

"I show a wolfish grin to my enemy,
I bare my rotten shatters,
But the snow, tattooed with blood,
Reads: we're wolves no more!"
V.S. Vysotsky. The End of "The Hunt for the Wolves"
The Song of the Leader

1.

"Wake up!" Andrey slightly pushed his wife, who was lying at his side. She mumbled something in her sleep and then snored quietly again. *It's for the better,* thought Andrey, huddling from morning chill, and he got out of the tent. It was very early—four in the morning, at most. Silence, gray morning twilight, and things wet with dew.

He quickly started a fire, put a pot with water above it, and went to the lake to wash up. The water in the lake was bitterly cold, and it braced him up. Having washed up, Andrey woke up completely. A cup of hot tea with sandwiches, and he's good to go. Returning to the fire, he saw with pleasure that the water in the pot was already boiling. Andrey took off the pot, put some tea into it, covered it with a lid, and left it near the fire to steep. Meanwhile, he got busy with sandwiches.

Well, one with butter and cheese, one with ham. Well, enough! I'll have a bite while fishing. He made a couple of extra sandwiches for the fishing, wrapped them in a plastic bag, and put it on a table, on the foreground near the thermos. He didn't want to leave them.

"Tea isn't ready yet. Let's check the gear, just in case—just to be safe. Well, I did check them in the evening, but I should really do it once more. It's the last fishing, after all. It would be a shame if I left anything. Well, spinner, landing net, fish lines 0.3, 0.4... I'm gonna take one more coil of 0.03 I'll need it; you never know. If I strike a fucking brush, I will tear everything apart. Well... jigs... Too few, yeah, too few! Well, okay! 'Too few, too few!..' - I'm carrying a whole bag with this metal stuff, and what's the point of it? Alright. Enough or not, I'm gonna take it. I'm gonna grab a couple more. Yeah, this one and this one, well, and that one also. And a couple of these small meters with feathers. That's it. That's it! Now it's really enough, and I can worry no more.

Alright, let's assume that plunkers are okay... they are dealt with. What next? Now wobblers, wobblers—floating, diving ones—should I take the rest, as well? It's the last day, anyway. What if I catch something with them? And? Why the fuck do I need them? How would I drag all this stuff? Nothing struck these wobblers, however hard I tried. Am I really going to learn to do it today? On the last day? That's it! I'm gonna take this one for the conscience's sake—it's too beautiful!—and close the box. Well, shads, of course.

Enough? Oh! Sure, there's a whole box of them! Should I salt them away or what? What else? Snoods, hooks—everything's here. Right That's it. Have I forgotten anything? Plunkers, wobblers, shads, lines, snoods, and hooks. That's it! Now that's it! Oh, well, together with spinning and landing net—that goes without saying! Well, now that's it. I'm good to go.

Andrey grabbed the bag with the gear from the table and proudly put it on a path that led to the boat. *Well, well! I don't want to go without the gear! I've been there. 'And where's the gear?' I left it! If you stumble over it, you won't leave it!* He returned to the fire, poured some tea in a cup, grabbed one of the sandwiches that he had made, and, trying to make no noise, started eating it quickly.

Oh, God! Help me! If only no one woke up—that would be a disaster! They get out, start making noise, rustling with bags, talking 'Where is this? Where is that?' They start making sandwiches, too, but not like I did it—without haste, but with feeling, wit, and punctuation. With loud calls. And then other guys would wake up, smelling the scents and hearing the noises. They would gather like flies.

Women, to begin with... If the women wake up, that would be a disaster—the game is over. They pack up for the half of the day, washing up and stuff, endless tea drinking. 'Oh, I forgot that! Oh, I need to change, I'm cold! Ouch and I... Ouch, and here.' Well, it's 'oh-ouch, fucking shit!' That's it! Broads are a fucking disaster. It's the end of a nice morning.

So, you can actually head to the nearest pine tree and hang yourself or go the tent and sleep. They won't be ready until twelve, and then they may still change their minds. 'Oh, I have a headache... I think I'll stay.' No, we won't be able to catch Abdullah with these women! Actually, we won't fucking catch anything. Why do people take their wives with them? Ugh... 'Take'!.. And what about you? Well, that's not it. What did I tell you? That's not it. Maybe that's it. That's not it! Alright, forget it.

As a matter of fact, Andrey didn't know why he had taken his wife with him this year. However, why take? It was her who took. She just went with him.

"But why? What are you going to do there? It's cold, there are a lot of mosquitoes, and the climate is very tough. You'll have to live in a tent under unsanitary conditions. Washing up with cold water. I don't want you to catch a cold and get sick. Very precious parts of you may get sick. It's no south. It's Karelia. It's north. What are you going to do then?"

"I won't get sick."

"What if you do?"

"Why would I get sick? What about other people?"

"Other people are other people—they go there every year. What are you going to do there, anyway? I just can't imagine that. I'm going to go fishing for the whole day, and what about you?"

"And why are you dissuading me? Why do you care what I'm going to do there? I won't be a nuisance, don't worry about that!"

I won't be a nuisance, thought Andrey gloomily. *Right!*

It seemed that his beloved wife wanted to check, one day, what her dear hubby was doing at the fishing. What kind of fish was he catching there? And, with a thoughtlessness which is a usual thing for many women, she decided to check that with her own eyes. She wanted to sort it out, so to say, to control the whole situation. And all his inescapable arguments, reassurances, and calls for sense just added oil to the flame. They only spurred and whetted her. They made her unexpected suspicion stronger. So, all said and done, why wait? She caught the train and set out.

'Set out'!.. The time in the train was very merry. Two more young couples, new acquaintances, jokes and booze! And then a night in a real country cabin of one of the locals whom they had known for ages and in whose house they had always stayed upon arrival. Baths, vodka with salted mushrooms and fish which is produced out of the huge glass cans. So romantic!

And then a four-hour motorboat trip on a wild but picturesque northern lake, in the maze of endless islands, small and huge. It was very interesting and entertaining. And, at last, their destination. A nameless bay, which they had been visiting for many years. Andrey couldn't even remember for how many. The guide unloaded them, wished them nice fishing, and left at once, talking about pressing business. He promised to come back for them three weeks later, as he had usually done during all these years.

And there were six of them left. When Vera, Andrey's wife, realized where she was and what she'd got herself into, it was too late. She couldn't leave by herself. It was a one-week trip on a canoe, and nobody really knew the way. The locals used to get them here and then pick them up. And canoeing was dangerous. Wind, waves, and huge open space—it was easy to turn over, and the water was icy cold. Forget canoes.

All in all, it was impossible to leave. One would have to wait for three weeks. And, meanwhile, such woman as Vera had nothing to do here at all—nothing at all. Other wives were gathering, salting, and stewing all day long. But Vera wasn't interested in all that, not in the least. She wasn't interested in this cooking. And there were no other entertainments here. It was impossible even to bathe in the sun. The climate was inappropriate. And the mosquitoes…

So, eventually, she began fishing with Andrey. Or she would ask him not to go anywhere tomorrow and stay with her. "Dima and Kostya aren't going anywhere. We'll stay near the fire, drink a bit, and have a talk. Kostya will play a guitar."

Dima and Kostya! The problem was that, unlike Dima and Kostya, Andrey was really an ardent fisherman, a real fishing fan. He wasn't interested in anything else here. Mushrooms, berries, evening talks, drinking, and singing near the fire - nothing!

Kostya and Dima were not real fishermen; they just thought they were. They would go fishing one day and then sleep off for the next three days. "What's the point of getting up early and going somewhere? The fishing is good during the day. Right here, near the camp."

Andrey met them quite accidentally. It happened several years ago, here in Karelia, in that very bay—they had their camp here—and, from that time on, he came here only with them. They were alright as companions. He could have come here alone, but three weeks' time! And here he had some people around, he could talk to them, and that was great. He had the minimum of communication that he needed. Well, he would sit with everyone for half an hour in front of the fire, talk to them and that would be enough. And it was even for the better that Kostya and Dima were not fishermen. Just the thing! Andrey liked to go fishing by himself. And the guys would follow him from time to time; that was alright. First, it didn't happen so often, and second, they couldn't endure the whole day. At best, they would stay with him until afternoon. And then, "it's time to go to the camp."

In general, they didn't burden him. As a matter of fact, they had a kind of mutually profitable, stable symbiosis. Everybody was okay with it. Andrey was supplying the camp with fish, and the others were cooking, running things, housekeeping, and simply providing the minimal level of communication for him. Such was the state of things for the last years. They all got used to it and felt comfortable; every member of this small society knew the habits and life regime of the others in the smallest detail. In brief, these three weeks used to pass peacefully and undisturbed, to the pleasure of everyone. And after that, they parted until the next year.

Now, suddenly, this small comfortable world was shaken. The appearance of Vera changed everything. It disturbed the stable balance that had been created before.

Vera was actually a typical cityish young lady from Moscow. Moreover, she was a spoilt, tender creature, and she was not fit for the camp life. Naturally, she couldn't do anything, but, what was even worse, she wasn't going to learn it. She would sleep until two in the afternoon, then get up slowly, stretch, get out of the tent, and, as if nothing had happened, sit behind the table to drink tea which was made by someone else. And she would take that for granted.

Andrey tried to talk to her about that a couple of times, but it was useless. "Would you just wash up dishes with everyone?"

"I can't do it in cold water."

"And how does everyone else do it?"

"Their skin is different. I have very sensitive skin."

And that was it.

All in all, the situation wasn't normal. It turned out that, out of the six people who were living together, one didn't do anything and, what's more important, didn't want to do anything. The others wouldn't say anything, of course, and would just pretend that they didn't notice anything, but, as a matter of fact, they did notice it and would say something sooner or later. But, surely it couldn't last like this forever.

In the end, Andrey had to abandon his fishing a couple of times. He stayed in the camp, chopped the wood, did the dishes, etc. Thus he tried to improve the situation and compensate for the idleness and laziness of his beloved wife. He had to make up her public debts, so to say. Though, frankly speaking, that was not good at all. There was no casual work in the camp—one had just to work a bit every day. Making some tea, scaling fish, and doing the dishes. All in all, one had to participate in public life. And what would you do it just one day?

Well, he gathered and chopped wood which would last for three weeks and what then? Could he now be idle and do nothing at all? As if he had already done his part? No, that was not the way they did it in the camp. *You chopped some wood—attaboy!* And tomorrow there would be something else to do; please do it with everyone else. All this casual 'making up' was not good at all. They were creating a bad atmosphere and petty calculations of who did more than everyone else. And, as one of his familiar criminals used to say, "it was fucking bullshit."

Exactly, thought Andrey gloomily, eating his last sandwich quickly and silently. *Fucking. Bullshit. Exactly. There are no other words for that. It's a fucking idiom. A camp one. Actually, a camp and prison idiom. There are probably such situations there as well. Thank God, we're leaving tomorrow. Several days more, and it all would fucking explode like an overheated steam boiler. Everyone would just fight. And I'd have no one to come here with!*

He decided firmly that he would never bring his wife here again. *She may do what she wants. She may stand on her head, if she wants to. No, under no circumstances! And she probably won't come herself. But if she wants—no—and that's it! Basta. No, no, and no!*

Andrey was cheering and screwing himself up with these tough words, but he clearly knew deep in his soul that if his Verochka wanted anything... He didn't want to take her with him to fishing today. He was dissuading her. It was the last fucking day!

"Why would you go with me? Why would you wake bright and early to the swamp mosquitoes? Have a sleep, stay in the tent. Then you're going to get up have a nice breakfast .Take some rest before leaving."

"No! I'm going with you!"

Fuck! What should I do to her?

It was good that she overslept. Andrey had to leave quickly. That thought lashed him. Andrey swallowed the rest of the sandwich, choking on it. Then he drank up his tea, put the empty cup on the table, and stood up without a noise.

At this very moment, Vera got out of the tent, yawning. She was sleepy and disheveled. Andrey kept staring at her silently for some time, as if she were a ghost. He stood still, unable to utter a word and not believing his own eyes.

Oh, God! Why? Why is this happening to me? She usually sleeps until two in the afternoon! And it seems that yesterday she went to sleep past midnight!.. Andrey did it on purpose, hoping that she wouldn't get up in the morning. He wasn't worrying about himself. "I'll sleep for a couple of hours, and that's it. I've been there. I'm going to sleep off in the train."

Meanwhile, Vera stood up, gave a wide yawn, covering her mouth with her hand, and, looking at Andrey, asked him loudly, "Are you ready? Why didn't you wake me up?"

"Hush, you're gonna wake everybody," hissed Andrey at her and listened carefully. Everything was silent in the camp. Nobody seemed to wake up, at least for the time being. "So, you got up, eh?"

"Sure! And did you want to leave without me?"

"Bullshit," whispered Andrey with irritation. If only he could! "I tried to wake you up, but you kept sleeping."

"It's not true," his wife pouted.

"Alright, go wash up, and I'm gonna heat the tea," ordered Andrey. "We're late."

He realized that he wouldn't get rid of his wife, so he had to make her get ready as soon as possible and leave quickly while the others were still sleeping. It was time to go. Five in the morning.

With monumental efforts, constant urges, shouts, and calls—"Are you coming? How can you be so long? Are we going to set out, or not?"—he managed to do the impossible. Only half an hour passed, and they were in a canoe, entering a familiar channel covered with grass which led to the Black Lake—a small lake which was connected by the channel with the large one; they actually had come on this lake in the motor-boat. Andrey didn't know why it was called 'Black.' Was that its real name, or did the tourists call it that between them? Andrey never actually tried to find it out. It was simply Black. It was called so. All the more so, the water and the fish in there were somewhat black, indeed. It was probably because of the boggish bottom and shores. Peat bogs were everywhere.

Andrey's plan was to reach the end of the Black Lake—it ended with another narrow weedy channel which then disappeared in the swamp—leave the boat there, considering the spot was desolate, and then, together with Vera, who was following him, go on foot and look for other lakes which were many there. Small and desolate lakes, full of untamed fish. The very thought was like a drug for him. He was even wondering why he hadn't done it before. He was just going to do that - and he left it for the last day, as usual. It was all because of fecklessness and laziness.

Coming to the Black Lake... It's early... silence... everything's great... No one around... And he wouldn't want to go anywhere else. *Heh! I'm gonna go there tomorrow.*

Andrey left the first channel, crossed the still and silent Black Lake, which was smooth as glass and seemed to be steaming early in the morning, and entered the second channel. A few minutes more, and the nose of the canoe struck the weedy shore. It was impossible to go any further in the canoe. They had to get out and continue on foot. Andrey turned the canoe to its side skillfully, got out, helped his wife to do it, tied up the canoe slightly—there was no current, so it shouldn't be washed away—took the spinner, the landing net, the bag with the gear, and they went on. As a matter of fact, Andrey wasn't sure where they were heading; they just went at random. The locals said that there were a lot of small lakes there, so they had to find something with God's help.

Well, at any rate, we'll have a little walk without a load, and then turn back. Big deal! It's even interesting, the search for new places—waiting, anticipation.

They struck the first lake very quickly. Ten minutes later, they saw a wide glistening water-table with the shrouds of white fog flowing on it. Carefully and trying to make no noise, Andrey crept to the shore and, catching his breath, made the first throw.

Remembering his plan to visit as many lakes as he could, Andrey went further on an hour later. *Look at these places! I just don't want to leave them!*

The second lake was near at hand, and then the third and the fourth; it seemed that the lakes were everywhere. New lakes—desolate, unexplored, full of secrets, huge pikes, and fat bass. A fishing Mecca. El Dorado! However, he didn't catch any pikes or fat bass. Strangely enough, the fishing went bad. The spots were great—grass and bush, the time—early morning, the best time for fishing—but no! No fish at all, whatever he did! *Maybe the weather is changing?* Andrey didn't know what to think. *Is it the pressure?*

Nevertheless, pressure or no pressure, he caught only a couple of small basses. Vera was tired and, naturally, began hinting about going back to the camp. Well, she wasn't actually hinting, she was demanding it. As a matter of fact, she started moaning, "How long shall we drag in these swamps? All of this for two crucian carps?"

"It's bass," corrected her Andrey gloomily.

"Really? I thought it was crucian carp. The guys caught the same fish near the camp, with long line and hooks. The same fish—small and striped."

Fuck! 'Small fish,' Andrey looked gloomily at the bag with two lonely bass in it. It was a shame, for there were a lot of these small guys near the camp, indeed. And he could catch them any time. The same fish. 'Small and striped'. Same micro-bass. 'Micras,' as he used to call them scornfully. Or 'sailors'. With a long line and hooks—that is, with a simple cross line—it was possible to catch a lot of them.

Well, actually, he didn't have anything to say to his wife. Nevertheless, Andrey wasn't going to return to the camp. No way!

First, he was interested not in the result, but in the process of fishing. It wasn't important whether he caught anything or not. Of course, it would be better if he caught something, but that was alright! He would—skill and patience; he still had a lot of time. And second, what fucking camp? It's the last day!

"What's the meaning of this? We had a deal—you wanted to go with me!"

However, closer to noon, it became clear that they had to return. His beloved wife told him flat that she was tired and wouldn't take another step. "Get me to the camp, and then you can hang out here the whole day." Grinding his teeth, Andrey had to agree to that. What could he do?

Alright, he thought quickly. *I'm going to get her to the camp, have a bite, and then come back here. I still have a lot of time. It's only 1 p.m.*

However, he didn't want to go back at all. They were pretty far from the camp. They needed time to get to the boat and then to the camp; they would lose half of the day. And after that, he would still have to come back here. It was too long and unpleasant in a psychological way. It would spoil all pleasure. He wanted to go on and find new places. But he could do nothing.

"Alright," he said reluctantly, "let's go."

"I'm tired."

"And why did you come here? You should have kept sleeping. I told you at the very beginning, that this would happen! 'No, no!'"

Vera didn't say a word, which was very wise. Muttering curses, Andrey went back. Vera was following him. The soil under their feet was boggish, and they were falling in up to the knee into the deep moss. It was difficult to walk. They were still looking for new spots, for they hadn't had the feeling of the search before; and now, on their way back, Andrey felt tired, and he could believe that poor Vera was exhausted.

He glanced at his wife and pitied her. *What is she doing at this swamp, anyway?*

It's her fault! he thought with revenge. She'll be alright. It will be good for her—a walk and some fresh air. But she'll never come here again. He would never lure her to Karelia again. She wouldn't want to feed mosquitoes.

By the way, there were innumerable hordes of mosquitoes. It was creepy. The air was buzzing with them. There was a constant and endless ringing around them; they would have been eaten if it had been not for spray! Karelian version of the movie "Eaten

Alive." Fucking episode three, "The Terror of the Swamps." The spray helped them a lot, but soon its effect would fade. They had to zap constantly, almost every half an hour. Forty minutes later, Andrey began worrying. He couldn't see the previous lake which they were supposed to strike.

Fuck! he thought with bewilderment. *What the hell is that? Where are we heading?*

Ten more minutes passed. They still couldn't see the lake. There were sheer, dry bogs with stunted pines and lonely birches. The walking became even more difficult. They would fall in the deep moss up to the waist. Andrey felt the growing irritation. They obviously lost the path and were going the wrong way.

That's it! So, we're going to lose two more hours at least, he thought gloomily and gave a desperate sigh. *We need time to find the way, then to reach the camp. How could I come back then? Fishing's over! Shit! These women do no good! She's suffering herself, and she managed to make a fucking disaster for me on the last day.*

He looked at his wife again. Vera was enduring her sufferings stoically. Obviously, she felt guilty that her husband had to leave everything and get her to the camp, so she showed patience and kept silent, though it could be seen that she was miserable. She was out of breath, she was sweating and breathing heavily. Frankly speaking, Andrey wasn't feeling any better. He was sweating, as well, and was very tired. Moreover, he was carrying the bag with the gear, the spinning, and the landing net.

"Hey, Andriusha," said Vera suddenly, bewildered. "Are you sure that we are going the right way? Where is the lake? Aren't we lost?"

A good question, thought Andrey sadly and halted. He still couldn't believe the desperate reality of what was happening. *And what next? Should we go back? Should we double-back upon our tracks? Fuck, we've been walking for forty minutes! Do we have to walk back for forty minutes again in this fucking swamp? I'm gonna die here!*

"Well," he muttered at last, avoiding his wife's gaze, "listen, it seems that we're really lost. We have to go back."

"Back? Where?" asked his wife, perplexed.

"Where? Where?" mumbled Andrey with irritation. "She's cackling too much!"

"Well, back upon our tracks. We're not that far yet. Not that far!"

"So, what, do we have to walk back for an hour?" asked his wife distrustfully, not believing her own ears.

"And what else can we do?" Andrey shrugged his shoulders with deliberate calmness. Actually, he was not calm at all; quite on the contrary, he was very uncomfortable. He was a man who didn't justify the other person's trust. *Fucking Susanin! He led them in a swamp. Fucking pathfinder. A hunter and a fisherman.*

"I can walk no more," shouted Vera indignantly, realizing what was happening, "Are you nuts? Walking for another hour! I'm tired! I've got no strength left! I don't really know how I walked here!"

"Well, stay, if you want!" Andrey flew off the handle, as well, "'I can, I can't!' As if we have a choice. Let's stay in this swamp! What are you suggesting?"

"Alright, why are we shouting?" he said apologetically a couple of moments later. "Let's calm down, take some rest and walk back slowly. Well, things happen—what can we do? That's it. Don't worry, everything's okay. You're doing great!" Andrey smiled cheerfully to his wife. "You're really amazing me. You're walking without any complaints. Frankly speaking, I'm fed up with walking in this swamp!"

They stood for some time, resting. The worst thing was that they had nothing to sit on. The moss was damp; one would be soaked at once. So, they had to rest while standing. As soon as they halted, the mosquitoes came at them with great strength. It seemed that they flew here from all of the surrounding bogs. It was a fucking feast for them, a free treating. And every second, there were more and more of them. All the more so, Andrey and Vera were hot and sweaty after a long walk, so the spray wasn't helping them. It would just flow down with sweat.

"Well, let's go," said Andrey with irritation, slapping his cheek yet again." The mosquitoes went berserk. *They're going to eat us alive*. "Did you take some rest? Can you walk?"

"I don't know," Vera gave a desperate sigh. "I think I can."

"Well, let's go," nodded Andrey inquiringly.

"Let's go," said Vera sadly.

After the first couple of steps on that fucking bottomless moss, Andrey felt as if he hadn't had any rest at all.

What forty minutes are you talking about? he thought in panic. *I'm going to die in five minutes. I'm going to fall face down in the moss, and fuck it all! I can't walk anymore!*

Suddenly Andrey startled and halted abruptly, staring in wonder at a large footprint that could be clearly seen on the wet moss. The footprint was definitely fresh—very fresh! It seemed that it had been left just a minute ago. Someone clearly walked here. It seemed that the moss that had been trampled down was straightening in front of his eyes. And here was another one! Andrey looked at the footprint that was a couple of meters from the first. *"Oh, God! Is it a step, or what? Someone had such a huge step. And who would that be? Who? A dinosaur? A swamp one?"*

Andrey was quickly looking around, feeling cold fear rising in his heart. His weariness vanished. *A bear! A huge bear! Right, this is no zoo, where all the bears are so kind-looking, fluffy, and funny. A hunter said that the bears were one of the most unpredictable and dangerous animals. If a bear attacks you, it's a fucking disaster! You cannot hide from it. It's faster than a horse; and you wouldn't hide from it on a tree, it climbs the trees very well. And it swims! A complete fuck-up. Game over.*

And where would I run, climb, or swim? I've got my wife here. So, it's like in a popular movie. 'If they push you to the river—it's the end!'

"Why did we halt?" asked Vera, coming to him from behind and panting.

"A bear," Andrey couldn't but say that and showed her the footprint. "Here, see? And there's another one."

"It's so huge," said his wife with wonder, but fearlessly. It seemed that she wasn't scared at all. Andrey was even insulted by her indifference.

"Yeah, it's not small," he said acidly. "It may well attack us now!"

"What does it need us for?" Vera smiled to Andrey carelessly. "It's probably gathering berries here."

"Mushrooms!" mumbled Andrey even more acidly, smiling sardonically. He was a bit ashamed by the firm cold-bloodedness of his wife, and, at the same time, it helped him to calm down.

Why would it need us, indeed! he thought suddenly. *It's got its business, and we've got ours. And our business isn't good. We've got enough problems without a bear.*

"Okay, let's go," he waved his hand.

Half an hour later, Andrey realized that they lost their old tracks and were going in the wrong direction. He didn't know these places. Although, the deuce knows if they are the right places or not! A swamp is a swamp. Moss and other stuff. Everything here was dreary and monotonous. However, the last few minutes gave him the uneasy confidence that they hadn't been here before. They definitely didn't see that cloven birch on their way. And those two pines. Fuck, they should have done some daps, though he should have known that it would go like this. Well, it was a fucking disaster! "*Where should we go now? It's 2 in the afternoon already. Fuck! It's very unpleasant. I don't like it at all. The fishing's over. What fucking fishing am I thinking about, though? I must forget it. Beggars can't be choosers. What shall we do?*

Andrey halted again.

"Well? Is it far?" Vera was tired and out of breath, but she still was doing well. Andrey even shook his head to himself.

"Well, well! I didn't expect that from her!"

"Listen, it seems, that we're lost again," he said reluctantly. "I haven't seen this place before. We haven't been here."

"And what next?" asked Vera calmly, looking at him inquiringly.

Andrey's amazement was growing. *Is she really so strong, or doesn't she realize what's happening? Isn't she catching on? Umph... Wonders never cease! Well, that's really great, but what shall we do?*

Andrey looked around. Far off to the left there was a forest. Actually, it wasn't in the desirable direction, but that didn't matter.

"Well," he said confidently. "We shall head to that forest," he pointed to the forest, "and then we'll see. As a last resort, I'm going to climb a high pine—there should be a great view from it. The terrain here is even."

What about the view? he thought sadly. *It's going to be more than a one-hour walk. View! Well, we'll see. Maybe it's going to help. I need to say everything in a confident tone. I don't want her to panic.*

It took them almost an hour to get to the forest. It didn't seem that it was that far—it looked close—but they walked for a long time, and it was still far ahead. It didn't seem to come closer at all. Poor Vera was obviously exhausted but very calm, to Andrey's amazement. She wasn't complaining and moaning. But that made Andrey feel even worse. He felt somewhat guilty for what was happening, for all that crap. In the end, he was the leader here. His wife was just blindly following him, without any questions. She was going where he led her. And what was the result? He fucking led her somewhere! *Fucking pathfinder.*

Now I can't understand anything at all. Where are we? What are we? How shall we get out of here? Clear as mud! We have to find the direction, right? North and south? What's the right thing?

There's less moss on the trees on the north side. Or on the south one? No, on the north! It's colder there.

Andrey looked at the nearest pine. *There's no fucking moss here! All moss is on the ground. What the fuck should it be doing on the trees? And why do I care where north or south are? As if I knew where our camp is. Is it to the north or to the south? Hell knows. I don't have a clue. Well, what shall we do? Should I really climb a pine? I'm going to see a large lake; there's only one of its kind here. The others are pretty small. Well, we'll see! That large lake is miles from here. It's very far from here. We've been walking for two fucking hours in these freaking swamps! No, more than two—since the morning, and we could have covered a fucking huge distance during that time. We were walking in the wrong direction. We could have gone to the far off lands. Shit! Tough titty! What crap! I couldn't even imagine that it's possible to get lost here. Well, alright, we should get going.*

"Hey, let's go!" Andrey threw a hopper to the moss and stood up from the tree on which he and Vera were sitting. Vera heaved a sigh and stood up reluctantly.

Andrey went ahead confidently, and his wife followed him without a word. As a matter of fact, Andrey's confidence was artificial. He didn't know where they should go and was actually heading at random. They were walking up hill and down dale. *We should strike something eventually, right? Is it some kind of a desert?*

It was much easier to walk in the forest than in the swamps, for the soil was harder, and they were moving quicker and were not so tired. Nevertheless, two hours later, Andrey had to call a halt again. Vera was out of breath and exhausted, and she said that she couldn't walk any more. By that time, Andrey realized completely that they were in trouble. They were lost, and it was very serious. No familiar places around the corner here would appear, as he was hoping subconsciously—alas!

Actually, he didn't know what to do. Should they keep walking without purpose? Looking for something? It may well be that there's no cabin here. They didn't come here on a motorboat for no reason. They wanted to get into the wilderness, far from people, like Robinsons.

And they did it! Robinsons! It's no Africa! It's no equator.

Andrey scrabbled about on the ground, stood still, and stared at his feet, blanching. There was a cigarette end on the ground. His own! The same one that he had thrown away two hours before, sitting on that log. He and Vera walked a circle and came back to the same spot. And they were sitting on the same tree—that was two hours ago.

Andrey felt the hair on the back of his neck bristle. It was impossible. Surely he heard that, when a man is lost in a forest, he starts walking in circles, and he knew the explanation of that: the left step is shorter than the right one—that's why a man starts to steer left when moving—but that was too much.

It's all just a piece of crap, all these explanations. Well, approximately or something like it - that could be understood. But the very same place? Here it is, my cigarette, at my feet! I would never find it on purpose in an unknown forest, even if I wanted to. Holy Mother of God!

Andrey recalled the story of one of the locals, which he had told while drinking. He, too, had been lost in the woods.

"I've been living in this forest whole my life, and I know every tree here. And it's no real forest—just three pine trees. Fuck! I can't get out of it—that's it! Here's the stunted pine, and here's the birch. Then go straight for two minutes, and there should be the turn to the house. I take the turn, and there's the same spot! The stunted pine and the birch! Well, I'll be damned! What should I do? And that happened five times in a row. That's a wood spirit guiding you."

"Wood spirit?"

"Right, wood spirit. Put your shirt wrong side out, and it'll leave you alone."

"And what? Did you do it?"

"Yeah. I sat down and had a smoke. Then I put my shirt wrong side out and got out of the wood."

Ugh! Well, maybe I should try the trick with the shirt and get out at once, Andrey smiled sadly. *Well, the trick with the shirt can wait; it would mean that I touched bottom. Well, we'll wait on that. Though, actually...* He looked at the cigarette in awe and shook his head. *Well! God save us! Forget the shirt, but I should climb a tree. It's high time. Soon it will be dark.*

Andrey couldn't make himself believe the dreadful reality of what was happening. He was still hoping desperately in his heart that everything would be okay, that he would see the Black Lake and the channel with the boat from the top of a tree. He would come down and tell Vera about it with relief, and they would laugh merrily at their fears, look at each other as if it was some kind of conspiracy, wink, and, holding hands, head straight to the canoe. They would get in it, push off the shore, and go to the camp. The camp was an inaccessible, fantastic, and heavenly place for him now. It was the land of promise! Tents, people, fire, hot tea—home sweet home!

Well So, what? Andrey looked intently at the nearest pines. *Right! I should be able to climb this one if I do my best.* He sat for some time, looking appraisingly at the chosen tree. *Well, on second thought...* On the other trees, the lowest branches were too high. He wouldn't reach them. And here... *Well, I should try.*

"You know, Vera, I should climb a tree, just in case. I'll check where our lake is. How long shall we roam here? Soon it'll be dark," he said with deliberate cheerfulness and stood up, warming up.

"What tree?" his wife looked at him an amazement.

"What, what? Like this! I'm going to climb that pine—that's it," Andrey pointed at the chosen pine.

"And what if you fall down?" asked his wife with a doubt, looking at the tall pine and then at Andrey.

"Why would I fall down? Nonsense!" Andrey was already approaching the pine, thinking how it would be better to reach the lowest branches, which still were rather high.

Right! A nice hollow, a twig. Well, well! Shit! And thus... Andrey was already sitting on a branch. It was thick, so he didn't have to worry. It would hold three guys like Andrey. *Higher, higher, higher. Carefully, carefully.*

The ground was receding. At last, Andrey got almost to the top. *Well, well! Ooh! Fuck, I haven't climbed trees since I was a boy.* Then he looked down. *Fuck! It's better not to look there. Well, what do we have here?*

On the horizon, there was a dazzling water-glass of a huge lake glistening and twinkling under the sun. *Thank God! Now I know where we should go. Shit, it's very far! Well, it doesn't matter. We know the direction. Now we won't be roaming like blind kittens. Alright, time to get down.* Andrey began climbing down cautiously. A couple of minutes later, he jumped down on the ground, covered with needles.

"So, what?" asked his wife hopefully.

"Everything's okay," said Andrey merrily and gave her a broad smile "Great! Our lake is out there," he showed it with his hand. "We'll strike the shore and then go to the camp. It's pretty far from here, but it doesn't matter! We'll do it."

Should I put my shirt wrong side out? he thought suddenly. *It will be a fucking disaster if we make one more circle. We'll have to sleep in the forest. Alright, enough of this bullshit!* he checked himself. *Wood spirit! You're a wood spirit yourself. That local was probably drunk; that's why he was lost in broad daylight. Wood spirit! He was drunk beyond repair when he was telling me this.*

"Well, let's go," he nodded to his wife, picking up the bag. "Soon it's going to be dark."

He got his direction according to the sun, chose a landmark, and headed straight to it. Then he got his direction again, chose the landmark, and went on. He was acting very carefully, but nevertheless, in one and a half hours, he was staring bluntly at the cigarette end at his feet. They had gone in a circle, in a loop. They were completely lost.

The sun was low, and it was too late to keep going. They had to get ready for the night—the night in the forest, on the ground, out in the open. It was August, so the nights were rather chilly. It was good that it wasn't raining. Andrey ground his teeth, swore to himself, and turned to his wife.

"Shit! We'll have to spend the night here."

"But why?" asked his wife in astonishment. "And what do you mean by here? Where here?"

"Well, it's too late. Where would we go? We have to get ready for the night while it's not dark yet. We need to pick up a spot. We won't be able to do it in darkness. Don't worry," he smiled playfully, trying to comfort his wife, "I'll get some fir twigs, and we'll spend the night with comfort! The nights are warm." As a matter of fact, the nights were not so warm.

Andrey looked around quickly. *Well, where should we lie down? Maybe, in that hollow? Why not? That's a very nice hollow. There's moss there, and I'm gonna get twigs, and it would be a real bed. We'll have a nice sleep. Soft, comfortable. No,* he thought eventually, *no hollows. What if it starts raining? We would be soaked. Though, it shouldn't be raining," he looked at the clear and cloudless sky, "but still, it's better not to risk it. And we shouldn't sleep in the open spot. We need to hide under the largest tree in case it starts raining. Say, under this fir. Well, right...here we go.*

Andrey started to chip off the fir twigs from the surrounding trees and put it on the selected spot. *Well? Enough or a bit more? Well, a couple of twigs, and that would be enough.*

As he was doing that, the sun had already set. It became dark and gloomy, damp, cold. A bird started hooting in the forest. At first, Andrey was going to make a fire quickly, but now he decided not to mess around with it. *What for—just for the sake of it?* They had nothing to cook, anyway. They were exhausted after a whole day of walking. *We're gonna lie down and sleep like logs. We're gonna fall fast asleep.*

Fortunately, they had plastic wrap with them. In case it rained. And it could be handy for the fishing, as well. One could cover himself with it, and it would be like an improvised tent. And now it came in useful. It turned up just at the right moment.

He and Vera lay on the fir twigs and covered themselves with the wrap. It was rather warm and comfortable. Andrey closed his eyes and went out at once.

***

When he woke up, the day had already broken. It got very cold during the night, but it was not so very serious. It was drizzling, and that was very bad.

We're gonna get soaked. And how will we dry off? Thank God, we didn't lie in the hollow. I don't want to think, what would happen to us. Ugh!

However, there was no reason to be merry. The rain was rather strong, and the fir tree under which they were lying was soaking quickly. The branches had begun dripping already. Andrey didn't notice a big puddle that appeared on the wrap, and his careless movement made it spill down on him and Vera. The bigger part went down on him, of course, but Vera was touched by it, as well. She screamed and woke up.

"Yikes! What's up?" she yelled in panic, "I'm wet!"

"Come on! That's a puddle that appeared on the wrap," mumbled Andrey apologetically, hugging and cuddling his wife. "I spilled even more on myself. Fucking rain…"

Vera calmed down at once and even dozed off. It was very comfortable under the wrap. Soft, comfortable, and the rain was pattering monotonously on the wrap. He could lie here forever Andrey felt that he was falling into some kind of slumber. He shook his head and slightly pushed his wife.

"Wake up! We have to get up!"

"Why? What for?" his wife opened her eyes. "Why would we get out in that cold? Let's stay here."

"No lying! We have to go," said Andrey confidently, "unless we want to be soaked to the bone. What's the sense of lying here? This rain may not stop until the evening. And we have a long road to the lake before us."

I must put the shirt wrong side out, he suddenly remembered. *No kidding. We already had to spend the night in the woods.*

As a matter of fact, Andrey felt an inspiration. He was filled with energy and the will to act. That was usual for him in time of real danger. He would jump into a special state, as if a special, extreme program would switch on in him—a program of survival in extreme situations. And this program would switch off unnecessary emotions and feelings: doubt, fear, and weariness. He would turn into a kind of fighting robot who would act according to the principle that the whole organism is resources, the task is to survive.

Of course, he never checked it in real life; such situations happened to him just a couple of times—the first time near the underground when three bullies came at him, and the second time during an expedition, when he was drowning in the swamp—but he thought that he was able to do anything possible in that state. He would walk as long as was necessary—a day, two, three —without sleep and rest. He wouldn't feel weary at all until his body would have any strength left; he would swim in ice water and he would jump across the precipice—all in all, he would act without fear on a purely automatic and refectory level.

As a live mechanism. Cyborg. Clone. As long as his energy lasts. Or gas. Or a battery-accumulator. Well, whatever this clone is operating on. What's his energy source? It doesn't matter. As long as it has at least a drop of gas, it would keep running, swimming, and jumping—he would keep acting—non-stop, persistently, and tirelessly, he would act! He would try to perform the program set in him, a program of survival. Survival! He had to survive! Survive, survive, survive! At any cost."

And, probably save his wife. 'Probably,' because he didn't quite understand the priorities. What was more important? Surviving or saving his wife? The question wasn't that urgent, but Andrey already felt that everything had gone wrong. They were lost, the weather worsened, with cold and cursed rain.

And what if that's the wrong lake? How long would we last in the forest without water? Nobody will look for us. He recalled the indifferent phrase of one of the locals, "Tourists die here every year—five or six of them at least. If someone's missing for two days—say, he hasn't come back to the camp—consider him dead! Climate is tough here. It's the North."

So, he could count only on himself. He could clearly hear the familiar click inside him. A fighting program was on.

2.

"Wake up! Wake up, wake up, wake up! Wake up," Andrey was shaking his wife, who had already closed her eyes, by the shoulders. "We're getting up!" He threw off the edge of the wrap and stood up. It was cold and wet. The rain was chilly, and the wind was strong. Oh, God! Everything around them was moist, slippery, and nasty—trees and moss under their feet—everything!

"Get up quickly!" he shouted at Vera, who cowered under the wrap and was afraid to get out to the cold. "We have to go. We'll warm up while walking. I don't want you to catch cold."

His wife lingered a bit, then got from under the wrap, and stood up. "What weather!" she complained at once, shuddering. "It's so cold!"

"We're gonna warm up on the way," promised her Andrey and headed in the direction where he had seen the lake yesterday.

I forgot to put on the shirt—right, he thought suddenly. He halted at once and, giving no heed to cold and rain, stripped to the waist, put on his shirt wrong side out, and then put on the rest of his clothes. "Well, let's go," he turned to his wife, who was staring at him in blind astonishment.

"What did you do that for?" Vera was looking at him with fear. *Has he gone nuts from all these troubles?*

"The shirt is bristly. The label is so stiff, and I forgot to remove it," said Andrey fretfully. "Alright, let's hit the road! We're going to freeze."

Enough talking! We need to act! Act, act, act! Let's go—the clock is ticking. If we don't get to the camp today, it'll be very bad. We'll be completely soaked—and where shall we sleep if there's frost during the night? We're going to catch cold or even pneumonia. That would be very easy. And what then? I don't care about myself, but what if Vera gets sick? And what if she can't go on? Alright, it's better not to think about it.

The worst thing is that we don't have enough room for maneuvering. We don't have it at all, actually. It all depends on luck. Either we're lucky or not. Odd—even. Is it our lake or not? And if it's not, I just don't know what we are to do. Where should we go? In what direction? Actually, I can keep going—I have no problem with that, but what's the point of it? We don't know the direction, and we can't do anything. That's completely unbearable! If only there was a specific enemy—for example, a firedrake, which we can fight. If only we could do something! Win or die. But there's no one to fight with, save mosquitoes. By the way, they're all gone; they probably hid from the cold. That's right. Good for them. I would hide myself, if I were them.

I'm going to fucking roam in these swamps, like a moron, and go on as long as I have any strength left, until I fall down. And it all may be useless—in vain. All this strenuous heroism of yours would be in vain. For, ultimately, you can't change anything. You're going the extra mile - it wouldn't matter. Absolutely! It wouldn't matter at all. Alright, alright! Enough! Enough! Don't relax. Enough moaning—you're not the first. People were in these fuck-ups before you. Those were even greater fuck-ups. And they held on.

Drozdovsky wrote in his diaries, 'One may be stopped by insurmountable obstacles, but not of the fear of them.' That's it! And I got only the fears. There are no obstacles, but I'm already scared. Hell of a hero! A freaking one. "Well, that's it! Enough! Enough of this irrelevant stuff. Ahead! Ahead! ahead! ahead! Never look back. I need to get to the lake, and then we'll see. Maybe... Well, we'll see. We'll figure it out on the spot. First, we need to get there.

They went on. The time was passing, but they didn't see any lake ahead. Meanwhile, the weather was worsening. The sky was filled with clouds; the rain became stronger, and it was pouring down; the chilling wind was piercing their clothes and, in the open places, it was not wind, but some hurricane! The most important thing was the cold. Cold! It seemed that the temperature was dropping in front of their eyes. Yesterday evening, it had been more or less warm, chilly during the night, and rather cold when they got up - and now it was really cold. No kidding! It wasn't just cold; it was brass monkey weather! It seemed that it was not August but November. They were waiting for the snow to start falling. Even the walking didn't help. Their bodies were cold, let alone their hands and faces; they became numb because of the cold wind.

Of course, Andrey was feeling all of that with his organs of sense; he was feeling cold, rain, and wind but, as a matter of fact, he didn't care. He didn't give a damn. He wasn't troubled by that at all. His program was pushing him ahead. He had a goal toward which he was heading. He had to find a lake. He had to, whatever it took. That was the most important thing. The outside environment didn't matter. At least, not until it would become an insurmountable obstacle. And all these small inconveniences, like wind and rain—fuck it! It didn't matter at all. If he had to, he would go on completely naked.

Andrey halted, looked at Vera, who was blue with cold, threw the bag and the spinner to the moss, took off his sweater, and gave it to his wife. "Here, put it on - you're freezing. Come on, put it on," he added impatiently, seeing her hesitate.

Vera lingered for a second, and then put on the sweater obediently.

Andrey bent over and took the wrap which they had used as a cover during the night. Spreading it on the ground, he almost made a cut in the center of it; he wanted to make a kind of a cloak or rain-poncho for his wife, but, at the last moment, he changed his mind and stopped.

No, what if we have to spend another night in the forest in the rain? I don't want to spoil the whole wrap. I'd better save in for the night.

He folded the wrap carefully and put it in the bag. "Alright, let's go," he said to Vera, who was looking at him indifferently, but didn't even ask what he was doing. Andrey didn't like it at all. He looked intently at his wife. "How are you feeling? Everything's okay?" She shrugged her shoulders in answer.

Shit! If only she doesn't catch cold, thought Andrey, worried. *And what then? Shall I carry her on my shoulders? How much does she weigh?* he looked at his wife appraisingly.

"Can you walk?" he asked her aloud.

"Well yeah," answered Vera limply and apathetically.

"Well, let's go?"

"Let's go."

And they went on. Andrey was almost hopping with impatience; he wanted to run. He wanted to fly! At any rate, they were walking very slowly—very slowly. Vera broke up. She was breathing heavily, complaining that she was tired, taking frequent breaks, and saying that she 'felt shivery.' Frankly speaking, she looked sick. It seemed that the night in the open had taken its toll. She'd caught cold.

They walked, rested, and walked again. Finally, four hours later, when Andrey was desperate and thought that they were lost again and would come upon the same enchanted cigarette, they glimpsed long-expected water. Seeing it, Andrey felt relief and joy as if they had already returned to the camp, although nothing was clear yet. That could be yet another nameless lake, of which there were a great many, as locals said.

Yet it was there! Something fucking changed at last—a new turn of events. He was fed up with walking in the swamps and coming back to the same spot.

So what? asked Andrey malevolently of the invisible wood spirit. *Bite me! The shirt did work. That's it! You thought you were a smart one—you thought you could lead me in circles! Right! Now you may smoke that cigarette of mine. Go ahead.*

Strangely enough, such tilting and babbling with hypothetical wood spirits were not scaring Andrey at all—*You never know; you might make it angry! What if it exists, indeed? Particularly after that thing with the cigarette and the shirt inside out... one might believe in anything!.. but, quite the contrary, they are calming me down. They are filling me with vague hope. After all, it was a living creature that can help us, although it was evil. It didn't matter. The point was that we aren't alone. There was someone else.* That thought made him feel easy.

For the reality was terrible. *There were no living creatures around, good or evil—just the naked reality. Cold, indifferent, and heartless nature, immovable and apathetic. And it didn't care whether you were alive or dead. You may live if you want or die. It's up to you*

The wood spirit feels interest in you, at least. He's leading you in circles. And reality doesn't care about you at all! There are rules, and they're same for everyone. If you win, you live; if you lose, you die. That's it! You're going to be proclaimed a winner or a loser with the same indifference—no congratulations and no malevolence. And nobody's going to lead you in circles. Why would anybody care?

The fates play fairly. But what is its game? Dice or chess? The difference is essential. There's always a chance to win in dice. Even in the most desperate and hopeless situation, you've got a chance for a lucky throw, and then everything could change in a moment. Everything would turn around. That's why all these common cool and tough facts and hints: 'hold on to the last,' 'no trust, fear, and begging' have some sense on them. What if we get lucky in the very last moment?

The game of chess is simpler and tougher. There is no suddenly in it. You lose a pawn, and that's it. It's useless to continue a game with a strong opponent, completely useless. The match is lost. Hold on or not, fear or not, trust or not—there's no difference. A purely technical endgame. You may stop the clock and leave the match.

It's lost, anyway. You should have been thinking before. You shouldn't have lost the pawn. You should have played better.

And Andrey was losing two pawns already—the weather and a sick wife. The nights in the open, under rain, in this cold—it's, you know. Oh, right! Three, it's probably three already! He still didn't know where to go. Well, a lake—so, what? There are a lot of lakes here. What if that's the wrong lake? Now it's three pawns. And one is enough. Is there any sense in playing at all?"

Well, well, well, thought Andrey. *There's no need to exaggerate. It's not that bad yet. Why am I scaring myself before time? 'Insurmountable obstacles, but not the fear of them!' If that's our lake, after all...*

However, his hopes were not meant to be true. Having come to the lakeshore, Andrey was very disappointed. The lake was small. It was definitely not their huge lake-sea, at the shore of which their camp was. It was yet another puddle, of which there were a great many here. Andrey bit his lips thoughtfully. It was a very severe blow. Actually, that was the end; only a miracle could save them. If today they don't—well, at least, let's hope that they will survive the night—so, if today or tomorrow they don't find the camp or any lodging, at least. And how will they do that? Where? Andrey didn't have a clue where they were. Where could they be? Anywhere! *There's a shit-ton of lakes here. They're everywhere. So, generally...*

Andrey had Vera sit under the biggest fir—it was the best shelter from the rain he could find. And, in spite of great weariness, he went to the water to throw the spinner, although it was probably useless. He would catch no fish in this weather. Or maybe a miracle would help him?

And the miracle happened! The first throw got him a pike. Andrey stared at the wriggling fish at his feet and couldn't believe his own eyes. His weariness vanished, and he began throwing the plunker with tripled energy, being sure that the pikes would go to him one by one.

Why not? Things happen. Maybe there are a lot of them in that lake, and they're so hungry, that they go at the plunker in any weather.

However, a second miracle didn't happen. He didn't catch anything else. It was dead, completely dead, as it should be in such weather. Andrey threw the plunker for some time, just for conscience sake, and then decided to wrap up and return to his wife. *Enough of this bullshit!* And he had to cook the pike. He had to make a fire under the pouring rain. Well, enough of these games. He had a lot to do!

Vera was cold and soaked, and she was clattering with her teeth. She was shivering.

That's very bad, thought Andrey gloomily, looking at his wife and making a fire. *How is she going to spend the night? And the weather may be freezing during the night. A hell of a weather!*

He looked gloomily at the low gray sky filled with heavy clouds and shivered in his shirt. It was fucking cold! Probably, some northern cyclone approached. That could continue for the whole week. Or two weeks. The fire was flaring up. Andrew was putting small wet twigs into it and musing quietly, "Maybe I should keep the fire burning during the night? Then, I won't sleep and keep it going until morning. And Vera will sleep near it."

He looked at his wife again. She moved close to the fire, throwing her arms about her knees and staring at the flames.

Well, maybe I will do it, if we don't find anything until evening. We just have to start gathering wood before it gets dark. We need a lot of wood for the whole night. Alright, we'll see.

Andrey sharpened a thick stick from the both sides, making a kind of a rod. Then he put the fish on it, through its mouth, and stuck the other end of the stick into the ground near the fire. Half an hour later, a pike, cooked in fishermen style or on a rod, was ready. It was something between a baked and smoke-cured fish. Andrey took off the fish from the rod, cut off the third part of it, with the head, and gave it to his wife.

"Here, have a bite."

"What about you?" she tried to protest.

"Come on, eat!" said Andrey softly, but insistently. "You need it more than I do. You're getting sick, you need to eat something hot. I can do without it. It's just one day."

"No, you should eat, too. I'll give you some," his wife tried to convince him again.

"Listen to me! Eat!" shouted Andrey harshly. "I don't want it. I'm not hungry."

He wasn't hungry, indeed. Actually, he was, of course, but purely theoretically. He didn't care about hunger or cold. He just wasn't paying any attention to them. It seemed that his extreme-program had switched all human senses in him. He had only pure practicability left. No emotions. Optimal distribution of the current resources - and nothing more.

Now they had only the pike; that was all their resources. And he should give it to his wife in that situation. That's it! Not because he was such a loving and thoughtful husband; no, because it was wise. So, there could be no arguing about that. And he was just irritated by the silly phrases like "I'll give you some."

Human! Too human! And he wasn't a human now. He was a mechanism whose aim was to survive. He was a machine. Robot! 'I'll give you some' - *you can't give me anything! I'll take it myself, if I want. I told you to eat, so do it. Don't lose time. That is wise at this stage.*

And we'll see what's going to be next. Every day brings its bread. We need to move ahead. Ahead! Ahead! Ahead, ahead, ahead! While we've still got strength, while we've got chances. We have to use them. All of them. And we'll see what's going to be next. We'll see. Maybe we'll have to change the strategy. Maybe we'll have to make allowances according to new conditions. What does our program have in that case, in case of the most unfavorable outside environment and diminishing resources? Well, we'll see. There's definitely something in the program. We'll contrive something. It will come out in the wash!

Andrey had no doubts about that. He was sure that he'd deal with it. If he had to, he would crawl and carry his wife on him. A day, two, three... as long as he had the strength, until he died! Of course, if his wife's life had such a great priority for him, then he had to save her. Was it so? He didn't know that. He didn't give a thought to that. These thoughts and questions just weren't entering his mind. He had no time for them; that would be in future. And now was the present. *If it's God's will, it won't come to that. Maybe we'll find the camp.*

What did Pliny write about Carthaginians? 'A too quick disappointment in success?' Exactly! 'Too quick.' He didn't use all the chances. Nothing is lost! Ahead!

3.

Andrey carefully wrapped the remainder of the pike and put it in the bag. "Well, are you ready?" he asked his wife impatiently. She had already eaten her pike and now was sitting glowering near the dying fire. "Let's go."

They got up. Andrey didn't even put out the fire—what for? The pouring rain would quench it in a minute—and went into the depth of the wood. Ten minutes later, the trees gave way, and they came on the shore of another lake. It was big and vast. About a hundred meters from them, there was a hut in the forest.

Seeing it, Andrey caught his breath. They were saved! He quickly approached it. Alas! The hut was empty. It was a forest hunters' lodge. There are a lot of them in taiga, and here, in Karelia, they do happen from time to time, as well. They are usually visited only during a season, once every couple of months. There was no one in it. But still, it was a great luck. Actually, they were saved. There was a fireplace, bed, and wood in the hut, as well as an axe, a pot, salt, and matches. It was a kind of emergency ration. It seemed that the tourists were not visiting the hut. Everything was in its spot, according to the forest rules and laws.

The laws are simple. If you're leaving, chop some wood and leave salt and matches, if you have them. And sugar, too. Unfortunately, there was no sugar or tea in the hut. The conditions in the north were very tough, so the person who found the hut could have the need of anything. Maybe, he wouldn't have anything at all, so he had to be able to warm up or boil some water. In his thoughts, Andrey thanked everyone who had been here before him and then fired the stove. Dry wood cracked merrily, and it became warm and comfortable at once. Andrey grabbed the pot and went outside to bring some water. The chilling wind and rain smashed him in the face. The weather was worsening. It seemed that a cyclone was coming from the north, indeed.

Oh, God! How can we be walking in such weather?" He went out just for a minute and was already freezing and soaked to the bone. Andrey ran to the shore and looked around quickly. To the left, there was a creek that flowed into the lake. He couldn't see anything interesting. A usual gloomy Karelian view—wood, moss, and stones. He scooped some water with the pot—the water was icy cold. Ugh! His hands were even cramped!—and then ran quickly back to the hut.

Vera was sitting motionlessly and looking at the fire. It was very warm in the hut—almost hot—but she didn't take off her clothes. She was still in two sweaters.

"Why are you sitting in wet clothes? It's already warm," asked her Andrey, putting the pot above the fire. Vera started undressing obediently. Andrey approached his wife and put his hand on her brow. It was burning. Vera had a fever.

"Hey, you're sick!" said Andrey anxiously, staring at her intently. "You got fever. Don't worry, I'll make it hot inside. Drink some boiling water and get some sleep. You're gonna sweat in the night and in the morning you'll be as good as new."

Vera smiled softly, but said nothing.

"Shit!" Andrey swore to himself. "As if that wasn't enough. She's seriously sick! And what if we hadn't found the hut?"

He put more dry wood into the fire, grabbed the axe, and went outside. There was a lot of firewood near the hut—a whole wood-stack. Whoever had been here before him did his best. Andrey thanked this unknown man once more and began chopping the wood. Having chopped the whole stack of it, he brought it to the hut and threw it near the stove to dry off. The water in the pot was already boiling over and seething.

Andrey took the pot off the fire, grabbed the half-liter glass can from the table, ran to the lake again to wash it, and then poured into it some boiling water mixed with cold water. He waited a bit for the can to warm up and added more water. Then he waited again and slowly filled the can with the hot water.

The only glass we have! If it cracks, that will be the end.

"Here, drink," he gave the can to his wife. "Drink all of it. But be careful, it's hot."

Vera took the can with her handkerchief and began sipping, trying not to scorch herself.

"Now try to get some sleep."

Vera lay down on the bed and closed her eyes. It seemed that she had no strength left. You bet! They were walking for two days. They trudged along in the swamps yesterday and today. And the horrible night—a healthy man couldn't endure it, let alone a sick one!

Andrey kept chopping wood, drying it, and keeping the fire until the night. However, he wasn't tired at all. He was still tense and concentrated like a stretched string. It seemed that the inspiration that took him in the morning had become even stronger now.

Act! Act, act, act—while he still had strength. He had nothing to eat, so his strength would diminish with time, and he had to mind that. So, the time was limited, so he had to do as much as he could now, for he wouldn't have strength for it later. In other words, he had to act immediately. Right now, this very moment!

As a matter of fact, Andrey already had a plan of action. He was thinking about it for the whole evening and made some decisions.

The lake is big, so it's probably our lake. The same one near which their camp is. We'll assume that. Well, it doesn't matter. Even if it's not so, it doesn't matter at all. The plan is to explore the shore, as much of it as I can. I have to try to find our camp or something else—well, any shelter. I have the highest chances to find it on the shore. People used to stay near the water. And even of my chances were not so high, I can't withdraw from the water. I don't want to get lost again. I don't want to be lost completely. So, I'm going to walk along the shore as far from the hut as I can. And if I don't find anything, I'll just turn back and return here.

I will get Vera a lot of wood, for her to stay here and keep the fire burning. Though," Andrey glanced at the huge pile of wood near the stove, *that would be enough. Well, I'll set out tomorrow, when she wakes up. There are twenty-four hours in the day; well, she won't be able to sit for twenty-four hours—she's sick, and she will fall asleep, and the stove will get cold, freeze, and she won't be able to make a fire again. So, twenty-hours are too much; she won't last for twenty-four hours. Well, let her sleep for eight hours, so twenty-four minus eight—sixteen hours. Well, she'll have to hold on for a couple of hours and stay awake; we'll take eighteen. So, it'll take me nine hours to get there and nine hours to get back if I don't fucking find anything. I hope I'll find something, and I won't just be walking back and forth like a moron. Alright. That's clear. Well, I'll hold on for eighteen hours. No problem. Sure thing!"*

The only question is, where should I go? To the right or to the left? It appears that the camp should be to the left where the cursed river is. Shit! Shit, shit, shit! What shall I do? Maybe I should go to the right? And why would I go to the right, if I have to go to the left? I may stay here just as well. I may stay in the hut, in the warm hut. I may sit around and wait indefinitely. Alright, fuck it! Fuck it all! I will swim across that fucking river. Come on! Fuck, I don't want to drown, really. The water is icy cold! Well, I won't. It's not that wide. Ten meters at most. Big deal! I'll swim over it. I will.

Ouch! It's a fucking disaster! It's raining and snowing, and I'm going to swim. Fucking Karbyshev. A mixture of a walrus and a penguin. Fuck me! Well, okay, there's no snow, but it may snow tomorrow. It seems that the temperature is already subzero! Well, well! Motherfuck! Fucking hell!

Alright, I need to get some sleep before this fucking ice march. I need to doze off. Well, well... What about the wood? I mean, will it last? Oh! I got an alarm in my watch. I'll set it for fifteen minutes. It will last for fifteen minutes. And every quarter of an hour, I'm gonna wake up and add some wood and then sleep again! Go to nirvana! Alright. Will do. Let's go. The clock is ticking!

Muttering the last phrases, Andrey set the alarm for fifteen minutes and closed his eyes. The alarm started beeping at once.

Oh? What? What's up? Being unable to think straight, Andrey bluntly stared at the watch for some time. *What? Fifteen minutes have passed? It's impossible! Shit! No, it's true. Well, alright. Well, well. Fifteen minutes more. Fifteen minutes more. What would that make? I just can't get it. Thirty-seven plus fifteen. Plus fifteen Oh! Right. Well, okay Oh, the wood! Wood! Yeah! A couple of logs more. That's it. Well, I can sleep. Bye-bye! Bye-bye, my love, bye-bye!*

***

Strange as it was, he felt alright in the morning. He was rested and slept well. It seemed as if he wasn't waking up every fifteen minutes to keep the fire. Vera was still sleeping. Andrey touched her brow carefully. Shit! It was burning. It was even worse than yesterday. She was altogether burning! Andrey waited a bit—he didn't want to wake her—and shook his wife's shoulder.

"Vera! Wake up!"

His wife opened her eyes for a moment, looked at him, and closed them.

"Wake up," he shook her again.

"Come on!" she grumbled.

"How're you feeling?"

"Bad. I've got fever. I'm burning."

"Yeah, your brow is hot," said Andrey. "Listen, you may sleep. I will walk along the shore and look for our camp. You stay here alone. There's enough firewood here. You just stay here and keep the fire burning. I'll come back before the night."

"Where are you going?" asked his wife, perplexed.

"I'm going to look for the camp," repeated Andrey with irritation. "What's the point of sitting here? We need to find the camp. It shouldn't be too far."

"Right! Fucking shouldn't be!"

"Well, you wait for me and keep the fire. I'll be back until the night. Off I go!"

"Wait," said his wife.

"What?" Andrey asked her impatiently.

"Are you going to leave me alone?"

"Well, wait here until the evening, and then I'll be back. Or probably even earlier. What's the problem? There's enough firewood. Sit here and keep the fire. Just don't sleep. If the fire dies out, you will freeze here. The stove will get cold. Oh! Here's the pike. Eat it. There's hot water in the pot. But be careful when pouring it—the can may crack. Got it?"

"Yeah," said his wife with hesitation.

"Alright, then I'm gonna go. I don't want to lose time. I don't know how long it'll take to find the camp. See you," Andrey turned away and went outside.

The weather was ungodly. Wind, rain, and bitter cold—it was a real hell! What swimming was he thinking about? No, he would rather go back to the warm hut. Shivering with cold, Andrey quickly went to the left. He approached the river and, without hesitation, took off his clothes, put them into the plastic bag which he brought with him, put a small stone in it, and tied it with a rope. Now he had a compact but heavy bundle. Andrey made a wide swing and threw it to the other bank of the river. The bundle plopped on the moss.

Andrey approached the water and tried to feel the bottom with his foot. He didn't find it. It seemed that the river was rather deep, beginning from the banks. The cold water scorched him. *I don't need a cramp!* thought Andrey, sliding down to the icy cold river and pushing off the bank. At first, his breath was taken away by the unbearable cold, but he didn't stop and paid no attention to it. *I'm not going to drown! Fuck it!* A couple of strong strokes and he was on the opposite bank of the river. *Cold, wind, and rain—none of it matters. Ahead, ahead, ahead!*

The program was pushing him ahead. If he had to swim over ten more rivers like this one, he would do it without hesitation. Well, he'd just stop to think whether he had enough strength for that and whether he wouldn't drown because of cold and weakness, for he didn't plan to drown. No way! Quite on the contrary. He had to survive! Survive! At whatever cost!

And he would survive. Even if he had to cross a hundred rivers. Well, he will just make a fire after every tenth one in order to warm up. That's it. But he would survive by all means. *Ahead!*

Andrey climbed on the shore, grabbed the bag with his clothes, untied it with his teeth, and started to dress quickly. His frozen fingers didn't want to move. At last, he got dressed, put the empty bag in his pocket, and, with his teeth clattering, walked, or even ran, along the shore. Fifteen minutes later, he almost warmed up and began walking slowly, trying to respire. After all, he hadn't eaten anything for two days—he had left the pike to Vera. And he still had an eighteen-hour walk and swimming over the river before him. So, he had to save the strength. That would help him.

***

Eighteen hours later, Andrey stumbled into the hut. He was deadly tired, exhausted, and blue with cold. It was rather chilly inside, as well. It seemed that the stove had gone out some time ago. Vera was sleeping, swept on the wide bed, and breathing heavily with some hoarse sibilation. She had a strong fever.

Andrey rekindled a fire with his disobedient hands, sat down, and stared at the red flames which were dancing on the dry pine logs. He was tired and sad. He hadn't found the camp. He hadn't found anything at all. No traces of people or shelter. The shore was completely empty. He hadn't even seen any tin cans or empty bottles. It seemed that these were uninhabited places. It blew his mind. Where were they? On the moon, or what?

And Vera felt worse and worse. Andrey didn't like this rattling. *Fuck, and she's got temperature about forty! She's burning! Can she have pneumonia?*

4.

For the next several days, Andrey stayed in the hut, treating his wife. As a matter of fact, the treatment was actually him giving her some hot water to drink. He couldn't do anything else. There was no medicine or food—nothing! They could only sit and wait.

At first, he tried to look for mushrooms or berries—red berry or fen-berry—but nothing grew in this deadly place. Unbelievable! Everywhere else there was something, but not here, as ill luck would have it! The red berries were everywhere, but not here. No mushrooms and no berries! At any rate, there was nothing near the hut, and he didn't want to go deep into the forest. He didn't want to get lost. He knew how it might go! *Fuck it!* He tried to walk in another direction to use all his chances, but he struck a swamp, a real bog, a hundred meters further. *A fucking disaster! A trap.*

Vera got worse and worse. She was burning, raving, and tossing about in her sleep. Her coughing and rattling were so bad that Andrey was scared.

She's gonna die, realized Andrey on the eighth day. *She will definitely die without medicine and food,* he looked at his wife. *She'll last only for a few days.*

Andrey looked at Vera intently again. He didn't have any doubts. Vera had lost a lot of weight and grown lean during recent days. It even seemed to Andrey that her nose became sharp. *She's a goner already!* he thought with detachment. *This is the end!*

Andrey strained his ears sadly. Nothing was changed outside. The same icy cold rain and the howling wind. *How long will it last? How long will that cursed cyclone last? Until hell freezes over! Maybe a week or two. Even if it ends—what then? Maybe people come to this hut only once a year, in spring or winter. We're gonna die of hunger a hundred times by that time—both of us.*

Well, maybe I'm not gonna die. I can walk all around this fucking lake, if necessary. From the fucking beginning to the end, even if I need a whole month for that. Or I will swim over it on a log. I don't fucking care! I don't give a damn about the cold water!

Somehow, Andrey was completely sure that he was really able to do all of that. He could do all these feats. He would go around the lake or swim over it. And nothing would stop him. Except for the exhaustion of his body. But that wouldn't happen; he would definitely find mushrooms or berries, or use the spinner. That cyclone wouldn't last forever, right? Well, he would find something to sustain himself.

For people in such situations usually die not from objective reasons or inability to fight the outer circumstances—'insurmountable obstacles'—but from despair. Despair and disbelief in their own strength. And he had no problems with that. No problems at all! He didn't feel any despair or doubts. He was still in his fighting mode. He was still calm, focused, tough-minded, and confident, like during the first days when it all had begun. The survival program that was activated by the emergency circumstances was still on. He even didn't feel any weariness or weakness, in spite of the fact that he hadn't eaten or slept in all these days.

Apparently, his body, when in that mode, burned ruthlessly all its internal resources, taking them from some forbidden and usually sacred places, like with doping. The principle is everything for the victory. Everything for the victory! Victory! At any cost! The winner takes it all. And what is the sense of saving then?

Andrey recalled that he had read that people don't get sick during the war. The soldiers never catch cold, in spite of the fact that the conditions of war are very unfavorable—trenches… cold… dampness... Probably, the same happens to them as to me—mobilization of the hidden resources of the organism, activation of the extreme-program, switching of the fighting mode.

And, like the soldiers at war, he felt that his survival program had a system of priorities. It was not survival for the sake of it, but survival for a higher goal, survival according to the higher task. For the victory! A soldier, as a fighting unit, must not be sick; he must be healthy in order to act efficiently when needed. He must fulfill the task of the higher priority. He must close the hole of the bunker with his body, get under the tank with grenades, or batter down the enemy airplane.

Saving Vera!.. Andrey found out with surprise that this task had a very high priority in his program. The highest! The highest possible. Saving his wife!! Actually, not his wife, but a weak creature, a woman, who, for various reasons and circumstances, got under his protection. And it wasn't important what these circumstances were; it didn't matter. All that mattered was that she trusted him and he was responsible for her. That's it! He had to save this woman at any cost. At any cost—any! This was the task for which he had been preparing all his life. And now it had the highest priority. The absolute one! All the rest was not so important—even his own fate. Apparently, that was his nature. That was his program. Now was the time for the test.

If the woman died, he wouldn't live, either. That would be worse than death. That would be shame. How could it happen? She died, and you're alive? That question will be burning him the rest of his life. It'll turn out that he's not such a kind, brave, and fair man as he thought he was. He's just a coward. A nullity! A pigmy. And then all will fail. All his world will fail. And he's going to choke in its wreckage. He's going to lose himself.

No. That won't happen. 'Forbidden operation! Low code of access!

***

Andrey fingered his sharp hunting knife thoughtfully. As a matter of fact, he should have done it yesterday. *Nimirum hac una plus vixi, mihi duam vivendum fuit—'I live this day one day longer, that I ought to have lived,' as an ancient Roman said two thousand years ago in such situation. And he was right. So let's not make this situation worse. All the more so, that I don't know what's the Latin for 'two days longer'. That's why we'll stop at one—this day.*

And, actually, it's impossible to talk about two days in Latin. The heroes do not wait for two days. One day is enough before death. Then the hero can utter this historical phrase for the edification of his descendants. But two days? That's too much! That's over the top. That would be a comedy but not a tragedy.

So, let's not do it! Let's not ruin everything before the end. Fuck, it's so silly! Just to think about it—a couple of weeks ago, I... Well, alright. Enough moaning. No words are good where the deeds are present. It's time! The clock is ticking. It's time. 'It's time, my brother, it's time.' Andrey looked at the hut for the last time, took the knife and the pot, and went outside.

The weather was awful. It seemed that rain and wind had gone mad. Gusts—hurricane. A stream of ice water.

Oh, God, is it snowing? Right, it is. Wet snow with rain. Is this August? Well, well! Though, maybe it's a usual thing for Karelia. Well, let's do it.

Andrey's shoulders shook with cold. Suddenly, he felt something prick his thigh. He put his hand in the pocket and hissed with pain. Turning out his pocket, Andrey saw, with surprise, a small black jig with red tail that clung to the cloth. A Mepps fish lure.

Oh, God! How did it get here? Did it fall out of the box? Have I been walking with it all the time? What if it stuck into my body? Into my thigh? Well, that would be a tragedy! The thought made Andrey laugh and shake his head. *Well! Life is a merry woman. She's got a sense of humor, even in such situation! Well, enough joking! Time for business.*

He pulled the jig with some flesh on it and wanted to throw it away, but halted at the last moment, feasting his eyes at the beautiful steel toy in his hand. *It's a nice thing! I don't want to throw it away. I don't have the heart to do it.* He took the jig and stuck it into the wooden wall of the hut. *That's it! Maybe it'll come handy for someone.*

After that, he slowly went to the river, whistling. He wasn't in a hurry. Frankly speaking, there was no need to hurry. He still had time. One can't be late when visiting God. Even Vysotsky said that in his time.

Right, exactly! One can't be late. God is our friend. He's gonna wait, if necessary. No offense taken.

Andrey approached the river and looked at the spot intently. *Well, moss... water... great! Everything's going to sop in, I think. At least, let's hope so. And who will see it, anyway? It's far from the hut. And there's nothing to see, nothing to look for It's still raining; it's gonna wash everything out. 'The Rain Washes All Traces'. A stupid movie. Well, I don't remember it. All movies are stupid! Alright. Well, what else? Strap... bag... rope... That's it? Right.*

Andrey put everything in a pile carefully, put a stone onto it—so the wind not to take it away—took the pot and scooped some water. Then he returned to the hut and hung the pot above the fire which he had made under the shed. He squatted and struck a match, and a dry splinter in the middle of the fire blazed up. Yellow flames licked the pine firewood, and it smoked and hissed at once, as if with pain.

Andrey straightened and stared at the fire that was burning up quickly. When the water in the pot bubbled up, he moved the pot aside, put some more wood into the fire, and went to the river, to the stuff on the shore. Yeah, now he had to hurry. The wood would burn quickly. The most important thing was not to hesitate or think about anything. He had to act automatically. What is the point of thinking? Everything was thought about before that.

He had already spent another day. Or what did that Liberius—right?—Liberius say? What did he say? "Lived?" "Vixi." Right, 'lived'. "He lived another day."

Having approached the river, Andrey took off his pants, tied the pants in knots so they wouldn't dangle, put a large stone in it, and tied it up with the belt. Now he got had a compact and heavy bundle. Andrey went to the river, halted for a moment and hurled the bundle into the water. A soft splash, almost inaudible in the rain, and the bundle was gone in the bubbling water.

Andrey grabbed the strap and pulled it over his left leg as high as he could, almost to his groin. *What if the water is clean here?* he thought suddenly. *Come on, it's impossible,* he comforted himself. "It's no less than two meters deep, and the bottom is boggy. *Oh, God! Is it really happening to me?* the thought sparkled on the edge of his conscience and was gone instantly.

He hesitated no more.

No thinking! No thinking at all! He had to act without hesitating and halting. 'If you stop for a moment, beware—you won't be able to continue.' *This phrase belongs to a fucking Korean on Chinese who lived a thousand years ago. Umph! He was wise man. I can't stop. Let's go!*

Andrey took a sharp knife and sat on the ground, on the moss, stretching his right leg and bending the left leg at the knee. *It's alright,* he tried to calm down. *I read about a man who amputated his leg above the knee; he was sawing off the bone for half an hour! How about that? And what's this? Piece of cake... Just half a minute...*

He sized up and, with a single strong movement, made a deep and long cut on the inner side of his left thigh. The pain was very sharp, but he could take it.

Well, there it is! It's not that scary, after all!" he smiled to himself. "And you were afraid.

Meanwhile, the blood flowed from the wound and covered the leg and the wrap at once.

Fuck! Andrey panicked. *The blood is spilling like from a wretched pig! Fucking cord! What's the use of it! Shit! That's not good. This could end very badly. Very badly! I need to hurry.*

He pulled the upper left edge of the wound with his hand. He was filled with a feverish excitement. He felt that he was a man who had already made a fatal and irrevocable step. That was it! There was no way back. It was too late to change his mind. Now he had simply to finish what he had started, as quickly as possible. He pulled the edges of the wound apart and cut the bleeding flesh again, deepening the cut. This time, the pain was so severe that he almost screamed. But he didn't stop. A couple of sharp and sure movements of the knife - and a huge piece of bloody flesh was in his hand.

*"Well, I need to take off the skin...it goes off so easily! Where should I put it? Into the pocket it goes. Well, I need to cut it in parts, probably, in order to cook it quickly. And I don't want to go faint before time. Blood is flowing, and it doesn't fucking stop! Motherfuck! Did I touch a vein, or what? It's flowing hard! Fucking fountain! Alright. Alright. Let's try to get up. Ah, ah, ah! Hush! Hush! Fuck, I should have made a crutch or a stick. Fuck, why didn't I think about it? Okay, let's try once more. Without a crutch. On the right foot. Well, well Ah, ah, ah! Uh, uh, uh! Once more, slowly. Uh, uh, uh! Right! Well, let's hop on one foot. What can I do?"*Andrey couldn't remember how he got to the fire. He lost his balance a couple of times, fell down, hissed and swore with pain, but then stood up again and kept jumping. He stood up and jumped. He jumped, fell down, and stood up.

However, each time was more and more difficult. His head was swimming, and his eyes were blurred. He was losing strength. A ten-day starvation and lack of sleep, let alone huge loss of blood, took its toll.

The fire was already burning down. Andrey lay down for some time, then put a couple of dry logs from under the wrap into it, and started cutting the meat with shaking hands and throwing it into the pot. There was a red mist before his eyes, the whole world was swinging and throbbing in a bleeding mirage.

Fuck, it all went wrong! thought Andrey gloomily, breathing heavily and trying to focus his view. He couldn't do that. *It's all going to hell! All of my detailed plans are being ruined.*

Slowly, with stops, he crawled close to the fire, which was burning brightly again, and put the pot above it, spending the last of his strength. *How long should I cook it? Half an hour? An hour? No, an hour is too much, I'm not gonna last.*

He looked at his leg. It was still bleeding badly. It seemed that he had really touched a vein. *Well I'm not gonna last for half an hour, probably,* he thought. *I'm gonna lose consciousness, and that's it! I'm hanging on by the eyelids. Well, let her cook it herself, if she can. Or she may eat it raw. Well, she's gonna see the meat and know what to do with it. Let's hope so. Anyway, I can't do anything else. Otherwise, it will all be in vain, if I perish right here and now. I can't perish now! It's too early! Early, early—wound, wound, wound! I'm an idiot. I couldn't do it right. I even cut a vein. Moron!" he spat with anger and groaned with powerless fury at himself. "Idiot! You could have done it more carefully, dumb head!*

Alright! He had several minutes left. He had to hurry. Quick! He had to act quickly. Andrey growled and tried to stand up. Click! The program switched to its last, final level. *'The performing of the task is in danger! Use all current resources!'*

He didn't receive any energy; it seemed that there was none left in the body, but the pain was gone. Andrey didn't feel the pain. Something rewired in the chains of his nervous system, so nothing hindered the performing of the task. Neither pain, nor emotions—nothing! The organism switched off all the security systems, like when it's done during the shock. Act! The goal must be reached! At any cost! Any! Even at the cost of his death.

Then there were lapses in Andrey's memory.

Holding an unnaturally heavy pot to his breast, he crawled to the door of the hut, dragging his left leg. He pushed that cursed pot inside, put it on the floor by touch and closed the door. Blackout—he's lying face down under the cutting rain, in a huge cold puddle, near the doorstep, and trying to lift up his head—again and again—

and everything's reeling before his eyes. Blackout! He's lying and resting again, but is this the same spot or somewhere else? Another blackout! It seems that he's crawling somewhere, crawling. Another blackout! He's crawling again. Another blackout! He's crawling again, crawling, crawling long, infinitely. He has to get there at any cost, he has to crawl to the river! He has to! He has to! Blackout.

And the last image. He's lying on his back near the water, two steps from it; flocks of wet snow are flying and falling on his face, but they're not melting. He's almost reached the water, there are a couple of meters left, but he would never make it. He lost. He's dying.

The program's still working, emotions are off. He doesn't pity anything: himself, Vera, his or her life. It's a pity that he didn't have enough strength to finish everything like he planned, to perform the task, to slide into the water and dive under the moving boggish shore. Then nobody would find his body. Well, he just disappeared. He got some meat; well, he caught a hare in the woods, cooked it, and left for his wife, and went to look for the camp and got lost. Maybe he drowned in the swamp. Such things happen! It's the North. And now…

His eyes were drawing straws… his mind was racing… his thoughts were slow and thick, and they were rolling in his head like heavy stones. He felt a huge, enormous, and inhuman weariness. He wanted to close his eyes… close his eyes and go out, go out, go out… Take some rest… Go to sleep…sleep… sleep. Die—sleep.

He closed his eyes, and, at that moment the program switched off. A merciless hand, which had been holding his will in its steel fist, went loose. Its grip weakened. The tension disappeared. The string broke. At these last moments of his life, he became a human again. An ordinary human. Just a human.

So they're gonna find me, he thinks, going to eternal sleep. *Poor Vera! If she survives and understands what meat it was... Poor soul!*

Everything starts to reel before his eyes…it's reeling faster and faster, and it seems that his soul is leaving his body and going up, up. Higher, higher. He can see himself from above… he can see his body with an unnaturally bent left leg, a wide bloody trace going from the hut—a terrible red line which is quickly disappearing under the rain—his last tough and sure stroke in the book of life—but he pays no interest to that. It all remained there on the ground. He's going higher, higher, but something happens, and suddenly he's again below, on the snow, in his body—and he sees a strange and amazing image.

There's gray dense mist in front of him, and from this mist, from nothing, there materializes a dark, black creature - an angel, or a demon, whose appearance makes Andrey shook in terror. And it goes to him.

Death! realizes Andrey. *Angel of the abyss. I'm dying.*

But suddenly, between this terrible and hideous angel-demon and him, there appears, out of nowhere, another figure—a slim and slender figure of a boy with a long sword at his side.

"Back off!" says a boy to the messenger of eternity, drawing his sword. The messenger keeps staring at him for some time and then starts fading—slowly fading, fading and then disappears completely. The boy sheathes his sword with one swift move, turns around, glances at Andrey, and disappears, too.

Andrey woke up as if somebody pushed him. The stove had gone out. He was lying on the floor of the hut, rolled up. *Have I been sleeping?* thought Andrey, embarrassed. *Did I see it in a dream?*

He touched his left leg. Nothing! No wounds and cuts. An ordinary leg. *Unbelievable! Crazy! What a dream!*

He stood up easily. The bright sun was shining through the windows. Apparently, the rain had stopped. He looked at Vera. She was sleeping, and her breath was even—it seemed that her face had gotten its color back. He felt her brow. It was cool. The fever was gone. The crisis was over.

Andrey shook his head in wonder and suddenly heard a familiar sound. He strained his ears for some time and then rushed to the door and went outside. He saw two motor-boats on the lake. They were clearly coming towards the hut.

Andrey wanted to go back and wake up Vera, but suddenly, a wall of the hut caught his eyes. He reached his hand slowly and carefully took off the jig from the wall. It was a black Mepps fish lure with red tail.

And Lucifer said to His Son:

—Thou shouldn't hast interfer'd and depriv'd the man of his fate. He pass'd his last life test with hon'r and earn'd the right to die with dignity. And anon he'll hast to take it again.

And Lucifer was ask'd by His Son:

— But if he pass'd it once, wouldn't he pass it again, when his time comes?

And Lucifer said to His Son, shaking His head:

—Thou cannot wot it beforehand. And the people change with time. Thou shall realize that.

LUCIFER'S SON. DAY 14.

And the fourteenth day came.

And Lucifer said:

—Every man loves himself and thinks about himself, above all. And women— in particular.

SHOW—2

"Do not spend your strength on women."

Book of Proverbs.

Kolya (K): "Hello, hello, hello, dear listeners! And our show is live again. And with you are the hosts: Kolya!"

Olya (O): "And Olya!"

K and O: "Greeting to everyone who's listening to us! Stay with us!"

<Theme music playing>

K: "So, today's topic is Eternal Youth. It's well-known that everyone wants to be liked, to hear compliments, and to stay forever young and attractive. Especially women, of course."

O (dreamily): "Oh, where is my seventeen? I'd like to lose a couple of years. Every woman dreams about that, right?"

K (acidly): "How many? "A couple of years?" How many?"

O (with dignity): "Nothing! I'm still seventeen. Almost."

K (still acidly): "Really? And how long have you been seventeen?"

O (laughs): "Not much. But, well, I wouldn't mind losing a couple of years. Well, every woman wants that. Oh, youth! Youth! Everyone's dreaming about it. Every woman."

K (continues): "And that's what our today's show is about—youth, eternal youth. We will talk about youth. Our guest is Viacheslav. He's 35 and he works in a Moscow bank. Right, Viacheslav? Am I right?"

Vyacheslav (V) (a bit embarrassed): "Hi. Yes, you're right. I do work in a bank."

K (curiously): "And what do you do, may I ask?"

V: "Sure, that is no secret. I'm a manager of the credit office."

O: "Oh! So, I can get a credit from you?"

V: "Sure! Welcome to our bank. We'll try to help you. Our bank offers the easiest terms and the lowest rates."

K: "Alright, Vyacheslav, we'll certainly take your offer."

O (merrily): "Oh, I do have a need of money!"

K (reasonably): "And who doesn't? Okay, Vyacheslav, I think we'll definitely talk about that, but now, let's get back to our show. So, as we agreed the last time, now we shall listen to the recordings of the conversations with your wife, which we made during this week? I remind you that, according to the rules of the show, we can stop the recordings at any moment. But it will mean that you have lost, and you shall have as little chance of seeing out marvelous prizes as of seeing, pardon me, your own ears. And, mind you, these are very nice prizes! As our show has been very popular recently, we've gotten a lot of sponsors, and there are some very serious companies among them—very serious! Well, we'll talk about sponsors when we have time. And we'll talk about prizes, as well.

So, let's start the show! Well, Vyacheslav, are you ready? Shall we put on the recordings? Or do you refuse to listen to them?"

V: "No way! Let's hear it."

K: "Great! Attention! The recording is on."

<Theme music playing>

***

Record 1.

Man (M): "Excuse me, I'm from TV, the show 'Youth and Beauty.' May I ask you a question?"

Woman (W): "Yeah, sure."

M: "How old do you think this woman or, rather, girl, is?"

W (hesitating): "Well, I think, 18 or 19."

M: "Thank you. (With other intonations, in a well-defined voice): So, dear viewers! Just now you heard the opinion of the tenth person. And not one—not one! of them said that this woman is more than 20. No one—not a single soul! By the way, the real age of Evgenia Nikolaevna is 38! Right—you heard it right. Here's her passport. (Shows her the passport. Reads): Sveshnikova Evgenia Nikolaevna, date of birth (reads the date of birth). How is this possible? How can a 38-year-old woman look like an 18-year-old girl? Today we shall talk about that. Evgenia Nikolaevna? No! Can I call you Zhenechka?"

Girl (G) (merrily and saucily): "Yeah, sure! I don't mind that." (Laughs).

M: "Zhenechka! "Tell us your secret! Tell us the secret of your eternal youth. We're very curious. You know, I'm looking at you, and I just can't believe my eyes… I just can't believe that you're really 38. Some people look young, very young, but that's different. There are always certain doubts, and, when you find out their real age, you start to see small wrinkles, skin laxity, dark eyes, etc.; you start to see all these menacing and inevitable symptoms of the coming age. And it's coming very quickly! And later you start to see that the person is really that age. Yeah, he looks exactly his age. Well, maybe a bit younger.

"But you! Well, you're 20; that's it—or, maybe 18 or 19. But I just can't believe that you're 38! I just can't; you're simply a young girl! You're not young-looking, but young—you're 20. No exaggerating—without any "almost," without any doubts. If you were among the 20-year-old students right now, it'd be impossible to single you out of the crowd according to age. You're same as them. You're of the same age. How is this possible? What's your secret?

G: "You know, just a year ago I looked like a 38-year-old woman. Maybe I looked a bit younger, for I always take care of myself. And then something happened that literally changed my life. I met a woman on the train who sent me to an old woman, a healer. And she returned my youth to me. I became the woman who you see now."

M: "Unbelievable! That's impossible!"

G: "However, that's true. And my present looks are the best proof. You saw my passport, didn't you?"

M: "Right, of course And did you become young at once?"

G: "Well, not at once—a month later."

M: "Amazing! Well, I think that any woman would like to be in your place and meet that old woman, a healer. By the way, would you tell us her address or telephone number so our female viewers could meet her and become young in a month, like you?"

G: "Unfortunately, I can’t do that. She’s very old, and she doesn’t practice a lot. The woman on the train warned me about that straightaway."

M (subtly): "But she gave you her address, didn’t she?"

G (tentatively): "Well, yeah…"

M (aggressively): "So, maybe we could send a single female viewer to her, right? Well, we can’t send all of them, I agree to that, but could we choose one girl?"

D (still tentatively, with hesitation): "Well, possibly?"

M: "Great! So, let’s do it! Here we have a woman, a voluntary participant of our show whom we have asked about your age. She’s an ordinary woman who just happened to be here when we were shooting. So, let’s ask her to take part in our little experiment. If she agrees, I suggest we do the following. You give her the address of that miraculous old woman, and we shall meet in a month, in our studio, and look at the result. What will happen to her in a month? Will she become younger, as well? Will she turn into an 18-year-old girl like you? (Addressing the woman): So, are you in? If there are any expenses, our program will cover them!"

W (joyfully and distrustfully): "I’m in! Of course. Why not? (Laughs). Moreover, it’s for free. You say the studio will cover all expenses?"

M (enthusiastically): "Great! (Addressing the girl): And you?"

G: "Alright! So be it. Let’s try. I’m in."

M (in a professional and cheerful voice): "That’s great! Then, see you in a month. So, dear viewers, don’t miss our show. Don’t forget! Straight in a month we shall meet, and you will see if the secret of eternal youth exists. Youthification! Is it myth or reality? Stay with us, and you will see it with your own eyes. Bye!"

***

Recording 2.

Same woman (W): "Hi."

Old woman (OW): "Hello, sweetie."

W: "Excuse me, I need to see Grandma Nadia."

OW: "Well, that’s me, sweetie."

W: "I’m from Evgenia Nikolaevna. She took a course of youthification with you."

OW: "Oh! Zhenechka! Right! I do remember her. How's she doing?"

W: "Great! Everything's alright. She sends her best."

OW: "Right, right. She doesn't forget an old woman."

W: "Grandma Nadia, I've got a request. I'd like to become younger, like Zhenia. Is this possible?"

OW: Ugh. "That wouldn't be easy, dear! I don't really know what to say."

W: "Well, take it, please. Here's <says the sum>."

OW: "Right! Well, so be it. Are you married, sweetie?"

W: "I am, Grandma."

OW: "Right, right! I can see it. Your husband's name is Slavik, he's 35, he's got dark hair and a large mole on his back, to the right, a birthmark. (Crustily): Is it so?"

W (astonished): "Yeah. Yes, Grandma…"

OW: "Well, listen to me then, sweetie. Here, take this green herb, burn it (Mutters something inaudible, "Moon is on the wane… Saturn… Jupiter…" Loudly): During the night to Monday, straight at midnight; eat the ashes and drink cold water. And then write down how many years younger you want to be, tie that piece of paper with thin thread, and put in into your husband's pocket. Do you love your husband? Tell me!"

W: "I do…"

OW: "That's good. For there will be no result without love. You need a beloved one to do it. Well! So, put the tied piece of paper into his pocket. He must not see anything—no way! And let him go to work with this paper in his pocket, and you'll become younger as many years as you will have written. Right. But know this, dear—these years will be taken from your husband's life. If you write '2', you'll become two years younger; you'll have two more years to live, and he'll live for two years fewer. He'll die two years earlier than fate prepared for him. That's it, dear. Understood?"

W: "Yes, Grandma."

OW: "Well, then go. And remember this: the more you live, the less he has to live."

W: "Good-bye, Grandma. I got it. Thank you."

OW: "You are welcome, dear! Ugh! Just know—you can do it only once in life—only once. Youth. No repeating. That's it! Well, good-bye, sweetie."

<The sound of the closing door>.

<Theme music playing>.

K: "So, Vyacheslav. What would you say? Did you understand everything?"

V (embarrassed): "And how could this healer know about me? Name, age, and even mole? "

K (with merry reproach): "Well, you told me that the last time I asked you about that."

V (shyly): "Oh, yeah Oh, God! I'm just…"

K: "So, let's continue?"

V (confused): "What exactly?"

K: "Our show."

V: "Oh, oh?"

O (impatiently): "Well, let's look for the paper. "

V (without understanding): "What paper?"

O (mockingly and ironically): "The one tied with a thin thread which your beloved wife put into your pocket at midnight. Yesterday was the night to Monday. Well, moon on the wane… Saturn-Jupiter… Well, you know."

K (laughs): "Eating ashes of enchanted herbs and drinking cold water. Tap water. By the way, what herb did you give her? Wasn't that poisonous, by the way?"

O (shrugging): "How would I know? Ordinary dried herbs. Our cameraman took it from his son's herbarium. They have classes in botany these days."

K (addressing Viacheclav): :So what? Are we going to look for the paper?"

V (embarrassed): "Where? Is it supposed to be in my pocket?" (Apparently starts to look around and feel his pockets).

O (reproachfully and mockingly): "You get it, at last!"

K: "Hold on! Stop the searches! At first, according to the rules of the show, you must guess if there's a paper at all and what number is written on it. What age? Well, of course, if there's a paper. And that's our task for today. So, try to guess. How many years younger does your beloved wife want to become? By the way, how old is she?"

V (still embarrassed): "Thirty-seven."

K: Oh! So, she's two years older than you, right? So, how many?" (addressing Olya): And how many years younger would you like to be by means of your beloved one."

O (saucily): "Why would I want to become younger? I'm only 18!"

K: "But you said you were 17?"

O (immovably): "I just turned 18."

K: "I see. Congratulations! Well, really?"

O (proudly): "Well, I think that if a man truly loves—and my husband adores me, he worships me!—so, it is well-known that love needs sacrifice."

K (subtly): "And would you sacrifice your youth for your husband? Would you grow old for him?"

O (indignantly): "No way! Nonsense! He's the one who has to make sacrifice for me; I've already made sacrifices for him, with youth and everything else, when I got married. 'Grow old!' Get off with you! 'Grow young again!' That's another pair of shoes! So he would like me. It would be better for him. This fool will be glad that he has such a young and beautiful wife. 'Grow old!' Bite your tongue!"

K: "Hush, hush! No need for shouting. I get it. A woman has to be forever young and beautiful, and her husband has to sacrifice everything for her. I get it. Why are you nervous? (Olya snorts with irritation.) So, Vyacheslav? What's your answer? What number is written on the paper? Eh? What do you think?"

V (hesitating): "Well I think… What do you mean, 'on my account'? By means of my life! Well, I don't know… I think, three or four years… well, five… Though, five… is it five, really?"

K (impatiently): "So, how many? Three?.. five?.."

V (after a pause): "Three! No, five! No, three! Well, no, I think, there's no paper!"

O (interrupts): "Vyacheslav! We're live! Say a number, a specific number—make a decision. Is there any paper or not? And if there is, what's written on it? So?"

V (confidently): "There is! There is a paper!"

K (asks curiously): "So, there is a paper, right?"

V (still confidently): "Yes. There is a paper! And the number is five!"

K (with curiosity): "Five?"

O (snorts loudly): "Umph!"

K: "Well, Vyacheslav! you made your choice. There is a paper in the pocket, and the number is five. Great! We'll get back to you after a commercial break and listen to the opinions of our listeners. And then we'll compare them to yours and to the real one, of course. If there's a paper, certainly. Maybe there's no paper at all!"

O (interrupts, with clear doubt): "It may well be."

K: "So, we're waiting for your calls! Call us and give your opinion. What number is written on the paper which is in the Viacheclav's pocket? Or you may send the messages to our beeper.

Our number is <says number> for the subscriber <says the subscriber>. Well, we're waiting for your calls and messages. We'll get back to you after commercial."

<Commercial>

K: "Well, there are calls and messages. The whole package! We've got 12 messages! Well, we're going to read them later. And now, Vyacheslav, look into your pockets—it's time! Look for the paper with a thread. (After a pause): Well? Did you find it?"

V (with a halt): "Not yet Oh! Here's a paper with a thread. That's it?"

K (confidently): "Right! That's it!"

V (inquiringly): "Should I open it?"

O (excitedly and impatiently): "Of course, open it! I can't wait! I'm dying to know what's on it! And I'm sure that all our listeners want to know it, as well! (After a pause): Well? What is it?"

V (rustling): "Hold on (Reads): 22. (Bewildered): 22? What does it mean—22?"

K (tutorially): "It means that your wife wants to become a 15-year-old girl again."

V (completely embarrassed): "This is nonsense! What girl? Our daughter is sixteen! What for? (After a pause): What's the meaning of that?"

K: "Exactly! It means… Well, you already realized that it means—it means that you lost. Alas!"

O (admiringly): "Well! Atta girl! Even I didn't expect that! Frankly speaking, I thought that it would be 14 or 15. Well, 17, at most. But no more! But 22! Well! Though, such a chance; it happens only once in life. The only one… Well, Vyacheslav, take it easy. It's just a game, a joke. All your years will stay with you, and no one will take them from you. Fortunately, it's simply impossible."

K: "Exactly! Fortunately. Then! Oh, women, women! Treacherous and ungrateful!"

O: "Come on! Women? Men are no better. We're all the same. We're tarred with the same brush and cut from the same cloth. Males and females alike. We're just humans. Weak humans…By the way, what's the situation with the messages? What did the listeners think? Did someone guess?"

K: "Well, what can I say? We got only three calls, but there are twelve messages on the beeper, as I've already said. Three calls: two women and a man. The women said the numbers 17 and 20, and the man said 3; well, a silly and naïve guy. The beeper? Well, let's see... Well... seven women and five men. Women: 17, 19, 19... right! 20! Oh, we even have 22! So, one of them did guess. Men: 3, 2, 2, 10! And one message, 'Trust people, Vova'. Well... It's not clear, Vova, what's the meaning of it? Is there no paper? Well, it doesn't matter. So, our show's over. That's all for today. We'll see you next Monday! Again, you were entertained by the hosts Kolya..."

O: "And Olya!"

K and O: "Good-bye! See you!"

<Theme song playing>

And Lucifer was ask'd by His Son:

—Did that woman love that man?

And Lucifer answer'd to his son, smiling:

—Certainly. Otherwise, she wouldn't hast written aught on the paper. F'r she was warn'd that she couldst doth that thing only with a belov'd one. Otherwise, nothing would hast betid. Thou can betray only the one, who trusts thou.

LUCIFER'S SON. DAY 15.

And the fifteenth day came.

And Lucifer said:

—Generosity is the path of the strong. The weak doth not wot of it.

If a woman thinks that she is right—her cruelty is truly infinite.

VOODOO

"Oh my dove! Let me see thy countenance,
let me hear thy voice;
for sweet is thy voice, and thy
countenance is comely."
The Book of Song of Songs.

Host: "Hi! Welcome to our weekly show, 'A view from behind the scenes'. Today's topic is 'Cruelty and love'. Actually, today's show will be a bit unusual. Now we're going to watch a special film, and then I'm going to ask the audience to share their impressions and tell us their opinion on the film. Alright? So, begin—let's watch the film.

<The lights in the studio go out. A screen appears. There's the same host on the screen (H).>

H: "So, we're in one of the Moscow apartments. Its owner, Lyudmila Ivanovna, <the camera shows a smiling aged woman with pleasant looks> is going to play the role of the fortune teller and sorceress in the fifth generation—well, the role of a kind of mystical and mysterious person who possesses some secret and unnatural capabilities. We need that for our program. You see, she's prepared—she's dressed in all black, she's got various magic rings. All in all, she's in her character!"

<The camera gives a close up of the owner's hands with different rings and then of a massive necklace with a pendant in the form of the skull, on her neck.>

"Look at these curious things which cover the walls; our prop department did its best and made a lot of different stuff."

<The camera shows various strange garlands, masks, insignia, amulets etc.>

"All of these are aimed to impress, so to say, our client. And the client is about to appear. We placed an ad in several newspapers. By the way, here it is."

<Camera gives a close up of the advertising page.>

"See: 'Returning husbands. Free. 100% guarantee'. That's us! Well, as you understand, the ad is very tempting! "For free!" "100% guarantee!"—so, I'm sure that there's going to be a lot of clients. Actually, we got a lot of calls, and now we're waiting for the first visitors. Female ones. By my reckoning, they must appear soon, actually… <The host takes a look at his watch> any moment.

"While we have some time left, let me bring you up to date <A door-bell rings> Well! Here are our dear clients. Well, we have no time for briefing; you'll get everything as we progress Well, attention! Here we go. We want to warn you—as the cameras are hidden, and the conversations will be rather private, so the faces and voices of the participants are changed. Well, the voices are changed, and the faces are blurred. Here we go!"

<The camera shows an empty room. Female mumbling can be heard from the other room. Then the mistress enters the room together with another woman. The woman is middle aged, well-dressed. It's impossible to see the face behind the sparkling spot, and the voice is changed, too.>

Mistress (M) (points at the chair): "Please, have a seat".

Woman (W) (looks around shyly and distrustfully, halting her gaze at the various scary and grinning masks and other props covering the wall): "Thank you. <Sits down.> You see, I don't really know where to begin. Are you a sorceress, indeed?"

M (calmly): "Yes."

W: "Umph…Well… There it is…"

M (still calmly): "Come on, tell your story! Don't be shy. What happened to your husband?"

W (amazed): "And how? Umph... Well, there it is… I do have problems with my husband… Recently… I think…"

M (finishes the phrase immovably): "That he's got a lover. Rival. Marriage wrecker."

W: "Right! Well, no. Right! I think… I couldn't believe it for a long time, but facts... little things…<And she bursts out>: It's impossible! Unbelievable! Are you getting it? How could he? How? After we've been together for so many years? Love! We have children. I'm ashamed to look into their eyes! How could he? He betrayed everything—vulgarized, disgraced. He ruined everything! He ruined our love, our relations! Our marriage, for God's sake! We had a church wedding! I just can't understand it. It just doesn't make sense! Leaving family and children for some... some…"

M (still immovably): "Do you know her?"

W (passionately): "Sure! Of course, I know her! It's definitely his new secretary. <With hatred> Her! That randy painted doll in a mini-skirt! I saw her make eyes at him and move her ass lustfully. And he's a married man! She's got neither shame nor conscience! And that old fool let himself be duped. She needs only his money! Money! Nothing more. How can he not understand it? All these modern young people, all these young chicks! They're thinking only about money!"

M (asks immovably): "So, she's young? Younger than you?"

W (grievously): "Yes… She's younger, much younger… She's an eighteen-year-old kid… But how could he?!.. How could he?!.. "

M (soothingly): "Hold on! Let's start from the very beginning. As far as I understood, you suspect that your husband is having an affair with his new young secretary, right? You don't know that for sure, but you suspect that. Right?"

W (still grievously): "Right. What do you mean 'Can't know that for sure'? Am I blind, or what? He's rarely at home—and when he comes home, he mutters something and then goes to bed. He's always busy, he's got constant meetings. Meetings! What kind of meetings are held in the evenings? And he smells of French perfumes after them! Meetings! Well! I can feel it. He's changed, as if he's not himself. We're not close as we used to be. I don't know what to do."

M (supportively): "And did you try to explain yourself? Did you try to talk?"

W (waves her hand sadly): "Sure, I did. Several times. With no result. It got even worse. 'You're making it up. Don't bother me with your nonsense. Get off me, I'm tired!'—that's it! He wouldn't say any more. Just 'get off!' and 'leave me alone'! <Bursts>: And this scum! She almost laughs at my face! I'm afraid to visit him at work. I'm ashamed! I used to go there a lot—the company is small, and we were all like a big family. And now it seems that they're all gossiping behind my back."

M: "So, what do you want me to do? Get your husband back? But it appears that he hasn't left you yet."

W (passionately, haltingly, and confusedly): "Let it be like it was before! He must leave that girl and come back to me. And let him fire her tomorrow. Let him chuck her out! And I want him to come home on time."

M (uncertainly): "Well, well, well!"

W (with hope): "Can you do that?"

M (still uncertainly): "Well, it depends Surely, I can do that, but the thing is that all these curses and love spells are not forever. They work during a short period of time, and then they become weaker. And he can go back to his young secretary, and then it'll be forever. He'll leave you forever. For good! Yes! See, I'm not charging you, so I can tell you everything in detail. I tell you everything about our sorcery. Others would never tell you that; they would only play games with you and take your money. But I'm laying it out for you. I have no secrets from you. I'm a sorcerer in the fifth generation, so you can trust me. I know what I'm talking about."

W (embarrassed): "So what shall I do?"

M: "We need him to cease loving this girl. Truly! Without love spells and curses. Or she has to disappear. That would be even better. The effect would be greater."

W (without understanding): "What exactly do you mean by 'disappear'?"

M (lowering her voice to a whisper, as a conspirator): "There's means—a sure one—very sure! Did you hear anything about the voodoo cult?"

W (in scared whisper): "What voodoo?"

M: "Well, did you watch any movies about zombies? Living dead?"

W (in terror): "Jees!"

M (confidently, dropping formalities): "Do you want to get your husband back?"

W (still scared): "I do."

M: "So, listen. I have a very powerful enchanted amulet. I brought it from Haiti; I went there to learn from the local priests. Here it is. <Shows a figure of a white idol.> It's an ancient god—the main protector of voodoo."

W (astonished, staring at the idol warily): "Have you been to Haiti? And you learned from that cult? Waking the dead?"

M (aggressively and convincingly): "What do the dead have to do with it? What are the dead? That's just a part—and not the most important one. That's just for the audience. Showing off. The movie makers made it popular for a reason, all this stuff about the dead. Trying to make a sensation. As a matter of fact, voodoo is a very ancient cult. A secret one. No one knows everything about it. The priests keep their secrets very well! And they don't tell anything to just anyone. They told me some stuff just because I shared with them our ancient Slavic secrets—in exchange, so to say. I gave them the witchcraft and spells. Well, that's not important! That's none of your business. You're not supposed to know that. It's a scary knowledge—a forbidden and secret one. Only a few people can perceive it. You should do the following. Take this amulet <Gives her the amulet. The woman hesitates, not taking it.> Take it, don't be scared! <The woman takes it shyly>. Here we go! And now go with it to the next room, over there. <Points to the door>. There's a table with a figure made of paper on it, a needle, an ash-tray, and matches. Put the amulet in front of you and, looking at it, imagine that girl, a secretary. Try to see her well—in detail—as best as you can. And then take the figure and pierce the spot in which you want her to be sick. If you pierce the arm, her arm will wither; if you pierce the leg, the same with her leg. If you do it with the eye, she will be blind. And if you pierce the heart, she's going to die.

"She will become a mud duck, and your husband will love her no more! He'll grow cold to her. Who would need her with her looks? Then burn the figure in the ash-tray and throw the ashes out of the window. And then everything will be as you wish. Your husband will come back to you, and your rival will disappear. Well, go!"

W (completely embarrassed): "I don't really know…"

M (imperatively): "Go! Do it for the sake of your children. They need their father."

<The woman stands up slowly and goes to the next room, hesitating. The camera switches to another room. The woman enters the room, looks around and slowly approaches the table. Then, still

slowly and hesitatingly, she puts the amulet on it, sits behind the table, and starts staring at the amulet. Then she reaches her hand and grabs the paper figure of a human from the table, gazes at it for some time, puts it into her left hand, and takes the needle with her right hand. She hesitates for a couple of moments, and then sticks the needle in the figure. Straight in the heart! She takes it out, freezes for a moment, and then sticks it a couple more times. Again and again! She squeezes the figure, crumples it, throws it into the ash-tray, and burns it. When the paper burns completely, the woman goes to the open window with the ash-tray. Yuck! And the ash-tray is clean again. The woman places it carefully on the table and goes back to the room, where the mistress waits for her.>

<Next shot. Another aged woman. She's plainly dressed and belongs to common people, obviously>.

W: "Fucking Mashka! Scum! Whore! Fucking cunt! I would strangle her with my own hands… I would scratch her shameless eyes out!"

<Next shot. The same woman holds the figure in her hands and pierces it with a needle. Into the first eye, and then into the second. A pause—and then into her heart. Heart, heart, heart! Again and again. Cut-in. A hand, that puts the empty ash-tray onto the table.>

<Next shot. A new woman. To be exact—a girl. A young girl.>

Girl: "My best friend—I hate her! "

<A hand that sticks a needle in a figure. At first, in the underbelly, and then, in the heart. Heart, heart, heart!

<The same hand puts the empty ash-tray onto the table. The appropriate music accompanies the row of shots, which are changing with growing speed.>

An elegant woman's hand, sticking a needle in a paper figure several times. Heart, heart, heart! The same hand puts the empty ash-tray onto the table.

Again! again! again!

Hand—needle—ash-tray!

Hand—needle—ash-tray!

Hand—needle—ash-tray!

A semi-transparent burning-paper figure appears on the background of this sequence, a series of changing shots. The figure becomes thicker and thicker and then fills the whole screen, pushing out the sequence. It stays on the screen for a couple of moments, the flame devours the paper, then the background music ends, and the screen goes out with the last accord.

THE END.

<The lights in the room go on.>

H: "So, we've just seen the film. Now I'd like to know the opinion of the audience. And mind that the audience is purely female! Usually I just put questions for participants of the show, but, as today's topic is rather delicate, I probably can't count on getting ~~the~~ honest answers. Few of the people who are present here would dare to say into the camera, 'That's right! I'd pierce the heart, if I were her!' That's why we shall do the following. I have 20 forms with a single question: "Were the women in the film right, piercing the figure?" Well, do you agree that you may fight your rival by any means necessary? There are two answers in the form: yes and no. Underline the appropriate one—that's it. So, if you think that it's right, underline "yes," and if it's wrong, underline "no." That would be it. Let's hope that these anonymous questionnaires will get sincere and honest answers, and we'll get the real opinions of the participants of today's show. We'll find out what they're really thinking. Do they support the actions of the women from the film or not? So, let's begin. Please hand out the forms."

<The assistants take the forms and go to the audience, so the participants can fill them in. After that, they bring these forms to the host. He looks through them quickly.>

H: "Well what have we got? Let's see. Right! 'No'—only two forms. The other eighteen say 'yes'! The score is 18 : 2. <Murmur in the room.> That's it, dear ladies. Love is blind. And it's cruel. We were convinced of that today. That would be it. Our show has come to an end. See you next Tuesday. All the best!"

<Theme song playing. The host and his assistants leave the room.>

And Lucifer was ask'd by His Son:

— 'Tis said in the Bible: "All is vanity of vanities!". Is it so?

And Lucifer answer'd to His Son:

— If all is vanity of vanities, what is the point of talking about it? For, then all these words art nay moo, than vanity. Doth not hark to all these Bible sages! These art dead words of dead people. The words of slaves. A slave invites thou to slavery. A dead invites a living to the grave. "All is going ashes to ashes...", "All is vanity of vanities...", "The end is same f'r everyone..." Right, the end is the same, but the paths art different! And not all is vanity of vanities f'r a man! Hon'r is nay vanity, and loyalty is nay vanity, and generosity is nay vanity. All that makes man a man is nay vanity. And freedom is nay vanity! Otherwise, it's nay man, it's a slave.

LUCIFER'S SON. DAY 16.

And the sixteenth day came.

And Lucifer said:

—Why does man worship God?

Because He is stronger?—So what?

Because He is more powerful?—So what?

Because He can help or punish?—Become free! Do not wait for help and do not be afraid of punishment—and you shall be like God. And you shall need no other gods.

FORUM

"You will not certainly die," the serpent said to the woman. "For God knows that when you eat from it your eyes will be opened, and you will be like God, knowing good and evil."
Genesis.

Nemox: "Hi to everyone! What's with the fit of hysterics with the Gibson's movie about Christ? Suicides, heart attacks? What's with this stuff? Actually, I don't get it. Well, take me. I'm an ordinary man. A modern one. Surely, I'm no scientist, but I do watch TV and read books, and I don't understand how it's possible to discuss such matters now, in the 21st century. The Bible, Christianity… science has already proven that it's nonsense, right?

"Well, according to the Bible, God created the world six thousand years ago, but the Earth is millions years old. And the stars are billions years old! And so on. And here they talk about God… the devil… I don't really know. It seems like a conspiracy theory. Everyone pretends that they believe in these tales. It's just unclear—what's the point of that. Science is on its own, and religion is on its own. Maybe we should pick one thing, shouldn't we? Either/or?"

Paul 23: "Science uses facts. But if God created the world, so He created these facts. So, science cannot prove or contradict the existence of God. No 'scientific' facts can do that, for these facts are actually God's facts. Just like science itself. Again. If there's a Creator, then He created everything. He created the facts 'proving' or 'contradicting' His existence, science with all its 'proof', and us, all of our thoughts, and doubts. He is everything! The question is—does He exist? But that's a matter of faith. Science cannot solve that problem. P. S. And the pure logic and sense cannot do it either. That was observed by Kant."

Alex to Nemox: "I agree with Paul 23 completely. I just want to add something about the 'facts'. Read, for example, Jonathan Sarfati's 'Refuting Evolution'. There's a lot of interesting stuff about these facts in the book. But it's not that simple. As a matter of fact, even from science's point of view, there are no specific facts. All of them are thin and unconvincing. Say, evolution and Darwinism.

"Did you know, for example, that the images of embryos of different animals—they show that they're very similar to each other—which are shown in all textbooks are fake? They were made by Ernst Haeckel, the defender of Darwin's ideas. The detailed study, dated 1997, conducted by Mike Richardson and his group, using the real photos of various embryos, showed that embryos of different kinds ARE VERY MUCH DIFFERENT.

"In his letter to 'Science Magazine', Richardson says explicitly: 'The pictures of Haeckel, dated 1874, are fake, for the most part. Proving this point of view, I must say that one of his first pictures—fish—consists of parts of various animals, including mythical ones. It's nothing else than a fraud. Sadly enough, but these pictures that are dated 1874 are, in spite of their shameful reputation, still to be found in many books on biology'. Let's take mutations. New species are created through accidental mutations, which are confirmed by natural selection after that. Well, that's what Darwin says. Well, during mutations the information is lost. So, nothing new can be created through this mechanism.

"Let me quote, for example, a biophysicist Dr. Lee Spenser, a professor of information of connection at Johns Hopkins University, 'In all studies on biology and related sciences, I haven't met any example of mutation, which would add new information to the current one. All isolated mutations, studied on the molecular level, appear to be decreasing the genetic information, but not increasing it. Mutations do not collect information—they just cause its losses.' By the way, didn't you think what would be, if Darwin was right, and the evolution was constant, with all species turning into other ones? There would be no complete species—just intermediate ones! Every species would turn into another one, and this process would last forever. Constant accidental mutations, natural selection. Well, like Darwin taught.

"As a matter of fact, the real picture is different. Complete species exist, and they do not change. So what? Nothing at all! There's no God—that's it! Mutations! In general, this Darwinism is a piece of crap! It's such gibberish that it passes understanding how the scientific world could embrace it and still accept it, in spite of everything! Actually, the whole story with Darwinism is a vivid example of the 'objectivity' of science. When, for some supreme goals—there's no God, there's no creator, everything appeared on its own, by natural causes—everything is sacrificed—logic, facts, and even sense. Everything! Even pure manipulations are used, like with the embryos. That's it! Science!

"Boyce Renberger was absolutely right, saying, 'The scientists are not that objective and impartial as they want us to think. Most of the scientists build up their own ideas of the world structure—and these ideas are based not on the accurate and logically connected processes, but on the guesses and speculations, which are sometimes very weird. A scientist, as a personality, very often comes to the conviction of the truthfulness of something long before he collects enough evidence of his guess. Being guided by the faith in his own ideas and by the ambition to be acknowledged in the scientific world, a scientist would work hard for many years, strongly believing that his theory is true, and he would undertake endless experiments which have, as he thinks, to prove it'.

Gene to Nemox: "Listen, Nemox. Do you actually believe in God?

Nemox to Gene: "Well, I think that God exists. There's something supreme. But I don't believe in the Bible or in Adam and Eve."

Alex to Nemox: "Have you heard about the term, 'mitochondrial Eve'? The similarity of the DNA mitochondria inherited only on female line shows that all people on Earth are descended from one woman. Even the evolutionists called her 'Eve'—to be exact, 'mitochondrial Eve'. At first, they were glad, for they thought that they had undoubted evidence against the Biblical annals, for 'mitochondrial Eve' lived presumably 200,000 years ago. But the results of the recent studies showed that the speed of the mitochondria's DNA mutations is much faster than it was considered. If we apply these new data to 'mitochondrial Eve', it becomes clear that she must have lived only 6000-6500 years ago. Of course, that conforms to the Biblical age of the "mother of all living," but it still remains a riddle for the evolutionists who believe in the million-year history of the world.

"It's curious that similar evidence exists for men, as well: the data received from the Y-chromosome proves that all males are descended from the one forefather. This data conform to the proofs of the fact that 'Adam of Y-chromosome' lived just a little while ago.

Nemox to Alex: "Is it true, really? Adam-Eve? Of course, I didn't know that. I haven't even heard of it. Well, well! So, all men are brothers?"

Jacki: "Right! And sisters. And all our life is a sheer incest—marriages with relatives. All in all, sheer equality and brotherhood."

Igor N: "What does equality have to do with it?"

Jacki: "Well? All men like brothers… they're equal. Are they not?"

Igor N: "It's nonsense! 'Equality'… 'they're equal'… What's the meaning of it? How are they equal? One is smart, another is dumb. One is white, another is black. One likes the priest, another likes the priest's wife. And the third likes pork. How could they be equal? It's the mentality of the weak. They wish to be in a crowd, to level everybody up. They try to regulate us. They try to put us in a line. Why? What for? Where are we going to parade?"

XYZ to IgorN:"What's all this cheap pathos for? On an empty spot. Why do we need that storm in a teacup? It means that everybody has the same rights. We're all equal under the law. We're all humans. That's it."

IgorN to XYZ: "As a matter of fact, that is wrong concerning rights. There are no 'obligations'. It's just one of the fundamental 'truths' which everyone is so tired of. These truths are so strongly pushed into the heads of the modern people that they take them for granted and don't even think about them. Right, we're all humans. So what? What? A globally renowned scientist, a prize winner is a human, and my neighbor, a cursed drunkard who's lying every day in his own vomit near my building, is a human, too. So what? Why would they have equal rights? Do they carry the same value for the society? Another thing is the attempts to define "grade of quality" and make the selection of people. It can bring the social disruptions. And that's why one must choose the lesser of evils and accept the compromise. One must declare that all people are equal. But it's a desperate measure! It's a compromise but not a great achievement of humanism and civilization, as they try to show us. People are not equal. We simply do not have the scales to weigh them, their advantages, and disadvantages. We cannot measure their social rating."

Jacki: "But that's what the Bible teaches us, right? Christ. All people are equal, they're brothers, etc.?"

Igor N: "The Bible, Christ, and what is Christianity? The religion of the slaves. We're all slaves. Slaves of God. And how does one treat slaves? Carrot and stick. Hell or paradise. If it were not for the stick, or fear of hell, there would be no believers left tomorrow. We keep the commandments not because we believe in them or deem them just, but because we're afraid to break them.—like animals in circus are afraid of the tamer's whip and pretend that they like to jump through the hoop and play with a ball. As a matter of fact, they like to hunt, kill, and fight for females. They love to be free! We're no more than tamed bears, dancing on their hind legs. We're dogs, running after sops."

Vasl: "Hey! Let's observe the rules and stay mutually polite. I, for one, don't like being called a dog."

Igor N to Vasl: "Alright, I'm sorry. I overreacted. By the way, one more question regarding the faith. Why do whole nations and countries believe in one god? They're all totally either Christians, or Muslim. How is this possible? So, it appears that we're not so free in the choice of religion as we think. We're born in Russia, we're Orthodox. If we were born among the Papuans or were taken there in the early childhood, we would worship the demons. It's all the same. So, it seems that a man doesn't care what he believes in. He does what others do. They just care that they have something—a god or an idol. And it doesn't matter what it is! As a matter of fact, that's a very interesting moment. Try to convince girls that they have to love only old men and impotents...you wouldn't be able to do it. Nature will take its toll. The powerful protective mechanisms will be at work—maternity, reproduction, birth of healthy descendants, etc. But you would easily convince them to believe in whoever you want—be it Christ or Buddha. Simple as that! They're following the others. And they would believe in them sincerely. Vigorously!

"It means that, actually, there are no natural protective mechanisms in the matters of faith. Be it god, or devil—the nature doesn't care. And so, we have an involuntarily question. Do they exist at all—God and devil? You may believe in them or not. Nature doesn't interfere with it, and there's no instinct. The instinct of maternity does exist—but there's no instinct of God."

Vasl to Igor N: "But you just said that a man has to believe in something, right? So, a need of faith—well, and instinct, if you want—exists in a man. It was put in a man originally. And in whom would a man believe? That's a freedom of choice, freedom of will."

Igor N to Vasl: "Of faith! Instinct of faith! It does exist. Not of God or Christ - but of faith! Faith, in general. Faith in anything!"

Vasl to Igor N: "Freedom of will! What do you want?"

Igor N to Vasl: "No, you don't understand me. Actually, I doubt in that. Does 'freedom' exist? Or is it yet another myth, like 'all are equal'? If it existed, there wouldn't be such solidarity of a nation, when all around you believe in one god. But when people change their country and surroundings, they change their beliefs, as well. They do it very easily. Then everyone would have his own god, chosen according to the need of his heart. And they would believe vigorously. And beliefs of the others are their private matter.

"However, it's not that simple regarding a simple matter. What is religious tolerance? "We have to respect the faith of the others." What's the meaning of "respect?" They're all wrong. They're all heretics and worshippers of idols! What should one respect here? If I truly believe that Christ exists, how can I respect the faith in some Buddha? Who is Buddha for us? Idol! Fake god! And Christ cautions us against it, "Worship the Lord your God, and serve him only." Him only! If I do believe in Christ, how can I respect someone who doesn't believe in him? It's huge insincerity! If people of a certain country invent their own arithmetic in which twice two is not four, but five, then I must either try to dissuade them, explaining that they're wrong, or just stand aside. But I wouldn't "respect" their arithmetic or participate in the meeting of these fools—no way! Count me out! I don't want to become a fool among them! Stupidity is foul.

"But that's fair, if I truly believe that twice two is four. That Christ really exists. And if I have the slightest doubts left, then I would have religious tolerance. Who knows? Maybe it's really five? Well, it was a lyrical digression. An introduction. The tale follows. So, regarding freedom—I think that there are laws, like physical ones, in the human relations. It's just that they're not explored at all. Have you ever paid attention to certain, rather interesting thing? Why are the wives of many famous people not so beautiful?

"Let's take the Beatles, for example. Millions of female fans, ready for everything, girls who are crying at their concerts—and what do we have? Who are their wives? Lennon's Yoko Ono is as ugly as death, and McCartney's Linda is past her best. If truth be told, she's no beauty at all—and she's got a child from her first marriage. And we're talking people who could choose any girl! Out of millions! Obviously, there's something unnatural and unclear in this—a secret, a riddle. For a normal guy instinctively tries to choose a beautiful girl; that's quite natural, and it's established on a genetic level, a desire of woman's beauty. And here we have a strange, dry Japanese—a very ugly one. Well, hell with Lennon—he was an odd and extraordinary man with his peculiarities. Same with everyone—same with a lot of people. Even with our pop-morons, who cannot be suspected in having any originality of tastes! All these 'Ivanushkas'. The same picture. Crowds of fans, crying with happiness—and ordinary, plain, or even ugly wives. Why is that? What's the meaning of this dream? What's the matter?

"I, for one, think that there is a law of sexual attraction of humans—men and women—well, like gravitation. Or like opposite charges in electronics. Like the Coulomb's law. I think that the strength of attraction to each other is in direct proportion to their beauty and magnetism (sexual charge) and in indirect proportion to the degree of distance between them. Degree! Squared or even cubed—as in the Coulomb's law. Or even more. In the fourth or fifth degree. That explains everything. The strength of attraction grows quickly with the distance. So, if a woman can approach you closely enough—that's it! Game over! Consider it done; you cannot escape. The strength of attraction becomes too strong, and you cannot escape. You cannot get out. You shouldn't have let her close to you. Other women, however beautiful they are, may be attracted, as well, but they are too far. They cannot help. Distance matters more than beauty. A plain woman next to you has a much greater influence on you than a beauty across the ocean. That's why ugly women are able to achieve a lot. You're not afraid of them, and so you let them close to you. You think that they're not dangerous. For they're so ugly, and their sexual charge is so low! But the distance, distance! They are women—so they're predators, and their law of attraction influences you, as well. Here! And you're wriggling in their little sharp steel claws.

"In brief, you can fall in love with any woman. The one who's closer to you, who's near. Even Romeo and Juliet. How many Juliets were there for Romeo? Thousands? Millions? But this one was near him. Thinking that she was the only one in the whole world, and she was living at that moment in the house next to him is a complete nonsense! It's like with Little Prince—the whole garden of red roses. All of them are similar. Equally fair. Choose any. But on his planet, there was only one. And it wasn't fair. And here there are many! The whole field. They're thick on the ground. And all of them are fair. All of them are yours. Just reach your hand. The same with faith. You can believe in anyone. And in anything. You may believe in that which is near you at the moment, that which everybody around you believes in. They believe that the cow is sacred, and you're gonna believe it, too. A tree? Be it a tree. A stone? Be it a stone. What would you do? Very strong self-persuasion mechanisms will come into action. Like, "It's impossible that everybody around me is wrong, isn't it?" These mechanisms influence each individual, each member of society. If you live in a society, you must embrace it. And if you communicate with the other members, you consider them equal to you. It's impossible to live among people and consider them idiots. Such a situation is uncomfortable for yourself. You wouldn't feel good in these conditions. You'd be an exile. And what about "idiots?" Are you smarter than them? More talented? No. So, what's your exceptional nature? And all these smarter and more talented people—scientists, etc.—believe in stone. So, how can you not believe in it? That's it. That's all your freedom!"

Vasl to Igor N: "Hold on! You have said—well, written—a lot, so it's impossible to get it at once. Without a drink. You've put everything in a pile—the Beatles, love, faith Romeo and Juliet. Religious tolerance. Enough! Hold on. Well, you write that one may believe in anything. Well, let's assume that. But religions of the nations change. Well, we were heathens once. And now we're

Orthodox Christians. How's that? So, there's a hidden process going on, right? Will the truth triumph? The truth ousts the lies."

Igor N to Vasl: "It's not that the truth ousts the lies, it's the new ousts the old! Religions and ideas incorporated in them grow old with time. They wither—like everything in the world. And they need a change. Like a worn dress. But then, it's a general process for everyone. Everybody starts believing in Christ. Yesterday, they believed in Perun, and today, they believe in Christ. Yesterday, no one had heard of Christ at all, and today—here you go! Everybody around you believes in him. Well, why do you care? Let it be Christ. Ultimately, everybody should believe in him. Still, what's the difference? you should do what the others do. Let the truth triumph! And let defeated Perun weep. All in all, the above supports my thoughts. In society, in human relations—like in physics—there are certain laws of strain—magnetism and repulsion—and, being in the force field of the whole society, you, like an individual, cannot resist it and have to obey and follow it. Or find yourself the other society—the one where you're going to be more comfortable. It's impossible that everybody around you is charged positively, and only you are charged negatively. The society and its force lines will simply push you out. If you live in a society, be like everyone else. Or leave. These are not human laws, but rules of nature. Social laws. The objective reality which is given to us in the feelings. If you don't want to go, you will be ousted. Because then, everybody else is uncomfortable around you. You should go to the likes of you; you should go to your pack."

Vasl to Igor N: "So, you began with the fact that only the weak create the packs, and finished that we're all members of the pack. Our pack. One or another. You gave a bad ending to a good start. Congratulations!"

Igor N: "Of course, we're all weak. We're ordinary humans. And why is it surprising? Do you think that there are only geniuses and Titans here, on this forum? Prometheuses, who can only fight the gods, though, without any success."

SATAN: "The necessity of struggle is not determined by the chances of success. Nor by their absence."

IgorN to SATAN: "Wow! By what, then?"

SATAN: "If you ask that, then there's no point in answering."

XYZ: "How can one fight God? For God is almighty and all0knowing, right?"

SATAN: "If God is all-knowing, then why is he constantly asking Adam in Paradise, 'Where are you? Have you eaten of the tree, etc.?' Isn't he supposed to know all that? And why does he ask Moses to mark the houses of the Israelites? 'Then they are to take some of the blood and put it on the sides and tops of the doorframes of the houses; the blood will be a sign for you on the houses where you are, and when I see the blood, I will pass over you. No destructive plague will touch you when I strike Egypt.' Exodus. Why would an all-knowing creature need any additional information, a sign? A simple marking on the doorframes. If he's all-powerful, why did he need the whole six days for the creation of the world and not a single moment? And then he needed time for rest. 'So on the seventh day, he rested from all his work.' Genesis.

"Need of rest means the loss of strength. So, on the seventh day, God was weaker than on the first one, right? Therefore, he's not all-powerful. Omnipotence is absolute. It cannot be stronger or weaker. And the most important thing— what was God scared of, when he said, 'The man has now become like one of us, knowing good and evil. He must not be allowed to reach out his hand and take also from the tree of life and eat, and live forever?' Genesis. How can an all-powerful and all-knowing creature be scared of anything? There can't be anything all-powerful in the world where time exists. For time is development. Dynamics!

"And an all-powerful creature is a thing in itself. It's out of the time. Out of the world. It doesn't have any goals nor can it have any. For all his goals are realized at once, in the moment of their appearance. Otherwise, it wouldn't be all-powerful. There are no dynamics in the world of the all-powerful creature. Its world is static. The world is adjusted for that creature once and for all, in the most optimal way. For it's all-powerful. If there's any process, a struggle—then the power has its limits. 'And there was a great battle in heaven, Michael and his angels fought with the dragon, and the dragon fought and his angels: And they prevailed not.' Apocalypse. Battle. Fought. Yeah, God was stronger and more powerful than the Dragon—that's it! He was a little more powerful. But only at that moment. The final result of the struggle is not clear. It's unpredictable.

"One more thing. If God is all-powerful, so he created Dragon, Devil, and Satan, right? Or is the Dragon a mistake? So, God can make mistakes, right? And what is the freedom of will? Independent of an all-knowing God? Is it a process which he cannot control?

Igor N: Well…curious… strange questions. What's with your name? 'SATAN'? Is it somehow connected to the Satan?"

XYZ: "'And there was given to him a mouth speaking great things, and blasphemies'."

Igor N: Oh! Apocalypse. Antichrist. 'He that hath understanding, let him count the number of the beast. For it is the number of a man: and the number of him is six hundred sixty-six. Here is wisdom'. Is it right?"

XYZ: "Almost. 666. Well… Actually, numbers are an interesting thing. Seven days of a week, seven notes, seven colors of rainbow."

Igor N: "Seven angels of Apocalypse, pouring seven vials of God's wrath upon the Earth."

XYZ: "Right. Seven is a mysterious number. However, three and six are even better. Holy trinity. THREE sixes. Cursed 666! Probably, it's the most mysterious and mystic number! A lot of people have tried to solve it. Count. But—'here is wisdom'. By the way, if the number of the Beast exists—the number of Apocalypse, of the world's end, of the future—then logic suggests that there should be a number of the present."

IgorN to XYZ: "What present?"

XYZ: "Well, of present time. The one that is in action now, while the kingdom of the beast is not yet come. The intermediate one. Between Christ and Antichrist. The number which has to contain everything. Present and future. 'Wisdom!' And with the coming of the kingdom of the beast, it will somehow turn into the number of the beast—666."

IgorN to XYZ: "Well! There you go! That is too much! Really! 'Number of present'! And what's this number, eh? Maybe you know it, if you're so smart?"

XYZ: "How can I know it?"

SATAN" "366"

XYZ to SATAN: "Why 366?? Why is this number so remarkable?"

SATAN: "Oh, oh, oh! 366 is a very interesting number! A three and two sixes—366 days in the leap year, which is traditionally regarded as unlucky—and Antichrist has to appear in the world, according to the prophecies. The Beast, according to the Apocalypse; 36.6 is a temperature of a human body. Body of the Son of Men, Christ and Antichrist. Further on. 'This is the genealogy of Jesus the Messiah the son of David, the son of Abraham. Thus there were fourteen generations in all from Abraham to David, fourteen from David to the exile to Babylon, and fourteen from the exile to the Messiah." Gospel of Matthew. So, 14x3 makes 42 generations. 36+6. And, finally, 42 months is 36+6."

XYZ: "What about '42 months'?"

SATAN" ""And power was given unto him to continue forty and two months'. Apocalypse. The kingdom of the Beast. Apart from that, according to the Apocalypse, the heathens will be violating the sacred city for 42 months, too. A woman, 'clothed with the sun, with the moon under her feet, and on her head a crown of twelve stars', after the birth of 'a male child, destined to rule all the nations with an iron rod', 'could fly to her place in the desert, where, far from the serpent, she was taken care of for a year, two years, and a half-year'. And 1,260 days are 42 months. The authors of the Apocalypse simply intentionally divide the devilish and the divine. The devilish is measured in months, and the divine in days, though the real time is the same. Same 42 months—36+6. And, finally, the two prophets of the Apocalypse, who will be slain by the Beast of the abyss, which 'they that dwell upon the earth shall rejoice over them because these two prophets tormented them that dwelt on the earth', who will come back to life in three-and-a-half days—they divined 1,260 days, too. 42 months—36+6."

XYZ to SATAN: By the way, why in three-and-a-half days? What's that time? Neither three, nor four—but three-and-a-half?"

SATAN: "42 months is three-and-a-half years. Accordingly, they will come back to life in three-and-a-half days."

Igor N: "Curious! Very curious! A year of life for a day of death. By the way, Christ was raised to life in about three days like he divined—'that he must go to Jerusalem that he must be killed and on the third day be raised to life'. Gospel of Matthew. And so it was. He died on Friday and was raised to life on Monday And he was preaching, it seems, for three years. 'Now Jesus himself was about thirty years old when he began his ministry'. Gospel of Matthew. And, as you know, he was crucified at the age of 33. Umph! The same numbers. A year of life for a day of death. It's interesting, indeed."

SATAN: "It's even more interesting that Christ had to follow and obey these numbers. Son of God! It seemed that he simply couldn't leave hell before that. That's regarding the omnipotence of God."

IgorN to SATAN: "What are you pointing at?"

XYZ to SATAN: "Wait a second! Let's get back to numbers. Well, how does 366 turn into 666?"

SATAN: "The first digit is a number of the Son."

Pat: "What son?"

XYZ: "Well, he talked about Christ, I think. God's Son. And other two?

SATAN: "The Holy Spirit and the Father."

XYZ to SATAN: "And why is three a number of the Son?"

SATAN: "For God is tripersonal. The symbol of the trinity."

Pat to SATAN: "And why are the Father's and the Holy Spirit's number six? They should have three, as well, shouldn't they?"

SATAN: "You're forgetting Satan."

XYZ to SATAN: "Hold on, hold on! What does Satan have to do with it?"

SATAN: "He rules the world, too. Christ calls him 'Prince of peace'. Gospel of John. And he is tri-personal, too."

XYZ to SATAN: "Why is that?"

SATAN: "It's written so in the Apocalypse. Dragon, Beast, and False Prophet. Father, Son, and Holy Spirit. The three of them are immortal, and so they will be 'cast into the lake of fire and brimstone, and shall be tormented day and night forever and ever'. Cast by the merciful and forgiving God."

Verochka: "Hey, guys, stop blaspheming! What are you talking about today, eh? Let's talk about something else."

XYZ: "Get lost, hen! Stay out of men's conversations! It's none of your business. Read a women's magazine about the jam rags. This stuff is not for you! Hey, SATAN! Well, let it be so. Dragon, Beast, and False Prophet—a trinity, too. Satan rules the world and is triune, as well. So what? Still, why do the Father and the Spirit have six and the Son three?"

SATAN: "Because Antichrist, Lucifer's Son, hasn't yet come into the world. Thus, the Son's number is a number of Christ only. God's Son. Three. Trinity. And the Father and the Spirit are two threes. Two trinities. God and Devil. When Antichrist comes into the world, the circle will close. The Son's number will double up. The three will become the six. Son—Spirit—Father. 6—6—6. Three sixes."

Pat: "Well, well! I've never heard anything like this!"

XYZ to SATAN: "And what then? Armageddon? The battle of good and evil? The end of the world?"

SATAN: "The battle of old and new. The end of the old world and the birth of the new one."

XYZ to SATAN: "What new one?'

SATAN: "That depends on men. Either the old wins, the time stops, and the slaves of God forever resound praises to their master under the guidance of twenty-four elders in white robes, or..."

XYZ to SATAN: "Or?"

SATAN: "Or slavery to God falls, men become free, and turn into gods, like it was said by the Serpent in the Genesis when he offered Eve a taste of the fruit of the Tree of Knowledge. That's what God was scared of."

XYZ to SATAN: "And then? What then? What shall I, a weak man, do with this freedom? From whom shall I seek comfort? Eh, SATAN?"

IgorN to XYZ: "If you ask that, there's no point in answering."

XYZ: "SATAN?"

XYZ :"SATAN?"

XYZ: "Hey, SATAN??:

Verochka: "Come on, guys, stop it! Let's talk about something cheerful!"

And Lucifer was asked by His Son:

—Am I Antichrist? The beast from the abyss? Has the circle closed?

And Lucifer answered His Son:

—Not yet. Thou hath to decide Yourself.

LUCIFER'S SON. DAY 17.

And the seventeenth day came.

And Lucifer said:

—A man can always remain a man. Whatev'r happens. He can remain free. Freedom is an internal state. Condition.

LETTER

"There is an abasement because of glory;
and there is that lifteth up his head from a low estate."
Wisdom of Jesus,
The Son of Sirach.

"If you falter in a time of trouble
How small is your strength."
Book of Proverbs.

Hi, Seriy!

I received your letter; thank you for writing to me. Yeah, interesting stuff is going on outside. Though, what interesting things can be there, anyway? Everything's the same… endless stir and crumby sessions. It's all bullshit, empty crap. Oh, right! Pardon me.

Actually, my friend, I wanted to say that your so-called pastime isn't worth detailed description, believe me. For it's all the same—resorts and presentations, saloons and chicks. Money, money, money… Boredom.

Or, shall we switch to French? That is more elegant. For Russian is somehow uncouth, don't you think? En general, mon ami, je voudrais dire…

Alright, relax! Forget it. I'm just kidding. I have an interesting sense of humor now—a prison one. For I'm in prison, after all. In close fucking custody. So, it drives me mad. It carries me away. Well, psychological problems—you should understand that. Nervous breakdown. Oh! It's a pity I don't have *sal ammoniac* at hand. You know, I've been thinking about lots of things during this year. I probably haven't done this much thinking my whole life! Of course—for here, I've got a lot of time, and outside, I was always busy. Fucking business. I was always busy as a bee. I was running like a pony in a circus—with blindfolded eyes, in circles. The whip is cracking, and the horses are running. Where? What for? Only God knows. They're running, like everyone. The tamer knows! All of them are running; they don't have time to think."Here we go! Wheel in a wheel. And I'll get to the final point." So I got there, to the final point! Eh-heh-heh.

Well, anyway, let's not talk about that. Why should I bother you with this crap? You have problems of your own. Forget it! We shall not talk about sad things. Enough grieving! Enough of poetry! Now we'll have only the prose. Frankly speaking, it's not that bad in prison—at any rate, as it goes for me. I mean it! Sometimes I even like it. Occasionally, of course. Well, "like" may be too a strong word—but, in any case, I'm quite comfortable here. Why not? I'm fed, dressed, and booted. I have a roof over my head. And no troubles. So, I have an opportunity to think; I have a lot of thoughts. By the way, sometimes they are very strange—about things to which you do not pay attention outside with all this fucking fuss. Probably, that's the way of life. Merciful and wise. Life prevents you from thinking too much outside. So you can spend your whole life without thinking. And you have to get to prison to start thinking; you have to get into extreme conditions.

Well, what was I saying? Oh, right! There you go. Do you know what comparison I've been thinking about? A figured one. How should I represent it? Express it?

Well, I think that human life is similar to ascending the summit. A storm! And the moment of the ascent of the summit? Triumph! The peak of the ascending is, at the same time, the beginning of the descending, of the end. And the more successful and stronger a man was, the faster he reached the summit and got to the very peak, then the faster he started rolling downhill. Freaking dialectics! The law of the negation of negation. Is it the right scientific name for it? Well, it doesn't matter. What is the sense of our life? What is its goal? Well, not an esoteric and philosophical one, but an earthbound goal? The goal of life of any normal man is, first of all, material benefits, whatever the appearances. First, way of life—and then everything else. First, one should solve all domestic problems and then indulge in mental ones when there's time. Social being determines consciousness. That's what they taught us at school. Creating the most comfortable and profitable conditions for you and your family; adjusting and adapting the surrounding world to yourself—that's what every man aspires to, and he's acting according to his perception of happiness. Certainly! And what else could it be? A home—full cup, the children are studying in prestigious colleges, etc. That is happiness for him.

And if a man is successful and lucky enough, then everything ends for him by the time he's thirty or forty. He has achieved it. He's caught the happiness and put it in a cage. Here it is—look and be glad! The world is adjusted to you. The system is closed. Home, wife, children—you've got everything. Everything!

And what then? What exactly? Nothing. Surely, you can attend to the mental problems—you've got means for that—but the scary thing is that there are no problems! And how could there be? You never had time to solve the mental problems; you were busy with the domestic ones! You were catching the happiness. And you caught it; you got what you wanted. The problems are formed by the needs, and what "needs" can you have? Watching a poor action movie on TV—even that is too difficult for you. It's better to hang out with chicks. So, you got to a dead end. Swamp, stagnation, decay. Degradation. Boredom! Boredom! Boredom! Boredom! Hellish, deadly, unbearable. Every next day is as similar to the previous one as two peas.

You don't want anything, and there's nothing to wish for; you got everything, you achieved and received everything in full. The business is working, the wheels are rolling, and the money is flowing. Cook is cooking, maid is cleaning, guard is guarding. Everybody's at work, everybody's on the alert—only you are the fifth wheel! Everything's boiling around you, but you're like the center of a typhoon, dead calm. Everybody's busy, and you're the only one who's not! The house is clean, everything's washed and ironed, dinner is served on time. Your everyday life is adjusted like a Swiss watch.

Well, what next? What? What are you living for? Only to have dinner on time in a clean apartment? After that, there will be nothing. Nothing at all. Nothing's happening. The main problem is that there are no problems. At all! Life is a damned wretch, and it has tricked you again. It seems that you've always won and achieved what you wanted—you were so strong, bold, and lucky—however, it came to pass that you are on a roadside. It went forward, laughing—young and careless—and you kept sitting in embarrassment, without understanding how it happened and what evil sorcery did it.

With a passion of youth and too much strength, you rushed to storm the summit, but it appeared to be not so high. There! And you're already on it. You came at life furiously, burning with desire to take, to grab your part, to snatch it out of life's hands, and, suddenly, you found out that, as a matter of fact, it doesn't resist that much. "Quite, monsieur! Calm down. What would you want, anyway?"

"This! This! This! And this!"

"Alright, alright! Here you go. Would that be all?"

"Yeah, all…"

"Great! Farewell. All the best."

A cellmate told me that he had been living abroad for some time, somewhere in Europe. He had a business there—it doesn't matter. That's not important. He said that, after two or three months, you start to go nuts. You have nothing to do at all. Well, if you don't have money or something else—it's alright. It's good. You're doing something, and time flows. But if there are no problems—that's it! FUBAR. You wake up in the morning, and you don't know what to do. You can go up the wall with boredom!

I tell my wife, "Let's go to Budapest?"

"Alright!"

It's not so far—a couple of hours on the train. Well, we're there, and I'm calling my friends.

"What are you up to?"

"Nothing."

"Wait for us!"

We buy stuff and go to our friends. We stay there for several days and then go back. Well, we were fooling around with boredom. The same with us. We're fooling around with boredom. We're contriving various entertainments, each in his own way. And what entertainments can a man have if he can't do anything except making money? The one who hasn't read a single book during all his life? (Like the most part of my cellmates, and they were very wealthy in the past.) What can he contrive? Well, a summary. Conclusion.

If a man is successful in life, then he adjusts the surrounding world to him by the time he's thirty or forty. He creates a closed, autonomous system. He cocoons. His circle of acquaintances is strictly determined, his interests are stable, and his everyday life is adjusted in detail. That's it! There are no goals left. He's got everything. Besides, the luckier and wealthier he is, the better he does all that—the closer his system is, the more reliable and impenetrable his cocoon is.

Well, if, say, he has to go to work, that's alright. That's not very bad. That's a ray of life, a breath of fresh air. But if he's a master, a boss, and he's got his own business, that's it! The end. Finish. Epic fail. He's too lazy to go to work, and, actually, there's no need of doing it; everything is functioning very well without him. He'd just be in the way. And he's got nothing to do. He can't do anything else in life, and it's too late to learn. What can a man learn at 40? And what for? He's got money. It's nonsense. Fooling around, playing. He's too well off, and he starts buying football clubs and collecting black squares. Well, right! Nature doesn't like vacuum. It has to be filled, and you have to occupy yourself. With some fuss. You have to fling yourself into the fuss and create a life, an image of life, if not a real one—appearance, phantom, illusion. A pseudo-life, a homuncule.

It's impossible to artificially create a real, authentic life. Life within a cocoon is anabiosis—eternal sleep, a half-life. You need some external events in order to wake up. Uncontrolled processes—only they can give birth to something new, something real. Something that makes the sense of life. Cream of life. Life contains troubles, too. And there can be no troubles in an artificially created world, in a cocoon. It's always warm and comfortable there. No one would invite disaster sincerely, right? If a man really doesn't want to do something, he would certainly never do it. They say you can make yourself do something. That's not true! You can do it for the sake of someone. So, you do want it deep inside—well, indirectly, in a roundabout way.

For example, you don't want to get up early in the morning and go fishing, but you have to, because you want to go fishing. So you make yourself win over the laziness. But, say, you want badly to watch the final of Champions League—you've been waiting for it a whole month—and here your mother-in-law comes on an unexpected visit and she wants to watch yet another idiotic, endless show, "Poor Douche." That is the simplest example of the uncontrolled external influence which you would gladly delete, if you could. For you really don't want that! And there are no mothers-in-law and TV shows in your artificially created and adjusted world. If push comes to shove, you're going to buy her a TV.

Why am I spelling this out? Because prison, incredible as it may seem, is the only real chance for a man of our level and circle, in his middle years, to come back to life, to resurrect, to wake up from slumber. To tear the cocoon, to burn the old life, and to build the new one on it. Starting everything anew, plunging into the struggle, feeling its taste, and living a real, authentic, full-blooded, and unlabored life. In prison, there's always something happening to you, some external events which do not depend on you and which you cannot control—that which you forgot in real life. Shakedowns, reshuffles, switch of cellmates, their problems and so on and so forth. As a matter of fact, these events are mostly unwanted and unpleasant, but that's not so important. Above all, you're in the middle of the whirlpool of life, in the thick of things; you're constantly struck with a gust of new information, and you're the one to decide how you're going to use it—whether you can reconsider and process it, whether it does good or bad, whether you eventually become better or worse. The most important thing is that this information exists. Here we are!

They say for a reason that the weak are ruined by the troubles, and the strong are hardened. The weak become weaker, and the strong become stronger. As usual. At any rate, this, if truth be told, is much better that the swamp outside, the one from which you can't get out on your own. As it's impossible to pull yourself out by your hair. Only Baron Munchausen could do that well. And the others need help from outside. Someone has to grab you by the hair.

For example, cellmates here are constantly switching. By the way, as a rule, it happens unexpectedly and unpredictably, when you don't expect it at all. A sudden command—"Name, grab your stuff! Out!" and that's it—a transfer to another camera or even to another jail. There was a man, and he's no more. And you don't know if you're gonna see him in this life. Most likely, you aren't. But you've been living with this man for a couple of months in one cell, sleeping on a bed (bunk) near him, eating at one table, and you know him as well as you know yourself.

Of course, it's unpleasant; it's a real shock—for him, for you, and for everyone else. You don't want to part, as you've become used to each other. And you don't know who's gonna take his place. Maybe a fucking moron, and he's gonna ruin the old way of your simple cell life. He's gonna drink your blood. Well, that's when someone's being taken from the cell. And if you're transferred, that's blue murder! Shit. Where do they transfer me? What kind of people are there? You may be sent to some awful place with scums!

Well, it's an important event. Shock. For you and for your cellblock. And it's an event from which you cannot get anything good. And if it were up to you, you certainly wouldn't go anywhere and wouldn't transfer anyone from your cell. You get used to people eventually, even if you had some disagreements. And what are the new ones? And, actually, you have to get used to them. Well, it's better to leave it as it is. It's more comfortable. But no one asks your permission. And that's a distinctive and essential peculiarity of prison. You can't do anything; everything goes on beyond your will. The decisions are being made for you. And, strange as it may seem, it's a good thing eventually.

Looking back, I see that I've gotten acquainted with a lot of people and learned a lot during this year. And, if I had lived in the same cell all that time and stewed in our own juices with the same individuals (and it would have been so, if I'd had my way! and any of us would have wished that if you had asked them), what would have been then? The same swamp and stagnation, the same as outside. A closed system, a small world. Degeneration, the absence of fresh blood. In order to create something new, you must destroy the old. And it's always painful. That's why you don't have the guts for that at the beginning. Therefore, it's great, wonderful, when others do it for you. For it's necessary. Otherwise, it's a no-go!

All right, I've probably told you too much. I must have bored you with this primitive philosophy. Right—hold on! I've saved the most interesting part for the end, the most piquant part. A surprise, a little surprise. You know, I have a very interesting thought. It just came to me. Imagine a hypothetical prison, an unusual one—let's say, an experimental prison. A cell for two: man and woman. They are constantly switched, like in a regular prison.

Just imagine—you're in a cell with a woman. What would your relations be? Loosely speaking, she's not obliged to sleep with you, and you can't make her do it by force; it's a prison. The guards will interfere—lock-up and so on. However, it's quite obvious that, after a while, you'll have everything figured with her in a natural way. For both of you are companions in misfortune; you're in the same boat, you need comfort. And, actually, life's gonna take the cost.

Nature's gonna do it! But, whatever you have, whatever wonderful and fair relations you build, however passionately and ardently you get used to each other, eventually you're going to be separated. Sooner or later. "Name! Grab your stuff!" That's all of your prison love. And no one knows when it's going to happen, neither you nor her. But it just adds flavor to your relationship, additional passion. It could be in a moment. Or in a month. Or in three months. Nothing is clear. Every moment is the last one.

You would never leave her in real life; you like her, you've fallen head over heels in love with her. She's your fate, but it's prison. No one asks your permission, and nothing depends on you. It's your doom, merciless and unavoidable. Such an unexpected breakup is dramatic for both of you, a Shakespearean tragedy; but, an hour or two later, you are joined by a new female companion, and everything is repeated from the beginning. The same scenario: acquaintance—intimacy—relationship - breakup.

And this forced changing of partners—not even sexual ones; it doesn't have to do anything with sex—is the looked-for, in the full sense of the word, ideal relationship between the different sexes, between man and woman. Well, at any rate, from the man's point of view. There's no routine, no addiction, no monotony; this is an elusive newness and dynamic which everyone's seeking and which is inaccessible and always slips away outside, under the usual conditions. It always seeps through the fingers. It disappears without a trace, like water, or sand, and you can't hold it. For the thing is that nothing depends on you at all. You're being made happy against your will, whether you want it or not.

Such a prison cannot be artificially created, like an attraction, a game, an entertainment, or a paid show. For, in this case, you can always interfere; you always have this possibility, and you know it deep inside. However elaborately it is created and organized, if you meet your Juliet, you can always tell the "guards," "That's it! Game over! This time, no jokes and no games! I want her to stay with me. I pay for this comedy, so do what I say." Well, at the very least, you can find her after the game. Though, the very thought that these Juliets are just whores with a salary… So, it's a poor fake, a stand-in, an imitation—nothing more! It's all unreal. You have to pay a real price for something that is real; you have to pay with your life, with your blood, with your fate—money won't help you here.

In other words, life teases, fools, and tricks you and laughs in your face. You think, "here is an icon, the bluebird of happiness, a magic recipe of happiness which everyone's seeking." Well, now you know it. Go for it! Bake your holiday cake. Well, come on! But here, you find out that it's impossible to bake it. In order to have a nice crust, you have to put it on a free fire; you have to hurl your own life into it, and you don't even know the result for sure. Not that you're gonna receive it. It's impossible to artificially create such a prison; that's not it, it's not worth the trouble, and no one would go to a real one for this. Moreover, there are no such prisons. It's just a game of imagination, a result of my idle fantasies.

There we have it! That's it. Well, there's no happiness in life at all, neither in jail nor outside—just boredom. I'd like to get to such a prison, eh? Right? Would you mind it? Well, I have to finish. I hope that you're going to like my ideas or, at least, to find them amusing. No? Are they not amusing? All right—waiting for your answer.

With kind regards, Frol.

P.S. You asked me if I regret anything. No. Nothing at all. Do not regret anything ever. There's no reason for looking behind. There's nothing except for ruins and dead memories. There's nothing alive. Why should it matter, what was before? It's the past, and it's dead. And today, we have the present. Every day, life starts anew. And that's great! Ahead! Hail to morning!

P.P.S. One more thing—most of the people just don't imagine how close jail is. They think that it's somewhere there, in another world, on another planet. And it's here at hand, around the corner. A neighbor made a tip-off, or you got yourself in silly trouble on the street… A man thinks that he's got stable floor under his feet, but it's no more than thin sticks. And under them is abyss, above which he's walking carelessly. Walking above the abyss… We are all the walkers above the abyss…

And Lucifer was asked by His Son:

—According to the New Testament, Christ began his ministry at the age of thirty. And before that, he was an ordinary man living an ordinary life. So, where are his friends of childhood and youth?

And Lucifer answered to His Son:

—He never had any. What friends can a man have if he easily abandoned his own mother and brothers, only to astound a crowd? To make an impression.

"While Jesus was still talking to the crowd, his mother and brothers stood outside, wanting to speak to him. Someone told him, "Your mother and brothers are standing outside, wanting to speak to you."

He replied to him, "Who is my mother, and who are my brothers?" Pointing to his disciples, he said, "Here are my mother and my brothers. For whoever does the will of my Father in heaven is my brother and sister and mother."

Gospel of Matthew.

LUCIFER'S SON. DAY 18.

And the eighteenth day came. And Lucifer said:

—Chinks dost not make a man happy. It makes him free.

MONEY

"Rich and poor have this in common:
The Lord is the Maker of them all."
Book of Proverbs.

"Gold hath been the ruin of many,
and their destruction was present."
Wisdom of Jesus the Son
of Sirach.

"Come on in!"

A huge guard stepped aside reluctantly, staring dubiously at a plain and poorly dressed man. Gorbalyuk entered with hesitation, looking around him shyly. *Well! The enormous hall is very impressive—marble, carpets, mirrors, plants everywhere, strange sculptures, and there is a fountain bubbling. Well!*

"This way, please!"

Another guard opened a door before him.

"Hi, Gorbal!" a plumpish balding man with a face often seen in numerous newspapers stepped cheerfully towards him and reached his hand. Zaychenko Petr Vasilevich was a former fellow student and a sworn friend. Now he was a billionaire, a business magnate, owner of factories, palaces, ships. Gorbalyuk hadn't seen him since the institute, so it happened—but, yesterday, he had appeared himself; he had called and offered to meet for no obvious reason.

"We'll have a drink and talk like in old times. Let's reminisce youth. Tomorrow's good?"

Of course, it was good. You bet—meeting with Zaychenko himself! Gorbalyuk was so excited that he even couldn't sleep that night at all; he tossed and turned until morning. He was expecting a lot from this meeting. He didn't know what exactly, but he was sure that something would change in his life, by all means. For Zaychik—the institute nickname of Zaychenko—had only to move his finger in order to!.. Having his possibilities and money! *He didn't call me for no reason, right?* He had found Gorbalyuk and had found time for a meeting. He probably had a very tight schedule, for a year to come. And every minute is worth a thousand dollars. A grand or maybe even more.

However, even a thousand dollars per minute was a huge sum of money for Gorbalyuk. Empyreal. Astronomical, it was like infinity, something like the speed of light. So, it didn't matter whether it was more or no more. Infinity is infinity.

"Hi, Petya!" Gorbalyuk answered Zaychenko's greeting with a halt. He almost said "Zaychik," as he used to, but he didn't have the heart to do it. He couldn't get his tongue around it. *He's no Zaychik now—he's Zaychenko. He's a respectable man and a very important one. He meets with the president in the Kremlin and appears on TV. Zaychik!* It was hard enough to call him Petya. He forced himself to do it. He just felt intuitively that it was right, and they didn't need any formalities. It would have been awkward. It wouldn't be the right tone; it would be unpleasant for Zaychenko himself. They were institute friends, after all, close ones. It appeared that Zaychenko had invited him as a friend, an old friend. He just wanted to talk to him in private, recall their common friends and pick them to pieces while having a drink. *And where's that one? Well! And this?" Freaking nostalgia. Idle curiosity. We're all made of flesh and blood, after all. Tycoons or no tycoons... Well, we'll see.*

"Well! You look good, by the way. Have a seat," Zaychenko pointed to one of the two massive carved chairs and sat on the other one. Now they were sitting opposite to each other behind a luxurious table, generously served and laden, which was groaning with food and drinks. *Viands,* Gorbalyuk suddenly thought. Now it was the most appropriate word. Caviar, all kinds of fish, cheese and wurst, salted and smoked meat—all in all, a wealth of fruits of the earth. Cognacs and vodkas—sure thing, as it should be.

"Well, let's drink to the meeting. Let's get cracking!" Zaychenko took a bottle with transparent liquid from the table—it appeared to be vodka—took off ("cracked") its head and filled the glasses.

Gorbalyuk snorted to himself, looking at these plain manipulations. He knew them very well. It seemed that the time went back, and in front of him there was sitting his old and loyal pal Petya Zaychenko, aka Zaychik. And they're warming up with vodka or porto, waiting for chicks who should be here any minute. If, of course, they don't give the string—and that happened a lot. Well! It was a good time. And where are those chicks now? Where are vodka and porto, Kavkaz and Agdam? They sank into oblivion. They went into the depths of hell, together with that life. Now even the vodka is different, let alone the chicks. They disappeared as a kind. It's good that vodka remained.

Gorbalyuk looked carefully at the dim glass bottle. Or was it crystal? You never know; who knows what to expect from these tycoons? What if they are loath to drink from glass bottles? It doesn't befit them. *No, it's probably made of glass, an ordinary Absolut, it seems. Yeah, we tasted that, we drank that. We've been there—not that often, but still. So, the billionaires drink it, too, don't they? It's a pity. I'm ashamed to say, I hoped to try a Billionaire's Special, Tycoon's—a million bucks per bottle. I opened my mouth too wide. It's a pity it didn't work out again. Well, alright! Absolut isn't bad. Moreover, it's probably original, not fake—a real one. I suppose it was delivered straight from Sweden on a charter flight.*

"Well?" Zaychenko reached his glass to clink. Gorbalyuk took his, looking at the table at the same time, trying to find an appropriate chaser. The choice was huge.

Well, I'm like a lion seeing a troop of antelopes, thought Gorbalyuk. *Well, what's the difference, actually? That fish would be okay for a start.* The vodka was icy cold. Gorbalyuk didn't even feel its taste. No, he did; it was great!

"Have a bite! Come on!" told him Zaychenko, chewing already. "Don't be shy."

"I'm not shy at all," muttered Gorbalyuk, filling his plate with different stuff. "Why not? I have to try it. When shall I have another opportunity to eat with a billionaire?"

"Well, let's have a second one!" It turned out that Zaychenko managed to fill the glasses again.

"Hey, wait a bit," Gorbalyuk almost shouted like he used to but bit his tongue in time. Alas! They were no longer young, cheerful, and careless students who were struggling from stipend to stipend. And it was no careless twenty-year-old Zaychik sitting in front of him. The short-lived illusion disappeared. Gorbalyuk was uncomfortable again in his old cheap suit. He remembered what he was and what his friend was—and who was calling the shots and what this show of plainness and the over-familiarity were worth. *Now the master is in a good mood, so he's a plain fellow, as easy as an old Tilly. And if he becomes sad in a moment, he grieves and says, for example, 'Dance a trepak for me, man!' And you're gonna dance like one o'clock! There's no way out. Yeah, you are! And what did you come here for, if not for dancing the trepak? What if he likes me?"*

Gorbalyuk swallowed his vodka and put something into his mouth without looking. *I shouldn't have fucking come here," he thought bitterly. "What a life, fucking life. Wife, children. Ah-ah!* He wanted to fill the glasses for the third time himself and even started to, but he didn't have the courage. He was sitting, despising himself, but couldn't take the bottle without permission.

"Well, how are people living?" asked Zaychenko meanwhile, idly. It seemed that he didn't bite up the third glass. He simply drank something from a wineglass—juice, maybe—and that's it. "Do you stay in contact with anyone?"

Gorbalyuk started to tell his story obediently. Actually, there wasn't much to tell. Everybody had the same plain, gray, and ordinary lives of plain, gray, and ordinary men. Work—wife—children. That's the whole life. Misery. Hard labor. Zaychenko was the only one of them who achieved something. And it wasn't something; against the background of his phenomenal and fantastic achievements, the results of the others were rather poor. And, frankly speaking, there were no special results. All of the girls got married straightaway, and the guys... "Well," Gorbalyuk said, continuing with his story. "Val is still working at the institute with their department; Azarkina got divorced for the second time,"

Zaychenko was listening absently, yessing lazily. "What if we made a poll of our batch? Well, who's going to achieve the most? No one would bet on Zaychenko! Never! Well, same with me. We were obvious outsiders, castaways, exiles—potential drunkards and, according to the others, burnt-out guys. Worthless and without prospects—all in all, sure losers.

"And what's the result? Where are all those winners, those young and brilliant talents who were so promising? Where are those averins-gusarovs? The one went on the bottle, and the other's working in a research institute for a dab of money. And they were really talented, especially Gusarov. I remember winning my diploma from him in poker. It was an epic battle—four of kings against a royal flush! He asked for trouble himself. Tough luck!"

Gorbalyuk felt that he was a bit drunk. His tongue began tripping, and his mind was racing As a matter of fact, he felt somehow different—better. He felt relaxed; he was merry. Even his shyness was gone. "Listen, Petya, let's drink from the wineglasses!" he offered in a drunk excitement, halting his endless and boring story. "These small glasses are no good with such food."

"Why not?" agreed Zaychenko at once. "Let's take these," he picked up a glass from the long line of various glasses. Gorbalyuk took some time to find the same at his side and moved it to Zaychenko. He filled them with vodka at once, both to the brink. There was a very interesting word in Dal's dictionary for that. They were laughing a lot when they read it, but then it turned out that it was used only with fill materials or liquids, but they didn't care. The word was still funny. "Well, let's go! What's the toast?"

"To everything good. Let everything be well with us!"

"Come on!"

They drank. Gorbalyuk screwed up his face and started eyeing the table. What haven't I tried yet? Oh, that! And what's this?"

"Should I tell them to serve the hot appetizers?" asked Zaychenko with full mouth.

"It's up to you," waved Gorbalyuk. He was drunk and merry. He felt very easy. "*Well, let him be a millionaire! Or even a billionaire? Why should I care? I don't give a fuck!"*

"Listen, Zaychik," said Gorbalyuk, unexpectedly even for himself, "you're a billionaire, right? Why wouldn't you give me some money, eh? For old times' sake."

"Money?" asked Zaychenko, stopping chewing and looking at him with interest, "And how much do you need?"

"Sure, how much do you need to be happy?" Gorbalyuk remembered the immortal lines at once and even laughed at his thought and the similarity of the situation. "Well, I'm not sure," he said after a pause, continuing to laugh. "What your soul tells you. But keep in mind that I won't be able to give it back. I'm poor as a church mouse."

"Alright," said Zaychenko sharply, filling the glasses and clanging with Gorbalyuk. "Come on."

Gorbalyuk drank the full glass in a couple of sips—*Fuck, how much is here? Two hundred grams, at least*—and then drank quickly the juice that was near him. He was rather drunk. And Zaychenko was drunk, too, it appeared. He was red, and his forehead was covered with sweat.

What were we talking about? Gorbalyuk tried to remember. His thoughts were escaping him like flies on a table. *About something interesting Oh, about the money!* "Hey," he said aloud. "Well, you're a billionaire. You're on TV, you're hanging out in the Kremlin and such fucking shit—a real fucking tycoon. So, what's it like to be a billionaire, having so much money? Everything's in your power—what you see around you. Chicks, cool cars… Do you remember how we picked up chicks in a tram?" he started laughing again, being drunk. "And how you were mad, because they gave us a runaround? Things are different with them now, right? If you want a top-model, you just beckon her, don't you?"

"No runarounds now," smiled Zaychenko thoughtfully and somehow sadly, "but I don't want to beckon them anymore. I don't fucking need them! Well, it's bad timing, as usual."

"Why is that?" wondered Gorbalyuk. "No boner?"

"That's about you, moron!" Zaychenko pretended to be insulted. "I've got a very nice boner, as good as ever!"

"So, what's the matter? What's the problem? If not a boner…"

"What do you mean?"

"I mean the top models!"

"Oh, god! Forget about them," shouted Zaychenko discontentedly. "They're all the same! 'I need money'—that's what it is. They're like usual stuff, but a bit more expensive."

"Well, right," Gorbalyuk was even more surprised. "Sure! What were you expecting? Getting her with your looks or what? With your great mind? Of course, it's about money! So what? Why do you care? So, give her some, if she asks. Are you greedy? Can't you help a girl? You give to her, and she gives to you, and everything will be sorted out. Everything's going to be great; everybody's satisfied."

But I asked him to give me money, too! thought Gorbalyuk with fear, *"like everyone else. What could he be thinking about me? 'I need money.' That's all there is to our prostitute friendship. 'Usual stuff, but a bit more expensive'."*

Gorbalyuk darkened, poured some vodka, and drank it up without tasting anything. He even forgot to fill up Zaychik's glass. However, Zaychik seemed not to notice that. He tipped back in his chair and stared in front of him, fingering his empty glass. It was obvious that his thoughts were hovering somewhere far away.

"You know, Gorbal," he said slowly at last and bit his lips thoughtfully, "it's not that simple. All this money…."

"Are you having any psychological problems?" wondered Gorbalyuk greatly, looking distrustfully at the billionaire and tycoon who was well-known in the whole country. *It would never strike me!* he thought. "Because of these broads? Because they need your money and not you? Right?"

"No!" he waved with irritation. "That's nonsense! That doesn't have anything to do with it! What do you mean, 'your money and not you'? That's the same as your legs and not you. Or your arms. Money is a natural part of me, of my personality. If I didn't have it, then I would be different; there would be someone else in my place. Present me includes money, as well. Saying 'they love you as long as you have money' is the same as saying 'they love you as long as you have legs'. And when you lose them, they will love you no more. Or, didn't they cease to love you? Well, then, we can try to chop off arms. Me is me! It's not only body, head, arms, and legs, but everything that belongs to me. And, as a whole, it is my personality, which you can love or not, but only as a whole. And all the attempts to separate—I am here, money is there—is nonsense!"

"Alright! Calm down, calm down!" Gorbalyuk waved his hands apologetically. "Why are you so excited? That's a whole tirade!" However, the conversation was interesting him. "Well, all right," he said after a pause. "If you realize that very well, then what's the problem?"

"What problem are you talking about?" said Zaychenko with irritation.

"Well, you started talking about money," reminded him Gorbalyuk, "It's not that simple, all this money.' So, why are you dissatisfied?"

"Dissatisfied? Dissatisfied? I'm completely satisfied! Listen, let's have a drink," suddenly offered Zaychenko. "You already had a fucking drink, but didn't offer me one," he added with a slight reproach.

Shit! He noticed, thought Gorbalyuk discontentedly, feeling kind of shy. *I should have poured him a drink. It's not good to drink alone. It's against the code.* "Well, you were so serious and all in your thoughts," he tried to excuse himself awkwardly, and turn it into a joke "You were dealing with the universal problems, probably. No shit. Why would I bother you?"

"Universal, right!" grumbled Zaychenko, clinking. "Drink! Universal! Well, you see, Gorbal," he returned to the conversation which he had started. "Money is a good thing, but only to a certain point, as with everything in this world. It's good to be tall, because then girls will like you, but not when you're three meters tall; that's deformity. The same thing with money. It's good when you have a lot of money, but it's bad when it's too much."

"And how much is too much?" asked Gorbalyuk with idle irony. The conversation ceased to interest him. It was too abstract for him. Speculative matters. "A lot, too much!"

You should live like me, he thought with sudden jealousy, *"from paycheck to paycheck. And not that I get it on time! You should feel what it's like when you have no money to raise your children. Then you would change your tune! Well, a wealthy personality—'Money is an essential part of me.' It's not essential at all; you're just lucky, that's it. You got into stride, you were there at the right time and place, so you became rich—accidentally, as is everything in life. It's all the same with us—just luck. Pure chance, lucky or not. Well, you're lucky—attaboy! Sit quietly and be glad. Why would you pretend to be a great one? 'Titan of thought! Father of Russian democracy.' Who's watching you, anyway? Me! 'Me is me?' Exactly—you are you! Do you think I don't know you? I know you through and through. We drank tons of vodka and fucked tons of women together—chicks! You're the same as me; you're no better. But somehow I... Ah, let it go to hell! I shouldn't have come here!"*

"Billions are a bad thing," he heard Zaychik speaking, meanwhile. "Millions are all right, but billions are a bad thing. Everything's within your power; that's why you don't want it—not even for showing off, for there's no one to show off for. They're all behind you. An ordinary man has a golden dream, like buying a Mercedes S-Class. And when you are able to buy a thousand Mercedes tomorrow, it turns out that you don't fucking need them! Crashing bore."

"Well, you have serious problems!" said Gorbalyuk with clear irony, chewing a bit of tasty fish. It was good. "By the way, an ordinary man has limited dreams; it would be a used car, at best. A Mercedes S-Class is something fantastic for him. That's tales—Arabian Nights, djinn, houris, amirs. Mercedes S-Class! Well, for you to know…"

"I realize it, of course!" said Zaychenko guiltily and lowered his eyes. "As the saying goes, 'someone has everything, and someone has nothing at all'. Is it the right saying? Surely, poverty is much worse. It has its problems. But money is, believe me—you know, money is no cure at all. At any rate, it doesn't make you happy. Believe me, you know!"

"Listen, Zaychik!" Gorbalyuk interrupted his old friend unceremoniously and stared at him. "Why did you invite me here? Eh? I haven't heard from you for so many years, and now... Did you want to show off? To take delight in yourself? Did you want to tickle your vanity? Did you want to feel yourself a great man yet another time?"

"Well that's not quite it," answered Zaychenko with a strain, after a long pause. His face became like a stone, and he gritted his teeth. He clearly wasn't used to someone talking to him that way.

Fuck you! thought Gorbalyuk carelessly, observing him with a curiosity. The world around him was shaking a little. Gorbalyuk felt easy and relaxed. *You can take it! Are you a touch-me-not princess? You're not made of sugar, so you're not gonna melt! And fuck your money—you can shove it up your ass!*

"Why would I take delight in myself? I passed that period long ago. And I know my worth," Zaychenko came to his senses, and his talk became more confident. His face relaxed. "You just get tired of the hero worship when everyone agrees with you at once and hangs upon your words. I just wanted to talk to someone who's an equal, like in the old times."

"Come on," Gorbalyuk waved his hand and filled his glass to the brims with vodka. He topped it up, then he lingered a bit and filled Zaychenko's glass. He didn't mind. "Come on!" they clinked glasses and drank. "What conversation between equals can we have?" he paused to swallow a huge piece of ham and drink some juice and continued. "What am I, and what are you? You realize that very well, so don't play a fool. To talk, equals, like in old times? Right! So, maybe we should split the check? Like in old times?"

"Hey," Zaychenko raised his voice, too. It seemed that he was really mad. "What do you want of me? Why did you fucking freeze to me like a fucking cunt? I invited you kindly."

"Oh, you should say that you really made me happy; you've descended to me, oh god! You came down from your Kremlin Olympus!" Gorbalyuk couldn't stop and, actually, he didn't want to. As a matter of fact, they had had about 1.5 liters for two of them. Or maybe even more. *Which one is this bottle? We had seven hundred for one!'* he suddenly remembered verses of a famous song. *And what next? 'And then we did some porto...'* "Listen, Zaychik!" Gorbalyuk interrupted his convictions, "Do you happen to have Kavkaz?"

"What Kavkaz?" Zaychenko looked at him in surprise. He even forgot that he was mad.

"Well, like Vysotsky sings," laughed merrily Gorbalyuk. "'And then we had some porto'. Do you have Kavkaz? We could drink it."

"I don't have any Kavkaz," grumbled Zaychenko. "Drink vodka; you don't need anything else! You're good already; you've had your fill, pig!"

"You're a pig," Gorbalyuk was insulted. "You're a teetotalist..."

"Who?" Zaychenko screwed up his eyes merrily.

"Teet... teeto... well, it doesn't matter! Well, all right, I raised hell. Let it be so! But listen to what I'm going to tell you!"

"What's the point of listening to a drunkard?" muttered Zaychenko, trying to pour himself some juice. Half of it spilled on the tablecloth. Zaychenko didn't pay any attention to it; he was rather drunk too.

"Hey, listen to me!" repeated Gorbalyuk with a drunken insistence and he even tried to grab Zaychenko's hand.

"What?" Zaychenko looked up at him.

"You know how the stores give away prizes to their jubilee buyers? Well, a hundred thousandth, a millionth?"

"So what?"

"Well, you just became such a buyer in the shop of life—a jubilee moron, one hundred thousandth! You came into that shop by chancel you just wanted to buy beer to cool your coppers, and suddenly you were given a prize. Money, position in society, palaces, yachts! And now you're trying to say that it was no accident and that it wasn't by chance; you were so smart and cunning, you knew everything beforehand and decided to buy beer at that moment! And, actually, beer was just an excuse. And really! Wow! Ugh! Wow! Ugh! I hate looking at you... I'm gonna throw up! You're acting high and mighty, and you teach us how to live from TV. And what can you teach? Going to the store to buy beer? Becoming the millionth moron?"

***

Gorbalyuk remembered no more. It seemed that they kept drinking, fighting, shouting at each other, and they even almost had a fight. Or maybe not "almost;" maybe they really had a scuffle. God knows! However, he woke up at home, in his bed.

***

"Two polite young men delivered you at three in the morning," his wife told him in a soft voice. "You were drunk as a hog!" she added acidly.

"As a pig," smiled Gorbalyuk to himself, recalling Zaychik's remark from yesterday. Thank God, Gorbalyuk's wife didn't know that he had been at Zaychik's the day before. Gorbalyuk hadn't told her because he was afraid of her acting like in the tale about the Goldfish—'ask her a tub '! He just said he was meeting with an institute friend. Meanwhile, it was almost twelve. He had to go to work in the afternoon. He could only get half the day off.

Zaychik is probably sleeping like a log! thought Gorbalyuk with jealousy, freshening the nip with a second bottle of beer, which he had thoughtfully bought beforehand. *He doesn't have to go to work, right? Good for him, cursed tycoon!*

"Hey, don't drink too much!" said his wife, worried. She saw two empty bottles on the table. "You have to be at work today."

"Come on," waved Gorbalyuk, wondering if he should drink another bottle. He felt very bad after yesterday's talk. It was good that he had snubbed Zaychik and showed him who he really was and what he was worth, but what had that changed? What? They both kept their beliefs. Zaychik remained with his billions, palaces, and villas, and he...

Zaychik doesn't have to go to work! thought Gorbalyuk sadly again, opening the third bottle. *And he doesn't have a fucking headmistress.* Gorbalyuk hated his headmistress with fierce hatred in every fiber of his soul. That was the bee in his bonnet. For him, she was the incarnation of the hopelessness and injustice of his wretched and unlucky life.

And she despised him, considering him a loser, which made Gorbalyuk hate her all the more. He hated this strong, smart, well-groomed and confident woman because she read him like a book, all of him. She saw what he was indeed. Nobody—null, zero. Empty space. A small, timid, and intimidated man.

She was okay with him as an employee; that's why she tolerated him and didn't fire him, though she definitely knew his attitude towards her. But it didn't seem to bother her. Why should it matter what this insect is thinking and feeling? Or if it's feeling anything at all? It must work; that's what matters!

When drunken Gorbalyuk tumbled in the room with a silly smile on his face, the headmistress gave him an icy look and, without saying a word, went to her office.

The bitch notices everything, thought Gorbalyuk indifferently, flopping in his chair. Well, the third bottle was too much. He was drunk. Gorbalyuk shifted in his chair, not knowing what to do. What can a man do in his state? And it was still a long time until the end of the day… too long—it was two o'clock now.

He couldn't remember anything from yesterday; it was like a dream. Zaychik, palace, fountain guards…

"Excuse me, Boris Anatolievich, can I talk to you for a minute?"

Gorbalyuk looked at the door in surprise. A tall, athletic, young man with short hair was smiling at him. Gorbalyuk stood up, perplexed, and, shaking, left the room, followed by the curious looks of his colleagues.

"This is for you, from Petr Vasilievich," Zaychik's guard—Gorbalyuk knew that for sure—gave him a briefcase.

"What is it?" asked Gorbalyuk in wonder.

"I don't know," the guard was very polite. "I was asked to give that to you; that's it."

"All right, thank you," Gorbalyuk shrugged his shoulders in his thoughts and took the briefcase. It was rather heavy.

"Good-bye."

"Good-bye."

The guard turned around and left. Gorbalyuk lingered for a second and then headed to the men's room. Stepping into a stall, he clicked the lock and opened the briefcase. He saw packs of dollars wrapped in plastic. There was a short note on the top. Gorbalyuk read it automatically: *'To the millionth moron from the hundred-thousandth one!'*

He stared in amazement at the contents of the briefcase for some time and then carefully took out a pack. Actually, it was a brick wrapped in plastic. Centuries—hundred-dollar bills. He counted the bricks. There were ten of them. How much would that be? *The pack has…umm... en, no, not ten—a hundred; right, a hundred thousand! So, it makes a million, right? A million dollars?*

And what's that? What the hell is that? Stuck between the hundred-thousand-dollar blocks, there was a lonely bottle of beer, which was quite amazing. It seemed that the beer was Russian. Without a clue, Gorbalyuk took the bottle and looked at the label. 'Khamovniki'. What the hell? What does beer have to do with it? *Did he send it to me so I can freshen the nip? A bottle of Khamovniki?"*

Oh! Gorbalyuk recalled the fragments of their talk yesterday. *You just became a jubilee buyer in a shop of life; you wanted to buy a beer. The hundred-thousandth moron…* He looked at the note again. *'To the millionth moron from the hundred-thousandth one!' I get it!*

'Millions are a good thing', he remembered. *Well, I see. So, our Zaychik is entertaining himself in this way. It's a joke. Why would he care with his billions? Just another million. A million more, a million less. An old institute friend, you see. It's nice to make him happy. We've been through a lot together. Yeah, he's the one! Well, thank you, anyway! I mean it. With all my heart!*

Gorbalyuk closed the briefcase and put it on the floor. Then he took the keys out of his pocket, opened the beer, and drank the whole bottle. The world around him flashed and sparkled with bright colors. Everything was great, wonderful. "Everything's gonna be okay, everything's gonna be okay, that's for sure!" he sang in his beard and wiped off his sweating forehead. *Well, first, I should quit this fucking job! Now! At once! Immediately!*

"I don't come to work on Friday, I screw my bosses!" he sang softly but with emotion. *Yeah, that's right! Straight from the shoulder. Concerning screwing—quitting my job is not enough. I have to…*

Gorbalyuk thought about his arrogant, proud, and confident lady mistress and smiled malevolently. *All right, highly-regarded Antonina Ivanovna. We'll see what Sukhov is!* He grabbed the briefcase and left the cabin. Approaching the wash stand, he poured some cold water on his face and looked in the mirror. *Well, you look awful! Well, it's for the better!* Gorbalyuk took the briefcase off the floor, left the men's room and headed to the mistress's office.

***

"Hold on," howled the secretary, Zinochka, scared to death and trying to stand up. Gorbalyuk paid no attention to her, gave the door handle a twist, and entered.

An elegant, exquisite, and business-like woman who was sitting behind the table, lifted up her head discontentedly and froze, seeing the drunk, wet, and disheveled Gorbalyuk. He halted for a second, too, staring at her with a keen and painful curiosity as if he tried to remember her forever.

A real fucking business woman! Margaret Thatcher and Hilary Clinton in one, he smiled cynically to himself and stepped to the table. He was very amused. "Hello, I'm Monica Lewinski!"

He must have uttered the last phrase aloud, for the eyes of the woman in front of him opened widely, and a strange expression appeared on her face—a mixture of distrust and fear.

"Dear Antonina Ivanovna," said Gorbalyuk slowly, softly, suavely, with pauses and punctuation, looking straight into the eyes of his ex-boss, taking delight in this moment, and doing his best to extend this moment, to prolong it as much as he could. "You're a business-woman…" (A little pause) "... and, correspondingly, I have an offer for you…" (Another little pause) "…which is purely business." (Pause.) "Nothing personal!" (Pause.) "Well." (Pause.) "The offer is the following." (A long pause.) "I want…" (A very long pause) "…to fuck you here and now!" (A long pause.) "For a million dollars, in the ass!" he added after another long and final pause, recalling the verses of a song.

The woman turned deathly pale. "Are you drunk?" she hissed in a spitting, menacing half-whisper, raising, leaning forward, and staring at Gorbalyuk, as well. "Leave my office immediately! You're fired!" she reached to the intercom with her hand.

Gorbalyuk threw a briefcase on the table and, without a word, opened it wide. Antonina Ivanovna's hand froze halfway. Her mouth opened a bit.

"What is this?" she muttered in embarrassment, as if to herself, gazing into a briefcase and being unable to draw her eyes off its contents.

"A million dollars," said Gorbalyuk slowly and quietly, too, staring at her and almost devouring her with his eyes. It seemed to him that he was already poking her, fucking her. And he was doing it in all the possible ways and in all the holes at once! Actually, that was true. He even thought for a moment that he would cum, for the pleasure was so unbearable, so keen, and so sweet. For a brief moment, everything around him reeled.

"How did you get it?" Antonina Ivanovna still couldn't draw her eyes from the packs wrapped in plastic.

"It doesn't matter. So what?"

Antonina Ivanovna's face was covered with red patches; it turned ugly and lost all its sleek arrogance.

That's it! thought Gorbalyuk, looking at her scornfully. *Now you're a bitch, even if you refuse.*

The woman breathed heavily and fitfully. Then she swallowed convulsively and made an effort to slowly raise her eyes at Gorbalyuk, who was standing near the table.

"I… I… I'm not sure. This is so unexpected." She looked at the dollars again, then at Gorbalyuk. Dollars. Gorbalyuk again.

"What do you mean by here? And what if someone comes in?"

Gorbalyuk was staring at her and smiling. Antonina Ivanovna took a deep breath and tried to gather herself. Then, with a confident and sharp move, she pressed an intercom button.

"Yes, Antonina Pavlovna?" said a worried secretary's voice from the loudspeaker.

"I'm busy. Don't let anyone in my office until Gorbalyuk comes out!"

"All right, Antonina Ivanovna," answered the secretary in wonder. Obviously, she was perplexed.

Antonina Ivanovna switched off the connection and turned to Gorbalyuk. She had already calmed down and came to her senses.

That was quick, thought Gorbalyuk with even greater scorn, *you didn't play hard-to-get for too long. The music didn't play long; prostie, prostie, prostie! I'm in a mood for singing today.*

"All right!" said Antonina Ivanovna coldly, still staring at Gorbalyuk. "Where? On the table?"

"You mean sex?" asked Gorbalyuk. "So, you agree, right? In the ass?"

"Yes, I said that already," said the woman abruptly, boiling.

"Great!" Gorbalyuk closed the briefcase with a careless move and took it. "All the best!"

"What's the meaning of that?" Antonina Ivanovna's face turned red.

"I changed my mind," Gorbalyuk turned away and left the office without looking back. "Please, come on in," he said kindly to a girl who was waiting in the reception area, "Antonina Ivanovna is already free."

And Lucifer was ask'd by His Son:
—Can anyone be bought with chinks?
And Lucifer answer'd to His Son:
—Aye. Chinks is the most reliable and sure method to get from a man what thou want. It's all very simple and thither is nay ne'd to make it complicat'd. Exceptions prove the rule.

LUCIFER'S SON. DAY 19.

And the nineteenth day came.
And Lucifer was told by His Son:
—I'm beginning to give up hope on men.
And Lucifer answer'd His Son:
—Nay. Thou simply begin to wot them better—with their strengths and weaknesses. And 'tis difficult f'r a man to enwheel this knowledge.

GENIUS

"Never send to know for whom the
bell tolls. It tolls for thee."
E. Hemingway "A Farewell to Arms."

"Love your neighbor as yourself."
Gospel of Matthew.

1.

The blow was so heavy that Kubrin passed out. Coming to his senses, he found himself lying on the grass. A huge branch that had fallen down on him was lying at his side. Kubrin felt his head carefully. There was no blood, but there was a huge lump—very huge, like an orange. Kubrin kept fingering it with fear and painful bewilderment, as if he couldn't believe that it was real.

That's ridiculous! He went for a picnic, sat down on the grass, under the tree, and a branch fell down on him as if it had been waiting for him. And it was no small branch; it was a huge branch, a log. Just look at it! He looked again at the huge pine branch that was lying near him. The sight was really impressive.

Unbelievable! It's lucky that it didn't kill me! Fucking picnic and barbecue; fucking nature. At last, I found time for that. Fuck me, fuck nature! I should have stayed home and drunk beer without any fucking lumps. No! "Let's go! Let's go! Clean air!" Why the fuck do I need all that?

Kubrin would probably have been sitting, touching his head, and swearing for quite a long time if two sedans hadn't appeared around the corner. Going through the pits and bumps, they approached Kubrin and stopped. In the first one, there was Valka Bobrov, and in the second, Andriukha Reshetnikov. Naturally, they were with their wives.

"Hi, where's Natashka?" asked Valka at once, getting out of the car and stretching.

"Ah! She's sick," Kubrin waved his hand. "She caught cold."

"How come she allowed you to come?" saucily laughed Zinochka, Bobrov's wife, and playfully snapped her eyes at him. "Doesn't she care?"

"Well, it means that she trusts him," Andriukha's Kapa joined the game—Kapitolina Evgrafovna Reshetnikova, nee Varivashen.

"Is this your family stuff?" Kubrin asked her once when he was drunk.

"What do you mean?" she didn't get it.

"Well, giving such names to your children? Evgraf Varivashen? Nice!" Kapa took huge offense and didn't talk to him for a long time. Andriukha even had to bring them together.

"And she's right. Kolian is a rock!" supported her Andriukha. "Hey, where's the firewood?" he startled, looking around him intently. "Rock? We had a deal, right?"

"Here," Kubrin pointed at the branch near him.

"Where here?" Andriukha stared at him uncomprehendingly. The others looked at Kubrin inquiringly.

"This very branch fell down on my head just before you came here. And I regained consciousness a couple of minutes ago. Before that, I was lying under the tree unconscious!"

"Are you kidding?" Everybody was staring at Kubrin distrustfully.

"Come here and touch it," Kubrin tapped his head slightly, inviting them. "Come here—I've got a lump as huge as a ball, as a chicken egg," he added, seeing the semi-smiles appear on the women's faces.

"Do you have a headache?" asked Andryukha, compassionately and clumsily and, putting his hands on his waist, he leaned back, stretching and warming up his stiff body.

"No, it seems," answered Kubrin tentatively, listening to his senses. Thank God, he didn't have a headache, indeed. And, what was more important, he didn't want to throw up.

Well, I don't have a concussion, thought Kubrin with relief. He read that people are sick when they have concussion. *So far, so good!*

"Well, then, let's go get some firewood," ordered Valka confidently and spat out. "Why are we wasting time?"

After that, everything ran its course. Fire, barbecue, beer and vodka. However, they were not drinking a lot, for they were driving. And Kubrin wasn't drinking at all. He was scared—*No way; what if I've got a concussion, indeed? In such case, I'm not allowed to drink*—and, actually, he didn't want to. *Fucking branch!* Kubrin found it with his eyes and swore indistinctly. *Confound it! I don't need any concussion. I broke my legs and arms once, but I've never had a concussion There you go! Shit!*

Arriving home, Kubrin immediately looked in the mirror. No, he couldn't see anything, and he thought that everybody saw his lump and that it really was as huge as an orange, like in a 'Tom and Jerry' cartoon. *Well, that's all right. Maybe, I should put something cold on it, although, what's the point? I should have done it earlier, just after the blow. And now, it's useless. Well, to hell with it! It'll vanish in a couple of days.*

2.

About a week later, Kubrin suddenly found out that something was wrong with him. The world changed. It became stupid—all of it, the whole world at once. His wife, friends, colleagues, books, mass media. It seemed that he was in a land of fools, and they were everywhere, at every corner. Even fox Alice and cat Basilio, who, obviously, had brought him here with some witchcraft, were gone. They brought him here and then left him. They vanished. He would be even glad to see them, and he would give them all his gold, so they got him out of here, saved him! Alas! They were not here. They disappeared without a trace. They were really gone.

They were gone, but the fools remained. And he couldn't escape them. He couldn't even read, let alone watch television. Kubrin couldn't understand how he had been watching it before. And he seemed to like it sometimes! What could he possibly like there? Drabness, primitivism, no talent at all, vulgarism and platitudes; lack of taste and elementary politeness. *Silly people, uttering silly words with smart look. It's our TV. A movie...*

Right, but on the other hand, thought Kubrin suddenly, *what's going on in the West? The same. All these Hollywood movies—they are a complete disaster—pieces of shit. And, while our problems often have a purely technical character—lack of financing, of professionalism—they've got it on a high level. And mind you, television and cinematography are just business for them. And if this business exists and prospers, its products are in demand. And if Hollywood produces stupid movies, these movies are demanded by society. So, it's the level of the society, the level of the modern society. Comics and action movies. And one should be critical not of Hollywood, but of society as a whole. It turns out that it's so silly and primitive. Vulgar!*

Kubrin suddenly recalled Pugacheva singing at her recent jubilee concert—*was it in Kremlin Palace, indeed?*—very vulgar and stupid verses; something about a hand from a toilet bowl that is giving her roses. Well, that meant that she had such inescapable and intrusive fans, they got to her. Well, she went to the ladies' room, and, as soon as she closed the door of the cabin, the toilet-bowl... Well, horror of horrors. *And the whole audience was applauding her—men in expensive formal suits and women in furs and brilliants—all of our home-bred* ***beau monde****, actually. I was there. I checked in.*

I'm the same!.. I like that! I like these poo jokes. I'm into it!.. I'm just pretending to be stately, educated, and refined. I attend smart concerts with smart looks, but really? Hoo-oo!" As a matter of fact, Lady Diana is just a beautiful pseudonym, a nickname, and, according to her ID, she's Dunka Tolstopyataya from Tetyushy. She always was one, and she remained her, in spite of her chinchilla fur coats and brilliants. I rely on your good offices. Well...

Kubrin suddenly recalled with unpleasant surprise that he had been laughing, too, while watching it on TV together with his wife. They thought it was funny at that time. *Why is it funny? It's horrible, not funny. Sure, one can talk about anything, on any subjects, for there are and there can't be any moral and aesthetic taboos. Take, for example, Barkov—the most important thing is how one talks. That's the trick. That's essential. And it's dangerous to talk on the forbidden topics not because they're forbidden, but because it's very difficult. One can easily turn to vulgarity and the usual obscenities. One wrong step, a wrongly chosen word... Have a limit; walk along the edge. That demands a great talent, good taste, and a perfect sense of delicacy. Even Pushkin and Barkov couldn't always do that, let alone the others—especially our modern performers, singers and entertainers. So, dear Alla Borisovna, woman who sings. It's been a long time since you were a woman."Now you're a simple broad—strong-voiced, banal, and vulgar, like a fishwife. Just...*

Oh," Kubrin suddenly checked himself. *What was I talking about? What do I want from poor Alla Borisovna? Why did I freeze to her, anyway? Oh, God! What am I thinking about? These are not my thoughts, not at all! Hollywood... Pugacheva... modern society... I've never thought about this before! Well, people sing. Music playing... concerts... it's fun... And here you go! Oh, God! What's wrong with me?!*

It seemed to Kubrin that he was a prodigy in a boarding school for mentally retarded children. Everybody around him was doing something,—playing silly games and living their silly lives. And pray tell, what does a normal child can do there, let alone a prodigy? What games can he play? And, above all, with whom?

The world around him withered, bleached; it lost color, grew dim, and lost all its beauty. There was nothing to read, nothing to watch, and no one to talk to. Boredom and melancholy—are sad and hopeless. There's nothing to count on. He can't hope that everyone around him would get smart at once, right? Kubrin thought about Brant's "Ship of Fools": *You have one cure, fool—/ A cap! Wear it and be grateful. Well, there's no cure for stupidity. A thought, there is one—I was hit by a branch! It could be good for others. Well, funny, very funny. It's so funny that I want to cry. To be precise, I want to howl like a wolf, like a werewolf howls at the moon. For I am a werewolf. Outside, I'm a man, and inside, who am I, anyway? I'm not a human, that's for sure. At least, I'm not an ordinary man.*

Degenerate. Monster. 'Not ordinary'—that's degenerate whichever way you slice it. Inhuman.

All around me are humans, and I'm inhuman. And they feel it in their guts, they smell it! Strange tones appear in relationships with friends and my wife, although, they're not my friends anymore. What do we have in common? Nothing! It seems as if I've come from another planet, an alien. How did we communicate before that? What did we talk about? I can't really imagine! Well, damn it! Damn it! Isn't it funny? Silly line of Mironov—"darn it" from "The Diamond Arm." So, I do like something, don't I? Well, some movies?.. books?.. is there anything left? Well, something, something may be left, but this something is too few...

Well, what should I do? I don't want to be smart—I don't! Turn me into a fool again, like I was before. Well, not a fool, but an ordinary man like everyone else. Why the fuck do I need the intellect? What shall I do with it? It's as useless as teats on a bull. It has disadvantages only. Grief! Like Chatsky said. Well, I realize now that he wasn't that smart either. As a matter of fact, we're in the same position. Absolutely—you're the smartest one, but there's no use of it at all. Being so smart is stupid.

Well, I realize that very well, too, thought Kubrin. *That's why I always wondered why these smarty-pants were so poor and wretched. I mean it. Well, they were poor, at least. And now, when I'm too smart myself, it all becomes clear to me. It dawned on me.*

Intellect is good for simple tasks, the ones that have clearly specified conditions, like proving a theorem or inventing something in physics or chemistry. But, in real life, in super-sophisticated systems, which is our human society, it's almost useless. You can't count everything, so, you can't become a huge success with it and build a career. For that, you need completely different skills. Super-sophisticated systems are best known for the fact that consequences of the influence from them can't be calculated at all. That is, you can't tell beforehand what the incoming signal is going to turn into and what is going to be at the outcome—a promotion or a dismissal. Too many factors are at work here; for example, whether the boss had a fight with his wife in the morning or not.

So, you may be as wise as Solomon or as Einstein, like me; the result is the same. It doesn't matter. You may be as wise as anyone. Not to mention that, at some point, you would be no human at all; you would be a walking nightmare—everyone shrinks from me! And you're going to have other, completely different, problems like a change of interests, priorities, new scale of values and so on. You wouldn't care about this at all, about success and careers, about the rat race. And the world would, probably never find out about you; you would remain unnoticed. Your interests and the interests of the world would never meet. Well, what common interests can a man have with rats? All in all, it's a closed circle. At first, you don't have an opportunity, and then you don't have a dream. Fucking dirty trick, as usual.

Thank God, I do have a dream—money, social position and stuff. Though, actually, Kubrin took thought. *Do I need all that? Hmm! At least, I'm not that sure. And what do I need at all? A good question, indeed. What do I need from this colony of the primary creatures? I don't fucking need anything from them; I don't need anything now! Well maybe, a little bit.*

I don't need much —
Hunk of bread and drop of milk.
And this sky,
And these clouds.

....Khlebnikov, Velimir...

Well, well! It turns out that I do remember it. Not that I have to, but... Hold on! Verses are a good thing, but I was thinking about something important. Right —what I need and what I don't need. And I came to the conclusion that I don't need a damn. I don't give a fuck! I'm free," like in a song. And why, anyway? Why don't I need it? Well, I became smarter, so what? Did my feelings change, as well? Did they become smarter? My mental outlook? Hmm! Well, my mental outlook did change. All wishes are somehow connected with humans. How would they like me, how could I show off and make an impression? Well, making a fucking impression on whom? On this eating and breeding protoplasm?"

Kubrin scowled. He shouldn't be thinking about humans this way. *It's bad; it's wrong. Wrong—and what is right? What is right? What is right? Only God knows what is right. If he exists, of course. Shit! I wish I were hit harder; then maybe I could become a god. Or a psycho. Actually, that's the same. I would be in nirvana, in the clouds; screw it all! Screw all these earthly problems. Fuck it!*

But he was stuck in the middle between heavens and earth like a kite. Like he was underfoot, between hay and grass—neither fish nor fowl, good for nothing. *I've got no wings, but I can still fly. I can fucking hover. I can glide like a flying squirrel. A fucking genius! What is that? Eh? Genius What kind of animal is that? A very smart man, right? He's smart enough, but he can't screw everything. He's smart enough to suffer but not enough to do something and change something. He's no god and no titan. He's just a man. Nothing human is alien for him. And that's the problem. Oh, god! Why did that branch choose me? Why? What's my fault before you, God? Why am I having these idiotic thoughts? Ingenious thoughts?"*

3.

Next day, Kubrin came across a volume of Chizhevsky. It had been lying on a shelf for so many years, and Kubrin had never opened it, but now, he was curious. It seemed that someone moved his hand. Devil. He opened the book and looked through it.

As a matter of fact, he had known the theory of Chizhevsky concerning clear correlations between peaks of solar and human, or social, activities. Actually, the author had created a huge piece of work, an incredible one—tables, graphs, a lot of statistical material; all of it was very impressive. But Kubrin had seen it before. He was looking through the tables carelessly and comparing the graphs. Well! Very interesting—an apparent correlation, an apparent one, and an explicit correlation. However, why should he wonder? The sun is the nearest star, and it's quite natural that all processes that happen there influence the earthly life. And they influence a man as well. They influence his mentality, mood, and cerebration. That's a natural correlation. What's the wonder? It would be strange if there were no such correlation. And now, that's normal.

Hey! Hold on, hold on! What is that? What is that graph? Well, well, and this one, too. What the hell? What's the meaning of it? Kubrin looked through the text quickly. *Well, right. Right, here.*

'Though the fact of correlation was evident and beyond doubt, however, some data showed that the graphs are shifted relative to each other in the wrong direction, and the peak of human activities was in advance of the corresponding peak of solar activity, usually for a year or two. And logic suggested that it was absolutely impossible. For it turned out that the result was in advance of the reason. Chizhevsky couldn't explain this incredible fact.'

Hmm, it's really interesting No, I mean, how is this possible? Kubrin looked through the book quickly one more time. *Well, well; the correlation is apparent. But still... hmm... it's strange, very strange!* A guess that flashed suddenly in his mind was so incredible and astounding that Kubrin even closed his eyes for a moment. *"Shit! No, it's nonsense! Though. though—why is it nonsense? A usual scientific hypothesis, and it's very easy to check it. Let's do it right now. And we'll check, if I'm a genius."*

Kubrin turned on the computer and started surfing the Web. *Well, well, what events were there during the last years?.. Oh, here we are... let's take Kampuchea, Khmer Rouge, Pol Pot. Well, here it is... 'More than a million people were executed...' And when exactly was it?.. Well, and what happened to the sun then? Eh?.. Where is it?.. Probably, it's here... Well, right... let's see... right, that's it. A one-year difference, as it should be—just what the doctor ordered. Well, here we are... just look at it. Great Scott! I'm a genius, indeed. No shit! A perfect score!*

Kubrin leaned back in his chair and spun a couple of times. He had a strange new feeling, a kind of excitement. Well, it was the feeling of a man who just made a discovery. Apparently, being a genius did have its positive side. However, his euphoria didn't last long. Suddenly, Kubrin realized clearly and distinctly what he had turned into. He realized what genius was. He knew that, from that time on, he was doomed to solitude, solitude, and solitude only! He was an alien among men. This thought pierced him and appeared before him in its horrible nakedness and desperation, in its obviousness. It didn't leave any place for hopes or doubts. He knew that very clearly then.

The solution that he had just found so easily wouldn't come to the mind of an ordinary man. Ever! A human mind just works in another way. One had to look at the task from the different angle in order to assume what he had assumed. One had to absolutely abstract away from the situation, leave the limits of human logic and human mentality. An ordinary man would never do that. And Kubrin did! He did that! He was able to assume the existence of the feedback. He assumed that possibility. He assumed that, maybe, not only the solar activity stimulated the human activity, but, vice versa, the human activity stimulated the solar activity, sunspots, etc. And why not? Social disasters, deaths—maybe, the deaths release some kind of emanation or energy which initiates the processes on the sun. And they, in their turn, amplify the social activity. That would mean new casualties, emissions, death emanations, new splashes of solar activity. And so on. The snake biting its tail! A classical process with feedback, like a speculative increase of prices on the stock market—shares, for example. The increase of prices stimulates the demand, and the demand, in its turn, stimulates a new turn of price increases.

Suddenly Kubrin remembered the Bible. 'They will throw them into the blazing furnace.' Into the blazing furnace...into hell—blazing furnace. What if the sun is Hell? Blazing furnace? And emanations of death are the souls of sinners who go there after they die. With huge numbers of sinners, special processes begin to happen in Hell; figuratively speaking, Hell triumphs, and it influences the Earth. Well, the people feel it, become nervous and excited, and that, in its turn, leads to new social conflicts, wars and revolutions, to new casualties, to more souls of sinners, and, correspondingly, to the new triumph of Hell.

Kubrin smiled to himself. *Hmm, the Bible says that, all right, but now it's clear, at least, why there are no super-civilizations. It's the main paradox of either cosmology or xenology. What is xenology? Oh, it doesn't matter; what's the difference? I should be thinking about other stuff. And what was I thinking? Oh, right, about super-civilizations. Shit! I've become rather absent-minded! So, what about super-vicilizations? Super-vicilizations, super-vicilizations. Oh! Why are there no supercivilizations? If space is endless, then it should contain countless numbers of super-civilizations which outran us for millions years of evolution and which should have been discovered long time ago. Or, at least, we should be seeing traces of their activities. However, in practice, nothing of that kind is happening, as we know. The impression is that there are no supercivilizations. Why?*

Well, now it's clear why it is so. Evolution and progress are accompanied by the rise of population, and that means a rise in the death rate and a rise of the intensity of death emanations. And it initiates more activity of the nearest star, the local sun. And eventually, there is a huge burst from the sun which sterilizes the whole planet. The end—apocalypse; the civilization dies, and everything starts anew. 'And I saw a new heaven and a new earth: for the first heaven and the first earth were passed way; and there was no more sea.' Right, there would be no sea. Seas and oceans would evaporate at once.

Moreover, as the civilization's level of development doesn't allow it to protect itself from such disasters, the mechanism has a really universal character and works smoothly. It cannot be fought. Well, I understood it. So what? First, no one would believe me, for it is just a hypothesis, and it cannot be proved; and, second, even if they believed me, what is to be done? Stop the progress? Limit the birth and death rates? Forbid wars and conflicts? It's nonsense! Well, the very nature of civilization foredooms it to death. It seems that nature doesn't need super-civilizations.

A pun! Actually, it's a slip of the tongue, but a very distinctive one. The word 'nature', in its both meanings, withstands civilization, even the inner nature of itself. Well, all right, I need to check what has been going on with the sun recently. Does its activity grow with time, according to the rise of intensity of the death emanation? It seems that it does; I think I read or heard about that. Oh, whether it grows or not—it doesn't fucking matter. Why should I care? I would definitely not live to see it, the general sterilization. This sun of ours isn't going to explode tomorrow; we've still got time—a couple of thousand years, at least. So, live and enjoy the warmth! And then? And then, let the chips fall where they may. And then—soup with hen. 'And then soup with a hen and a dick in your mouth!' Blast it all! Let it burn with cleaning and devouring fire. And it will burn. Amen.

3.

That night, Kubrin had an incredible dream. He was in a room with a strange man—an elegant and exquisite man in his forties—and he was disputing with him. To be precise, the man tried to explain something to Kubrin, and Kubrin was listening carefully and trying to contradict him. All in all, they were arguing. Kubrin tried to recall the details of the argument and was surprised to find out that he remembered everything vividly and clearly, word for word. It seemed that it hadn't been a dream, but reality. It seemed that it had happened to him for real. He just concentrated a bit, and all details of the dream, all words and phrases of the argument, came to his memory.

He closed his eyes and went back to that room; he could hear the hoarse, soft, indifferent, patronizing, and lazy voice of his night companion, the voice of man who was absolutely self-assured, who knew everything, understood everything, and who had been living on Earth for several thousand years. Kubrin even shivered from these memories and felt uneasy. It seemed that he felt the cold breath of an unknown dark abyss.

"Oh, here you are, Nikolay Borisovich!" he heard in his ears. These were the first words that he heard in the dream.

"Where am I?" Kubrin was overwhelmed with a feeling of great astonishment and even fear which he had experienced at that moment.

"In a dream," explained his companion kindly. "You're sleeping and dreaming."

"A dream?" Kubrin was looking around him in surprise. However, there was nothing to look at. It was an ordinary room, nothing special. Actually, everything was kind of blurred; everything was shaking, twinkling, and teasing—everything was hazy and vague. It was a kind of mirage. He could clearly see only his companion. He was real, and the words that he said were real. Definitely real.

"So how do you like it in your new status? Do you like it?" Kubrin heard again.

"What are you talking about? What new status?" Kubrin stared in surprise at the man sitting opposite him.

"Well, of genius!" he laughed. "You're a genius now. Do you like being one?"

Kubrin stared silently at his companion, unable to utter a word. "Listen," he said with difficulty, at last.

"Yeah!" the man smiled in answer and nodded. "You're absolutely right. Branches do not fall down on one's head for no reason and with such luck."

"So?" Kubrin even opened his mouth in astonishment. The man didn't answer but looked at him with the same semi-smile. "Who are you?" asked Kubrin softly, struck with superstitious awe. He startled, recalling his feeling at night.

"Alien!" answered merrily his companion. "Humanoid! Overmind. Oh, right—you know now that there are no aliens, no overminds and super-civilizations. A sun burst, and game over, global sterilization of a planet. Simple and effective, isn't it?" the man laughed, staring at Kubrin. However, his eyes were not laughing. They were staring at Kubrin coldly, intently and inquiringly, as if Kubrin was a new and interesting specimen in his strange collection.

"What about a collection?" Kubrin thought in a dream. He was perplexed and wondered why that word came to his mind. *What collection? Collection of what? Or whom?*

"Concerning solar activity," continued the man, cutting his laugh abruptly. "Tomorrow or the day after tomorrow, there may be a huge burst on the sun, probably the greatest in the history of such observations." He fell silent, looking at Kubrin with expectation.

"What does it have to do with me?" he shrugged his shoulders automatically after a pause. He didn't understand anything. "Hold on! Hold on!" he suddenly came to his senses. "How do you know that tomorrow there will be a burst on the sun?"

"I said there *may be*," Kubrin's companion corrected him calmly.

"So what? What do you mean by ***may be***?" Kubrin still didn't understand anything. It was a strange conversation—a wild one, as if he was talking to the Lord himself. *Tomorrow there may be a huge burst on the sun—so what? What should I say to that? And how should I react? Oh, so, there was an announcement, wasn't there?* he realized with belated relief.

"No," answered the man calmly. "There was no announcement at all. Nobody knows about that."

"Then how do you know?" In spite of everything, Kubrin felt a growing irritation. *What's the meaning of it, really? Is he kidding me?*

"Well, I do," an ironic smile appeared on the man's lips. "You're not very quick-witted for a genius. Well, all right," he checked his smile at once, "let's get to business! You are familiar with nonequilibrium thermodynamics, right? Well, in general, at least?" the man looked inquiringly at Kubrin.

"With what?" Kubrin didn't know what to say, for the transition was too sharp.

"Fluctuations, bifurcation points," said the man. "You can remember this—'When a system, in its evolution, comes to the bifurcation point, the deterministic description does not apply. The fluctuation makes the system choose the branch, through which the further evolution of the system will go. The transition through bifurcation is a random process, like a flipping of a coin,'" quoted the man in an instructional tone, as if he was delivering a lecture. "Well, do you remember now?"

"Hold on! Hold on!" Kubrin began to get it slowly. "Bifurcation points are critical points, right? When any minimal amount of influence can lead to a completely new behavior of the whole process, right? In particular, to a disaster. A cistern with dripping water, standing on an inclined platform. The last drop turns the cistern over. A butterfly flying on the edge of the origin of the typhoon which is causing a tornado somewhere in California. Did you mean that?"

"Well, there you are!" the man smiled broadly and nodded his head, "you remembered! 'Magnification of microscopic fluctuation, which happened at the right moment, leads to the preferential choosing of a certain development path from the row of paths, which are a priori equally possible.'"

"Okay, let's assume that," Kubrin still couldn't understand anything. "So what? What does the sun have to do with it?"

"Tomorrow is the 'right moment', said the man softly, "a critical point, bifurcation point when microscopic influences can cause or cause not a disaster."

"So what?" Kubrin almost cried. "What do I have to do with it? Why are you telling me all this? What do you want of me? Can you explain it to me clearly at last?"

"Well, you grasped it yesterday!" the man shook his head reproachfully. "Well, Nikolai Borisovich? What's the matter? Well, do you remember now? Souls of sinners, death emanations—well?"

"Wait a bit," Kubrin rubbed his forehead. "Okay, right—death emanation. So, you mean that?"

"Right, Nikolai Borisovich," the man said softly to Kubrin. "Exactly! That's right. Yet another life or death may decide everything, whether there will be a burst on the sun or not. And the burst means thousands and thousands of new deaths. Magnetic storms, chronically ill people who react to them sharply, etc. Well, you know all of it very well."

"All right, all right," Kubrin tried to concentrate. "Let's assume that I've got it. Still, what do you want of me? Why are you telling me all of this?"

"Why?" the man was truly surprised. "Don't you want to save thousands of innocent people? Save their lives, become a hero? Tomorrow, you will have such an opportunity, although you'll become a secret hero," he added and smiled, staring at Kubrin. "No one will ever find out about it. But what's the difference, anyway? You're not doing this for glory."

"What exactly am I doing?" hissed Kubrin, trying to check his fury. "Can you tell me clearly what you want of me? Eh? Come on!"

"All right," the man began talking in a business-like tone and moved in his chair. "I offer you the chance to become a savior of humanity tomorrow, to become a hero. First, you have to save one person—a child; you have to pay for his surgery, $15,000. It will save his life and, maybe, the lives of thousands of other people. For, maybe, it will prevent the burst on the sun, the microscopic fluctuations happening at the right moment." The man intentionally emphasized both "maybes" in his speech. He uttered them with greater stress and emphasis.

"Are you serious?" Kubrin stared at his companion in astonishment. He was expecting anything but this. "You're saying that I have to spend all my money because of some stains on the sun? Goodness knows why and for whom? And goodness knows what's going to come out of it! You're saying all the time 'maybe, maybe.' So, there are no guarantees, and there can't be any, and you know that very well. And indeed," he shouted in complete bewilderment and abashment, "that's not important! That's nonsense, a piece of crap, guarantees or no guarantees! I'm not going to spend my own money! And why should I believe you? Who are you? What is this comedy for? It's just a dream!"

"Nikolay Borisovich!" said the man and stood up. Kubrin did the same automatically. "Tomorrow, in a newspaper, you will see an ad—'Help needed! Money for child's surgery. Urgent!' That's the person whom you have to help, a sick child. It's up to you. All the best."

"But…" said Kubrin, and he woke up.

Right, I woke up with that stupid 'but', scowled Kubrin. Hero and genius. Fucking bullshit! Savior of humanity from the stains on the sun. A hero, right! But not a hero of my novel! What crap! I don't want any such dreams!

4.

Groaning, Kubrin got off the bed, moved his stiff neck, and went to the bathroom. He washed up, took a shower and had breakfast. He tried not to think about his dream and was driving it away from his memory. He did his best, but nothing helped. The dream was fiercely entrenched into his head like the famous pink elephant which you are not supposed to think about. At last, Kubrin gave up and started thinking with rage which was surprising, even for him.

Well, all right, what do we have? I had a dream about some bullshit. It's totally unbelievable, a piece of crap! Gibberish! And why is it bothering me, then? Eh? Well, a dream, so what? Because it's not gibberish, he answered himself, *and I know it very well. It was too coherent and logical to be gibberish. 'Nonequilibrium thermodynamics.' Fuck! I really don't know such words! Or do I? Actually, we studied something like this in the university. We had lectures. I don't remember anything, but what does it mean, 'I don't remember?' It seems that I don't remember, but, as a matter of fact, I do, at the back of my mind. So, it could be just my imagination, all these universal disasters. I read too much of Chyzhevsky, got overexcited, and my subconscious played Old Harry with me.* He stopped, took breath, and looked around him sadly, as if waiting for help. He didn't want to think any more.

Well, and what about a child? he thought reluctantly. *An ad in a newspaper? If it's my own nonsense and deformed imagination, then there's no ad, and there can't be any. Provided that, except this fucking genius, I have a gift of foresight. I can fucking unveil a curtain of the future with my shaking hand, I can guess the ads in newspapers. Fucking Cassandra,* he smiled joylessly. *Cripes! Damn! Why is this happening to me? Millions of people live their normal, vegetative lives, and they don't have any prophetic dreams; no monsters come to them in their sleep. Branches do not fall on their heads." Kubrin gave a heavy sigh and looked around the kitchen sadly. "I'm the one who's so lucky. So, what shall I do now? Eh? Look for an ad? Why the fuck do I need it? If it exists, of course," he corrected himself quickly. "There's definitely no ad! It's all my fantasies and imagination!"* Kubrin stood up and, stepping heavily, went to the window aimlessly. He stared outside, then approached the fridge, and opened it without a goal. He gazed inside it for some time, then closed it, and sat down. *Well, what? Shall I read the newspaper or not? I won't!* he made a decision.

"I'm off," his wife quickly chattered, rushing into the kitchen. "Food is on the oven. Here's a newspaper," she threw the paper on the table. "Bye!"

His wife left, and Kubrin kept sitting and staring bluntly at the newspaper that was lying in front of him. Then he sighed desperately, reached out his hand, and moved it closer. He had almost no doubt that there was the ad in it. *Yep, here it is. 'Help needed! Money for child surgery. Urgent!' Word for word, just like that one from the dream said. Who was he, by the way? A demon? Or, quite on the contrary, an archangel?*

Well, he didn't look like archangel, Kubrin smiled softly, recalling the sardonical smirk of his night guest. *Although, you can't know for sure with these archangels! I don't know what they look like usually, at peace and in ordinary life. Maybe they do have such scoundrel-like mugs. Maybe they usually embarrass good people and demand some incredible good deeds from them. Probably, a demon wouldn't want me to do something good. What the fuck would he need it for—me saving someone? Quite on the contrary, he would take delight in the fact that a million or two morons are going to bite the dust because of the burst on the sun and go straight to hell to bake in the sun, to fucking warm up.*

It's nice to deal with demons. It's quite comfortable; you understand them completely. That's because I'm a demon myself!" *he thought suddenly. "There's much more devilish stuff in me than divine. There's much more evil than good. That's why I don't like to deal with angels. It's more convenient to deal with devils. I get on well with them. A child? What child? Are you nuts? You can't save everyone! Hell of a savior, Christ-like. Mind your own business! Exactly! Everything's simple and clear, easy to understand. Well!* Kubrin scowled and scratched his head with his finger. *There now! I was honored to see an angel or a demon, and I'm not surprised at all. Well so, what shall I do? Shall I make a call or not?* He already knew that he would make a call. With the same acid look, he reluctantly dialed the number from the newspaper.

"Hello?" answered a worried female voice.

"Well, hi," mumbled Kubrin, not knowing what to say and why he'd called at all. "I'm calling concerning the ad." *Moron!* he thought discontentedly. *Concerning the ad! Are you selling a recorder? Idiot!*

"Yes, I'm listening!" shouted the woman, and Kubrin even started back, so great was desperation and reckless hope coming from her "Can you help?"

Kubrin hurled the phone and sat for some time without moving, breathing heavily and looking at the phone, as if waiting to hear the woman's voice which was entering his soul and tearing his heart into pieces. *How terrible!* he took head in hands. *What the fuck did I call her for?* It seemed to Kubrin that some invisible threads appeared between him and that woman after the call—bonds. He wasn't a stranger anymore; he had a responsibility, and he would be guilty in the death of her child. He could save her, but he didn't.

"*I'm not giving her money,"* he came to his senses suddenly. *I'm not, I'm not, I'm not! Let a hundred children die! A thousand! A million! Tomorrow, there will be new ones, new monsters. These from a cartoon—potstickers, Beavis and Butt-head. Pepsi generation—the ones shouting and sucking. Fuck all those bursts! Let it all explode, the whole world! Why should I care? The fewer people, the easier it is to breathe. It's no concern of mine. Here we are. Sympathy? Please. Pity? No problem. But no money, sorry. I've got children of my own, as well as a wife. And they need to eat and drink. Well, so, good day to you!* Kubrin stood up confidently and, without looking at the phone, left the kitchen, whistling.

***

Towards evening, Kubrin got a call from his wife, who was scared to death.

"Mom just called from the summer cottage. Sashenka had a severe asthmatic attack!" she shouted in the phone. "And they can't call the hospital—there's a strong magnetic storm. No connection. Everything's dead. She's going die! She's going die! Do you hear me? Do you?"

"I do, I do, I do," answered Kubrin monotonously and bluntly, like a broken record. He was staring in front of him with an empty look, unable to stop. "I do, I do, I do, I do, I do."

Down from heaven, there came to Him an Angel - strong, with great power, and shrouded in a cloud; a rainbow was above his head, and his face was like sun, and his legs were pillars of fire.

And Angel told him:

—If Thou wish good for men—bereave the world of evil.

He answered:

—If there is no evil in the world, how men shall tell good from evil? They shall become humble and speechless domestic animals. Adam and Eve.

Then Angel said:

—Truth cannot be built on lies, and good cannot be built on evil. Tell the people who Thou art. Let them know that Thou art Enemy's Son, Lucifer's Son.

He answered:

—What difference does it make, who I am and whose son I am? It is said: "By their deeds you will recognize them." My deeds shall stand for me.

And Angel said again:

—It is said: "Worship the Lord your God, and serve Him only." Worship God - and He shall forgive Thou.

And then He said in great wrath:

—It is also said: "And His servants shall serve Him." Come away, servant of God, and let Me follow my Path. The Path of a free man.

LUCIFER'S SON. DAY 20.

And the twentieth day came.

And Lucifer was ask'd by His Son:

—Can one rely on aught at all in this ordinary?

And Lucifer answer'd to His Son:

—Nay. Thou can rely on thee only. Such is the nature of the ordinary.

DIAGNOSIS

Lucifer's Son

"Take and eat; this is my body."
Gospel of Matthew.

"What are you willing to give me if
I deliver him over to you?"
So they counted out for him thirty pieces of silver."
Gospel of Matthew.

1.

"Do you have any relatives?" the doctor was nervous and didn't look him in the eye.

"Yes, my wife," said Chilikin in amazement. "Why?"

"Please tell her to come see me soon …"

"What's the matter?" Chilikin became cold. He didn't understand anything but felt that something was wrong.

"I'll explain everything to her," the doctor was still hiding his eyes.

"Well, all right," Chilikin shrugged his shoulders, while dressing calmly and coolly. Yet, he wasn't calm deep inside. He could imagine a little of what it could mean, what all these evasive answers could mean. He was there but in a bit different role. He had to play the role of a relative, who was asked 'soon'. Like when his mother was diagnosed unexpectedly—liver cancer.

It was almost the same way. She was leading her life without any complaints; she submitted documents for her pension, she was about to see a medical board, then bam! Here you go! This is it! She didn't last for a year after that. Beginning from that moment, she started fading, withering. That was mysticism, illusion. It seemed as if she gotten ill at that moment, and before that, she was absolutely healthy. Like, if she hadn't visited that cursed hospital, nothing would have happened to her. She would still be living without knowing that she'd gotten cancer. It seemed that they didn't make a diagnosis but infected her with cancer. Chilikin understood with his mind that it wasn't true but couldn't help himself. It just seemed so likely. No wonder many people were afraid of hospitals and hated consulting doctors—probably for the same reasons. Well, you just live a life without any knowledge whatsoever; maybe, you're gonna live for a hundred years, and what if they find anything?

Well, so it seemed that they had found something with me, something unusual. That's for sure. What exactly? Well, we'll find it out without any wife. Why would I scare her? And if there's anything to be scared of, all the more reason I shouldn't tell her. First, I have to deal with it. And then we'll see what's to be done.

Chilikin told the doctor good-bye with exaggerated politeness and left his office.

"Well?" his friend who had been waiting for him in the hall stood up. It was he who made Chilikin start all of it—all this fucking checking of his precious health. His mother was working in that fucking center; she was a manager or a clerk, the mother of his friend. "Come on" and "Come on, you live around the corner. And we'll do everything we can for you, on the VIP level. They're going do the overall check-up. Completely, from top to bottom." *Well, I did fucking check. I checked too much. 'Do you have any relatives?' Well, I'll be damned! Are they going to bury me or what?*

"Listen, Dima," said Chilikin, suffering from inner embarrassment, "it's unclear. It's a mess. They didn't tell me anything, but they want my wife to see them. Would you talk to your mother? Let her ask them?"

His friend was taken aback for a moment, but then looked at Chilikin in surprise. "All right, wait here," he ordered at last and went to the office. Chilikin was left alone in the hall.

***

When his friend came out of the office ten minutes later, he had a strange look on his face—actually, the same one the doctor had. He stared at Chilikin as if seeing him for the first time.

"You know," he said haltingly and coughed, "they said that you should submit the tests anew."

"Listen, Dima," said Chilikin softly and patiently, trying to make his voice sound convincing. "Are you going to play hide-and-seek with me, as well? Tell me what they said."

"Umm," his friend was hesitating and didn't know what to do in this situation. Then he resolved. "Well, they said that there's suspected cancer. But that's not for sure!" he said hastily. "You should have the tests again."

"What kind of cancer?" asked Chilikin softly. He realized that he'd been ready for that deep inside. Well, not for cancer, exactly. Maybe, for some other filth, a similar one; there are a lot of diseases in the world. Well, it was clear that everything was serious. Otherwise, why would they want to talk to relatives?

"Liver," mumbled his friend and glanced at Chilikin. He still was very calm. It seemed that someone else was diagnosed with a mortal disease. Liver means the end. Fucking disaster. Six months at most. No surgery would help. Lesions would start spreading through the whole body, or maybe they already did—through all the organs. All the blood flows through liver.

He went through that with his mother and his father who died swiftly from cancer, too. Lung cancer. So, Chilikin had a very nice inheritance—a corresponding one. The most appropriate. He could as well get into the coffin!

"So, how much time have I got?" asked Chilikin with the same cold calmness. "Well, Dima, you should understand," he explained to him softly, seeing that his friend didn't have the heart to tell him. "I must know it. I have to put my business in order. And, in general, that's serious stuff, you know."

"They said half a year, at most," Dima was perplexed by this inadequate behavior of Chilikin. It seemed that he had been waiting for something else.

"I see," said Chilikin thoughtfully. *There you go, I guessed it right!* He smiled to himself. *I had a gut feeling.* "Well, that's all right. I have enough fucking time."

His friend startled and looked at him with an anxious fear. He must have thought that Chilikin had gone crazy because all of this or that he couldn't fully understand what was happening and was simply shocked, that he was prostrated and couldn't grasp the situation.

"Well, Dima, see you!" Chilikin offered his hand. "Sorry, but I have to be alone. Don't tell anyone yet, neither my mother nor my wife. Okay? *Although, my mother will find it out, that's for sure*,: he thought at once.

"All right," his friend was embarrassed and didn't know what to do next.

"Well, see you!" Chilikin was about to leave, but suddenly halted. "But why didn't they tell me anything?" he asked. But he already knew the answer.

"You see..." his friend Dima was completely embarrassed, "People usually react differently in such situations. Some of them try to commit suicide at once. They jump out of the window, straight from the doctor's office."

2.

Leaving the hospital, Chilikin lit a cigarette and headed home. Actually, it was a long walk from there—about an hour or so—but, now, it was for the best. Summer—nice weather, calm—through Moscow alleys, you may walk slowly and look around without haste. No need to hurry—now he had no need to hurry at all. All his mundane affairs had come to an end. He had a lot of time in the future. The whole eternity, six months long.

Though, I seem to be wrong about mundane affairs, the thought flashed through his mind. *What's ended? Nothing has even started."* He saw an empty teetering board near a building, sat down on it, bending his legs, and, keeping his feet on the ground, started to swing back and forth. *My family is going to be left destitute. Actually, they're going to lose shirts. Well, my wife will be okay; she's an adult. But what about the child? How is she going to make it with the kid? Where will she go, what will she do? It's impossible to find a job now, and what can she do anyway? Who will she leave the kid with? Nursery? Does it still exist? I doubt it.*

Chilikin's wife didn't have a job—she stayed at home with the child and they subsisted on his salary. Chilikin was doing quite decently but not enough to save any money. He didn't have any savings. He just didn't have enough time to make them. So, with his death, his family's small world was going to ruin, and his wife might as well start begging. She could start begging with an outstretched hand, or she could go on the streets. This thought made Chilikin sweat. He became wet.

Well... he carefully exhaled at last, *a nice conversation... I've been living and got to this. Now I'm going to send my wife on the streets. I seem to be a normal guy; I'm smart and hard-working—and what's the result? I guess I've hit rock bottom. Why has it come to this?* Deep in thought, Chilikin looked up at the sky, at the clouds. *The clouds are drifting. They're drifting slowly. They must be warm. And I..." Well, here we go—that was kind of unexpected.*

Chilikin snapped away the cigarette which he had smoked to the very filter tip and stood up from the teetering board. He sighed and went home. He felt incredibly sad, dreary, and heavy—sheer hopelessness, desperation. As a matter of fact, he wasn't thinking about himself. He already kissed himself goodbye. Well, he's going die—big deal—everybody dies in this world." But his family, his child—well!

Maybe I should kill someone, he thought lazily, *or rob someone. I've got nothing to lose, anyway. A bank or cash-in-transit car? Although, can I really do it?* Chilikin sighed heavily again.

How? With what? It's nonsense, a piece of crap—baby talk and daydreaming. 'I wish that...' I wish I could do that, but how? I'd have to buy a gun first, and where would I do that? Who should I contact? I don't know where to start. And indeed," Chilikin spat out angrily. *I have a month or two, at most, while I still can do anything. And then it will begin quickly. It will be constantly worsening. Faintness, pain and other stuff. I know it; I've been there. Weapon—what fucking weapon are you talking about? Fucking gangster. Al Capone. What can I do in a month? And I won't be able to do it. I won't! It's not my style! It'll all end with me getting shot, and that's it. And I won't get any money like this. If it was so easy, everybody would be robbing the banks.* With these sad thoughts, Chilikin came to his building.

Well, well, he wondered indifferently, entering the cold hall. *So quickly! Usually you just walk and walk, and now, it seems that I have just left the hospital. Did a whole hour pass?"* He glanced at his watch. *Indeed, an hour. Hmmm, that's curious, so quickly Well, from now on, everything's gonna be quick. Hours, days, weeks, and months. And then, all right,* he came to his senses. *Here it goes! It's very easy to go nuts, if I think about it all the time. I don't want to get stuck on it. I need to catch a break. And what should I be thinking about?"* He kicked the wall of the elevator angrily. *How could I catch a break? Break or no break, the end is the same. You can't miss it. Six months top. Well, what six months am I talking about? I have to do something in a month already. I have to make a decision. Well, six weeks, at most. Why would I torture myself and the others? When pain starts, it will be a fucking disaster. That will be a different me. When you have terminal cancer, no painkiller can help. I need to do something while I still have strength left and the will. Maybe I should jump out of the window How else? Well, all right. We'll think about it Why hurry? I don't want to rush into hell before my father. I'm not gonna be late!"*

Chilikin entered his apartments, changed his shoes, and went into his room. *What about some tea?* he thought while changing. *No, I'd rather not. I don't want tea—drinking tea is a sign of despair. Well,* he looked in the mirror. *How is this possible? I feel no pain, everything is good. And yet, I've got cancer. 'You've got six months to live.' How is this possible?* But he knew that he could. He could—no mistake! *Well! So, where s this cancer, anyway? In my liver? It's a pain in my liver!* joked Chilikin to himself. *And where is it, anyway? Where's the liver? To the right side? Left side?* Chilikin lifted his shirt and touched his right and left sides. He felt no pain. *There you go,* he tucked the shirt and lay down on the bed. He lay on his back with his hands behind his head and stared at the ceiling. *Should I turn on the TV, let it babble? No, I'd better lie here in silence. I need to think. Well, what's the point of thinking? It's as clear as day. I'm jumping out of the window, my wife is going on the street, and it's unclear what's gonna happen to the baby. Well, it's gonna be okay. My wife is going support her with her pussy. Fuck it!* Chilikin gritted his teeth at his helplessness. *And that's the best option,* he smiled cynically at once, wishing to drain the cup of grief and humiliation to the dregs, at one draught. *That's the most optimistic and idealistic option for supporting herself and the child. There's fierce competition there. Nobody's waiting for her with outstretched arms. They have enough volunteers, young and fresh. There are even too many of them.*

Shit! I'm beginning to change already! Chilikin turned cold. *I'm beginning to rot alive. It seems that this cursed tumor gnaws my body and my soul, as well. The lesions appear in the soul, too. What am I thinking about my own wife? She's the mother of my own child. Why am I considering her as a potential whore? Why am I evaluating her in this respect? Well, I'm guessing what level she's gonna be at. How many bucks is she going to get? What could she do? Is she competitive enough? Is she young enough? What's wrong with me? Maybe I should jump out of the window right now while it's not too late, before I turn into something awful, into a monster!*

The phone rang suddenly. Chilikin startled and stared at it with painful embarrassment. Do phones still work? Hasn't the world collapsed yet? Is life going on?

"Yeah?" he picked up the phone.

"Hi!" it was his wife. "It's me. What's up? You were supposed to go to the hospital, right?"

"Yeah," hesitated Chilikin. The question took him unawares. He didn't know yet how he should talk to his wife. Should he tell her everything or not? He just didn't expect her to call so soon. "Well, everything's all right."

"Why is your voice so strange?" asked his wife suspiciously, after a pause. "What's wrong?"

"Nothing," answered Chilikin indifferently. "What can be wrong with me?"

"But I can hear it!" his wife was obstinate. It wasn't easy to trick her. "Something's wrong with you."

"You're making stuff up!" interrupted Chilikin with irritation. "By the way, where are you?" he asked after a pause, just to change the topic.

"What do you mean 'where'?" his wife was surprised, "I'm in a child health center. Did you forget? What's wrong with you today?" she asked anxiously after a pause.

"Nothing!" shouted Chilikin, being really irritated. "Nothing," he added calmly, "I'm sorry; you just chose wrong time for the call. I'm busy with work. My boss just called."

"What's wrong with work?" his wife bit at this simple bait at once, becoming worried. Chilikin's work was very important. It was the foundation and basis of the well-being of the family, after all. "Are there any problems?"

"No, there are no problems," Chilikin tried to calm her at once. "Usual routine. Well, I need to work. I don't have much time. See you at home."

"All right, get to work. Bye," said his wife and hung up the phone.

Chilikin listened to the dial tone for some time and then put down the phone. It rang again. Chilikin almost jumped with surprise.

"Yeah?" Who could that be?

"Andrey Pavlovich?" the voice was rather pleasant, although Chilikin didn't know its owner.

"Yeah," said Chilikin, perplexed.

"Hi. I'm calling regarding your diagnosis. We have to meet as soon as possible."

"Excuse me," Chilikin was embarrassed. "What's the matter?"

"Andrey Pavlovich! We shouldn't discuss that on the phone. I'll tell you everything when we meet."

"Well, all right," said Chilikin, still having doubts.

"Great!" the man was clearly self-assured and used to giving orders. Chilikin could feel that. "Let's meet immediately, if you don't mind. I'm near the hospital. Tell me the address. I'll be there soon."

"Are you in a car?" asked Chilikin.

"Yes," briefly answered the man.

"Write down Street Building Wait near the first entrance; I'm going to come down. So, you'll be here in about 15 minutes?"

"All right—in 15 minutes, near the first entrance," repeated the man. "Black BMW 7, plate number, in 15 minutes. See you,"

Chilikin heard the dial tone. He held the phone in his hand thoughtfully.

That's curious. Who could that be? And what does he want of me? Maybe he wants to buy my organs? A liver! I don't need them anymore. Though, what organs can he buy from an oncology patient? It's all infected. Blood takes cancer cells through the whole body through the lymph. No, that's not an option. Maybe it's some illegal stuff, eh? What if it's for third-world countries?.. They're just going to sell it a healthy one. Well, I'm not sure I've never heard about that, although, what have I heard? I don't know nothing in this sphere; I'm completely ignorant. I can't know how they do business. What if that's a normal practice? A usual fucking business? And everything happened so quickly—too quickly, I'd say! Only one hour has passed or even less. I've just come home. Well, slick; that's for sure. Hell of a doctor! Are they all in it? In that center of theirs?

Shit! What if they told me the wrong diagnosis? he thought suddenly. *What if it's all a setup? They tell a man that he's got cancer and then buy his kidneys on the cheap! How could he fucking appear just in an hour? Like a gray wolf from the tale. In a black BMW—angel of death! Did he wait for me near the hospital? What the fuck is this? That's very strange!"* All these thoughts made Chilikin's head reel. He felt desperate hope appearing in his soul. It was yet weak and faint, but it grew with every second. It was growing stronger. *Shit! Is it indeed a setup? A normal performance? Really? So, maybe I'm healthy, eh? What if this cancer is fucking bullshit? What if they just want to get money from me? Bastards! A healthy man!* Chilikin almost persuaded himself. He had no doubts. *Of course, I'm healthy! Why not? I've never had any problems, and here you go!*

"My father never had any problems, either," grumbled a gloomy voice at the back of his mind, but Chilikin waved it off discontentedly. *Get lost! Indeed, they just couldn't diagnose it so quickly; one must be thoroughly examined. Right. Well!*

Or maybe, he could be a kind of a healer? he thought suddenly. *A fucking psychic, sorcerer and magician. 'Traditional medicine can't help you, but there's no need to despair, Andrey Pavlovich! No, by no means! We're going to save you. Though, as a matter of fact, your case is rather serious, but...' Well, and so on and so forth,* Chilikin felt as if someone spilled a tub of cold water on him. *Shit! Well, of course, that's possible—very likely. That's a working version. They've got the doctor on a payroll; why not? That's right!*

That's a business attitude. If a man was given a death sentence, it's clear that he will do anything, especially, if he's got money. But here you're wrong, dear sirs. Right—you're not going to get anything from me! I'm poor as a church mouse; I've got nothing at all. So, you're showing off in vain, and there's no need to burn expensive gas. There's no need to spend your precious time for me. 'In 15 minutes! Black BMW 7!' Fuck you! Find some other fool—I'm not one! I've got nothing to give you."

Chilikin looked around the room. *Maybe I shouldn't go, eh? It's just gonna kill my mood. No, I made a deal, and, anyway, I should listen to him. That's all my imagination; what if he tells me something else? Although, what can he tell? It's clear—'we'll help you.' What else can he tell the sick'? Well, I probably over-exaggerated the stuff with organs; I overreacted. It's too scary. Still, I should probably do some research about a fake diagnosis. That wouldn't hurt. And I think they're going to double-check it a lot of times. What if...?"*

"Oh," Chilikin waved his hand desperately. *"I'm just grasping at straws. All sick people start persuading themselves that it's a mistake. My mother and father did the same. Don't you remember? Well, I need to go. It's not polite to be late, especially when all you have to do is to go down. The man will come to you himself. He will drive to your building.*

Chilikin stood up slowly and began changing.

***

Thirteen minutes later, he was standing on the street. And, two minutes later, a luxurious black BMW drove along a narrow path to the entrance. It was shining as if it was new—a BMW 7 with the right number plates.

Healers make a nice living! thought Chilikin with jealousy, looking at the expensive interior and greeting an elegant man in his forties who was sitting behind the wheel. *I'd say they make an excellent living, excellent! Well, let's say that I didn't come down in vain. At least, I get to sit in an expensive car in the end. One for the road.*

"Andrey Pavlovich!" Meanwhile, the potential magician started the conversation. "Unfortunately, I know your diagnosis." *How come?* smiled Chilikin softly to himself. "I sympathize with you, but it's the nature of life." *And it's the nature of death,* Chilikin continued the phrase with the same faint irony. "And it's the nature of death," said the magician, as if overhearing his thoughts. Chilikin startled and looked at the man in astonishment. *What the hell is that?*

"Therefore, I have a rather unusual offer for you concerning death." *What else? Is it really organs?* thought Chilikin quickly. The man went silent and stared at Chilikin. Then, after a long pause, he continued. "My offer is the following," he halted for a moment, "You commit suicide in front of the camera—you hang yourself. All the details of your suicide will be shot by a camera—from the moment of preparing and putting your head into the noose to the agony and the subsequent death. For that, I'm going to pay you," the man paused again and, still staring at Chilikin, said calmly, "100 thousand euro."

"What?" Chilikin even rose a bit in his leather seat. "How much?"

"One hundred thousand euro," repeated the man softly. Chilikin swallowed convulsively. Blood was throbbing in his ears. His head was completely empty.

"And when do I have to do that?" he asked at last, trying to talk calmly.

"In a week or two at most. Well, you must understand…" the man looked at Chilikin meaningfully.

"Yes, I do," he smiled wryly. "The client must have a market condition."

"It's a pleasure to deal with a smart man!" the man smiled, too, and added unexpectedly. "You know, Andrey Pavlovich, you're a fine fellow!"

Strangely enough, it was pleasant for Chilikin to hear that compliment. He was astonished by this thought. A man is indeed a strange creature, a paradoxical one!

Right, Andrey Pavlovich! Say yes! Hang yourself! You're a fine fellow! Thank you! Andrey Pavlovich smiles shyly and happily, being utterly flattered. *I'm a moron,* thought Chilikin to himself, *the biggest moron there is.*

"Well, we should talk about technical details," the man smiled kindly to Chilikin, "concerning money, in particular."

"Sure," Chilikin suddenly realized. "Of course."

"So, if you agree, I'll give you half of the money at once," Chilikin caught his breath, "and I'll give the second half to your relatives when everything's finished. To your wife, right?" the man looked at Chilikin inquiringly. He kept silent, embarrassed.

"The same day," the man didn't get any answer, so he continued. "Well, if you want, we can put the other half in a safe-deposit box, luggage locker or something like that," he shrugged his shoulders. "If you wish, you can secure it yourself. But, frankly speaking, I wouldn't, if I were you," the man kept silent for some time. "In case of an investigation, it might become known, and then your family would have unwanted problems. With the authorities, I mean," he specified, seeing Chilikin startle. "They're going to ask, 'What is that? Where did it come from?' And what will your wife tell them? They're going to embarrass and scare her, and it's all going to end with them taking the money from her—confiscating it to the profit of the state until the end of investigation. Well, you know how they do it!" the man smiled to Chilikin sympathetically.

"All in all, Andrey Pavlovich, here's my advice—the simpler, the better! That's why I recommend to you the simplest and most reliable option. At any rate, I'm going to need a suicide note from you, a standard one as they usually write in such situations. 'No one is to be blamed in my death,' or something like that. You will give it to your wife, and then she will exchange it for the second half of the money. Mind you, that would be the cleverest option; that would be convenient for everyone. If, of course, you agree," the man went silent, looking at Chilikin inquiringly.

"I agree," he squeaked. Then he coughed and repeated in a normal voice. "Yes, I agree."

"All right," the man reached his hand, took five bank packs of 10,000 euro each from the glove compartment and held them out to Chilikin carelessly. "Fifty thousand even; no need to count."

Chilikin took the money with his shaking hands.

"Here, take this," the man gave Chilikin a bag, seeing that he had nothing to put the money in; he was about to try to stuff it in his pockets. Chilikin put the money in the bag without a word. "All right, Andrey Pavlovich, I have to go," the man glanced at his watch, which was incredibly beautiful, and scowled a bit. "I'm running late already. So, we have a deal. I'm going to call you in a week, and we'll talk about the details. You should be ready by that time, just in case. Put your business in order"—Chilikin startled; he remembered that he used this phrase word for word with Dima in the hospital an hour-and-a-half before that, "I have to order my business and do other stuff concerning my mental state."

"Excuse me!" Chilikin resolved to ask at last. "Please, don't get me wrong," he hesitated. "What if I change my mind?" burst out Chilikin, plucking up his courage. "Well, I'm not going to change my mind," he tried to explain at once, although his companion didn't react whatsoever to his remark and continued to look at him calmly and kindly. "But, you see, I have to talk to my wife What if she's against it?" *Oh, God! What am I talking? What does my wife have to do with it?* "Or if the diagnosis doesn't prove correct—such things happen!" he added quietly, just to say something, and lowered his eyes. He was very ashamed of his weakness. *Happen? Happen! Everything happens. And it could happen that nothing happens at all. Happen! Oh, what a shame! I'm a nicey-nice!*

"You know, Andrey Pavlovich, let's make a deal." As if nothing had happened, the man smiled softly at Chilikin, pretending that he hadn't heard anything. "A week is a long time. It's enough time to talk to your wife and have another test. So, please, make a decision by the time I call you next time. All right? If you change your mind, you'll just give the money back, that's it, but without any further delays. And don't change your mind after that. You have to understand me," he shook his head sadly. "I have to make some preparations, as well—renting the building, hiring the men, renting the equipment It's a lot of expenses. And what if you change your mind after that? Well?"

"No," muttered Chilikin with a heavy sigh, "I won't. *If no miracle happens!* he thought sadly. *A-ah!* "I won't change my mind!" he repeated confidently and looked straight in his companion's eyes. His smile seemed to become wider. "You may be sure of that; everything's going to be like we agreed."

"Excellent!" the man offered his hand to Chilikin. "Then I'll call you on Tuesday."

"Right," Chilikin shook his hand and got out of the car.

3.

Arriving at home, Chilikin went to the kitchen and put on the kettle. Then he went to his room with the bag and put the money on the bed—five neat packs in bank wrappings. Chilikin even smelled them with pleasure, inhaling deeply the smell of newly printed money, which couldn't be compared to anything—the smell of freedom, of happiness, and of prosperity; the smell of life!

Of death, he thought suddenly. Squirming with disgust, he threw the packs away. He even felt an urge to wash his hands thoroughly. .for he smelled clearly the sickly, sweetish, and pestilent odor. It was elusive, but still could be sensed the odor of a tomb, a grave. a coffin. *Shit! I'm too nervous*, Chilikin took a breath, calming down slowly. *I'm a weak sister! Soon there will be hysterics and fainting.*

Nevertheless, it was unpleasant to look at the money on the bed. It seemed to be not the money; Chilikin couldn't understand what it resembled him and what association it triggered, but there was definitely something menacing and scary in it—a message from the other world, a friendly hand of a devil—his wolfish paw. An invitation to hell, a pass, a ticket with a notification about the safe arrival. The next five packs would mean that the client had arrived.

But I'm never going to see those five packs, thought Chilikin suddenly, and this simple and obvious thought shocked him *Ten packs would mean that I'm in hell already. Or, maybe, in paradise?* he smiled sadly. *Yeah, right! Sure, in paradise—in your dreams! Suiciders don't go to paradise. They go straight to hell, straight to some circle. I need to consult Dante about what circle that is. What should I be preparing for?*

Well, these are jokes, but...so, a week; I see. Why am I not happy, eh? Everything's so great with money, like in a fairy tale. And I'm sad, anyway; might as well cry.

By the way, concerning money, Chilikin bit his lower lip while making tea. *That's somewhat too simple and easy—no acquittances, nothing at all! He just took 50 grand out of the glove compartment and gave it to me. 'Here, Andrey Pavlovich, take a bag, for you have nothing to put it in!' A miracle!*

"What if I... what? What can I do with my disease? And what's the point? Yeah, that's right, but still. There are different people. There are complete idiots. He's just going to say, 'I didn't take anything!' and what are you gonna do with him? Moreover, he has his foot in a grave! He doesn't give a fuck!" Giving 50,000 euro to the man you've just met! Without any documents! That's strange! That's really strange! It's clear that it's strange. Well, why do I care, anyway? What's the difference? That's their problem. Maybe 50 grand is not a lot of money for them. Well, chicken shit—I don't give a fuck! Let them deal with it."

"Well, I'm just curious. Shit! The tea is very hot, I burnt myself! Why did he give me so much money? Moreover, he gave it to me at once, without bargaining; I would have agreed to 50—easily! Come on, what 50? I would have done it for 20, or even 10. I would have sold my soul to the devil. I would have given it away. Well!" Chilikin waved his hand in his thoughts. *"If he had tried, he could have bought me even cheaper. With guts. I'm worthless. I've got no money, and I'm leaving my family with nothing, with a naked ass.*

Fucking breadwinner. 'I, I, head of the family, my job, I'—fuck! Head! Dickhead! Ugh!" Chilikin sipped some hot tea and hissed with pain. *"Fuck! I burnt the whole roof of the mouth,"* he touched the shreds of tender skin with his tongue. *"Shit! So, concerning money,"* Chilikin indifferently tickled his chin with a thumb. *"Why am I bothering? Because they gave me too much? Why should I care? Too much is not too few. But they did give it to me. They didn't just promise, it's no trick; it's completely true! They did. There it is, in the room, on the bed! I can go there and take delight,"* the thought of the money made Chilikin squirm. *"So, why would I care? Everything's great—never better! Though, never worse, either. And if it is, it's not so often. All right, all right! Enough sulking enough scowling and grumbling. As the song says. The Angel of Death himself paid me a compliment, the one in the black BMW. He said that I'm a 'fine fellow.' I need to maintain my reputation."*

Chilikin finished his tea, washed the cup, and went to his room. He put the money into the bag, lay on the bed, turned on the TV, and began waiting for his wife. He wasn't bored—quite on the contrary. Time was flowing unnaturally quickly; it was rushing. A merciless chronometer inside him was counting minute after minute, and he was listening to it. Another minute passed; another one—shit!

4.

One hour, 42 minutes and 23 seconds later, his wife came back from the hospital. Chilikin heard the door slam and looked in the corridor.

Right. Oh, God, here it begins, Chilikin scowled. *Maybe I shouldn't tell her, he* thought faint-heartedly, realizing at the same time that it was absolutely impossible now. *Well, I could wait for the results of the second examination, but what's the point? That's nonsense—piece of crap! The probability of a mistake is very small—it's almost zero. What mistake am I talking about? They checked my blood, and they saw something on a screen. They saw it. Well, come on; I shouldn't be relying upon that. That's a shame. I don't want to lose faith. I'm not a child. And I'm not an ostrich that hides his head in sand. I have to face the truth. That would be fair Well, fair, fair,* Chilikin looked at the ceiling sadly. Still, he didn't want to tell her anything. *What if I tell her after the second examination?* he began convincing himself. *In a week, when everything is confirmed? 'Darling! Here's the money, and I'm gonna hang tomorrow! Remember me kindly.' Like this? I have to do it right. Humanely. I have to tell her beforehand. Discuss it. Talk to her and explain about other half of the money."*

"Or shouldn't I tell her? Eh?" Chilikin didn't know what to do. He was listening to all sounds and rustles which were coming from the corridor. *Here she comes; what shall I explain? I'd rather leave her a letter with detailed explanation. I'll write her everything—a set of fucking instructions. 'Exchange my suicide note only for...' And so on and so forth.*

Of course, she'll take offence, Chilikin sighed to himself. *Well, why do I care?* he tried to calm down. *I won't care by that time. I won't give a hoot about it! I'll be far away from here, in the afterlife. Then no one can demand anything from me, right?* Chilikin couldn't resolve to do it. He jumped up and started pacing the room in anxiety. *She should understand me,* he began looking for excuses. *It's not that pleasant to spend the last week of life as a seriously ill, as a condemned man. So, I want to relax before the end, as well as I can. Maybe I should go somewhere, visit some bars. I've got money.*

Right, I've got money! What if, Chilikin halted for a moment. *Well,* he waved his hand, *what if? Well, if it happens, then we'll think about it. We'll deal with it. But there won't be any problems. It's as clear as day. What if—it's about fucking disasters. Here you go. Pretty often. It appears in the twinkling of an eye. And the good stuff...*

No, I'm not gonna tell her, he said at last and felt an unspeakable relief. He even cheered up. *All these fucking conversations, tears; I have to go with honor, without crying.*

"You're here?" his wife was surprised, when she entered the room. "You had to go to work, didn't you?"

"I postponed it until tomorrow," carelessly said Chilikin, bringing her closer. "Come to me."

***

The next day, about 11, while Chilikin was still in bed, smoking thoughtfully and puffing smoke at the ceiling, the door slammed, and, in a second, his tear-stained wife rushed into the room.

"Why didn't you tell me anything yesterday?" she shouted as she entered.

Chilikin even dropped the cigarette on the bed in surprise and started looking for it, swearing. "What do you mean?" he said at last, lighting a cigarette and giving a sigh. He knew the answer.

"Your diagnosis," his wife started crying again. "What did they say yesterday?"

"Why, why?" mumbled Chilikin in embarrassment. How could he explain it to her? Why? Because. A nice answers—"because". "It's not for sure," he said at last. "I wanted to wait for the final diagnosis, after I take the repeated examination. Why would I bother you beforehand? I knew that you'd worry," he tried to wheedle his wife. "What if they're wrong?" *Sure!* he smiled sadly to himself.

"Why haven't you told me about the money? And the suicide?" asked his wife again.

"What?" Chilikin stood up in astonishment and dropped the cigarette again. "What?" he repeated in a moment, having pushed the cigarette to the floor and crushing it in an ash-tray. "How do you know that?"

"So, it's true?" his wife began sobbing.

"Wait a bit!" Chilikin yelled at her. "Answer me. Why do you know about it? And about the diagnosis as well? Did they call you from the hospital?" *How could they know my phone number* he thought at once.

"No, not from the hospital," sobbed his wife, wiping her eyes with a handkerchief.

"Then how do you know?" Chilikin sat up on the bed. "Who told you?"

"Well," his wife gave a sigh, trying to calm down, "that man whom you met yesterday who gave you the money? I was at Vera's."

Chilikin was staring at his wife in astonishment and couldn't believe his ears.

"Did he call your friend?" he asked distrustfully. "And how?" Chilikin wanted to ask, "And how could he know the phone number?" but realized that it was useless. How could she know that? How, how? Duh! It seemed that the organization whose representative he had met yesterday was more serious that he thought. As a matter of fact, he didn't think about that at all. He didn't have time, and he was busy. And if he had given it a little thought, he would have guessed it, with such money. Well, it's clear how he knew the number.

It's not clear why the fuck he called her at all. What the fuck is that? He should have warned Chilikin. He didn't tell him anything and just called her… He pinned him down to facts. *Fuck! What if I don't hang myself? What an arrogant guy! And what for? What for? We already had a deal. Why did he contact my wife?*

"What did he tell you?" Chilikin attacked his wife, who was still sobbing. "Tell me what he said—word for word."

"Well, he asked, at first, if I knew what they diagnosed you with?" babbled his scared wife, looking at Chilikin with wide eyes. "I said that I didn't; you didn't tell me anything."

"Well," Chilikin cheered her up, "And then?"

"Then he said," his wife wept again, "that it was liver cancer!"

"Stop crying!" said Chilikin discontentedly. "What was next?"

"Then he said that he had offered you the money, and you had agreed."

"Did he explain in detail? Oh, well," Chilikin remembered the beginning of their conversation. "Hold on!" he thought suddenly. "Did he tell you everything on the phone?"

"No," sobbed his wife again, "in a black car…"

"Fuck!" Chilikin swore to himself. "So, you met, right?" he asked patiently, ready to burst.

"Yeah," said his wife, as if it was something normal. "He drove straight to Verka's place. Verka must have been shocked!" she added acidly, with women's anomaly.

Chilikin ground his teeth and closed his eyes for a second, trying to calm down. "Yulia!" he said in a calm voice. "Can you tell me everything in detail? How did it happen—from the beginning until the end? Can you? Is this so difficult?" he shouted, being unable to restrain himself.

Well, they truly say that all women are stupid,: he thought in wrath. *Stupid, stupid, stupid! Stupid and witless hens! Her husband is going to hang himself in a week, and she's babbling about her friend Vera! Same idiot as her. I don't give a fuck if she was shocked or not! I don't fucking care!*

"But I told you everything!" said his wife in an injured voice, ceasing to cry.

"And now tell me everything again, from the very beginning," asked Chilikin persistently. "You were at Verka's, he called there. What then?"

"He wanted to talk to me."

"How? Did he say your name? Just "Yulia?" Or by name and patronymic? By surname?" interrupted her Chilikin.

"How would I know?" he heard slight irritation in his wife's tone. She obviously couldn't understand what he wanted from her and what this interrogation was about. Well, he wanted to talk to her; he said something, name or no name. What's the difference? He stuck like a bur! "Verka said, 'it's for you'—well, I took the phone."

"Alright!" Chilikin continued, "You took the phone. And what did he tell you?"

"Well, what?" his wife shrugged her shoulders in irritation. "Hi, Yulia Vladimirovna!"

"Oh! So it was actually name and patronymic," noted Chilikin with pleasure. He then decided not to interrupt her. He didn't want to have a fight with his wife.

"I'm calling concerning your husband's diagnosis, concerning his examination yesterday. We need to meet as soon as possible," his wife halted, trying to remember. Chilikin waited. "'I'm not far; come down in 5 minutes, I'll be waiting near the entrance.' Then he told me the number plates."

"So, you didn't even tell him the address, did you?" asked Chilikin in amazement. "He knew where to go?"

"Yeah," his wife wrinkled her forehead. "I think I didn't. And I don't know the address, anyway."

"Well, well," thought Chilikin. He didn't know, why he was questioning her so thoroughly, but he felt that it was important. "So, it appears that he knew my address yesterday. He asked me, in order not to scare me; he didn't want to frighten me away. I see."

"Well, all right. And what then? You got in the car, and what did he tell you?"

"Well he told me that," tears appeared in the woman's eyes, "about your diagnosis and about your deal," she cried again. "How could you agree to that?" she said weepingly. "That is a sin—suicide!"

"Come on, a sin," said Chilikin in embarrassment. *I know that! And what the fuck can I do? Sin! And leaving the family without money—isn't it a sin?* "Yulia," he said carefully after a pause, "you do know our situation. We've got no money. How are you going to live with the baby? What are you going to eat, the Holy Spirit? I want my baby to be healthy; I want him to live like others. And I want you to be okay. So what can I do? Sin or no sin, I've got no choice!"

Would it be better, if you went on the street? he wanted to add, but checked himself. "Sin!"

His wife didn't say anything but wept again. Chilikin lit a cigarette with trembling hands and stared straight ahead. His head was empty. He felt very gloomy and sad.

"Well, one day is gone, he realized clearly. *Six days are left... 'Life is flowing like goose down...' 'Meter's clicking constantly—you'll have to pay at the end of the road!' You'll have to. We'll pay, if we have to... all right.*

"By the way, did he say why he told you all that? Did he explain that to you?" asked Chilikin, just in case, although he didn't expect to hear anything new from her.

His wife kept sobbing for some time, and then, sniffling, answered in a choking voice, "He said that with such money, there should be no surprises, and he had to be sure that all concerned parties stay informed," her voice faltered. "That's what he said," she added after a pause.

"Bastard!" swore Chilikin angrily to himself. "Heartless wretch!" *Although, why do I yell at him?"* he realized suddenly. *That's just business for him. He's risking his money. And, as a matter of fact, he's acting like a gentleman with me. I can't complain. No acquittances, cash in advance. That's it! What else do I want from him? Compassion? Here you go, with an extra charge. Hang yourself, not for a hundred grand, but for thirty grand, and I'll weep over your body—sob violently, before or after, according to the deal. Well. Business is business. It's just money, nothing personal. And, actually, no additional stuff—it goes for extra charges only. Well...*

Yulia is tough! I'd been questioning her for a whole hour before I got something. Although, what can I demand from her, a woman? She's got only curlers on her mind. Me too, though; I didn't act nicely! I attacked her like a vulture; I started an investigation. What and where? "Word for word." And what did I find out, what important stuff? That the Volga flows in Caspian Sea? That they don't need any surprises, and they want to secure themselves and to be sure that my wife knows everything and has nothing against it? That she won't sue them and go to the police? That was clear from the very beginning. Chilikin could have realized that, he could have grasped that with his wretched mind. *Fucking Pinkerton! Sherlock fucking Holmes.*

"Did he really give you 50,000 euro?" Chilikin heard his wife ask. Deep in his sad thoughts, he didn't understand at once what she was talking about.

"What?" he asked her.

"I said, did he really give you 50,000 euro?" his wife repeated his question.

"Yeah," said Chilikin reluctantly. He produced the bag and put the money on the bed. "Here it is."

His wife stared at the packs on the bed with fascination. She had never seen such a sum of money in her whole life. Then she took a pack and fingered it tentatively.

"Is it really 50,000?" she asked softly.

"Yeah," said Chilikin. "There's 10 grand in every pack. Here, hundred euro bills in every pack, 100 euro, 100 bills in a pack, 100 times 100—10,000."

"Well." said his wife quietly, staring at the pack. "Every bill is 100 euro! And here's a whole pack of them! One—100 euro; one—100 euro! I can't believe it!"

"You'd better believe it!" muttered Chilikin, taking the money away.

His wife followed it with her eyes. Then she looked at her husband. "So, you really want to do it?" she whispered very quietly. She was about to start crying again. "What about me?"

"Yulia, come on!" Chilikin was sad enough without that. "Well, it's no use plowing the air. You're a grown woman; you must understand everything. If I got cancer, I have six months to live, at most. You know that my parents died from cancer, and I saw it all with my own eyes. I saw how it went. Drugs and attendance. And do we have any money? I want to leave something for the family, for the child," Chilikin felt a lump rolling up his throat. "Hey, let's not talk about it anymore," he asked her quietly, taking hold of himself. "All right?"

"But it's a mortal sin!" his wife was staring at him in horror. "I won't be able to live, knowing that you did it because of me.»

"Come on," interrupted her Chilikin in grief. "Don't blame yourself. Consider that I'm doing it for the child. Let's change the subject, all right? I feel bad about it. Really!"

5.

The next six days went by in a twinkling for Chilikin. First day, second, third. It seemed that it was Tuesday yesterday, and today is Tuesday again. Since the morning, Chilikin felt ill at ease. His wife was gone on her business; truthfully, Chilikin had lied to her, saying that they would call him on Wednesday, and he was smoking ceaselessly in the kitchen, looking out of the window, and waiting for the call. Now, here it goes!.

Deep inside, he couldn't fully believe the reality of what was happening. Well, how come that he has to die today or tomorrow? What's the meaning of this?

So, I'll just cease to exist, or what? How's that? Forever? World, sun, earth, water, trees, sky, wind, birds, and people around—will it all remain, when I'm gone? Forever? Forever? That's not possible!

Chilikin imagined himself hanging. He stands on a stool puts his head in a noose, tightens it a bit, then a short movement of his legs, and... ugh! Chilikin remembered that he had read about a doctor conducting experiments on himself. He hung himself, and his assistant saved him from the noose. The doctor wanted to know what a hanged man felt. And how do people manage to hang themselves when they are lying on a bed? It seemed that the self-preservation instinct should turn on at the last moment and make a man get out of noose when he starts choking. Moreover, it's so easy in this situation. No way. According to the doctor, when the noose starts to tighten, a man cannot move at all. Either the aorta gets squeezed or something else, but the fact remains. A man is filled with a great weakness, his body turns to jelly, and all his essence is filled with a wave of unbearable, deathly horror.

It seemed to Chilikin that he clearly saw indifferent body lifters take his blue, dead body from the noose, put him carelessly on a stretcher, and take him to the morgue. There, they undress him completely, put the tag on his toe, and heft him onto the zinc table. And nearby, there are same tables with same naked bodies, male and female; hideous yellow corpses of ugly withered old women, hobos, drunkards, etc.

Then they roll the table with him for the autopsy: they rip open his chest and his skull and rummage in his bowels. After that, they sew him up. During all this time, he's lying there indifferently, feeling and not feeling all of it at the same time. He can't move, and he feels no pain, for the body doesn't belong to him anymore, but some of his senses remain. He is a kind of animated stone or a piece of raw meat. He's impassive to what they do to him, but, somehow, he feels it.

Then he's dressed again, put into the coffin and taken to cemetery. They close the coffin with the lid, nail it closed, and put it down into the damp and cold grave. They cover it and leave.

Forever. And he lies underground, in this narrow, small, and stuffy coffin without air; he can't breathe, move, or turn over. He's pressed down by a heavy, solid, and thick layer of soil, deep underground, in the coffin.

The phone rang loudly. Chilikin startled and grabbed it quickly, unable to understand anything. "Yeah?"

"Andrey Pavlovich?" he heard a familiar slow voice.

"Yes, it's me."

"Hi. We need to meet urgently." Chilikin felt his heart sink.

"Hi. When?" he asked in a faltered voice.

"Now would be great, say, in 10 minutes, at the same place. Is it okay with you?"

"Sure," Chilikin halted. "And then what?"

"It won't take long, Andrey Pavlovich. Half an hour."

"All right," said Chilikin with a huge relief. "Phew!" He felt a load lift from his mind. *So, not today. Phew! Of course. We had a deal—a week or two. So I should be able to bargain for another week, and then we'll see. What's the point of guessing? What's the point of thinking about it? A week is almost an eternity.*

"And bring the money with you," said the man suddenly, "the money that I gave you last time."

"Excuse me?" said Chilikin.

"Andrey Pavlovich! I'll explain everything to you in person," the man interrupted him. "Come down. and we'll have a talk," Chilikin heard the dial tone on the phone.

Chilikin's high spirits vanished without a trace. "Oh, God! What's happened? Did he change his mind? Why?"

Chilikin got dressed, grabbed the bag with the money, and went outside. At exactly appointed time, to the minute, a familiar BMW drove to the entrance. Chilikin took delight in it before he got inside. *Beautiful!*

I'm curious how many people hung themselves, so this man with the cold face could buy it—10, 20, 100? Chilikin shivered.

The man seemed to feel his mood and smiled softly. Then he looked intently, straight into Chilikin's eyes and said after a pause, "Congratulations, Andrey Pavlovich! You're healthy; your diagnosis proved wrong."

"What?" Chilikin didn't get it at first. For some reason, he wasn't thinking about that. "What did you say?" he almost shouted a second later. "How do you know?"

"Well, you did take another test," explained the man calmly, looking at Chilikin with interest. "And the results came up this morning."

"Eh? Oh, right. I see. And what about the first time?.." asked Chilikin after a pause.

He still couldn't realize what he had heard. *What does he mean by 'healthy'? Everything's ended? All this horror is ended, as simple as that?*

"Your organism has a very rare peculiarity, and the doctors were deceived by it," explained the man calmly, still looking intently at Chilikin. It seemed that he could read him like a book. Chilikin kept silent, not knowing what to say. "Andrey Pavlovich!" continued the man calmly after a pause. "As you must understand, our deal automatically ceases to be effective. Although, if you want…," he joked suddenly and smiled.

"No, no!" Chilikin supported his humorous tone and broke into a broad smile, too. "God forbid! Here's your money! All of it."

"Excellent!" the man took the bag with the money from Chilikin and put it carelessly into the glove compartment, without checking. "One more thing, Andrey Pavlovich," Chilikin was staring at his companion, grinning cheerfully. "Please read this," the man gave Chilikin a piece of paper folded into fourths.

"What is that?" asked Chilikin automatically, unfolding the paper and looking through it quickly. "What is that?" he repeated in a shaking voice, in a moment, lifting up his eyes. His smile froze on his face, as if it was glued.

"Read it," his companion shrugged his shoulders.

Chilikin read it again, quickly at first, and then slower and slower, halting, stumbling at every word

Promissory Note

I, Chilikina Yulia Vladimirovna, do allow the use the body of my husband, Chilikin Andrey Pavlovich, as an object of sexual acts (necrophilia), and allow video recording of these acts, for 20 (twenty) thousand euro.

Date.Signature.

Ten thousand euro received.

Date.Signature.

"What's the meaning of this?" he said at last, slowly lifting his eyes at the man sitting near him.

"Well, you read it!" he shrugged his shoulders slightly. "It's your wife's promissory note."

"What's 'necrophilia?'" asked Chilikin heavily. Although, he knew it very well.

"Copulation with a corpse," explained his companion immovably. "You know that, Andrey Pavlovich. Why do you ask?"

"Did she sell my corpse so it could be fucked in front of the camera when I hang myself?" Chilikin just couldn't realize that. *That's absurdity! Necrophilia! Yulia wouldn't even know such a word! She probably never heard of it! And she's a believer, after all! If suicide is a mortal sin, so what's that? It's not even a sin, it's...there are no words for that in human language! It's beyond the limits of morality—maltreatment of her husband's corpse. It's nonsense! Nonsense! Piece of crap!*

"You must be wondering, Andrey Pavlovich, why I'm showing you all this," asked the man politely.

"Yeah," Chilikin could hardly think at all. His head was a complete mess. Only the shreds of some thoughts were fleeting through his mind—cancer, death, money, child, necrophilia, money. Money, money, money. Too many things happened to him. Too much news. His wonderful comeback and now this note Wondering? Indeed, why?" he froze tensely, waiting for an answer and staring at his companion. *What if that's a stupid joke? A trick? What if all of it is not real?*

"Because it seems that Yulia Vladimirovna is not going to give the money back," explained the man kindly. "Therefore, I had to approach you with this matter."

"What matter?" Chilikin asked him bluntly. He couldn't understand or perceive anything. His forehead was burning, his temples were throbbing, and the world was shaking, trembling, and flowing somewhere—somewhere far away, in some magic and unknown lands, in the fairy land of Oz, where the fairies fly above the flowers, where there is no cancer, no necrophilia, no money, and no treachery. Where he could forget about all of this. Forever and ever! Forget! Forget! Forget! 'They say there are islands, Where the forget-grass grows...' *I wish I were dead*, he thought sadly.

The man looked at Chilikin more intently and explained to him with a kind of compassion, "Concerning the return of the money. Your wife received 10,000 euro from me—see, here's the note—and it seems that she doesn't want to give it back. Or she can't," he added after a pause.

"Why doesn't she want to?" Chilikin made a great effort in order to concentrate. "Or, as you say, she can't. What does it mean, she can't? Why?"

"Well, I suppose she already spend some of it," the man smiled. "You know—a woman…"

"How could she spend it? Didn't she realize that she'd probably have to give it back? Hold on!" Chilikin came to his senses. "We'll get back to the money. Don't worry, I'll give it back, that's for sure!" Something flashed in his companion's eyes—probably the last words of Chilikin amused him. "Let's change the topic. When did you make her the offer? Well, about me," Chilikin faltered, trying to find the right words. "My body? Did you do it when you first met her? When you told her about my diagnosis?"

"Don't say that!" the man wondered and even shook his head reproachfully. "I didn't do it then. I told her the next day."

"So, did you just call her and…?"

"And offered to meet," the man was looking at Chilikin as if he was a slow-witted child, "and to discuss some financial matters. And I told her not to say anything to you."

"And she agreed?" asked Chilikin sadly.

"Sure, she did," the man was looking at Chilikin with curiosity. "Of course, Andrey Pavlovich, she agreed. Any woman in her place would agree. Any daughter of Eve."

"Son of a bitch!" Chilikin swore to himself involuntarily. "'Sure! *Of course!" That's my wife, by the way!*

"And then?"

"And then we met," the man smiled again, looking serenely straight into Chilikin's eyes. "I explained to her what I wanted and gave her time to think. I told her I would call the next day. I have to say that the initial reaction of Yulia Vladimirovna to my offer was very wild and painful, but as you see," the man threw up his hands. "Time and reason…"

"And the next day, you met again, and you gave her the money," finished Chilikin for him. The man nodded with a smile. "And why did you have her write a note?" asked Chilikin. "That's a worthless piece of paper. It doesn't have any legal force."

"The usual counter-insurance," the man smiled. "First, it's a purely psychological effect; it's unlikely that your wife knows the law. Second, it's not that useless in practice. I don't think that a woman who wrote such a paper would dare to complain. I think she'll keep her mouth shut. For such deeds are not approved by the society—quite on the contrary."

"I see," said Chilikin slowly. He got it all, indeed. He got it so good that he wanted to hang himself! Come on. But now for free. "So, she…? All these days? She showed her compassion, pitied me, cried, comforted me, and whispered the words of love, the tenderest words in the world! We were intimate—with her having sold my corpse for sexual acts and bought rags for this money?"

The man kept silent, looking at Chilikin inquiringly.

"Oh, yes! Money," he came to his senses. "So, you say that she isn't giving the money back?"

"That's right, Andrey Pavlovich," the man shook his hand sadly. "Unfortunately, that's right."

"So, does she simply refuse to do it?" asked Chilikin, being unable to believe it. "What's she saying?"

"Yulia Vladimirovna doesn't say anything to me," the man sighed dramatically. "She's just hiding from me. We were supposed to meet today, but she didn't show up. And she's not at home. And, you know, I have neither the time nor the wish to look for her in Moscow. I'm a busy man."

"Yes, sure," said Chilikin politely and gave a frozen, still smile. "I understand you completely. Of course, I'll give you the money back. How long can you wait? Well, considering the current situation?"

"Sure," the man sighed again and took a quick thought. "Is one week okay with you?" he looked inquiringly at Chilikin.

"Yeah, sure," he answered automatically. *And where shall I get it?* he thought at once. *As much as 10 thousand euro?* "If I do have problems, shall we be able to renew our contract?" asked Chilikin with calm that surprised even himself.

"Of course, Andrey Pavlovich, of course," the man smiled leerily. "Of course. Any moment."

"But, you know," Chilikin halted, looking straight in his companion's eyes. "I wouldn't like my body to be raped in front of the camera, even if my wife didn't mind it."

The man sitting near him looked into Chilikin's eyes silently for some time and then said slowly, "All right, Andrey Pavlovich. I promise you that."

***

Chilikin followed the departing black BMW with his eyes and reached for his cigarettes. He looked at the sky, at the people and the cars which were hurrying somewhere. He had nowhere to hurry; going back home was out of the question. The very thought that he would see that woman and hear her voice was making him shake with disgust. He lit a cigarette and headed slowly to the metro. There were shreds of some half-forgotten song in his head: "There are islands somewhere/ Somewhere, there are islands/ Islands somewhere/ Islands, islands, islands."

And Lucifer was ask'd by His Son:

—Wherefore art the commandments of Christ bad? Art they not good and just?

And Lucifer answer'd to His Son:

—They art commandments of a master f'r his meiny. Be kind to each other, don't mortal arbitrament, follow the rules of social life."Love thy neighbor", "thou shalt not kill", "thou shalt not steal"...

All of this is right, but what is it for? What is the final goal? Thither is nay goal. These art just instructions f'r the crowd not to push and mortal arbitrament. Only the master hath a goal. Meiny and crowd doth not hast goals—and they cannot hast them. The only "goal" of slaves—not to create any troubles f'r the master.

And Lucifer was again ask'd by His Son:

And what are Your commandments?

And Lucifer answer'd to His Son:

- Be free! Stay what ye are! Stay humane! This is the higher goal. That is the most important thing!

And f'r that, one may doth aught. Killing and lying. One can kill a guard to escape a prison, and one can lie to an foe to save his family, children, lov'd ones, country, and people.

And Lucifer was again asked by His Son:

—So, the end justifies the means?

And Lucifer answered to His Son:

—Freedom needs not justification.

LUCIFER'S SON. DAY 21.

And the twenty-first day came.

And Lucifer was asked by His Son:

—Why do men willingly call themselves "servants of God?"

And Lucifer answered to His Son:

—Servitude deforms and corrupts a soul so much, that a servant begins to like his bonds. Freedom is, first of all, responsibility, a necessity to decide for yourself. And a servant cannot do that. "It's all in God's hands," "God shall see," "God sees everything" and so on and so forth.

Lucifer's Son

Man likes to be a servant. And it is very difficult for him to overcome the mentality of servant and to "become like gods."

BOOK

"And he spake like a dragon."
Revelation of St. John the Divine (Apocalypse).

"Didst thou not obey the voice
of the Lord?"
First Book of Samuel.

1.

"Amen!" Kurbatov put the exclamation mark at the end, pressed 'Save', and stretched with pleasure.

Well, I did well, he thought with pleasure, looking at the twinkling screen of the computer, at the even lines of the text. Now he could go to bed. The job was done.

***

About a week ago, Boris Vladimirovich Kurbatov, a humble clerk of one of the Moscow banks, began experiencing strange things. He began having nightmares. Or, rather, he began seeing visions. He didn't know what it was and what he should call it, for there was no name in the human language for what was happening to him. It all began when he had an incredible dream. Well, it wasn't really a dream; it was some strange stuff—nonsense. Normal people do not have such dreams. They just don't; they don't. That dream came out of nowhere.

Summer, steppe, Russian Revolution, civil war—1919 or 1920. He—Kurbatov, B.V.—takes part in a bayonet assault. But he had a different name then. What name? And title—what title did he have? What rank in that other, pre-revolutionary life? Staff-captain, it seems? Well, it's not important. Now he is clad in a black uniform, and, as a soldier of officer volunteer regiment, he walks in the steppe, burnt by merciless sun, with his rifle atilt. It's hot, with no wind.

Coming from the opposite direction, still distant, there are even, thick ranks of the Reds. There are a lot of them. Their number is many times larger than the whites. They march confidently and quickly, with a light and somehow flying pace. Red cadets, the elite of the red army. The troops come closer to each other. Suddenly the Reds start to sing "The Internationale." Taken up by thousands of people, it goes wide across the steppe and sounds very formidable. "Arise, ye prisoners of starvation!" roar thousands of mouths in one outburst.

The Whites keep silent. Soldiers of Markov always attack silently. And they never fall back, no matter who the enemy is, even if they are outmanned. The Reds know that very well. The sides come closer; the tension grows. The ranks of both sides start to tighten. Somehow, Kurbatov knows that it always happens during the bayonet attacks. You must feel that you're not alone, you're not abandoned to the whims of fate, you're not left to face the endless wave of heavy glistening bayonets which are coming towards you, bringing death. You must feel that there's someone near you; you want to feel your comrade's elbow. That's why you're looking involuntarily for the comrade, you come closer to him, although you know very well that you shouldn't do that, you shouldn't break the formation. But you can't help it. Nobody can help it. Nobody! Neither the Whites nor the Reds.

The sides are closer, closer. The song of the Reds breaks down. The tension is so high that it's impossible to sing. You do everything you can to not turn away and run; you make yourself go forward. Ahead—towards death. One more step, another one; it seems that you can't take it. Enough! We're going to run, now! And, at that moment, the Reds start running.

Kurbatov startled and woke up.

***

"What was that?" he asked himself in amazement. "Dream or reality? Where did it come from? How do I know all this? Markov, black uniform, Red cadets, how people behave during a bayonet assault? What kind of miracle is this? I felt it all very vividly—the sun, heat, sweat pouring from under the cap, the intoxicating smell of the steppe. Fear, despair, wrath, confidence of that man. It seems as if I really was there, as if I took part in that fight in that village in the steppe. Did we take it, by the way? Oh, God! What village?" he came to his senses. "Who are 'we'? What's wrong with me?"

But that was just the beginning. After that, Kurbatov saw a row of images and recollections of that kind. They were haunting him constantly—every second—day and night. While in the metro, he would see in his mind burning walls of a fortress, torches, swords, ladders, people climbing them, mouths open in fierce cries. While talking to his boss, he would choke with horror, seeing himself chained to an oar in a sinking Roman galley. He would be dying with Spartans of Leonid under the clouds of arrows of Xerxes' archers at Thermopylae. He would endure the horrible strike of heavy Roman infantry while in the ranks of light-armored Gauls at Cannes, in the very center of formidable Hannibal crescent; he would freeze while in the Great Army during the severe frost at the Smolensk road... He would drown, be burned alive, he would be chopped by swords and pierced by pikes… He would be tortured, hung, and crucified innumerable times…

He lived a thousand lives during that week. He faced thousand deaths, and felt pain, torments and grief, pleasures and delight of thousands of people. Soldiers, assassins, rapists, heroes and prophets, butchers and their prey. It seemed that hell released all its souls, so they could go through Kurbatov, so he would feel and sense all that they felt and sensed. So he would understand them, realize what they were living for, why they were doing their feats and mischiefs. And what they were dying for.

When it ended a week later, Kurbatov was already a different man. He was wiser by a thousand years and thousand lives. The truths in which he had believed sacredly and without question—or, maybe he just hadn't given them any thought—suddenly shook and trembled. Black became white, and white became black. With the cold and merciless light of his thousand-year experience, his world began to look different. Visions disappeared, mists were gone, and universal truth shined again in its cold, indifferent, and dispassionate beauty. The truth was in its clean, primary, and original state. Good became good again, and evil became evil. Treachery became treachery, lies became lies, and betrayal became betrayal, whatever masks and veils they were clad in and whatever cloths they wore. In those lives, he had been liar, scoundrel, and traitor a thousand times, and now he could see through them, he could see them at the first glance.

He realized again what dignity and honor were, how beautiful a victory was, and how bitter and horrible a defeat was, who was friend and who was foe, and what was love. This new knowledge was overwhelming him, and he simply didn't know what to do with it. And then he decided to write a book, a novel. He had never written anything before, and he didn't know what he should do and where he should start.

But everything turned out to be simple, even too simple. He didn't even correct anything in the text and didn't know at the beginning what he would be writing about and how it would all end. The words were born in his soul, as if someone else whispered them to him, and he had just to manage to write them down, to print them, to put them in the computer. In less than three weeks, the book was finished. It was a rather strange work. It was neither novel nor story It could be called fiction only by a stretch of imagination. There was no plot and no main heroes; there were just separate, isolated pieces, shreds, shards, and fragments of different lives and fates, of someone's notes, diaries, and thoughts.

Nevertheless, it was undoubtedly a single work. It was filled with one design which was not comprehended completely even by the author in the process of writing. It certainly made an impression of integrity and monolith. After reading, its pieces, which had seemed not to be connected at all, would somehow take the shape of something single and whole, and that whole thing would have a truly magical effect on a reader; it would influence his soul directly. It would intrude there, easily passing endless walls, barriers, and filters of conscience and subconscious—moral, ethical, and religious.

As there was no single plot, a reader was unable to resist and oppose a great infusion, for he didn't understand until the last moment what he was convinced of. The author went along in small steps which seemed to be random and chaotic, in various and even opposite directions. Every step didn't spawn doubts; it didn't cause any antagonism, rejection, or repulsion—neither a religious nor moral one—and a reader would agree with him easily and accept him willingly. More unexpected was the finale, the destination point, where a reader would get together with the author. A reader was taken there by the author very warily, slowly, and secretly.

Kurbatov actually understood what higher, real, and genuine art was; he perceived its great, overwhelming power. Since the ancient times, the traditional church had a good reason to consider it a devilish temptation, a seduction for a weak human soul which can't resist man-made beauty without God's help. It gives the opportunity to convince a man of anything while breaking all barriers easily and playfully—moral, ethical, and religious barriers. It depends only on the power of an author's talent. Empathizing with hero, a reader would become him for some time. He would accept and find excuses for his life values and approaches. And they could be really strange for him before he read the book. And now, when he read it…

It was a completely new morality; a new, another system of values. It was secretly entering, penetrating, and sliding like a silent shadow, straight into the soul. It was well-shaped and logically faultless, cold and ruthless, the Tower of Babel, going to the very sky with its peak. It was something like a code of honor or a statute of a secret order—commandments, like the Biblical, but completely different in essence—opposite. No humility, no fear of God. Don't fear anything. Be a god yourself. Decide for yourself. God reports to no one, fears no one, and asks no one's advice. His only judge is Himself. Do the same. Let your conscience be your only judge.

The only commandment—don't lie to yourself. Scrupulously weigh your deeds on the scales of your conscience. Act justly; do not betray you divine nature. Do not turn into a demon. But if you think that you're right, act. Act—you can do anything; you can kill and betray. You can kill a betrayer and betray a murderer. There are no wrong deeds, there are wrong goals. Within the limits of right goals, any deed is right. And do not fear anything, neither in this world nor in the afterlife, neither hell nor paradise, neither God's trial nor that of man's. Fear humiliates man. It turns him into a servant. If you have no fear, you're invulnerable. But if you falter, fear or quail, that's it—you're not yourself anymore. You've chosen your path. Amen!

2.

Kurbatov saved the text on the floppy disc, turned off the computer, and went to bed. That night, he had yet another nightmare. During three weeks of writing the book, he hadn't seen any horrors, and now, it seemed to begin again. But that new nightmare was a bit different. It wasn't like the previous ones. It wasn't like those medieval horrors. That one was quite modern, from our world, so to say. It was probably for the sake of variety.

He saw images of a horrible Apocalypse that began in the world after the publication of his book. New York, London, Paris,

Moscow—hundreds and hundreds of other cities, towns and villages. Street demonstrations with thousands and millions of people. Torchlight processions—long, endless fiery serpents, going somewhere in the dark of the night. Men, men, men, clad in dark robes and hoods, with frozen and immovable faces. They're singing something or rather chanting. Men and women. Children. Innumerable, immense, and uncountable crowds, thick masses, lots of people Dark and still, filling all space, stretching as far as the eye could see, all the way to the horizon! Fanatics—they're everywhere. The crowd shook and, obeying someone's harsh and shrill cries, slowly went ahead towards the policemen and the army barriers. Women with immovable faces, throwing their infants under the trucks of tanks and armored vehicles. Soldiers, backing in terror.

***

Kurbatov woke up. He was covered with cold sweat. He turned on the nightlight and lit a cigarette with his shaking hands. He did it with the third attempt only. Then he leaned back on the pillow, took a deep pull at the cigarette, and stared at the ceiling. Horrible images of the end of the world were still before his eyes.

What about their faces? he thought and shivered involuntarily. *They're robots, not humans. Zombies! Where did it all come from? There's nothing like that in my book! Quite the contrary! Dignity and honor—freedom. Freedom! And what is that? Fanatics, fanaticism. Fanaticism is incompatible with freedom; fanaticism is always limited. It's equal to slavery, after all Shit!* He put out a cigarette nervously and lit another one. *"Shit, shit, shit! Devil! I had very good intentions, natural intentions! I wanted to publish a book and have people decide whether it's good or bad. They should decide for themselves. And what now? Am I not allowed to publish it? But this is nonsense! Heresy! Zealotry! How is this possible? I can't publish a book? That's bullshit. Right, but look at their faces! Ugh!"* Kurbatov squirmed involuntarily again.

What if the devil dictated it to me? he thought suddenly. *Satan? What if he exists?*

Until recently, Kurbatov was an atheist. He was a doubting Thomas, a cynic, and a skeptic. To be precise, he somehow didn't give any thought to that, to all those matters. *God, faith. Does he exist or not? Who knows? Maybe he does or maybe he doesn't. Well, there's definitely something, but what exactly?*

Well, what's the point of thinking about that? No need to bother. Anyway, I can't find anything out or invent something.

Nobody thought anything up before you. Is there no one else? I'm busy without it! Well, there is someone. Thank God!

During the last month, his ideology changed very much!.. Well, he tried not to think about that, but deep inside him, in his soul… At any rate, he truly believed that there's something out there—no doubts! And he didn't just believe, he knew!

That's a given! One would definitely start believing after all those real miracles, Kurbatov smiled gloomily. *All right, all right! God or no God! We're modern people, after all, we're living in the 21st century with science, computers; we're used to looking for scientific and logical explanations for everything, even for miracles. All right, all right! Let's assume that. Here, it may be some genetic memory induction of biofields reading of information directly from the matrix of the global universal profile; well, I don't really know! I can come up with a lot of this pseudo-scientific nonsense if I want, and I can explain everything very well. I don't know! Inductions fuck deductions!*

But all those things did happen to me; that's a fact. Matrix or no matrix, but I was in all those people—I was! I looked at the world with their eyes, I felt what they felt, I grieved and loved with them. All of that happened, it did! And indeed! After all, what's the difference—god or matrix? It's clear that something's happening to me, something unusual, strange, and wonderful. Call it what you wish. These dreams are not without a reason. And these are not fucking dreams, nice dreams, Kurbatov remembered when he had been soaked with boiling resin during the storm of Kaifeng in 1234, and shook. *Fuck it! I still have goosebumps, and my breath is taken away! I just imagined that—fuck! Fucking power! Dreams! Shall I drink some cold water or, even better, pour cold water on myself, take a cold shower? Pfft! Dreams! Well, so! Pfft! So, dreams or no dreams, I mean, matrix or no matrix. Fuck, I lost the thought! Fucking resin… fuck it!*

Well, that's it! These dreams are not just dreams. There's something behind them. These dreams are fucking real—they're prophetic. Ugh! I need to be careful with these spells. I don't want anything wrong! If I'm really somehow connected to that fucking global-informational-universal matrix, then I don't fucking know how it works. I could as well call a Sivka-burka before me, a fucking little hump-backed horse. And what am I going to do with it? Shall I mount it and gallop fucking away from here, to the Far, Far-Away Kingdom. 'Take me, fox, behind the dark wood!' Although, that is from another tale, the one about a cock with a fucking golden crest.

And it's not take, but taking! 'The fox is taking me.' Well, the cock is fucking dead. Same with me. And all other cocks. Together with the fox. That's probably the way my subconscious works. Whatever you think, it all goes to a fucking disaster.

And where would I go? Apocalypse remains Apocalypse, even in Africa. It's everywhere, even in the Far, Far-Away Kingdom. Behind dark woods and behind light woods—everywhere! That's apocalypse—the end of the world. The end of everything! But why am I so sure in that? It was just a dream. People have different dreams. Right, different—exactly! That's what we're talking about. It was me who had the dreams, and they were very odd. That's the point; they are fucking strange dreams! Whether God sends them to me or the devil or I read them from the universal matrix through induction and deduction—fuck it! It doesn't matter! The most important thing is that it's reality. It's the most real reality! Well! New horrible recollections flashed through Kurbatov's mind, but he drove them away and kept thinking. *"Well, and I have to reckon with this reality. And if I suddenly saw apocalypse in a dream...*

So what? Should I not publish it? Maybe I should just destroy it and that's it. Delete it? Should I press one button on the computer?"

But the thought filled Kurbatov with a keen feeling of sadness and pain. He was even surprised with that. He got attached to that book. He was constantly drawn to it. He wanted to read it; it filled his soul and satisfied his eternal and inescapable spiritual hunger. It gave sense to his life. Kurbatov remembered that he had read that only God could fill a soul. It appeared it was not so. The book did it with the same result. It calmed him. It comforted and acted as a balm to him. It had answers to all questions; it seemed as if it contained all the wisdom of the world. Reading it, he was communicating with a Higher Being which knew and understood everything in the world, even that what you couldn't understand in yourself.

I need to read the Bible, thought Kurbatov. *What does it say about that? About the soul, Satan, concerning Apocalypse?* He put out the cigarette in the ashtray and went to wash up.

Well, I'm gonna wash up, have breakfast, and then we'll see. I'll be able to delete it at any time. It's no pressing matter."

3.

Kurbatov went outside, lit a cigarette and slowly headed to the metro station, looking around him lazily and blinking from bright morning sunlight. For a whole month, while writing a book, he stayed inside and didn't breathe fresh air, and now the walk gave him a lot of pleasure. Sun, wind, greenery grass - he didn't have to hurry anywhere. He felt good!

What's the time? Is it twelve already? No? Good. I've still got time. Bookstores have a lunch break from 2 to 3, so I have a lot of time. After some thought, Kurbatov decided to go to a bookstore and buy the Bible. He wanted to read it at leisure. *Well, not actually at fucking leisure, but at once, today! Why would I linger? What if I find something interesting in it?*

***

The night's dream left a heavy aftertaste in him. He felt himself a man who must involuntarily make a very important decision, a decision which may influence the fates of a lot of people. Well, not really a lot of, but all of them; all the people in the whole world. For, if that cursed dream comes true… As a matter of fact, there were two opposite feelings fighting inside Kurbatov. He both believed and doubted the seriousness of what was happening. On the one hand, he believed his dream, of course; he feared it and realized that he should take it seriously and that it was no joke. But, on the other hand, thinking seriously that a book, however ingenious it might be, would bring such cataclysms in the world, that he, Kurbatov B.V., was deciding the fates of the world and the whole of humanity. *Be it as you wish, but somehow all of this is… Yikes!.. A cheap horror movie. Bless me! With Antonio Banderas in a leading role. For sensitive teenagers. Well, that's not serious stuff—Stallone and Schwarzenegger will appear and save everyone. They will shoot the bad guys with machine guns, with silver fucking bullets!*

Kurbatov felt awkward from these thoughts. He was ashamed, as if someone else could overhear them. *If my friends should find out what I'm thinking right now,* he shook his head with a wry smile, *and what I'm doing! That would be a fucking disaster! I'm going to buy the Bible; I need to find some advice in it. They would think that I'm insane! Well, what else would they think? Visions… Apocalypse… It's clear!.. He's already pale!.. he's burning!*

The nearest bookstore was not far, just a couple of stations by metro. Kurbatov entered the store and halted, at a loss. *Where should actually I go? What department? Where are the religious books? I can't see them; should I ask? I feel awkward. A young man, a Bible—did he decide to become a monk? Oh, well, I should ask about religious literature.*

"Excuse me, miss, where is the department of religious literature?" he asked a young shop assistant.

"I think with the fiction department," she said hesitatingly. "Try there."

"Are you interested in religion?" Kurbatov suddenly heard a question addressed to him and turned around in surprise. A middle-aged, medium-sized man was looking at him kindly and smiling. Kurbatov saw thick tattoos on the man's arms. At his side, there stood another man, taller and broader; he had a lot of tattoos, as well. For some reason, Kurbatov felt ill at ease. Not that he was scared; he was in a store, and there were people around, but still. *What do these two morons want from me?*

"Yeah," he smiled forcedly, wishing to leave at once. But he couldn't do it. He just wanted to turn away.

"There it is, dude! Come on, I'll show you," the man beckoned to him. There was nothing for Kurbatov to do but to follow him without a word—actually, them. *What do they want from me, anyway?* Kurbatov's anxiety was growing. His attempts to get rid of his uninvited companions in another department were not successful at all.

With the concerned look of a very busy man, he asked a shop assistant about the price of the book, got the receipt, and quickly headed to the counter, trying not to look around him. "Bible, please!"

His dry and business-like tone didn't leave any doubts that he was in a hurry, in a great hurry. He was late to a very important meeting. But his new acquaintances didn't react to this simple comedy, it seemed.

"Hey, dude!" a stubby guy with tattooed arms lazily called to Kurbatov, who almost turned away and was about to leave. "Can I talk to you for a moment?"

Kurbatov felt a slight panic. He was actually a simple guy—peaceful, harmless, and a bit cowardly—and the insistence of these nuts was worrying, and, frankly speaking, scaring him. He felt as if he was a sheep who became an object of interest of wolves. *What do they want from me? And what can wolves want from sheep?*

"Yeah?" Kurbatov lifted his eyebrow with surprise, turning around again. And how would a man behave when complete strangers start talking to him in a public place? Slight and calm surprise, strong confidence? "Yeah? What's the matter? How can I help you?"

"Hey, are you a believer?" the stubby guy was waiting for an answer. "The reason I'm asking is that I saw that you bought the Bible," he explained, seeing Kurbatov's embarrassment. He really was taken unawares with such a question.

"Well, you know," said Kurbatov tentatively. He was at a loss. He didn't consider himself to be a believer, but what if they don't touch the believers? *I'd say, "No," and they say, "Oh, so you're not a believer? You're the right guy!"*

"Have you believed in God for a long time already?" asked the stubby guy with the same curiosity. He seemed to understand Kurbatov's behavior in his own way. He saw it as the modesty and restraint of a true believer, which were worthy of utmost respect. It was an unwillingness to talk in public about such purely intimate matters.

"Yes," answered Kurbatov in short. He decided to answer all the following questions laconically, hoping that soon the conversation would die away on its own.

"There now!" the stubby guy was surprised. He looked at Kurbatov thoughtfully. "I thought that people started to believe in God only in prison Hey, dude! Are you in a hurry? Let's go outside and have a talk, eh?"

The stubby guy was looking in Kurbatov's eyes so calmly and serenely that he had to sigh desperately to himself and agree. Actually, he didn't have the guts to refuse. What could he do? How could he refuse such a fucking invitation?

The stubby guy went straight to the luxurious Mercedes S-Class that was parked near the store. He said to Kurbatov, "Let's get inside. What's the point of staying outside?" Near the Mercedes there were a couple of SUVs with solid, shaven-headed guys in them. Kurbatov got scared. He had no doubts that this conversation wouldn't end well for him. He just couldn't guess what they wanted from him. What could these hardened criminal sharks want from such a small, plain gudgeon as Kurbatov B.V., a humble gray bank clerk who was always sitting in his hole?

Did it concern his work? Do they want to rob his bank? Well, he wouldn't help them. He just wasn't able to. He didn't know anyone and didn't decide anything. *So, you're wrong, dear criminals, you're very wrong—you've got the wrong guy. I'm as worthless as teats on a boar. I'm no use for you. So you should learn it as soon as possible and let me go to the four winds. Let my soul go to confession. For, somehow, I feel uncomfortable with you; I don't want to talk to you in your criminal SUVs and Mercedes. Screw you!* All these thoughts flashed through Kurbatov's mind while he was walking towards the car. They cheered him up.

Well, what can they do with me, anyway? he tried to calm down. *They're going to sort everything out and let me go. There you go, Vasya! What the fuck do they need me for?*

"Well, you read the Bible. And do you go to church?" the stubby man got at the back seat together with Kurbatov. His friend got in front, half-turning to them.

"I do," Kurbatov lied confidently. He had never been to a church.

"Have you ever taken the sacraments?" the guy was staring at Kurbatov with a tense curiosity.

"Well, yeah, sure." Firstly, Kurbatov didn't know exactly what a sacrament was and, secondly, he didn't understand anything at all. *What stupid talk is that? Church sacrament or no sacrament?' Have you said your prayers tonight, Desdemona? Have you ever taken sacrament, Kurbatov?' Well, I don't really like these edifying conversations about churches and sacraments. I don't want to take sacraments here! Before I...*

"And?" the stubby guy was looking at Kurbatov.

"Good!" he shrugged his shoulders, waiting. When are we going to talk business? Why am I sitting here, anyway?

"Relax, dude," the stubby seemed to see his condition. He leaned to him and slapped his knee with his hand. "Why are you so tense? Do you smoke?" he offered Kurbatov a pack of Marlboro.

"Thanks," Kurbatov took a cigarette and lit it up with the stubby guy's lighter, who smoked, too.

"You know," said the stubby guy after a pause, as he looked in the window thoughtfully, "though I've been baptized, I've never believed in all that."

"In church and the sacraments?" asked Kurbatov irrelevantly. He just wanted to say something and fill the pause.

"Church has nothing to do with it," said the stubby guy with irritation. "There are only rogues in church. Once we had a get-together in Danilov Monastery, in the residence of patriarch; my mate, thief in law as well, was sitting in patriarch's seat, in his chair. Can you imagine that? And the patriarch came in, saw it, blessed all of us, and left. How's that? Well, actually in the patriarch's chair!" the stubby guy went silent, looking at Kurbatov and waiting for his reaction.

"Well!" Kurbatov muttered indistinctly, twitching his eyes. He still didn't understand. *What kind of crap is this? What's going on? What does the patriarch have to do with it? Why the fuck does he have to know these scary secrets of the life of high ministry? He's a small man. Oh! So this dude in front of me is a thief in law? As well!" Jesus! That's bad. I'm in a jam. Oh, Lord and Holy Mother in heaven, save and protect. Hallowed be Your name! Well, I'm done!*

"And do you know what's going on in monasteries?" It seemed that the stubby guy had an urge to unmask someone. "I was doing business in a convent and talked to guys. You know, there's no problem fucking any nun. But who the fuck needs them? They've all got clap or even something worse. So, these new Russians come there to fuck young nuns. They like it, fucking them when they're dressed in a monk's habit. Well, they're idiots."

"Shit happens," the stubby guy went silent, took a pull at the cigarette, let the smoke out of the window, and continued. "The guys talked to ostiaries; they say they even had to dig the graves! If a man goes to a monastery, he's done! It's impossible to find him. They'll just say he moved to another monastery, and that's it. They have no registration, no passports, nothing. And nobody's going to look for him. Well, there's no need to talk much; the church has a lot of money—millions—and cigarettes, vodka. And where's money, there's murder and other stuff. Churchmen seem to think only about the money. No faith at all!"

Kurbatov was paralyzed with fear. All that was happening began resembling some wild phantasmagoria, yet another nightmare of the kind that he had seen. Fuck it! He just wanted to buy a Bible in a bookstore. *Fuck it all! I'm in deep trouble. The devil made me do it; I wish I stayed at home.*

"Well!" he mumbled indistinctly again, trying painfully to squeeze something out of himself to keep up the conversation. He didn't want the guy to be insulted. He'd think that Kurbatov was not interested. Meanwhile, Kurbatov's head was filled with ringing emptiness—vacuum, no thoughts at all. "So, you don't believe in God, do you?" Kurbatov said something sensible at last, something that resembled human speech. Well, he didn't want to mumble and bleat all the time.

"I do now," the stubby man looked at Kurbatov again. "Listen, dude. I'm gonna tell you what happened to me recently. My right hand got swollen; can you believe it? I went to the doctors, but they couldn't help me. Well, they said that they didn't know what it was. But it got worse. The guys said that I had to go to the sacred spring.

Well, they brought me there, but I already felt very bad; the lump went up into my throat, I just couldn't breathe. I shouted, 'Give me the pills; I've got special pills with me. I got them from America.' And the monks told me, 'You don't need any pills; bathe in the sacred spring.' Well, they took me to the place with that spring, and it was fucking cold there. The water was icy cold. I screamed, 'I can't bathe in such water!' And they say, 'No, you have to.'

"Well, they left, and I just sprinkled myself with water. I got out and said that I had bathed. They looked at me and say that I hadn't. Do you get it? They saw it straightaway!" the stubby man took a pause.

Kurbatov couldn't come up with anything better that to bleat his favorite "Well!"

"Well, I went to that pool again," the stubby guy continued his story. "All right, I was going to bathe in it. I didn't like lying like a child. I took my clothes off and went into the water. And I started to feel myself healing! I felt it at once! The swelling began to go; I was choking no more Well, they healed me. It took them several sessions, then they brought me to the hallows, and they healed me! Everything was gone. The swelling got smaller and smaller, and it disappeared. And then they came to me with a cross, took it to my forehead, and my body curled. I jumped up! My wife was at my side, she saw everything."

"And what did you feel at that moment?" Kurbatov couldn't help but ask him.

"Well, it seemed as if an electrical charge went through me," the stubby man paused. "Then the monks told me that someone had put an evil eye on me. Someone had hexed me. I thought about one girl at once. Well, I was dating a 20-year-old girl from Serpukhov, and then I saw that I had problems at home, and my family began falling apart, and I left her. I thought that it was her; no one else could do that.

"I sent the guys to her. They searched all of Serpukhov, found all the witches, and one of them confessed that she had done it. She recognized me in the photo. At first, she didn't want to say anything; but then they took her to a cemetery at night, and she got scared that she would be killed, so she told everything. She had done it. But she said that it was a love spell, not a curse. She said the problem was that I was too strong, thus the effect. And she said other fucking stuff. And then she told that she would never be doing such stuff in her life."

Kurbatov caught his breath and listened to him. As the story went on, he realized that no one was going to kill him, and no one was going to ask him about bank secrets. There was too much talk—abstracted talk. Moreover, he suddenly thought that all that was happening had a reason, that it simply was an incredible continuation of the strange events that had been happening to him. Part two or even three. Nightmares, the book—and now this. *And how, pray, should I take it? As an incredible coincidence? At the very moment when he...*

"Hey, dude!" he heard again. "And I saw a strange picture there. A woman was being dragged to the sacred spring by force, and she was resisting, as if something held her! And she was being pushed there by force! And then I'm sitting near a man— they had separate sessions for men and women—and he sees my tattoos and asks, "You were in prison?"

I looked at him and asked, "So what? Why are you asking?"

"Well, I was with SWAT."

"So what?" I ask him. "Have you seen that woman?"

"'That's my wife'. She had been working with him in that system. And it seemed that they had fucking done something wrong! Well, they had too much blood on their hands; he told me that they had been haunted by strange visions. Then they quit and began visiting the sacred spring. He told me that it was really helping them. And before that, it had been really bad," the man took a pull at the cigarette, and Kurbatov saw with surprise that his hands were shaking.

What's wrong with him? Kurbatov felt ill at ease. *Why is he confessing to me? I'm a complete stranger, right? Thief in law! I assume that this is a continuation of my miracles, but I really need to fucking get going, in good time, out of harm's way.*

"Well, the reason I was asking you about the sacrament," the man took a pause. "I saw a woman leaving the line, the line to the sacrament. She was just standing there and suddenly turned around and left the church. I asked the priests, 'What's wrong with her? Is she sick'? Well, I saw that she was okay. She entered the church; everything was all right," the stubby man halted and then went on, lowering his voice. "And I was waiting in the line with another guy. I was OK, but when there were only three people left, he turned around and left the church.

I go outside; he's standing and smoking. 'What's wrong, dude'?"

"'I don't know. I don't remember anything. It seemed that something took me out of the church!'" And he wouldn't lie to me, that's for sure. So, I just wanted to ask you," the stubby guy gave a sigh. "Well, dude, we took your time, sorry."

"No, no, it's okay!" answered Kurbatov automatically.

"Do you need a lift to metro?" asked the stubby guy.

"No, thanks, I have some business here," said Kurbatov quickly. *What metro? Let me out!*

"Oh, as you wish!" the stubby guy offered him his hand.

Kurbatov shook it, then quickly shook the hand of the guy sitting in front, said warm goodbyes, and got out of the car. Having followed the departing Mercedes and SUVs with his eyes, he caught his breath and wiped his forehead, which was wet with sweat. He felt as if he had somehow escaped a great peril, as if he had successfully passed through the pit with lions. He got lucky—coincidentally, the lions were not hungry.

Well, thought Kurbatov sadly, *teaching others not to fear is one thing and doing it all yourself is quite another thing! For how many times have I been a warrior and hero in my dreams? And what's the point of it? I didn't become a hero. I was a coward, and I remained one. Eventually, like that thief said. But I became a wise coward, and that's worse. Wise as a serpent—a creepy one. I know very well that one must fear everything, and I know how it goes in life. I have felt it all on my skin. Bother it!*

"Hi! Look who's here! Borka, is that you?" he heard a loud call and nearly jumped with surprise. At first, he thought that it was those two morons whom he had successfully parted with. again, those criminals.

Of course, it wasn't them. It was his old school friend, whom he hadn't seen for almost ten years; he hadn't seen him since the prom. Well, he hadn't seen him, and now here you go—he saw him exactly today. Well, things happen—a lucky coincidence.

After initial merry greetings, they started to talk about their common friends; "and where is that one? And this one? Oh! Well, well!" They were talking about their former classmates, of course. Who else?

"Listen, Dima, and where's Dan?" asked Kurbatov suddenly. "You used to be close friends, right?"

"He was murdered," his friend got gloomy and gritted his teeth.

"Murdered?" Who did that?" Kurbatov didn't understand anything.

"Well, he was just murdered," said his companion, as if it was a normal thing. "By some scums."

"For what?" Kurbatov still couldn't understand anything.

"Business matters," said his friend unwillingly. "We were working together."

"Jesus Christ!" Kurbatov stared at him. Another mafioso! Is today a special day for them or what?"

"Are you reading the Bible?" his friend pointed at the thick book with a golden cross on the cover in Kurbatov's hands. And he continued, without waiting for an answer, "You know, he came to me after that. After his death."

"Who? Dan?" Kurbatov froze in astonishment. "What do you mean 'he came?'"

"He did!" said his friend slowly, looking strangely at Kurbatov. "At first, my dog began howling; it howled for the whole day. It would just stare at the corner of the room and howl. And then I found out that Dan had been murdered that day. The dog never howled before or after that. It's a mastiff, and their kind is calm. And then, on the thirty-eighth day I was in the bed with my wife. I woke up, as if someone pushed me. and I saw him standing near the bed. He was dressed as usual, as I saw him last time.

"I got up, and we went to the kitchen. We sat opposite each other and he said: 'Dima! Remember—don't trust anyone!' And I said, 'All right, I've got it.' And he says, "No, you didn't get it. Don't trust anyone!' 'All right, I won't, I get it.' 'No, listen to me. No one!' 'All right, I get it. No one!' 'All right. Now you get it.'" Well, we stayed there for some time, then I blessed myself, and he disappeared.

Kurbatov was staring at his friend, unable to say a word. That was too much! At first, thief in law leads pastoral and moral conversations about the saving of the souls while sitting in a Mercedes with him, and then his school friend appears out of nowhere after 10 years and starts talking the same way, teaching and instructing him! And, moreover, both of them speak of absolutely incredible things! Strange things—these are true miracles!

So what? Believe or not? They don't have any need to lie, and they couldn't have an agreement; they don't know each other, they have never seen each other, but at the same time... Umph! And all of this happens exactly when I have to make a decision—what I should do with the book. Should I publish it or not?

And thinking about his visions and how he actually wrote the book—*oh, oh, oh! If this is not a miracle and a sign from above, then what's a sign? Maybe an archangel with a flaming sword should come to him? Or a devil with horns? But that could be considered a mirage as well, a hallucination, a nervous breakdown. Then it turns out that there are not, and there could be no signs, right? It's all a coincidence. Any miracle is a coincidence.*

"All right, Borya, I gonna get going!" his friend glanced at his watch and was about to leave. "We'll stay in touch; we've got each other's telephone numbers Don't get lost!"

Kurbatov's friend waved his hand and vanished in a crowd. It seemed as if he had never been there. Kurbatov stood for some time, then gave a heavy sigh, and went slowly to the metro. *Well! There you go!* He somehow had an impression that his friend had just appeared, done his job—a secret mission, his providential purpose—and disappeared. He had appeared only to tell Kurbatov about the death of Dan and about Dan coming to him after his death. *Well, well! It seems that those from the high spheres are seriously interested in me, and that's for a long time. Well! It would be great if they gave a sign, a distinctive one. What if this is all the wiles of devil?*

Kurbatov sighed again and looked sadly at the sky. He seemed to hope indeed to see there an angel who would wink at him kindly from behind a cloud. Right! Angel—with the wings of a batfish. He went into the underground, came down the escalator, waited for the train, and plumped into the vacant seat. There were just a few people in the train.

So what? he thought lazily, looking around him indifferently and glancing at the passengers. *Is the limit of the miracles used for today? Or is someone going to face me with more conversations? If so, let it be a pretty chick, a nice birdie. That one, for example. A good one! Pretty eyes! Oh! She's snapping them! Hell of a girl! Angel and demon in one!*

Enough of these nightmares! I'm already afraid of everything. Be sweet and tender! 'Oh, darling,' let her say. 'Don't you publish that filthy book! And for that, I'm going to...' Or, on the other hand, 'Darling, you have to publish it! For sure! And for that, I'm gonna...' Well! So, what should I do? Should I publish it or not? What the fuck should I do?"

4.

Entering his building, Kurbatov first checked the mail-box as he used to do. *Wow! A letter! From whom?* He hadn't got letters for donkey's years. *Why would people write letters when it's possible to make a call from any place?*

Oh! Yudin A.F., Biriuch, Novousmank region, Voronezh oblast. I see! That's clear now! Why would he write me?

Kurbatov looked at the letter. *There now! It's rather thick, an epistle. What's he writing, eh? From his village Biriuch. I hope, it's not about religion. Is that him?*

Kurbatov quickly changed, opened the letter, and began reading it avidly. He felt a keen, even painful, curiosity. *Oh, God! Here as well? That would be too much!*

Well, well... 'drinking...'. Umph! 'For a whole month! Forgot about everything!..' Well! They have a good life in the village of Biriuch. I'd like to forget about everything as well, with great pleasure! Instead of... well, here! I see, I see... interesting... 8 kilos! He's lying. Is that a crocodile? 'For a whole hour... the spinning bent!.. I nearly fell off the boat...' Interesting!.. Well, fuck... I want it, too! I want such a pike perch! 'For a whole hour'! Well, people are lucky! He's living in the country, drinks as much as he wants, and catches 8-kilograms pike perches. And here! Oh! Kurbatov looked out the window sadly and continued reading. "*Well, I see... right. And this?!.. Oh?.. Oh?.. What the hell is that?!*"

> ***"By the way, Lena always prays for you; she became a believer in the last seven or eight years. She goes to church, visits sacred places, reads religious books and wants to steer me onto the right path. By the way, I got baptized on August 26th. I'd never been baptized, because my mother never baptized me or my brothers, and she's a true believer now. She thinks that a man has to be baptized consciously. And I've been believing in the ideas of communism, of social equality, and it's all taken from the Bible. And Volkov Semen Timofeevich, my friend, died a while ago. He was a smart and educated man in his prime. He was my teacher and mentor both in life and work. A day before his death, we talked about God, life after death—he wasn't baptized ,either—and came to the conclusion that a man needs baptism and faith in God, in spite of his political views. But he didn't manage to do it and was buried unbaptized. So, I made a decision to get baptized. The day I was going to do that, I woke up in the morning and couldn't open my mouth. My whole body was swollen. I wanted to stay home and call a***

doctor, but everything was already arranged with a priest, and a car was waiting. So I was swollen, and I set out. People told me that the evil one didn't want to let me go. Well, we came there—I was baptized in a river; I don't remember its name—and waited for the priest for three hours. He was probably tempting me, too. Thank God, I got baptized. The next morning, I went to the church nearby to take Communion. And the next day—it was Monday—I was going to go to the doctor concerning my swollen mouth, but everything was all right, as if nothing had happened. Miracles! Well, that's not all. God sent me another test."

Kurbatov laid the letter aside and stared in front of him. *So, let's summarize. Thief, friend, and this letter. So, does God exist? Or the devil? I don't understand what they want of me! What should I do? Well, today I heard about some supernatural stuff; I even got evidence that God and the devil exist. Let's assume that. Let it be so! So, what should I do? Is it a good book or a bad one? I can't really understand. Who sent me the dream about an apocalypse so I wouldn't publish anything. God or Devil? Is God guiding me, or is the devil misleading me? Who dictated that book to me? If the devil did it, what was God doing at that time? That's blasphemy; that's not for me to decide. Let them deal between themselves. Oh boy! Oh! It's all useless! What should I do? At any rate, it's me who has to make a decision, with my own brain and wits.*

All right, be it wits. Let's think logically. Nightmares or, rather, visions—whatever they're called. Could God send them to me? Of course, he could! Why couldn't he? God can do anything. Right, I see. And here I can stop the thinking. I won't be able to find anything out by logic. Eventually it comes to the fact that if God is almighty, then he can do whatever he wants. And what for? God knows! The ways of God are inscrutable. All in all, I can't discern God from the devil with logic. I won't be able to tell wings from horns. Well, well, well, well, well! What should I do?

Oh, right! I've got the Bible. Should I read it? Kurbatov looked at the Bible doubtfully. Frankly speaking, he didn't want to read it. For him, the Bible was associated with something boring and wearisome—morals and commandments, a shaggy dog story. He opened the book at random.

"In the western foothills: Ashtaol, Zorah, Ashnah, Zanoah, An Gannim, Tappuah, Enam, Jarmuth, Adullam,

Sokoh, Azekah. Shaaraim, Adithaim and Gederah (or Gederothaim) - fourteen towns and their villages."

What the hell is that? What can I find here? What can I read here? If there's some divine wisdom here, then it's hidden so deeply that I won't fucking find it. Blasphemy again! Oh, fuck it! God will forgive. And I need to perform great deeds. Fucking feats! It's a subtle matter. If I guess it, they will forgive me everything, and if I'm wrong, it will be a fucking disaster for everything. So, I can omit the little things. I need to think about serious stuff. "Right! Logic is a great thing. I unscrambled all of it. I really like it. Right, that's great. So, what should I do? What am I to do?"

By the way, speaking of guess—can I read a fortune on the Bible? I read about it somewhere, or someone told me; I should think of a page and a line at the top of it. And then I should find it and read. That's a prediction. Well, that's a sin, right? Concerning the situation.. Well, let's try it, sin or no sin! Well What do we have?

Well, let's assume Page 673, 13th line from the top. Well, let's see. It's gonna be some crap, anyway, like all those horoscopes, Well, page 673... one, two, three...

"Then the Lord put forth his hand, and touched my mouth. And the Lord said unto me, Behold, I have put my words in thy mouth."

Fuck it! What the fuck is that? Book of Jeremiah. Who the fuck is Jeremiah? And what then?

"See, today I appoint you over nations and kingdoms to uproot and tear down, to destroy and overthrow, to build and to plant."

Well! And then?

"The word of the Lord came to me: 'What do you see, Jeremiah?' 'I see the branch of an almond tree,' I replied."

Well, no need to read any more. That's a hit! Right in Jeremiah! Well, let's try one more time. Let's secure ourselves. Well, well. Let it be 200, Page 200. And Line 16—Page 200, line 16. Let's find it. Well, I'm fucking tired of counting! It's okay; let's count. Shit! I lost it! One more time. Well, well, well—here it is!

"...but a prophet who presumes to speak in my name anything I have not commanded is to be put to death."

What the hell is that? What death? Who is to be put to death? Me? Why the fuck do I need all that? I'm not gonna say anything! Fuck you with your prophecies! Let someone else be a prophet! Some half-witted Jeremiah! Although, I really want it. Well, that's the truth. I want it! I want to show them that I'm so smart. I want to show it to the whole world! Even if the cost of it would be apocalypse. It would be a pleasure to know that I started it with my wonder-book.

All that brings us death,
Brings to a mortal heart
Inexplicable pleasures.

Here are the flush of battle,
And of the abyss on a brink,
And in the whirling ocean...

Well, 'hail to plague!' 'We're not afraid of darkness of the grave.' That's right! We're not fucking afraid! Right! But just look at it! Two hits in a row! Well, it's no surprise after the events of the day, but still... Well? One more time? One last time? Or is it enough? I don't want to strike something strange, a chestnut from the fire. All right! Let's risk it. Come on! Well! 923! And the line, the eighth one—it's easier to find.

"He that believeth in the Lord taketh heed to the commandment; and he that trusteth in him shall fare never the worse."

Great! Excellent! That's what I was looking for! We came to where we started, where we finished. Fuck! "Trusteth in him." Well, you must decide on your own. There will be no help. Nice! Thank you very much, Lord, for good words and advice! For care! For.. Well, enough! Blaspheming? Making it worse? Although, I want to do it Really, I do want it! Well... Let's see somewhere here! At random. Without turning the page! 924, 11.

"For dreams have deceived many, and they have failed that put their trust in them."

Fuck it! That's enough! Enough of these prophecies! Enough! The farther in, the deeper. The more I want it. I'm completely lost. Who am I? Prophet Jeremiah, false prophet, or sensitive moron who has seen too many dreams and imagined some bullshit? Well, I wish it was the last one. Right! What about the visions? And today's events? What should I do with them? Imagined? You wish! Imagined! Sure! That's a pretty fine imagination!

In your heart! I feel in my heart that I want to publish it! That's it! I want it very much! I just can't help it! And the wish becomes stronger with time. The farther in... Feeling myself God! Or Devil! Well, that's actually the same, in brief, an idol, a fetish, an object of general worship. And if the whole world goes to the depths of hell, I can go with it. For company's sake, together with everyone! I'll do what the others do. Misery loves company. 'Where there was table with viands, there is coffin now. And the pale death stares at everyone.' Oh, come on! 'The hour of our death shall be light'! But I can be God before the end! A head of this universal sect. Well, or Antichrist, antigod. Oh, oh, oh! For that!

And if it's all my imagination, it's even for the better! Then I have no reasons to worry. And, thus, I have no reasons not to publish it. No one's gonna notice anything. A lot of trash is published every day! Yet another pulp-writer, thinking that he's a genius! Come on! I'd be glad to know that myself. No problems! No problems at all!

Well, here's the deal. Either I'm a genius, and my book is great, and then I'll become antichrist and Antigod—yo-ho-ho, and a bottle of rum—or I'm just a hack writer, and it's all fucking bullshit, and it's not important at all. And all my current tortures and excruciations are not worth a tuppence. Well, it's for the better. That's good. I'll just continue to lead my ordinary life. Well, I'm okay with both variants. And that means that I have to publish it—I have to! Well, it's as simple as that. Easy as a damn. A piece of cake!

Right! But there's one more variant, a small one. How could I omit it? It's the most unpleasant one. Well, the book is ingenious, it's a hell of a book! Actually, the devil himself dictated it to me; why should I lie to myself? Did I write it myself? 'Genius'! But all of it is a trial, sent to me from above. A trial of genius and fame! Shall I pass it or not? If I don't, there would be no Apocalypse, of course; God shall not let it happen! But me? I'm going straight to hell. That's for sure! To the last circle of hell! Into Satan's mouth, together with Judah and others. I don't really know what I'm given such honor and fame for, and why my humble personality is so interesting for the supreme forces, but maybe, it's exactly because of the modesty and humbleness, the mediocrity. How would an ordinary, plain man behave in such an extraordinary situation? Well, I don't know! That's not for me to decide. What matters ...

Ha! One more! Not one—there's a third one. Actually, a fourth one. This book is a good book. It brings good and light. And the dream is evil, the intrigues of Satan to convince me not to publish it. What did the Bible tell me?"

"Do not believe the dreams!" *Decide yourself! Read it in your heart! That's the only criteria. Well, that's a wonderful option, a great one! The book is good, and I'm good and kind, as well. I'm white and fluffy. I'm no Antichrist—quite the contrary, I'm Messiah. Almost Christ. A fucking prophet Jeremiah. Why not? Why can't I be him?*

Right! Right. That's the point! Temptation and trial—I don't fucking care if the book is good or bad—I mean, whether it brings good or evil; I just want to know what would become of me? In person. Shall I become a star, an idol, or not? I'm ready to do anything to become one! I'm ready to do anything right now. I'm fine with any villainy. Let them be! Genius and villainy are incompatible, he remembered the warning line which he had heard back in school. *"Come on! "Incompatible?"*

Well, I mean abstract villainy, of course, the one that doesn't concern me directly. Well, let millions and billions die on the other side of our globe. I don't care. It's even interesting. It's the same as watching TV. Pah! Everything's burning, exploding, and being ruined, and you're sitting in a cozy chair, drinking cold beer, and listening to the indifferent voice of the speaker. 'As a result of the bombing, thousands of civilians died—mostly old people, women, and children.

Well, so they died. Let them be in peace. Let's drink for the peace of their souls. But then imagine!

"New riots caused by the book of Kurbatov B.V. Throughout the whole world, millions of people came onto the streets with the portrait of Kurbatov in their hands! New sects are appearing everywhere; they claim Kurbatov is their spiritual leader, Messiah, and living God. As a matter of fact, we're seeing the birth of a new cult, a new religion."

Well! It's breathtaking! My head is swimming from these perspectives. Fuck me for that! Even if the scale is smaller...Still, why would I hesitate? That's it! That's it! I've made a decision. Fuck it all! I don't give a damn! Be it as it may!

Shaking with pleasant anxiety and expectation, Kurbatov rushed to the computer. His plan was very simple. He was going to post the beginning of the book on his homepage, tell about it on several forums, and see what happened. For some reason, he was sure that he wouldn't have to do anything more, that it would go all by itself. It would develop itself. Well, in case of urgency, it didn't matter. He just wanted to post it. He wanted to show it to the world!"

The first thing that he saw on the provider's web-page was the huge colorful ad in the foreground:

"SENSATION!

The site with an incredible book by Ishutin V.S. sets new records of views! You must read it!"

Chilled with an ominous foreboding, he left-clicked on the word "book". At once, the text appeared on the screen. Kurbatov felt that he couldn't breathe. It was his book! His book! How did that Ishutin V.S. get it? That was impossible! Suddenly he was struck with a guess. *Oh, God! Could that be true?*

Kurbatov left the internet and started an antivirus program. Could that be true? Several minutes of weary waiting and…

Infected files17
Total size KB

Virus! Someone hacked his computer! Fuck! But he had checked it two days before that! A day before! It was all clear! With-out any hope, he slowly pointed the arrow at the "My documents" icon. Pause Click! Nothing! It was empty! The book was gone. It had disappeared.

Fuck it! This faggot not only copied the text, he also deleted it from my computer! Scum! Douchebag! Well, it's no use swearing. The ship has sailed. There is no use crying.

And what about the disc? I have a copy of the text on the disc, right? Although, what would that change? Still, what if it's a better version? I think that I've been doing the last proofreading on the disc. Shit, I don't really remember!" Kurbatov feverishly put the disc into the computer. Well "My computer," "Disc…" Well?

The text was completely ruined. Some scrappy pieces, shreds, lines, and separate letters. Suddenly Kurbatov remembered that, recently, he had put the disc into the computer when he searched something on the Internet. Automatically. He got used to it for the last three weeks while he was working with the book. *So, when that fucker Ishutin hacked his computer, the disc must have been in it. I get it! I get it.*

Kurbatov scrolled through the file aimlessly. Gibberish, a mixture of letters, empty again, some meaningless crap. Suddenly his attention was drawn by two lines. Just two. Two short sentences.

"There are no bad deeds, there are bad goals. Everything is allowed. Within the limits of the right goal, any deed is right."

Kurbatov leaned back in the chair, licked his dry lips, and giggled hysterically. *That's what I was teaching. Why should I be offended now? Well, here is my first student! Ishutin V.S. Please accept him! 'There are no bad deeds!..' 'Everything is allowed!..' If you need your teacher no more, just step over him and move on to your own, private goal. 'Within the limits of the right goal, any deed is right!'"*

He sat for some time, staring with unseeing eyes in front of him, then slowly looked at the screen and reached his weak and sluggish hand to the keypad.

Nothing. Nothing. Nothing. Again. That's it! No. One more page. The last one. Empty. Almost. In the middle of the empty screen, there was flashing one line. Just one phrase.

SEE YOU IN HELL!

Kurbatov felt his hair move on his neck. It seemed to him that there was someone in the room, a horrible, hideous monster from his nightmares. And that someone was sending regards to him through the ages.

"But why?! Why??!!" he shouted in a whisper with his frozen lips. "I didn't do anything!.. I didn't!!! It's unfair!.. For what???!!! For what? For what???????!!!!!!!"

~*~*~*~

Lucifer's Son

And Lucifer was ask'd by His astonish'd Son:
—Can a word hast such power?
And Lucifer smil'd and answer'd to His Son:
—"In the beginning was the word"...

Made in the USA
Lexington, KY
11 June 2016